PROLOGUE

Sunday, May 15, 7:11 a.m.

Their hands were cuffed and gags were winched behind their teeth. They were half lifted, half shoved into the back of an unmarked van. It felt like they'd stumbled into a *Law & Order* episode, but without a soundtrack to know when the scene was going to end.

She hadn't managed to scream. She'd been too shocked. In the distance, the constant thrum of traffic on I-40 sounded almost like water. Birds twittered mindlessly in the trees. She kept thinking someone must have seen, someone would call for help, someone would come.

No one came.

But these backwater Tennessee roads were empty even at the busiest times. Seven in the morning on a Sunday, there was no one on the road; it was too early even for the church crowd.

No one but the men in the van, with their hands slick

as machine-gun barrels and their orders to obey.

At least the men hadn't shoved their heads into burlap sacks. She'd seen a movie like that once, where a rich woman kidnapped for ransom was placed in a sack and had inhaled fibers and was asphyxiated, and then the criminals had to figure out how to dump the body and conceal the crime.

Maybe she, too, had been kidnapped for ransom.

But she knew, deep down, that she'd been taken for a different reason entirely.

It was because of Haven.

It was because they'd escaped.

She tried to listen, to keep track of where they were heading as the van picked up speed, bumping them down the road. The potholes threw them so high before slamming them down again that tears came to her eyes when her tailbone hit the van floor.

The ride smoothed out once they were on the highway. It was thunderously loud, like huddling under the bleachers while a homecoming crowd drummed their feet in unison. She felt like a slab of bacon stuck in somebody's hold. With no sunlight, she quickly lost track of time. Her throat was sore and it was difficult to swallow. The fibers from whatever they'd gagged her with tickled her nose and tonsils. It tasted like a sock.

Maybe they'd bought a pack especially for this purpose.

LYRA

LAUREN
OLIVER

RINGER

LYRA

HARPER
An Imprint of HarperCollins*Publishers*

PART I

ONE

LYRA HAD STARTED COLLECTING THINGS. When she saw something she liked, she pocketed it, and usually by the end of the day she was weighty with the sloughed-off skin of someone else's life: losing lottery tickets, Snapple bottle caps, ATM receipts, pens, chewed-up foil that came off the cheap bottles of wine sold down at Two Brothers Beer & Liquor.

In the privacy of her small room in the double-wide trailer gifted to them by Gemma's father, which to Lyra, formerly known as 24, felt very luxurious, she shook out her new belongings on the comforter and tried to listen, tried to hear them speak to her of this new world and her place in it. Her old belongings had spoken: the bed at Haven had whispered, and the Invacare Snake Tubing asked questions, the snobby syringes had insulted her with their sharp little bite, and the long-nosed, greedy biopsy needles used for marrow extraction had always wanted gossip, more and more of it.

But these new objects told her nothing, spoke of nothing. Or maybe it was just that the outside world was so noisy she couldn't hear.

She was no longer a human model. She was a she, not an *it*. But it was now, here, with a room of her own and photographs from her earliest childhood Scotch-taped to the walls, that she didn't know who or what she was.

Here she could wake when she wanted and eat what she liked, although since she'd never prepared her own food, she and Caelum, who had been 72 until she named him, mostly subsisted on cans of soda and granola bars Rick bought from the grocery store. They did not know how to fry an egg. Rick taught her to use a can opener, but the microwave bothered her; its humming energy reminded her of Mr. I.

Caelum spent hours sitting cross-legged on the couch, watching whatever channel happened to be on when he first pressed the power button: news channels, movie channels, and his favorite, the Home Shopping Network. Lyra had learned to read. Caelum learned how to watch. He learned the world through the things it bought and sold.

He did not want to learn how to read.

There were sixty-two trailers in the Winston-Able

Mobile Home Park, and the whole thing could have been slotted down comfortably in two of Haven's wings. But to Lyra it seemed infinitely bigger, because it was unknown, because of all the things she'd never seen before: wind chimes and old Halloween decorations and cars on cinder blocks and pink plastic flamingos; lawn chairs and barbecues.

Caelum stayed inside and watched the world through the pinhole of the TV screen, and Lyra walked for hours a day and put things in her pockets and sorted through them like an archeologist trying to decode hieroglyphs. They were both trying to learn in their own way, she thought, but she didn't like it even so. Sameness was the only way she had ever understood who she was. What she was. Now, everything had changed. He was inside, and she was outside, and that made them different—at least, during the day.

Night came again and again like a tide foaming over the trailers and the cars and the scrubby trees, and turning it all to the same smudge of darkness, rubbing shapes into shadows. The night broke Lyra and Caelum's separateness. It collapsed the space between them; they fell into its depth and landed, blind, together.

Rick worked the graveyard shift, and when he didn't, he went to bed early, still sweating a faint chemical smell. Every night, Lyra and Caelum walked down to the unoccupied trailers on lots 57 and 58. He found a garden hose, and in the sticky air they'd let it flow, drink from it, throw water between their hands at each other just for the fun of it, because fun was new.

They kissed. They kissed for hours, until Lyra's lips were sore and tender to touch, still heavy with the pressure of his mouth. With her tongue she found the ridges of his teeth, and the soft rhythms of his tongue in response. She touched the vault of his mouth and the strange slick texture of the inner side of his cheeks. She let him do the same, let him learn her through his tongue. Sometimes it was kissing, and sometimes it was something like learning, like collecting seashells, the way Cassiopeia had, turning them over and over to memorize the miracle of ridges and whorls built by thousands of years of soft water.

They played a game where their eyes stayed closed and they had to see with their mouths instead. Lyra knew bodies for what they did and what they failed to do, and her only feelings had been in sickness or in pain. She learned the soft wonder of the human body on the planes of his chest, and on the angles of his shoulders, and in the soft fuzz of hair, like the gentlest kiss, below his belly button. She learned it on his scalloped ears, and on his kneecaps, and on his long and gentle fingers.

She learned his body, and she learned that her body

was a strange and watery thing that pooled and flowed and turned all at once to a current; the pressure of his tongue, on her neck, on her nipples, on her thighs, turned her into a million other things. She became air and the electric possibility of lightning. She became a furred animal, howling in summer. She became his mouth, and she existed in his mouth. She poured her whole body into the radius of the circles he made with his tongue. And at the same time her body became huge, like a long shout of joy hanging in the quiet.

They had a game to kiss each other on every scar, slowly, starting from the neck. They had a game to find the darkest place they could and touch each other until they couldn't keep track of whose body was where. *Your knee or mine?* he would say. *Your hand or mine?* They had a game to act like the night when it came, and erase all the space between them, to lose their bodies entirely, until they didn't know who was holding and who was being held. She didn't have a name for some of the things they did, only a melody, a rhythm that hummed in her skin after they were done.

She wanted things she hardly understood: to be closer, closer, closer than bodies could ever be. She wanted to take her body off and for him to shed his, too, and to stand like two shadows overlapping with not a shiver of space between them.

And she wanted to keep her body, so he would keep kissing it.

She learned how to tell time, and every morning, she counted the hours until dark, when Caelum was no longer Caelum, and she was no longer Lyra, and both of them became each other.

She was terrified that one day it wouldn't work, that the distance would put up a hand, and hold them apart.

TWO

AND THEN, ON THURSDAY, IT happened.

At Haven, Lyra had been bored so often that, paradoxically, she had almost never been bored at all. Little things consumed her attention: the petty squabbles she imagined between her belongings; the replicas who went to the Box or were disciplined by the nurses; her small missions, planned and executed with all the precision of a military invasion, to steal words from medicine bottle labels or even the nurses' cigarette packs.

But now that there was so much to see, so much to do, she was often bored. On Thursday, a bright day of puffed-up clouds, the world beyond her windows looked dizzy in its own light. But when Lyra suggested to Caelum that they take a walk, he looked at her with eyes burned like wounds in his face.

"No," he said. And then, looking back at the TV, "This isn't my place."

Caelum had wanted to escape. He'd been Code Black. And now when Lyra thought of Haven and what had happened to it, her memories were intertwined with him, with the moment she'd slipped through the fence past the drums of old construction litter and biohazard signs and where he'd first touched her wrist. If she had known about the world, about space and time, she would have known that matter bends the universe around it. But even without knowing that, she saw how Caelum had bent her universe, and made everything change.

He had wanted to be free, and to see how real people lived. But now they were free and he wouldn't go outside except at night, when there was nothing at all to see. He learned the world only from what he saw on TV.

"It will never be your place if you don't try," Lyra said.

"It will never be my place even if I do," he said.

She went alone. Going anywhere by herself thrilled and terrified her, no matter how often she did it. At Haven she had almost never been alone. There were nurses to accompany them everywhere, and researchers to watch behind glass. There were the silhouettes of the medical machines themselves, and the doctors to operate them. And of course, there were thousands of replicas, all of them dressed identically except for their bracelet tags. They ate and bathed and showered together. They moved together as a single mass, like a swarm of gnats, or a thundercloud.

"Hey. You. I'm talking to you."

Lyra turned around, still unused to people who addressed her directly, who looked in her eyes instead of at her forehead or shoulder blades. Something strange had happened to her in the outside world: she had begun to forget how to stay invisible.

The girl outside lot 47 was chewing gum and smoking a cigarette from something that resembled a pen. After a closer look Lyra recognized it as the kind of e-cigarette some of the nurses had smoked. "You're new here," she said, exhaling a cloud of vapor.

It didn't sound like a question, so Lyra didn't answer. She put a hand in her pocket, feeling her newest acquisition: a cold metal bolt she'd found half-embedded in the dirt.

The girl stood up. She was skinny, though not as thin as Lyra, and wearing low-waisted shorts and a shirt that showed off her stomach. She had a birthmark that made a portion of her face darker than the rest. Lyra had once seen something similar, on one of the infants in the Yellow crop before they died in the Postnatal wing.

"My friend Yara thinks you're a bitch," the girl said calmly, exhaling again. "Cuz you never talk or say hi to anyone. But I don't think you're a bitch. I think you're just scared. That's it, isn't it? You're scared because you came from somewhere else and never expected to end up here, and now you're wondering if you'll ever get out."

Once again, Lyra said nothing. She didn't know what a bitch was, although she thought, years ago, she might have heard the word—something to do with Nurse Em, one of the other staff members complaining about her.

"So?" The girl's eyes were a dark, rich color that reminded Lyra of the mud along the banks in the marshes, teeming with invisible life. "Who's right? Me or Yara?"

"Neither," Lyra said. She was startled by the way her voice rolled across the short distance between them. Even though it had been weeks since she'd left Haven, she wasn't in the habit of speaking. When Caelum came out with her at night, or when he snuck into her room and slid into bed beside her, they rarely spoke out loud. They breathed and touched, communicating through language of the body: pressure and touch, tension and release. "I never thought I'd end up here. I didn't know there was a here to end up. But I'm not worried about getting out. This *is* out." She stopped herself from saying anything she shouldn't.

To Lyra's surprise, the girl smiled. "I knew you weren't as dumb as you looked. Half the people round here could double for shitbricks, so you never know. I'm Raina. What's your name?"

Lyra almost said *twenty-four.* Rick always called her Brandy Nicole. But she had lost so many things in her life; she wasn't ready to lose her name, too, and the memory of the woman who'd given it to her.

"Lyra," she said.

Raina smiled. "You drop out of school or something?"

Lyra didn't know how to answer.

"School's dumb anyways," Raina said. "I finished last year and look at me now, on the nine-to-five shift at Fantasia." She tilted her head and Lyra thought of the funny, knob-kneed birds that used to scuttle through the gardens at Haven, looking for crabs as small as the fingernails of the infants in Postnatal. The only part of her that wasn't skinny was her stomach, which had the faintest swell, as if there were a tiny fist inside of it. "You want a Coke?"

Lyra almost said no.

But instead, almost accidentally, she said yes.

Lyra was with Raina, and then she was home, and she couldn't remember anything that had happened in between. She'd obviously fallen down. Her palms stung and there were flecks of gravel in her skin. Her knee was bleeding.

It was happening more frequently now, these jump cuts in her mind. She knew that what they'd done to her at Haven, what they'd grown in her, was to blame, and remembered that Gemma had said prions made holes grow in the brain, slowly at first, then faster and faster.

That was exactly what it felt like: like holes, and hours of her life simply dropped through them.

Rick's car, tawny with dust, was parked in front of lot 16, and the lightning bugs were up, as well as swarms of no-see-ums that rose in dark clouds. She heard raised voices as she came up the porch steps, but it wasn't until she was standing inside, under the bright overhead lights on a secondhand *Welcome Home* mat, that she saw Caelum and Rick had been fighting. Their last words slotted belatedly up to her consciousness.

It's enough now. You can't stay here if you don't find a way to help.

Both of them turned to look at her. Caelum she couldn't read. But Rick's eyes were raw, and his expression she knew from the youngest researchers at Haven whenever they accidentally messed up an IV and blood began to spurt or the replicas cried out: guilt.

"What's going on?" she asked.

"Nothing," Rick said quickly. Patches of scalp showed through his hair, shiny and bright red. "Nothing. Just having a family talk, that's all."

"You're not family," Caelum said. "You said so yourself."

Rick stared at him for a long minute. Then he shook himself, like a dog, and moved for the door.

"I'm working a double," he said. "I just came back for

a bite. I'll be home later tonight." He stopped in front of her and reached out two fingers to touch her shoulders. This was a gesture they'd agreed on, an expression of affection she could tolerate. "Will you be all right?"

"Yes," Lyra said. She knew he wanted more from her but wasn't sure what or how to give it to him. Sometimes Lyra tried to see herself in his nose and jaw and smile, tried to climb down a rope of feelings to get to one that made sense, but he still looked like a stranger, and felt like one, too. He had given her photographs from when she was a baby, but they felt like images from someone else's life.

"Okay. Good. Okay." He dropped his hand. The noise was loud in the quiet. Then he was gone, leaving Caelum and Lyra alone.

The room smelled faintly sour, as it always did. Another thing Lyra had not gotten used to was the dirt in the corners and the insects that tracked behind the faucet, plates and pans half-crusted in the sink when Rick went to work, fruit flies that lifted in clouds from the garbage, and the giant water bugs that came up from the drains in the shower.

Caelum stared at Lyra for a second, then turned back to the TV, although he didn't sit down.

"What happened?" she said. It wasn't the first time that Caelum and Rick had fought. Several times she had been startled into awareness by the sound of raised voices, or come out of her bedroom to find them standing too close together. "What did he say to you?"

"Nothing." Caelum turned up the volume. Words flashed on the screen, but they were gone too fast for Lyra to read them. "What happened to your knee?"

So he'd noticed. Lyra bent down and thumbed the blood off. She'd heard at Haven that blood was only red after it oxidized. Strange the way everything changed on contact with the world.

"Nothing," she said, since that was the answer he'd given her.

"You were gone for a long time," he said. It wasn't exactly a question, but Lyra nodded. "Where were you?"

"I made a friend," Lyra said, and nearly regretted it when Caelum looked up, his face seizing around a quick spasm of pain. "She invited me to a party on Saturday. You're invited too."

"A party," he said. He said the word as if it were in a different language, the way the birthers had said *water* or *help* or *doctor,* if they spoke English at all. "Why?"

"There's no reason," she said. She didn't have an answer. But this made her defensive, not embarrassed. "It's what people do."

"People," he repeated. Now he made the word sound like a medicine that turned bitter as it dissolved. "*Your* people."

"Don't," she said. They had gone through this before, when Gemma had first told her that she had a father, that she wasn't really a replica. *I thought we were the same. But we're not. We're different,* Caelum had said, but she hadn't believed him then.

But now a new voice began to whisper. *Maybe he was right.*

"I can't stay here much longer," he said. "*He* doesn't want me here." Caelum refused to use Rick's name. "And you don't, either."

"Of course I do," Lyra said.

Caelum just shook his head. "You have a new life here," he said.

All the anger she'd been keeping down broke free. It was like a rope whipping up words in her chest. "Why did you leave Haven?" she burst out. "Why did you run away? What do you *want*?"

"I got what I wanted," he said, and with a quick step came closer to her. In an instant everything stilled and went white, and she thought he was going to say *you*, and wings of feeling lifted in her chest. But instead he said, "I wanted to do something on my own. For myself. I wanted to choose."

"So you chose. Congratulations." In words, now, she heard the echo of Raina's voice, the edge of her sarcasm. "Are you happy now?"

"Happy." He shook his head. "You even talk like one of them now."

"So what?" She hated him then. More than she'd hated any of the doctors or the nurses or the sanitation teams who'd bundled up the dead replicas in paper sheaths, making jokes the whole time: *How many clones does it take to screw in a lightbulb?* "So I talk like them. So maybe I have a friend. What's wrong with that?"

"It's a lie, that's what's wrong with it," he said. "You're sick."

"You don't seem sick," Lyra said automatically, and only registered a split second later that he hadn't, in fact, said *we're sick*. And with a kind of yawning horror she realized that what she had said was true. Caelum had been so skinny when they met that his collarbones stood out like wings. But he had put on weight. He didn't get nauseous, not that she could see, and he never got confused, like she did.

There was a long, terrible moment of silence.

"You're not sick," she said at last. She could barely get the words out. Then: "What cluster were you in?"

He looked away. She closed her eyes, tried to picture him as she'd first seen him, his wild eyes and dirt-encrusted fingernails, the wristband looped around his dark skin . . .

He said it at the same time she remembered. "White."

It was stupid she'd never wondered, stupid she'd never asked. It was all her fault.

White was *control.*

And control meant that he was fine.

"Lyra . . ." He tried to reach for her and she backed away from him, nearly toppling the table in the front hall, bumping against the door. "I'm going to find a way to fix it. I promise. I'm going to find a way to help."

When he tried to touch her again she lurched past him, knocking a coat from the rack pegged to the wall. She felt like she would cry. She hardly ever cried.

Maybe this too was something that had *oxidized*: her feelings had changed color, and flowed more quickly now. She imagined that inside of her, the prions pooled like dark shadows, waiting to swallow her up.

"You can't help me," she said. "No one can."

THREE

FOR TWO DAYS, SHE HARDLY saw Caelum at all, and she felt nothing but terrible relief, like after you finally drop a glass that has been slipping for some time from your fingers.

Caelum was her tether to Haven, but he was also her anchor. Around him she felt stuck in her old life, stuck in her old name. 24. The escaped replica, the human model, the monster.

Rick told her that he'd put Caelum to work. There was little he could do, because in order to become someone in the outside world, you *already* had to be someone, which required pieces of paper and numbers from the government and identification that neither Lyra nor Caelum had. But Rick had met a guy who owned a tow company and impound lot and needed help on the graveyard shift, from midnight to eight a.m. He was prepared to pay cash, and he would ask no questions.

Money, Lyra was learning, was a source of near-constant worry in the outside world, as it had been in Haven. At Haven the staff had talked constantly about budget cuts and even the possibility of having funding cut off completely. But it surprised her to find out that money everywhere was so difficult to get and hang on to. Gemma's father had offered them a large sum of money, but Rick had refused it, and when Lyra asked him why, his face darkened.

"Blood money," he said. "It's bad enough I have to lean on him for a roof. I won't take a dollar I don't have to."

She had a hard time thinking of Rick Harliss as poor, since he had a car and his own TV and his own narrow house, a bathroom only the three of them shared, multiple sets of clothes—all things that to her seemed rich.

But they *were* poor, at least that was what Rick said. And while Lyra was his daughter and it was his duty to protect her, Caelum was freeloading—*stealing time from the clock,* Rick said—and would have to figure out how to make his own way in the world.

Lyra should have heard the threat in those words: that Caelum would have to leave, sooner or later.

On Friday and Saturday morning, after his first two shifts, Caelum left piles of dollar bills on the small kitchen table, secured beneath a can of Hormel chili, and Rick took the money wordlessly and bought more Hormel chili from the store, more toilet paper and toothpaste, more pairs of socks and books for Lyra to read, all of them with creased pastel covers and heroes who always arrived at the right moment.

For two days, Lyra was happy—despite the holes dropping hours of her life, despite the fact that she and Caelum had had their first fight ever, despite the way she had to pick through the boredom of the day on her own, collecting ever more pieces of trash, arranging them and rearranging them as if they would someday yield a sentence. She visited with Raina, and was absorbed in an endless funnel of people, ideas, and places she'd never heard of—Los Angeles, the neo-Nazis in lot 14, veganism, YouTube, Planned Parenthood, the Bill of Rights.

She was angry at Caelum for lying to her, even though she realized he'd never said he was sick and she had never asked. Still, she was angry. He resented her for becoming something he could never be, but there was no greater abandonment than this: she would die, and he would live.

Even so, she never thought she might lose him for good. He had been absorbed into her life, into the constellation of her reality now growing to include the small trailer on lot 16; moths beating against the screens and spiders drowning in the sink, Raina and her parties, clothing purchased from the Salvation Army by the pound. Her whole life she'd experienced as a series of circles, days that repeated themselves, procedures that happened again and again weekly or monthly or yearly, birthdays that passed without celebration to mark them. Even the fence at Haven had been a rough circle, and Spruce Island had been bounded by water on all sides.

Things didn't change. They just returned to what they were before. And she and Caelum would return, again and again, to each other.

She should have learned, by now, that nothing was ever so easy.

On Saturday, she didn't see Caelum at all. In the morning, she found his mattress—concealed behind an ugly fuchsia curtain Rick had strung up from a shower rod—empty and the bed neatly made. But he'd come home at some point: she saw that he'd left money for Rick. Next to the bed was a shoe box he used for his belongings, and when she opened it, she felt like someone had just tapped the center of her rib cage. He, too, had obviously been collecting things when he went out: old coins, a bus schedule, an empty cigarette pack, a brochure, a receipt carefully unfolded and weighted beneath a tin labeled *Altoids*. She felt a sudden, hard aching for him. At Haven, she had once had an Altoids tin, had kept it stashed carefully in her pillowcase.

He wasn't home by the time she left to meet Raina, and she couldn't leave a note for him. She didn't know how to write and he wouldn't be able to read it. She wasn't sure what she would say, anyway.

She and Raina walked together to Ronchowoa, a town lobbed down in the middle of nowhere as if it was made by God's spit. (That's how Raina put it.) Lyra still didn't like being out on the road, and got jumpy whenever she saw a sedan with dark-tinted windows. But it was hard to be nervous when Raina was around. She never stopped talking, for one thing. Just listening to her took up all of Lyra's attention.

"The Vasquez brothers will be there for sure, they think they're hot shit because their dad has four car dealerships in Knox County. Watch out for Sammy Vasquez, he'll have his hands down your pants before he even knows your name. . . ." She laughed. She had a laugh like a solid punch. "I don't know. Maybe you should let him. I hear you got caught tonguing your own cousin."

Caelum and Lyra had said they were cousins when they first arrived, because Rick had said it and then they'd repeated it, if anyone asked. "He's not exactly my cousin."

"Yeah, I got some *cousins* like that." Raina smirked. "What is he, anyway? Chinese or Korean or something? He's all mixed-up-looking. Cute, though."

"I don't know," Lyra said. Many of the replicas had

been grown from stem cell tissue purchased on the sly from clinics and hospitals, and no one knew exactly where the genotypes had come from.

"It's all right. My first was a Haitian. My mom nearly flipped her shit. You know, you could be pretty if you weren't so *basic.*" This was another thing Raina did: slid sideways into new thoughts without any warning. "You ever think of cleaning up a bit?"

They went to the big Target, whose bright-white look and antiseptic smell reminded Lyra painfully of Haven. In the cosmetics aisle Raina opened tubes of lipstick and little plastic-shrouded tubs of eye shadow, experimenting with color on Lyra's cheeks and on the back of her hand, keeping up her nonstop stream of conversation.

"You got big eyes, that's good, and your lips are decent too. . . ."

She'd almost finished with Lyra's eyes when a woman in a red polo shirt came to yell at them. "What do you think you're doing? Those aren't for sampling."

"Well, how was I supposed to know?" Raina made her face go blank and dumb, and Lyra had a sudden memory of some of the Yellow crop back at Haven, a bad crop full of replicas who *failed to thrive.* After the Yellow crop, God mandated that all the newest replicas needed at least two hours of human contact a day.

"Don't give me that duff. I've seen you in here before."

The woman had a name tag, S-A-M. "I've half a mind to call the cops on you myself."

"Don't," Raina said. "We'll pay for everything. We always meant to, anyway."

The woman shook her head again. But she said, "All right. Follow me."

They were halfway to the checkout lanes when Raina gripped Lyra's elbow and steered her instead toward the exits. They were almost at the door before S-A-M realized they were no longer following and shouted.

"Run," Raina said, and keeping her grip on Lyra's arm, she and Lyra hurtled toward the exit. An alarm screamed. Memories lit up flash-like in Lyra's head: Code Black, the sweaty heat, a spring storm that knocked out the power and forced the generators on. They were in the parking lot. They were laughing, and the sky was spinning overhead, and Lyra was dizzy with a sudden happiness that punched her breath out of her chest. She had never laughed like that—she was surprised by how it came, in waves that rocked her whole body and made her feel fizzy and bright and airless.

Raina's trailer was the same size as Rick's but even more cluttered, and Lyra felt a pang to see so many possessions worn and used and taken for granted—family photos hung crookedly in plastic frames, throw pillows shaggy with dog hair, mugs holding a crown of pens. By comparison, Rick's trailer was as cold and impersonal as the hallways of Haven.

On a side table sheeted with mail, she noticed the same glossy brochure she had seen in Caelum's shoe box of belongings. This time she focused on the letters until they ran into meaning: *Nashville Elvis Festival.*

Raina caught her looking. "Don't tell me you're an Elvis freak too?"

Lyra didn't answer: silence, as always, was like a corner for retreating.

"My mom goes every year. Can you believe she met her boyfriend there? Look. He even made it into the brochure." Raina shook out the folds of the brochure so it opened suddenly into a fan of narrow pages, and Lyra lost her breath.

Replicas. Dozens of them, all men, identically dressed in white, but not in hospital gear: in suits with beautiful detailing.

They looked well-fed. They looked well, period.

"That's Mike," Raina said, and plugged a finger on one of the replicas in the third row. "He won two years ago. My mom saw him perform 'Hound Dog' and walked right up to him and asked him out." She rolled her eyes. "It's been true love ever since."

"I don't understand." Lyra's voice sounded distant to her. "Where is this place?"

Raina shot her a puzzled look. "You've never been to Nashville?" When Lyra shook her head, Raina frowned. "Where did you come from, again?"

"Florida," Lyra said, although she had never known where she was from until Gemma had told her. She knew only Haven, and Spruce Island, and Barrel Key. She hadn't understood the world was so big it had to be endlessly divided: into countries, states, towns, neighborhoods. Was it possible the world was so big it included places, like this Nashville, where replicas were made and lived happily, in the open? "We—we had replicas there too."

Raina squinted, like she was trying to see Lyra from a distance. "Impersonators, you mean?"

Lyra shook her head; she didn't know. Her body had turned to vapor. She was suddenly overwhelmed by a sense of all the things in the world she didn't understand coming toward her, a hard high wave she couldn't duck or ride. But she clung to the idea of a place where replicas could smile and be photographed in the open: it was a reedy, ropy line of hope.

"I think the whole thing's stupid," Raina said. "A bunch of grown men dressing up like some dead rock star from a thousand years ago. I mean, his music isn't even that good."

"What do you mean, dressing up?" Lyra asked.

"Well, you know, dyeing their hair, growing sideburns,

shopping for costumes and stuff. I mean, it's just make-believe. But Mike acts like he really *is* Elvis." Then, seeing Lyra's face: "Don't tell me you don't know who Elvis is."

Lyra, miserably confused, said, "He's like the God in Nashville?"

She was reassured when Raina laughed and agreed. "Oh, for sure," she said. "He is definitely the God in Nashville."

In the bathroom, Raina finished Lyra's makeup, and then dressed her, too.

"You look nervous," she said, when she stepped back to evaluate her work. "Are you nervous?"

Lyra shook her head. In her mind she had already passed through the party and returned home; Caelum would for sure have come home by now. She didn't know whether he'd collected the brochure by chance. She didn't know whether he'd even looked through it—surely he would have told her. And that meant that *she* could tell *him*. She would give him this enormous gift, and he would understand that she had forgiven him and that they were still, after all, the same.

"You ever been to a party before?"

There had been a Christmas party at Haven every year, but only for the nurses and researchers and staff. For weeks, administrative staff bolted garlands of sweet-smelling greenery to the walls and lumped colored tinsel across the security desks and strung big red ribbons in the entry hall. The night of the party only a skeleton staff remained, and they were blurry-eyed and rowdy, wearing crooked fur-trimmed red hats and strange bulky sweaters over their uniforms.

Then, the Choosing: a handful of male doctors who came staggering into the dorms sweating the smell of alcohol swabs.

"Not exactly," Lyra said.

"Didn't think so," Raina said. "You'll love it. Trust me."

Raina put cream in Lyra's hair—which was longer than she'd ever had it, feathery and thin, the color of new wood—and set a timer for fifteen minutes. By then the sting of chemicals made Lyra's eyes water. Lyra bent over to rinse out the dye and afterward Raina finger-combed it and set it with gel.

"Don't look," she said, when Lyra started to turn. "Not yet."

She sprayed Lyra down with something called Vixen. She reached into Lyra's shirt, and hoisted her breasts in their borrowed bra, and laughed when Lyra didn't even flinch. Then she spun Lyra around to face the mirror.

The girl looking back at her was a stranger, with white-blond hair and smoky eyes and a tank top that barely cleared the bottom of her breasts. Tight stomach, hips suctioned into their jeans.

"How do you like that, Pinocchio?" Raina slung an arm around her shoulders. "I knew I'd turn you into a real girl."

FOUR

IT WAS NEARLY EIGHT O'CLOCK when they set out, and the sun was low. Lyra had always liked this time of day, when the light turned everything softer and edged it in gold. Even the Winston-Able Mobile Home Park looked beautiful at this time, all the slinky cats sunning their final hour and patchy gravel roads deep with shadows and everyone coming back from work but not drunk or angry yet. She felt new, walking with Raina, her friend, side by side, smelling like a stranger, in borrowed clothes. She *felt* like a stranger, as if she'd put on not just someone else's clothes but a whole identity.

All her life she'd been smoothed and blunted down to an object, had her body handled, touched, manipulated without her permission, until even she had come to see it as a kind of external thing, a stone or a piece of wood. For the first time she felt her breasts and legs and hips as *hers*, truly hers, a delicious inner secret like all of her belongings, tucked away for safekeeping in her room.

They stopped by lot 16 to see whether Caelum had come home yet, even though Raina made fun of her for having a kissing cousin. ("That's some real hick shit," she said. "Too hick even for us out here.") But he hadn't returned. His bed was still neatly made. Lyra didn't know whether to be relieved or disappointed and was a bit of both.

Eagle Tire was a big factory on the other side of the weigh station. To get there, Lyra and Raina shimmied beneath a fence and skirted between enormous trucks, then had to pick their way over a trash-strewn lot.

Inside, and despite all the blown-out windows, it was hot. It smelled like smoke and urine, and the walls were soot-blackened from a decade's worth of fire pits, since transients and homeless people squatted there when it started to get cold. Almost immediately, Lyra regretted coming. All the kids knew one another, and half of them snickered when they saw Lyra, as if they could also see 24, sticking out at awkward angles, underneath. Some of them were from Winston-Able, and a few girls asked her where her *cousin* was, lingering on the word and making it sound like something bad Lyra had done.

"Ignore them," Raina said, as if it were that easy. Lyra didn't see how she could ignore them when *they* were everywhere. There were more people massed into the empty rooms of Eagle Tire, more people crunching over broken glass and shouting through the cavernous halls, than she had ever seen outside the Stew Pot at Haven.

At Haven there had been rules, the explicit ones—rise at bell, listen to the nurses and doctors, stay out of all the doors marked with a circle and a red bar, don't bother the guards—and hundreds of secret rules, too, that grew invisibly and were absorbed like mold spores through the skin. She'd thought it was because Haven was an institute, but out here there were just as many rules, as many codes and ways of behaving. And Raina's explanations only made Lyra more confused.

"There are those bitches from East Wyatt; just because they got rezoned into PCT now they think they're hot shit," she said. "Oh. And check it out. Those are the McNab sisters; don't talk to them, whole family's cursed, their grandfather killed himself and that's what got it started. You know, because of it being a sin and everything." In the dark, Raina looked much paler, like one of the silvery fish that finned through the shallows near the beach at Haven. "Now every generation, someone dies in a freak accident. They lost their mom to a fluke at Formacine Plastics last year."

What was rezoning? Or a bitch, for that matter? What did it mean to be cursed? She knew what sins were—Nurse Don't-Even-Think-About-It had often quoted from the Bible—but not why it would be a sin to commit suicide. At Haven, it was only a sin because the replicas were expensive to make.

But regular people came cheap. Didn't they?

Before she could ask, Raina seized her arm. "Don't look now," she said. "Remember those Vasquez boys I was telling you about?" She got no further. Two boys shouldered through the crowd, one tall and skinny with the crowded eyes of a fish, the other shorter, more muscular, his arms dark with tattoos.

"Oh no," one of the Vasquez brothers said to Raina. "Who let the dogs out?"

She crossed her arms. "Same person who let you out of your cage, I guess."

Lyra found herself standing next to the other brother, the shorter one with the tattoos. "Cool hair," he said. He lit a cigarette that didn't smell like a cigarette. It was stronger and reminded her not unpleasantly of the smell of the marshes when the tide was low. "You know what they say about girls with short hair?"

"No," she said.

"Freaks in bed." He exhaled. It was so dark she could hardly see his face, just the wet glistening of his lips. "Is it true?"

"Go suck on a tailpipe, Leo," Raina said, and put a

hand on Lyra's arm to steer her away. "I *told* you they were retrogrades," she said. "Their mom's a boozehound. Must have dropped them one too many times on their heads, that's what I think."

The next room they came to must have been an office once: it was smaller and reeked of cigarette smoke. Someone's belongings were piled on a mattress in the corner. All the walls were covered with writing, but she couldn't make out what the words meant. Tendrils of wire punched through the walls and ceiling. Someone had brought speakers and people were dancing. A boy offered her a drink in a can and she took it, thinking it was soda. Then she took a sip and immediately spat it out, wetting Raina's shoes.

"Oh, for fuck's sake," Raina said, and for a quick second, a new face dropped into place over her old one and she looked annoyed—annoyed, and embarrassed.

All at once, Lyra knew she shouldn't have come. Raina didn't want her there. Lyra could see it. She recognized the look on Raina's face; it was the way the nurses looked when they discovered that one of the replicas had wet the bed or gnawed the edge off a pillow or been eating paint chips from the windowsill, like 108 had done when she was hungry.

"I'm sorry," Lyra whispered.

Raina's expression softened. "That's okay. I hate Bud Light, too."

But it was too late. Lyra, ashamed, knew how Raina really felt. She was Raina's project, and she was failing, and they both knew it.

She shoved her way back through the room, which had only gotten more crowded. The echo of so many voices had invaded her memory, so all the shouting seemed to be coming from some old association; she was worried she might throw up, or drop into a hole and lose minutes, hours. Someone grabbed her and she nearly screamed, but it was just a girl with hair sculpted high and breath that smelled like hand sanitizer, saying, "Watch where you're going, bitch."

Lyra pulled away. Somehow she made it outside. She crunched over the vacant lot, watching for needles, as Raina had instructed her to do. She passed between cargo trucks at the weigh station next to the fizz and hiss of highway traffic and ducked beneath the loose fence. Her eyes burned. She rubbed them with a fist, smearing her makeup.

She'd been stupid to believe, even for a second, that she might someday belong in this world, among these people. She belonged only to Haven, now as ever. Caelum was right all along.

She was cutting between the straggly overgrowth that had reclaimed the abandoned trailers at lots 19 and 20 when she heard the murmur of voices. Edging past the water hookup across a splinter of exposed concrete, she saw through a web of blistered tree branches an unfamiliar sedan parked directly in front of lot 16, not ten feet away. A man and a woman stood together on the porch. The woman was trying to see in past the slat of drawn blinds that covered the window.

Lyra froze. Although they were dressed in normal clothing, she had no trouble at all recognizing them. She had spent her lifetime around Suits. She read power from minor details, from small differences in the way people stood and spoke and acted. And on the strangers, power was like an oil slick. It darkened everything around them. She could see it, dark and wet, everywhere they put their hands. She felt suffocated by it. Her breath was suddenly liquid and heavy.

"Think someone tipped them off?" the man said. He spoke quietly, but it was late and for once, no one was shouting or playing music. The sound wouldn't have carried far, but it carried to her.

"Nah. Doubt it. They're probably out with Harliss."

"At midnight?" The man shook his head and reached in his pocket for a cigarette pack, then shook one out into his mouth. "Nice family gathering. What do you want to do?"

"What can we do?" The woman took a seat on the porch, resting her elbows on her knees. Next door, their neighbor had rigged a floodlight to deter thieves—he imagined anyone under the age of forty was a would-be thief—and the artificial brightness hacked her face into exaggerated areas of hollow and highlight. It was a good thing, though. She would be blind, or almost—and hidden in the shadows, Lyra would be practically invisible.

She thought about trying to backtrack, but she was worried her legs would betray her, too scared they would hear her cracking through the undergrowth. Instead, she lowered herself carefully to the ground, hardly daring to breathe. Though she didn't know where the strangers had come from, she knew plainly enough that they were here to take her away. Caelum was still missing. Where was he? And where was Rick? She hoped he was still at work, and safe; it didn't look like the strangers intended to leave anytime soon. If they would wait, so would she. She could only hope that Caelum didn't come home in the meantime.

"What a mess," the man said. When he exhaled, he tipped his head to the sky, exposing a dark ribbon of throat. Lyra fantasized about putting a bullet right through his skin, sending it back through the architecture of his spinal cord. Why wouldn't he just let them be? "Sometimes I envy the paper pushers."

"You'd lose your mind."

"One more all-nighter and I might lose my mind

anyway." Then: "It doesn't make any sense to me. If CASECS wants to go public next month, why wipe out the old specimens?"

"The DOD's got Saperstein's ass to the wall. It isn't CASECS that wants to clear the slate. They've got nothing to do with it." She put her hands through her hair and looked up. "Besides, they were smart about it. They did the lobbying first. They got the Alzheimer's lobby, the cancer lobby, the MS lobby—everyone's lining up. They're going to go at it from the direction of public interest."

Hearing God's name was like a wind. It made Lyra shiver.

The man came down off the porch. For minutes, he and the woman said nothing. He smoked. She picked at something on her pants.

Then she looked up. "You know Saperstein's supposed to be ribbon-cutting in Philadelphia on Tuesday."

The man coughed a laugh. "Bad timing."

"Sure is. Danner told me that UPenn might disinvite him. The students are rioting. They want the name Haven stripped off the goddamn water fountains."

"They don't know the half of it."

"Sure. That's the whole problem."

The man shook his head. "Count no man lucky till he's dead, right?"

They were quiet for a bit, and Lyra was terrified they would hear her heartbeat, which was knocking hollowly in her throat. Then the man spoke up again. "You ever think it's wrong? Making them in the first place?"

Though her face was still a cutaway of shadow and light, the woman's posture changed, as if she were hoping the idea would simply slide right off her. "No worse than anything else," she said. "No worse than the air strikes last year—how many civilians killed? No worse than shooting soldiers up with LSD to watch what happens. No worse than thousands of kids slaving to make those sneakers you like. The world runs on misery. Just as long as it's not ours, right?"

"Just as long as it's not ours," he echoed. Then: "Those shoes aren't stupid, by the way. They're classics."

Lyra didn't know how the woman would have responded, because a car was approaching. Tires crunched on the gravel, and a sweep of headlights appeared. The man put out a second cigarette and stood up, dusting himself off, neatening his cuffs as if he were there for an interview.

Lyra recognized Rick's car from the sound the engine made, a growl-spit that Rick was always complaining about. She hoped he would see the strangers and know what she knew, and turn around. Regular people knew so much and yet so little; they had never been taught to scent danger the way she had, to smell the metallic sharpening of tension on the air, the same odor as an approaching scalpel.

He didn't turn around. He cut the engine and climbed out of the car. "What do you want?" was the first thing he said, and Lyra's stomach tightened. You did not speak to Power like that. Power spoke to you.

The man responded, with exacting politeness, "Mr. Harliss?" But Lyra wasn't deceived. At Haven, Dr. Good Morning always spoke gently, and asked questions in just that kind of voice. But he liked to find all the replicas' weak spots—their poorly healed scars, their new abrasions—and plumb them with his fingers, as if manually drawing out the pain.

Then he would take notes on the way they screamed. Private research, he called it. To see whether their brains experienced sensation the same way.

Rick said nothing. He concentrated on feeding a cigarette from his pack to his mouth. Now it was the woman who tried. "Are you Rick Harliss?"

"Depends on who's asking."

"We're detectives with the county PD. We're investigating a pattern of B and Es and we have reason to believe your daughter"—she pretended to consult a piece of paper, or maybe she really did—"Brandy-Nicole, may have been a witness on the latest scene. We need to speak with her."

There was a long, heavy silence. "Bullshit," Rick said finally.

This was obviously not the answer they had expected. "Excuse me?" the man said.

"You heard me. Bullshit." Rick got a cigarette lit, came a little closer, and blew a long plume of smoke directly in the man's face. Lyra couldn't have come up with the words herself, but in that moment a strong web of feeling knitted together in her chest, and she came as close to loving him as she ever would. "Who sent you?"

There was another short silence. When the man spoke again, his voice was harder, and Lyra felt the impact of the words like little metal hammer blows to the base of her spine.

"You violated parole. You were caught with an illegal handgun. You assaulted a police officer. You jumped bail."

"I didn't jump bail," Harliss said. "They let me go."

"Our records say you jumped bail. That makes you a fug-i-tive." He drew out the syllables, stretching them taffylike between his teeth and his tongue.

Rick froze with his cigarette halfway to his mouth. Then, to her surprise, he started to laugh. But the noise was awful, and reminded Lyra of the way Nurse Don't-Even-Think-About-It used to cough up phlegm when her allergies were bad.

"Shit. He turned on me, didn't he? Fucking Ives. Piece

of shit. Well. It's my fault for trusting him."

"We need the kids, Mr. Harliss. Where are they?"

"Fucked if I know." He took another long drag and spoke with smoke ribboning out from the corners of his mouth. "You don't believe me?"

"We don't want any trouble."

"Neither do I. But it sure as shit seems to find me." He shook his head. The light was a lurid yellow, and in its glow he looked exhausted, washed out, like an old photograph. "I don't know where they are, I'm telling you. The boy took off sometime last night. Stole a thousand dollars out of a lockbox from the impound lot and made off with it. As far as I know, he hopped a plane to Mexico."

"With no ID?"

"You can buy IDs, same as you can buy anything else. Ain't nothing and no one in this world isn't for sale. But you know all about that, don't you?" He smiled narrowly, through another mouthful of smoke.

"Careful," the woman said. But Lyra could no longer follow their conversation, or the shifting currents of insult and threat that eddied around their spoken words. Caelum was gone. Caelum had stolen money and run off. She knew both that it was impossible—he would never leave her—and that it was true. It explained why he had consented to the job in the first place, and the bed he hadn't disturbed last night, and why he still wasn't home.

He had done what he did at Haven: he'd split.

"And the girl?" the woman said. But at that moment, Tank, the fluffy white dog Angie Finch kept in lot 34, started to yap, and Angie Finch's voice, thick with sleep, hushed him sharply. Something thinned on the air; Lyra had the impression of a drawstring cinched suddenly tight, squeezing out the possibility of escape.

"Look, why don't you come with us, get in the car, come on and talk about it," the man said—in that fake lullaby voice, the kind Dr. Good Morning used when he was knuckling new bruises until the pain sharpened to a kind of obliteration.

"I ain't going nowhere with you," Rick said. His voice had changed too, and Lyra heard the warning in it. He took a last drag of his cigarette, fanning his fingers, making a show of it. "Not unless you make me. And I can kick up a pretty big scene."

He flicked the butt. Lyra watched it flash the distance between them, spinning through the web of old shrubbery—by bad luck it landed on her foot, a half inch from the sandal strap that would have protected her.

She swallowed a short cry, shuffling backward and disturbing a rustle of old leaves. Both strangers whipped around—and for a second, before she retreated farther into the shadows, she could swear that Rick's eyes landed on her. Or maybe he only sensed her presence.

She sat there, sweating in the darkness, stomach cramping from an agony of fear.

The woman took a step in her direction. "You hear that? Something moved back there."

"I wouldn't, if I were you." Rick's voice was louder now, and froze the woman before she could come any closer. Lyra could see, now, the woman's heavy jaw and penciled-in eyebrows, her hair showing its real color at the roots. "Not if you like your fingers. Had a lot of problems with coons these last few weeks. Had to shoot one myself. Rabid."

Now she was sure he'd seen her. It was a lie. They'd had no trouble with raccoons, other than catching one rooting around in the garbage can one time they forgot to put the lid on overnight. Caelum had chased it off by shouting.

Angie Finch's dog was barking again. Angie's voice was muffled by the trailer walls. "Shut up, you filthy animal!"

"Look," Rick said. "I don't know where they went. Like I told you, they could be halfway to Mexico. If you want to find them, you're wasting your time talking to me."

The woman seized on this. "You think they're together?"

Rick scowled. "I'm done talking," he said, as if they'd

caught him out in some kind of lie. She understood it was all an act. A show, so they would leave, so Lyra would have a chance to escape.

The strangers exchanged a look. The man cleared his throat. "You know what I think?" He didn't wait for Rick to answer. "I think you're hiding something."

Rick said nothing. Lyra searched his face for the resemblance or the history he'd promised her was there, the story where she was a baby, loved, swaddled, wanted. But she couldn't find it.

Still, for the first time ever, she had the urge to call him *father.* She wanted to tell him to run.

"We can help you," the woman said. "Get those charges in Florida dropped once and for all. Clear your record, even."

Rick appeared to be thinking about it. He gnawed the inside of his cheek.

"She isn't your baby girl anymore," the woman said softly. "It was a terrible thing that happened to her. Terrible. But all those kids raised out there on that island . . . they're all screwed up in the head. They're made all wrong. They're dangerous. You understand that, don't you? They're putting good people in danger."

"She would never hurt anybody," Rick said—but weakly, as if he wasn't totally convinced.

And he was wrong, anyway. Several times in the past

few weeks, Rick had walked her out behind lot 40, where someone had pinned paper targets to a rotting fence, and shown her how to shoot his gun. She had seen the guards aiming at waterbirds for target practice back at Haven, and had even heard some of the other replicas boast about trying it out for themselves—some of the male guards would let them do that, hold and fire guns, for exchanges Lyra understood only distantly. Haven was, in a way, like a large-scale replica of the minds it had grown: things needed to be neatly locked away, certain areas inaccessible, the whole place kept clean and bright and orderly so it could function at all.

Rick told her she was a good shot. She liked to imagine Dr. Good Morning's smile wrapped around the aluminum of a beer can. She tried to picture God pinned to her targets, but whenever she did, her hand faltered. He was cruel and he had filled her with disease. He had done terrible things.

But he was still her God.

"She doesn't have to want to. She's sick. She's got a bad sickness inside her. If word gets out . . ." The woman shook her head. "Can you imagine the panic? Can you imagine the protests, the violence?"

Rick stood there some more, acting out his uncertainty. Finally, he said, "All right. All right. I'll come with you. But you gotta help me out, okay? I'm talking clean slate."

"That's a promise," the woman said, and the lie was like a long metal tongue, something smooth and slick and easy. When, Lyra wondered, did people learn to lie, so often and so well?

She wanted to scream, *Don't go.* But it was too late. He was getting into their car already.

The woman got behind the wheel, and the man took the passenger seat. Just a few seconds, and they might as well never have been there at all. Headlights dazzled Lyra as the car reversed. She was seized by the sudden memory of lying flat on an observation table, disembodied voices and hands touching her. She could see her father's face, framed briefly in the car window, and the sweep his eyes made as they looked for her again in the darkness.

A sudden panic overwhelmed her: wrong, wrong, wrong. It was like the alarm that had gone off during the Code Black, except this time the sound was inside her, in her chest, shaking her lungs. She had barely thought about Jake Witz and how she and Caelum had found him hanging from a door with a belt around his throat, but now she did; she saw Rick's face in place of Jake's, his skin a mottled purple and his eyes enormous with fluid. She had seen many corpses in her life, had watched countless replicas bundled and packaged onto the freight barge for disposal, but Jake's was different. Rick would die too, she knew that. That was what Power was—to decide who lived and who didn't.

Dad. The word rose in her chest, and pushed the breath from her lungs with its weight. *Dad.* She thought of running after the car, rocketing out from the shadows, and offering herself in his place.

But she stayed where she was. The taillights dimmed and then disappeared, and the growl of the engine quieted to a purr, and finally became the soft tutting of the crickets, singing endlessly from ten thousand hidden places.

Inside the trailer, everything looked the same way it always did. The warped mirror and the framed needlepoint *Home Is Where the Heart Is* were in place. The TV was still on. An open can of soda had left rings on the old wood coffee table, and next to the sofa the makeshift curtains were still drawn around Caelum's mattress.

He might have been sleeping. He might have been only moments from strolling through the door, wearing a salvaged T-shirt and jeans that hung below his hipbones, showing off the muscles, like wings, above his waistband.

She had traced those muscles with her fingers. She had licked them to know the taste.

She wanted to scream, to break something. Now she understood the replicas who spent hours knocking their heads against the walls, or who picked all the skin off their arms.

Rick was gone. He was as good as dead, and it was her fault.

Caelum had left her.

Was she still the same person without him? Who *was* she? Brandy-Nicole? Lyra? 24? Someone or something else entirely? She touched her face, her breasts, her thighs. She didn't seem to have cracked anywhere. Nothing had broken off. And yet she felt that something *had* broken, that there was a big gaping hole somewhere inside her, and air blowing through it.

She knelt on his sheets and put her face to his pillow. It smelled like him. She took the shoe box and carefully laid out the belongings he'd collected, placing them side by side on the mattress, as if they were runes and by some magic she might call him back. The brochure from the Nashville Elvis Festival. Bus schedule. A receipt. The plastic wrapper that had enclosed a utility knife. Several miniature Snickers, uneaten. Old batteries.

And then she blinked and the objects blinked too and became something else, something meaningful: not trash but a sentence written earnestly and urgently, just for her.

She smoothed out the receipt and read the list of things he had purchased from Able Hardware: one utility knife, one pocketknife, one flashlight and four packs of AA batteries, a butane lighter, a can opener. The bus schedule was from something called the Knoxville Transit Center. Her heart jumped. Someone had circled all the buses running between Knoxville and Nashville for Caelum.

Caelum had left her. That was true. Probably, like he'd

said, he thought she didn't want him around. He thought she'd be better off without him. But he'd also left her clues, just in case, and they all pointed to Nashville, where another God named Elvis had made hundreds of replicas.

Caelum had gone home, and she was going home with him.

FIVE

IT DIDN'T TAKE HER LONG to pack. There wasn't much she owned, and almost all of it had been owned by others first and would, she assumed, be owned by new people later: a bright-pink sweatshirt, a pair of sneakers and one pair of flip-flops, three T-shirts. Even the backpack Rick had purchased for her, red nylon and blotchy with old stains, was doodled over with someone else's notes and pictures, like a skin covered with faded tattoos. But she was careful to pack all the belongings she'd found, all the things she'd salvaged from the dirt: pens, metal soda tabs, loose coins.

She debated whether to bring Rick's gun with her, in case the man and woman—Suits, even if they had been dressed casually—caught up. But after weighing it in her hand, the metal oily like a slick of pollution, she put it back. She was afraid not that she wouldn't be able to use it, but that she would. That she wouldn't be able to stop.

Maybe, she thought, the strangers who'd taken Rick away were right. Maybe all the replicas were broken. Maybe they didn't have souls, like the nurses had always said. Maybe they were like the shells that Cassiopeia had sometimes collected, abandoned by whatever had once lived inside of them, full of nothing but a hollow rushing.

But if Caelum was broken, then she was broken in the same way. And she didn't know much, but she knew that had to count for something.

She was eager to set out as soon as possible, but her body was heavy with exhaustion and waves of dizziness kept tumbling her. She meant to close her eyes just for a minute, to catch her breath, to get her strength back, but woke up hours later in a panic, just as the sun was poking through the sagging blinds. Dawn already.

She shouldered her backpack and slipped outside, fiddling with the door handle, which was loose, to lock it. It gave her a brief pain to think of what would happen to the trailer with no one there to care for it: soon, she knew, it would be reclaimed by squatters, and the other residents of Winston-Able would strip it of its good furniture and sheets and dishware. Or they would gray the walls with cigarette smoke and carpet the floor with a surface of broken bottles, like in lot 48, where people went to get drunk and worse.

But she let this worry slip away from her, like a kind of smoke. She had learned long ago to let things go, to let them pass, to allow all her worry and hurt and need to simply drift, cloudlike, until it had left her behind.

Tank was barking, as usual, as if he knew where she was heading and wanted to be sure she didn't get there. She turned in the direction of the highway. She would cross through the truck weigh station again and have to pass Eagle Tire. She hoped she wouldn't see Raina but had no idea how long parties lasted. One time she had woken up at dawn after the Haven Christmas party to the sound of laughter and the crack of gunfire: a few doctors and some of the guards were taking turns hurling bottles and trying to shoot them in midair.

She heard a familiar voice call her name, but knew she must be imagining it: sometimes, in her dreams, she heard Dr. O'Donnell call her voice in just that way. Only the second time did she notice a sharpness to the voice that didn't sound like dream or memory—and didn't sound like Dr. O'Donnell, either.

She turned and saw Gemma and Pete. Gemma, flushed and pretty, was wearing clothes that struck her as exotic and reminded her of some of the birds that landed, occasionally, on Spruce Island: elaborately colored, sleek, showy.

"What are you doing here?" Lyra asked them. She

thought Gemma's house was far away, but she couldn't be sure. The journey from Florida to North Carolina, the meeting between Rick Harliss and Gemma's parents—seeing parents up close, even—was a hole all of its own. She felt if she got too close to the edge, she might fall into a place that had no bottom.

"You're in danger," Pete said. "The people who killed Jake Witz are tracking you and Caelum. They're probably on their way now."

"I know," Lyra said. She thought of Rick, and the way his eyes had swept the dark for her, trying to latch on. She thought of his pink scalp and his blunt fingers and his slow, shy smile, all of it soon to be reduced to nothing but skin cells and decomposition. A long rope of hatred coiled around her throat. "They were here already."

Gemma was sweating. "Is Caelum . . . ?"

"Gone." Lyra hated to hear the word out loud. It was like something rattling inside an empty tin can.

Gemma closed her eyes and opened them slowly, as if she was trying to pry herself out of a dream. "They—they got him?"

"He was already gone." She thought of telling Gemma and Pete where he had gone—that there might be others like them, free, and living happily in Nashville—but she was afraid that they would discourage her and that saying the words out loud would burst them like small bubbles, and make her see how silly she was to hope.

"I saw them come, and I hid until they left."

"They'll be back. They'll be back any second. You have to come with us."

"I can't," Lyra said. "Thank you. I'll be careful." She knew they were trying to help. Rick had taught her to say thank you, like he'd taught her to say please, to look people directly in the eyes and say hello, too.

She turned and started off again, but before she had gone four feet, Gemma called her back.

"Wait." Gemma's face looked unexpectedly altered, her eyes startlingly bright, as if they'd grown. "What do you mean, you *can't*?"

"And where's Caelum?" Pete's whole face was pinched with exhaustion, as if someone had sewn his skin on too tight. "Where did he go?"

"Home," Lyra said, and ignored the way Gemma and Pete looked at each other. She knew they couldn't understand. The world had grown too big. She had to shrink it back to manageable size, back to the slender weight of the secrets that she and Caelum could carry together. "I'm going after him."

"I don't think you understand." Gemma was trying to be nice. Lyra knew that. But her voice was razor sharp, as if at any second it would fall off an edge into hard anger. "The people who came here won't just quit. They'll look until they find you, wherever you are."

"They're looking for *Caelum* and me," she said. "They

won't expect us to split up. And they won't expect us to get far. They don't think we're smart enough." She thought of the way the nurses and doctors had always spoken over their heads, had avoided their eyes, had joked and laughed about things in the outside world—never understanding that Lyra had been listening, learning, *absorbing.* And it struck her as funny, now: they hadn't thought to watch what they said because they believed they had complete power over her. But as a result, their power had become hers. She'd eaten just enough to survive. "Besides, what other choice do we have?"

Lyra could tell that Gemma knew, immediately, that there were no other choices. Still, she said, "You could come with us. We could drive you somewhere far away. Maine. The Oregon coast. Canada. Wherever." Places that made Lyra feel uncertain again. Places she'd never heard of.

"Not without Caelum," she said. Caelum was a person, but he was a place, too. He was her place.

"You'll never find him," Gemma said. "Do you know how many people there are in this country? Millions and millions."

Lyra knew her numbers up to the hundreds, because there had been nearly twenty-four hundred replicas at Haven. But she didn't know what *millions* was. "You just said the people who came from Haven will find *us*."

"That's different. They're bigger than we are. Do you

understand that? They have cars. They have drones, and money, and friends everywhere."

Lyra was surprised to realize she felt sorry for Gemma. Gemma was so desperate to help. She didn't understand that Lyra and Caelum were beyond reach. They belonged to a different world.

"You forget what they made us to be, though." Lyra spoke gently. And then: "Invisible."

She managed to smile. Smiling had always felt strange, but now it was getting easier. "Thank you, though. I mean it."

"Please. Take this, at least." Gemma dug in her pocket and found a small wallet that was covered in a repeating yellow graphic of smiling faces. Lyra was momentarily breathless when Gemma handed it to her. It was the most beautiful thing she'd ever seen or held, its plastic slick and new-feeling, bulky with whatever it contained. She wanted to smell it, to nibble on its edges. "You'll need money. You know how to use an ATM card, right, to get money? The code's easy. Four-four-one-one. Can you remember that?"

She nodded. She had had to remember numbers for Cog Testing—words, too—and parrot them back for the proctors. She knew now that they had been testing the progression of prion disease, but at the time she had thought they only wanted to prove how smart the replicas had grown. She only wanted to do well.

"Thanks," she said. She couldn't bring herself to decline it. Already, the plastic wallet had warmed in her hand, pulsing there as if it belonged. She took a step forward, overwhelmed by feeling, and, before she could decide against it, brought her hands to Gemma's shoulders the way Rick had for her. Gemma's face reminded her so much of Cassiopeia in that moment that she felt an unexpected doubling of her life before and after. She was two Lyras and she was no one: she was a hole falling through the past. "See you," she said, stepping quickly away, because for a split second a terrible urge possessed her to hang on, to stay with her hands on Gemma's shoulders and never let go—an urge she thought she'd been rid of long ago.

She turned away. She knew she'd never see them again. Let go. It was surprisingly difficult to walk, to *keep* walking, as if the air was throwing up extra resistance. But there was no other choice. Let go. It was the rule that bound everything, as true in the outside world as it had been in Haven.

Let go, let go, let go. She thought of wind through the trees, and laundered white sheets, and the warm fog of anesthetic. Let go. She thought of clouds and shadows and waves; she thought of the ocean, bearing away a boat filled with the small bundled bodies of the dead.

SIX

LYRA KNEW FROM THE BUS schedule that Caelum was heading to Knoxville, and from there to Nashville. She knew that Knoxville was a large city less than an hour away by car, because that was where Raina's mom worked at a twenty-four-hour restaurant called Big Tony's.

But she didn't know how to get there. The first person she saw, a guy unloading cartons from a grocery truck, pointed her in the right direction and even offered her a ride. But she didn't like the way he looked at her. "Can't walk all the way to Knoxville," he'd called out, when she kept going.

The next person she asked, a woman counting change behind the gas station counter, told her she couldn't get to Knoxville without a car. But a third person had overheard the exchange and told Lyra, outside, that she thought there was a local bus station that had buses to Knoxville.

She was black, with very red lipstick, and so tall the light haloed behind her, as if she were cracking the sky with her head. She smelled like Dr. O'Donnell had, like lemon soap, very clean. Lyra thanked her and kept going.

It was a seven-mile walk along a bleak industrial road that kept edging close to the interstate and then away again. Stanton Falls was bigger than Ronchowoa but she didn't know by how much. She knew she was in town when she began to pass occasional strip malls of mostly shuttered stores. She saw a boat shop, too—funnily enough, since she had no idea where the nearest water was—with little motorboats displayed in the brown grass and covered with tarps. She couldn't have said what drew her across the yard and to the display, only perhaps that it reminded her of where she'd first met Caelum, in an overgrown section of Spruce Island, littered with old waste.

One of the tarps had been loosened and retied. She saw that right away. She tugged it free and knew that someone had slept there. On one of the benches the treads of a dirty sneaker had left marks. There was a crumpled Snickers wrapper, too, wedged between two seat cushions. Probably Caelum had arrived too early, before the bus was running, and had lain down to sleep for a bit.

She was catching up.

But in Knoxville, she lost hope again. Knoxville was by far the biggest place she'd ever been, full of so many people she couldn't understand how there was enough air to allow them to breathe, and the clamor of noise made the back of her teeth ache. Faces, faces everywhere—all of them looked the same to her.

The Knoxville Transit Center was huge, all glass and concrete and escalators rolling up and down, the loudness and the lights, and the *womp, womp, womp* of her own heart, like a fist punching her in the chest.

A man shoved her. A woman yelled at her for standing motionless in front of the revolving doors, unsure of how they worked. There were people in lines as if waiting to get medication, and big machines grinding out slips of paper, and numbers on big boards that blinked and changed, dozens of TVs, words everywhere, signs everywhere, the smell of sweat and perfume and bathrooms.

She found a bus after twice standing in the wrong line, and was handed a ticket and told by the girl who sold it to her that next time she could do it through the automated system and also that she had cool hair. "I went short for a while too," she said, "until my mom said she would boot me from the house." This gave Lyra a boost, however, as it always did when she went out into the world, into people, and *passed*.

Because at heart and despite what Raina or Rick thought, she knew the truth now: she wasn't one of them and would never be.

She had to wait because the bus wasn't ready to board.

She counted how many people wore red hats, and how many people wore black ones. She tried to close her ears to the unfamiliar voices, dozens of conversations that together sounded like the grinding work of one large machine, all stutters and beeps and sharp, hysterical alarms. Whenever an individual voice reached her, she was reminded of how the researchers had spoken, moving in packs down the halls as if they were cabled together invisibly, using English but somehow an English she didn't understand. A man sitting next to her on the bench picked dirt from his fingernails with a pen cap, and spoke in words that made her head ache for their foreignness. *Can't fault Walsh on that snap . . . you watch and see, Seattle'll blow holes in their defensive line. . . .*

Holes. She closed her eyes; she breathed carefully through her nose. She'd believed for a long time that the outside world might be as big as ten times Haven, and after escaping she knew it had to be at least ten times that. But a bigger vision was impossible. What she knew of Tennessee was Ronchowoa, and the walk to the Target and back, and the Winston-Able Mobile Home Park, and its grid of sixty-two lots.

In the end, she only knew the bus had arrived when a loudspeaker voice announced that it was getting ready to leave, and she had to run to the far end of the terminal, barely gasping through the doors before they shut behind her with a hiss that sounded ominous.

She lurched into a seat just as it began to move. The blur of landscape still made her dizzy. She leaned back, clutching the schedule she'd been given in one hand. It was already wet, damp with sweat. Three and a half hours to Nashville, with one stop at Crossville to pick up new passengers.

She got sick in the tiny, filthy bathroom once, twice, a third time, until nothing came up but bile. She couldn't rinse her mouth out. There was no water to drink. So she wiped her mouth with a sleeve, toweled off her face with a hem. An old woman seated near the bathroom shook her head and frowned, as if Lyra had gotten sick deliberately, when Lyra made her way carefully back to her seat. But she felt better. She was even a little bit hungry.

In Crossville, there was a layover of twenty minutes, and the passengers disembarked to use the bathrooms and buy food from the station. Lyra was feeling a little braver, so she showed the bank card Gemma had given her to a woman across the aisle.

"I need money," she said, since Gemma had said that was what the card did.

The woman gave her a strange look. "Well, there's an ATM right over by the bathrooms," she said.

Lyra shook her head to show she didn't know what that meant.

The woman squinted, moved her gum around in her mouth. "It's your card, isn't it? You've got a code?"

"Four-four-one-one," Lyra recited, and the woman put up her hands to cover her ears, laughing.

"Whoa, whoa, whoa. You're not supposed to say it out loud." She put her hands down again, and her son thought it was a game, placed his hands to his ears and down again, said, "Whoa, whoa, whoa," and cackled.

"Please," Lyra said, getting desperate now. The bus would leave in twenty minutes. She was hungry—she had not had anything to eat in twenty-four hours—and the station smelled like frying meat fat, like the Stew Pot in Haven but better. "I need money."

The woman let out a *shush* of air, like the sound when SqueezeMe had finished hugging. "Come on. I'll help you." She took Lyra's arm, exactly where SqueezeMe would have in order to read her blood pressure. Her hair was gray and brown, both. Otherwise, she looked a little like Dr. O'Donnell.

When they left Crossville, the bus was more crowded than ever, and Lyra's heart stopped when she saw that among the passengers was a replica like the kind she had seen in the Nashville Elvis Festival brochure: a slick of black hair and dark sunglasses, plus the same beautiful white jumpsuit with beading that caught the sun. She was desperate to ask him questions, but felt too shy; he was traveling with a large group and spent the whole time chattering with the other travelers, or crooning along to songs the bus driver piped from the speakers. At one point he stood, staggering a little to keep his balance, and danced along to the music, pivoting his hips and holding a soda bottle like a microphone. Everyone laughed and even applauded, and Lyra felt a vague sense of foreboding. It wasn't real. It couldn't be.

She was even more discouraged when the bus driver announced their arrival in Nashville. She had been hoping that Nashville would look like Haven: an orderly series of buildings contained by a fence. Instead, it turned out to be a city: stack-block buildings, signs puncturing the sky, roads like the serpentine trails left on the surface of the marshes by passing water snakes, the slow crawl of traffic. More people. Perhaps the world didn't end at all. Perhaps it went on and on forever. It occurred to her that if she didn't find Caelum, she wasn't even sure how she'd get back to Winston-Able, couldn't remember what bus line she had taken to Knoxville.

But maybe it didn't matter. Now that she knew the people from Haven were looking for her at Winston-Able, now that they had taken Rick away, she couldn't return anyway.

She followed the line of passengers off the bus, trying to work up the courage to speak to the man in the clean white suit. He moved quickly with a surge of other travelers toward the station doors, and she knew that as soon as he hit the street, she risked losing him. She was sure that she would find Caelum wherever the replicas were heading, and so she took a deep breath and jogged to catch up, with her backpack slamming against her lower spine and echoing the rhythm of her heart. She had to say *please* several times before he turned around. The people with him—regular people, none of them replicas, but none of them dressed as nurses or doctors, either—turned with him. Under the weight of their stares, Lyra felt suddenly shy.

"What's the matter, little lady?" he said. He had a deep voice that rumbled in his chest. "You want an autograph or something?"

She knew what an autograph was—it was when a doctor put down his signature on a piece of paper. The nurses were always asking the doctors to autograph one thing or another: disposal orders, cognitive evaluations, the reports generated by the Extraordinary Kissable Graph. This gave her confidence.

"No autograph," she said. "I'm looking for all the others."

"You're here for the festival, huh? You an Elvis fan?"

Raina had said that Elvis was the name of their God. "I need to speak to him," she said, which made the others laugh.

"Isn't she sweet," one of them said.

But another one frowned. "I hope she ain't on her own. She's too young for it."

The replica with the dark hair inched his sunglasses down his nose. "You want to talk to Elvis, do you?" he asked, and she nodded. "Come on. Let me show you something. Come on," he said, and gestured for her to follow him out the revolving door, into the bright afternoon sunshine, and the wet-tongue heat. In the distance, she could hear the faint roar of a crowd, like the break of ocean waves, and a cascade of music.

"You want to talk to Elvis, little lady, you just close your eyes and listen," the male said. "You hear that? That's Elvis talking, right there. You just gotta follow the music."

SEVEN

LYRA DID AS SHE WAS told. She set off toward the music, and when she got lost, she simply closed her eyes and listened for the drumbeat rhythm of applause, and the crackle of distant speakers, and turned right or left. She wondered whether Caelum had been here, had waited at the crosswalk for the light to turn green as she was waiting, had thought of her or worried about her or wondered whether she would follow.

The streets grew more crowded and funneled a mass of people down toward the music. Colored flyers fluttered from the lampposts. People drank in the streets and leaned over the balconies of their high-rises to wave. Lyra was overwhelmed by the crush of people, by the blur of strange faces and a celebratory atmosphere she couldn't understand. Was this another party? She had yet to see any more replicas. The music picked up the tempo of her heart and knocked it hard and fast against her ribs.

Then she turned a corner and saw them: hundreds of identical men milling around a stage elevated in the center of the plaza, all with the same oil-black hair and sideburns and sunglasses, many of them dressed the same, too, in heeled boots and spangly white uniforms. She cried out without meaning to, filled with a sudden, cataclysmic joy.

Replicas. Hundreds of them. Alive, healthy, drinking from red plastic cups, posing for photographs with eager tourists.

But then she got closer, and her heart dropped. She saw at once she'd been mistaken. The men weren't identical at all. Some were fat, some were dark, others were pale. There were even women among them, with sideburns pasted to their skin that in places had begun to unpeel. They weren't replicas at all—they were simply regular people, costumed to look the same, for reasons she couldn't understand.

The disappointment was so heavy she could hardly breathe. All of a sudden she felt trapped—squeezed to death in the vast open space by the pressure of all the strangers around her, by the chaos of so many unfamiliar things. Speakers blew feedback into periodic screeches. Laughter sounded like explosions. The air stank of fried food and sweat. Caelum must have come here, and seen what she had seen. But where would he have gone afterward? He could have wandered in any direction. He could have left Nashville entirely.

She would never find him now.

She was suddenly dizzy. Turning to move out of the crowd, she stumbled.

"Whoa. Take it easy, there, lady. Are you okay?" A woman squinted at her and her dark wig—that's what it was, a wig—shifted forward an inch on her forehead. "You need some water or something?"

Lyra wrenched away from her. She was hot. She couldn't think. She hadn't been afraid at all, not when she believed that in Nashville she would find more replicas. But now she was panicked, and her mouth flooded with the taste of sick. *Do you have any idea how many people there are in this country?* Gemma had asked.

You'll never find him, she had said.

She hardly knew where she was going. She just knew she had to get out, away from the noise, away from the music and the crowds. She was desperately thirsty, and whatever energy had carried her this far had abandoned her all at once.

She crossed a scrubby parking lot to a 7-Eleven, stepping onto the curb to avoid two boys smoking outside their car—when, just like that, in the space between one second and the next, she saw him.

Or not him, exactly, but a picture of him, taped to the

window of the 7-Eleven.

The picture wasn't very good, and most of his features were obscured. But it was definitely him. She recognized the hooded sweatshirt he was wearing, which they'd found together at the clothes-by-the-pound thrift store Rick had taken them to when they'd first arrived at Winston-Able Mobile Home Park.

There were words on the page, but she had to blink several times to make them come into focus.

Smile! You're on candid camera.
Thieves will be photographed, shamed,
and prosecuted. Just like this one!

She didn't know what *prosecuted* meant. But she knew what a thief was. Had Caelum stolen something? Was he in trouble?

Suddenly, on the other side of the window, a man's face appeared: an ancient face, tufted with hair in strange places, and eyebrows that ran to meet each other above the nose. She took a quick step backward before remembering there was glass that separated them.

"In or out?" he said. His breath misted the window, and his voice was faintly muffled. "Or you just going to stand there gaping?"

"I . . ." Before Lyra could think of an answer, he'd

turned, shaking his head, and stumped back toward the cash register. She followed him. Inside, the air smelled like a shoe box. Several customers stood at the counter, waiting to have items scanned. She detached Caelum's photograph from the window where it had been hung. The old man scowled when she approached him with it.

"Hello," Lyra said.

A guy so skinny his head looked inflated blinked at her. "There's a line," he said.

Lyra ignored him and spoke directly to the man behind the counter. "I know him," she said, and placed the picture of Caelum down on the counter.

The man just kept running items past the scanner. "That boy is a thief, young lady," he said. "Tried to lift a package of jerky and a Coca-Cola, right from under my nose. I been in this business a long time. I know a bad seed when I see one." He glared at Lyra as if to say that he was looking at one right that very second.

"Sorry," she said—a default word of hers, a word that had always helped at Haven with the nurses and doctors. *Sorry I made too much noise. Sorry I'm in the way. Sorry I breathe, that I'm here, sorry I have eyes, sorry I exist.* "I'm looking for him. That's what I mean. I need to find him."

"You should stay far away from him, is what I think," the old man said. He'd finished ringing up the skinny guy and gestured the next customer forward.

"Please," Lyra said. Her palms were sweating. The overhead lights were very bright. Remembering the lie Rick had coached her on, she added, "He's my cousin."

The old man shook his head again. But this time, his voice was a little softer. "I'm not in the business of giving handouts, young lady," he said. "It's a store. Not a church. Besides, if I'd let him get away with it, who's to say someone else couldn't just waltz on in here and strip the place?"

"Do you know where he went?" she asked. Fortunately, her voice didn't shake. She had gotten very good at that, at hiding, at burying things deep inside of her.

The old man blinked at her as if she'd just appeared. "Where do you think he went?" he said, scowling again. "The cops took him down to the station. And if I were you, young lady, I wouldn't hurry to bail him out."

EIGHT

IT WAS EASY ENOUGH, IT turned out, to find a police station, even if you had no idea where you were going. All you had to do, Lyra discovered, was start walking—and eventually, when it started to get dark, the police would find *you*.

She walked down a long street empty of cars. Lyra couldn't exactly be considered lost, since she did not know where she was going: still, she very definitely did not know where she was.

At some point, it had begun to rain. She crossed an empty playground darkened by shattered floodlights. Next to the swings, several guys paused to watch her, the happy rhythm of their conversation abruptly silenced. A woman with a big metal cart piled with plastic bags wheeled slowly down the sidewalk, her feet swollen with rags instead of shoes. Lyra saw a rat picking at trash bags piled on the street, and the gutters were knotty with empty bottles and old sandwich wrappers and cigarette packs.

She had been walking for at least an hour, wondering whether she would recognize a police station if she saw it, and if so, whether she would have the courage to go inside it, when a dark sedan pulled up beside her.

"Are you all right?" A man leaned over to squint through the passenger-side window. His skin was very dark, and his hair was threaded with gray. He was wearing a dark suit.

Lyra's immediate thought was to run. She knew sedans, knew the look of the Suits who drove them, knew that they carried smiles along with their guns. But she was trapped: he could easily follow her if she took off running down the block, and there was nowhere to hide, and no possibility of cutting across a nearby park that was hemmed in by a tall chain-link fence.

"This isn't a good place for you to be walking this late," the man said. Lyra backed up, shivering, until the fence punched her between the shoulder blades. She wondered if she should scream. But who would help?

"Hey." The man's voice got softer. "It's all right. I only want to make sure you're safe out here." Then: "It's okay. You're not in any trouble."

Lyra was confused by the tone of his voice—none of

the Suits had ever spoken to her like that, or looked at her the way he was, as if his eyes were something warm he wanted to give her. And he hadn't come at her with a gun or tried to force her into the car.

Maybe, then, he wasn't a Suit.

Still, Lyra was frozen. The man didn't move, or get out of the car. He just sat there, looking at her, his face touched with light from a streetlamp on the corner.

"Do you speak English?" he asked. And then: *"¿Habla español?"* Then: "My name is Detective Reinhardt. I work with the Nashville Police Department."

Finally, Lyra eased her weight off the fence. She was positive, now, that he hadn't been sent to find her. And she had to be brave, if she was going to find Caelum, which meant she had to believe him.

She hesitated. "I was looking for a police station," she said finally.

He stared at her a second longer. "Get in," he said, and opened the door.

His car was very clean, which relaxed her. A picture of three girls was mounted to the dashboard, and when they passed beneath a streetlamp, she saw two of them were identical and felt a kind of ecstatic relief: twins, she knew, not replicas, but still it seemed like a sign. The other girl looked older, and she had the policeman's long nose and the same enormous eyes. She wore a bright-red headband and had her arms looped around the twins. Her eyes were closed and she was laughing.

He saw her looking. "The twins are my nieces, my sister's kids. Jamie and Madison. And that's my daughter, Alyssia," he said, thumbing the girl in the middle of the photograph. "An old photo. She's in college now."

"She's pretty," Lyra said.

He smiled. "Don't I know it," he said. He had a little bit of an accent, like Nurse Curly, who'd come from a place named Georgia. "What's your name?" he asked.

"Gemma Ives," she lied quickly. Before leaving Haven she hadn't been a good liar, but this was a skill, she'd rapidly learned, that most humans had perfected; it was necessary to lie, living in the human world.

"Nice to meet you, Gemma Ives," he said. His eyes were big enough to root her in place: as if he wasn't just seeing her, but absorbing everything about her, her past and even her future. "You can call me Kevin."

"Detective Kevin Reinhardt," she recited, and he laughed.

"Just Kevin is fine, like I said."

Lyra was glad that his suit was rumpled, and smelled like soft old wool. Not sharp, like the suits the military men and women wore when they came. "Why don't you wear a uniform?" she blurted out.

He smiled. "I'm a detective," he said. "We travel under the radar."

Lyra nodded, though she didn't know what a detective

did, exactly. But she was glad he wasn't in uniform. Uniforms made her think of Haven and its guards, of the soldiers who'd pursued them out on the marshes. *You know how expensive these things are to make?*

"Now," Detective Kevin Reinhardt said, "why don't you tell me what you need a police station for?"

She wasn't used to being spoken to in that tone, as if she might have something valuable to say. She told him her cousin had been picked up for stealing.

"You know what precinct got him?" he asked.

She shook her head, and repeated what the man at the 7-Eleven had said: "He tried to lift a package of beef jerky and a can of Coca-Cola. They took him down to the station."

They were stopped at a red light. The policeman turned to look at her again. She felt the way his eyes moved from her hair, still shorter than most of the boys' she had seen since leaving Haven, to her bare arms, to the flimsy backpack with someone else's name written on it in marker.

"You know if you're in trouble, you can tell me," he said, still in that same low and gentle voice, as if he was singing instead of speaking. He wasn't like other police officers she had seen on TV, or even the few she'd encountered since leaving Haven. His face looked as if it had been dimpled permanently into an expression of understanding. "If someone's hurting you, you can just let me know right now, right here, and I'll help you out, and make sure you're safe and no one hurts you again. That's my job."

The darkened city outside their windows was a wash of blue tones and hazy cones of color from the streetlamps; then she realized, to her shock, that her eyes were leaking. That's what they'd called it at Haven. Never crying. *Tear duct inflammation, leaking eyes, overactive lachrymal production. Crying* meant feelings, and the replicas didn't feel, or at least the humans pretended they didn't. Probably that made it easier for them not to feel, either. That way they could do their jobs, draw their paychecks, and sleep soundly.

For a second she fantasized about telling Detective Kevin Reinhardt everything: about all the pills and medications and lies, the harvesting procedures and the testing and the MRIs, the small prions, deformed like bits of melted plastic, whirring through her blood and bone marrow. In the end, what came out was half-truth.

"I'm sick," she said. "I'm dying. My cousin takes care of me. He's the only person in the world who does."

"What about your parents?" the policeman asked. "Where are they?"

She thought of Rick and the dry skin around his mouth, the way he squinted through his cigarette smoke when they were target shooting. The smell of hot dogs and frozen soup. She thought of Dr. O'Donnell, her blond hair like a vaporous haze barely clinging to her head. She thought of Cassiopeia bleeding out in the marshes, of the Yellow crop bundled up for disposal, of Jake Witz hanging by his own belt.

"My parents are dead," she answered. "Everyone's dead. We came all the way from Florida on our own."

"Florida," he repeated. "Must have been a long trip."

"It was." Suddenly, she couldn't stop talking. Words skittered off her tongue like insects trying to beat a path home before they were trampled. "We lived on a small island and saw all the same people every day. There was water everywhere, in all directions. And alligators that lived in the marshes. There was a fence—" She sucked in a quick breath. She'd nearly revealed too much. "There was a fence to keep them out." She looked down at her hands, surprised at how badly she actually *missed* Haven. "There were birds there. Lots of birds. More birds than people."

"It sounds like a beautiful place," Detective Kevin Reinhardt said, and turned off the car engine. They had arrived somewhere she assumed was a police station: a one-story brick building, and big windows through which more police in uniform were visible. "How old are you?"

This lie came easily, too. "Twenty-one," she said,

because she had learned from Raina that this was a magic age, even if she didn't quite understand why. Raina had complained about not being twenty-one yet, about all the bars and concerts and parties that were twenty-one and over, about getting kicked out of someplace for not being twenty-one, so Lyra figured that once you turned twenty-one you got special rights to exist.

"My niece had brain cancer," he said finally. "Jamie, the one in the picture. Took her when she was fourteen years old. Cancer's what you're sick with, isn't it? But there are clinics. Treatments. You should be under the care of a doctor."

"I am," Lyra said. "That's where I'm heading. To UPenn in Philadelphia. To see my doctor." As soon as she said it, she knew it was exactly what they had to do.

Lyra and Caelum had been wrong about Nashville. There was no God here. Which meant they had only one option left: they had to find their original God.

They would ask him to help. They would *demand* it.

Detective Reinhardt's relief was obvious. She could almost smell it coming off him, like a particular odor of sweat. "My daughter almost went to UPenn. Opted for Columbia instead. Philadelphia's a great city. I know a guy at UPenn Hospital." He looked at her sideways. "Who's your doctor up there?"

This time, Lyra couldn't think fast enough to lie. She

said, "Dr. Saperstein," hoping he wouldn't recognize the name. Luckily, he didn't appear to.

He just gave her a quick pat on the knee. "I'll take care of your cousin, don't you worry. No one's going to jail for wanting a soda, all right? You just leave it to me."

They got out of the car. A rush of black overtook Lyra when she stood up. The rain had turned to a heavy, hot vapor that hung in the air. Who knew what would happen to her once she followed Detective Kevin Reinhardt inside? He seemed okay, but the doctors and nurses at Haven had seemed okay, and all the time they'd been filling her up with disease, tending not her but the disease inside that would eventually sweep away her memories and her words, seize her arms and legs, numb her throat until she couldn't swallow.

Still, she followed Detective Reinhardt inside, shy in the sudden brightness. Police officers wove between a jigsaw puzzle of wooden desks. The room stank of old coffee and new ink. A phone seemed to ring every five seconds.

"Don't be shy, now." Detective Reinhardt put a hand on her shoulder when she hesitated in the doorway. "You go on and get comfortable and I'll be back in a hurry. Now, what did you say your cousin's name was again?"

Lyra froze. She pictured her mind as a series of computer monitors, all of them darkened at once by a power surge. There was no way Caelum would have given his real name. But she couldn't think of the name he would have invented.

But she was lucky. Finally, she was lucky. Because even as she hesitated, she heard someone shout.

Turning, she saw Caelum rising from a plastic chair to greet her, trying as hard as he could not to smile, not to *grin*, and failing totally, so they stood together twenty-five feet apart in a police station in Nashville, Tennessee, at nine p.m. on a Sunday, and laughed.

NINE

DETECTIVE KEVIN REINHARDT KEPT HIS word and made sure that no charges were filed against Caelum. By the time he announced that Caelum was free to go, it was nearly midnight, and Lyra had fallen asleep in one of the plastic chairs in the waiting room with her head on Caelum's shoulder, directly beneath a large framed poster of the singer named Elvis she had originally mistaken for another Dr. Saperstein.

Detective Reinhardt volunteered to drive them back to the Greyhound bus station, although he warned them it was likely the buses to Philadelphia wouldn't run until morning and that the neighborhood was a bad place to go wandering. Lyra told him they planned to wait inside the station, that they didn't mind spending the night on the floor.

"You got somewhere to stay once you get up to Philly?"

he asked them, once they arrived at the station. "You got friends up there? People you know?"

"Oh, sure," Lyra said. "Lots of people. It'll be just like home to us."

It wasn't exactly a lie. Lyra had told Caelum that they would find God there, at a place called UPenn.

It was a slim hope—Dr. Saperstein might simply put them in a cage, as he had done back in Haven—but their only one. He had filled Lyra with sickness. He might, she thought, be able to remove it.

"You need help or run into trouble, you just give me a call," he said, and gave her a small white card with his name printed on it, and more numbers she now knew must connect to his telephone. "I want you to study that number. Memorize it, okay? Promise me."

Lyra nodded, overwhelmed. Other than Gemma, Detective Reinhardt was the first person to give her a number, his number, to call. She felt, holding the card, as if she were holding something fragile, something sacred and beautiful.

She blinked to clear her eyes of tears and watched the numbers sharpen and flow into a pattern, make a sentence in her mind. "I promise," she said.

Climbing out of the car, however, she felt a strong pull of dread. She thought again of Jake Witz; of finding him swinging from a doorjamb, his face swollen and discolored, and the cleanup crew who'd come afterward to make sure that no one would ask questions. He, too, had offered help. Rick had helped, and she was sure that by now the people who'd taken him in their car had murdered him.

She hoped this man, Detective Kevin Reinhardt, wouldn't end up hanging from a rope.

It was by then after midnight, and no buses would run for hours. Several people lumped on the benches to sleep might have been distant rock formations. It was quiet, and still, except for an old man pacing and muttering darkly to himself.

She wanted to ask Caelum why he had gone off without her, but she was worried about what his answer would be. Besides, she felt sick again. A seesaw was starting in the bottom of her stomach, back and forth, back and forth, slowly tossing acid up in the back of her throat.

They went in search of ginger ale: the vending machine at the station was out of everything but Coke. At Haven, she had had ginger ale regularly, because along with the antinausea drugs that got delivered orally or piped in through an IV, the nurses distributed warm ginger ale in small paper cups. The taste of ginger ale reminded her in equal measure of Dr. O'Donnell and of the Box, and so she loved and hated it, also in equal measure.

Nothing was open this late. They kept walking. Lyra's

legs felt strange and sticky, as if they were made of metal that had rusted. She was exhausted. Her relief at being reunited with Caelum only made her aware of how lost she would have been without him; it wasn't, therefore, exactly relief. Though Detective Reinhardt had said it was a bad place to walk, she felt that with Caelum next to her, nothing bad could ever happen again. But several blocks from the bus station, Lyra became aware of a change in the shadows around them, a subtle rearrangement of the nighttime noise of that foreign city.

They were being followed. They'd been herded, actually. Unconsciously trying to outpace the voices even before they knew what the voices meant, they had wound up on a narrow one-way street that contained nothing but a shuttered auto-parts supply store and a vacant warehouse.

Before Lyra had a chance to warn Caelum, they were surrounded. Five men, not much older than Caelum was, and one girl who hung back, keeping her eyes on her phone. The light from the screen made strange shadows on her face.

The five boys tossed Lyra's backpack and took the wallet Gemma had given Lyra, which held Gemma's bank cards and all of her money. But what really made Lyra angry was the way they scattered her stuff: the bottle caps and old plastic bags filled with clinging browning plant matter and coins and a rusted pin shaped like an apple, all the things she'd collected and cared for at Winston-Able.

"You a trash lady or something?" one of them said, and hurled away a pen, her favorite pen, its end deformed by chewing.

They made fun of Caelum for the knife he carried—"You need more than a pair of tweezers, you swag around here like we're supposed to know you"—and insisted he hand over his money (stolen, Lyra knew, from the cash box at work) and even his belt, which one of the boys wanted. Caelum did what they said without a word. Still, Lyra could feel anger like heat ticking off him, subtle waves of it that made her light-headed.

When one of the guys moved to touch Lyra's cheek, Caelum began to growl. At first the boys thought this was funny, and they laughed.

"Look at this guy. He's like a cat or something." A second guy stepped forward and tried to push Caelum.

Quickly, even as a passing car threw light briefly onto the brick wall behind them and then darkness crowded in after it, Caelum changed. He was a person and then he was something less, something animal and old. He lunged, snapping his teeth.

The guy wrenched his wrist away, finally. "Freaks," he said. Though Caelum and Lyra were drastically outnumbered, the power had shifted. "Freaks," he said again, and when he met Lyra's eyes, he looked afraid. "Come on. Let's get the fuck out of here."

After they were gone, Lyra bent to retrieve her scattered belongings. But she couldn't distinguish her things, her special things, from the trash in the gutter, little knobby strangers that meant nothing to her—snub-nosed cigarette butts, tongues of gum stuck to their wrappers.

"Are you all right?" Caelum asked her. It was practically the first thing he had said to her directly since they'd laughed together like idiots in the police station.

She didn't answer him. She was nauseous, and tired, and they had nowhere to sleep, and no money to buy a bus ticket, either. She hated the group of boys who'd followed them and laughingly upended her backpack to shake her things into the gutter. She hated the girl who stood there with her eyes stuck to her phone screen, the girl who couldn't even be bothered to look. How could they be people the same way that Detective Reinhardt and Gemma and her friend April were people? The difference between people and replicas was one of ownership. Real people owned, and they took, and replicas *were* owned. A difference of action and object.

"Lyra," Caelum said, when she didn't answer. How to sort out her things from the flow of human waste? Where did all these things come from, and who was discarding them so easily? It seemed to Lyra that the whole human world was built on waste, and trash, and things manufactured just so that they could be tossed out afterward. She couldn't save it all. She could never rescue everything.

"Lyra, please. Talk to me."

"You left without me." It wasn't what she had been planning to say, but once the words were out of her mouth, she knew that she was still furious at him. "You were just going to leave me behind. You didn't even say good-bye."

"I thought I was doing you a favor," Caelum said. "You seemed happy."

"I was happy because we were together," she said. "I thought we would always be together, at least until . . ." She found she couldn't think about her sickness. She couldn't say the words out loud. At Haven, death had never seemed particularly scary. It was a bald, natural fact, like the transformation of food through the digestive tract. Replicas were born, they got sick, they died, their bodies were bundled and burned. Someday she would be ash sifting through the ocean waves, to be consumed by half-blind deepwater fish.

"I'm sorry." He knelt so she had no choice but to look at him. "I didn't want to leave you. I didn't," he said, reaching out to touch her face, so she couldn't turn away. He placed a hand on the back of her neck, and her body responded, as it always did, as if she were something hollow—a husk, a leaf—and he the wind lifting it. "I thought it would be best. I thought I was protecting you."

Another passing car threw up a quick wedge of light. Caelum looked so beautiful it was almost painful. She was relieved when the darkness chased the car away again.

She stood up. "What are we going to do now?" They had nothing of any value, and Lyra knew by now that everything in the real world cost money. You needed money to eat, and money to sleep, and money even to use the bathroom in public places, which were *for patrons only.* Caelum was quiet. "We'll find a way," he said.

"What if Dr. Saperstein won't help us?"

Caelum's smile was as thin as a razor. "We'll make him."

They backtracked to the station, thirsty now, and moneyless, and ticketless. They hunched down in a dark alcove near the men's bathroom, with its smell of armpits and old urine, and waited for morning to come.

Lyra balled her pink sweatshirt up beneath her head for a pillow. She closed her eyes and felt the nausea rise and fall like a swell of water, and she was scared. She pictured her own body like a night sky, a web of black tissue, and small disease cells burning like stars inside it; she closed her eyes and saw instead of darkness a blinding light, the compression of all that light, all that energy, into a single blazing explosion.

She woke up swallowing a scream that came up in the toilet with splatter. In her vomit: small comet trails of blood.

Whether she made it to Philadelphia or not, she was running out of time.

PART II

TEN

BARELY SIX HOURS AFTER HE let the skinny girl, Gemma Ives, and her cousin off at the Greyhound station—regretting, on the one hand, not keeping them for more questioning, and on the other hand himself exhausted, eager to believe that they were indeed heading to see someone who could help her, that they were not just two more junkies busing toward their next high—the police commissioner in Nashville, Sarah Rhys, called Detective Kevin Reinhardt's supervisor, Captain Basher, to say that Mr. and Mrs. Ives would be coming by the station.

The day before, Gemma Ives's debit card had been used to purchase a one-way ticket to Nashville from the Knoxville Transit Center, and hours later she'd withdrawn two hundred dollars from an ATM at a rest stop in Crossville, suggesting she had, indeed, boarded a bus. It had been less than the requisite forty-eight hours since Mr. Ives's daughter had gone missing. Nonetheless, Rhys was issuing an Amber Alert: the girl wasn't yet eighteen years old.

She was thought, perhaps, to be traveling with a boy.

Detective Reinhardt knocked his chair over in his hurry. He didn't even double-check the girl's likeness: her parents had sent the Crossville PD a series of photographic attachments, and Crossville had forwarded them on. Buses started running at six a.m. But she might still be there, he might have time to catch her, she needed sleep, there was still time. . . .

"Where you going with your pants on fire?" Officer Cader was checking her teeth in her computer monitor, working a fingernail between her incisors.

Christ. He should have been a dentist.

He should have been a bus driver.

He should have been something, *anything* else.

He was already through the revolving doors, into air swollen and thick with the promise of more rain, and sprinting to the car, thinking there was still time to catch her.

He plunged through the revolving doors at 6:17 a.m. exactly—record time—into the echo chamber of cell phone conversations and squeaky-soled sneakers, into a colorful foam of faces and rolling luggage. Any other person would have been overwhelmed, but Detective Reinhardt had been a cop for a long time, and his dad had been a cop, and his uncle was a cop, and so was his cousin

Rebecca. So he looked not where all the color and sound was but where it wasn't: the negative spaces, the empty corners and hallways and alcoves that regular people were trained to ignore.

His eyes leapt over the crowd. He let himself drift. He released the station so that it floated away from him, like a boat unmoored from the shore. The girl, the funny soft-spoken kid with the eyes made slightly bulbous from being too thin and the bright-red backpack, was the only thing he could have clipped onto.

Nothing. Nothing. Nothing.

"Now boarding, Gate 3, 405 north to Boston."

And then: a glimpse of red, a flash of platinum-blond hair, a girl who moved like she was drifting.

Almost at once, the crowd re-formed and he lost sight of her. It didn't matter. He was shoving his way through the funnel of people churning toward the gates, swirling around the big departures board.

Someone stepped in front of him, and Reinhardt nearly went down over the wheels of a hideous green faux-alligator suitcase. The man looked outraged, as if it were an actual alligator and Reinhardt had just trampled its tail.

Only then did the loudspeaker voice touch his consciousness.

"Now boarding, Gate 3, 405 north, destination Boston, with stops in Washington, Philadelphia, and New York . . ."

ELEVEN

"NOW BOARDING, GATE 3, 405 *north, destination Boston, with stops in Washington, Philadelphia, and New York . . .*"

Lyra came awake to a booming electronic voice. A cop was frowning down at her.

"Can't sleep here," he said. He had to speak loudly above the echo of so many voices. Spokes of sun, a blur of people holding briefcases, women in sneakers that went *squeak-squeak* and reminded her of the nurses, children shouting.

She got to her feet, leaning hard against the wall for support. Caelum was gone. Standing, she was even taller than the police officer. Sweat dampened her underarms, and she could smell herself.

The cop squinted at her. "You all right?"

"Fine," she said quickly. Her voice sounded like it had

been chewed up. "Just waiting for my bus."

He nodded as if he didn't quite believe it but moved off anyway. She stood there breathing hard—even the effort of standing had made her dizzy—and tried to think. She couldn't remember why she was there, only that Caelum had been with her and now he was missing. The pattern of travelers was dizzying. Strangers threshed the lights into shadow patterns. A gigantic clock on the wall with tapered iron hands pointed to 6:09. She was going to be sick again.

She closed her eyes and leaned her forehead against the wall, grateful for the coolness of the stone. *Think.* But she couldn't think. She couldn't remember a thing. Images came to her in flashes: Detective Reinhardt's big cow eyes, throwing up in the toilet, the veins of blood.

When she opened her eyes again, she thought for a moment, through the thick haze of sun, she even saw him moving through the shifting crowd of travelers. But then the pattern changed shape and instead she spotted Caelum, dodging the crowd without appearing to notice anyone else.

"Here," he said, when he reached her. He was holding a paper bag. From it, he produced a can of ginger ale. Cold.

"I thought you'd gone," she blurted out. She lowered her mouth to the soda can, sucking along its rim, comforted by the taste of metal. This was a Haven taste, of tongue depressors and tubes behind the throat, even of Thermoscan, though that had been made of plastic.

He just shook his head. He looked happier than she'd seen him in a month. "I bought us tickets, too. The bus is boarding." She remembered now, dimly: those boys moving out of the dark, an impression of wet mouths and the harsh birdlike cries of their laughter. She remembered kneeling in the gutter, trying to sort out her things from the collection of trash.

"How?" she asked.

He shrugged. "I told you I was going to get our money back," he said. "And I did. Some of it, anyway."

She still didn't understand. She could hardly remember what they looked like: to her they now seemed a blur, their faces eaten up by shadows, and all their mouths identical and grinning. "You found those boys from last night?" she asked, but knew immediately, from his face, that wasn't what he meant.

He took her free hand, pressing something into her palm. She opened her hand and found a battered leather wallet. She saw a flash of wadded bills before he took it back again.

"They're all the same, Lyra," he said. "That's what you have to understand. Even the ones who say they'll help are the same."

Her head was pulsing, like the rubber pump of a stethoscope when it was squeezed.

"You stole it," she said.

"They took from us," he said. "So I took back from them."

It was wrong to steal. Lyra knew that. Once Calliope, one of Cassiopeia's genotypes, had stolen a cell phone from the nurses' break room. Even though they'd found it tucked inside Calliope's pillowcase, Nurse Swineherd had insisted that *all* of her genotypes be punished. Privately, Lyra believed that that was when number 8 had gone so soft in the head, that maybe she'd been knocked too many times. Although the truth was that she had always been smaller than the others, and much dumber, too, so maybe she'd simply been born that way.

Caelum was right: Why should they have to give so much, and never take anything in return?

If everyone believed they were monsters, shouldn't they at least be allowed to have teeth?

She could feel Caelum watching her, felt a question hanging between them like a very fine curtain of fabric. 6:20 now.

"Last call, Gate 3, 405 north, destination Boston, with stops in Washington, Philadelphia, and on to New York . . ."

She looked up. The curtain parted. "We better hurry," she said, "if we want to catch the bus."

They slipped easily through gaps in the kaleidoscope of people, like rats, like shadows. All the people Lyra passed did look the same. Their skin and hair and jaws began to blur into a smear of indistinguishable color, into people who were simply not like them.

But then, for half a second, her eyes snagged again on a vision of Detective Reinhardt pushing frantically through the crowd. This time, she was sure she hadn't imagined him.

She nearly lifted a hand to wave.

But then Caelum took her hand in his, and together they sprinted the rest of the way to the bus, slipping inside just as the doors were closing.

TWELVE

LYRA AND CAELUM ARRIVED IN Philadelphia just after eleven p.m., and still a crush of people poured with them into the station. Every time she thought she must have seen all the people there were in the world, all the buildings and cars, they kept coming: it was a little like watching distant waves in the Gulf of Mexico, as she had sometimes done at Haven, to see the way each wave in fact hauled dozens, hundreds, thousands more on its back.

Lyra knew that Dr. Saperstein was going to speak on Tuesday at a place called UPenn—that was what the people who had taken Rick Harliss away had said. She had been keeping careful track of the days, as Rick had taught her to, and knew that they were a day early. Still, she was nervous.

Remembering how helpful Detective Reinhardt had been, Lyra suggested that they ask a police officer for directions. Caelum was less certain—the day before, he'd been shunted between holding cells, and desks, and grim-looking officers for hours, waiting to be booked—but after two hours of wandering, he finally agreed.

They circled back to the bus station, where there were plenty of cops. But the first one just shook his head.

"If you're here for the protests," he said, "you'd be better off just turning right around. This country's got bigger things to worry about, and we've had guys down there clearing the roads for two days. Besides," he added, narrowing his eyes, "it's almost midnight. Don't you have somewhere to be?"

The second one, a woman with her hair in tight braids, like Dr. Fine-Yes had worn back at Haven, just stared at Lyra for a long time, up and down, as if her eyes were a broom and Lyra a bunch of dust.

"How old are you, honey?" she asked, and Lyra grabbed Caelum's hand and hurried away without answering.

By then, Lyra was too tired to continue: exhaustion kept rolling up and crashing over her, hauling her down into brief, blinking moments of darkness, so she would come alert and realize she didn't remember crossing a park, or she didn't know how they'd ended up inside a neon-bright restaurant that sold hamburgers flattened like palms.

They found a Motel 6. They had no ID, since Lyra's

wallet had been stolen, but the desk clerk just shrugged and handed over a key anyway.

"No smoking in the rooms," he called out after them. "I'm serious."

In the room was a carpet the color of vomit, and ancient wallpaper that still exhaled the smell of old cigarettes and booze, two twin beds and an old, blocky TV, a bathroom where mold inched between tiles and decals on the tub floor peeled like brittle leaves. It was the prettiest room Lyra had ever seen, except for the one in the little white house where they'd first been taken by Gemma—she couldn't believe how big it was, how spacious, that it was all theirs for the night. How many rooms, she thought, must there be in the world: How many rooms like this one, folded across the vast space of the world, pretty and quiet and safe, with doors that locked? It was a beautiful idea.

She showered first, taking her time, letting herself imagine that her body didn't belong to her at all, that it was just an object, a broken-down chair or a table full of surface cracks, and that she herself was somewhere different, that she would not be affected if her body gave out entirely or was discarded. Afterward she stood in the cloudy bathroom, listening to the muffled noise of the TV from the bedroom, feeling suddenly nervous. She had been with Caelum countless times in vacant trailers and behind the supply shed, and played a game of kissing each other's scars, and the thin, fragile skin on the inside of the elbows and the back of the knees. But that was in the dark, at Winston-Able, in a room musty with spiderwebs and the smell of bike tires. That was washing up accidentally somewhere, and clinging to each other because there was nowhere else to go.

This was different.

She knotted a towel around her chest. Before Caelum could even turn to look at her, she'd slipped into the bed closest to the bathroom, shivering when the cold sheets touched her bare skin. She pulled the covers to her chin.

"Are you finished?" he asked, and she saw his eyes move down to her shape beneath the blanket, and this made her shiver, too.

The drumming of the shower in the bathroom, the murmur of TV voices—soon she was asleep, falling off the edge of sound into quiet.

She woke to movement, the rustle of sheets and the sudden touch of cold air. She'd fallen asleep in her towel, and she was cold. The lights were off, and the TV was off, and it was quiet except for the faint hum of an air conditioner. For one disoriented second, she didn't know where Caelum was: she had a vague sense of his outline standing beside her, watching her sleep.

"What are you—?" she started to say, but then Caelum

was sliding in next to her in bed, naturally, as if there was no other place to be. He looped a heavy arm across her waist. He wasn't wearing a shirt, only a thin pair of boxer shorts. She could feel his chest rising and falling, his breath on her cheek, his anklebones when he moved, and immediately she wasn't cold anymore. She was burning hot.

"Lyra?" he whispered, but before she could say *what*, he put his mouth against her neck. Then she realized that it hadn't been a question after all. He found a gap in the towel and slid his hand to her stomach. He touched the architecture of her hips. He moved a hand, carefully, gently, between her thighs. "Lyra, Lyra, Lyra," he said again, singsonging it, as if he were learning how to speak through saying her name.

She wasn't a human. She wasn't a replica. She was a star trail, burning through the darkness, lighting up the room in invisible spectrums of color.

"Caelum," she said, turning over to him, and opening her mouth to his, letting him pour this new language inside of her, letting it transform them together into music.

THIRTEEN

IN THE MORNING THEY SHOWERED together, soapy, touching each other with slick-fish fingers, filled with the joy of the new. They packed their few belongings, and Lyra took a pen from the nightstand. She left behind the Bible she found there; she associated it too much with Nurse Don't-Even-Think-About-It, with quick and blinding sideswipes to the head.

They had better luck than the day before. The desk clerk didn't even blink when they asked for directions to UPenn. She just slid a paper map across the desk and charted the best route with a little ink line.

"It's a hike, though," she said. "You might want to Uber."

Lyra just thanked her and said a quick good-bye.

It *was* a hike: an hour of slogging next to a sluggish gray river and a grid of barely flowing traffic. Lyra marveled at the look of the houses on the river, enormous and colorful, in a style she had never seen before. Caelum puzzled over the map, charting their progress carefully, inching a finger along the ink pathway when Lyra read out the names of the streets they were passing.

Finally, when his finger was almost directly above the little star indicating they had arrived, Lyra saw something that took her breath away. A group of boys and girls came toward her, singing. There were so many of them that Lyra and Caelum had to step off the sidewalk to avoid being bumped.

"Caelum," she said, and pointed.

Several of them wore T-shirts marked with a logo she recognized. An electric thrill traveled her whole body. *The University of Pennsylvania*. Lyra knew it. Caelum knew it. Everyone at Haven knew it.

It was a place both Dr. Haven and Dr. Saperstein had come from. The bust in the entryway of admin wore a blanket bearing the same logo for a cape. On certain days, certain *game* days, God went into his office and didn't come out. Sometimes the staff members drank beer on those days, carted from the mainland in coolers on the boats, and sat for longer than usual in front of the TVs, watching sporting events whose rules Lyra didn't understand.

"UPenn," she said out loud, and began to laugh as

the group of strangers raised their fists and shouted, "Go Quakers." Finally, she understood: UPenn meant the University of Pennsylvania, where both of the Gods of Haven had started.

Where the second God, Dr. Saperstein, was soon due to return—and where she and Caelum would be waiting for him.

She'd assumed that UPenn was a single place, almost like Haven, that had produced both Richard Haven and Dr. Saperstein. But once again the outside world smashed itself into a thousand different visions, into dozens of buildings, hundreds of people, noise and color and rhythms she didn't understand.

Kids sat cross-legged with homemade signs in front of the looming stone buildings, chanting. Others, ignoring them, lay out on blankets in the grass or played a game that involved a flat plastic disk and lots of running.

"I don't understand where they all come from," Caelum said, and she knew exactly what he meant: How could all these people have been made if not on purpose?

"Come on," she said, and took his hand. Caelum was agitated by the crowds. She remembered, suddenly, seeing an eclipse when she was younger, how the nurses had let them file out into the garden to look. Caelum became like that when he was nervous, like something dark that swallowed the light around him.

Lyra was anxious too. The swell of voices from every direction made her head hurt. The blur of colors reminded her of the starbursts that crowded her vision when, stretched out on the examination table, she looked too long at the ceiling lights. If Dr. Saperstein was here, did that mean that other people from Haven were here, too? Guards with guns? People like the ones who had killed Jake Witz, and had come most recently for Rick Harliss?

To her surprise, the first person they approached didn't hesitate when they asked whether she knew where to find Dr. Saperstein.

"He's not coming," the girl said. She was wearing lots of rings, and violet eye shadow that made Lyra think of Raina, and of the strange party where people stood in the half-dark together and also somehow alone, like the individual patches of land submerged in the marshes that only from a distance looked like solid ground. "I mean, they haven't officially announced it yet, but he won't."

Lyra's palms began to sweat. "What do you mean?" she said, and repeated as faithfully as possible what she had overheard. "He was supposed to be here Tuesday, for the ribbon-cutting."

"Yeah, but that's probably not happening either. Have you been to the protests? There's, like, two thousand people outside."

"Where?" Caelum asked.

"Over by the Haven Center. Or *whatever* they're calling it now." The girl rolled her eyes. When she saw that Lyra and Caelum had no idea what she was talking about, she sighed. "Next to the medical school and PCAM. You know where PCAM is, right? The Perelman Center for Advanced Medicine? It's right next to the Haven Center. You can't miss it, it's right on Civic Center. You students here, or incoming?"

Lyra said nothing.

"Well, you'll get a real view of Penn, anyway. Protesters and crusty alums and all. Whose side are you on?" She smiled in a way that might not have been friendly.

"No one's side," Lyra said, though she had no idea what the girl meant.

At the same time, Caelum said, "Our own side," and squeezed Lyra's hand even tighter.

They found PCAM and the medical school—an enormous modern complex, all steel and glass, which reminded Lyra of the real Haven—and next to it, the brand-new Richard C. Haven Center for Regenerative Research.

"He was here," Lyra whispered excitedly. "The first God was *here*."

It seemed impossible that God, the first God, could have existed here, so many hundreds of miles away from Spruce Island. That here, too, in this busy city, he'd put a thumb in the soft clay of reality, he'd existed, people knew his name.

If there were a single place in the world where she would find help, it had to be here, where the Gods of Haven would be once again reunited.

Despite the crowd gathered in front of it, the building itself had the whistling, empty look of an abandoned shell. The revolving glass doors were roped off behind a thick red ribbon, and Lyra's heart picked up—this, then, must be the ribbon Dr. Saperstein was expected to cut. But the podium positioned directly in front of the doors stayed empty, the microphone crooked uselessly toward the open air, like a finger beckoning to no one. Police sawhorses kept the crowd a safe distance from the building.

Hundreds of people eddied around the steps, blocking the entrance. Lyra kept hold of Caelum's hand—she wasn't sure she would have been able to loose herself, he was squeezing so tight—as they edged along the periphery of the crowd, puzzling over what it meant. From the fact that the girl with the violet eye shadow had asked them whether they were students, she now knew this must be a school. Maybe this was simply how schools looked, how teaching took place.

Many of the students carried signs that said *Not Our Penn*, *Take Haven to Hell*, *Penn Students for Awareness*. Others waved school flags, or carried signs that said *Penn Pride* or *Penn Students for Science*.

Between the two groups there was obvious tension. A makeshift line divided them, like the finger of an invisible current had divided the crowd in two, and as they watched, two boys began pushing each other and one of them ended up on the ground, his glasses shattered.

Finally, she worked up the courage to ask a girl what all the shouting was about.

The girl, red-faced and sweaty, wearing mismatching shoes and thick glasses, was resting on a stone wall with a cardboard sign tucked between her legs. Because of the way it was angled, Lyra couldn't read what it said.

"You go here?" She squinted at Lyra and Caelum in turn, and when they shook their heads, seemed to relax. "Oh. I was gonna say. What *planet* are you from?" She bent down to retrieve her sign, propping it on the wall next to her. This one said *Not Our Penn.*

Lyra tried a different tack. "Do you know where to find Dr. Saperstein?" she asked. The sun was too bright. In its glow she felt as if all her holes were visible, all the defects in her brain obvious.

"Oh, the ceremony's off for sure. They're just too spinecheese to tell us. You heard about what happened in Florida, right? I mean, you're not *actually* from Mars?"

"Don't be a dick, Jo." This came from a boy sitting next to her.

"Florida." Lyra swallowed. "You mean what happened at the Haven Institute?"

The girl, Jo, nodded. "Richard Haven was a professor

here, like, a million years ago. He's been dead for, like, a whole decade." She paused to let this settle in. "Anyway, he went off and made fuck-you money doing biotech and who knows what, and he bought his name onto this building."

"It wasn't biotech," the boy said. "It was pharmaceutical stuff."

"No one knows what it was, and that's the point. No oversight. Typical one percent stuff, too big to fail. And Saperstein's just as bad." That she addressed to the boy, and he raised both hands. "Anyway"—she turned back to Lyra and Caelum, exhaling heavily, so her bangs moved across her sticky forehead—"the Florida meltdown is, like, the worst environmental catastrophe *ever.*"

"Since the BP spill, at least," the boy chimed in.

"Since the BP spill, for *sure.*" Jo glared at him. "There are clouds of pollution, like seriously chemical clouds, practically *poisoning* everyone within eighty miles—"

"Not eighty miles," the boy put in mildly. "You're exaggerating."

The girl didn't seem to hear him. She was getting worked up now. Her glasses kept slipping. Every few seconds, she thumbed them higher on her nose. "They're saying there might be generational damage, plus it turns out Saperstein was *completely* skirting federal regulations, they're saying he was *cloning* people. . . ."

"*One* person is saying that," the boy interrupted her again, and nudged her. "Didn't your mom ever tell you not to believe everything you read on the internet?"

Finally, she turned on him. "Whose side are you on, anyway?" He shrugged and went quiet, picking at a pimple on his chin. "The point is"—she said, rolling her eyes—"I'm premed, and I don't want this guy's name on our buildings. How about Marie Curie? How about a *woman*? Richard Haven doesn't represent me. Not my Penn." She pointed to her sign.

"But where is Dr. Saperstein?" Lyra felt increasingly panicked. In the distance, she spotted a man uniformed in dark blue, wearing mirrored sunglasses: a guard, sent to collect her. Then he was gone, dissipated in the sweeping motions of the crowd, and afterward she wasn't sure whether she'd imagined him.

Jo blinked at her. "I told you. He's not coming. He'll be lucky if he doesn't end up in jail."

"Thank you." Lyra remembered, just barely, to say it. Thinking of Rick, and the way he'd tried to teach her about manners, and how to talk to people, brought on an unexpected spasm of pain.

They turned away from the girl and her sign. Then Caelum pivoted suddenly.

"He *was* making clones," Caelum said.

Both the girl and the boy stared.

"I'm one of them," he said. "I'm number 72."

"Ha-ha," the girl said flatly. An ant was tracking across her sign. She frowned, took it up between two fingers, and squeezed.

In the short time they'd been speaking to Jo, the crowd had grown even denser. Now the protest spilled up the steps, toppling the sawhorses, and as she watched, several students charged the podium and brought it crashing down. Lyra saw a blur of police uniforms among the crowd and felt suddenly as if she were going to faint. Reality slipped slowly toward darkness.

"We have to get out of here." Caelum sensed the change at the same time: the current had tipped over to one of fury. The crowd seemed to pour into a single roiling mass, like a tight-knit cloud condensing on the horizon.

"He still might come."

"You heard them. He's not coming. He's not—" But Caelum was whipped away from her when people surged suddenly between them, a wall of people pulsing together like an enormous organ, walls of breath and hair and sweaty skin.

Someone grabbed Lyra's wrist, hard. She turned and a scream throttled her, lodging somewhere in her throat.

Though she had seen him only from a distance, in the harsh glare of the floodlight, she recognized him: he was the same man who had come for Rick, but dressed up now like some kind of local security guard. But she would have sworn it was him. She recognized the flatness of his eyes, like the dead stare of a fish.

Are you okay? his mouth was saying. But she couldn't hear the words. Instead, she heard him laughing. She heard the guards on the marshes weeks and weeks ago, laughing as they toed their way through the blood of dying replicas.

You know how expensive these things are to make?

She wrenched away from him. She spun around—she had a brief impression of open mouths and shouting, a boy with blazing eyes shouting at her. A backpack caught her in the chest and she was knocked off balance. She was on the ground. Someone stepped on her fingers. Sneakers and legs, so many bodies—she was momentarily overwhelmed, she couldn't breathe.

Even as a girl reached to help her, the crowd moved. Suddenly everyone was shouting and she couldn't get up. Someone kneed her in the ribs. Through a rift in the crowd, she spotted Caelum, flying at the guy with the backpack. A girl screamed. Caelum was a sudden frenzy of motion; there were three guys fighting him now, and blood on his teeth. As she watched, trying to find the breath to shout, one of the boys caught him on the cheek and then another one on the back of the head, and then a third kneed him in the stomach. Then he was on his knees, spitting up blood, but she couldn't get to him—still they were separated by a hard blade of moving bodies.

Someone hooked Lyra by the elbows and got her to her feet. Air touched her lungs like a burn. She gasped and tears came to her eyes.

"Are you okay?" the guy shouted. He was wearing glasses with only a single lens. She recognized him as the boy who'd gone down before, shoved by someone. He kept a hand on her arm, even as Caelum finally pushed his way toward her. "Animals," the boy kept saying. "You're all *animals*."

Now Lyra could see the guards carving the crowd up, dispersing it. But the man with the dead fish eyes was gone.

Caelum's face was swollen where he'd been hit. Lyra could tell how much pain he must be in. His cheek was cut. One of the guys who'd hit him must have been wearing a ring.

"Goddamn. *Tell* me you aren't prospectives." The boy in glasses looked furious. "Come with me. Let's get out of here before these psychopaths start a riot."

FOURTEEN

HIS NAME WAS SEBASTIAN, AND with his help they elbowed their way free of the crowd. From a distance, it resembled an organic mass, a seething, hungry creature.

Lyra was still having trouble breathing. She kept scanning the street for the man with the fish eyes, or the woman who traveled with him. She felt the weight of invisible observers watching their progress, the way she had always felt the Glass Eyes at Haven.

"Animals," Sebastian said again, when they were several blocks away, and the noise of the chanting had faded. Lyra was surprised that it was still early afternoon, still sunny; that the cars still churned by slowly, that nothing else had stopped.

Caelum hadn't spoken at all. His left eye was swollen shut. When he leaned over and spat up a gob of blood, the boy shook his head.

"You should really get some ice on that. And clean the cut, too, so it doesn't get infected. I'm in med school," he added, in response to a look from Lyra. "If you want, my apartment's right around the corner."

Lyra hadn't exactly recognized it as an invitation until he started walking again and Caelum, to her surprise, followed.

Sebastian lived in a small, bright apartment on the third floor above a sandwich shop. The whole place smelled like the inside of a book. Books sagged the built-in shelves lining the wall. The sun caught thick swaths of dust in the air and striped the room vividly in golden light. She couldn't see anything in the haze of sun.

"My roommate's a lit PhD student," Sebastian said, when he caught Lyra pacing the shelves, running her fingers over the spines. "Can you believe he still reads *paper* books? It's so nineteenth century."

The sun made black spots in Lyra's vision. The room began to turn, slowly, and to stay standing she had to grip the table. Side effects. No. *Symptoms.*

"Do you have a bathroom?" she asked him. Sebastian had so many things it made her dizzy: paper clips and mugs, framed photographs and bundles of wire, coins and little porcelain trays to hold them. She could hear all of it screaming, crying out in neglect; she wanted to open her mouth and swallow the whole room. She wished she could stuff all of his belongings down inside her, like some kind of magical potion that would turn her human, totally human, at last.

Like some kind of magical potion that could make her well.

"Are you all right?" He squinted at her, and for the first time she noticed how nice his clothing was compared to theirs, how well it fit him, how healthy he looked.

"Bathroom," she managed to say again, even as she felt bile biting off the edge of the word, making acid in her throat.

In the bathroom, she turned on the faucets and opened her mouth and let the black come up, waves of sickness that brought with them a sharp antiseptic burn in her throat and Haven's smell. They had failed to find Dr. Saperstein, like they had failed to save Rick Harliss, or Jake Witz, or Cassiopeia in the marshes. Everywhere they went, they had left nothing but death behind them.

And she had nothing but death to look forward to.

She sat back on her heels, waiting for the rise and fall of the room to go still. Her face was wet. She was crying. A green toothbrush with its bristles splayed, tweezers, a scattering of clipped hair, an empty tissue box gathering dust, a straw basket piled with magazines and paperback books. She wanted things. She wanted a phone, an apartment full of books, tall glasses and ice cube trays and mugs for tea hanging from nails beneath the kitchen cabinets. She wanted a space she could fill and fill with her belongings, until no one could touch her, no one could even reach her past all of her beautiful things.

She took a paperback from the basket and opened to inhale its pages. She tore off a piece of paper, and then another, and fed the pieces one by one into her mouth until she felt well enough to stand.

She hadn't brought her backpack to the bathroom and that was a mistake. But she tucked the paperback into her waistband and found her T-shirt concealed it perfectly. She washed her mouth out. She felt better, with those pieces of paper pulsing their small words out from somewhere deep in her chest.

Hers.

Caelum and Sebastian had moved into the kitchen.

"I should have known the whole demonstration would be a disaster," Sebastian was saying. Without his glasses, he was beautiful—not as beautiful as Caelum, but still beautiful. He had dark skin, high cheekbones, and eyes the same color as the afternoon sunlight on the wood floor. "But people never listen to reason. They don't care about facts. They read one think piece in the *Times* and they get hysterical about everything. I swear, you can't even fart on this campus without someone screaming environmental policy at you nowadays. You want some water or something? Beer? I have wine but it's old."

"Water's fine," Lyra and Caelum said, at the same time.

"I'm not a conservative," Sebastian said. He poured water from the tap into tall glasses, and Lyra marveled at how comfortable he was touching everything, as if the whole space was just an extension of his body. "I understand we shouldn't have theaters named after Ponzi scheme billionaires, or slave owners—and in our country, that excludes more people than you'd think. But Richard Haven?"

He shook his head. "His work on stem cell regeneration was pioneering. Do you know he built a lab in his room when he was in elementary school? He isolated his first nucleus when he was *nine*, using a kitchen spatula, basically. I'm exaggerating, but you get the point. He was a genius. You think Steve Jobs made people feel warm and fuzzy? Benjamin Franklin was a total prick, and so was Edison. He *bought* the idea for the lightbulb, by the way. He was basically just the licensor."

He paused to take a breath and Lyra too felt breathless: so many words, ideas, names she'd never heard.

And she realized, then, that that was what being raised at Haven truly meant, and why she would never be entirely human. It wasn't that they'd inserted needles to draw bone marrow or fed her a diet of pills, that they'd called her "it," that she had never been held or cuddled, that her head had been shaved to keep out lice, and small fatal disease cells had been introduced into her muscle tissue just to watch what would happen. She'd been completely torn away from the human timeline, from a vast history of events, achievements, and names spanning more years than she could think of.

She had no context. She was a word on a blank page. There was no way to read meaning into it. No wonder she felt so alone.

"Actually, that was one of the reasons I was hoping that Dr. Saperstein would show up today—other than taking a stand, I mean. I'm interested in medical tech, and I'm curious about the IP aspect. They're saying Cat O'Donnell might be up for a Nobel Prize. But she wouldn't have a career if it weren't for Haven. The whole idea of individual-specific stem cell regeneration . . . It seems obvious now, but that was a revolutionary idea."

The name O'Donnell touched Lyra like the electric zap of the Extraordinary Kissable Graph: one of the machines she'd loved the best at Haven, which read her heartbeats and then drew them, vividly, in climbing green lines and vivid peaks that recalled the mountains she'd seen only on TV.

"You . . . you know Dr. O'Donnell?" she asked.

"I mean, not personally." Sebastian gave her a look she didn't know how to decipher. "I just know her because of what she's doing at CASECS. I heard she used to work with Dr. Saperstein at Haven," he added, almost as an afterthought. "That's why he's suing her. I guess he thinks she stole some of his research. Meanwhile O'Donnell won't say a word about it. Still, pictures never lie."

He pulled out his cell phone and made adjustments to it, tapping and swiping the screen. Then he spun it across the table to her and she lost her breath.

There, in miniature, was Dr. O'Donnell, stepping off one of the trash ferries that used to travel back and forth to Haven. She was wearing regular clothing, and her head was angled toward Dr. Saperstein, who was next to her, but Lyra would have known her just from the geometry of her ear where it joined her jaw, by the color of her hair, by the way her mouth flattened when she thought.

Dr. O'Donnell had given them names from the stars, and so she had given them a whole universe.

And in a single instant, Lyra realized how wrong she had been, how stupid.

Dr. Saperstein wasn't God.

Dr. O'Donnell was.

FIFTEEN

LYRA DIDN'T LIKE TO STEAL from Sebastian. He was nice. He had helped them. He had resurrected Dr. O'Donnell, and shown them where CASECS was, only a short distance away in a place called Allentown.

But she was beginning to understand that those things didn't matter. Whether he was nice or not, he had a phone that she wanted, and so she took it when he wasn't paying attention.

Richard Haven had a whole building. He had his name above beautiful glass doors. And he was not nice.

Being nice didn't matter. Only taking did, the way animals took.

They wouldn't get far, Lyra knew, before Sebastian realized that Lyra had stolen his phone.

But they didn't need to get far. They didn't need distance to disappear.

Being invisible had benefits: it was easy to shoplift, as long as you picked a crowded store (Caelum's mistake in the 7-Eleven had been to steal when there was no one around to deflect the clerk's attention; when he had, for a brief, flaring moment, become visible); to edge a little too close, or lean a little too hard, and come away with a phone or a wallet; to pass into a restaurant and then stand up and leave again before anyone could ask that you pay.

Lyra was now throwing up almost everything she ate, but that was all right, that didn't stop her.

They'd agreed their best chance of getting into CASECS to see Dr. O'Donnell was at night. They were thinking, of course, of Haven's security and of Caelum's escape, which could never have been accomplished during the day. By evening Caelum had two cell phones and a new wallet of his own, plus more than fifty dollars he'd skimmed from the tables of restaurants and cafés, and Lyra had a leather billfold and several credit cards, plus a necklace she'd found coiled at the bottom of a woman's purse when she'd dropped her hand casually down inside it.

Everything she added to her backpack made her feel better, less nauseous, less dizzy. She didn't understand gravity, but she knew intuitively every bit of weight, no matter how small, slowed her, made her mind turn less quickly, made her feel less as if she might drop down into a place where no one could find her.

It wasn't yet dark when they hired a car to take them to Allentown: their first time in a taxi. Though they didn't have an address for CASECS, the driver managed to locate it easily enough on his phone, and told them the route would take roughly an hour and a half in traffic.

Maybe she should have felt bad. Maybe she should have felt sorry for all the things they'd stolen. She wondered whether Sebastian was angry, whether the woman with the bright-pink lips from whom she'd taken the necklace would be sad.

But she didn't feel bad. They were going to see Dr. O'Donnell, and Dr. O'Donnell would make it all better. She was happier than she'd ever been, sitting in a sticky backseat that smelled like bubble gum, her backpack heavy on her lap, Caelum's hand occasionally brushing her thigh, her hand, her shoulder, like a bird exploring the territory. She felt human. Didn't humans, after all, take what they needed? Wasn't that what humans like Dr. Saperstein, like Richard Haven, had always done?

They reached Allentown just as dusk lowered like an eyelid. From one minute to the next, streetlamps blinked on, and buildings lost form and instead became beaded strings of lit windows. They wheeled off the highway into long bleak alleys of car lots, parking garages, blocky office buildings, industrial complexes with names like Allegra Solutions and Enterprise Data. Lyra lowered the window and smelled gasoline and tree sap, frying oil and a faint chemical tang.

The taxi driver slowed, leaning over his steering wheel to squint hard at every street sign. Finally, they turned down a street identical to all the other streets except in name. On the corner, a Kmart showed off a cheerful block facade that reminded Lyra of Haven. A good sign. They kept going, past a fenced-in parking lot and a flotilla of bright-yellow school buses, all sickly in the fading light and pointed in the same direction, like fish suspended in the deep.

Several blocks later, the street dead-ended in a scrub of thinned-out, trash-filled woods. But as they approached, a narrow drive appeared behind a low stone wall, moving out of the shadow of the trees like some kind of optical illusion.

CASECS was marked by a single sign planted low in the grass. The *No Trespassing* sign next to it was leaning at an angle, and half-swallowed by a hedge that had begun to lose its shape. There were no patrolling soldiers, no guard towers, no obvious security measures: just a long, narrow sweep of driveway that pointed to a simple guard hut. The institute itself was concealed by the curvature of the drive, but the distant lights winking through the overhanging trees suggested a building much smaller than she'd been expecting.

Her heart began gasping, and she imagined the organ like the bird she and the other replicas had once found near A-Wing, sucking in frantic breaths.

"Here," Lyra said.

The driver met her eyes in the rearview mirror. "Here? You sure?" When Lyra nodded, he said, "You want me to wait?"

"No," Lyra said. Suddenly her happiness broke apart. It lifted into her chest and throat, and beat frantic wings against her rib cage. What if Sebastian had lied? What if he was wrong? What if Dr. O'Donnell didn't remember her?

The driver turned around in his seat to peer at Caelum and Lyra, as if he'd just noticed them. "You sure you gonna be okay getting back?"

"We're not going back," she said, and he just shook his head and accepted the money they gave him. Too much, probably—Lyra was too nervous to count and let Caelum do the paying.

They waited until the cab light became distant and then blinked out. From where they stood, Lyra could see one of Allentown's major arteries. But this road, sloughed off by the main thoroughfare, was totally without movement, except for the occasional approach of a car toward the Kmart. Haven's security had depended on its remoteness. But CASECS was hiding in plain sight. No one would ever believe anything of importance would happen here, down the street from the school bus depot.

They went parallel to the driveway, on the shadowed side of the stone wall that continued along its length, concealed by a vein of trees that ran parallel to the pavement. They moved in silence, stopping every few feet to wait, and listen, and watch for security. But there was no movement, no distant voices or footsteps. Lyra should have been reassured, but instead, she only grew more anxious: she didn't understand what kind of place this could possibly be.

They stopped a short distance from the guard hut, edging closer to the stone wall in a crouch, hoping to be mistaken for rocks. Now they had a clear view of the CASECS complex. It was a fraction of the size of Haven: three stories high, blocky white and bleakly rectangular. Security was tighter than it first appeared. A fence ringed at the top with barbed wire marked the periphery and made climbing impossible. Lyra noted, too, the presence of Glass Eyes everywhere, and small glowing pinpricks, like the burning embers of cigarette butts.

That left only one option: they would simply have to walk in, and hope they wouldn't be shot.

They crouched, and they waited, learning the rhythm of the traffic in and out—almost all of it, at this hour, *out*. A sweep of headlights, the occasional patter of conversation as the guard—a woman with a sweep of blond hair and a booming laugh—leaned down to greet the driver. The mechanical gate clanked and shuddered open, then closed again. They counted seconds: twelve, thirteen, fourteen. The gate was open for anywhere from ten to twenty seconds. More than enough time to run, if they were quick, if Lyra didn't stumble.

Still, they would be heading for the guard directly, and Lyra was sure that she had a gun. She thought she could even see it: a dark bulge on the woman's hip.

For the first time the whole thing struck her as funny, that they were risking their lives to get back into a facility like Haven after risking their lives to escape in the first place.

"Let me go alone," Lyra said to Caelum. Suddenly it seemed important to her, critical, even. She would die anyway, whether pulled apart by the ricochet of bullets or by falling into holes that got ever deeper and harder to escape. Caelum was White. He could go anywhere—he could continue stealing wallets and cell phones, he could drift and disappear and reappear again. There would be other girls who loved him, and saw him as beautiful: human girls, who never knew where he came from and didn't care. They would do what Lyra had done with him in the hotel room. They could turn themselves into living strands of music that played together.

“Don’t be stupid,” Caelum said. “We’re together.” He stood up. When she hesitated, he reached back and took her hand again. “Come on.”

They moved a little closer, until they were only a few feet from the perimeter fence and another, larger sign that announced *CASECS* to visitors. The headlights of a departing car made Lyra throw a hand up, momentarily dazzled. The gates clanked open again and then closed. The car swam past them, so close that Lyra could make out the silhouette of a man behind the wheel, turning to fiddle with the radio.

“Next one,” she said. She was suddenly having trouble breathing, and after only a few seconds her feet and legs felt numb and bloated, as if they’d been submerged in freezing water. What if she ran into the driveway and then froze, couldn’t remember where she was or where she was going? She hoped Caelum would hold her hand the whole way, but she didn’t want to ask.

“No,” Caelum said. “We wait for a car going in. The headlights will give us time. The guard will go blind for two, three seconds.”

He was right. They waited. She squeezed her toes. She named all the bones she could think of—ankle, clavicle, tibia. She would have looked for the stars, too, but they were invisible behind the light-smear from the city.

Lyra lost track of time. Minutes went by, or hours. The

parking lot continued to empty. All the traffic flowed the wrong way. But at last a car approached from the direction of the Kmart, its headlights skimming the stone wall and then latching on to the guard hut, the fence, the harried-looking trees.

"Now," Caelum said, as the gate began to grind open and the rhythm of conversation reached them—*how ya doing, another late one, huh?* Suddenly Lyra found that she could not remember how to stand. She tried to shout the urge to her legs, but they didn't hear her. She was stuck where she was, and as Caelum tried to get her to her feet, she simply landed knees down in the grass instead, barely missing the stone wall with her chin. It was as if her ankles had been bound together by invisible cording. *Stand, run, walk,* she thought, but her body remained blankly unresponsive, filled with a useless static.

It was too late now: the car was passing inside the complex, tires fizzing on the pavement. Lyra's heart was so swollen with fear she could feel it in her head, in her mouth, in the bottom of her stomach.

"What happened?" Caelum's face was unexpectedly illuminated: fluid cheekbones, dark eyes. He was so perfect, so alive, and she was so broken. White cluster. Control. His blood, she imagined, was a deep and royal blue, hers dark and sludgy. "What's wrong?"

Then she realized why she could see him so clearly,

why every eyelash was drawn so vividly: yet another car was coming. This time she didn't even have to tell her body to move. She didn't have to think at all. She was on her feet. Caelum cursed, but he was right behind her. She made it over the fence but tripped getting over the curb.

The guard had once again moved into the light to greet the driver, and she was so close Lyra could see the blunt bob of her hair cut to her chin, see her uniform straining over her breasts and revealing a narrow slice of her bra. Lyra couldn't believe the guard didn't see them, that she didn't begin to shoot, but Caelum was right: with the headlights in her eyes, she *couldn't* see.

They came at an angle, scuttling low around the back of the car—a sleek and silver thing, like an elegant fish—until they were pressed up against the passenger side. Lyra thought even if the guard couldn't see them, she would surely hear the way Lyra's breath tore at her throat. A second woman's voice, high and laughing, touched off a nerve inside of Lyra's whole body, like the memory of something bad that had once happened to her. The smell of exhaust made her dizzy.

"You have a good night." The guard was retreating to her hut. The gate churned open and the car eased off its brakes.

Lyra tried to keep pace, flowing through the gate at the same time the car did—but even as she stood up, the darkness stood too, the sense of vertigo and falling. She was pulled up and down at the same time. She was trying to leap over holes burning open at her feet. Her mouth tasted like gravel, like chemicals, like metal. Someone was shouting. She was at Haven and coughing blood.

"Get up, Lyra. Get *up*."

Her ideas rotated. They pivoted and suddenly the true picture emerged: she was on the ground. She'd tripped. She wasn't at Haven. She was here, at CASECS, in Allentown, Pennsylvania, and the person shouting wasn't a doctor but a guard, *the* guard, who must have heard her fall.

The silver car had stopped. A woman leaned out the window to shout. *What happened, what's the problem, I can't understand you.*

"Not you, not you," the guard said. But the woman in the silver car was still confused, and the car exhaust kept stinging Lyra's eyes. "Those two, behind you, two kids, out of the way."

Caelum grabbed Lyra by the elbow. The guard was running, and Lyra, still on her knees, saw the shiny polish of her boots, the walkie-talkie strapped to her belt, the gun holster. "Hey, you. Hey, stop."

Lyra made it to her feet, finally, just in time. But Caelum's hand was torn free—she lost him, they started off in different directions. Now she heard the crackle of radio interference and the guard shouting again and at the same time Lyra hurtled to the left, the car decided to turn too: she was blinded by a funnel of white light, she saw the grille leap toward her shins and she couldn't turn, she had no time.

The car hit her or she hit it. She cracked against the hood, rolled off an elbow, and went down.

A woman screamed. Caelum shouted to her but she couldn't call to him. She was on her back now, breathless beneath a starless sky. She couldn't move at all, couldn't feel her arms or legs. Maybe her spine had snapped, maybe her head had rolled off her body.

A car door opened and slammed closed. Footsteps, muted voices, an explosion of radio static and distant voices communicating in a slang patter. The headlights made a halo of her vision. Someone came toward her—Caelum? the guard?—but in the high beams faces became formless shadows.

"Look at her. She's just a girl." It was the driver, her voice like a hand that tugged at an ancient memory. Haven and clean sheets and pages that turned with the soft *hush-hush* of wind through the grass. Then: "Oh my God. My *God*."

The guard was talking into her radio, so many words that they themselves became static bursts. "That's right, just two kids, some kind of prank, the girl's down, the boy beat it when I tried to grab him, looks like he headed into the parking lot—"

"I know her. Do you understand? I *know* her."

Fingers cool on Lyra's cheeks. The woman slid like an eclipse across the blinding bright lights. Her hair was dirty-blond and gray and loose, and tickled Lyra's face where it touched her.

"She belongs to Haven. I'm sure of it, I'm absolutely positive. . . ."

Lyra fell. She sank toward a warm and forgiving darkness. The pavement softened beneath her back, the night dissolved into a memory of other nights and other places.

"Can you hear me, hon? Can you hear my voice? Open your eyes if you can hear me."

She thought she opened her eyes. It didn't matter anyway. In the dark behind her eyelids she saw a face, so familiar, so often recalled: the freckles and the wide, flat mouth, the smile that said *welcome, I love you, you're home.*

"She must have hit her head bad. . . ."

"Her name . . . I wish I could remember. . . . She was one of the earliest ones. . . ."

"What?"

Dim voices, trailing across her mind like distant comets. One a flinty blue. One the soft white dazzle of a shooting star.

"We named them. Some of the replicas. It was a game

we played. They only had numbers before. It wasn't Cassiopeia . . . what was her name?"

Lyra, Lyra thought. She opened her mouth. Her words evaporated into bubbles of air.

"Jesus. Looks like she's trying to talk."

The woman leaned closer. Her hair tickled Lyra's cheekbone. "What's that, honey?" she whispered.

"Lyra," Lyra managed to say, and the woman cried out softly, as if the word was a bird, some soft thing that had landed in her palm.

"Lyra," she said. "Of course. Can you open your eyes, Lyra?"

Lyra did, surprised by how much effort it took. The pavement hardened beneath her again. There was pain in her ankle, a sharp pain behind her eyes. Her mouth tasted like blood.

"Do you remember me, Lyra? My name is Dr. O'Donnell. I knew you at Haven. Remember?"

She reached up to touch Lyra's face. Her fingers smelled like lemon balm.

SIXTEEN

LYRA WOKE UP AND FOR a confused moment thought she was back at the Winston-Able Mobile Home Park: in the distance she heard the thud of music and people laughing, the scattered catcall of loud and joyful conversation. But it was too clean, and it didn't smell right. When she moved, she thumped her head on the arm of a sofa.

"Sorry for all the noise." When she heard Dr. O'Donnell's voice, Lyra remembered: the car, the driver, the cones of light, and Dr. O'Donnell's hair tickling her face. She turned and a flock of birds took off in her head, briefly darkening her vision. She must have cried out without meaning to, because Dr. O'Donnell reached out and touched her cheek.

"Poor thing," she said. "We wrapped your ankle up nice and tight. It doesn't look broken to me, thankfully."

Lyra noticed then that her ankle had been wrapped

tightly in tape, and various cuts and bruises had been treated with CoolTouch: it had left a shiny film on her elbow and shins.

"Is this CASECS?" she asked. The room looked nothing like a hospital. There was a desk cluttered with belongings in one corner, and shelves filled with books. A miniature fridge hummed in the corner, and a stuffed bear wearing a *Number One Boss* shirt gathered dust on top of it. Lyra was lying on a scratchy dark-wool sofa. There were framed posters on the walls, giant posters of people she didn't recognize. There was a clock on the wall, and a paper calendar with cats. There were no keypads on the door and the only lock was the handle variety.

"This is part of it," Dr. O'Donnell said. She wasn't even wearing a lab coat—just jeans and boots and a light sweater. Maybe that was why Lyra felt so shy around her—that and the gray in her hair, the lines around her eyes, the sharp angle of her nose, all features Lyra hadn't remembered. She had changed or she was different from the start, and either way, Lyra was nervous. "We're a small operation. We keep a staff of just under a hundred and fifty. That includes the cleaning crew." She smiled.

Then Lyra remembered Caelum, the way he'd veered off in the darkness when the headlights swept him, and the guard radioing for backup. "Where's Caelum?" she asked, sitting up and blinking at another rush of birds in her head.

"Caelum. Is that what you call him?"

"That's his name," Lyra said, and felt anxious for reasons she couldn't exactly say. The laughter, the distant drumming of music, a faint smell of alcohol—maybe it all stirred memories of Haven Christmas parties, when the researchers would remove their shoes to slide down the halls in their socks, and the air was edged with a taut, superficial tension, like the lip of water in a glass about to overflow.

"Don't be afraid," Dr. O'Donnell said, and that, at least, reassured her: Dr. O'Donnell still had that skill. She could look at something, or someone, and understand. "He looked hungry. Sonja—she's my research assistant—went for pizza. Caelum's probably halfway through it by now." Her smile made new wrinkles appear and others collapse. "Are you hungry?"

Lyra shook her head. She was dizzy, and nauseous, and thirsty. But not hungry. *I'm sick,* she wanted to say. *Help me.* But she was too shy. She wished Dr. O'Donnell had been wearing a lab coat. Wished she'd looked more like a doctor, and that the room looked more like a hospital. Here she felt her sickness was a stain, that it would be terribly out of place.

Dr. O'Donnell got a bottle of water from the miniature fridge, which was also stocked with Diet Cokes.

"Drink this, at least," she said, once again as if she'd read Lyra's mind. She took a seat, and Lyra was aware of how closely Dr. O'Donnell watched her drink, no doubt taking note of the way Lyra's hand shook. But Dr. O'Donnell didn't comment on it, and she didn't offer to help, either. "I still can't believe it's you. Number twenty-four, wasn't it?"

Lyra nodded. It was strange to hear the words out loud, even after only a few weeks, strange to think of herself again that way, *one of a series,* something that could be stacked or arranged.

Dr. O'Donnell was watching her. "A Green. Is that right?"

Lyra nodded again, this time because her throat seized.

"And Caelum," Dr. O'Donnell said, "is he a Green, too?"

"Caelum is a control," Lyra said, surprised the words brought a bad taste to her mouth. She was expecting Dr. O'Donnell to look sorry for her and was glad she didn't. But she was also confused. Did Dr. O'Donnell know what that meant? Did she know that meant Lyra was dying, and Caelum had to watch?

Dr. O'Donnell was good, but she had known about the sickness. She had known about the variants and the prions and the holes opening up in Lyra's brain, and she had lied, like all the others, and claimed that Haven existed for the replicas' protection.

But maybe Dr. Saperstein had forced her to lie.

In the silence, she heard a new swell of music. Someone shouted, "turn it up, turn it up," and there was laughter.

"Is there always music here?" she asked.

Dr. O'Donnell laughed. "Sometimes. Not usually so late, though. Some of the staff members are celebrating tonight." She seemed to hesitate. "We had some good news today."

Lyra waited for her to go on, but she didn't. It was, she realized, the longest conversation she'd ever had with Dr. O'Donnell. "What kind of good news?"

Dr. O'Donnell looked surprised. She didn't know that Lyra had learned how to ask, how to say please and thank you, how to put on mascara and speak to males. *Boys.* "We'll be able to continue our work here," she said carefully. "We had—well, call it a contest. CASECS was up for an important award. And we won."

"Award." Lyra held the word on her tongue, and found it tasted like coins. "You mean like money?"

Again, Dr. O'Donnell looked startled. But almost immediately, she was serene again, and Lyra thought of a stone disappearing beneath the surface of a still pond. "Yes, like money." She pronounced the word as if it were unfamiliar to her. "But more than that. Support. People who believe we're doing the right thing."

Lyra wanted to ask her about a cure, and about whether Dr. O'Donnell knew how to cure the twisted shapes deforming her brain. But before she could, Dr. O'Donnell leaned forward and took her hands, and Lyra was startled by their dryness, by the coolness of her touch, both familiar and totally foreign. For some reason she thought of Rick and felt a strong impulse to run, to backpedal into the darkness, to rewind the miles they had covered and return to Winston-Able.

But almost immediately, the impulse passed, and she couldn't have said where it had come from. Rick was gone. The past was gone. Dead. You had to sever the lines and let it float off on the ocean, or you would simply sink with it.

"Tell me what happened to you, Lyra," Dr. O'Donnell said softly. "Tell me everything that happened. It's important."

"Haven burned down," she said simply. "Everything burned."

She waited for Dr. O'Donnell to express surprise, but she didn't.

"I heard," she said finally, when Lyra said nothing more. "It was in the news. And besides, Dr. Saperstein—well, we stayed in touch, in a manner of speaking." But a shadow had crossed her face and Lyra knew enough, now, to read Dr. O'Donnell's unhappiness. They had always been fighting, Dr. O'Donnell and Dr. Saperstein. Most of what they'd said was above her head, full of scientific words that had washed over her like breaking water. But there had been one memorable fight about the rats, and whether or not the replicas should be allowed to have some toys and games.

Still—if Dr. O'Donnell had left Haven because she wanted to help, why hadn't she come back when she heard about the fire?

Lyra was having trouble pinning her ideas of Dr. O'Donnell down onto the face in front of her. That was always the problem with faces, with bodies: they told you nothing. Like the genotypes who looked the same but acted completely different. Cassiopeia was proud and strange and angry, but she collected seashells, she scooped insects from the path so they wouldn't be stepped on.

Then there was Calliope, who would catch spiders just to pull their legs off, one by one. Who'd once stepped on a baby bird, just to hear it crunch beneath her shoe.

"Caelum escaped with me," Lyra said. "We ran and hid. We didn't want to go back to Haven. They were making us sick."

She waited for Dr. O'Donnell to apologize or say that Dr. Saperstein had forced the doctors to obey. But she just said, "That was weeks ago. Where have you been all this time?" She seemed truly curious. "Who fed you? Who gave you clothes? Who brought you here, to see me?"

It annoyed Lyra that Dr. O'Donnell assumed someone

else had brought them. She didn't want to tell Dr. O'Donnell about Gemma, or about Rick—they were hers, she decided suddenly, like bed number 24 had been hers, like *The Little Prince* had been hers after Dr. O'Donnell gave her a copy.

"No one," she said. Her voice sounded loud. "We came ourselves. We took the bus and a taxi. We slept where we could. And we took what we needed."

"You mean you stole it?"

"We took it." Lyra was more than annoyed now. She was angry. "Everybody else has things. Why shouldn't we?" Dr. O'Donnell's cell phone was sitting there, on the counter, next to a coffee mug ringed with lipstick, and this infuriated Lyra more: it was evidence. Proof. "People take things all the time. They took what they wanted from us at Haven, didn't they? Didn't you?" She didn't mean to say it, but the words came out and she wasn't sorry. She was happy when Dr. O'Donnell released her hands, happy to think she had caused Dr. O'Donnell pain.

But when Dr. O'Donnell spoke, she didn't sound upset. She actually smiled. "You're tired," she said. "You're sick. And, of course, you're right. You're *right*." And Lyra couldn't understand it, but Dr. O'Donnell began to laugh.

SEVENTEEN

AFTER A DINNER OF SALTY soup and crackers that dissolved in the broth, Lyra worked up the courage to tell Dr. O'Donnell what she had come for: she wanted to live.

Dr. O'Donnell listened in silence, resting one hand lightly on Lyra's knee. Lyra should have felt happy, because Dr. O'Donnell was obviously so happy to see her.

But a shadow had attached itself to her thinking; everything dimmed beneath it. Why hadn't Dr. O'Donnell come to help? Why did she allow the doctors to make all the replicas sick? What was CASECS, that there were no hospital beds but only sofas and armchairs and corkboards, where the doctors wore jeans and sneakers and music played at midnight?

She was reassured, however, when after a long pause, Dr. O'Donnell stood up. "Wait here," she said, and slipped out the door. When she reappeared, she was holding a

RINGER

small, unmarked bottle of fluid, along with one of the long-snouted syringes Lyra had despised back at Haven, for their cruel curiosity. Now, she was relieved to see it.

“What is it?” Lyra asked. Dr. O’Donnell found a pair of medical gloves at the bottom of a desk drawer and cinched them carefully on her fingers.

“A new medicine,” Dr. O’Donnell said. She drew the liquid carefully into the syringe, keeping her back to Lyra. “Very rare. Very expensive.”

“Will it cure me?” Lyra asked. Hope buoyed her, swelled her with air, and made her feel as if she might lift off toward the ceiling. “Will it make all the prions go away?”

“With any luck,” Dr. O’Donnell said. Then: “Hold out your arm for me.”

Dr. O’Donnell offered Caelum a couch in the office next to hers, which belonged to a beautiful woman named Anju Patel. But in the end, since Caelum insisted on sleeping next to Lyra, Dr. O’Donnell and Anju maneuvered a second couch into Dr. O’Donnell’s office instead.

“Sorry if there are any crumbs in the cushions,” Anju said. She had appeared suddenly, practically careening through the door, wearing sweatpants and an inside-out T-shirt, as if she’d dressed in a hurry. Lyra had overheard Anju tell Dr. O’Donnell she’d been in bed when someone had rung her up to share the news of Lyra and Caelum's arrival.

The medicine had filled Lyra with a kind of happy warmth: already, she could picture the prions breaking apart, like mist by the sun.

"Cupcakes are my coffee. I need at least one a day just to keep moving." Anju turned to Dr. O'Donnell. "Sorry, I don't—I mean, do they understand me?"

"We understand you," Caelum said. "You like to eat cupcakes?"

For some reason his voice made Anju startle. Then she began to laugh.

"Oh God," she said. She had tears in her eyes, soon, from laughing, though Lyra didn't know what was funny. "Yeah, I do. I really do."

After Dr. O'Donnell had cleaned and bandaged the cut on Caelum's cheek and set him up with an ice pack to help reduce the swelling around his eye, she left in search of Advil and something to help Caelum sleep. Anju Patel stayed, staring. Her eyes, dark as the nicotine candies Rick had sucked sometimes, were enormous, and Lyra had a sudden fear she would be spiraled down inside them, like water down a drain.

"Are you a doctor too?" Lyra asked, both because she was curious and because she was slowly learning to dislike silence. At Haven, silence, her silence, had not been a choice but simply a condition.

Anju Patel laughed again. "God, no," she said. "I can't even get my blood drawn. I'm a baby for things like that." Lyra didn't know what she meant, or why anyone would be unable to have blood drawn—for a second she thought Anju meant there was something physically wrong with her, that she couldn't. "I'm in sales. Licensing, really."

"What's licensing?" Caelum asked. Lyra, too, had never heard the word.

Anju Patel's face changed. "Do you like to ask questions?" she asked, instead of answering. "Are you very curious?"

Caelum shrugged. Again the shadow swept across Lyra's mind, like a dark-winged bird brushing her with its feather.

"When we don't know something," Lyra said, "we ask to know it."

Anju nodded thoughtfully, as if there were something surprising about that. Maybe Anju was just very stupid. She took a long time to answer.

"Licensing is about rights," she said finally, very slowly. "It's about who has the right to do what. It's about who has the right to own what."

A chill moved down Lyra's body and raised the hair on her arms. It always came back to ownership.

"Let's say you have an idea, a good idea, and you want

to share it. To make sure other people can use it. But it was your idea, so you should get rewarded." Anju was talking very slowly, like the nurses at Haven always had when they were forced to address the replicas directly. Maybe because they had known all along of the holes that would eventually make shrapnel of their brains; maybe they had already zoomed forward in time and seen the replicas idiotic, unable to control their bodies, paralyzed and silenced and then dead.

But didn't Anju know that Dr. O'Donnell had given Lyra special medicine? Didn't she understand that Lyra's brain would be saved?

"You mean paid," Caelum said, and Anju nodded.

"Exactly. So *licensing* takes care of that. We license a thing so that we can then replicate it all over"—she caught her use of the word, and smiled at them as if they were all sharing a joke—"and make sure that no one uses it illegally, for free."

In the outside that was the most important rule: that nothing was free, and everything would be paid for, one way or another.

Then something occurred to her. "Were the replicas licensed?"

Anju barely moved, but nonetheless Lyra was aware that everything, even her skin, had suddenly tightened. "What do you mean?"

She *was* stupid. She must be. "Were the replicas licensed?" she repeated. "Is that why the Gods"—an old habit, to think of them that way—"I mean, why Dr. Haven and Dr. Saperstein were allowed to make so many of them?"

Anju seemed to relax, and Lyra wondered why the first question had bothered her. "No, no," Anju said. "You can't license human beings. Licensing is for . . . well, for ideas. Techniques. Methods. Let's say I invented a new way to manufacture a chair, for example. I might patent that, and then sell it through a licensing agreement, so other people could use my method when they made their own chairs. Do you understand?"

Lyra did understand, at least in general terms. Licensing was a way to make money off replicating ideas, as far as she could tell. But she *couldn't* understand why CASECS needed a person like Anju Patel. Haven had never had a licensing department. She would have heard about it.

"Can you license a medicine?" Lyra asked, trying to puzzle out why CASECS, with its nest of cluttered offices and the smell not of antiseptic but of old carpet, made her uneasy.

"Oh, sure," Anju said, and Lyra felt instantly better. That was all right, then. CASECS made cures and licensed them because in the outside world money was everything. "You can patent a medical technique, too.

About a hundred medical patents are issued per *month*—"

Anju broke off suddenly, and glancing up, Lyra saw that Dr. O'Donnell had returned. In the split second before she knew Lyra's eyes had landed on her, she appeared baldly angry: it was like a raw, hard flush had ruined her complexion, even though Lyra didn't think her color had actually changed. The stain was invisible, and as soon as she saw Lyra she smiled and her face smoothed over.

"You must be so tired," she said. "All the way from Tennessee, all by yourselves."

"I can have Sonja round up some blankets," Anju said.

"Already did." Dr. O'Donnell didn't look at Anju, and her tone swept a thin band of cold through the room. She was obviously angry at Anju for speaking with the replicas, but Lyra didn't know why.

Anju left without another word. A moment later another woman appeared, this one even younger than Anju and with the stoop-shouldered look of someone who got tall very young, carrying an armful of blankets.

She also seemed as if she wanted to speak to Lyra and Caelum, but Dr. O'Donnell intercepted her before she could even step foot in the room.

"Thank you, Sonja," she said, in the same tone she'd used before on Anju. Lyra didn't remember this tone of voice. It reminded her of someone she knew, someone not from Haven but from outside, but she couldn't think who. More holes, maybe, or she was simply tired. Her whole body ached. Her mind felt like a bruise, throbbing with a single message of pain and tenderness.

Dr. O'Donnell had small white pills for Caelum that Lyra recognized as Sleepers. She felt a rush of sudden affection: the Sleepers were everyone's favorites, those small soldiers that herded you off into a mist of dreaming. But when Lyra reached out for her dosage, Dr. O'Donnell shook her head.

"It isn't safe," she said. "Not when you cracked your head. I'll have to wake you every few hours. Sorry," she said, but any regret Lyra felt was outweighed by the sudden pleasure of Dr. O'Donnell's expression, which softened into the one she remembered so well. Instead Lyra got reddish Advil pills, slick and sugared on her tongue.

Caelum settled on the couch next to Lyra's. He hadn't said much since Anju had first appeared, except to say he wouldn't leave Lyra, and when Dr. O'Donnell tried to place a blanket over him he caught her wrist, and for a moment they were frozen there, staring at each other.

"I'll do it," he said. But already Lyra saw him relaxing, as the Sleepers did their work.

"I'll be here all night," Dr. O'Donnell said. "Just shout if you need something." She smiled at Lyra, and momentarily the changes to her face, the new wrinkles and the slightly thinner skin, were erased. "And I'll see you in a few hours."

She turned off the lights. It was surprisingly dark. The window was covered by thin slat-blinds but must have been facing away from the parking lot, toward the fence and beyond it, the woods. The only light at all came from a tissue-thin crevice around the door, which appeared as a result like a faint, glowing silhouette. But Lyra could still hear the muffled rhythm of music, although after only a minute, it cut off abruptly. Then: footsteps ran like water, and whispered voices outside their door soon flowed away.

"Caelum?" Lyra whispered. Then, a little louder: "Are you awake?"

He didn't answer for so long she thought he wouldn't. When he did speak, the edges of his words were round and soft, as if they were melting on his tongue. "I don't trust her," was all he said.

Lyra wanted to be angry with him. CASECS and its unfamiliar sounds, its dizzying arrangement of cubicles and ceiling tiles and cluttered desks and new names, had exhausted her. "You don't know her like I do," she said. "That's all."

Caelum didn't respond. After a minute, she heard his breathing slow and realized he was asleep. She closed her eyes, expecting to drop quickly into a dream, but instead she found her mind cycling, insect-like, landing quickly on old memories, on visions of Haven, on quick-splice images she'd thought she had forgotten.

She was still awake when the door opened again. She thought at first it was because Dr. O'Donnell was coming to check on her. A band of light fell sharply across her eyes. She squeezed her eyes shut, and was about to ask for water when she heard an unfamiliar voice and froze.

"Are you sure they're sleeping?" It was a boy's voice, totally unknown to her.

"Positive. O'Donnell was hunting around for Ambien."

Because of the lightening of the colors behind her eyelids, Lyra knew they were standing there in the doorway, staring.

"It's weirder in person," the boy said, after a minute. "They look so . . . normal. Don't they?"

"What did you think? They'd have three heads or something?"

"Shut up. You know what I mean." Then: "Do you think . . . do you think they dream and everything?"

"I don't see why not. Dr. O'Donnell says they . . . like we do," the girl whispered, so softly that even the rustle of Caelum's blankets when he turned blew some of her words away. "She never had proof before. So many of the others were morons. She told me some of them couldn't even use the toilet. But these . . ."

Caelum rolled over again, and so the boy's response was

lost. When he finally settled down, the girl was already speaking.

". . . depending on what you use them for." There was a long stretch of quiet, and Lyra feared, though she knew it was impossible, the girl would hear the knocking of her heart and know she was awake and listening. "Everyone always thought AI would come from computers. But we did it first. Biology did it."

For a long time, they didn't speak again.

"It's kind of sad, in a way," the boy said at last.

"You can't think of it like that," the girl responded. "You have to remember there's a purpose."

"Cha-ching," the boy responded. Lyra didn't know what it meant.

"Sure," the girl said. She sounded annoyed. "But that isn't the only reason. We can save hundreds of thousands of lives. Maybe we'll even cure death."

"Who knew," the boy said, "eternal life would spring from a cooler in Allentown, Pennsylvania?"

He closed the door, sealing out the light. Lyra's heart was beating fast. She rolled over to face Caelum, trying to slow the frantic drumming of her pulse, listening to the sound of their intermingled breathing. She thought about what she had overheard: the talk of AI, which she didn't understand; licensing, the key to eternal life. She had misunderstood many things, but she had understood that: the key was here, somewhere in CASECS, locked in a cooler. Perhaps the key was in the medicine that Dr. O'Donnell had given her. Or perhaps it was a real key, or a kind of medical equipment.

Though it should have been an electrifying idea, instead it made her uncomfortable. At Haven, they had tried to be gods by making life: and so the replicas had suffered for their miracle.

She wondered what it would look like to cure death, and who would have to suffer for it.

As her mind wandered through strange corridors that bordered on dream, she thought for some reason of a bird they'd found on one of the courtyard pathways when she was a child: a scrawny brown thing, smaller than her palm, it must have mistaken the reflection in one of the windows for an aerial pathway and flown straight into the glass.

She remembered the way it had tried to hop to safety as the replicas had crowded around it, and her sudden lurching awareness of death all around them, not just in the clean white folds of the Box, not contained or containable. And then Calliope, who was then only called number 7, had stepped forward and driven her foot down on top of it, so hard they all heard the *crunch*.

It was broken, Calliope had said. *It's better to kill it. It's the right thing.*

But Lyra had suspected, had known, that she had just

wanted to know what would happen. She was curious to know what it would feel like, that small fragile second when a life snapped beneath her shoe with the sharp crack of a flame leaping to life from the head of a match but in reverse: the sound of darkness, not light.

EIGHTEEN

WHEN SHE FINALLY SLEPT, SHE had a dream of standing in the middle of a large metal chamber that vibrated like the interior chamber of Mr. I, while Anju spoke over the roar, explaining how to license chairs.

Leaning forward over the railing, Lyra saw hundreds and hundreds of chairs lined up along the tongue of a conveyor belt, and for some reason she was repulsed by them, by their jointed design and the crooked look of their spindly legs—until, looking closer, she saw they weren't made out of wood or plastic, but out of human arms and legs, human feet, thousands of bodies hacked up and rearranged and made available, Anju was saying, for sale on a large scale.

She woke up sweating. The morning, which should have been filled with a buzz of activity and voices, was instead profoundly quiet. Caelum had opened the blinds, and his face was cut into horizontal stripes of light.

"How are you feeling?" he asked her, without turning away from the window.

She sat up, shaking off the sticky remnants of her dream. Her whole body was sore and her legs were purpling with enormous, flower-shaped bruises. But her head was clearer. Maybe the medicine was working already.

"Better," she said. "What are you doing?"

He turned to face her. "The windows are barred. It doesn't make any sense. There's nothing but telephones and office rooms and computers. So why bar the windows and put up the fence? Why security?"

"They want to keep people from getting in," Lyra said.

"Why? If they're making medicines, if they're curing diseases, why all the secrecy?" He shook his head. "They're hiding something."

Lyra was annoyed. Caelum saw danger in everything and everybody. But it was easy for him to doubt. He wasn't the one who needed a cure.

And what bothered her most, deep down, was that she knew he was right.

"Maybe they don't want anyone stealing from them," she said. She was about to tell him what she had overheard in the night—about the key to eternal life, about the magic cooler—when the door opened and a girl came in with a paper bag that said *Dunkin' Donuts*. Her face was shaped exactly like a circle, her eyes like two exclamation points of surprise.

"Dr. O'Donnell said you might want breakfast." She looked nervous, Lyra thought—as if she were the one who felt out of place.

"Where is Dr. O'Donnell?" Lyra asked.

The girl looked startled, as if she hadn't expected questions. "Putting out fires," she said, and Lyra frowned. "I don't mean real fires," the girl added, seeing that Lyra didn't understand, and she giggled a little. "It's just an expression."

"It means there's been an emergency," Caelum said. Lyra looked at him, surprised. "I heard Rick say it."

Thinking of Rick and the people who had taken him made Lyra feel nauseous again. She wondered whether they were still out there, searching for her and Caelum. She wondered whether she really had seen the man at UPenn or only imagined it; she wondered if they could track her to CASECS. But Dr. O'Donnell would protect her.

She'd promised.

"What emergency?"

Now the girl definitely looked nervous. "Dr. O'Donnell says you have to eat something," she said, avoiding the question entirely. "I have some water for you, too."

She deposited the bag on top of the mini fridge and, as

she went to root around inside it, toppled the small vial of special medicine that Dr. O'Donnell had left, stoppered, for Lyra's morning dosage. Lyra shouted and Caelum made a dive for it.

But it was too late. It hit the ground and opened, liquid seeping out into the carpet. For a second, Caelum stayed there, his hand outstretched. Then he drew back, and Lyra felt a sharp pain: as if something hot had gone straight through her lungs. Unexpectedly, tears came to her eyes.

The blond girl stared from Lyra to Caelum and back. "What?" she said. "What is it?" She followed the direction of Lyra's gaze then, and gave a quick laugh. "Oh," she said. Carelessly, she snatched up the now-empty vial and tossed it once, catching it in her palm. "Don't worry. It won't stain." Lyra could only stare at her.

"I *mean*"—the girl sighed and slipped the vial into her pocket—"it's just saline, anyway. Salt and water never hurt anybody."

"She lied to me."

They were alone again. The girl had left them, promising to get Dr. O'Donnell, frightened perhaps by Lyra's stillness. This hole was worse than any yet, because she was conscious, she was aware, she was remembering. But she felt that enormous walls of darkness had grown to enclose her. She was shivering at the very bottom of a pit. Caelum was speaking to her from somewhere very far away.

"We have to go. Lyra, listen to me. We have to find a way out of here, now."

"Why did she lie to me?" She was so cold. Her hands and lips were frozen. Corpses grew cold, she knew; she had touched one before, the day that she had found number 236 dead, her wrists cabled to her bedposts. "It doesn't make any sense."

"Of course it does." Caelum grabbed her shoulders. "They're all liars, Lyra. Didn't I tell you? Each and every one of them is the same."

She didn't want to believe it. But when she closed her eyes, she saw memories revolving, taking on new dimensions. She had overheard Dr. O'Donnell fight with Dr. Saperstein, and had always believed it meant that Dr. O'Donnell loved them. But if she'd really loved them, why hadn't she tried to end the experiment? She had once tried to convince Emily Huang to stand up to God. But she hadn't stood up herself. She hadn't exposed Haven.

She had just left.

She had left to do her own experiments, to do whatever it was they really did at CASECS. To *license*. All the times that Dr. O'Donnell had read to Lyra and the others, had taught them about the stars—was that simply its own experiment?

Maybe all people were the same—they all wanted different things. But they all demanded the *right* to want whatever it was they wanted. They all thought of it as their birthright.

Caelum let Lyra go. He turned back to the door and tried the handle: locked, from the outside. He aimed a kick for the door and Lyra didn't even startle at the noise. Dr. O'Donnell had lied to her.

All people were the same.

There was nowhere to go, nowhere for them to run, no time left for her. What did it matter whether she died here or somewhere else?

"We shouldn't have come here." Caelum's voice cracked, and Lyra wanted to tell him it was okay, that it didn't matter anymore.

"What choice did we have?" Everywhere Lyra turned she hit walls and more walls. "I'm running out of options, Caelum. I'm dying." It was the first time she'd ever admitted it to Caelum.

When had she become so afraid of dying? For most of her life, she'd seen death as deeply ordinary, almost mechanical, like the difference between having a light on or off. She was afraid that death would be like falling into one of the holes, except that this one would never end, that she would never reach the bottom of it.

She couldn't stand to look at him, at the angular planes of his cheekbones, at his beautiful eyelashes and lips, all of it undamaged, pristine, *beautiful.* She was unreasonably angry at him—for being so healthy, for being so beautiful.

Because she knew, of course, that Caelum was the reason she was afraid. She'd never had a reason to care about whether she lived or not. Caelum had given her the reason. Now he would continue, while she would end.

"Don't," she said, when he tried to touch her. But he got her wrist before she could turn away from him.

"Hey," he said, and put a hand on her face, resting his thumb on her cheekbone, forcing her to look at him. "Hey."

They were chest to chest, breathing together. His eyes, so dark from a distance, were up close layered with filaments of color. She felt, looking at them now, the way she did when looking up at the dark sky, at the stars wheeling in all that blackness.

"I would trade places with you if I could," he said. He moved his hand to her chest, and her heartbeat jumped to meet his fingers. "I would trade in a second."

"I know," she said. She was calmer now. He had that effect—he softened her fears, blunted them, the way that when night fell it softened corners and edges.

"I'll stay with you, always," he said. "I want you to know that. I'll never leave you again. I'll go with you anywhere. Anywhere," he repeated, and then smiled. "You tamed me, remember? Like the little prince tamed the fox in the desert. And you named me and made me real."

She wanted to tell him she loved him. She wanted to tell him she was afraid. But she couldn't get the words out. Her throat was too tight.

Luckily, he said it first. "I love you, Lyra," he said.

"Me too," she managed to say.

He kissed her. "I love your lips," he said. "And your nose." He kissed her nose, then her eyebrows, then her eyelids and cheeks. "I love your eyebrows. Your cheeks." He took her hand and gently brought her pinkie finger into his mouth, kissing, sucking gently, and now the distinction between her body and his began to erode. She was his mouth and her finger, his breath and her heartbeat, his tongue and her skin, all at once. "I love your hands," he whispered, moving finger to finger.

"Me too," she said, and closed her eyes as he knelt to kiss her stomach, explored her hipbones with his tongue, naming all the places he loved, all the inches of skin, the seashell parts spiraled deep inside of her, filled with tides of wanting.

But her wanting wasn't a right. It was a gift. It was a blessing. She came to it on her knees, holding out her arms.

"Me too," she said, and every place he kissed her, her skin came alive, and told her she had to live.

NINETEEN

THE LOCKS AT CASECS HADN'T been made to keep people prisoner—especially people like Lyra and Caelum, who were only half-people, raised in a place where a thousand different locks controlled the motion of their daily lives. Lyra and Caelum knew locks that beeped and locks that spun, locks that clicked and locks that jammed. Each of them had its own language, its own clucking tongue.

They rooted in Dr. O'Donnell's desk. Lyra turned up a business card like the kind the Suits had carried into Haven, dropping occasionally like scattered jewels for the replicas to collect: this one carried the name Allen Fortner. She knew this must mean that Dr. O'Donnell had business with the Suits, or wanted to, even before she turned up a to-do list that included the item: *Call Geoffrey Ives.*

Rifling through a notepad, she found many to-do lists, and many calls to Gemma's father.

She wondered whether he was already on his way.

More likely, he had simply sent someone to take care of Lyra and Caelum; he was the kind of person who spoke through his money.

She stuffed her pockets with paper, with Post-it notes, with business cards and scrawled reminders. Evidence, although she still wasn't sure what it proved. But every piece of paper, every scrap, hardened a sense of rage and injustice.

If she had any time left, any time at all, she would take the words and light them on fire so they would explode everywhere; they would drift like a cloud and blacken Dr. O'Donnell's name, and CASECS's name, and Geoffrey Ives's name too. Even if she died, she would find a way to make the words live.

In the bottom drawer, behind a rubble of loose pens, they found a handful of bobby pins. Caelum straightened out one of the bobby pins and inserted it into the keyhole, wiggling until he heard it click. In less than five seconds, they were free.

The hallway was empty, and branched in both directions. Lyra saw no exit signs and couldn't remember which way to go. The night before, she'd been too overwhelmed to pay attention. Caelum had been brought in by security and was distracted by a small cluster of people who had gathered to watch, but he thought they should turn left, and so they did.

Caelum was right about the rest of CASECS: it was

all carpeted hallways and offices marked with unfamiliar names, conference rooms and cubicles. Lyra saw signs of the previous night's celebration: a bottle of wine, uncorked, and plastic cups that had pooled liquid onto a conference table. There were coffee mugs still exhaling steam at empty desks, and abandoned jackets, purses, and cell phones everywhere, suggesting their owners had, indeed, come to work only to be spirited away.

Fear moved like a film of sweat across Lyra's body. The hallway seemed to keep unrolling extra feet, stretching endlessly past the same bleak workstations, as if it were expanding. She kept spinning around, thinking she heard footsteps on the carpet, expecting to see Dr. O'Donnell bearing down on them. But they saw no one but a guy wedged into a cubicle, fiddling with a grid of numbers on his computer, ears obscured beneath palm-sized headphones. He didn't see them.

Finally, the hallway dead-ended and they turned right, startling a girl holding a bakery box. She nearly dropped it, yelped, and turned to hurry away—as if *she* had reason to be afraid of them.

"We have to hurry," Caelum said, as if Lyra didn't know. But she spotted a set of double doors where the girl had whipped out of sight around another turn, and she and Caelum grabbed hands and ran.

Lyra's heart was gasping. As they got close she thought

it might burst; she saw a keypad like the kind they had used at Haven, which required an ID to swipe. But the doors had been propped open with an old paperback book, and beyond them was a stairwell and a sign pointing the way to further levels.

The stairs went down, and twisted them around several landings, past a level called Sub-One, which was unlit. Through a set of swinging doors, Lyra saw a vast room filled with nothing but old machines, abandoned workstations, and freight containers. The double doors opened at her touch.

"In here?" she whispered to Caelum. But just then, a patter of footsteps passed overhead, and he shook his head and pulled her on.

As they descended, the air got noticeably cooler. Lyra remembered what the boy had said about a refrigerator. She pictured an enormous, chilled space, like a dead heart, filled with endless chambers.

The stairs bottomed out at a heavy metal gate; this one was closed and required a digitized code to open. Beyond it was a plain white windowless door, fitted with yet another keypad and marked with a small sign that simply said: *Secure Area—Live Samples.* Lyra's blood rushed a frantic rhythm to her head, and in its rhythm she heard the certainty of dark secrets. Whatever CASECS made, whatever Dr. O'Donnell built with all her wanting, it was here.

They had no choice but to backtrack. The climb left Lyra winded and she had to rest on the landing, leaning heavily against Caelum, before they slipped once again through the propped-open doors at the top of the stairs. Maybe, Lyra thought, there was no exit. Maybe Dr. O'Donnell had trapped them, the way in the early days Haven had placed rats in mazes that didn't lead anywhere, to test how long it took for the sick ones to learn all the dead ends.

They turned again, and this time Lyra's heart leapt: an exit sign pointed through a set of doors only twenty feet away. She was so happy she failed to register the sudden swell of voices. She slipped easily away from Caelum even as he tried to grab her.

"Lyra, wait."

But she had started toward the sign already, hooked on the glowing comfort of its syllables. *Exit.* A funny word, and one she had only lately come to love. At Haven, she had always thought the exit signs were taunting her.

She was halfway there when the wave of voices finally broke across her consciousness; as if the sound was a physical substance and she had mindlessly stepped into its current. Forty or fifty people were gathered in a conference room to crowd around a wall-mounted TV. Had they been turned to face the hallway instead, Lyra would have been visible. She was rooted directly in the middle of the doorway, frozen with sudden terror.

Dr. Saperstein was staring directly at her.

For a confused and terrified second, she mistook the image for the real thing and thought he was really there, staring bleakly over all the CASECS employees, pinning her with his eyes. But of course he wasn't. It was just an old picture, an image made huge by the television. Almost immediately, Dr. Saperstein vanished, and a female newscaster with stiff black hair and an even stiffer smile took over the screen.

The rush of blood in Lyra's ears quieted. But just for a minute.

". . . confirmed that Dr. Mark Saperstein was indeed found dead this morning at an undisclosed location . . ."

A microwave beeped. No one bothered with it. They were all still. Lyra felt as if the air was being pressed out of her lungs.

"Though Dr. Saperstein had just undergone a spectacularly public fall from grace, culminating in this week's protests at his alma mater, the University of Pennsylvania, the police have denied reports that his death was a suicide. . . ."

Dead. Dead. Dead. The word kept drilling in Lyra's mind. Dr. Saperstein was dead. God was dead. She should have been happy, but strangely, she was just frightened. It had never occurred to her that God would die, or that it was even possible.

She was less than fifteen feet from the exit. No one had seen her. And yet she couldn't move, and even Caelum hesitated, teetering on the edge of the doorway as if it were a river he was worried about crossing.

Eight seconds, maybe ten. Twelve at a stretch.

God had died, and with him, the replicas' only reason for being.

Was a terrible reason better than no reason at all?

"There they are. Get them. *Get* them."

Lyra turned and saw Dr. O'Donnell charging them and trailing a small crowd of people behind her; among them were three guards and the girl who'd dropped the bakery box.

And at the same time, in response to her shout, everyone in the conference room turned and spotted Lyra.

She ran. Caelum was shouting over the sudden chaos, and though she couldn't hear him, she could feel him a step behind her. They had a small advantage, but it was enough. They were steps from the door, inches, they could get outside, they would be free—

But even as Lyra reached for the door, it opened forcefully from the other side. Caelum managed to pull up, but Lyra was thrown backward by the blunt collision, as with a hard and hollow smack the door caught her in the side of her jaw. She landed on her back, breathless and dizzy. Through a fuzz of dark shapes she saw a whip-thin man, soaked with toppled coffee, gaping at her.

Caelum tried to get her to her feet but by then Dr. O'Donnell had caught up, and the guards drove him to his knees, and Lyra saw a thicket grow above her: a nest of mouths and unfamiliar faces, long arms that looked like weapons. Cold fingers locked her wrists in place. Someone sat on her ankles.

They look so real, somebody said.

You'd never know.

Be careful how you handle them, please. That was Dr. O'Donnell. *It looks like they may be the last ones.*

TWENTY

THIS TIME THEY WERE PLACED in an unused office whose only furniture was a set of metal filing cabinets and two chairs brought in for Caelum and Lyra to sit on, although Caelum remained standing. The door required a key. Dr. O'Donnell had locked them in herself.

"Give me a minute," she'd told them, almost apologetically. She couldn't stop pretending that she was on their side. She probably didn't know the difference.

Standing with her ear to the door, Lyra could hear Dr. O'Donnell speaking to someone in the hall.

"She says they came here on their own, with no help. I doubt she knows a thing."

There was only silence in response, and Lyra realized that Dr. O'Donnell was talking on the phone. Her skin tightened into a shiver. Dr. O'Donnell knew the Suits. How long would it be before they arrived?

"She hasn't mentioned Gemma at all, but I can ask." Another silence. "You think she ended up there by mistake?"

Lyra leaned so hard against the door, sweat gathered in the space behind her ear. For a long time, Dr. O'Donnell said nothing, and Lyra worried she might have hung up.

But then she spoke again. "I'm sure she's okay, Geoff. I'm sure she made it out." Then: "No, I understand that. But she's a smart girl. You've said so yourself."

Lyra put a hand on the door and pressed, imagining she could squeeze her rage out through her fingertips, harden it into blades that would slice them free. Geoff meant Geoffrey Ives. Though she didn't understand much of the conversation, she understood that something bad had happened to Gemma.

Something had happened to her by mistake. She was in trouble. And Lyra knew, without question or doubt and without knowing how she knew, that it was because Gemma had come to warn her.

Had Gemma, like Rick, been taken away?

She thought of Jake Witz hanging by his belt, and the purple mottle of his face.

The memory brought back a roar of sound, a memory of Haven exploding into flame, and the char of burning skin carrying over the marshes. She nearly missed the next thing Dr. O'Donnell said.

"I see. So how many of them escaped?" Then: "We can still use them, you know. If we could spin it—" She broke off. After another minute, she spoke again, this time so close to the door that Lyra startled backward and could still hear her clearly. "Well, maybe it's for the best. Public support will be the trickiest. If word gets out that they can be violent . . ."

The last thing she said was, "I'm praying for Gemma."

Lyra couldn't help but wonder whether anyone in the whole world was praying for her and for Caelum. She doubted it.

Then Lyra had to stumble out of the way, because Dr. O'Donnell turned the key in the lock and opened the door. For a half second, Lyra didn't recognize her: the lines of her face had converged into a baffling question mark.

"Sit," Dr. O'Donnell said. Neither Caelum nor Lyra moved. "Go on. Sit. Please. I won't hurt you."

"You're a liar," Caelum said. "Everything you say is a lie."

Dr. O'Donnell sighed. She must have gone home at some point to change; she was wearing different clothing than she had been last night. Lyra hated her for this—that she would think to go home, that she would think to shower, that Lyra and Caelum were so small in the orbit of her life they hadn't even caused a ripple in her routine.

"I wasn't lying when I said I could help you," Dr. O'Donnell said. "I'm sure I don't need to tell you this, but you're in a difficult position. You're not supposed to exist."

Although she said the words gently, Lyra knew them for what they were: sharp, weaponized things, knives designed to make her bleed. She wouldn't argue, or cry, or show that they had landed.

"What happened to Gemma?" she said.

Dr. O'Donnell looked momentarily startled, and Lyra was glad: she had an advantage, however brief.

Dr. O'Donnell recovered quickly. "You're very observant," she said. "I'd forgotten that."

"There wasn't much to do but observe at Haven," Lyra said. A wave of dizziness clouded her vision, and she wanted to sit down but didn't want to give Dr. O'Donnell the satisfaction. "What happened to Gemma?"

"I don't know," Dr. O'Donnell said, after a short pause. "No one knows. It seems she disappeared on Sunday morning."

So. It *was* Lyra's fault.

Dr. O'Donnell moved away from the door—slowly, as if Caelum and Lyra might startle, as if there was anywhere for them to go. "Can I ask you a question?" She held up both hands when Caelum started to protest. "Then you can ask me anything you want, and I'll be honest. I promise to tell you everything you want to know."

Caelum's eyes locked briefly on Lyra's. She shrugged.

"Go on," Lyra said. Finally, she took a seat, hoping that Dr. O'Donnell hadn't noticed her relief. Caelum, however, stayed where he was. "But then it's our turn."

Dr. O'Donnell called up a smile with obvious difficulty. "I promise," she repeated. Since Caelum wasn't sitting, she took the empty chair instead, and drew it across from Lyra, so they were almost knee to knee. She leaned forward, and Lyra was sure she would ask about Gemma.

But instead she said, "Do you know how many replicas escaped Haven after the explosion?"

Now Lyra was the one who was surprised.

"Why does it matter?" Caelum asked.

Dr. O'Donnell barely turned her head to give him a tight smile. "You said you'd answer first."

Lyra shook her head. "I don't know," she answered honestly. "Caelum and I were hiding. We got under the fence. . . ." When she closed her eyes, she could still see the zigzag of flashlights, and hear the rhythm of helicopters threshing the smoke beneath their propellers. Dozens of them, passing back and forth, back and forth. She remembered screaming. "There were rescue helicopters, though. So there must have been some. Dr. Saperstein survived, didn't he?" Dr. O'Donnell nodded. "The explosion happened in A-Wing. But there wouldn't have been replicas there."

Dr. O'Donnell was quiet for a bit. She clutched her hands, making her knuckles very white. Were they really the same hands, Lyra wondered, that had smuggled books onto Spruce Island, had touched Lyra's forehead when she was feverish?

"Why?" Caelum asked again. When she looked down at her hands, he said, "You promised to answer."

Dr. O'Donnell shook herself, as if she were passing out of a rain. "I never liked what Dr. Saperstein was doing at Haven," she said. "Research of that magnitude . . ." She cleared her throat. "Secrets breed violence. The bigger the secret, the bigger the violence." Suddenly, she stood up, moving not toward the door but to a barred window with a view of nothing but a blight of straggly trees. "Dr. Saperstein is dead. His secrets killed him. And it's possible—it's likely—that the replicas he brought up from Florida managed to escape."

"Where?" Lyra asked.

"I don't know." Dr. O'Donnell turned to them when Caelum made a noise in his throat. "That's the truth. I don't know. Somewhere in Lancaster County, only an hour or so south of here. That's all I know. We weren't exactly on the best of terms."

"He was suing you," Lyra said, parroting back what

Sebastian had told her. Again, Dr. O'Donnell looked surprised.

"You were always very smart," Dr. O'Donnell said. Lyra wanted to hit her.

She gripped the sides of her chair, as another wave of dizziness nearly took her sideways. "What do you make here, if you aren't making cures?"

Dr. O'Donnell turned back to the window. She waited so long to answer, Lyra began to think that her promise had also been a lie.

But finally she did. "Dr. Haven and Dr. Saperstein were convinced that their work could only be done in secret," she said. "That was wrong."

"You said that already," Caelum said.

"Just *listen*." A sigh moved from Dr. O'Donnell's shoulders down her spine. "I've spent years doing nothing but speaking to people—scientists, engineers, politicians, even—about how important this research is. How important it should be."

Lyra decided she hated that word—*important*. The way Dr. O'Donnell said it made her want to spit. As if it were a beautiful piece of glass, as if Dr. O'Donnell was beautiful just because she carried its syllables around on her tongue. How many people, Lyra wondered, were dead because of someone else's importance?

"That's what we do at CASECS. We promote research.

We give hospitals, facilities, even governments the chance to do their *own* research. That's where you come in." Dr. O'Donnell turned away from the window again. She wasn't smiling. "There's nowhere else for you to go. I know you understand that. If you leave, you'll eventually be caught by the same people who wanted to erase you in the first place."

"I'm dying anyway," Lyra said. "Aren't I?"

Dr. O'Donnell winced, as if Lyra had fired something sharp at her forehead.

"You lied about a cure," Lyra said, although the words curdled in her mouth and left her with a bad taste in her throat. "Admit it."

Dr. O'Donnell looked down. "There's no cure," she said softly. But Lyra thought, unbelievably, that she really sounded sorry about it. Still, the words fell like a thin knife, Lyra felt, slicing the world in two. She remembered the moment that Caelum had grabbed her wrist and she'd seen his mud-coated nails and felt the strange warmth and newness of his touch, and then a rocketing blast had driven her off her feet. She had thought, then, the world might be ending.

Instead it was ending here, in this room.

"We hardly understand prions," Dr. O'Donnell said. "Dr. Saperstein understood them better than anyone in the world, probably, and he wasn't looking for a cure. The whole point was to study a class of disease that we knew hardly anything about. To see how it could be manipulated, to understand it by making different variations and observing their effects." She shook her head. "He was collecting data. It *had* to be incurable."

Lyra thought of all the replicas she'd ever known—Lilac Springs and Rose and Cassiopeia and the hundreds of numbered ones they'd never named—standing in a vast row against a blinding sunshine, looking like pen strokes on a page. Looking like data.

"So why does it matter?" Lyra said. "Why does it matter, if I'm just going to die?"

Dr. O'Donnell looked up. "I'm offering you more time," she said.

Years collapsed in a second. Just for a second, Lyra fell back into the fantasy of Dr. O'Donnell as her savior, as her mother, as her friend.

"We don't want anything from you," Caelum said.

At the same time Lyra asked, "How?"

Dr. O'Donnell spoke in a quiet rhythm Lyra knew from their Sunday readings. "Most people in the world—the vast majority of people—don't even know it's possible to clone human beings. They've heard about cloning sheep, and cloning human organs, even. Dogs, apes, cows, on rare occasions. But Haven's work was kept so confidential—secret, I mean—that most people, if you told them a single human clone was alive in the world, eating, breathing, thinking—*they wouldn't believe it.*" When Dr. O'Donnell spoke, it was like the soft touch of a Sleeper. Lyra's mind turned dull and soft and malleable. "You're our proof."

She could have laughed. She wanted to cry. "I'm not proof."

"I didn't mean it that way," Dr. O'Donnell said. "I only meant—"

Lyra cut her off. "No. You don't understand. I'm not proof. I'm not even a replica. I wasn't made at Haven. I wasn't made at all." She felt both satisfied and sickened at the fault line of disappointment that shook Dr. O'Donnell's face. "You didn't know? I have a father. His name is Rick Harliss. I had a mother too, but she didn't want me, so she gave me over to Haven and then she died." Saying it out loud gave her the good kind of pain, like digging in the gums with a fingernail. "I wasn't made by anything except accident. No one wanted me at all."

That was really what had made Caelum so special to her: he wanted her. And not just because of her body and what he could do with it, but for her, something inside neither of them had a name for, the stitching and the thread that held her whole life as a spiderweb holds even the sunlight that passes through it. "There were more of us at Haven. Not just me. Replicas are expensive." She remembered that day on the marshes, the soldier saying, *You know how expensive these things are to make?* "I guess that means I was cheap."

Dr. O'Donnell shook her head. "I'm sorry," she said. Lyra wanted to ask whether she was sorry for Lyra or for herself. "I . . . heard rumors. But that was all before my time."

It was the most dangerous kind of lie: the one the liar believed. "That's convenient for you," she said. She felt a hard, ugly pull of hatred. Was this all the world was? They'd escaped Haven only to find that Haven existed everywhere.

Dr. O'Donnell stood up. She stared down at Lyra as if from an enormous height. But when she spoke, she sounded calm. "If you understand anything, I want you to try and understand this," she said. "We're all doing our best. We always have been." But her mouth twisted around the words, and Lyra wondered if on some level even her body knew that was a lie—or at least, that it wasn't an excuse. "Haven was a crazy place—such a crazy time for everyone. . . . I posted there for three years and I remember I would leave for the holidays, step off that launch, and hardly remember how to be human. . . ." Bad choice of words, and she seemed to realize it. Lyra and Caelum had no idea what any of it meant: the holidays, family, Haven as a fluid world that allowed passage in and out. "Some people might think what we did was wrong.

Maybe it was. But it was also a miracle. It was, maybe, the first scientific miracle." She almost looked like she might cry. "You make choices. You make sacrifices. Sometimes you make the wrong choices. Then you work to correct them. That's what science is about."

Lyra wanted to argue, because she knew there was some problem of logic there: there had to be. Anyone could give names to anything—Dr. O'Donnell had taught her that, when she'd given Lyra her name. If you could do anything you wanted and then call it *doing your best*, you could invent anything, excuse anything. There had to be a center somewhere. There had to be a truth.

But suddenly, Lyra found she couldn't bring up the words she wanted to say. The word *center,* for example. She could picture it, see it as a hard little seed at the back of her tongue, but she couldn't find the word. This was a hole of a different kind. She wasn't dropping into it. It was reaching up to swallow her. Lyra thought of the pages she'd eaten in Sebastian's bathroom, and the words all dissolving into her blood. She wished she hadn't: now she was nauseous and thought that they were the things poisoning her, saw the letters reconfigure themselves into deformities, like little mangled prions, and float carelessly toward her heart. Words could make anything: that was their great power, and their great danger. Lyra saw that now.

Dr. O'Donnell had already started moving for the door

when Caelum spoke up again.

"I have another question."

She turned around, keeping her hand on the door.

"Someone blew up Haven because of their idea of God," Caelum said. "You know that?"

Dr. O'Donnell frowned. "I'd heard."

"And Haven was for science, and it killed people, too."

Dr. O'Donnell said nothing.

Caelum took a step toward her, and then another. Dr. O'Donnell's whole body tensed.

"My question is this." He stopped when he was no more than four inches away from her, and Lyra could see how badly Dr. O'Donnell wanted to flee, how hard she was trying not to throw the door open and run. "If it's okay to kill people for science, or for God, is it okay to kill people if you think you need to?"

"Of course not," she said sharply.

"Why not?" He spoke the words softly, but she flinched.

"I—I don't expect you to understand." She couldn't control herself anymore. She wrenched the door open, forcing him to step back. "The world isn't black and white. There are no easy answers."

Still, Caelum wasn't done.

"You said the world isn't black and white. But the world isn't like you think it is either," he said quietly. Dr.

O'Donnell froze. "I watched and I watched. There were days I watched so much I thought I wasn't even a person, just an eye. And even I know that when you push, and you keep pushing, someday, sometime, someone is going to push you back."

Dr. O'Donnell turned to face him, very slowly. "Are you threatening me, Caelum?"

"I don't need to," he said. "That's just the way the world works." He smiled, too. "We all do our best, like you said."

Dr. O'Donnell opened her mouth, but Lyra couldn't hear her response. A sound filled her ears like the sifting of wind across a desert, a sound of huge emptiness, and her body disappeared, and Dr. O'Donnell and Caelum and the room disappeared, and darkness lifted up and swallowed her like a wave.

TWENTY-ONE

SHE DIDN'T EXIST AND THEN she did again: she was drinking water, and as the cold touched her lips and tongue and throat, it poured her back into herself. She was so startled she nearly choked.

Dr. O'Donnell was gone.

So was Caelum.

She couldn't remember where the water had come from—it was in a mug, and there was writing on the mug, but she couldn't seem to bring it into focus; the letters were meaningless geometry. She couldn't understand where Caelum had gone, or Dr. O'Donnell, and in fact she couldn't remember their names or what they looked like but only that there had been other people with her, a sense that she'd been left behind.

The room smelled bad, and in a lined plastic trash can there was vomit mixed with a little blood. She knew it must be hers, but for a long time she stared at it, revolted and uncomprehending: she didn't remember throwing up. She tried to move to the window but found that she was instead pushing on the door, pushing and trying to open it. The door was locked.

She turned around and the room also turned, swung and changed direction, and just as the letters had disintegrated, the whole place had ceased to have any meaning. She saw lines and angles skating in space like the cleaved wings of birds in the sky, and she couldn't tack any of it down or make sense of it. *Help,* she wanted to say, but she couldn't find the word for help. There was a sound in her ears, a hard knocking. And after a bit she recognized that she was hearing her own heart, and the idea of a heart came back to her, four interlocked chambers webbed with arteries.

At the same time, words loosed themselves from the dark hole and soared up to her consciousness: *room, chairs, rug.* Every time she found the word, the shape of the thing stopped struggling and settled down and became familiar.

She was still in the unused office. Caelum had been with her but he had argued with Dr. O'Donnell and now he was gone. Outside, the light had been reduced to a bare trickle that bled through the tree branches: it was evening. But Caelum had argued with Dr. O'Donnell in the morning.

She had lost a whole day.

Think. Someone had brought her the mug of water. She was sure it hadn't been there earlier. That meant someone must be close, and in fact when she went to the door again and leaned up against it, she could hear the murmur of voices.

Dr. O'Donnell wouldn't hurt Caelum, not when she wanted to use him to show off. So Caelum must have been removed either to another room in the building, or somewhere else entirely—which meant first that Lyra had to find him.

Second that they had to escape.

Another wave of nausea tipped her off her feet and she sat down and bent over, waiting for it to pass. At least she didn't throw up again.

When she felt better, she moved to the file cabinets and opened all the drawers one by one, hoping to find something she could use to get out. But they were all empty—she didn't find so much as a pen cap. Even if she could slip out into the hallway, she would need an ID to swipe in and out of doors. But Dr. O'Donnell, wherever she was, had of course taken hers along.

Think, think. Along with the water, someone had left her a pack of gum, probably because she had been throwing up. Lyra got a small, electric thrill.

An idea, a very small one, a very desperate one,

condensed through the fog of her brain.

She fed a wad of gum into her mouth and gnawed, then went to the door again; the murmur of voices, probably from an adjacent office, continued uninterrupted. Someone was watching TV. She lifted a fist and banged several times, and after a brief and muffled discussion, footsteps came toward the door. She quickly spat her gum into one hand, and thumbed it into two portions.

The door handle jumped around while someone took a key to it. When it opened, Lyra saw a girl with chunky black stripes in her hair and very thick glasses.

"Oh," she said, and took a step backward, as if she hadn't expected Lyra to be there. "Oh," she said again. "I *thought* I heard you knocking."

"I need to pee," Lyra said. The girl tried to step in front of her, but she shoved into the hall, wedging the gum right into the locking mechanism, forcing it in deep: a trick Raina had taught her.

The girl took a few quick steps away from her—Lyra realized she was frightened, and didn't want even accidental contact. The halls were dim, and Lyra knew most of the employees must have gone home for the night, although she could hear the ghost *clack-clack* of invisible fingers on keyboards, and a few offices still spilled their light onto the carpets.

In a narrow office across the hall, a boy was hunched

over a laptop, watching something. He quickly thumbed off the volume. Lyra's heart swelled: his ID was lying next to his computer, coiled inside its lanyard at the edge of his desk. Her fingers itched to take it.

"What does *she* want?" the boy asked, jerking his head toward Lyra, and even though he sounded tough, Lyra knew he was afraid also, and just trying not to show it.

"She has to use the bathroom," the girl said, in a desperate whisper, as if it was a secret. "Where's O'Donnell?"

"Still on the phone," he replied. "She said she might be half an hour."

So: Dr. O'Donnell was still here. That was good. It likely meant she hadn't taken Caelum somewhere else, somewhere that would require a car. But Dr. O'Donnell had said she'd be back in half an hour; that didn't give her much time to look.

"Should I . . . take her?" the girl asked, still shying away from Lyra as though she were diseased.

The boy blinked. "Well, *I'm* not going with her."

"Dr. O'Donnell said not to go anywhere. . . ." The girl trailed off uncertainly.

Fear could be used. The nurses at Haven had been afraid; they had acted as though the replicas had something sticky on their skin, something that might spread through contact and turn them into monsters. But back then, Lyra had not known how to use this to her advantage.

Things were different now.

"I threw up in the trash can," she said. "There's some on the floor, too."

"We heard," the girl said. She avoided Lyra's eyes. Lyra knew the girl was afraid she wouldn't be able to find the difference between them, the reason she had the key to the room where Lyra was getting sick and not vice versa.

"Did Caelum get his medicine?" she asked. This made the girl and boy turn to stare at her. "The other one," she clarified. "The male."

The girl looked worried. "What medicine?" she asked loudly, as if Lyra might otherwise fail to understand.

"He has medicines," Lyra said. "He always takes them. Otherwise he'll get sick worse than I did." She held her breath as the girl chewed on her thumbnail. If she went to get Dr. O'Donnell, Lyra would have to admit Caelum didn't take medication.

She counted heartbeats, one, two, three.

"Can you go and get Sonja?" the girl said finally, turning to the boy. Lyra let out the breath she'd been holding. "Can you ask whether the other one said anything about medicine?"

"Now?"

"Just ask," the girl said. "I don't want to get in trouble."

The boy leaned to hoist himself to his feet. He grabbed

his ID, winding the lanyard between his fingers, and Lyra's heart skipped down into her fingers. "In one of the cold rooms?"

The girl nodded. "Sub-Two," she said, and Lyra had to bite her lip to keep from smiling. Now she knew where Caelum was.

But she was careful to keep her face blank, to look as dumb as they thought she was. To watch without seeming to pay any attention at all.

She saw: the way the boy slipped his ID in his back pocket when he stood.

"I really need to pee," Lyra repeated.

She saw: the girl relenting. "Come on. Make it quick."

Lyra followed her into the hall, head down, obedient as a cow. Dumb, docile, harmless. The boy glanced at her with barely concealed pity before turning to lock his office door.

She saw: the loop of lanyard visible above the stitching.

All she had to do was hook it with two fingers as she was passing.

Harmless.

In the bathroom, she used the toilet and washed her mouth out in the sink. There was no time to waste. Once Dr. O'Donnell returned, Lyra would lose her chance.

The girl had waited in the hall. When Lyra emerged,

she saw the boy retracing his steps, making a search of the hallway.

"I had it right here," he was saying. Another sleepy-looking employee had come to her office door, blinking and yawning, as if she'd just been napping. "Right here, in my pocket . . ."

When he looked up and spotted Lyra, he blinked, and Lyra was seized by sudden panic. But his eyes traveled through her down the length of carpet.

Of course. He wouldn't think to check her or look in her pockets. They thought she wasn't capable of it. Too dumb to lie. Too dumb to plan.

Lyra followed the girl back to the empty office, taking a seat quietly as the girl tried, and failed, to make the key work. She made a face when she saw the gum jamming the lock. "I don't *believe* it," she said. Suspicion tightened her face. "Did you do this?"

"Do what?" Lyra asked stupidly.

The girl rolled her eyes. "Worst night ever. Just stay here."

Lyra nodded, dozy as an animal.

She counted the girl's footsteps until the carpet had absorbed them completely.

She stood up, steadying herself against the wall. She had to be careful, to stay clear of any holes that might grab her.

For the moment, the hall was clear. She went quickly, scanning for hiding spots, checking door handles lightly with her fingers, looking for open offices. She ducked into the bathroom again when she heard voices, but the sound of a closing door quieted them. They had gone into an office, whoever they were.

She found her way to the stairwell without seeing anyone else. The doors were still propped open by the same book, its pages furred with moisture and age.

The first basement level was still dark, still full of the lumpy silhouettes of old equipment. She kept going, listening carefully for footsteps, since the turns concealed the landings beneath her. The girl with the striped hair had probably already discovered she was missing: Lyra had a minute, maybe two, before the girl panicked and launched an all-out search.

She reached Sub-Two, and the gate locked with a keypad. She nearly cried when she saw that it required a numbered code: she'd forgotten all about it. Her palms were sweating and dizziness rose like a sudden swarm of insects. She leaned against the gate, sucking air into lungs that felt like paper.

She imagined her whole body strapped with fear and anger. She imagined burning up with it, like the woman who, arriving at Spruce Island, had detonated the dozen homemade explosives lashed to her body. She imagined screaming so that all the windows shattered, so the roof blew off, so that everyone above her was consumed in flame.

She imagined fire.

She wheeled away from the gate and backtracked up the stairs, leaning heavily on the railing, until she spotted what she wanted: on the landing of Sub-One, directly across from the swinging doors, a small red-handled fire alarm. At Haven the alarms had been enclosed by plastic, surfaces warm and smudgy from the fingers of all the replicas who'd touched them for good luck and connection.

Pull down, the alarm said.

She pulled.

The noise made her teeth ring. It vibrated her eyeballs. Immediately, the stairs filled with the echoes of distant shouting. She rocketed across the landing and hurtled past the swinging doors, into the dark recesses of the empty basement level.

From where she stood, she could see a steady flow of people up the stairs from Sub-Two. But not Caelum. She kept waiting for him to pass, but all she saw were strangers made identical by their confusion, by the quick-flash way they passed behind the glass.

She counted them all, the way she'd counted beads of IV fluid from the drip bag: *two, seven, nine, fourteen, fifteen, sixteen.* Still Caelum didn't come.

The blur of people slowed. She counted three heartbeats when no footsteps rattled the landing, when the window stayed empty of passing faces.

Hardly thinking, she pushed once again from her hiding place through the swinging doors and hurtled out into the open stairwell. She sprinted down the stairs, no longer thinking of being caught, thinking only of Caelum, of reaching him, of losing her chance.

As Lyra crashed around the corkscrew of stairs, she saw the gate at the bottom of the stairs was only just swinging closed. She saw the inch of space between lock and gate as a narrow tether. She leapt, shouting, reaching for it the way she might have reached for a rope, and got a hand through the gate just before it clicked shut. Her mouth tasted like iron relief, like blood. Beyond the gate was the door marked *Secure Area—Live Samples*, which she opened with the stolen keycard.

It was very cold.

For a moment she stood with goose bumps lifting the hair on her arms, suddenly confused by a vision of Haven unrolling in front of her, by the collapse of past and present. But it was just an illusion: this hall looked almost identical to so many hallways at Haven.

There were no offices here. There was no carpeting. Just a long linoleum hallway and windows overlooking darkened laboratories, doors barred and marked with

Do Not Enter signs, cameras winking in the ceiling. Her stomach turned. She'd forgotten all about the Glass Eyes, and she felt a pull of both homesickness and revulsion.

Almost as soon as she started down the hall, a man with an Afro and a goatee turned out of one of the laboratories, shouting something. She froze, thinking he was angry, or that she'd been caught. Then she realized he was just asking her a question.

"Is it a drill or what?" he said, and she realized, too, that he had no idea who she was. Dr. O'Donnell had told her there were one hundred and fifty people who worked at CASECS: he must simply have mistaken her for one of them.

"Not a drill," she said, and had to repeat herself twice over the noise. "Everybody out. I'm making the rounds," she added, when he started to respond, and she continued past him down the hall. Maybe that was the secret, and why at Haven the doctors and nurses had been able to lie for so long. People were trained to believe.

Lyra counted two laboratories, each of them a fraction of the size of Haven's. Some of the pieces of equipment were familiar. She recognized them from the vast, brightly sterile rooms where the doctors had done all the making, had with a shock of electricity made an egg swallow the nucleus, the tight-coiled place where DNA nested, of another person's cells.

But CASECS didn't make replicas. Dr. O'Donnell had said so herself, and Lyra didn't think it could be a lie. If there were other replicas, Dr. O'Donnell wouldn't be so desperate to use Caelum as evidence.

Dr. O'Donnell had said CASECS helped other places do research. But Lyra hadn't thought to ask what kind of research she meant.

Or maybe she *had* thought to ask. Maybe she had known, deep down, and she didn't want to hear the answer.

Understanding was like its own kind of alarm—so loud, so overwhelming, that the only choice was to ignore it altogether.

There were just three other doors in the hall, and one of them wouldn't open. But the second one did and inside she found Caelum, sitting on the floor, knees up, head down on his arms. She called his name at the precise moment the alarm was silenced, so her voice echoed in the sudden quiet.

"Are you hurt?" she asked. A stupid question. When he stood up and came toward her, his face was pale, and she noticed new cuts and bruises on his cheek.

"The guard," was all he said.

He didn't hug her, but from a distance of several feet he lifted his hands and touched her face and smiled.

"We have to go," he said, and she nodded.

But she hesitated when she registered all the industrial freezers, the careful labels and printed signs. The whole room was full of them. Storage freezers, of the kind that kept embryos cold, on ice, until they were ready for use.

And suddenly she knew.

Who knew eternal life would spring from a cooler in Allentown, Pennsylvania?

We give hospitals, facilities, even governments the chance to do their own *research.*

"They're not making replicas," she said. "They're selling them."

"They're selling *how* to make them," Caelum said. Lyra remembered what the woman Anju had said to explain how licensing worked: *Let's say I invented a new way to manufacture a chair . . .*

"They're making new Havens all over the place." He even smiled, but it was a terrible smile, like a new wound. "They're replicating Haven all around the world."

PART III

TWENTY-TWO

AS A COP, REINHARDT KNEW lies, but he also knew coincidence. Coincidences happened all the time, everywhere. Plenty of rookie cops wasted time giving too much weight to the kind of background coincidence that blew through every life, every death, every case.

Coincidences happened everywhere, all the time: but they didn't happen in the *same* place, at the *same* time.

That was called a pattern.

The girl who'd called herself Gemma Ives, that skinny little thing with eyes eating up her face, wasn't any of his business. He had plenty of other cases to worry about, *actual* cases: three other missing-persons cases had landed on his desk in the past six months alone, two of them teenagers from the same low-income district where he'd grown up, one of them a forty-five-year-old stay-at-home mom on the board of her children's PTA who'd disappeared in February on her way to the gym. No signs of violence, but no activity on any of her credit cards, either, nothing to indicate whether she was alive or dead. Only yesterday he'd found her in Florida, living with an ex-con who'd retiled her roof last summer. Reinhardt still hadn't figured out a way to tell her husband.

As far as he knew, the girl wasn't in any trouble at all. Just because she'd lied about her name didn't mean she'd lied about heading for Pennsylvania to see her doctor.

Of course, she couldn't have been headed to see Dr. Saperstein, since Dr. Saperstein was dead. It had been all over the morning news. That was coincidence number one.

Maybe she'd lied about his name, too. But it was funny she'd chosen his name in particular, and funny she'd chosen Gemma Ives's name, too. Because after Detective Reinhardt had seen the real Gemma Ives's picture, and after he'd Googled around a bit, he found that Geoffrey Ives and Dr. Saperstein, now deceased, knew each other, from a place called Haven, a research institute off the coast of Florida.

The girl, the skinny big-eyed girl, had said she came from Florida.

And if you were counting—which Detective Reinhardt wasn't, because it wasn't his business, because what did some skinny, desperate stranger matter to him?—but if you were, you would count coincidences two and three.

And you would know that three coincidences were two coincidences too many.

Of course, anyone could imagine meaningful connections where none existed. It was all a question of wanting. If you wanted to find a thread between JFK's assassination and a UFO sighting in New Mexico, you could be sure you would hit on one eventually.

But Detective Reinhardt didn't want to find a thread. He didn't want to see a pattern. He wanted to forget the girl, and forget Gemma Ives, and the smell of moneyed lies that leaked off her father, and the skittish look of his wife, like someone awakening in an unfamiliar room from a terrible nightmare.

He certainly didn't want to find significance in the presence of federal investigators on a missing-persons case. He didn't want to find it strange that they'd grilled him about the girl and her cousin—or whoever he was—he'd picked up Sunday night, though Mr. Ives had said previously that Gemma knew no one of her description.

He didn't want to find it suspicious that his captain, usually so forthcoming, shut down Reinhardt as soon as he'd thought to question their participation.

He didn't want to see, and he didn't want to care, and he sure as shit didn't want to spend Wednesday, his only day off, making the twelve-hour drive to Philadelphia.

He would have to stop for gas on the way out of Nashville.

TWENTY-THREE

THERE WOULD BE NO THIRD chance to escape. Maybe Dr. O'Donnell would lock them in cages, or cuff them to a bed, as some of the replicas at Haven had been cuffed. Or maybe she would simply grow tired of protecting them, and hand them over to one of the Suits who wanted Lyra and Caelum dead.

You aren't supposed to exist, she had said.

Whose fault is that? Lyra should have asked.

Every second they delayed brought them closer to disaster—and yet they went through the laboratories, smashing everything they could, knocking equipment from the countertops, shattering microscopes, dumping out chemical samples. Lyra knew Dr. O'Donnell and her staff would recover soon enough—they could buy new equipment, order new chemical samples—but it made her feel better. Every test tube that shattered, every hundred-thousand-dollar piece of lab equipment that crashed and splintered into pieces, seemed as it broke to simultaneously split open a kind of joy inside of her.

Finally, there was nothing left to destroy.

The hallway carried distant echoes, footsteps overhead, voices shouting words she couldn't make out. People looking for them.

They were halfway up the stairs when the rhythm of footsteps narrowed above them: in her head, Lyra saw sound like a cloud that had collapsed into a single dark stream of water. She recognized Dr. O'Donnell's voice, and the panicked response of the girl who'd escorted her to the bathroom earlier.

"In here," she whispered to Caelum, and she pulled him past the swinging doors into the vacant offices on the basement level. Through the cutaway window, she saw Dr. O'Donnell pass, followed by the girl and the boy whose ID she had stolen. There were other employees with them, brown and white and tall and short, but all with the same identical expression of tight-cinched panic.

They didn't dare turn on a light and so they went slowly through the dark space, feeling their way, toward an emergency exit sign that floated up through the murk of shadows.

More shouts, increasingly urgent, vibrated through the ceiling and floated up through the floor, like a dust they disturbed with their feet. It seemed they weren't getting any closer to escape, as if the darkness kept unrolling.

"Wait," she said. She couldn't breathe. When they reached the emergency exit, a barred door, she was so dizzy she had to stop, leaning heavily against it. "Wait."

Suddenly she wasn't sure. Dr. O'Donnell was right: there was nowhere for them to go. She wondered how much time she even had left. One week? One month? Two? Would they spend the rest of her time simply running, like this, in the dark, trying to stay ahead of the people who wanted to erase them? And what would happen to Caelum once she died?

It was terrible to think that he would go on, and terrible to think that he wouldn't.

"We have to go," Caelum whispered to her. "They'll find us here."

Lyra still couldn't breathe. The room was spinning, and ideas began losing their shape: Rick was warming soup in the microwave; there were men passing through rows of beds, touching the replicas with their fingers. She recalled the strange, sweet stink that had sometimes carried back to Haven from the ocean, when the winds were right and the disposal crews hadn't gone far enough to burn the bodies of the dead. Time, the present, was like a hook; she struggled to hang on.

"Where will we go?" she said. Caelum's breath was hot

on her cheek. The dim light of the exit sign gave shape to his shoulders and neck. "Dr. O'Donnell was right. No one can help us."

"It doesn't matter if she's right or not," Caelum said. His hand found hers in the dark. She was shocked by the sense that her heart had traveled down her arm into her palm, and that he was holding that instead, fragile and alive. "She doesn't have the right to say," he said. "She doesn't have the right to choose."

Lyra swallowed. She felt like crying. "I'm going to die," she whispered. "Aren't I?"

He leaned forward. His lips bumped her nose and then her jaw and finally her lips. "Sure," he said. "But not yet. Not today."

Elbowing open the door, they found instead of stairs a cavernous loading bay. They ran together, even though the effort made her gasp, and she kept fearing they would hit some obstacle, a sudden wall that would surprise them, although there were dirty bulbs set in the ceiling that switched on with their movement and she could see there was nothing to stop them.

Caelum found the switch to control the rolling doors and the noise rattled her whole body: it seemed to take forever before they'd inched high enough for Caelum and Lyra to duck beneath the gap.

Either her sickness or her fear began to cut things into clips: a short stretch of pavement and a fence they couldn't climb. Dumpsters to their right. To their left, a sweep of red light: a fire truck had come, although as Lyra watched, the lights went dark and the truck began to shimmy itself into a turn. She couldn't see the parking lot or the front gates they'd snuck through; they'd come out the back.

They skirted the building, looking for other gates, or places the fence wasn't reinforced. But the only way out to the street was through the manned gates. And the fire alarm had driven the staff out into the parking lot; there were still a half-dozen people milling around in front of the double glass doors.

They could wait for the crowd to break up, but that just meant it was even more likely that Dr. O'Donnell would catch up. The only other option was simply run for it. Charge straight through the lot and count on surprise. The fire truck was just nosing toward the driveway. They might even be able to hitch a ride out through the gate when they opened it.

"Think you can make it?" Caelum asked her, and she knew he was thinking what she was: Why stop now?

She nodded, although her legs felt wobbly and she knew that there was always a hole waiting for her, waiting like a long throat to swallow her up.

He took her hand again, and she was glad. A sudden,

strangling fear made her want to cling to him, to tell him that she loved him. But she couldn't make the words come up. They were stuck behind the fear, which glued her lungs and made it hard to breathe.

"When I say go," he said. "Go."

It was a good thing they were holding hands. She wasn't sure her legs would have started moving if he hadn't yanked her forward. They came around the side of the building, charging straight toward the group of people still milling outside, texting, one of them smoking a cigarette; but by the time anyone thought to look up, they were already blowing by the crowd, weaving through the few cars in the lot and sprinting to follow the fire truck as it approached the gate.

Everyone was shouting, and touching off explosions in her head. The gate was opening to let the fire truck through. They were too slow. They wouldn't make it. But Caelum wouldn't let go of her hand.

Almost there. The truck had slowed to maneuver through the gates. They were ten feet away, then closer. They were going to make it.

"Stop, stop, *stop*."

Dr. O'Donnell's voice was high and clear: it rang out like a bell. The fire truck braked abruptly, and Caelum threw out a hand to keep from cracking into the bumper. One of the firefighters leaned out the driver's-side door and cranked around to see what all the noise was. Lyra saw his mouth moving, saw the way his eyes darkened when they landed on her.

Stop. Lyra was screaming, too, or she thought she was. Then she realized she had only been screaming in her head. She threw her voice as hard as she could, hurled it like a stone. "Stop! Please! Help!"

He retreated, yanking the door shut; she didn't know if he'd heard. The fire truck jerked forward another few feet, and that did it—Lyra gave up, she dropped, her knees gave out and she stumbled. Caelum caught her and tried to draw her in another direction, toward the parking lot. But she could barely stay on her feet. She was too tired—of running, of hiding, of hitting walls, of finding that every face concealed a sharp set of hungry teeth.

Then Dr. O'Donnell threw herself between them and the truck.

"Wait," she said. Her hair was slicked by sweat to her forehead. "Just wait a second, okay?"

Caelum had to put an arm around Lyra's waist just to haul her backward. Her feet had stopped obeying her. Her whole body felt as if it were as flimsy, as weightless and useless, as an empty sheath of skin.

But Caelum wouldn't give up. "Come on, Lyra. Come on. Move." He was still shouting, although it was suddenly very quiet.

And then, with a start, she realized why: the fire truck's engine had stopped growling. No more exhaust plumed from its tailpipe. And almost as soon as she noticed, the door opened again, and the firefighter dropped to the pavement from the cab. Another one followed, a woman, this time from the passenger side. Both of them wore heavy rubber suits that made funny squirting noises when they walked—that was how quiet it was.

"Is there a problem?" The firefighter who'd been driving had sharp eyes, placed very close together, as if they'd been made that way just to notice every detail.

"Please," was all Lyra could say. She was still winded, still gasping for breath—partly from the run, partly from a dizzying sense of relief.

Dr. O'Donnell pivoted neatly to face him. "There's no problem." In an instant she transformed. She had been begging them to listen, begging them to stop. But in a split second, she shimmied into a new skin, and Lyra was seized by a sense of dread. "I'm sorry you had to come all the way out here. Honestly, we didn't expect them to react like this."

He looked from Dr. O'Donnell, to Lyra and Caelum, and back again. "What do you mean, 'react'?"

"They're patient volunteers," Dr. O'Donnell said smoothly.

"She's lying," Caelum burst out.

But Dr. O'Donnell didn't miss a beat. "Sometimes our volunteers get anxious. Sometimes they get paranoid. It's the first time anyone's ever tried to stage an escape, though."

She slid over the words as if she'd been waiting for years to use them. And Lyra hated her so violently, the hatred blew her apart into a thousand pieces.

Because the worst part, the absolute worst part, was that Dr. O'Donnell truly believed she was good. She was surprised that Lyra and Caelum weren't grateful; that they didn't see the way she wanted to use them as a kind of gift.

Because deep down she thought, of course, they didn't deserve it. Because she thought that it was *obvious* they didn't.

And that made her worse, even, than Dr. Saperstein. Saperstein had treated the replicas like objects, but at least he never pretended.

Dr. O'Donnell thought the replicas should love her for helping them pretend that they were worth something, when it was so obvious they weren't.

The woman's coat was folded down at the waist. She thumbed her suspenders. "So it's some kind of medical research?"

Dr. O'Donnell smiled. Lyra couldn't believe she'd ever loved that smile. "That's exactly right," she said. "Medical research, pharmaceutical testing. All voluntary, obviously."

"She's lying." Lyra could finally breathe, but the effort of speaking, of trying to be believed, made her words come in hard little bursts. "She's been keeping us locked up. She won't—she won't let us go." Then: "You can't believe her."

Dr. O'Donnell didn't even glance at Lyra. "Paranoia, like I said."

The firefighters exchanged a look. "They seem pretty upset," the man said doubtfully. But Lyra could tell he was wavering.

"Of course they're upset. They're having a bad reaction to a new SSRI." Dr. O'Donnell grew taller, swelled by her lies, or maybe the world shrank around her. She sounded calm. She looked calm. Lyra couldn't imagine what she and Caelum looked like. "And I can't help them unless we get them inside. They should be monitored. We should be watching their heart rates."

Lyra saw at once that Dr. O'Donnell had won. She watched the firefighters tip over into belief; she saw them shake off their doubts, like a kind of irritant.

"Please—" Caelum tried again. But his voice broke, and Lyra knew that he, too, had seen.

"Thank you for coming out here," Dr. O'Donnell said. "We really appreciate it."

The firefighters had already turned back to their truck. Though they were only a few feet away, Lyra saw them as though from the bottom of a pit, as if they had already vanished into a memory.

"Wait." She cried out from the bottom of a long tunnel of anger and fear. "Wait," she said again, as both of them turned back to face her.

Dr. O'Donnell showed her irritation, but only briefly. She was busy playing a role. "Really, we should get them inside—"

"She said she would let me call my mom," Lyra blurted out. Caelum tensed.

But Dr. O'Donnell looked at her with blunted astonishment: it was as if her polish was only a mask, and someone had elbowed it off.

"She promised," Lyra said, feeling her way into the lie. If Dr. O'Donnell was going to make up a story, Lyra could get in there, could hook her hands around it and make it hers. "She said I'd be able to call if I got scared."

Dr. O'Donnell licked her lips. "I never—"

But this time, the firefighters were on Lyra's side. "For God's sake, let the kid call her mom," the man said.

For a half second, Dr. O'Donnell and Lyra locked eyes. Dr. O'Donnell squinted as if they were separated by a hard fog, and Lyra wondered what she saw. That Lyra was small and young. That she was stupid. That she was *dying.* Just like Calliope, all those years ago, and the bird. *It was broken,* she'd said. *It's better to kill it.* For weeks afterward Lyra had dreamed of the bird coming back to life, but enormous, and swooping down through the dorms to peck their eyes out, one by one.

Dr. O'Donnell even looked vaguely amused. Of course she knew that Lyra had no mother.

Of course she knew, or thought she knew, that Lyra had no one to call.

Maybe that was why she didn't put up more of a fight.

She shrugged. "Okay," she said. She took her phone out of her pocket, and, after punching in her code, passed it wordlessly to Lyra.

She'd been trained to memorize number series, of course, so that the doctors at Haven would be able to collect data points, would be able to track how quickly her mind was breaking up. And she'd been trained to observe, too: not intentionally, but she had been trained.

And in the real world, she'd been trained to lie.

Lyra pressed the numbers very slowly, making sure she got them right.

Now Dr. O'Donnell was frowning. "Honestly, this isn't standard. . . ."

But the firefighters said nothing, and stood there, watching.

Lyra brought the phone to her ear. She pressed it hard,

the way she had with those seashells Cassiopeia had collected long ago, and her breath hitched. It was ringing.

Once. Twice.

Answer, she thought. *Answer.*

Dr. O'Donnell lost patience. A muscle near her lips twitched. "Okay. That's enough."

"Wait," Lyra said. Her heart was beating so loudly she lost track of the number of rings.

Answer.

And then a fumbling sound, and a cough, announced him.

"Reinhardt." His voice sounded rough, but also comforting, like sand.

She closed her eyes and watched his name float up from the darkness, resolving slowly, like a distant star captured by a telescope.

"Detective Kevin Reinhardt. Hello," she said. Her throat was tight. It was painful to speak. When she opened her eyes again, Dr. O'Donnell was staring at her. Shocked. Hands hanging at her sides, limp, like old balloons. "You picked me up in Nashville. You gave me your number and told me to call if I ever needed help."

It seemed that everyone was frozen: Caelum, watching her, and the firefighters, watching her, and Dr. O'Donnell, slack-faced and dumb. Only the insects sang, a noise that sounded to her like a motor.

She took a deep breath. She had never been taught how to pray, but she did pray, then, without ever having learned it.

"I need your help," she said.

TWENTY-FOUR

FOR A SHORT TIME, THE firefighters waited with them on the road, pacing in the quiet and talking into their radios, casting cautious glances at Lyra and Caelum from a distance, as if they were fish and too much attention would cause them to startle away.

Then a cop arrived to replace them, a woman with a high forehead and a long nose that reminded Lyra of a hanging fruit. She wanted to talk, to understand, to hear Lyra's side of the story.

But though the woman was kind to her, and though Lyra liked the look of her face and the slope of her nose, she didn't want to talk to anyone but Detective Kevin Reinhardt. She didn't even want to get into the police car: she was tired of strangers and their doors.

So instead, she and Caelum sat on the curb, with the police car parked a dozen feet away, watching the last trickle of car traffic out of CASECS. Dr. O'Donnell and the other CASECS employees weren't in trouble, exactly, because the trouble couldn't be reported or understood when neither Caelum nor Lyra would talk, as the policewoman explained to them more than once.

But they weren't exactly not in trouble, either. CASECS wasn't invisible anymore. She kept her hands in her pockets, touching the drift of words, notes, telephone numbers. Proof.

And so the employees who had lingered to work late, or to catch a glimpse of Lyra and Caelum, spilled into their cars and flooded the exit gates, and tried to vanish. Lyra thought of cockroaches flooding from a clogged drain.

She tried to pick out Dr. O'Donnell's car in the sixty or so that passed. But the cars looked the same, and the drivers, inside of them, looked the same too: hunched shadows, leaning over the steering wheels as if that would make them go faster. As if they could escape whatever was coming, just by leaning forward.

He arrived an hour or so before sunrise, when the darkness was like a scowl that had folded deep into itself.

They waited for him in the car while he spoke to the policewoman who had by then sat with them for hours. It was hot. An empty cup of coffee in the cup holder had scented the whole car with hazelnut.

Finally, he returned, and put the car in drive without saying anything except, "I brought you snacks." At Lyra's feet was a bag of gas station food and water. Caelum ate three bags of beef jerky, and Lyra drank two bottles of water.

Then Detective Reinhardt said, "Do you want to tell me your real name, at least?"

Inexplicably, the question—how kind it was, how gentle, and how difficult it was to answer—made tears come to Lyra's eyes.

"Which one?" She turned to the window, swiping her tears away with a palm. "I've had three so far."

And then, after hours of silence—after years of it—she talked. Detective Reinhardt was listening quietly, not saying anything, not interrupting to ask questions, just listening. She told him everything: Haven, all the replicas, Jake Witz, Nurse Emily Huang, Gemma Ives and how she'd saved them. Dr. O'Donnell and CASECS; a world full of places where people could be manufactured, like furniture, for different uses. About Rick Harliss, her real father, and the people who'd taken him away.

Afterward, he was quiet for a long time. Lyra couldn't tell whether he believed her, and was too tired to ask.

When he finally asked a question, it wasn't the one she expected. "Do you have any idea where Gemma might be?"

Lyra shook her head. "I heard that she was missing."

"Missing," he said. He appeared to be choosing his words carefully. "And in quite a bit of trouble."

Caelum spoke up for the first time. "What kind of trouble?"

Detective Reinhardt appeared to be chewing the words. Lyra liked that about him. Too many people used words without thinking. "I'm out of my element here," he said finally. "I'm flying blind."

"What kind of trouble?" Caelum repeated.

"The Lancaster County Sheriff's Office is looking for Gemma," he said, with some difficulty. "I got a call about an hour before we talked. Because you'd given me her name," he added, and sighed. "Funny coincidence."

Lyra looked down at her hands. "It was the only name I could think of." Then: "Gemma's my friend."

"That's what the sheriff's department figured, too. They thought you might be a clue."

"A clue to what?"

Detective Reinhardt hesitated. "Several people were hurt—badly." He cleared his throat. "They were killed. There was a witness. He described a girl Gemma's age, matching her description."

"It wasn't her," Caelum said, and leaned back.

"The witness got a good look at her," Detective Reinhardt said. "He was very specific. And—" He broke off. Now his whole face corked around his mouth, like there was a wrestling match between them.

"And what?"

He shook his head. She noticed then how tightly he was holding the wheel.

"Dr. Saperstein and the Ives family have history. A long history."

"Because of Haven," Lyra said.

"Okay." He exhaled. "Okay. Because of Haven." He didn't believe her, not totally, not all the way. But he didn't disbelieve her, either. "Dr. Saperstein was found not far away from where the victims were discovered. And the Iveses are there, now, in Lancaster. They drove straight from Nashville. Look, like I said, I'm flying blind." He held up a hand as if Lyra had argued with him. "But where there's smoke, there's fire."

"But Gemma wouldn't hurt anybody," Lyra said. "She couldn't."

He shook his head. "Sometimes people can do a good job of hiding who they really are," he said, as if Lyra didn't know that. "Some people put on their faces the way you and I put on clothes."

"Exactly." She was growing impatient. "The faces don't mean anything." But when he glanced at her, puzzled, she could tell she'd misread him. He *didn't* understand. He had listened to her without really absorbing it. Maybe he thought she was making it up. "It's like you said—people can wear different faces. And different people can wear the same face, too. It's not Gemma," she repeated, a little louder. "So it must be one of the others."

"One of the others?" Detective Reinhardt's voice cracked.

"Yeah. I already told you." She pivoted in her seat to look at Caelum. "At CASECS, Dr. O'Donnell said some of the other replicas might have escaped. Wherever Dr. Saperstein was, they couldn't have been far off."

Detective Reinhardt was quiet for a bit. "So you're saying that Gemma Ives has—has replicas? That she was . . . cloned?"

"Of course." Lyra was too tired to be polite. "Were you even listening?"

"I was, I just—" He broke off. "Bear with me, okay? It's a lot." He took a hand off the wheel to rub his temples. "So you think—you think one of Gemma's replicas is responsible?"

"I know it," she said. She leaned back against the headrest. She thought of Calliope, number 7, squatting to nudge the broken bird with a knuckle before straightening up to smash it beneath her shoe. Lyra had thought at first she intended to help it fly again. "I bet I know which one, too."

TWENTY-FIVE

THE DAWN CAME, WEAK AND watery, bringing a patter of light rain. Lancaster was long spools of dark green, fields and forests: at any other time, Lyra thought, it would be peaceful.

But now, helicopters motored down over the nature preserve and hovered there like giant mosquitoes. Unmarked, but obviously military grade. There were snipers wearing camouflage visible inside.

"You're sure you want to be here?" Detective Reinhardt asked, and Lyra realized she'd been clenching her fists so hard she'd left marks.

She nodded. "I want to help Gemma," she said. "Gemma helped me." But she was afraid. She was afraid she would not be able to help. She was afraid of the Suits, afraid Detective Reinhardt wouldn't be able to protect her, afraid that he would try.

But she could no longer be invisible.

Detective Reinhardt drove slowly, showing his badge whenever they were stopped, which was often. The interstate was completely blocked off between the exits to Loag and Middletown, as were all the local roads bordering the Sequoia Falls Nature Preserve. Police had come from all over the state, some of them on their days off.

Detective Reinhardt had said little since they'd reached Lancaster, and had ordered Lyra and Caelum to stay in the car with the doors locked when he climbed out briefly to speak with a cluster of police officers. But she had picked up rumors, whispers, words carried back to the car like a kind of contamination.

There were *kids*, dozens of them, maybe even more than that, running loose.

Not normal kids, either. Twins, triplets, even quadruplets. Skinny. Feral. Covered with blood.

"Creepy as shit," she heard one cop say, when Reinhardt swung open the door. "Everyone's saying that guy Saperstein must have had them in juvenile lockup, but I never seen a juvenile lockup makes kids like these. It's like something from a horror movie. You can't make this shit up."

You can make up anything you want, Lyra felt like calling out to him. *Even horror.*

But of course, she stayed quiet. She imagined the

whispers blowing like tiny seeds from one person to the next. Words were little things, of no substance at all. But they were curiously stubborn. They rooted.

They grew.

It was easy enough for Reinhardt to get through the various cordons. All he had to do was show his badge. Only one trooper seemed interested in Lyra and Caelum, and leaned down to stare at them in the backseat.

"Picked 'em up ten minutes ago trying to hitch a ride," Reinhardt said easily, before the trooper could ask. "Must have come from Saperstein's JDC—they won't say where they've been, got no ID on them."

Wordlessly, the trooper backed up and waved them through the line, shouting for another trooper to move the sawhorses out of the way.

After that it was easy enough; they pulled over and Reinhardt nosed his car into a thick entanglement of growth, so it was partly concealed. As they climbed out of the car, Lyra could hear the distant whirring of the helicopters, and felt the hairs rise on her neck.

Reinhardt had gotten a copy of the map the search teams were using to organize their efforts. He had marked the approximate location of each of Gemma's sandals, which had been located several miles apart with a piece of fabric that might have come off her clothing.

Caelum immediately pointed to several shaded-in

squares a fingernail's distance away from where a search crew had turned up her second sandal.

"What's that?" he asked Reinhardt.

"Those are farmhouses, turn-of-the-century settlement. I'm talking turn of the *last* century. Three cabins, totally run-down. But the police checked the cabins early this morning," he added. "I heard it over the radio. Apparently some kid from one of the Amish farms rang up to tip them off about the cabins—he'd walked seven miles just to find a pay phone." Reinhardt smiled. "He was scared his parents would find out. I guess the place is popular with teenagers around here when they want to be alone. Some things are the same from Lancaster to Miami, huh?"

"She couldn't have gone far without any shoes," Lyra said.

Reinhardt looked at her. "She made it more than two miles with only *one* shoe," he pointed out. "Besides, the police were already there. They cleared the cabins."

"Maybe she hid," Lyra said. "She wouldn't know she could trust them. She might think they were coming to get her for what happened on the farm."

"I thought you said she didn't do it," Reinhardt said. "That it was one of the other—the others." He still couldn't say *replica*.

"She didn't," Lyra said. "But she wouldn't know that

they knew that." That was what people did when they escaped: they found a place to hide. Caelum had hidden successfully on the island for several days when he was 72, even though there was an armed military guard on the perimeter, even though there must have been fifty people looking for him. It was because he'd stayed on the island, exactly in the middle of where he was supposed to have escaped, that no one had found him.

Besides, places had feelings to them, just like objects did: they whispered things, absorbed secrets and quietly pulsed them back. But most people didn't hear. They didn't know how to listen.

Lyra listened, and she heard a whisper even in the lines on the page. A lost and abandoned place, for lost and abandoned people.

"She could have planted the shoes," Detective Reinhardt said. "She might have wanted to throw people off her trail."

"Why would she plant them so far apart?" Lyra shook her head. "She might be underground. She might be in a basement or—or hiding under a bed."

She could tell that Reinhardt didn't think so. But he folded up the map. "Someone's going to find her. They'll stay at it until they do. The dogs will get a scent."

"The dogs look for dead bodies," Lyra said. She remembered how the soldiers had brought dogs onto the marshes after the explosion to scent the trails of blood. She didn't hate dogs, though: she knew it was just their training. "Besides, it rained." She and Caelum had slid into the water to avoid being caught, and Cassiopeia had been located instead—located, and then permitted to die, flagged for collection later.

Reinhardt said nothing.

"There," she said, and pointed again to the ghost-silhouettes of the long-abandoned settlements. The paper dimpled beneath her finger, and hissed the smallest of words. *Yes.*

It was still raining when they set off into the woods, using a compass Reinhardt had on his phone. If they kept straight north from where they had parked, they would eventually hit the old settlement.

It was harder going than Lyra had expected, and she had to stop frequently to rest, overwhelmed by sudden tides of vertigo.

She was falling more. It was like there was a wall up between her brain and her body, and only some of the messages made it through. This was, like the holes, a symptom of the disease as it progressed: she'd seen it at Haven, even, though at the time she hadn't known what it was, and had believed it was just a problem in the process going wrong. Replicas got sick. They forgot their numbers and then how to use the bathroom and then how to walk and swallow.

She was glad neither Reinhardt nor Caelum asked her if she wanted to go back, though. Caelum just helped her up, every time, without saying a word. And Detective Reinhardt went ahead, scouting the easiest routes, and trying to break apart the growth where it was thickest to make it easier for her to pass through.

It took several hours, but at last they saw, through the tangle of natural growth, the hard sloping angle of a roof and a little stone cottage. The settlement had been made in a literal natural clearing, although growth had reclaimed the area, and one house was little more than rubble, punctured by the hardy fists of oak trees that had grown straight up through a collapsed portion of the roof.

As soon as Lyra saw the place, her stomach sank. It was obvious that Gemma wasn't here. It took only a few minutes to check the two standing houses: they were each a single room. Inside was a litter of cigarette butts and empty soda cans. But no Gemma. She was glad, too, that Reinhardt didn't gloat about it, or say he'd told them so.

Instead, he said, "I'm sorry."

"I thought she'd be here," Lyra said. Her stomach felt like it had coiled itself around her throat. "I really did."

"She'll turn up," Reinhardt said. "I promise."

Lyra just shook her head. She knew he was trying to

make her feel better, but she knew, too, that it was a promise he had no ability to keep. In the distance, she heard a faint hollow clacking—the noise of a woodpecker, or maybe a squirrel, cracking two stones together. An empty sound.

Lyra was reluctant to leave. Though Gemma was obviously not here, she kept feeling that she'd missed something, kept turning around to stare even as they began to retrace their steps. The houses, dismal, lurching on their feet. Piles of rot and leaves. The trees puncturing the beams. An old circle of stones. Maybe a fire pit, or a garden.

And not a single sign of movement, nothing but the hollow drumming that made her heart ache with loneliness.

They started back the way they'd come, and Detective Reinhardt took the lead again. They'd barely left the cabins behind when they heard him shout. Caelum put a hand on Lyra's elbow, to help her go faster, and they pushed forward through a leaf-slicked trail marked by the detective's footsteps in the mud. The rain was coming harder, beating its percussion through the trees.

She saw Reinhardt, moving through the mist toward a girl in a filthy dress, and from a distance, for a second, even Lyra was confused: Gemma, it was Gemma, they'd found her.

But immediately the vision passed. The girl's body was wrong, and her hair was wrong, the way she stood with her arms very still and tight at her sides was wrong, all of it just a small but critical distance off, like a door hanging an inch off its hinges.

Not Gemma. Calliope.

Caelum realized it too. He dropped Lyra's arm and started to run, an instinct, as if he could physically get between Calliope and Reinhardt. Lyra started to call out but it was too late, Detective Reinhardt had crossed the distance. He reached out to put a hand on her shoulder even as Caelum shouted, "No!"

Calliope moved quickly. It was like a sudden pulse of electricity had brought a statue to life. From an angle Lyra saw only the quick motion of her hand and then Reinhardt, leaning heavily on her shoulder, so it looked as if he would pull her into an embrace.

Then he released her and stumbled backward, and Lyra saw the knife handle stuck in his abdomen, and blood already darkening his shirt. He reached for the gun holstered to his belt, but only grazed the grip before pulling away again quickly, as if it had scalded him.

For a split second, just before Caelum reached her, Calliope met Lyra's eyes. Lyra was shocked by the feeling; she stopped moving; it was like running into a wall, a huge hand of immovable stone. She thought then of the statue of Richard Haven, which had been built from the wrong stone, so that quickly its face had begun to dissolve in the rain; by the time Lyra was named, its eyes were gone, and its nose, and even its lips, so it looked like the blank face of a clock without numbers or hands: like a warning of some terrible future to come where no one could see or speak or hear.

Then Calliope turned and ran, wrenching away from Caelum when he tried to grab her. Caelum hesitated. Lyra knew he was torn between the urge to go after Calliope and the desire to stay with Detective Reinhardt. But they couldn't let Calliope get away.

"Go," Lyra said to Caelum. And then, when he still didn't move, *"Go."*

Finally, he took off after Calliope. She had a head start, but she was weak; he would catch her easily.

Lyra dropped next to Detective Reinhardt when he sat down heavily.

"I'm okay," he said. But he was chalky-looking, sweating. The good news was that Calliope had stuck him in the stomach, not the chest; she'd missed his heart by a mile. "I'm okay."

"You have to keep pressure on it," she told him.

"I know. I'm a cop, remember?" He tried to smile, but pain froze his expression into something horrible. "God. When I saw her standing there . . . She looked so lost. . . ."

“That was number seven,” Lyra said. Calliope didn’t deserve her name; Lyra couldn’t stand to say it out loud.

“Poor kid.” Detective Reinhardt coughed and then cursed, his face screwed up with pain. Lyra couldn’t believe it: Calliope had stuck him with a knife, had caused him all this pain, and still he felt sorry for her. “Do me a favor. Get my belt off, okay?”

She unclipped his duty belt, which was heavy. The gun he carried in his holster was the same as the one Rick Harliss had taught her to fire, only a little heavier. A Glock. Lyra thought the word fit. It was a loud, angry word, and it sounded like an explosion.

Lyra was suddenly furious. “You should have killed her,” she said, thinking of the way Detective Reinhardt had fumbled for his gun. “She would have killed you.”

Detective Reinhardt shook his head. “She’s just a kid,” he said.

“She’s a replica,” Lyra said, but Detective Reinhardt shook his head again.

Lyra saw then that he really, truly didn’t understand the difference. That to him, there *was* no difference.

She had been told she was supposed to love Rick Harliss because he was her father, and because he loved her. But she had never felt as if she loved him, and she had worried simply that she didn’t know *how.* Even the way she felt about Caelum, she thought, might not be love at all, but something different, something she had no name for. Hadn't she heard again and again at Haven that the replicas weren't all-the-way human, they weren't real people, they were simulations of people, precisely because they *couldn't* love? Damaged, monstrous, soulless—these were all different words for the same thing.

But in that moment, and though she hardly knew him at all, she knew absolutely that she loved Detective Reinhardt. It was complete and undeniable, and it changed the whole world around her, like being submerged in a warm bath for the first time. If she could have chosen a father, she would have chosen him.

The gun was cold in her hand. But its grip felt familiar.

"Stay here," she told him. "I'll be right back." He didn't say anything, and she wasn't sure he'd heard. His whole face was screwed tight around his pain now, as if it too had been winched around the knife.

She'd been right: it hadn't taken Caelum long to catch up to Calliope, and Lyra found them quickly. He had gotten her facedown in the wet leaves and pinned her arms behind her back. But she'd obviously fought him. There were deep scratch marks from his cheekbone to his jaw, and a bite mark on the back of his hand.

When Lyra approached, Calliope tried to lift her head. But she couldn't manage it. She thudded down into the dirt again, one cheek flat to the leaves, the other catching the drive of the rain. But her eye, swollen with rage, rolled toward Lyra, like the eye of a spooked animal.

Except that Lyra didn't feel sorry for Calliope, not one bit.

"I thought you were dead," Calliope said. Because of the way her head was angled, her voice was distorted. It was a terrible version of Gemma's voice: it was the same 15 percent wrong as the rest of Calliope.

Lyra ignored that. She knew Calliope likely meant that she thought Lyra had died on the marshes, but she couldn't help but feel, too, that Calliope had seen immediately how little time she had left, that the disease was starting to show on her skin. "Where's Gemma?" she said.

"I don't know any Gemma," Calliope said, and Caelum gave her a nudge with his knee. Her tongue appeared quickly to wet her lower lip. She was nervous, and Lyra was glad. "I don't know where she is."

Lyra didn't know whether to believe her, but it didn't matter, anyway. Calliope would never tell her the truth.

"Why'd you do it?" she asked. "You killed that family. You left Gemma to take the blame."

"I didn't know what would happen," Calliope said. Then: "Why do you care, anyway?"

"Gemma's my friend," Lyra said.

Calliope's pupil was so large it seemed to swallow all the color in her eye. "Friend," she said, and the rain suddenly changed its pattern through the leaves, creating a ripple sound like laughter. "You were always one of the dumb ones. They'll kill you. You know that, right? They're all the same. They'll pretend to help you and then they'll hurt you, again and again, just like they did at Haven."

Lyra had always felt anger as a kind of heat burning through her. But now she was freezing cold. As if from the grip of the gun her whole body was turning to metal very slowly. Calliope had known the truth about Haven, just like Caelum had. But not Lyra.

Was it true, then? Was she really just stupid?

Was she being stupid now?

"Let me go," Calliope said. "You're not going to kill me. So let me go."

"Not until you tell me why," Lyra said. The trees chittered under the pressure of the rain. They threw the question back at her, and made it sound ridiculous.

"Cassiopeia was dead," she said. "Number six was dead. Numbers nine and ten, too. They never made it out of the airport. And number eight doesn't count. Even if she did escape, she couldn't last long." Calliope pulled her mouth into a smile, exposing an incisor tooth, graying and sharp. "I wanted to be the only one."

Lyra closed her eyes. She stood and listened and thought of her whole life like a single point of rain, falling down into nothingness. Calliope was still talking, wheedling now, sounding young and afraid. But Lyra could barely hear her. *Let me go, Lyra. I'm sorry. I'm so sorry. I didn't mean to. I was so scared.* It was the strangest thing, as if Calliope wasn't talking at all, as if Lyra was just remembering something she'd said years earlier.

She thought of Detective Reinhardt and Gemma lost forever, and those people on the farm, lying in one another's blood. Detective Reinhardt had said that some people could wear faces, could slip them on like masks.

Lyra opened her eyes. "Do you remember the baby bird that flew into the glass?" she asked. Funnily enough, she felt calm. "It flew into the glass and broke a wing. I thought I could nurse it."

Calliope frowned. "No," she said. But Lyra could tell she was lying.

She could see it so clearly in her mind: the way its tufted feathers fluttered with every breath, the shuttering of its tiny beak, how scared it was.

"You stepped on its head to kill it," Lyra said. The barrel of Detective Reinhardt's gun was slick and wet but she felt it, slowly, warming in her hand. "You said it was the right thing to do, because of how it was broken. Because there was no hope of fixing it."

Calliope went very still. The whole world went still. Even the rain let up momentarily and seemed to gasp midair, deprived even of the will or energy to fall. Calliope's fear smelled like something chemical. Lyra saw her calculating: right answer, wrong answer.

"I don't remember," Calliope said finally, and all the rain unfroze, all of it at once hurtled down fast and thick to break apart, as if trying to blow itself back into elements purer than what it had become. The feeling came back to Lyra's hand, warmed her fingers and wrist and arm as she raised the gun. It spread down through her heart, opening and closing like the wings of a bird in her chest.

"Funny," she said. "I never forgot."

She didn't need more than one shot, but she fired three anyway, just to be sure.

TWENTY-SIX

THE WARMTH FLOWED AWAY FROM her as quickly as it had come. She didn't feel sorry, or sad. She didn't feel anything at all. The bullets had ruined Calliope's face, and forever destroyed her resemblance to Gemma. There *would* be only one now: the right one. Still, she wasn't sure whether she had done the right thing, or why she felt so little. Maybe there really was something wrong with her—with all of them.

"What's going to happen?" she asked suddenly. She was too afraid to meet Caelum's eyes, so she stared instead at the leaves turning to pulp in the rain.

"I don't know," he answered. Caelum was always honest. It was one of the things she loved about him.

Suddenly she felt like crying. "I'm a replica, really, aren't I? I'm more replica than anything else."

He touched her face. His fingers were cool and damp.

She blinked at him through the rain webbed in her lashes.

"You're Lyra," he said. He smiled, and she fell down into his love for her, touching every layer, and this kind of falling was like its opposite, like flying instead. "That's all. That's enough."

Lyra was relieved to find that Detective Reinhardt was on his feet, leaning heavily against a tree. When Caelum reached for him, he said, "I'm okay, I'm okay," and even managed to smile.

They had no choice but to give up their search for Gemma. Detective Reinhardt needed help, and it would take longer for someone to find them out here than it would for them to make it back to the car on their own.

Slow. One foot in front of the other. Stop to rest. Lyra turned her face to the sky and whispered an apology to Gemma, for leaving her behind. For failing.

The rain had dropped off, faded to a bare mist, and the leaves shook off their moisture, so it sounded as if high above them, in the cage of the branches, tiny feet jumped from branch to branch. Lyra smelled mulch, rot, growth, and the pure wet sweetness of new blood, of life.

Lyra smelled her old life burning. Every day, the past was burned and you became something new from the ashes.

Lyra smelled burning.

No. She smelled *fire*.

Detective Reinhardt must have smelled it at the same time, because he winced and grunted, ordered Caelum to stop. But Lyra had already turned. She'd already spotted a thread of smoke unwinding above the trees, back in the direction of the cabins, and she'd already started to run.

TWENTY-SEVEN

DIMLY, LYRA WAS AWARE OF shouting: the gunshots must have drawn the attention of the searchers. She had been worried about coming across police officers in the woods; she was worried they would ask questions that Detective Reinhardt didn't know how to answer.

But now, she thought of nothing but Gemma, her *friend*.

She saw through a break in the trees the architecture of the old cabins, and the smoke coming from somewhere beyond them. She had approached from the back and had a view of collapsed stone timbers and a ruined hearth.

She circled around to the front, completely mindless of the way her heart was jumping arrhythmically in her chest, mindless of the little moments of dark that shuttered her vision for seconds at a time. *Gemma, Gemma, Gemma* was the only rhythm she could hear. The long finger of smoke was all she could see.

The ground was smoking. Or at least, that's what it looked like to her from a distance. But as she drew closer, she saw a blackened door laid flat over a lip of stone, and the smoke flowing out from an opening beneath it.

She dropped to her knees, soaking her jeans. She got her fingers around the old door and pushed, recoiling as the column of smoke thickened, carried up by a surge of air. Blinking to clear tears from her vision, she spotted a mass of uniforms coming toward her through the trees—troopers, police officers, firefighters.

"Here," she screamed. At the bottom of a long well, Gemma was curled up next to a smoldering fire, which blew its thick smoke into the air. Lyra felt as if she were falling, and leaving her body behind. "Here. Here."

It seemed to take forever for her to lift her hand. She saw it waving there, tethered to the narrow cable of her wrist, and it looked like a distant balloon, like something that didn't belong to her at all.

"Here, here, here," she shouted, again and again, as all the uniformed men and women came toward her through a scrim of smoke. Maybe it was a trick of the smoke, or maybe not: but funnily enough, all those strangers fractured in her vision into a kaleidoscope of different angles, and she saw them coming toward her not as a wave, not as a group, but as individual points of color, as individual hands reaching to hold her, as individual arms that caught her just before she dropped.

TWENTY-EIGHT

LANCASTER GENERAL LOOKED LIKE THE Haven from her dreams: full of windows that let in long afternoon sunlight, when the clouds eventually broke up; full of the reassuring squeak of footsteps, and the smell of floor polish and fresh flowers. Lyra was placed in her own room and hooked up to an IV to deliver fluids and Zofran to get rid of her nausea. Her window looked out onto an interior garden, just like the one at Haven, except there was no faceless statue here. Just flowers, and benches where visitors sat in the sun.

The IV fluids made her feel better right away, and she began to drift, rising and falling through different dreams: in one, she and Caelum lived in a white house that looked just like the one at April's grandparents', and Detective Reinhardt brought them mail, but every single one of the letters he delivered turned into a white bird and flew away.

She woke up because she thought a bird wing swept across her face; it was dark already, and she was startled to see Kristina Ives, Gemma's mother, draw away.

"Sorry," she said. She looked embarrassed. "You were so still—I wanted to make sure you were all right."

Lyra sat up in bed. For the first time in days, she wasn't nauseous, and movement didn't give her vertigo. A reading light was on in the corner, and Kristina Ives had obviously been sitting there: her purse was on the floor next to the chair, a magazine rolled up inside of it. "Where's Caelum?" she asked.

"He went to check in on Detective Reinhardt. Both of them are fine," Kristina said, before Lyra could ask. "Detective Reinhardt was very lucky. The knife missed all his major organs." She smiled. She looked very tired, but she was still extremely pretty. Lyra thought she was a little bit like the rose in *The Little Prince*. She'd been sheltered behind glass for a long time. But she was loyal. She knew what love was. "I want to thank you," Kristina went on. "You found Gemma. I can never repay you."

"You don't have to," Lyra said. "Gemma found me once. We're even."

To Lyra's surprise, Gemma's mother reached out and took her hand. Her skin was incredibly soft, and Lyra was shocked to recognize the scent. Lemon balm. Her expression changed, too. When she smiled, it was like light passing into a room through an open door.

"I want you to know I'm your friend," she said. "You can trust me to help you however I can. Do you believe me?"

Lyra nodded. She was overwhelmed by the tightness in her throat, and by the feeling, at the same time, that paper birds were winging up through her chest.

The door opened, and Lyra turned to see Caelum and Detective Reinhardt. The detective moved slowly, and a bulk of bandages was visible beneath his shirt, wrapping his abdomen. But he was smiling.

"You shouldn't be up," Kristina said, releasing Lyra's hand with a final squeeze.

Detective Reinhardt waved her off. "I'm good as new. The surgeon said so himself."

Caelum came right to the bed. "Hey," he said. He put a hand on Lyra's face, and she turned so she could kiss his palm. "How are you feeling?"

"Better," she said. For once, it wasn't a lie. "Much better."

"I'm going to go check on Gemma," Kristina said. She picked up her purse and hugged it.

"I want to see her," Lyra said, sitting up a little straighter. "Can I come and see her?"

"Of course." Kristina smiled. "She's just down the hall. You were the first person she asked about—you and Caelum, both."

After she had left, Detective Reinhardt moved to the

window, parting the blinds with a finger. Lyra thought he was giving Caelum time to lean forward, quickly, and kiss her.

"You get some sleep?" Reinhardt asked, and Lyra nodded. "Incredible how different the world looks on the other side of a nice sleep, isn't it?"

She wanted to tell him about her dream, but she was too embarrassed. He eased into the chair in the corner, wincing a little.

He waved off Caelum's help.

"I'm okay," he said. But he sat for a long time with his chin down, eyes closed, breathing hard. Lyra even began to think he'd fallen asleep. Then, at last, he looked up. "I'm afraid I have some news about your father."

Lyra knew just by looking at him what he was about to say.

"He's dead, isn't he?"

"Yes." He looked her directly in the eyes. She liked that about him. That he wouldn't look away, even though she was sure he wanted to. "Found at home, at the trailer park, only yesterday. Looks like an overdose."

"That's impossible." Caelum's voice leapt almost to a shout. "It's a trick."

"Caelum, please." Reinhardt sighed. "I'm on your side, remember?" Caelum wheeled away and went to stand by the window. Lyra wondered whether he was thinking about how he and Rick had fought. She knew he would be sorry he had never had the chance to apologize.

She was surprised that she was the one who couldn't make eye contact with Detective Reinhardt. She looked down, blinking back her tears.

"I promise you, Lyra, I'll make sure your father gets his justice. I'll make sure you do. Do you believe me?"

She nodded. For a long time, he said nothing. She liked that about him too: he wasn't afraid of silence. He had learned to find comfort in it.

"They've still got those vultures by the main entrance, waiting to pounce," he said. There had been a crowd at the hospital when they arrived: police officers but also men and women holding phones, video equipment, cameras that went flash-flash. "I don't imagine any of us are getting off easy."

The nurses had sworn that no one would be able to get to Lyra so long as she was in the hospital—she'd been worried, initially, that Geoffrey Ives or one of the other Suits would simply creep in and murder her while she was sleeping. There were even police officers monitoring every visitor to and from this portion of the hospital. But what would happen once they left?

Detective Reinhardt seemed to know what she was thinking. "They're going to want to ask you questions," he said. "There's going to be a lot of nosing around. I expect a department inquiry. Well. I *asked* for a department inquiry."

Lyra had worried that Detective Reinhardt might be disappointed when he found out she had stolen from Dr. O'Donnell's desk drawer. But instead, he had hugged her. He had lied for her, too, and told the state troopers who found Calliope's body that he'd been the one to shoot her, after she rushed him with a knife.

There's no hiding this anymore, he told Lyra on their way to the hospital, as she drifted in and out of consciousness. *There's no covering up.*

"I don't blame you," Detective Reinhardt went on now, "if you had other things on your mind. Things you wanted to do, for example."

Detective Reinhardt was looking intently at his cuticles. That was how Lyra understood: he was giving them a way out. He understood she didn't have much time left.

"I like buses," she said. Caelum took her hand. "I wouldn't mind riding some buses again."

Detective Reinhardt heaved out of his chair, using both arms for leverage. "Amazing things," he said. "You can go coast to coast on the Greyhound bus line, from Maine to Santa Monica. Did you know that?" He started limping toward the door. "'Course, they won't discharge you yet. Not without wanting to know your story. And the front entrance is crawling with press." He paused by the door, turning back to smile at Lyra, and she saw in his expression love, actual love, the kind she'd felt for him in the woods. She barely knew him at all, but he was family. "Of course that's the problem with hospitals. Always have to be a million exits, because of fire regulations. You can't cover them all. I saw a stairwell right by the ladies' room, led right down into the parking lot and not a single person standing guard."

"Thank you," Caelum said.

Detective Reinhardt nodded. Then he turned around and fished something from his pocket. "Oh," he said. "I had one of the nurses run out and pick this up. Thought it might come in handy. Pay-as-you-go. No code." He tossed a cell phone in the air and it landed at the foot of Lyra's bed. "Don't worry. My number's already in there."

It was brand-new, made of plastic, and had little numbered buttons. It had a fake-leather case, which snapped closed and could hook to a belt.

Lyra's throat closed up entirely.

Thank you, she tried to say. But she couldn't get the words out.

Detective Reinhardt seemed to understand. He touched his fingers to his forehead, once—a kind of salute—and was gone.

Lyra didn't need to ask where Gemma's room was; all she and Caelum had to do was listen for the babble of April's voice. Though Lyra didn't know April well, she knew her voice right away.

April was sitting at Gemma's bedside. With her were two women Lyra assumed must be related to April. One of them had April's warm brown eyes, and the same nest of curly hair. The other one kept a hand on April's shoulder.

"Looks like you have some more visitors," Kristina said, when Lyra and Caelum entered. She, too, had drawn a chair up to Gemma's bedside.

"You're awake," Gemma said, sitting up. She was pale but smiling.

"You're *heroes,*" April said through a mouthful of candy, pivoting around to face her. "Twizzler?"

Lyra shook her head. But Caelum took one.

"Come on." The woman with the curly hair gave April a nudge. "Let's leave them alone for a bit, okay?"

Kristina took the hint and stood up. "I could use a cup of coffee, actually."

April frowned. "Yeah, sure. But we'll come back, right?" She pointed a Twizzler at Gemma. "You can't get rid of me that easily."

"I wouldn't dream of it," Gemma said, and rolled her eyes.

Kristina bent down to kiss her daughter's forehead. "I'll be right back," she said.

Lyra almost laughed. And she nearly cried, too. The sun through the blinds looked almost solid. It was beautiful, she thought. It was all so beautiful.

She would miss Gemma.

Maybe Caelum knew what she was thinking, because he reached for Lyra's hand and squeezed.

"How are you?" Gemma asked, after the others had left. "How are you feeling?" That was so like Gemma: she was the one who had nearly died, and still she was worried about Lyra.

"We're fine," she said. Caelum's hand was warm in hers. It was both true and not true, of course. She was still dying, of a disease for which there was no cure.

But it was like Caelum had said: she wasn't dead yet.

Not today.

Already, the words she'd taken from Dr. O'Donnell were beginning to turn, to flow, to do their work.

"April was right," Gemma said. "You're both heroes. I can't believe you found me."

Lyra wondered whether anyone had told her about Calliope. She knew that Gemma would be sorry, even though Calliope was broken, even though Calliope had killed people. That was the kind of person Gemma was.

"That's what friends do," Lyra said. "They find each other."

Gemma beamed. It was like her smile split her face

open, and sunshine poured out of it. "Exactly."

The look on Gemma's face, the way she smiled, the understanding that Gemma would mourn Calliope even though Calliope had never mourned anyone—all of it warmed Lyra's whole body and moved her forward, to Gemma's bedside, compelled by an instinct that for years had remained buried. But now it broke free of its casing. She made her body into a seashell and gathered Gemma in the curve of her chest and spine. She didn't think about doing it. Her body just knew it, remembered the impulse, the idea of warmth and closeness, as if all along the knowledge had been there, working through her blood.

And for the first time ever, Lyra and Gemma hugged.

"Thank you," Lyra whispered into Gemma's hair, which still smelled, faintly, like smoke. Words were funny things, she thought. The best ones carried dozens of other words nestled inside of them. "Thank you," she repeated.

I love you, she thought. *Good-bye.*

RINGER

TWENTY-NINE

THEY COULD HAVE BEEN ANYONE, going anywhere. There was a joy in that, in the absorption: they were caught up in the great big heartbeat of the world. They were infinitely large and infinitely small. They were a single vein of feeling, an infinitely narrow possibility that had somehow come to be.

They could have vanished, right there, from the bus stop, and who's to say whether anyone would have noticed, what would have changed, and whether somewhere in the rippling universe a wave would turn or fall or change directions.

But they didn't vanish.

They sat in the sun, sweating, holding hands, and avoiding the gum on the underside of the bench when they moved their legs. They breathed the smell of exhaust. They saw people pass, a wash of sneakers and colors and cell phones. They sat for hours without speaking, without moving, without impatience or desire. Their hands were so tightly intertwined that looking at them you could not immediately say whose was whose. The sun wheeled through the sky; it turned its infinite cartwheel and blinded them when they stared directly.

And Lyra, sitting there, knew at last that she had found her story. It was not, after all, a story of escape and fear and fences. It was not a story about power, and so, after all, she did not have to play the role of sacrifice.

The story, *her* story, was about a girl and a boy on a bench, holding hands, watching bus after bus arrive and leave again. And because it was her story, that was all right: there was no hurry, no rush to get anywhere. The universe slowed, and both the past and future fell like a shadow flattened beneath the sun. The girl and boy sat, and watched, and time dropped a hand over them. It held them there, together, safe, and in love.

And in her story, they stayed that way.

ALSO BY LAUREN OLIVER

Before I Fall

Liesl & Po

The Spindlers

Panic

Vanishing Girls

Replica

Curiosity House: The Shrunken Head

Curiosity House: The Screaming Statue

Curiosity House: The Fearsome Firebird

THE DELIRIUM SERIES

Delirium

Pandemonium

Requiem

Delirium Stories: Hana, Anabel, Raven, and Alex

FOR ADULTS

Rooms

This is a work of fiction. The characters, incidents, and dialogues are products of the author's imagination and are not to be construed as real. Although many of the larger geographical areas indicated in this book do, in fact, exist, most (if not all) of the streets, landmarks, and other place names are of the author's invention.

Ringer

 For information address HarperCollins Children's Books, a division of HarperCollins Publishers, 195 Broadway, New York, NY 10007.
www.epicreads.com

ISBN 978-0-06-239420-0

Typography by Erin Fitzsimmons
18 19 20 21 22 PC/LSCH 10 9 8 7 6 5 4 3 2 1
❖
First paperback edition, 2018

To the incredible staff of Glasstown Entertainment,
some of my favorite human beings,
for their support and inspiration:
Kamilla Benko, Lexa Hillyer, Adam Silvera,
Jessica Sit, Alexa Wejko, and Lynley Bird

Her wrists hurt. She wondered whether handcuffs came in extra large, for heavier inmates, the way that condoms came in Magnums, which she had learned only last week, when April gave her a box as a joke. *For your very first boyfriend.*

Your boyfriend.

His chest was moving fast, as if he was having trouble breathing. His eyes were closed and he'd scooted back against the trunk. His head knocked against the doors every time they hit a bump.

She nudged his ankle with a foot to make him look at her. There was a small bit of blood at his temple where one of the men had hit him, and looking at it made her queasy. She counted the freckles on his nose. She loved the freckles on his nose.

She loved him, and hadn't known it until that instant, in the back of the van, with cuffs chafing the skin off her wrist and blood moving slowly toward his eyebrow.

She tried to tell him that it would be okay—wordlessly, with her eyes, with noises she made in the back of her throat. But he just shook his head, and she knew he hadn't understood, and wouldn't have believed her, anyway.

GEMMA

LAUREN OLIVER

RINGER

GEMMA

HARPER
An Imprint of Harper Collins *Publishers*

PART I

ONE

"PICK," APRIL SAID, AND THEN leaned over to jab Gemma with a finger. "Come on. It doesn't work if you don't pick."

"Left," Gemma said.

With a flourish, April revealed the bag of chips in her left hand: jalapeño-cheddar flavored. "Sucker," she said, sliding the chips across the table to Gemma. "Maybe if you'd been paying attention . . ." She produced a second bag of chips, salt and vinegar, Gemma's favorite, and opened it with her teeth. She offered the bag to Gemma. "Good thing I'm so nice."

This was a tradition dating from midway through freshman year, when the school had for whatever reason begun stocking various one-off and weird chip flavors—probably, April theorized, because they got them on the cheap in discount variety packs. They'd made a game of picking blind—one good bag, one bad—even though

they always split the salt and vinegar anyway.

But Gemma wasn't hungry. She hadn't been hungry in weeks, it seemed, not since spring break and Haven and Lyra and Caelum. Before, she'd always been hungry, even if she didn't like to eat in front of other people. Now everything tasted like dust, or the hard bitter grit of medicine accidentally crunched between the teeth. Every bite was borrowed—no, stolen—from the girl who should have come before.

She, Gemma, wasn't supposed to be here.

"Hey. Do I have to get you a shock collar or something?" April's voice was light, but she wasn't smiling.

Gemma reached over and took a chip, just to make April feel better. Across the cafeteria, the Bollard twins were huddled over the same phone, sharing a pair of headphones, obviously watching a video. Brandon Bollard was actually smiling, although he didn't seem to know how to do it correctly—he was kind of just baring his teeth.

"Did you know some twins can communicate telepathically?" Gemma asked suddenly.

April sighed so heavily her new bangs fluttered. "That's not true."

"It is," Gemma said. "They have their own languages and stuff."

"Making up a language is different from communicating telepathically."

"Well, it's both." It was weird to see Brandon and Brant together. Brandon was dressed all in black, with a fringe of black hair falling over his eyes and a sweatshirt that had two vampire fangs on it. Brant was wearing blue Chucks and low-rider jeans, and his hair was brown and curly and kept long, supposedly because Aubrey Connelly, his girlfriend and the most coldhearted of all the coldhearted pack wolves, loved to pull it when they were having sex in the back of her BMW.

It didn't make a difference: they had the same slouch, the same lips, the same wide-spaced brown eyes, the same way of slugging through the halls as if the destination would come to them and not the other way around.

"Did you know that sometimes twins, like, absorb each other in the womb?" Gemma went on. "I watched this thing online about it. This woman thought she had a tumor and then they found teeth and hair and stuff inside. Can you imagine?"

April stared at her. "Eating," she said, except she had just taken a bite of her sandwich and it came out *eaffing*.

"Sorry," Gemma said.

April swallowed and took a huge sip of coconut water, eyeing Gemma the whole time, as if she were a bacterial culture in danger of infecting everybody. "You're not hungry?" she said.

Gemma moved her sandwich around on her tray a little. "I had a big breakfast." She wouldn't meet April's

eyes. April always knew when she was lying.

April shoved her tray aside and leaned forward to cross her arms on the table. "I'm worried about you, Gem."

"I'm fine," Gemma said automatically. She must have said it a thousand times in the past few weeks. She kept waiting for it to be true.

"You are *not* fine. Your brain is on autopilot. You're hardly eating anything. Suddenly you're *obsessed* with the Bollard twins—"

"I'm not obsessed with them," Gemma said quickly, and forced herself to look away from Brandon, who was slouching toward the door, so pale he could have been the ghost of his twin brother.

"*Obsessed*," April repeated. "You talk about the Bollard twins more than you talk about *your own boyfriend*. Your new boyfriend," she continued, before Gemma could open her mouth. "Your new *awesome* boyfriend."

"Keep your voice down," Gemma said. At the next table, she caught a group of sophomore boys staring and made a face. She didn't care if they thought she was crazy. She didn't care about any of it.

April shoved her hands through her hair. April's hair was like some kind of energy conductor: when she was upset, her curls looked like they were going to reach out and electrocute you. "Look," she said, lowering her voice. "I understand—"

"You don't," Gemma said, before she could finish.

April stared at her. "I saw it too," she said. "Pete saw it. We were there."

It isn't the same, Gemma wanted to say. But what was the point? Just because they had seen the same things didn't mean they felt the same way.

"Haven isn't your problem anymore. It's not who you are. Lyra and Caelum are safe. There are people, major top-level people, investigating Dr. Saperstein. Your part is done. You wanted to know the truth and now you do. But you can't let it destroy you."

Gemma knew April was trying to help. But something black and ugly reached up out of her stomach and gripped her by the throat, a seething anger that had, in the past three weeks, startled her with its intensity.

"I mean, plenty of people have seriously screwy backstories." That was April's big problem: she never knew when to stop talking. The anger made Gemma's head throb, so she heard the echo of the words as though through a cloth. "You know Wynn Dobbs? The sophomore? I heard her dad actually tried to *kill* her mom with a shovel, just lost it one day and went after her, which is why she lives with her aunt. . . ."

April couldn't understand what it meant for Gemma to be a replica, and she didn't *want* to understand. Gemma was well and truly a freak, and though she and April

had joked for years that they were aliens in high school, Gemma might as well have been from a different planet. In fact, she almost wished she were an alien—at least then she'd have somewhere to go back to, a true home, even if it was millions of light-years away.

Instead she'd been cloned, made, manufactured from the stem cells of her parents' first child, Emma. She was worse than an alien. She was a *trespasser.* It felt now as if she were living her whole life through one of those vignette filters, the kind that eats up the edges and the details. As if she'd hacked into someone else's social media accounts and was trying to catfish. Emma should have been sitting at this table, happily crunching through a bag of chips, stressing about her precalc exam. Not Gemma.

Gemma should never have been born at all.

"Gemma? Hello, Gemma?"

Somewhere in the deep echoes of the past, her lost twin, her lost replica, cried out soundlessly to be heard.

What was the point of trying to explain *that*?

Gemma forced herself to smile. "I'm listening," she said.

On days that April stayed after school for chorus, Gemma had always taken the bus, refusing her father's offer of a driver because it would only make her more of a target. But now Pete drove her home, at least on days when he

wasn't working behind the register at the Quick-Mart.

It was Wednesday, May 11, nearly three weeks since she'd last seen Lyra. Pete had gotten rid of the eggplant-colored minivan they'd driven down to Florida. He said it was because of the mileage, but Gemma suspected it was because of the memories, too. Even when they were riding around in his brown Volvo station wagon—the Floating Turd, he called it, although it was definitely an improvement over his last ride—she imagined dark-suited men and women passing her on the streets, tailing her in featureless sedans.

Paranoia, obviously. Her dad had taken care of it, he'd promised her, just like he'd taken care of springing Lyra's dad from jail and setting him up with a job and a mobile home in some big Tennessee trailer park Gemma had never known he owned. April was right, at least about that part: Lyra and Caelum were safe, and staying with Lyra's father. Dr. Saperstein had survived the explosion and subsequent fire at Haven, but he and his sick experiments would, her dad assured her, lose their funding after the disaster at Haven. She couldn't bring herself to ask what would happen to all the replicas who'd managed to survive, but she liked to believe they would be placed somewhere, quietly fed into the foster care system or at least moved into hospice care before the disease they were incubating chewed them up for good.

Pete always held her hand on the way to the parking lot, and even though the drive was only fifteen minutes, it often took them nearly an hour because he was always pulling over to kiss her. Whenever Gemma's mom was home, she invited him in for sweet tea made by their housekeeper, Bernice, who came in the morning. The whole thing was so normal it hurt.

Except that it wasn't, because *she* wasn't, and they weren't, and the more she tried to pretend, the more obvious it was that something had cracked. Meeting Lyra and Caelum, knowing they were out there, knowing Haven and the people in charge of it were still out there somewhere—it had knocked her life off its axis. And Pete and April thought they could make things right just by *acting* as if they were all right. Gemma felt all the time as if they were circling a black hole, bound by the gravity of their denial. They would fall: they had to.

"What is it?" Pete brought a hand to her cheek. She loved the way he did this, touched her face or her lips with his thumb. They were parked at the very end of her driveway, the final quarter-mile stretch through graceful birches and plane trees whose branches interlocked their fingers overhead. "What's wrong?"

She wondered how many times he'd had to ask in the past weeks. "Nothing," she said automatically. "Why?"

"Your eyes were open," he said. "Like, staring. It was like kissing a Chucky doll."

That made her laugh. That was the amazing thing about Pete, his special talent: he could make anyone laugh. "Thanks a lot."

"Let's try again, okay?" He leaned into her. She closed her eyes. But she couldn't relax. Something was digging into her butt. She must be sitting on a pen. This time, she was the one to pull away.

"Sorry," she said.

For a split second, Pete looked irritated. Or maybe she only imagined it. The next moment, he shrugged. "That's all right. We should probably keep it clean for Ms. Leyla over here." He reached out and flicked the hula girl on the dashboard, who promptly began to shimmy. Then he put the car in drive again. Gemma was relieved, and then guilty for feeling relieved. What kind of monster didn't want to make out with her adorable, floppy-haired, freckle-faced, absolutely-scrumptious-kisser boyfriend?

A monster who couldn't move on. A monster who felt like moving on was giving up, even though there was nothing, anymore, to fight for.

"Where'd you get this thing, anyway?" She leaned forward and gave the hula girl another flick. Her face was chipped away and the only thing left was a small, unsmiling mouth.

Pete shrugged. "Came with the car. Your dad thinks she must have good engine juju."

Gemma got a weird prickly feeling, like a spider was

walking on her spine. "When did my dad see your hula girl?"

"When he dropped the car off." He shoved the gear-stick into park as they pulled up to the house, which never failed to emerge suddenly, enormous and unexpected, from behind the long column of trees. If a house could pounce, Gemma's would have.

Pete caught her staring at him. "What? He didn't tell you? His friend was selling the car and he knew we were looking to cash in the Eggplant. He offered to make the trade. It was *nice*," he said, frowning, and Gemma knew she must have been making a face.

"Sure," she echoed. "Nice."

This time, he was definitely annoyed. He rolled his eyes and got out of the car without waiting for her to unbuckle her seat belt. Already the front door was open; Rufus bounded outside, as quickly as he could given his age, and began licking Pete's kneecaps. Gemma's mom, Kristina, appeared in the doorway, waving overhead with a big, beaming smile, as if she were heralding him from across a crowded dock and not from twenty feet away.

It was a stupid thing. Tiny. Minuscule. So what if her dad had a friend selling some shitty old turd-colored Volvo? Her dad had friends everywhere. Friends in the police department. Friends at the Formacine Plastics Facility, where Rick Harliss was now employed, a short

ten-minute bus ride from the Winston-Able Mobile Home Community and Park, where he, Lyra, and Caelum were living.

Still, she didn't like it. She'd told her father weeks ago she would come home only if things changed. It would be her rules. Her life now. And yet weeks later she was as trapped as she'd ever been. They were trying to soothe her, appease her, distract her, make her forget. Even Pete wanted to forget.

It's too big for us, he'd said to her, shortly after they returned home. *It's too heavy for us to carry.*

Gemma knew exactly what he meant. She felt the weight too, the constant pull of something deep and black and huge. Except she wasn't carrying it, not even a little.

It was carrying her. What would happen, she wondered, when she fell?

TWO

"NO WAY WILL WE PUT troops on the ground." Gemma's father talked through a mouth full of half-chewed tenderloin. Geoffrey Ives believed strongly in table manners—for other people. "No way will the American public stand for it." He leveled a fork at Ned Engleton, an old friend of his from high school, now a detective with the Chapel Hill Police Department. "Patriotic outrage is all well and good, but once you start shipping out these poor kids from Omaha, Des Moines, wherever, it's a different story. I've seen robotics stocks go up tenfold the past month. Everyone's gambling on drones. . . ."

"May I be excused?" For the past few weeks, Gemma had seen her father for dinner more than she had in the previous ten years. Usually, Gemma and Kristina ate take-out sushi in front of the TV in their pajamas, or Gemma was left to scour the refrigerator for whatever Bernice had

left her while Kristina floated between various benefits and social obligations.

But after Gemma had come back from Florida, and Lyra, Caelum, and Mr. Harliss had been packed off (*protected*, Kristina said; *given new life*, her father said, although Gemma thought it was more like out of sight, out of mind), Gemma's parents had determined they needed more *together time.* As if everything Gemma had learned, everything she'd seen, was just a nutritional deficit and could be resolved by more home-cooked meals.

It turned out Geoffrey Ives's idea of family time was simply to bring his business home. In the past week alone they'd had dinner with a professor of robotics at MIT; a General Something-or-other who'd helped Ives land a lucrative consulting contract with a biotech firm that did work for the US government; and a state senator on recess whom Gemma had surprised later on that night in her kitchen, standing in his underwear in the blue light of the refrigerator, staggering drunk.

"You may not." Geoff forked some more steak—home-cooked by Bernice, of course—and barely missed a beat. "But I don't think air strikes are going to get the job done, not when these psychos are so scattered. Warfare keeps evolving, but have our methods evolved with it?"

Gemma felt a sudden hatred light like a flare inside her. She turned to Kristina, who had said next to nothing.

Normally she didn't pill-pop when they had company. But Gemma thought she was getting worse. Two, three, four glasses of wine, a Valium or two, and by bedtime she could hardly speak a word, and her smile was blissed out and dopey, like a baby's, and made Gemma sick to look at.

"I'm thinking of going to visit Lyra this weekend," Gemma said loudly, and there was a terrible, electric pause, and then Kristina let her wineglass drop, and suddenly Geoff was on his feet and cursing and Gemma felt sorry and triumphant all at once.

"I spilled," Kristina kept saying dumbly. Red wine pooled over her plate and made a handprint pattern on her shirt. "I spilled."

Geoff was shouting in staccato bursts. "For God's sake, don't just sit there. The carpet. Gemma, get your mother something to clean up with."

In the kitchen, Gemma wound a long ribbon of paper towel around her hand like a bandage. She was shaky. It felt as if someone was doing a detail number on her insides, vacu-sucking and carving and hacking her raw. Muffled by the door, Kristina's words took on the bleating, repetitive cadence of an injured sheep.

Before she could return to the dining room, the door opened and Geoff appeared. She was sure he was going to yell at her for mentioning Lyra's name in the presence of a guest—not that anyone could guess who she was.

But he just took a step forward and held out a hand for the paper towels.

Feeling bolder, she took a deep breath and repeated herself. "I want to see Lyra this weekend," she said. "You promised I could." For a second, their hands touched, and she was briefly shocked. They almost never touched. She didn't think her father had hugged her more than once or twice in her life. His fingers were cold.

"This weekend is your mother's birthday," Geoff said. "Did you forget about the party?"

"I'll go Sunday," she said, unwilling to give up. She half suspected that he was filling her time with celebrations and dinners and obligations precisely so she *couldn't* see Lyra.

"Sunday we're going to church," he said, and his voice was edged with impatience. "I've told you we're going to do things differently from now on, and damn it, I meant it."

"I'll go after church," Gemma said. She should have dropped it. She knew her dad was getting angry; a small cosmos of broken blood vessels darkened in his cheeks. "I'll get Pete to drive me. It'll only be a few hours—"

"I said no." He slammed a fist on the counter so hard that the plastic kitchen timer—untouched by anyone but Bernice—jumped. "Sunday is a day for family, and that's final."

Gemma turned away from him, balling her fists tight-tight, as if she could squeeze out all her anger. "Some family."

"What did you say?" He got in front of her, blocking her way to the stairs, and for a moment she was gutted by a sudden fear. His eyes were hollowed out by shadow. He looked almost like a stranger. She could smell the whiskey he'd had at dinner, could smell the meat on his breath and the way he was sweating beneath his expensive cashmere sweater and she remembered, then, seeing her mother once sprawled at his feet after one of their arguments.

She tripped, he'd said. *She tripped.* Gemma had never known whether to believe it or not.

And in that second, weirdly, she felt time around her like a long tunnel, except the tunnel collapsed, and became not a road she was traveling but a single point, a compression of ideas and memories; and she saw her father with a dead baby, his first and only born, and knew that he'd done what he'd done not from grief but because it offended him, this natural order over which he had no control, the passing of things and the tragedy of a world that whip-snapped without asking his permission. He'd done it not for love but to restore order. Nothing would break unless he was the one to crush it. People didn't even have the right to die, not in Geoffrey Ives's house.

"Whether you like it or not, you follow my rules,"

he said, and she wanted to cry: this was her father, who should have been both a boundary and a promise, like the sun at the edge of every picture, the thing that gave it light. "You're still my daughter."

"I know," she said, and turned away. But in her head she said *no.* In her head, and in the deepest part of who she was, she knew she wasn't. She was born of the sister, the self, who had come before her. She was the daughter of a silent memory, except the memory wasn't silent anymore. It had reached up out of the past and taken Gemma by the throat, and soon, she knew, it would begin to scream.

THREE

GEMMA COULDN'T REMEMBER THE LAST time her father had been home for one of Kristina's birthdays, or for one of hers. Last year, she had been patched through to the Philippines by his secretary so that he could wish her a happy fifteenth. She dimly recalled a party when she was five or six at a petting zoo, and crying when her mother wouldn't take her closer than ten feet from the animals, fearing Gemma would catch something.

The guests began to arrive midafternoon. For a short time, she forgot about Haven and poor Jake Witz, who had died trying to expose the truth about Haven and Spruce Island; she forgot about the feeling that she was sleepwalking through someone else's life. Her parents often hosted parties, mostly to support one of Kristina's dozens of causes—the Mid-Atlantic Breast Cancer Prevention Society, the North Carolina Nature Refuge, the

Equestrian Society, the Garden Club—or a political dinner for some local candidate Geoffrey was supporting. Those parties were stiff-backed and yawningly boring, and usually Gemma stayed out of the way or hung out in the kitchen stealing leftover nubs of filet mignon from the caterers and anxiously tracking how often Kristina came into the kitchen to refill her glass in private.

But this was a real, true, honest-to-God party.

The theme was Hawaiian, a nod to the bar that Kristina had been working in after college, where she and Geoffrey had met; Geoff liked to tell people that he'd never seen a girl make a grass skirt look so classy. Fifty or so of her parents' friends had been invited, including April's moms, who both showed up wearing coconut bras over their regular clothing. April's mother Diana was a computer programmer and software engineer who designed malware detection systems for big companies; Gemma had hardly ever seen her in the daylight hours. April's other mother, Angela Ruiz, was now a renowned prosecutor for the state. Watching them swish around with leis and fruity cocktails gave Gemma the same dizzying upside-down feeling of trying to do a cartwheel. Meanwhile, April stomped around, looking absolutely miserable, dressed pointedly in all black.

"What happened to aging gracefully?" she muttered, gnawing a pink cocktail spear she'd been using to stake

olives from the bar. But Gemma thought it was funny, all her parents' friends in ugly Hawaiian shirts and plastic flower crowns, getting drunk on piña coladas and rum punch.

Kristina had suggested she invite Pete, and he came dressed up, as she'd known he would, in a loud-print Hawaiian shirt he proudly announced he'd purchased from the gas station during a week of random travel promotions. Gemma couldn't understand how he pulled it off, but he did. The shirt showed off his arms, which were long and tan and just muscle-y enough, and deepened his eyes to the rich brown of really good chocolate.

There were ribs smoking in a rented barbecue, honeyed ham with grilled pineapple, coconut shrimp circulated by waiters wearing grass skirts over their jeans. The grown-ups set up a game of bocce, but Gemma and April soon took over, making up their own rules so they wouldn't have to learn the real ones, and Pete refereed and narrated through a fake microphone, using made-up terminology like *the looping cruiser* and *the back-switch hibbleputz* that made Gemma laugh so hard she nearly peed.

Gemma had determined that at the party she would ask April whether she'd had any luck getting into Jake Witz's computer. April was sure Diana could get past Jake's security measures and had come up with a convenient excuse to get her mom on board: the computer, she claimed, had

been left at the public library, and they needed to get into the system to find a registration and return it.

Gemma had bugged April for days after turning it over, until April threatened to karate-kick her spleen if she didn't stop. That was ten days ago. Gemma had figured she would slip it into conversation when April was relaxed, when they were having a good time, after she had proven she wasn't obsessing, like April said she was.

But somehow, she couldn't. For the first time in weeks she actually *felt* normal—she felt happy, and she wasn't faking it. Neither Pete nor April was staring her down like she was in danger of morphing into a feral animal. Geoff and Kristina were actually *dancing*—there, on the deck, in front of everyone—as the sun broke up into layers of color and the fireflies lifted out of the dark. Pete had his hands around her waist, humming into her neck to the cheesy eighties music her parents still adored. His breath was warm. The sky was big, the stars new and shimmering, and though the world was large, she was safe inside it.

Standing there, she even thought that maybe, just maybe, she could choose to forget after all. April was right—lots of people had fucked-up childhoods—and Pete was right, too, that what had happened at Haven was too big for them to make better. Lyra and Caelum had a place to live, and her father had promised he would figure

out a way to get Caelum papers so he could be legal, so he could exist. It wasn't like they'd been trying to reach her. They hadn't called her, not even once, since they cleared off. Maybe they were doing just fine—maybe they, too, wanted to forget.

If they could, she could: forget where she'd been made, and how. Forget about Emma, her little lost shadow-self. Maybe there was nothing to being normal except the decision to do it. You had to simply step into the idea, like wriggling into a sweater.

She should have learned, by now, that nothing was ever so easy.

Pete had moved off to check out the party's main attraction: a full-on spit-roasted pig to be wheeled out and served before the hired Hawaiian dancers shimmied and hip-jiggled their way through dinner. But he came back and found her, his hair smelling sweetly of smoke, his hand warm when he interlaced their fingers. He was wearing half a dozen leis around his neck, on his wrists, even looped around his head.

"Come with me," he said.

"Where are we going?" she asked.

He turned briefly to bring his mouth to her ear. "Somewhere we can be *alone*," he said, and his eyes were bright and alive with reflections. Her stomach dipped,

not the way it usually did when they began to kiss and she felt herself seize up with panic, but like when riding a roller coaster: like good things were about to happen.

He pulled her up the stairs onto the deck and toward the sliding doors. Luckily, all her parents' friends had the sleepy-blissful look of tipsiness and were too wrapped up in their own little dramas to do more than wave. In the kitchen, Bernice was hustling the caterers around. When she spotted Gemma, she winked.

The hall felt even cooler after the dampness and warmth of outside, and when Pete stopped her and pushed her up against the wall to kiss her, she could smell charcoal in his hair and on his fingers. For once she didn't feel like a monster, didn't feel ugly or badly formed, and she stepped into him. He put his hands on her waist, slid them up her stomach, fumbled at her bra. . . .

Down the hall, a bathroom door opened, and Gemma heard the sharp rise of a woman's voice—Melanie Eckert, one of her mom's country club friends, sounding drunk. "I *told* her too much filler would split her like a pumpkin. Have you seen her now?"

Gemma launched herself across the hall and yanked open the door to the basement, practically shoving Pete down the stairs before Melanie could see them. For a second they stood together on the landing, breathless and giggly, until Melanie's voice had faded.

"Is this where you murder me?" Pete whispered, bumping his lips against her neck in the dark.

She knew he was kidding, but a sudden vision of Jake Witz returned to her the way she'd last seen him, standing at the door, angling his body so she couldn't get inside, trying to warn her. Trying to save her. *Jake Witz is dead.* She was glad she hadn't seen the body but had read, anyway, that people sometimes choked on their tongues when they were hanging, or broke their nails off trying to loosen the noose.

She hit the lights, relieved by the bland normalcy of the carpeted stairs leading down to the basement.

"You wanted to be alone," she said, taking his hand, eager to get back the good feeling she'd had only a minute ago.

The basement was a clutter of old furniture, dusty table tennis equipment, a pool table with stains all over its felt (Gemma's father kept a second, nicer pool table in the library upstairs), and old toys. Metal shelves, like the kind you might find in a library, were packed with massive jugs of bottled water, Costco-sized packages of toilet paper, cartons of canned soup, enough ketchup to fill a bathtub.

"Nothing says romance like industrial-sized rolls of toilet paper," Pete said, and she laughed. "Are you guys preparing for the apocalypse or something?"

"Prepared. Past tense. In case you haven't noticed,

my dad's kind of a freak." She drew him between the shelves, moving deeper and deeper into the basement. It was like a spiny city built out of boxes of shredded wheat and stacks of Dove soap. And despite the musty smell of the basement and the bright overhead lights and the cheap gray wall-to-wall carpeting her parents would never have allowed anywhere else, Gemma felt in that moment, with Pete's hand in hers, that it was the most beautiful place she'd ever been.

They started kissing again: first they stood, and then, when Pete bumped her against one of the shelves and nearly toppled it, they lay down together. He got on top of her. Her whole body was breathless and hot, as if she were nothing but breath, nothing but the inhale-exhale of their rhythm together. He was struggling to get her shirt off and fumbling with her bra, and for once she wasn't worried about anything or even wondering how far things would go. Her nipples touched the air and he pulled away to look at her, to look at the long Y-shaped scar on her sternum that had earned her the name Frankenstein at school.

"Beautiful," was all he said, touching her scar gently, with a thumb. She was liquid with happiness. She believed him. Weeks ago, someone had thrown a Frankenstein mask through the window. She knew now that it had been a warning from Lyra's father, Rick Harliss, but

at the time she'd been convinced that it was from Chloe DeWitt and the pack wolves.

But maybe everyone was wearing a mask. Maybe no one was completely normal.

Maybe she *was* beautiful.

She wanted him. The want, the desire, was so huge she felt it incinerate her in a split second, burn her up to a single driving instinct: closer, more. She loosened his belt and undid his jeans without any trouble; it was as if she'd been practicing her whole life, as if she'd carried the knowledge of him in her fingers.

Suddenly, the basement door opened and footsteps came down the stairs.

"Glad you could come. Thought you might've gone back to town already . . ." Her father's voice. Of all the stupid luck. She'd never once *seen* her dad use the basement.

"Shit." Pete pulled away, his face almost comical with panic. *"Shit."*

She sat up. Her fingers turned clumsy again, stubborn with disappointment. She struggled to get her bra reclasped, and put her shirt on backward the first time. At least they were concealed behind several aisles of shelving, which, through a kaleidoscope of different supplies, gave them a patchwork view of the stairs.

Allen Fortner, a military guy her father knew from

West Point ages ago, passed momentarily into view, and suspicion scratched at the back of Gemma's mind. Fortner was FBI, and he and her father hadn't seen each other in years.

So what was he doing here, at Gemma's mom's party?

". . . wasn't sure what side of the fence you were on," Fortner was saying. "Trainor never thought you could be bounced this way."

"Trainor's an idiot," Geoffrey said easily. They had moved out of sight, but Gemma could still hear them perfectly. "Besides, it's not about loyalty. It's about future growth."

Pete made a movement as if to stand, but she grabbed his arm to stop him.

"Aren't you worried about exposure?" Fortner asked.

"It's my wife's fiftieth birthday party," he said. "You're an old friend of the family. What's to expose?" Then: "You didn't think we invited you for the pig roast, did you?"

In the long pause that followed these words, all of Gemma's earlier good feeling collapsed. She knew that this conversation, this man and her father standing between old furniture and rolls of extra toilet paper, was the true reason for everything: the skirts and the music and the honeyed ham and her mother's happiness.

A cover.

"All right," Fortner said at last. "Talk, then."

Geoff's response was immediate: "I know where they are," he said. And then, when Fortner was silent, "The subjects. The missing ones."

Gemma's heart was a balloon: all at once, punctured, it collapsed.

"Christ. It's been three weeks."

"Your guys lost track. I didn't."

"We didn't lose track," Fortner said, and he sounded irritated for the first time. "We were dealing with containment issues. Civilians, data leaks—"

"Sure. Harliss. I know."

Next to her, Pete shifted. His knee knocked a shelf containing dozens of bottles of water. They wobbled but didn't fall. Gemma held her breath.

Neither Fortner nor her father seemed to notice, because Fortner went on, "You were the one to spring him." He must have been pacing, because he passed into view again. Through the shelves packed with Christmas ornaments and old memorabilia, Gemma saw Fortner bring a hand to his jaw. It was like he was a robot with only a few preprogrammed modes. But when he spoke again, he just sounded tired. "I should've known."

"That's the problem with your end of the business, Allen. No local connections. A guy down at the precinct in Alachua County played basketball with me at West Point. It wasn't hard."

"Why now? Why not before?"

Again, silence. Gemma felt a finger of sweat move down her back. She was in a crouch, and her thighs were beginning to shake.

"I made a promise to my daughter," Geoff said, and Gemma heard the words as if they had glanced off the lip of a well high above her.

Allen Fortner obviously didn't buy it either. "Come on," he said. "You can't be serious."

"I promised her I wouldn't be the one to hand them over," Geoff said. "And I won't be. That's what your people are for. And I wanted to make sure the Philadelphia team was ready. I did some digging in DC, too, felt out the lobbies. Saperstein's done, even if he won't admit it. But that doesn't mean there won't be a place for the tech. I've spoken to Miller, and he thinks we're ready for a big policy push."

Pete reached for Gemma's hand. She pulled away, balling her fists instead, squeezing until she felt pain. She couldn't touch him. Her whole life was a lie, and it had festered and turned poisonous.

She didn't want to infect him, too.

"What's the end goal?" Fortner said. "Talk quickly, now. Your wife will be expecting a cake and her sing-along."

That almost killed her, right there. She was still breathing, though. It was amazing the little deaths that she had lived through.

"We get the contract. Simple enough." Through the shelves, Gemma caught only quick glimpses of her father, still wearing his party outfit, his colorful Hawaiian shirt. All show. "Triple the size and change the objective, at least in part. There will be a medical aspect, sure. That's where Miller and our friends in Congress come in. But there's a bigger endgame, too, to get costs down and make mass production viable. Saperstein bled money out of that place for a decade. His focus was too narrow and his production was too small."

"We got functional variants. We got real-world observation."

"You've got billions of dollars sunk into that shithole, a containment mission on your hands, and a PR shitstorm that will take a quarter of Washington. Come on, Allen. You know as well as I do that Saperstein's interest was ideological, not functional. He just wanted to prove he could make test subjects from scratch."

From scratch. Gemma felt like she was going to throw up. *From scratch.* Like pancake batter, or Lego kingdoms.

After a pause, Fortner cleared his throat. "Keep talking."

"I'll give you the location. Everyone feels good. The mess is cleaned up, no one's in trouble, we move on." Geoff leaned on the TV console that had once been upstairs. He looked almost bored. "It's like making toy soldiers," he

added. "Think of how many lives we'll save."

Fortner was quiet again. Gemma's heart was emptying and filling, turning over like a bucket. She felt as if she might drown.

"You said you promised your daughter," he said finally, and just hearing the word made her body go tight. "What made you change your mind?"

"I kept my promise. I won't be the one collecting. Besides"—he threw up his hands, a gesture Gemma knew well, like, *what does it matter, Kristina, kale salad or arugula, it's all a bunch of rabbit food*—"what would it have done before now? I knew Saperstein would hang himself by his own rope. The Haven team has proved its own incompetence. Billions of dollars down the drain, and enough cleanup to keep a thousand crisis managers employed for a decade."

"Where?" Fortner asked finally. For a split second, Gemma still held out hope that her dad would lie.

"I put them up in a trailer on one of my investment lots. Winston-Able, right off Interstate 40. Lot sixteen, a double-wide. Not far from Knoxville. Didn't even remember I owned the damn thing until the federal government reminded me in April." This made Fortner laugh. It sounded like a cat trying to bring up a hairball. "Pulled some strings and got her dad working at Formacine Plastics out there. You know it?"

Fortner sighed. "I'll talk to my guys about Philly. See what strings I can pull."

"I'm sure you'll figure it out. Saperstein shot himself in the dick. He doesn't listen. This is a new age, Allen. We got the chance to change the world here. ISIS, the Taliban, Al Qaeda, you name it—they don't follow the old rules."

"You're preaching to the choir."

"They're gonna brainwash their army of human IEDs, no reason we can't *make* ours."

"Like I said, preaching to the choir. But I'm going to have to go up the chain on this one."

"I believe in you," Geoff said, sounding faintly sarcastic.

Gemma had lost the thread of the conversation, but it no longer mattered. She understood everything that mattered: her father had betrayed Lyra and Caelum. He'd betrayed her, and his promise. She should have known he would.

Finally, Fortner and Geoff moved toward the stairs together. She could have cried from relief. Gemma's feet and legs had gone numb.

But at the last second, Fortner hesitated. When he turned back to Geoff, Gemma saw his face—cold and long and narrow, like an exclamation point—before he passed once again out of view.

“Your daughter,” he said, and Gemma’s blood turned thick and heavy. “She was made at Haven. One of the first.” It wasn’t a question, but Gemma could hear a question layered beneath the words, like a knife angled up through a fist.

“She was born there, yes,” Geoff said, and Gemma heard the importance of the correction—*born*, not *made*. But did it matter? Made, spliced, implanted—she might as well have been a fast-growing variety of bean sprout.

Fortner coughed. “You ever wonder what makes the difference?” When Geoff said nothing, he went on, “You want to put the replicas to good use, and I’m with you. But what makes them any different from your girl?”

“What do you think makes them different?” Geoff’s voice had turned cold. “Someone wanted her.”

Someone. Gemma noticed that he did not say *I*.

FOUR

THE PARTY WAS STILL GOING. Of course it was. They'd been in the basement for probably an hour. And yet somehow Gemma had expected to resurface and find the whole party incinerated, like Pompeii, vaporized in just a few seconds of suffocating ash. She wouldn't have been surprised to walk through empty rooms filled with cast-off trash, to find everything grayed with decay, to see her parents' friends transformed by the alchemical power of disaster into skeletons.

Now she saw the party for what it was: packaging. Pretty lies packed, beveled, and neatly shaped together, like an intricate sand castle, teetering at the edge of a creeping tide. The leis, the guests, the vivid cocktails colored like drowning sunsets: all of it an excuse for her father to see Allen Fortner, to negotiate with him. Even the cake was bullshit. When was the last time her mom

had eaten cake, let herself consume a single thing that wasn't low-calorie, high-protein, grass-fed, non-GMO?

They were only playing parts, and Gemma had been playing right along with them.

Again.

"Gemma. *Gemma.*"

She'd made it outside before Pete caught up with her. The air was alive with fireflies. Someone had lit the tiki torches; even burning could be made pretty, so long as it was contained. Gemma was struck instead by how insubstantial it all looked, the shadows and the light, the women in their bright dresses: like the scrim that dropped during a play so all the stagehands could get the furniture into position. She spotted her mother and father at the center of a group of dancers. It made her sick, that he could dance like that, arms up, not a care in the world, while in the background a faceless army prepared the audience for the next illusion.

"Talk to me," Pete said, and put his hands on her face. "Please."

Before Gemma could answer, April shouted her name. She came ripping out of the crowd, and Gemma had the impression of a curtain swinging aside to release her.

"Where have you been? I got stuck talking to—" She caught sight of Gemma's face and broke off. "What happened? What's wrong?"

"My dad lied to me." She felt as if she had to say the words through a fist. "He gave Lyra and Caelum up."

"Gave them up?" April repeated the words very slowly, as if Gemma were the one in danger of misunderstanding. Gemma felt her anger, so poorly buried, give a sudden lash.

"That's what I said. He gave them up. He sold them out." She felt like screaming. She felt like taking one of the stupid tiki torches and lighting the whole place on fire. "Haven's a PR crisis. That's what he said. And they're the biggest leak." The worst was that she couldn't even be angry at her dad, not really. He was a liar, and lying was what liars did.

She was the bigger idiot. She'd actually believed him.

April's eyes passed briefly to Pete—so briefly that Gemma almost missed it. *Almost.*

"I'm sorry," April said, and reached out, as if she wanted to touch Gemma's shoulder, or maybe pat Gemma on the head.

Gemma took a step backward, out of reach. All at once it was as if she was the torch: she was burning with rage, combusting. "You're *sorry*?" As if that was it, end of story, too bad. As if Gemma's favorite toy had just been stolen. "You know what this means, don't you? You remember how they *cleaned up* Jake Witz?"

"Keep your voice down," Pete said, although it hardly

mattered. Everyone was so drunk she could have been shouting.

Gemma spun around, stumbling a little on the grass, too furious to look at either of her friends. But April and Pete caught up to her almost immediately. Pete tried to take her elbow, but Gemma shook him off.

"Gemma, please," Pete said again. "Can you just . . . I mean, can we all stop and *think*?"

But she couldn't stop. There was no time. She closed her eyes and saw Jake Witz, the geometric perfection of his smile, the way he neatened his silverware, the intense stillness of his gaze, as if his eyes were a gravity trying to hold you in place. Already, her memories of him were fading. Too often, she saw him now as she did in her nightmares: half alive, half dead, lisping details about the constellations with a swollen tongue.

She kept stumbling on the grass, and nearly twisted her ankle when her wedge drove down into a soft bit of soil. She kicked off her shoes and didn't bother picking them up. She didn't have a plan, she didn't know what she would do now that Fortner had a head start, but she knew she had to keep moving, she had to go fast, she had to outrun Jake and her nightmare vision of his face and the sly orbit of Lyra's and Caelum's faces, moving eclipse-like to hang in his place. Pete and April could easily outpace her, but she was first to the narrow path that interlinked

the front and back yards, and that was so hemmed in by growth they had no choice but to fall back. They were maybe a step behind her, but she heard them the way she heard the distant twitter of birds in the morning—all noise, all background.

"Christ, Gemma, will you *wait* for a second?"

"Can someone please just tell me *what the fuck happened*?"

She broke free of the tangle of azaleas. The cars in the driveway looked like a freeze-frame of a collision about to happen. But before she was halfway to the driveway, Pete had his hand on her arm.

"Jesus *spitballs*." He was practically shouting. She'd never seen him mad before, not like this, and a small, distant flare of love went up through the smog of her own pain: you could count on Pete to make up a curse like *Jesus spitballs*. "Will you talk to us for a minute? Will you actually *listen*?"

That word, *us*, extinguished the flare right away. April and Pete were on the same side, which meant Gemma was left out. Alone.

"What?" she said. "You want me to listen? So go on. Spit it out," she prompted, when he said nothing. A floodlight came on automatically, triggered by their movement. In its light, Pete looked hollow and exhausted, and for just a moment, she felt guilty. Then she remembered: it was

two against one. All her life she'd felt as if she was trying to play a game from outside the stadium, trying to intuit the rules from brief and distant snapshots. But at least April had been with her, and Pete.

By learning the truth, she'd gone somewhere they couldn't follow. And that was just a fact.

April rocketed out of the growth looking as though she'd done personal battle with every inch of it. There were leaves in her hair, on her shirt, clinging to the wet of her shoes. "I won't," she panted, "ask"—more panting—"again." But she did anyway. "What. The. Hell. Happened?"

Pete still wouldn't meet Gemma's eyes, and for some reason that alone made her queasy: it meant for sure he had something to say that she wouldn't want to hear.

"Lyra and Caelum are in trouble," she said, keeping her voice as measured as she could. "I have to help. It's my fault, don't you get it? I walked them into this. I hand-fed them to my dad. If anything happens to them—" She broke off, suddenly overwhelmed.

In her dreams, Jake spoke to her even with the rope around his neck, puckering the skin around it. In her dreams, they were back on the marshes, and sometimes when he opened his mouth, he had beetles on his tongue.

Would he still be alive if she hadn't shown up to ask for his help?

"It isn't your fault," April said. "You couldn't have known."

"Let's hope I get a big *E* for effort, then," she said.

Pete looked at her then, and she wished he hadn't. His mouth was like a zipper stuck hard in a bad position. "If the *military* is going after Lyra and Caelum, like you said, you can't stop it. You're in danger, too."

"I don't have to stop it," Gemma said. "But I can warn them. I can give them a head start."

"How?" Pete's tone sharpened. "You don't even have a car." *Bang, bang, bang.* Little shrapnel words.

"You can't even drive," April added. This felt like a low blow. Her parents wouldn't let her learn to drive: another way they kept her bubbled off in glass, like one of those dumb ballerinas at the center of a snow globe.

"I'll take the bus," she said, and turned around again, so Pete and April had to jog to keep up with her.

"You don't know where you're going," Pete pointed out. "It's almost eleven. It isn't safe for you to travel on your own. Besides, I doubt they have all-night service to Rococo."

"Ronchowoa. So I'll hitchhike. Or I'll take a bike. I'll take a horse." But Gemma's throat was all knotted up. She turned away, swiping her eyes with her wrist.

"Jesus, Gemma. Will you listen to yourself? You aren't thinking." He wasn't shouting—not even close,

not compared to what Gemma's dad could do—but still, Gemma pulled up as if she'd reached an unexpected cliff. "If the military or the feds or whatever are trying to do a cover-up job—if they're willing to kill people to make sure the truth never leaks—you're a target. You were a target before, but you'll be a bigger target now. I won't—" His voice broke. "I'm not going to risk you again, okay? Not for Lyra. Not for Caelum. Not for any fucking person on the planet. I won't do it."

She started to cry, obviously. Trying not to cry was like trying to hold on to water by squeezing it. She cried until she gasped. "Don't you see? I have to *do* something. I have to help them. They're my people. They're like me. . . ."

But by then she couldn't go on. Fear and guilt came down on her mind like a veil, rippling all her words into distant impressions. In the house, Rufus began to bark, as if he was determined that she not cry alone.

And, weirdly, just when it felt as if she could cry until she drowned, she felt a sudden pressure, an invisible presence. It was as if an unseen person had just stepped up to place a hand on Gemma's shoulder and whisper in her ear. *It's okay,* this other person said, and Gemma recognized in the silence the voice of Emma: the first, the original. *It's going to be okay.*

Pete came forward to put a hand on her back. "It's okay," he said, and Gemma startled, turning around to

face him. Her impression of Emma's voice broke apart on the wind. "I'll drive you."

Behind him, April's face was narrow with worry, but she didn't argue. And Pete even managed to smile. He didn't look angry anymore.

"We're your people too, you know," he said. "We'll always be your people, if you let us." He ran a thumb over her lips. His skin tasted like smoke.

FIVE

THE WINSTON-ABLE MOBILE HOME PARK was just under six hours away, forty minutes outside Knoxville. Pete and Gemma drove mostly in silence, with the radio off and the windows down, except when Pete asked whether it would be all right to stop and get coffee.

The drive, the tension, the wind blowing in the wake of passing semis and the windshield dazzling with headlights: it all felt like they'd tripped over a wrinkle in time and wound up back where they were three weeks ago. Gemma tried to sleep but couldn't. Whenever they passed a cop on the road, she got jumpy. Gemma had told her mom she was going to sleep at April's house, and Pete had told his parents he was sleeping in one of the Ives's guest rooms, and April had, after much protestation, gone home so that she could run interference if Gemma's mom called the house before Gemma got back. April's moms

had left the party early, so there was no reason to think her cover story had been blown so quickly. Still, if worse came to worst, Gemma hoped her mom would assume she had merely lied in order to sleep over at Pete's house (which Kristina seemed to suspect Gemma was always angling to do—seemed to *hope* for it).

But she knew, too, that anything was possible. Her dad might have gotten suspicious. He might have radioed friends in the force, friends at the tolls, friends even now crawling dark highways, waiting to stop her and bring her home. A network of owed favors, backroom deals, contracts and alliances: the whole world was a spiderweb and all the threads were made of money.

Geoffrey was the spider. Which made people like her, and like Lyra and Caelum, the flies.

It was just before six o'clock when they spotted a sign for Ronchowoa, a dump of a place whose claim to fame was one of Tennessee's largest privately owned plastics manufacturers. By then, the darkness was letting up a bit, but the air was smudgy with chemical smoke and had its own gritty texture. Gemma remembered that her dad's brother, Uncle Ted, had helped restructure the Knox County debt, but she was still surprised to see a strip mall—containing a hair salon, a liquor store, a check-cashing place, and a local bank—sporting the name Ives.

It made sense. The Ives brothers loved nothing so much as ownership.

The trailer park was at the end of a long dirt road that badly needed paving. They went so slowly it felt as if they might simply be rolling in neutral. Gemma was itchy with anxiety, as if she were wearing a full-body wool sock. She saw no sign of Fortner or whoever he had sent to do his business. There were no other cars on the road, no strangers lurking around in the early morning shadows. Then again, she knew there wouldn't be. People like Fortner worked fast and clean.

Most of the time, at least.

What if they were too late?

She wished for the millionth time that Lyra had called her, and wondered for the millionth time why she hadn't. Gemma had told her to call first thing after their phone got set up, and had spent hours watching her cell phone, as if she could will it to ring through the pressure of her eyeballs.

Despite the grid of dusty, dirt-rutted streets, none of the trailers seemed to be in numerical order. Gemma's father had said that they were in number 16; she assumed that the unnumbered trailer between lots 15 and 17 must be the one they were looking for. But then she spotted the plastic children's toys scattered in the patchy yard. This wasn't it—couldn't be.

Still, they got out of the car, moving slowly, quietly, so they wouldn't startle anyone. Gemma wasn't in the mood for a showdown about trespassing—and besides, it was possible that even now they were being watched. Spiders had eight eyes, enough to see in all directions. But human spiders had hundreds, maybe thousands, more.

She was almost relieved to hear a dog barking. Everything until then had been so still, so silent, she might otherwise have thought they were too late, that the whole damn place had been rounded up.

Gemma was turning to shush the dog when she saw movement from a dingy white trailer set behind a scrub of balding bushes across the street. A girl or a boy—she couldn't tell from a distance, not in the half-light—slipped outside and turned to lock the door.

As soon as the girl started down the stairs, Gemma knew her.

"Lyra," she said. Her voice sounded hoarse. It was the first time she'd spoken in hours. "That's Lyra."

She and Pete jogged to catch up. Lyra was already moving away from them, head down, as if she was afraid of being followed. Did she know she was in danger? Where was Caelum? She must have heard them approach, because suddenly Lyra whirled around, hands on her backpack straps, elbows out like miniature wings.

"Lyra." Gemma felt out of breath, though they'd gone

barely one hundred feet. Lyra was more beautiful than she remembered. Funnily enough, she was wearing eye makeup. Not just a little, either. Shimmery, smoky, purple eye makeup, the kind April applied to Gemma when she was "practicing her technique." She'd dyed her hair, too, a platinum blond. She had gained badly needed weight.

"What are you doing here?" Typically, Lyra didn't smile or even seem that surprised to see them.

Despite having come to warn her, Gemma found at the last second she couldn't say the words—couldn't admit to Lyra that everything her father had promised was a lie.

Instead, it was Pete who spoke.

"You're in danger," he said. "The people who killed Jake Witz are tracking you and Caelum. They're probably on their way now."

Lyra hardly even blinked. "I know," she said. "They were here already."

Gemma's heart fell through a hole. "Is Caelum . . . ?"

"Gone." She frowned a little, as if the word carried an unexpected taste.

The world tightened around them. Even the air seized up and grew too heavy to breathe. "They—they got him?"

Lyra shook her head—a quick, spastic movement, like an animal trying to shake off a fly. "He was already gone. I saw them come, and I hid until they left."

"They'll be back," Gemma said. She could barely understand what Lyra meant—Caelum gone, but not taken, and Lyra now alone. But she knew for sure they would come back. "They'll be back any second. You have to come with us."

"I can't," Lyra said abruptly. And then, an afterthought: "Thank you. I'll be careful."

She turned and started walking again. For a second, Gemma was so stunned she could only stare after her. Then she registered the red backpack Lyra had on, bulging with belongings. Where was she going, at just after six in the morning? Where had Caelum gone?

"Wait," she called out. Lyra turned around, still with that same blank expression, a little bit patient, a tiny bit irritated, too. Unexpectedly, Gemma was furious. That was the good thing about anger: it was always bigger than fear, always bigger than guilt or disappointment. You could count on anger. "What do you mean, you *can't*?"

"And where's Caelum?" Pete was on Gemma's team again, bound to her by exhaustion and frustration. "Where did he go?"

"Home," Lyra said, as if that made any sense at all. "I'm going after him."

"I don't think you understand," Gemma said. The long night was starting to catch up to her. Whenever she closed her eyes, she saw starburst colors, quick explosions in the dark. "The people who came here won't just quit. They'll

look until they find you, wherever you are."

"They're looking for Caelum *and* me," she said. "They won't expect us to split up. And they won't expect us to get far. They don't think we're smart enough." Her expression changed, just for an instant, like a plate shifting deep undersea and causing ripples at the surface. "Besides, what other choice do we have?"

"You could come with us," Gemma said. But she knew that Lyra had made her decision. Gemma was fumbling for a way to convince her, hauling at a line stretched thin to a breaking point. "We could drive you somewhere far away," she said. "Maine. The Oregon coast. Canada. Wherever."

"Not without Caelum," Lyra said simply.

"You'll never find him," Gemma argued. "Do you know how many people there are in this country? Millions and millions." But there was no way to explain to Lyra how big the world was, and how far it went. Until a few weeks ago, her world was by the water, by a fence that ringed her off into a few square miles.

"You just said the people who came from Haven will find *us*."

"That's different," Gemma said. "They're . . . bigger than we are. Do you understand that? They have cars. They have drones, and money, and friends everywhere."

Lyra's face changed again. A new current swept away all the feeling, shutting her down to a perfect blank. "You forget what they made us to be, though," she said—softly,

gently, as if Gemma were the one who needed to understand.

Gemma shook her head. Her heart was beating through her whole body. Every minute the sun leeched away more cover.

"Invisible," Lyra said, so softly Gemma almost missed it.

Then she smiled. Gemma thought it was the first time she had ever seen Lyra smile, and the effect was dazzling, like watching the sun slide behind a prism and light it up in various colors. "Thank you, though. I mean it."

"Please," Gemma said, as Lyra turned away. "Take this, at least." Gemma took her wallet from her back pocket. It was cheap, plastic, and covered in smiley faces, and April had bought it for her as a joke their sophomore year. There were probably sixty bucks inside, plus an Amex tied to her parents' account, a debit card, a non-driver state ID, a folded-up note April had given her on their first day back in school after break—*This note certifies I give zero fucks*—and, in the little coin pouch, a nest of unspooling thread she'd picked off Pete's pocket the first time she'd worn his sweatshirt to school. She could get new cards, and even an ID wasn't that difficult, especially since she didn't drive. She had only a few hundred dollars in her bank account, anyway. She mostly regretted that bit of thread. "You'll need money. You know how to use an ATM card, right, to get money? The

code's easy. Four-four-one-one. Can you remember that?"

"Thanks." Lyra managed to smile again. Then she did something funny: she reached up and placed two hands on Gemma's shoulders. "See you," she said.

That was it. She turned and disappeared. At least, to Gemma it seemed like she disappeared, even though of course Lyra was actually visible for a while, moving between cars, heading in the direction of the highway, and finally passing into a thicket of disease-blighted trees. The sun had finally come up for good, and Gemma found her eyes watering in the sudden bright. She should run after Lyra. She should beg her, or scream at her, or force her to come with them.

But she knew it wouldn't do any good, and she didn't move, and couldn't breathe. She knew they would never see each other again. Lyra would be cleaned up, like Jake had been. Caelum too.

"Gemma?" Pete found her hand and held it tight-tight, as if she was in danger of falling off a ledge. "You tried, okay? You did everything you could do."

Gemma said nothing. It didn't matter if she'd tried. She'd failed. And that was the only thing that counted.

"You can't feel guilty about this, okay? You can't save her. You can't save any of them. I want you to say it."

She was surprised when Pete pulled her into a hug. His

shirt still smelled a little like the tiki smoke, his skin like the sweet punch they'd been drinking. She felt like crying again. But she kissed his collarbone through his shirt, and tilted her head to catch his Adam's apple, too.

"I tried," she said. "I can't save them." As quickly as the urge to cry had come, it was gone. It wasn't that she believed it, exactly, but that it didn't matter anymore. What she had said to Lyra was true: the people working against them were too big. They were too strong.

Lyra and Caelum would die by their will, just as Gemma had lived.

The hand of misery that had been squeezing her for weeks unclenched. She felt light. Free. She saw now that her only mistake had been in thinking she had a choice.

There was evil everywhere in the world. Liars outnumbered truth tellers, probably by three to one. So what did it matter, one more or less? She might even be able to look at her father again. "Let's go home," she said.

For the first time since they'd left the party, Pete smiled. "Now you're talking," he said, and kissed her hand even as he interlaced their fingers. He seemed happy. He thought she was happy.

She didn't have the heart to tell him the truth. There was no need, anyway. Happiness never lasted, because happiness didn't pay dividends.

That was just the way the world worked.

SIX

THEY WERE ONLY A FEW miles out from the dump of run-down fast-food restaurants that counted for the center of Ronchowoa when they came across the accident: a big delivery truck and a sedan nosed together at a right angle so they blocked the road entirely. The truck driver was visible in his cab, hunched over the phone. The woman was pacing, and when she spotted Pete and Gemma she flagged them down, as if they might otherwise have any choice but to stop.

"Don't get out," Gemma said, when Pete unbuckled his seat belt. "There must be another way home."

"She could be hurt," he said.

Gemma was too tired to care, and too tired to feel guilty. "She isn't hurt," she said. "She's walking. See?"

And she was—the woman was heading straight for them, gesturing for Pete to roll down the window. When

he did, she leaned down to squint into the car. She had the washed-out coloring of an old T-shirt, but her eyes were dark and Gemma didn't especially like them. They were the kind of eyes that worked like specimen pins, as if they were trying to nail things down in their proper place.

"Sorry to bug you," she said. "Do y'all have a cell phone I could borrow? Mine's out of batteries. And this guy won't give me his info, won't speak a word to me."

Gemma's phone was also dead, so Pete handed his over. Gemma did feel a little guilty then. The woman's hands shook badly when she tried to dial the police, and it took her several tries before she could get the number right. She moved away from the car, plugging one ear with a finger, while the truck driver climbed out of his cab and glared at her. Gemma didn't like the look of him. He looked big and ropy and mean.

The woman hadn't even hung up before the police were on the scene: two of them, a man and a woman, who arrived in an unmarked sedan.

Every minute it got hotter. Gemma and Pete sat and watched the woman and the truck driver argue and the cops look on impassively—they were too far to hear what was being said.

"Should I ask for my phone back?" Pete asked. Gemma shook her head and said nothing. She was too tired to

think. When he keyed on the engine so they could use the AC, the female cop turned in their direction, as if seeing them for the first time.

"Great," Pete said. Now it was the cop's turn to approach. "Just great."

"Step out of the car, please," she said, in the flat drawl of someone extremely bored by her job. Gemma could see the sky mirrored in the woman's sunglasses, and she straightened up as fear twinged her spine.

"Hang on a second," Pete said. "We didn't do anything."

"Please step out of the car." She showed her badge—a flash of gold, and then it retreated.

"But we didn't do anything," he insisted. "We were just driving home and we came across the accident."

"I understand. If you would both just step out of the car, we'll get you on your way in a minute."

"Just do it," Gemma whispered to him. Now the other cop was sauntering over, hands on his belt, working a piece of gum in his mouth.

They got out of the car. The backs of Gemma's thighs were slick with sweat from where they had stuck to the seat leather. It was bright and very quiet. A dozen cows stared dolefully at them from behind a rotting fence. From their perspective, Gemma and Pete were the ones fenced in.

"You see what happened?" the female cop asked.

Pete was getting agitated. "No. I already told you. We had nothing to do with it."

Now the male cop chimed in. "You from around here, then?"

Pete hesitated. His eyes slid to Gemma's. Once again she felt a pinch of worry—could they be sure these were real cops? She'd only seen the woman's badge for a second. They weren't driving a squad car, and though they were in uniform, it wasn't like she could pick out a fake. Still, she knew they were safe so long as there were witnesses.

"We're from Chapel Hill," Gemma said. Right away, she knew she'd made a tactical error.

The male cop's eyebrows blew up to his hairline. "You're quite a little ways from home," he said. "Whatcha doing in Tennessee?"

"It isn't any of your business," Pete said. Gemma nearly told him to calm down, but she didn't want to make things any worse.

The cop gnawed his gum some more. "You two got some ID?"

Gemma's heart sank. She didn't have ID—she'd given Lyra her wallet. Pete seemed as if he might argue the point, but at a look from Gemma, he turned and moved back to the car, muttering. Gemma waited in the agonizing

silence, half wondering why the truck driver and the woman he'd smashed were being so patient. If she'd been in an accident, if the cops were wasting their time on two nobodies instead of helping, she would have lost her shit. But they just stood there, dumb and practically silent, as if the cops' arrival had turned them into statues.

Pete was taking too long. He searched the front seat. He appeared to crouch, as if searching the floor. When he straightened up, his face was hollowed out with fear.

"I—I can't find my wallet," he said.

Gemma felt the ground buck like an animal beneath her. "What do you mean?"

"What do you *think* I mean?" He threw open the door to the backseat and disappeared again. "I can't find it. It's gone."

"That's—that's impossible." But as Gemma closed her eyes, she remembered that they'd stopped for coffee a few hours before dawn. She saw Pete, juggling a Styrofoam cup and a water bottle, slide his wallet on top of the car so he could reach for his keys. What if he'd left it there? They'd been so tired.

It was possible.

Pete slammed the door shut. Then, suddenly, he aimed a kick at the rear tires. Gemma shouted. The cops started toward him and he backed off, holding up both hands. "I'm all right," he said. "I'm all right."

"Why don't you have a seat here on the curb?" The male cop reached for his belt—Gemma saw a flash of metal handcuffs.

"What—are you going to arrest me now? We. Didn't. Do. Anything."

"Settle down, son. No one's accusing you. No need to get so defensive."

"I'm not defensive—"

"Early in the morning, wearing party clothes, maybe you been drinking some, decided on a little joyride—"

"Jesus Christ. This is *insane.* We weren't *joyriding*—"

"Pete." Gemma's voice cracked. Everything was happening too fast. Gemma felt as if she were listening to a song at triple, quadruple speed. There was a high ringing in her ears, like the sound of electricity through a live wire. Danger. "Please. We weren't joyriding. And we haven't been drinking. We have . . . we have friends nearby."

"Friends?" Too late, Gemma knew she'd made another tactical error. "These friends have names?"

Pete jumped in again. "We don't have to tell you anything. You don't have any reason to hold us." He was almost shouting. But for a second, the cops seemed to realize the truth of this, and froze where they were. "Can I have my phone, please?"

These words he directed at the female driver, the one

who'd originally flagged them down. Funnily enough, however, she didn't move. She didn't even blink. Again, Gemma had the impression of a statue.

No. Not a statue. An actor—a bit-part actor whose lines have come and gone, contentedly watching the rest of the play from the wings.

Too late, Gemma understood. Too late, Gemma knew there were no witnesses, and no one to hear them scream.

SEVEN

THE WORST THING ABOUT BEING kidnapped with your boyfriend, it turned out, was having to go to the bathroom. First Gemma thought she could hold it. Pete tried to get his hands free so he could at least pee in the corner, in a pile of rags or the empty water bottle that rattled across the floor whenever the van made a turn.

But he couldn't get his hands free.

She pretended to be asleep, choking on her own panic, on tears she couldn't even wipe away, while the van filled with a sharp metallic stink. Later it was her turn, and she felt a flood of shame that made her want to die, truly die, for the first time in her life.

Instead, she slept. Unbelievably, improbably, mercifully, she slept, with her head knocking against the filthy floor and the stink of ammonia everywhere.

Every hour or so, the van came to a stop: the drivers

were in no particular hurry. Every time, Gemma woke with a start, hoping they'd come to a checkpoint, or a roadblock—hoping, though she knew it was impossible, that someone had already realized she was missing, that police had been mobilized across fifty states—but no one came to let them out, and every time, after they lay there in the sweating quiet for agonizing minutes, the van simply started up again. Who knew whether the strangers who'd cuffed and gagged them were fake cops or the real thing, just paid off by somebody higher up? She understood that the truck had been brought, and the accident staged, specifically for the abduction. It was likely Fortner's friends had blocked off all the roads around Winston-Able with more fake accidents or fake checkpoints, scanning for a boy and girl traveling together, acting weirdly, no convincing story about who they were or where they'd come from.

By the time the van stopped for good, Gemma and Pete hadn't looked at each other in hours. Her jeans were wet. His, too. She was still wearing her party top, which had beaded sequins along the hem. He was in his Hawaiian shirt.

She nearly toppled over when she had to stand. The man who'd masqueraded as the truck driver took her arm, surprisingly gentle, as if they were on a date and she had caught a heel in the sidewalk. But the woman

who'd posed as a cop stepped forward and seized Gemma roughly.

"I'll take this one," she said simply.

It was dark except for a ring of headlights in the distance that might have been Jeeps, more vans, some kind of security cordon. There were streetlamps, but most of them were missing bulbs. People on foot patrolled with flashlights, and in the distance, Gemma made out a big, low, slope-roofed building, barely speckled with light.

Long runways of pavement, distant fists of furry trees, signs (A-32i, B-27a) blinking in the sudden clarity of the guards' flashlights. It was an old regional airport; she could even now make out a single hangar, illuminated by the temporary sweep of passing headlights.

Where were they? Not Tennessee. They must have been driving for twelve hours at least. She smelled running sap, tilled mud, even a very faint tang of fertilizer. Farmland.

Crickets cut the air into sound waves. Stars wheeled prettily above them. Ohio? Indiana?

Their abductors removed their gags at last; they were wet and heavy with saliva. Tears of relief burned Gemma's eyes, even though she still couldn't speak: her tongue felt swollen and painful, her lips were raw, and her throat dry. She wondered why they'd been gagged in the first place—whether it was just to keep them from talking to each other, or so they would be afraid.

Voices shouted in the dark. Someone called, "Hot shit!" and there was even a smattering of applause, as if the people who'd seized Gemma and Pete had instead won several rounds in a bingo tournament.

"Where are you taking us?" Pete's voice was hoarse, too. She wanted to reach over and squeeze his hands. But she was filthy, ashamed, and besides, her hands, still cuffed behind her back, were numb.

"Nowhere." The guy who'd been playing male cop sounded tired. Almost reproachful. Like, *hey, buddy, I've had a long day too. At least you didn't have to drive.*

"Don't answer it," the woman said. Hearing Pete referred to like that, like an *it*, sparked a new terror.

"My name is Gemma Ives." Gemma's words tasted a little like vomit. They were coming up quickly on the airport—too quickly. A few distant lights had swelled from fireflies to windows: in a few of them, she could make out concrete interiors, wires nested like intestines in the ceiling, banks of leather chairs still bolted to the floor. "I'm the daughter of Geoffrey Ives. My dad was one of the original investors in Haven. This is my boyfriend, Pete. You've got it all wrong. We're not who you think we are."

"I told you"—the woman sighed, speaking directly over Gemma's head, as if she were nothing but air—"not to talk to it."

"What does it matter, anyway? You want to know

where we're going, kid?" Her partner, or whatever he was, wouldn't look at Pete or Gemma, even when he was addressing them. "Nowhere. We're already here."

The old airport terminal rose steep-faced and ugly, like someone's blunt and splintered jaw. There was a faint hiss in the dark, and then the wheeze of rusted hinges: a door.

Gemma had known they were in trouble—big trouble. In the van she'd sat there grinding her teeth and trying to force her thoughts to settle, to pin them down whenever they flitted out of reach, like trying to catch horseflies by hand. They'd been followed. The military, or whoever was in charge, had figured out that they were trying to help Lyra and Caelum. Maybe they even knew that Caelum had managed to slip away, and somehow they blamed Gemma and Pete.

But now, for the first time, she understood. The people who'd abducted them didn't think Gemma and Pete had helped the replicas escape.

They thought Gemma and Pete *were* the replicas.

EIGHT

INSIDE: THE SMELL OF SHOE polish, sweat, gunmetal. Two soldiers wearing military fatigues straightened up at their post. They were in a tight corridor, carpeted and filthy. A narrow set of stairs, dirty with footprints, rose into the darkness. Gemma knew once she went up the stairs—wherever they led—things would be hopeless.

"You're making a big mistake." Gemma's voice cracked. How many hours had it been since she'd had anything to drink? "Call my dad. Call him."

"We should have left the gags on," the man holding Pete muttered. He nudged Pete toward the stairs. Unexpectedly, Pete broke loose, reeling like a drunk. His hands were still bound, but he cracked his head into the man's jaw; Gemma heard the impact of it, a hollow sound.

Suddenly, everyone was shouting. Gemma screamed as both soldiers launched for Pete at once.

"Don't hurt him! Please. *Please.*" She was too scared even to cry. For a second, she lost sight of him in the shuffle of human bodies. One of the soldiers accidentally caught her with an elbow and she bit down on her tongue.

"Easy, easy, easy." The two soldiers hauled Pete to his feet, pinning him between them. Still, he struggled to break loose. Gemma had never seen him look the way he did then, and she thought randomly of a video April had once shown her during her vegetarian phase: how fighting dogs were burned with cigarettes, beaten with sticks, until they were so angry and desperate they would tear each other up, actually tear each other into pieces.

The dogs in the video knew they were going to die, and that was what made them fight. They had nothing to live for.

"Let go of me." Pete's face was so twisted with raw anger, even Gemma was afraid of him. "Get your fucking hands off me."

"You better tell your boyfriend to calm down." The man who'd been holding Pete was massaging his jawbone. He glared at Gemma. "Or he's going to get his head blown off."

"Please." Gemma's voice cracked. "Please, Pete." At the sound of her voice, he finally went still.

"Good boy," one of the soldiers said. "We don't want to hurt you."

Neither Gemma nor Pete bothered pointing out that that was very hard to believe.

"Take him up," the man said, still rubbing his jaw and looking pissed about it.

This made Pete go wild again. "Let me stay with her." But the soldiers pivoted him, with difficulty, toward the stairs. "Let me stay with her. Please."

Gemma let herself cry then. She couldn't help it. She felt as if she were watching Pete through the wrong end of a telescope, getting smaller and smaller, though he was only a few feet away.

"It's okay, it's okay," she kept repeating, even as his voice splintered into echoes and then grew fainter, even though it was obviously not okay, nothing was okay, nothing would be okay ever again.

"Please." She tried one last time to make them listen. "Please," she said. "I'm telling you the truth. Geoffrey Ives is my father. Ask Dr. Saperstein, ask anybody—"

But she went silent as, down the hall, a door opened and spilled a gut of light.

"What's all the shouting for?" A woman's voice, low and surprisingly warm, floated out to them. For a moment, she was silhouetted in the light. As she came forward, Gemma experienced a shock of displacement: the woman looked like a soccer mom, like one of Kristina's lunch crew. She was even wearing yoga pants.

“Nothing.” The man finally quit massaging his jaw and straightened up. “Is Saperstein back?”

The yogi shook her head. “Tuesday,” she said.

Gemma’s mouth tasted like plaster, like the soft crumble of a pill. Saperstein knew her father. She’d been counting on the fact that he, at least, would be able to help. She’d comforted herself with the idea that wherever she was being taken, Saperstein would be there.

What would happen to her, and to Pete, before Tuesday when he returned?

“He didn’t go to Penn after all, did he?”

“No. Washington.” The yogi’s eyes swept Gemma. “Where’d you find her?”

“Where we were supposed to.” Gemma’s captor was squeezing her arm so tightly, Gemma could feel her fingernails. “She says it was all a big mistake. She says she doesn’t belong here.”

“Is that right?” The yogi was still watching Gemma curiously—not meanly, not with disgust or contempt, but with true curiosity. “Well, someone’s been feeding her, at least.”

A fist of hatred tightened in Gemma’s stomach. “I’m not lying,” she said. “I can prove it. Call Saperstein. Ask him yourself.”

Gemma couldn’t tell whether the yogi woman was even listening. She only looked puzzled, as if Gemma

were speaking in a different language. After a moment, she withdrew, and Gemma heard the murmur of distant voices: she was speaking to people out of sight. Gemma was dizzy with fear. What was she doing?

A minute later, several people wearing medical scrubs flowed down the hall and moved up the stairs without acknowledging either Gemma or the man and woman who'd brought them. They had the same look as all medical staff: harried, professional, too busy to be bothered. The colossal, patchwork strangeness of it all—the yoga pants and the doctors' scrubs and the soldiers with assault rifles and the reek of sweat—made a sudden rise of hysteria lift in Gemma's chest.

The woman in yoga pants returned, turning her face to the ceiling as if listening to the pattern of footsteps above them.

"Should I take her up?" Gemma's captor asked, and she shook her head.

"In a second. I'm going to bring them down first."

"Bring *who* down?" Gemma blurted out.

The woman didn't answer right away. Just then, the sound of footsteps above them grew louder. The door at the top of the landing creaked open, and the doctors, or nurses, or whatever they were, returned.

They had brought along three Gemmas.

Three Gemmas crowded the stairwell. Three Gemmas

gazed down at her. Three Gemmas, scalps shaved clean, wearing filthy T-shirts and pants that bagged from the hollows of their hipbones, chittered like small mice, as if at a fun-house reflection.

Gemma lost her breath. A hole opened up beneath her feet. She dropped straight through the floor.

Dimly, she was aware that the woman in yoga pants had turned at last to address her. "My proof," she said simply.

NINE

FINALLY, GEMMA WAS ESCORTED UPSTAIRS. The airport terminal was crawling with military personnel, but also people in medical scrubs, rendered identical by their dirty hair and look of shared exhaustion. One woman dressed in a pantsuit, who resembled a fashion mannequin on Fifth Avenue, kept massaging her forehead with perfectly manicured fingers. Gemma didn't even want to know what government agency *she'd* crawled out of.

The airport was dizzying not so much because of its size, but because of its regularity, the identical halls stripped of furniture, counters, vendors, arrivals screens. There were very few working lights, and new ribs of plywood divided room from room. The ceiling panels were missing.

Gemma was led to a bathroom with no stalls at all, just toilets bolted to the floor at regular intervals. A nurse was

summoned—she was wearing a shapeless medical smock over her street clothes, and had that blind-mole look of someone who'd just been asleep—to unbutton Gemma's reeking pants and underwear and haul them to her hips while Gemma peed, since her wrists were still bound.

The nurse's hands were cold. Gemma tried to blink away the sudden pressure of tears: the woman's fingers swept the place between Gemma's legs when she went to hitch up Gemma's underwear and then jeans.

"Sorry," the nurse whispered. "We'll find you something dry to put on in a bit." But Gemma felt something come down around her, some inner space collapsing.

There was no air-conditioning. If it wasn't obvious enough from the smell of must and raw wood, from the filthy corners and cables of dust visible through open gaps in the walls, it was clear to her now: whatever this place was, it wasn't like Haven. There was no experimentation here, no medical treatments or analyses. This was a holding pen, pure and simple.

Outside the bathroom, the woman in the pantsuit was waiting, yawning behind a hand. She straightened up and frowned briefly at Gemma. "Well?"

"Well what?" the nurse responded, keeping a hand on Gemma's elbow. Her touch was surprisingly gentle, as if she wanted to make up for what had happened in the bathroom.

“That’s the last of them, isn’t it?”

“How should I know?” The two women obviously despised each other. “That’s your business. What I’m supposed to do is keep them *alive*.” Gemma disliked the way she emphasized that. It suggested the other woman’s business was something else entirely.

“No need to get defensive. I was just asking. They all look the same to me, even the ones that aren’t doubled.”

“I bet.” The nurse’s voice was hard with sarcasm. “We still have bodies to match. Some of ’em no more than fingers—thanks to you.” She sniffed. “But if you say so, you say so.”

They moved again down the hall, cavernous with shadow, and half-splintered spaces suggesting their original purpose: countertops, old glass display cases where she imagined sandwiches withering behind glass.

Something smelled: a trash smell, an inside-of-the-body smell. The scent of urine was strong. They stopped to draw water from a long industrial sink: plastic cups overflowed a massive trash can. The nurse had to hold the cup while Gemma suckled at it like a baby, but she was too thirsty to say no. Then, to her surprise, the woman turned Gemma and released her handcuffs. Gemma nearly fainted from the rush of pleasure, of relief, when she could move her shoulders freely.

But she understood, as the woman gestured her on,

why the restraints weren't necessary: patterns of footsteps sounded softly on the linoleum, overlapping, like the drum of distant rain. Soldiers with guns. Even when they hung back in the dark she could see the barrels winking like animal eyes.

"Be a good one, now, and you won't get in any trouble," the nurse said. For the first time since being taken into the van, she felt a spark of hope. This woman wasn't evil. Maybe she could be made to understand. To believe.

"Please listen to me." Gemma spoke in a whisper. Her throat was raw from crying. "My name is Gemma Ives. I live in Chapel Hill, North Carolina. I have parents. They're looking for me."

She couldn't tell whether the woman was even listening. This part of the airport was almost completely dark: a runner of cheap battery-pack lights lit a narrow aisle of floor, like those on an airplane designed to help you find your way to the emergency exit. Around them furniture was lumped and piled and stacked in the darkness. It looked like a whole warehouse had been emptied. The smell was terrible, too. It was so bad it had weight, and form, and even movement. They paused briefly in front of a set of plastic shelves piled with cheap T-shirts and plain cotton pants, laundered to the point of stiffness.

"Laundry day's Friday," the nurse said. "You'll get a replacement soon as you turn in this pair."

“Please,” Gemma said. She found herself speaking in a whisper, as once again fear flooded into her, poured down her throat like the taste on the air, like the grit of human skin and nails. “I don’t belong here.”

Someone moaned. Then a cry in the dark, quickly stifled. But the sound seemed to find Gemma, to burrow deep in her chest, like a hook. And at the same time her eyes adjusted, she realized that what she’d mistaken for piles of furniture were really people, girls: hundreds of girls, dressed identically, some of them visibly wounded, others so thin they looked like a wreckage of bones; sleeping on the floor, on mattresses, on piles of fabric and tarps, on stacked blankets.

“Nobody belongs here, child,” the nurse said. She was holding her throat. Gemma saw a small gold cross nested between her fingers. “Not even the devil himself.”

PART II

TEN

KRISTINA IVES SPENT THE FIRST day of her fifty-first year crying, and picking the cuticles of her fingernails until they bled, and then shivering damply in bed, waiting for the Xanax to take effect, and the second day counting all the ugly things she could find on the way to Nashville, Tennessee.

A dead deer, mangled on the side of the highway. A house punched in by age and neglect, spilling its rot onto the porch, as if it had been gutted. Billboards advertising strip clubs, XXX stores, erectile dysfunction clinics.

Since having Gemma, she'd hardly ever traveled: she liked to be home with her things, in the beautiful house with the rugs that went *hush hush*, with Rufus and the cats and the pool in summertime where she could lie out with a book, her feet damp with dew and new grass, the hum of a lawn mower in the background like the pleasant buzz of one of her pills.

They had a house in Vail and Geoff hosted clients there several times a year, but she hadn't been, not since Gemma was a toddler. Though Geoff had urged her to learn to ski, she could never see the point in it, the suiting up and the rentals and the waiting in line to crank all the way to the summit only to plunge down the mountain again.

One time, only one time, he'd convinced her to put Gemma in ski school. She was maybe four years old, so young even she didn't remember the experience, and Kristina had stood with a crowd of other parents in the lodge while outside a group of fluorescent children made pie-wedges with their skis. No one else was worried—the other mothers and the scattered father drank spiked hot cocoa or went off on runs of their own—but Kristina had stayed at the windowpane, her breath misting the glass, watching the little gob of purple that was her only daughter, funny-faced and precocious with cheeks so fat Kristina had to stop herself from biting them.

She'd read once that during World War II many of the Jews had sewn their precious belongings, jewels and watches and things, into the lining of their coats before fleeing, and she'd immediately understood: Gemma was like that, like a secret, precious thing sewed not into the lining of her coat but into who she was deep down, at her core, as a person.

She saw it even before it happened. Saw Gemma's

puffy-coated arms begin flapping frantically, saw her teeter on her tiny skis. And she saw, at the same time, beneath Gemma's coat and beneath her skin, to the webbing of her narrow bones and all the fragile organs tucked among them, so easily punctured, ruptured, burst; and she was out the door and running, calling for Gemma to stop, be careful, stop, so that Gemma, looking up at her mother, lost her balance and fell.

So Kristina didn't go to Vail anymore. They had a place in the Outer Banks, but there, too, she rarely went. Gemma loved it, but Kristina could never keep down images of Gemma drowned in the waves, pummeled by sand, her lungs bloated with seawater. And she had another fear—that she would have to bring Gemma to an unfamiliar hospital, that blood would be drawn, or bones x-rayed, and somehow, the doctors would know. That evidence of Kristina and Geoff's crime might be encoded in every single one of Gemma's cells, embedded in the filaments of her DNA.

She'd been in the kitchen, rinsing out stray wineglasses that Geoff must have collected from the deck, when the call came in. Sunday: her favorite day. She never minded washing dishes, even though they had help to do that. She liked the sound of rushing water, the soap-steam clouds, the way the glasses chimed when she tapped them with her nails.

"Gemma?" she answered the phone automatically. No one else would be calling so early on a Sunday.

But it was April. And as soon as Kristina heard the sound of April's voice, she knew.

"Ms. Ives?" That was a tell, too—April never called her anything but Kristina, not since she was in third grade. "I'm worried about Gemma."

And then, in a rush, April had told her everything: that Gemma had not, in fact, slept over; that she had gone with Pete to see Lyra down in that tragic little shoe box her husband had shoved Rick Harliss into; that she should have been back already.

She wasn't back, though, and she wasn't picking up her phone, and Pete wasn't picking up, either.

By some miracle, Kristina had managed to locate a telephone number for Rick Harliss, scrawled on a notepad and wedged deep in the junk drawer, along with all the other miscellaneous things they couldn't stand to look at but knew might prove useful someday.

Rick's home number just rang and rang, and his cell phone went straight to voice mail.

She went right away to Geoff, as she always did, as she had been trained to do. He had the idea to check Gemma's debit card activity and see whether she had taken out any money. In the very early morning, Gemma had purchased tickets from Knoxville, Tennessee, to Nashville.

In the afternoon, she had taken out two hundred dollars from an ATM in Crossville, Tennessee. Around midnight, someone used her ATM card to check into a Four Crossings Motel in Nashville, and although by this morning that proved to be a false lead—the girl and boy in room 22 had obviously stolen Gemma's wallet, although they claimed simply to have found it.

Still, they must have stolen it *from* Gemma. Which meant she had gone to Nashville.

But why? For what reason? And why was her phone dead, and Pete's too?

Where, for that matter, was Rick Harliss?

You promise you know absolutely nothing about this? she had asked Geoff, after a terrible, sleepless night, half drowning in barbiturate dreams. *You swear you had nothing, nothing at all to do with it?*

Of course not. Geoffrey's answer was quick. *How could you even think that?*

And she believed Geoff because that was what she did, what she was compelled to do, the way the earth was compelled to go around the sun. They'd built the belief together, carefully, spinning turrets, ice-thin pillars, delicate vaulted ceilings alive with all the stories they'd made. Even a single crack would make the whole thing come down.

Now she counted: A truck overturned on the other

side of the highway. A highway memorial to someone who had died. A sign warning of a nearby maximum security prison. Ugly, ugly, ugly. Concrete sprawl and withered shrubbery baking in the heat. And Gemma, little Gemma, her small, glowing secret, somewhere out there. There weren't enough pills in the whole world to shave Kristina's fear into some manageable shape, a small white sphere she could swallow and let dissolve in her stomach.

A sign blinked, and disappeared behind them. Thirteen miles of highway left until they reached Nashville.

ELEVEN

"WHERE DID IT COME FROM?"

On Monday, those words had pulled Gemma from one nightmare into another: *mirrors,* she thought confusedly.

Three-dimensional, living mirrors: three Gemmas wore identical expressions of bland curiosity, three Gemmas had been split and fissured from a single central image. Unconsciously, she brought her hands to her face, her arms, her thighs, to make sure they were still intact. To make sure *she* was still intact.

"Which number are you?" asked one of the mirrors.

"You're not Cassiopeia," said another.

The third one said, "Cassiopeia is dead."

"I'm Calliope," said the first one. She added: "Number seven." In her eyes, Gemma was reduced to a narrow reflection. A reflection in a reflection in a reflection. Gemma thought of a double helix that mirrored even

as it turned and turned. Symmetry, but a terrible kind. She sat up, half expecting the other Gemmas to move in response. But they didn't.

"You think it's dumb?" one of the girls said.

"Dumb how?" one of the others asked.

"Dumb like number eight," the first one replied, and turned. "Like Goosedown."

Thud-thud-thud.

Only then did Gemma see another one, a fourth one, even skinnier than all the rest, crouched in the corner not far from them. Her legs were bare and covered with scabs. She was wearing a diaper. She was so thin her head appeared gigantic, her features too far apart, as if they were wrapped around a fishbowl.

Thud-thud-thud. As Gemma watched, she lifted her head and slammed it, once, twice, three times, against the wall; the sun caught a mesh of plaster fine as dust hanging in the air, sifting above her head, before slowly, it began to fall.

The sickest replicas were segregated from the rest of the population, concealed behind rudimentary curtains of burlap, kept mostly unconscious through regular dosages of morphine, at least according to what Gemma overheard. She might have been tempted to peek beyond the curtains and see for herself were it not for the smell.

Blood. Bodies in a constant state of hemorrhage, of organ failure, of beginning to turn.

Someone was always getting sick—in the toilet, in a trash can, on the floor when they couldn't make it to a trash can. Gemma knew that prions weren't contagious, at least that they couldn't be spread by breathing, but still she couldn't help but see prions turning invisibly on the air like sharp-pointed snowflakes, like dandelion fluff, like burrs that would stick in her lungs when she inhaled.

Diapered toddlers who had never learned to walk instead crawled among the wreckage of dirt, or simply sucked their fingers and cried.

Nurses still wandered the halls, like bewildered ghosts, as if questioning why on earth they couldn't just move on. They did the best they could to help, with limited supplies, dwindling medication, and power that failed regularly.

A single building, L-shaped, and boys and girls separated by security at the joint. Soldiers moved through crowds of standing cadavers—hollow-cheeked and fire-eyed, dizzy with disease and starvation—by parting them with their rifles. When one of the soldiers, a girl with tight cornrows, stopped to comfort a bawling replica, another soldier reprimanded her.

"You'll give them the wrong idea," he said. He was tall, with pale eyelashes and a burst of acne across his

forehead. "It'll only be worse in the end."

Gemma tried to find her way to Pete, to make sure he was okay, but was stopped by a redhead in full-on camouflage who looked like someone who might have been in her English class.

"Turn around," he said. "You speak English? Turn around."

Another soldier, a girl with her nails painted different rainbow colors, was sitting in a single plastic chair still bolted down in a waiting area otherwise empty of furniture. "They all speak English, dummy," she said softly. She was playing a video game on her phone. Gemma could tell from the sound effects.

"Doesn't seem like it, half the time." Gemma had turned away from him but not quickly enough to miss what he said next. "Shit. I don't even like *twins*."

She wanted to scream, but just like in her dream she couldn't. *Not me,* she wanted to say. *You've got the wrong girl.*

But how could she? Three other Gemmas tailed her. Three Gemmas who stood shoulder to shoulder, blink-blink-blink, breathing with *her* lungs, twitching with *her* hands, turning their heads on her own too-short neck.

No one would come to save her. Not a single person in the world knew where she was. Even when Pete's car was discovered—which she had no doubt it had been by

now—there was nothing to suggest where they had gone, not a trace of evidence, no ransom notes, no trail of blood.

Her only hope was that somehow, her parents would catch up to Lyra and Caelum and realize what had happened. That her dad would charge in here in his Big Suit way, threatening to sue everyone from Saperstein to the president of the United States, and she and Pete would be saved. But she knew, too, that would mean that Lyra and Caelum would have to take their place. Maybe the whole thing had a sick poeticism. After all these years, she'd finally ended up back where she started. Where she *belonged*.

It was better not to think. She gave up on trying to speak to anyone and didn't bother trying to get anyone to speak to her. When Dr. Saperstein came back, he would see her, know her, and realize his mistake—that is, if her dad didn't find a way to track her down first.

Until then, she simply had to survive.

TWELVE

THERE WAS NOTHING TO DO. No books, no magazines, no computers, no phones. Nothing but mattresses jigsawed on the floor and hundreds of girls sticky with injuries sitting or lying around.

Some of the replicas had made up their own games, rolling pen caps or stacking coffee cups. She even saw a girl, maybe three or four years old, playing with an old syringe. When Gemma tried to take it from her, the girl turned unexpectedly vicious, spitting in her face, going for Gemma's eyes. Gemma stumbled backward, and someone reached out to steady her. Again, Gemma had the sense of falling into a mirror: one of the reflections, one of her *clones*, had followed her.

"Don't worry about the Browns," the girl said. Her eyes were always moving—around and around, taking in Gemma's hair, and stud earrings, and fingernails, which

were painted yellow and green, alternating—as if trying to generate some centrifugal force that would pull Gemma closer. "They're all soft in the head."

Gemma went from feeling angry to feeling sick. She turned around again and saw the girl had resumed her play, pulling up wool fibers from a patch of dirty carpet. Another girl, identical to the first, had scuttled closer to watch. Looking at them side by side made Gemma dizzy.

"You're not one of us," the girl said. Her breath reeked, and Gemma felt sorry about being disgusted. "You were made somewhere else. There were only five genotypes at Haven. Numbers six through ten. And number six is dead."

"I know," Gemma said automatically. "I saw her." It made a twisted kind of sense that this girl could see what the people in charge couldn't, or wouldn't. To them, the replicas weren't people. They were lab rats. Or they were things, manufactured shells, like so many plastic parts cut from the same mold. It must be hard to keep track.

The girl leaned closer, and Gemma had to stop herself from flinching. At the same time, she was seized by an impulse to dig her fingers into the girl's eyes, to pull them out, to tear off her skin. She wanted her face back.

"Number six was named. We called her Cassiopeia. Dr. O'Donnell named me, too. My name is Calliope. Are you named?" Calliope's eyes were huge. Hopeful. April

called it Gemma's *sad kitten face.*

Gemma nodded. "Gemma," she said.

Calliope smiled. Two of her teeth overlapped. She hadn't had braces, obviously, like Gemma had. "Gemma," she repeated. "Where were you made?"

Gemma was exhausted again, though it couldn't be much past noon. She wondered whether the girl had ever met anyone new, at least anyone who would talk to her. "I was made at Haven, like you, but then I went somewhere else."

"Outside," Calliope said, exhaling the word as if it were the final piece of a powerful magic spell.

After that, Calliope wouldn't leave Gemma alone. She followed Gemma when she walked the 282 paces she could walk, between the curtained-off wing where the sickest replicas lay mangled, tethered weakly to life by grim-faced nurses working a dozen machines; to the two bathrooms, men's and women's, in the no-man's-land between the gendered sides.

When Gemma sat, Calliope sat a few feet away, watching her. At one point Gemma lay down and pretended to sleep. Still, she felt Calliope watching, and she sat up, finally, relieved to realize that she was angry, that there was another feeling elbowing in besides fear.

"What?" Gemma said. Looking at Calliope still gave her a terrible sense of vertigo, like being spun around

blindfolded and then discovering, with the blindfold off, that the world was still spinning. "What do you want?"

She'd meant to scare her, or startle her away, but Calliope kept staring. Gemma couldn't shake the feeling that Calliope had crawled into Gemma's body, that she wasn't another person but a shadow, a squatter. That would explain the tight, airless feeling Gemma had, as if when she breathed it had to be for both of them.

"I'm looking at you," she said, "to see what the outside looks like. You have hair like the nurses. And you're fatter," she added, but not meanly at all. Of course, Gemma realized, she didn't know that this was mean, like she didn't know it was rude to stare.

This made Gemma feel sorry for hating her face, for hating to see her, for wishing she would disappear.

Calliope tipped onto her knees and pulled herself closer, then rocked back on her heels again. She might have been Gemma's age, but she seemed younger. "Do you know Dr. O'Donnell?" she asked. "She's the one who named me. Then she left. A lot of them leave but most of them not for good. She's outside, too," Calliope clarified, as if Gemma might not have understood.

Gemma tried to swallow and couldn't. How to begin to explain? "I don't know Dr. O'Donnell," she said at last.

"What about Pinocchio?" Calliope asked. "Do you know Pinocchio?"

"Pinocchio?" Gemma thought Calliope must be joking. But she was completely serious. Her eyes were moon-bright, huge in that thin face—familiar and also totally foreign. It occurred to Gemma that she'd never heard Lyra make a joke. She'd never even heard her be sarcastic.

"Pinocchio's made out of wood just like a doll," Calliope said. She slid fluidly and without warning through different ideas, through fiction and reality, the past and present. "Wayne calls me Pinocchio, and I don't say how Dr. O'Donnell named me first. Names are like that. You have to be careful—once someone names you, you belong to them for life. Pinocchio wanted to go to the outside and be a real boy." Once again, she leapt to a new stream of thought: she had no meaning, no system to unwind them, to decide what was important and what wasn't. "He got ate by a whale but then he made a fire in the whale's stomach." She laughed and Gemma flinched. It wasn't exactly a laugh, more like the sound of a hammer against metal. "He made a fire just like the one at Haven. He lit it right in the whale's belly, right here." She pointed to her own stomach. She seemed to find this hilarious. "Wayne told me how he did it. And so the whale had to spit him up. I seen fire at Haven and I wasn't scared, not like some of thems."

Untangling Calliope's speech took almost physical effort. She nearly explained that Pinocchio was only a story, but stopped herself.

“Outside is huge,” she said instead. “Much bigger than you can imagine.”

Calliope hugged her knees, shrugging. “I know. I seen it through the fence and on TV, too. Who cares, anyway? It dies, it dies, it dies.” She turned and pointed casually to three replicas. “It dies.” She pointed to herself. Before Gemma could say anything, before she could deny it, Calliope was talking again.

“Haven is much bigger than where here is. Here is only the size of how A-Wing is at Haven. But there’s more doors at Haven, and more nurses, too. I don’t like the nurses, except for some of them are okay, because they feed us greens and blues for sleeping. One of the guards let me touch her gun.” She spoke quickly, hardly pausing for air, as if the words were a kind of sickness she had one chance to get out. “At Haven we can’t go in with the males because of their penises and how a normal baby gets made. So we have to stay away, except at Christmas for the Choosing.”

Something touched Gemma’s spine and neck, and made the fine blond hair April had always called her *goose down* lift on her arms, just like that, like bird feathers ruffled by a bad wind.

“What do you mean, the Choosing?” she asked, but Calliope wasn’t listening. She was pinballing between stories and ideas, feeding Gemma all the words she’d had to carry alone.

"Have you ever used a penis to make a baby?" she asked, and Gemma, stunned, couldn't answer. "The doctors still don't know if they can, I mean if we can, the its. Pepper got a baby in her stomach, but then she cut her wrists so afterward they all got more careful."

Gemma could hardly follow the story—Calliope combined pronouns or used them indiscriminately. She'd heard Lyra and Caelum refer to themselves as *it* at different times. All the replicas confused phrases like *want* and *ask, make* and *own.*

I owned it, one of the replicas insisted, when a nurse tried to take away a mold-fuzzed cup of old food remnants she'd been concealing beneath a panel of loose floor tile. *I owned it. It's me.* And some of the replicas couldn't speak at all—they could only growl and keen, like animals.

"So the doctors don't know." Calliope was still talking, working a fingernail into a scab on her knee; when the blood flowed she didn't even wipe it, just watched it make a small path down her shin, as if it was someone else's blood entirely. "Some of the its are too skinny for the monthly bleeding, but I have mine. Wayne said that means I'm a woman now."

Nausea came like movement, like the rolling of a boat beneath her. "Who's Wayne?"

"He's the one who told me about Pinocchio." Her

eyes weren't like eyes at all: they were more like fingers, grasping for something. "I always wanted a baby," she said in a whisper. "Sometimes I used to go to Postnatal and hold them and say nice things to them, like I made them instead of the doctors."

Blood was rushing so hard in Gemma's head she could hardly hear. Infants. Babies. She hadn't seen any since she'd been here. What had happened to all of them?

But she didn't have to ask. Calliope leaned forward, all big eyes, all hot little breath, all *need*. "Postnatal burned fast," she said. "The roof caved in and all my babies got smashed." Gemma turned away from her. But there was nowhere to go.

Nobody belongs here, child. Not even the devil himself.

Calliope pulled away again, smiling to show her teeth. "I like Haven better for most things. But here's better because of the males and how you can talk to them if you want." She said it so casually that Gemma nearly missed it.

"Wait. Wait a second." She took a deep breath. "What do you mean, you can talk to them?"

Calliope smiled with only the very corners of her mouth, as if it was something rare she had to hoard. "You can come with me," she said. "You can see for yourself."

Calliope came for her in the middle of the night. It could have been midnight, or four a.m.; there were no clocks in

the holding center, and since arriving Gemma had truly been aware of the rubbery nature of time, when there were no watches, phones, or activities to pin it down to.

"Follow me," she said, and took Gemma's wrist. Gemma had seen staff members guide the replicas this way, and imagined this was where she'd learned it.

They moved through the maze of sleeping replicas, most of them drugged up on sleeping aids distributed by the nurses before lights-out: pills for the replicas whose pain was greatest, and, when these ran out, simply plastic mouthwash cups full of NyQuil. Gemma had thrown hers out, as she assumed Calliope must have, too.

As they passed through the darkness, Gemma again had a strange doubling feeling, as if she and Calliope were two shadows, two watermarks identically imprinted. Or maybe she was the shadow, and Calliope the real thing.

Only one nurse, nodding to sleep in a swivel desk chair despite the lack of desk, jerked awake to ask where they were going. Calliope whispered, "Bathroom," and the nurse waved them on.

"Be quick," she said.

No-man's-land: the makeshift kitchen, the bathrooms, a plastic card table covered with scattered magazines and phone chargers, what passed for a break room for the staff during the day. A light in the kitchen was on, and as always the coffee machine was burbling and letting off a

burned-rubber stink. There was always coffee brewing, at every hour, although so far Gemma hadn't actually seen anyone drink from the machine.

Only a single soldier was on duty, the same red-haired guy with a pimply jawbone. He couldn't have been older than nineteen.

"That one never plays," Calliope whispered to Gemma.

"Plays what?" Gemma whispered.

But Calliope just shook her head. "He thinks it's bad luck."

Gemma saw a quick look of pain tighten the soldier's features, as if seeing them together hurt. He turned away again as soon as they veered right, toward the bathrooms.

At the last second, instead of going into the girls' bathroom, they simply went left, into the boys'. Unbelievably simple. Gemma doubted the soldier had even noticed. He probably thought the replicas were all dumb, anyway. It was reasonable to expect they'd make mistakes.

The bathroom was only half-lit. Most of the bulbs had burned out in the ceiling, and a sink filled with paper towels had overflowed, leaving puddles of water on the floor. The tiles seemed to pick up her voice and hurl it in a thousand directions. But the boys' bathroom had stalls, at least, as well as two puddly urinals.

"What now?" Gemma asked.

"We wait," Calliope said. "Come." She took Gemma's

hand and pulled her into one of the toilet stalls. She closed the door behind them and sat down on the toilet seat.

Less than a minute later the bathroom door opened again. Calliope held up a hand, gesturing for Gemma to be quiet. For a long second there was nothing but the *drip, drip, drip* of water from the faucet.

Then a boy: "Hello."

Calliope stood up then. "In here," she said, and opened the door.

He was younger—maybe twelve, thirteen. It was difficult to tell, since all the replicas, skinny as they were, with no concept of words they hadn't experienced directly, like *snow* and *cross-country,* seemed younger than their true age. But Calliope looked pleased anyway.

"A male," she said, as if Gemma might not be able to tell. The boy had very dark skin and perfect features and the kind of lips Gemma's mom's friends paid money for. He would grow up to be beautiful. *If* he grew up.

"What crop are you?" Calliope asked.

"Fourteen," he said. "A White."

This made her smile. "Like me," she said. "The Whites are the most important." She turned back to Gemma again. "Well? What do you want him for?"

"I need you to give someone a message for me," she said. He showed no signs of having understood. "Another male. Like me, from the outside. His name is Pete. Can

you ask him to come? Can you bring him?"

The boy looked at Calliope. She nodded, barely. "What's for me?"

She tilted her head to look at him. Once again, Gemma had the uncanny doubling sensation of watching herself in a fun-house mirror, the kind that elongated and thinned.

"Observation," she said, and held up one hand. "Five seconds."

He frowned. "I want to stethoscope," he said.

She shook her head. "Observation."

He looked away.

"Ten seconds," he said finally. "Five now, five when I bring him."

Finally, Calliope shrugged. Before Gemma could stop her, she lifted her shirt, exposing her chest: ribs visible, small pale nipples identical in shape to Gemma's, breasts stiff and small and hard, like little knots. Gemma was so horrified, she froze, and by the time she thought to grab Calliope's arm, to haul her shirt down, Calliope was already finished.

"Five seconds," she said. She didn't seem bothered at all, and the boy didn't seem all that interested. "Now go."

He turned and left the bathroom. As soon as he was gone, Gemma said, "You shouldn't have done that." She felt sick. They hadn't even cared that she was there, that she was watching. It hadn't *occurred* to them to care. She

supposed *observation,* for them, happened in front of lots of people. She wondered if they even knew what privacy meant. "You didn't have to."

Calliope looked puzzled. "It's only observation," she said. She smiled and showed her crowded teeth. "I've observed with twelve males so far. Only number forty-four is ahead of me. She's observed with fourteen. Plus, she lets anyone stethoscope with her, even the guards if they want."

She spoke matter-of-factly. There was no playfulness to it. It wasn't pleasure, just something to do. It wasn't at all like the party games people had played in middle school, Seven Minutes in Heaven, the stoplight game, all of them excuses to squeeze a nipple in a dark room and knock braces for a bit. All night, Gemma imagined, the bathroom would fill and empty with replicas meeting to touch and bargain and barter and stare.

Gemma leaned up against the counter, not even caring it was wet. The half-light made strange looping shadows on the walls and ceiling. "Stethoscope?"

"Like how the doctors and nurses do it," Calliope said. She placed a hand on her own chest to demonstrate, inhaling deep. Then she shifted her hand again, and again. Stethoscope: they'd invented their own term for second base. She dropped her hand. "Have you ever done stethoscope?" she asked.

"No," Gemma lied. She thought of being with Pete in her parents' basement, next to the rows of canned goods and bottled water, and how he'd traced the long scar between her chest and navel. It could have been a memory from someone else's life.

She had the crazy idea that maybe Calliope and her other replicas would take not just her skin and hair and freckles, but her past, her life, her memory. The longer she stayed here, the less she would have that would belong to her and to her alone.

She was losing it. She opened her eyes and fumbled to turn on the faucet, drinking from a cupped palm. Behind her, Calliope's face was a narrow shadow of hers.

"Then there's the full examining," Calliope was saying. Gemma didn't have to ask what that was. She could imagine well enough. "But I never done that yet. I tried one time with a Green, but he got sick right in the middle. Then one of the guards came in and yelled."

Gemma seized on this. "Didn't you get in trouble?" she asked. She didn't want to talk about *examining* and *stethoscope* and *observation* anymore. She didn't want to think about these broken kids playing doctor.

Calliope looked puzzled. "Lots of the guards play too," she said.

Gemma understood, now, what Calliope had said to her outside the bathroom, and why the red-haired soldier

had looked at them the way he did. He must know what went on at night, and what the other soldiers did with the replicas when they thought they could get away with it.

The door opened again. The boy, the White, had returned, alone.

Gemma's heart broke, actually broke—she felt it crumble in her chest, like a nub of chalk—but before she could ask what had happened to Pete, the door opened a second time and there he was.

Pete. He looked as if he'd been shocked into aging a hundred years. Feathery white eyelashes, hollows beneath his eyes, skin leached of color.

And yet, when he saw her, he smiled, and everything changed. Her whole world tilted, and slid her toward him, into his arms.

"Fancy meeting you here," he said. His voice was the same—he might have been teasing her during a long car ride, and she tasted salt before she realized she was crying.

"Hey," he said, pulling away to take her face in one hand. He wiped her tears with a thumb. "Hey, now. It's all right."

"Are you okay?" She couldn't stop crying. Both Calliope and the male replica were watching them, truly curious, and Gemma could almost see Calliope calculating, trying to understand the way she and Pete were holding each other, what it meant, and what kind of

examining this was. "Did they hurt you?"

"I'm okay, Gem. I promise. I *swear.*" He ducked a little to look in her eyes, keeping one hand beneath her chin. "The food sucks and this whole place could really use some body spray, but I'm *fine.*"

It was unbelievable that he could make her laugh, but he did. And then she choked again, and he held her, and she heard his heartbeat through his chest, and tasted her own breath on his T-shirt, and she lost track then of exactly who was who and where she ended and he began. It was like losing yourself in the softening of a warm bed you've been looking forward to all day.

Then Gemma felt Calliope's fingers on her arm—cold fingers, needy.

Only when Pete sucked in a breath did she realize how strange it must be for him to see both of them together, and when he took a quick step backward, something dark and heavy opened in the bottom of her stomach.

"We have to go now," Calliope said. "We had our turn." But Gemma couldn't shake the feeling that Calliope had merely wanted to interrupt. She didn't like how Calliope looked at Pete. Like someone starving who just wants to eat and eat and eat until she pukes.

"Christ." Pete exhaled and put a hand through his hair, tufting it like a bird's. They hadn't shaved it. That was one good thing, at least, that they were giving him that. He

managed another smile. "Sorry," he said to Gemma. He reached out and took her hand, but his palm was sweating now. "It's just . . ." He shook his head.

"I know," she said. "You don't have to say it." That cold, dark thing was still writhing at the bottom of her stomach, and Calliope breathed next to her, clinging to her like a film. She kept his hand in hers and pretended not to notice he was sweating. "You'll meet me here again tomorrow night?"

"Every night," he said. His eyes moved to Calliope and back again. Gemma pretended not to see that, either.

She took a step closer to him. "They're not going to let us out, Pete," she said, in a low voice, though there was no point in trying to keep it a secret. Calliope could hear everything. Maybe she could even hear inside of Gemma's head. "We know too much."

"We'll find a way," he said, and his eyes softened.

Then Calliope took Gemma's hand, and Gemma wondered whether she had just learned that kind of touch from watching Pete. How many of the other things she did and said were just imitation?

Simulacrum. *A slight, unreal, or superficial likeness.* Calliope's fingers were long and very bony.

"We had our turn," she repeated. "More of them get to go."

"I didn't get my second observation," the boy said.

Calliope turned back to him. "Next time you'll have stethoscope, then," she said, as if it hardly concerned her.

"Tomorrow," Gemma said to Pete, even as Calliope drew her toward the door.

"I promise." But he was looking at Calliope, not at her, and she felt a sudden dread. Now it was Pete doubling, splitting in two, and becoming a twin version of himself who looked the same, who talked the same, but was, deep down, a stranger.

THIRTEEN

SHE WOKE TO THE DEEP navy light of a predawn sky.

Already, the holding center was full of voices and movement, the scuffle of rubber sneakers, the tooth-chatter of heavy equipment scraped along the ground.

She sat up, edging away from Calliope, who had insisted on sharing the twin mattress. When she stood she was dizzied by a sharp, sudden hunger. She'd received a minuscule ration of spongy baked pasta for dinner, spooned from a tinfoil-covered catering tray of the kind Gemma associated with school fund-raisers.

Gemma knew that meant there must be civilization nearby—a restaurant, a deli, something. She'd even found a receipt for a Joe's Donuts in Windsor Falls, Pennsylvania, coasting on a surf of overflowing trash outside the bathroom.

But Pennsylvania or Pakistan, what did it matter? No

one knew where they were.

The sleeping replicas, motionless in the half dark, were so closely fitted together that they took on the quality of a single landscape: mounds of soft earth, ridged spines and shoulders.

A sudden light dazzled her and she turned to the window to see a van wheeling away, its headlights briefly revealing funnels of rain. More vans were arriving.

She saw soldiers jogging with rain slickers pulled down to protect their faces. Someone was using orange light sticks, like a real airport ramp handler, to indicate where the vans should park. And out of the airport came a constant flow of equipment: staff members passed in and out hauling plastic bins and waste containers, paperwork lashed into waterproof boxes, medical equipment, stacks of unused linens, snowy piles of plastic-wrapped Hanes T-shirts, hundreds of them, of the kind that were given to the replicas.

Gemma felt as if the rain had found its way inside. She was suddenly very awake and very cold.

They were closing up shop.

She picked her way between the replicas to the central corridor, full of a deep and driving panic, half expecting to find that she was alone, that the walls had been dismantled and the rug pulled up, that she had been left behind. Several nurses, bleary-eyed from lack of sleep,

pushed past her wheeling IV carts. The atmosphere was tense, almost desperate.

"What's happening?" Gemma asked, without expecting anyone to answer, and no one did. "What's going on?"

A patrolling soldier frowned briefly at Gemma before turning her attention back to several staff members trying to work a medical cart through a door down to the loading dock. "Careful," she said. "Stairs are wet." Gemma noticed her fingernails were painted pink.

She kept walking, feeling as if she were in the beginning of a nightmare. Even before anything bad has happened, you *know*, you're sure, that bad things will come. When guards in no-man's-land prevented her from going any farther, she went again to the window, mesmerized by the look of all the headlights through the rapidly ebbing dark. How quickly would it take them to clean the place out, to erase all the evidence that Haven had ever existed?

And what would they do with the replicas?

Why the sudden urgency? Why now?

But the last question, at least, was answered even as she stood at the window, squinting through a mist of condensation.

Because a new vehicle was arriving, not a van but a regular sedan, like the kind of shitty rental a budget travel agency might give you. From the driver's seat came a tall

man with a dark beard and glasses. He stood for a second, squinting up at the airport, his glasses, in the glow of the exterior lamps, so bright it looked like they themselves were glowing.

He grimaced a little as the rain hit him. Then he ducked and began to jog through a slosh of puddles toward the door, and Gemma saw a flurry of movement, flapping raincoats and umbrellas, as he was enfolded by staff members and hustled inside.

Dr. Saperstein was back.

A woman in a tailored pantsuit came for Gemma midafternoon. It was the same woman Gemma had pegged for a government slug when she had first arrived. As far as Gemma could tell, it was the same suit, too.

They went through a door marked with a sign that unnecessarily stated *Authorized Personnel Only,* guarded by two soldiers with long-range rifles. Down a set of stairs, the same ones they'd climbed Sunday night. Gemma knew they must be level with the tarmac, imagined phantom travelers hurrying with rolling suitcases and duffels toward waiting short-haul jets.

Through another door for Authorized Personnel, they reached what must once have been the airport's administrative hub, an inner funnel of connected rooms still showing the ghost-marks of old desks. The overhead

lights were out, and a few standing lamps left whole areas oily with shadow. There were tubs of plastic containers full of shrink-wrapped sterilized needles and miniature urine collection vials. Two fridges were marked with handwritten signs: *Live specimens, do not open.*

Hidden generators bled thick cables across the floor, and Gemma thought of bits of dark hair clinging to the damp floor of a gym. Stacked messily on a folding table were cardboard boxes full of translucent medical gloves and antibacterial cloths, cotton swabs and rubber thermometer tips, laptops wired to a single power strip, and three-ring binders. Here, she knew, must be the remains of Haven's record keeping, the experiential evidence it had accumulated over decades and had not yet had a chance to move elsewhere or destroy.

Another woman, this one a stranger, leaned knuckles-down on a desk, in the posture of a gorilla, peering over the shoulder of a red-haired guy at a computer. She immediately straightened up.

"Ah, shit." The woman had to step over the fluid ropes of electrical cable to get close. Her hair was cut short. She reminded Gemma of one of her favorite nannies, Laverne, a soft-spoken Haitian woman who'd come up from Louisiana and gave hugs that felt like being wrapped in a blanket. But the impression was over the moment she spoke. "What a mess."

"Hi yourself," said Gemma's escort.

"Not what you thought?" The red-haired guy was still lit faintly by the computer screen, and the glare in his glasses had the weird effect of erasing his eyes beneath them. There was something wrong with the skin on the left side of his face, and his chin beneath his lips. It looked weirdly shiny, as if it were covered with a layer of Vaseline. He'd been badly burned, Gemma realized, and her stomach yanked: he'd been at Haven.

Laverne-not-Laverne took two sudden steps forward and snatched up Gemma's chin, as if it were a fish that might otherwise dart away. She angled her face left and right before Gemma managed to pull away.

"I don't know where she came from." Her eyes on Gemma's face felt like mosquitoes, circling and circling without landing anywhere. "She's not one of ours."

"I *told* you," Gemma said, though it was obvious the woman wasn't speaking to her. She let her hatred narrow like a knife inside her. "You guys fucked up, big-time."

Not-Laverne was still staring. "Werner, pull up Sources, will you?" She pivoted, finally, and moved behind the computer again, leaning over to point. "D-101," she said. "See here? Some of our first donor tissue. And these are the genotypes that took. Numbers six through ten."

"Number six is Disposed," the man, Werner, said.

The woman in the suit was sweating. "You told us a boy and a girl. This one and her boyfriend fit the description."

"They aren't ours." Not-Laverne looked green. Werner was chewing on an unlit cigarette. Then: "Dr. Saperstein will nail you to the wall for this."

Gemma was sick of being spoken about as if she wasn't in the room. "My name is Gemma Ives. Ives," she repeated, and saw Not-Laverne register the name, saw it pass through her like a current.

"Ives." Werner nearly choked. He wet his lower lip with his tongue. "Is that like . . . ?"

But he trailed off nervously as behind Gemma another door opened and then closed firmly with a click. The sudden silence filled the room by emptying it of pressure. She felt a pop in her ears, as if they'd just dropped altitude on a plane.

She turned, knowing already what she would see: Dr. Saperstein, smiling, holding his glasses in one hand, shaking his head, like some kindly guidance counselor who'd discovered a mistake in her first-period schedule.

"The last time I saw you, you were six months old," he said. He looked shorter and older than she'd been picturing him—of course, the photographs she had were outdated, and she'd been a baby when her father had severed his connection to Haven.

She felt a surge of hatred so strong it scared her: it was a hand from the dark side of the universe that reached up to turn her inside out. "You've seen plenty of me," she

said, but heard her voice as if it was a stranger's. "Four, by my count."

"Looks can be deceiving, believe me. There is only one Gemma Ives." He smiled again at this. Patient, indulgent, very slightly embarrassed. *Sorry about the confusion. These little mix-ups do happen.* "Your parents, I'm sure, would agree."

"Dr. Saperstein—" The woman in the suit began to speak, but he cut her off.

"Later." For a split second she saw, from beneath the surface of his expression, something sharp and mean solidify: it was like the sudden vision of a very sharp tooth. But almost instantly, it was gone. He smiled at Gemma again and opened a door that led to a small and very ordinary-looking office. "Why don't you have a seat inside? I'm going to grab a soda. You want a soda? Or something to eat?"

Gemma shook her head, although she was desperately thirsty, and weak with hunger, too. But she didn't want to take anything Dr. Saperstein offered.

"Go on. Make yourself comfortable. I'll be right with you." When she didn't move, he hitched his smile a little wider—she could actually *see* the effort, watch individual muscles straining to achieve the right look. "Go on. It's all right."

"No," she said. She wanted to scream. She wished she

could open her mouth and let her rage come up like a sickness. “It’s not. It’s definitely not all right.”

“Well, that’s what we’re going to try and sort out.” He spread his hands. As if she were the one who’d screwed up and now refused to admit it. “Look, I highly doubt you want to stay here. Right? So go on and have a seat, and I’ll be with you as soon as I can scare up some caffeine.”

FOURTEEN

DR. SAPERSTEIN RETURNED WITH TWO cans of warm Diet Coke, even though she'd said she didn't want one. She didn't want to sit and planned to say no, but at the last minute she was worried about her legs, which had begun to shake. So she sat, tucking her ankles together, pressing her hands between her thighs, hoping he wouldn't see how afraid she was.

He poured his soda into a plastic cup, took a sip, and made a face. "Why does the diet stuff always taste like the back of a spoon?" He shook his head. "The real stuff always goes first around here."

Gemma felt more confused than ever. Dr. Saperstein didn't look evil. She tried to paste what she knew about him onto his face, to make the images align. Emily Huang, those photographs of the two of them together. Jake Witz and his father. Those hundreds and hundreds

of starved and broken people he treated like possessions, disposed of by burning them in the middle of the ocean after drilling their bones or opening their skulls for marrow and tissue and cell samples.

But she couldn't make it hang there. She couldn't make it fit.

He leaned forward. "I can't tell you how sorry I am that you're here," he said. Shockingly, she believed him. "I've been in Washington, DC, crawling around on my knees trying to save this place. . . ."

"What—what *is* it?" She had to swallow hard against the feeling that she would begin to cry. "What are you *doing* with all of them here?"

He shook his head. "Nothing, now," he said. "I drove straight from DC this morning. Our funding's been cut." This time, his smile never traveled up past his lips. "Twenty years of research. Twenty years of effort, incremental gains, mistakes and corrections. All of it . . ." He gestured as if to scatter something into a passing wind.

"And what happens to them?" Gemma said, through a hard fist in her throat. She was still too afraid to ask what she really wanted to know: What would happen to her? And to Pete?

Dr. Saperstein took off his glasses to rub his eyes. "How much did your father tell you about Haven?"

"He didn't tell me anything," Gemma said. Dr.

Saperstein looked surprised. "But I know that you've been using the replicas to grow prions."

"To *study* prions," he corrected her. "You make them sound like petri dishes."

"Isn't that what they are?" The pressure in Gemma's chest was so great she felt as though she was speaking around a concrete block. "It was all for the military, wasn't it? It was all to make weapons."

He raised his eyebrows. "I won't ask you how you know that," he said. She could tell she'd impressed him and, weirdly, felt happy about it. Then she hated herself. Why did she care about impressing him? "Look, you obviously know quite a bit about Haven. But there's a lot you *don't* understand. The US military gave us one of our biggest contracts, yes. But it wasn't our only one." Then: "You know the word *prion* wasn't even coined until I was in college? It's been more than thirty years since then, but until I took over the Institute, we'd discovered almost nothing more about the way prions work, or how they progressed, or how fast." The overhead light grayed the look of his skin. "Prion disorders share traits with some of the most crippling brain diseases we know—diseases like Alzheimer's, which affects millions of people per year. Diseases we can't cure or even help."

"I don't need a lecture," Gemma said. "I asked what happens to the replicas now."

"There are protocols," he said gently. "I'm sure you understand that. Haven deals with—dealt with—deadly biomaterials. We're talking about a major health hazard."

Deadly biomaterials. Otherwise known as: replicas. Gemma recognized the technique: every so often her father hid behind words too, not big words but acronyms, military slang, a patter she could never understand. But she knew what Saperstein was saying, and no amount of fancy vocabulary could make it any less horrible.

"You're going to kill them," she said. Though it was what she'd been expecting, it was terrible to say the words out loud. The room seemed suddenly to be filling with fog. Or maybe it was her head that was filling up. She couldn't make his face come into focus. "What about me? Are you going to kill me, too?"

"Kill you?" He actually laughed. "Last time I checked, that was still illegal in this country. I'm going to make some calls, and sort out some details, and get you home to your father. Then I'm going to hope he doesn't kill *me.*"

He didn't sound like he was lying. "What about Pete?" she asked. She thought, though she couldn't be sure, that for a split second he froze, and a sour panic rose in her throat. "If you don't let him go, I'll tell everyone. My dad will track you down and murder you—"

"Gemma, *please.* Of course Pete will go home." If he'd hesitated before, now he spoke easily. "I know you think

I'm some kind of monster, but I'm not. I'm a geek from Bethesda, Maryland, who fell in love with science and has loved it my whole life. I have a cat at home. Did you know that? He's a thirteen-year-old tub named Copernicus. Copper for short. I'm a Dodgers fan, God help me."

Could she have been wrong about Dr. Saperstein? Was it possible that Haven's work was, if not right, then at least justified? The idea made her head hurt.

"But what you've done is monstrous," she said. "What you're *talking* about doing is monstrous. It's murder."

"It's euthanasia," he said, a little more forcefully. "And it's standard practice. Labs all across the world do chemical testing on live animals. Cancer researchers inject rats with cancer cells. Ebola researchers shoot monkeys up with Ebola. Test subjects are routinely euthanized."

"But we're not talking about rats," she said. "Or monkeys." She thought of strange Calliope and her enormous eyes, Gemma's color exactly, only bigger in her thin face; she thought of the girl who'd nearly stabbed her with a syringe and the children who spent their days crawling around in oversized diapers, sucking their fingers and wailing if a nurse tried to touch them. How many graves would they need? Would they even be buried? Lyra had mentioned that the replicas at Haven were either burned or packaged up and dumped into the ocean, but there were no oceans here. Perhaps they would be stacked like

fish fillets in refrigerated trucks and shipped off to the coast. "We're talking about people. Human beings."

Saperstein squinted at her as if trying to see her from a distance. "You're what—sixteen? Seventeen? I remember being your age. Everything seems so certain. Black and white. Wrong and right. Good guys and bad guys. But the real world isn't like that, unfortunately." He leaned forward again, putting his elbows on the desk. His sweater, Gemma saw, was in fact filmy with a surface of cat hair, and it made her want to cry again. "Let me ask you something. What makes a human? Do you think it's our eyes, our ears, our capacity to walk upright?"

She nearly said, *All of those things*, when he went on, "It can't be. What about the blind, or people missing their ears, or paralyzed from the shoulders down? What about people whose faces have been burned off, deformed by war or birth? You would say that those people are humans, too, wouldn't you?"

"Of course," Gemma said quickly, embarrassed she had been on the verge of agreeing to something so stupid. "Being human isn't a trait, like having hair."

"Okay. So what is it?"

"That's a dumb question." But she realized she couldn't actually answer him. "It's how we think," she said finally. "It's our brains and what we do with them."

"But what about humans who've lost their capacity to

think and reason?" he asked. He sounded almost apologetic, as if he hadn't meant to trap her. "And what about computers, which can think and reason as well as any human? Are they people? Do they deserve to have rights and freedoms?"

"You're trying to confuse me," Gemma said.

"No, Gemma. I'm not. I'm trying to understand." Dr. Saperstein sighed and took off his glasses. Suddenly he looked strangely exposed, like a half-blind mole coming up from the ground. There was a splotchy ink stain on his cheek, and more on his fingers. "If it isn't legs or eyes or even how we think, what? Might it be the capacity to love, to be loved, to grieve and be grieved for by others? Friendship, connection, the ability to empathize, to walk in someone else's shoes?" She could see, now, why he had been the one to take over after Dr. Haven's death, why people had trusted him to lead. His voice was hypnotic, almost comforting—like the drumming of rain on a window. You wanted to curl up and go to sleep, let his voice do all the work.

"You're talking about a soul," she said. Suddenly, she was exhausted. She remembered, all at once, being at church when she was a kid, leaning against her mom, drowsy in the sunlight, while the priest droned on and on.

"Soul, sure. It doesn't really matter what you call it." Saperstein was still watching her. She felt he almost knew

what she was thinking. He spoke so softly she nearly missed what he said next. "Whatever it is, the replicas don't have it."

"So what? That gives you the right to use them how you want?" When had they stopped going to church, and why? It seemed important, suddenly, to know. Had her parents believed, like the replicas did, that because she wasn't made by God, she didn't belong to him? That she was excluded? "What about the Home Foundation? You stole kids. And you can't pretend they weren't loved by someone, somewhere. You can't pretend they aren't people."

For the first time, Dr. Saperstein looked uncomfortable. And this, more than anything, gave her a small jolt of pleasure. She sat up a little straighter.

"You didn't think I knew about that?" She thought of poor Rick Harliss, his stale breath and face rutted by years of desperation and loss, that shitty motel room when he'd first told her about how she'd been born, *made*, at Haven.

"What happened at the Home Foundation was wrong," he said firmly. Once again, she was surprised. "You have to understand, I had no idea what was happening until later. We were on the verge of shutting down. I was on a plane twenty, twenty-five hours a week, in different states and even different countries, trying to raise funds. I trusted the wrong people to manage. And believe me, I

put an end to it as soon as I found out."

Was it possible? In the letter Emily Huang had written to her friend, she'd made it sound as if it was all Dr. Saperstein's idea. But what if she'd lied? What if she was ashamed of her own role?

What if she *had* killed herself after all? Out of guilt and shame and a sense of remorse?

"You covered it up," Gemma said. "You lied and you made everybody else lie, too."

"What else was I supposed to do? We would have lost everything. Then there would have been no reason for any of it." He leaned forward and his eyes screwed onto hers like metal caps. "We're talking about research that directly impacts Alzheimer's research, research into what makes the brain deteriorate, how to stop it. We're talking about research that could have spared the lives of thousands of civilians stuck in hellish war zones, that might have been used in targeted attacks to prevent the horrific casualties of innocent people. We're talking about research critical to modern food supply. I regret some of the things we did—and some of the things done in our name. Of course I do. But we were fighting a countrywide campaign against reason—against *research*."

"That still doesn't give you the right," Gemma said.

He ducked his head and sat for a few seconds with his eyes closed, almost as if he were praying. When he raised

his head again, he looked even older, as if several years had elapsed. "Do you use shampoo?"

She was so startled by the question she couldn't even nod.

He went on anyway. "Do you take cold medicine when you're sick, or Advil when you have a headache? How about vaccinations? Been vaccinated for mumps, rubella, tetanus? Vaccinations are diseases, you know. They're nothing more than weak concentrations of the exact disease they're designed to prevent."

"What's your point?" She felt shaky, almost dizzy, as if she'd stood up too quickly, although she was still sitting across from him.

"How do you think those drugs came to market? How did the Advil get into your bathroom cabinet? How did the Sudafed land on your bedside table? How did we cure polio? Tuberculosis? Smallpox? How did we save hundreds of thousands of people, millions of people, from diseases big and small?" His smile was thinning. "Hundreds of thousands of mice, rabbits, primates killed. Humans, too, of course—volunteers, desperate people, sick people. Some of them dead because of side effects, unpredictable responses, bad science, or just bad luck. I'm one of only thousands of scientists and researchers doing similar work, dangerous work, work that requires living people to die, so that in the future, people can keep living.

A terrible paradox, but there you go. Did you know that a former staff member of mine is up and running in Allentown, Pennsylvania? All our funding will go to her. And the cycle continues."

The name registered dimly in Gemma's memory, but she didn't know why.

Saperstein wasn't done. "And those are just the medical casualties. Noble, really, by comparison to what we do every day, in thousands of places across the globe, all for cheaper products and more of them, new clothes every season, new cell phones, faster cars."

"That's different," Gemma said. But she couldn't think how.

"Is it?" He shook his head. "I don't think so. Everything we have, everything we know, everything we own, has been paid for in someone's blood. Once you understand that, you understand we're just talking about ratios. Percentages. Math."

He was confusing her, like her father always did, twisting things around somehow.

"How many people have to benefit from a cure before you risk the life of a single test patient? Ten? One hundred? How many people might live easier lives because of a new technology before you can justify disrupting the livelihoods of those who benefit from the old one? What does help have to look like? Do you have to help them a

little, or a lot? Help them now, or in the future? Tell me. If you have the formula figured out, tell me."

Of course she couldn't. There was no answer; she didn't know.

"What about all those children who work backbreaking hours for pennies at factories across the globe to make the T-shirts you and your friends wear, who die early of tumors caused by fumes, smog, chemicals? How about boys sold into slavery on fishing boats to haul smelt and plankton so that we can eat fresh shrimp all year round, how about girls half your age helping to make your shoes, your lip gloss, your phone covers, your accessories? What about children blown up mining minerals we use for the memory chips in your cell phone, and children eviscerated by drone strikes in countries we spent decades squeezing for their oil, whole countries decimated, populations starving to death slowly? What about them? Who's crying for them?"

Gemma *was* crying. She couldn't help it.

"We never cloned people at Haven. That's what you have to understand. That's impossible and always will be. We cloned genetic composition, fetal cells, *structure*." Gemma could tell by how easily and quickly the words came how often he had repeated them to himself. She could tell he really believed them. "You can't make people with science. We're all born a collection of cells and

senses and chemical patterns. We have to *become* human."

Gemma thought of Calliope, and the bulwark of her ribs beneath her skin, the way her hand, slick with sweat, had held to Gemma so tightly. A terrible sadness touched her.

"The replicas can't feel loss, or love, or empathy. When they die, no one grieves for them, and they grieve for no one else. Any one of them would kill you, or me, if it suited them, if they needed to. Any one would lie or cheat or rob you, and never feel bad about it. They wouldn't even know the difference. To them there is surviving and not surviving, and that's it."

Was any of it true? Did it even matter? "You make them sound like robots," she said.

"Not robots," he said. And for a brief second, a look of terror moved like a hard storm across his face. "Animals."

FIFTEEN

THERE WERE DIFFERENT SOLDIERS ON duty outside the bathrooms that night, a young man and woman, maybe early twenties. The card table was gone: it must have been packed up and shipped off. Gemma had lost count of how many vans had left throughout the day. Though the airport was still crowded with clutter, medical equipment, and mattresses, curtained-off alcoves and makeshift break stations, it felt incalculably emptier. It felt like being sunk at the center of an old ship while it was hollowed out by bottom-feeding fish.

The rain, still drumming the windows, filled the terminal with hollow echoes.

As soon as the female soldier saw them approaching, she stood up abruptly and vanished, as though by prearranged signal. The guy was older, maybe twenty-four or twenty-five, with a blunt jaw and a prominent forehead

that made his eyes appear to be hiding out in his face.

"That's Wayne," Calliope said. She had taken Gemma's hand again, and Gemma was both glad of and frightened by her grip. "Wayne was the one who told me about Pinocchio and how he got spitted up by the whale." A strange expression pulled briefly at Calliope's face: if Gemma hadn't known better, she would have called it joy.

They had to wait for Wayne—an ugly name, she'd always thought, made even uglier now by him—to acknowledge them. Calliope didn't tense up or even seem uncomfortable when he stared baldly at her breasts and legs, at the space *between* her legs. She was used to it, Gemma knew, and that was the most terrible thing of all: her body had never belonged to her, not for a second.

Animals, Dr. Saperstein had said. But animals had the urge to protect themselves, to protect one another. The replicas were like human photo negatives: like they weren't alive at all, only giving the impression of it, but always just a little bit off. Even tonight, moving through the darkened puzzle of bodies, Gemma had the strangest feeling that none of the replicas were sleeping at all—that this, too, was illusion, bodies laid down to rest while their spirits roamed elsewhere, hungry and awake.

"All right," Wayne said finally. "But quick. Fifteen minutes." As soon as they started toward the bathroom

together, he called them back. "See me after," he said to Calliope.

Gemma was surprised and relieved to find Pete already waiting for her, leaning heavily on the counter, head bowed. For a second, she hung back. His face was so serious, so sad, it made her ache.

But when he caught sight of her, his face rearranged into the one she knew so well, and it was like two plates slid together deep inside her and sealed off a rift. Her anger went, and so did her fear. If she could just stay with him, everything would be fine.

She was grateful that Calliope let her go, and even hung back when Pete hugged her, and kissed her gently, lips, nose, forehead, and lips again. It was funny: as soon as Pete had become her boyfriend, she had started being more careful about her looks, not less. She put on lip gloss and mascara; she always made sure her hair was blown straight; she agonized about what she wore. She told herself she wanted him to be proud of her, but it wasn't that, not exactly. Really, she wanted to make sure he wasn't *embarrassed.*

But here, in this place, even though she hadn't showered—a ritual that, like laundry day, occurred once a week, in which replicas were shuffled in and out by the dozen to hose off in a dim concrete room with open holes for drainage—even though the toothbrush she'd been

given had disappeared earlier that morning, even though she was braless, her breasts sticky-heavy beneath her shirt, she realized it didn't matter at all. She loved him and felt, in that moment, truly loved: the feeling of being saved, of coming home after a long night at a terrible party, and getting to wipe your makeup off and take off uncomfortable tights and slip into a pair of worn pajamas.

"Another day in paradise, huh?" Pete said, touching her face.

She could feel Calliope watching them, and was struck by Calliope's stillness, her complete absorption. She was reminded, then, of the way her cats, Bean and Ender, sat in the window seat to watch the geese that landed on her lawn on their way south. It was as if Calliope's whole body was funneled into her eyes, and the desire to consume.

She was going crazy. She was going to lose her mind in this place.

"You okay?" he asked. She tried to smile but saw her reflection thrown back at her, ghastly.

"I'm okay," she said. "I saw Dr. Saperstein today." She lowered her voice, hooked her fingers into the neck of her T-shirt. Hers, familiar, real. "It's all over. They're shutting down."

"Yeah, I kind of got the idea. I'm surprised they haven't shipped out the toilets yet." Then, unexpectedly:

"Three replicas died today. I saw them packed up. They were loaded onto a gurney like—like meat or something. All bundled in plastic." His voice was too tight, like fabric stretched thin by too much use. "There are children tied down in place. One of the nurses said that otherwise they'll try and chew their own fingers, or scratch themselves until they bleed. And the *nurses* . . ." Finally, the fabric snapped. His voice cracked. "Nurses, doctors, soldiers . . . everyday people, good people. It's like they've all gone blind. It's like this *place* has blinded them. How can they stand it?"

"Pete." She couldn't make it better. She couldn't explain. There *was* no explanation. They had to get out of here before they were poisoned. She took his hands. They were very cold. "Pete, listen to me. Dr. Saperstein is making arrangements with my dad," Gemma said quietly. "He's going to let us go."

His eyes were like windows, suddenly shuttered. She was aware of a strange tension, not just here but everywhere, as if an enormous underground rift was slowly widening, as if they might all drop.

"We don't have a choice," she added. She seemed to smell smoke. Memories that weren't even hers flowed to her, of Haven on fire, of the island burning and bodies bleeding out into the marsh. Maybe Calliope wasn't feeding off her. Maybe she was feeding from Calliope,

collapsing into her. "But the important thing is that we're getting out of here. They're letting us go."

He looked away. A muscle pulsed in and out in his jaw. "When?" he said finally.

"Tomorrow." Still he wouldn't look at her. She followed his gaze and saw that he was staring at Calliope in the mirror. But she wasn't looking back at him. She was standing, motionless, staring up at the ceiling with the strangest smile on her face, as if she was listening to a favorite song played far away. "I don't know when. I think Dr. Saperstein's scared. He'll have to . . ." *Negotiate,* she nearly said, but stopped. The word wouldn't make it out beyond a sudden tightness, a feeling of burning.

"I won't go," Pete said. "I can't." And she heard the crack of the fault line beneath their feet. She saw that they were already falling.

"You can't save them," she said, but she felt a rising panic as the dark rose up to reach them. She heard her own voice faintly and heard, too, the echo of Dr. Saperstein. "It's already done."

"I can't just walk out of here." He turned back to her but now she hardly recognized him. His eyes didn't seem brown so much as gray. Smoke-gray. "I can't just *forget.*"

"I'm not asking you to forget," she said. She realized she was going to cry and had to swallow fast. "But there's no other choice."

"There is," he said sharply. "There always is. There has to be."

"Would you rather stay here?" She was cold and hot all at once. She was losing him. "What about your parents? What about how worried they must be?"

Pete stepped away from her. "So that's it, we leave, and your dad's the big hero." He looked so different when he frowned, older and harder, somehow. She'd nearly always seen him smiling, had even begun to believe it was his natural state, like having blond hair or freckles like a scattering of brown sugar. "And then what? We go back to school? We hold hands after chem and I drive you home and feel you up in your driveway and that's *it*, that's all we have, that's all—"

He broke off, as if the words had driven the air from his lungs on the way out. "Sorry," he said, in a different tone of voice, and, turning back, tried to put his hands on her shoulders. "I'm sorry. I didn't mean that."

"Don't," she said. If he touched her, her skin would burn away, she would disappear into smoke. All along she'd been wrong. All along he *had* been ashamed of her—ashamed and disappointed, and trying to hide it only because she was the best he could do right now.

"Gemma, please. That came out all wrong." He looked truly upset but she didn't care, didn't feel sorry for him at all. "You know I didn't mean . . ." When again she

stepped away from him, he let his hand hover there for a second. "What I meant was I can't go back. I can't just rewind. Do you understand?" His voice was climbing registers, clawing up toward a point of panic. She saw him bloated by misery, choking on its fumes. "I can't unsee what I've seen, I can't unknow what I know. I *can't*."

"Keep your voice down," she said. Something really was burning. She wasn't imagining it. She could smell smoke now, for sure. Confusedly she thought Calliope must be smoking. But that was crazy—Calliope was still smiling her secret smile, still absorbed in her own invisible kingdom—and besides, the smell was too strong for that.

Pete hadn't heard or didn't care. He was talking louder than ever, as if he weren't so much speaking the words as letting them rattle through him. "I can't walk out of here and know that these people—people, Gemma, not experiments, not test subjects, human beings—are going to die. I—"

But then he broke off again, and she knew that he, too, had felt the change: the approach of danger that, like a storm, sent invisible messages ahead.

Just as suddenly as clouds might vault from the horizon, Gemma found the source of tension, grabbed it, and tracked it to its source. Calliope was laughing.

Gemma remembered going with her parents to their

house in the Outer Banks one summer and hearing coyotes shrieking in the night. They laughed when they killed, her father told her later, but she would have known anyway. It was cruelty set to music: it wasn't even the pleasure of the *kill*. It was the pleasure of pain, the pleasure of watching small things die slowly.

And now, here, in this bathroom in an old airport that might as well have been hell on earth, Calliope laughed just like that.

"You're wrong," Calliope said, and her words still carried the echo of something old and predatory and hungry. "You mixed it all up. You got it backward." She was still standing there with her head tilted, still staring vaguely at the ceiling. But by then, of course, Gemma knew. She wasn't staring. She was *listening*. And by then Gemma was listening, too: the shouts, the sharp punctuated cries, and footsteps vibrated the floor.

The stinging in Gemma's throat had been real. Smoke was texturing the air, giving it the appearance of a solid, and somewhere solid matter burned, and transformed to smoke.

"What are you talking about?" Pete asked, and Gemma could hear that he, too, was afraid.

"You said we would die. You said you don't want to leave us." She shook her head. She was smiling in a way that Gemma had never seen before. It was as if her smile

was actually consuming her face backward, trying to reveal her skull. "But you said it backward. The us won't die." She bit her lip, and Gemma tripped over the image of her own habit, her own nervous way of correcting herself. "*We* won't die."

In Gemma's head, she saw smoke trails plumed over Haven, saw men with rifles, working in the rubble; she saw fireworks leave tentacle trails of smoke across a bloody dawn sky. *Crack. Crack. Crack.* But these weren't fireworks. They were bullets that cracked sound in two when they leapt, explosively, from their long slick barrels. They were bullets that made a lot of noise and then killed silently.

People were screaming.

"What's happening?" Gemma asked. Her voice sounded like it was coming to her from the other side of a tunnel.

Calliope finally looked at Gemma. She was radiant. And in that split second, Gemma saw that both Pete and Dr. Saperstein were wrong. Calliope wasn't an animal, and she wasn't a human, either. She was something darker and older and far more dangerous, she was something *deeper*—a compression of matter and space, a possibility collapsed into the narrowest, narrowest place. Being, urge, energy—emotionless, unthinking, unfeeling—funneled so deep, for so long, that it became an explosion. She was a black hole that could take a planet apart forever,

in endless slow motion.

"It's starting," she said, and reached up to touch Gemma's face. Her fingers smelled like metal.

Her fingers smelled like blood.

SIXTEEN

THEN A BULLET BLASTED THROUGH the bathroom door, ricocheted off the counter, and blew the pinkie finger off Gemma's left hand.

It was the craziest thing. One second she had five fingers, and the next, her pinkie was missing and blood had patterned the linoleum. And yet at first she knew it had happened only because of how Pete began to shout. For a long, watery second she floated somewhere outside her body, and observed the blood and the missing finger and the raw exposed muscle of her hand with a kind of detached curiosity.

And then the pain came, like a gigantic rubber band that snapped her back into the bathroom, into her body. It was pain like nothing she'd ever known, like the kind of high vibration that could shatter glass, like a full-body flu that burned even in your bones. She couldn't even

scream. She couldn't try and stop the bleeding, couldn't move, could only stand there, staring like an idiot, as the blood kept pooling at her feet.

Somehow she ended up on the floor. She wasn't sure whether time had leapt forward or she'd simply, for a half second, lost consciousness. She no longer had the strength to stand up.

All this happened in three seconds, maybe quicker. When she did finally speak, she could only say, "My finger," over and over. By then Pete had found a roll of toilet paper—from God knows where, the girls' room never had any—and he was frantically unwinding it, half the roll at one go, and packing it against the wound. The pressure triggered a new surge of pain and brought her stomach into her mouth.

He wrapped a fist around her hand to stanch the bleeding. It hurt so much she wanted to pull away, to yell at him to stop, but the pain had her in a chokehold now, and she couldn't.

"It's okay, Gem, you're going to be okay," Pete kept saying. He looked as if he was going to cry. "Deep breaths, you're going to be fine, I know it hurts, but you're going to be okay. . . ."

Another bullet blasted through the door, this time punching out one of the overhead lights. Calliope ducked and scuttled beneath the sinks as a spray of plastic and glass

sifted down on them like a snow. Still keeping her injured hand wound tightly in his fist, Pete put an arm around Gemma, herding them inside one of the bathroom stalls. She leaned against the hollow of his chest, and he whispered *it's okay, it's okay, it's okay,* so many times the word and his heartbeat became confused in her head, until she heard in its rhythm that same exact message.

The initial shock had passed and already her body was working to absorb the pain, accept its reality, to find equilibrium inside it: a process she knew intimately after so many hospital visits, so many surgeries and scars. She missed her mom with a sudden sharpness even worse than the physical pain—how she sat next to Gemma's hospital bed, whispering *it's gonna be okay, I'm here,* just like Pete was doing now; how she'd climb into bed next to Gemma, making a seashell-curve of her body, and the two of them would fall asleep. She missed her mom and wished, more than anything, that she could say she was sorry. She'd been so angry with Kristina that they had barely spoken in weeks, and Gemma could see the way it was killing her mom, coiling her down around an internal misery like a winch.

And now it was too late. They would die here. She closed her eyes and tried to hang on to an impression of her mom's voice, soothing her to sleep.

"Hush, hush." It was Calliope's voice she heard instead.

During a break in the rhythm of gunshots, Calliope came toward her. She moved quickly, propelling herself with her palms and sliding belly-down on the floor with the sinuous grace of an eel. Gemma, still half-blind from pain and shock, was repulsed. The gunshots started again, and Gemma found herself briefly fantasizing about a bullet cleaving Calliope's head in two, or just evaporating her, as her finger had been evaporated.

Calliope crowded into the stall with them and began touching Gemma, stroking her arms, her wrist, her thighs. "Hush, hush, there's no reason to cry," she said. "It's a finger, just a little finger."

"We need to get out of here," Pete said. He hadn't let go of her injured hand, not for a single second, but already the toilet paper was nearly useless, soggy with blood. "She needs a doctor."

Calliope looked briefly annoyed. "She doesn't need a *doctor,*" she said. "I'll take care of Gemma, don't worry. Just as soon as it's over."

"This isn't one of your fucking games." Pete's voice edged toward a shout. "She's hurt, can't you see that? She needs *help.*" Gemma wanted to tell him to be quiet—they would be heard, they would be found, they would be killed—but she couldn't. She didn't even know who to be afraid of. She was as terrified of Calliope, of her strange little smiles and the light touch of her fingers, as

she was of the guards who were shooting, still shooting. She heard screaming and pictured hundreds of replicas simply mowed down where they were sleeping, a surf of blood rising, coming to drown them all.

"It's not a game," Calliope said, and she drew away from Gemma, looking hurt. "It was never a game. But you can't leave now, anyway, not until it's sure."

"Not until *what's* sure?" Gemma said. Her voice sounded as if it had been punched through with holes. Calliope chewed the inside of her cheek and didn't answer. She was angry, Gemma knew, because Pete had yelled at her. "Please, Calliope."

"It's like Pinocchio, like I told you," Calliope said, sounding almost bored. "He got swallowed up, so he started a fire to get out." She held up her left hand, turning it, admiring it from several different angles. Then she began to touch her pinkie finger, bend it and flex it, as if to see whether it, too, would evaporate now that Gemma's was gone. And yet each time she moved or stroked her finger, Gemma felt a phantom stirring in her own hand, and a new wave of triggered pain.

"You started a fire?" Gemma said, trying to hang on to the thread, to stay focused, to make sense of the nightmare. They'd been so close to being released.

"*I* didn't," Calliope said, still sulking. "Some of the other thems did."

Gemma remembered feeling, earlier tonight, as she and Calliope wove through a slum of bodies and filthy mattresses, that the replicas weren't sleeping, only pretending to. She felt suddenly dizzy. How many replicas were there in the airport? Five hundred? Six? More?

And maybe three dozen, four dozen guards, a handful of doctors and nurses.

"Wayne thought he taught me something about fire because of his friend Pinocchio," Calliope said, with new scorn in her voice that made her seem older. "But I knew about fire forever. When I was little, there was a kitchen fire, and we didn't use the Stew Pot for days."

"This . . . this was your idea?" Gemma asked. She remembered what Dr. Saperstein had said. *The replicas can't feel loss, or love, or empathy. To them there is surviving and not surviving, and that's it.*

Calliope ignored that question. "The people always think we don't remember," she said. "They think we don't pay attention, that we don't listen, that we're all soft in the head. But I've been listening. I know plenty. I know how to use a gun."

Immediately, as if in direct response to that statement, another quick-fire burst of rifle fire just outside the bathroom sent terrible echoes through Gemma's head and the back of her teeth. She heard a man's voice shout—a plea, a call for help, she wasn't sure—and then another gunshot.

But the voice was enough. She had recognized it, and her stomach pooled all the way down in her feet, a terrible, sick helplessness, like having to sprint for the bathroom.

It was Wayne's voice, Wayne on the ground, Wayne crying for help. And though Gemma couldn't feel sorry for him, she knew what that must mean: the replicas had taken control.

They were taking revenge.

"It's always fire, isn't it?" Calliope said then. "In all the stories, there's always a fire. Does it hurt to burn, do you think?" And she turned back to Gemma, eyes bright and big and curious, and not unhappy at all.

SEVENTEEN

THEY HAD TO MOVE. THE smoke had sniffed out the corners and ceiling, and it rolled down now in heavy waves, turning the air gritty. Gemma didn't know where she'd read that during fires most people don't die from the fire itself, but from inhaling too much smoke. Even now her lungs felt heavy, wet, like a towel soaked through with rain.

"It's okay now," Calliope said, and the words were so absurd that they came to Gemma like sounds in a language she didn't know. *It's okay now.* The pain in her hand was a rhythmic throbbing, and she thought it must be her pulse, beating out her blood. When they stood up she saw a butterfly pattern of blood, absurdly red, soaking the toilet paper, and so much of it: it was insane that it should all have come from her, that she would have so much to begin with.

She was freezing. She remembered, then, a bath when she was little, maybe eight or nine, and hearing her parents begin to argue. She'd stayed there, motionless, until the water was freezing: she didn't know why, in retrospect, she hadn't just drained the tub. But it hadn't occurred to her. If she didn't move, she'd thought, she wouldn't exist, and if she didn't exist, she could stop hearing them.

"You're okay, Gemma." Pete kept his arm around her, even when he bent to cough. His eyes were tearing up. "It's going to be okay. I promise." He was using the same sounds as Calliope, and none of them made sense, and she couldn't stop laughing, laughing and shivering. "She needs a doctor," he said—shouted it, actually, his throat raw from smoke, as if he expected someone to hear.

Calliope was at the bathroom door. She touched the handle lightly with a finger, to feel if it was hot. "There are no doctors," she said.

Only then did Gemma realize that there were no more shots, no more sounds of gunfire. Just the noise of fire getting fat on drywall and ceiling panels and support beams, gobbling up filthy rugs and mattresses, swelling itself with sound. They never told you that about fire, how loud it was, as if everything it touched started to scream.

Outside the bathroom, Gemma was relieved to find no fire. She could hear it close, though: the *pop* and *boom*

of things changing form suddenly, exploded from solid to gas, a noise that sounded just like terror. But the smoke was even worse, so bad she could hardly see, and a single breath made her choke.

"Get down," Pete said. He had to repeat it before she understood. In a crouch, he took off his shirt and wound it tight against her fist, since the toilet paper had begun to come apart. They went, crawling, Calliope in the lead. Gemma wanted to leave Calliope—she wanted Calliope to vanish, to disappear into the smoke like a mirage—but she was also terrified of losing her. She would never be able to find the exit. She couldn't think at all, didn't know which way the stairs were, thought that everything had burned already, the doors and windows and the way out, that they might be crawling their way to an exit that no longer existed.

In the stories, there is always a fire.

The floor was slicked with blood, and there were bodies everywhere. Gemma wondered whether one of them was Wayne's. She had the urge to shout for everyone to wake up, to run, to get out, although she knew they were all dead, replicas and soldiers, humans born by chance and by design, all of them sleeping together under a veil of smoke. She was glad that the darkness softened dead bodies into shapes: already, they were losing reality.

But she had to crawl around a dead replica who'd lost

half her head to a bullet. She still had a gun in her hand, and Gemma noticed her fingers, long and pale and lovely, and imagined that they still stirred, like underwater plant life moved by a current of water.

The stairwell was impassible. Even the door marked *Authorized Personnel* was warm, and Gemma could hear the fire beyond it humming, shredding the physical world into vibration. Calliope tested the door handle, then quickly pulled her fingers away and sucked them into her mouth.

Trapped. They'd waited too long to get out.

They headed back across the scrum of debris, of broken bodies and cotton drift. Everything was dark with ash, everything looked like the grit of burning, and even as they made it to the windows, the fire finally punched its way up to the second floor, collapsing a portion of the wall near the stairwell and tonguing its way over the blood-sticky floor.

A sudden sweep of fresh air made Gemma want to cry. Several windows were missing where people had crashed through them. Gemma, Pete, and Calliope leaned out into the night air, still fizzing with rain, and in the distance Gemma saw dark figures escaping into the trees, pouring through the open gate, shaking the fence to dismantle it: replicas, hundreds of them, making a run for it. Two vans were on fire and half a dozen bodies—soldiers

and replicas, it looked like—were scattered across the parking lot, like dolls abandoned by a careless child. Most of the usual Jeeps and trucks were missing. Probably the soldiers had gone, carrying their wounded, or maybe seeking reinforcements, and whisked Saperstein and the other staff to safety.

"We're going to have to jump," Pete shouted. "It's the only way."

Gemma nodded to show she understood. The drop was twenty feet, and almost directly beneath them two replicas lay, half-naked and entangled, their eyes unblinking, exposed to the wind and rain. She didn't know whether they'd landed wrong or been shot, but it didn't matter. She would have jumped if the distance was twice as great, would have catapulted into the air without looking back—anything to get out, to get away, as far from the chokehold of the smoke and the fire feeding off bits of skin and scalp and hair as possible.

She jumped.

She was screaming through the air, and her lungs were bursting with the joy of oxygen, and then she landed hard in a barren patch of dirt, next to a scrub of bushes. Her right ankle rolled and she knew right away she'd twisted it, but the pain was nothing compared to the red-funnel fire that burst in her vision when she drove her injured hand down into the ground for balance. It was like the

missing finger had instead folded up inside her and shot all the way to her throat; she nearly gagged.

Pete landed with a grunt and scrabbled quickly away from the bodies. Now that Gemma was closer she saw they'd been shot, probably from the air: there was a pattern of blood spatter on the exterior wall. It was Calliope, funnily, who hesitated, teetering on the windowsill, looking now not like the monster Gemma had seen in the bathroom but like a sister Gemma might have dreamed. Smoke undulated and roiled behind her.

"Jump," Gemma found herself shouting, though minutes earlier she'd been hoping Calliope might simply disappear. "Jump!" Her throat was raw from smoke, and when she tried to draw air again, she began to cough.

Calliope jumped, and for a second Gemma saw her framed in the air like a bird, arms flung wide and mouth open, suspended in the glitter of the fine rain.

Then she landed, gracelessly, but on her feet. Gemma felt the impact herself, whether from the vibration of the ground or because of the doubling effect, she didn't know. When she stood up and tested her weight, her ankle held, barely.

"What happened?" Pete had already moved to take hold of her injured hand again, but she drew away. It was too painful, too awful, and numbly she half believed she could make everything that had happened untrue again.

"I landed wrong," she said. "It's nothing."

"Keep pressure on your hand," was all he said. He'd always looked thin but now, in the slick light of the remaining streetlamps, covered in blood that wasn't his, he looked truly sick.

They moved across the parking lot, leaving the ruins of the airport behind. Gemma kept expecting to hear a ricochet of shooting, to be stopped, to have her legs eviscerated by bullets. But other than the sound of the fire and a few distant shouts, it was quiet. Why was it so quiet? The fire must be visible for miles. Shouldn't there be sirens already? Ambulances? Shouldn't someone have noticed and responded? It was as if . . .

As if they were miles away from anyone.

It felt to her that they were in the open forever, inching across that bleak expanse of gray pavement, with the painted silhouettes of old parking spaces still faintly visible and bodies flung at intervals facedown on the concrete. But finally they were at the woods, which would hold them and hide them: and at the far end of the woods would be roads, and gas stations, and telephone wires, and help.

Then an explosion made waves of sound that made the ground shudder and vibrated in Gemma's teeth as she turned around. A portion of the roof had collapsed, and flames shot suddenly to the sky, illuminating a

low-hanging covering of red-tinged cloud, before retreating again. Gemma and Pete stood stunned, watching the last of what had once been science's greatest experiment consuming itself.

Only then did Gemma see Calliope a short distance away, standing next to a sedan leaning on a flat tire, windshield shattered. It had obviously been heading for the gate. Gemma couldn't see Calliope's face, but she was strangely immobile, as if something inside the car fascinated her. And for whatever reason Gemma found herself backtracking, limping on her injured ankle. Forever afterward she couldn't have said why she was compelled to the window of that sedan, only that she was.

When she was still twenty feet away from the car, Calliope leaned in through the open window. Gemma couldn't see what she was doing, but she thought she heard a shout. This, too, she couldn't absolutely swear to afterward.

By the time Calliope withdrew, Gemma had come up beside her. It was brighter now: the burning airport had created an artificial dawn. When Calliope turned, Gemma nearly screamed: her hands, her wrists, her shirt, all of it was soaked in blood.

"I tried to help him," Calliope said quickly. "It was too late."

For a moment, Gemma couldn't make sense of what

she was seeing: a confusion of glass and blood and steel, the horrible staring face, and the metal finger jointed to its forehead. It looked like one of the cubist paintings her father collected, a nonsense-jumble of shapes.

Then, in an instant, she understood: the blood leaking from his mouth, the air bag pinning him to his seat, a steel rod that must have rocketed from the building just before the roof collapsed, whipped through the windshield, and punctured Dr. Saperstein between the eyes. His glasses were gone. In death he looked suprised, and vaguely puzzled, as if he'd come across an unexpected turn in a familiar road.

"Poor Dr. Saperstein," Calliope whispered, and almost sounded as if she meant it. What had she been doing when she leaned into the car? Why was she so covered in blood?

Gemma turned to look at her. Calliope's face rapidly shuttered into an expression of disgust. Like a mirror, it rearranged itself to reflect back what it saw. It was very fast and extremely convincing, but Gemma had caught her too early, had seen the truth nesting like an insect beneath her skin.

Of course, that was the problem with simulations. They were never exactly like the real thing.

EIGHTEEN

GEMMA COULDN'T HAVE SAID HOW far they walked that night looking for a road—miles, maybe, or maybe no distance at all, turning circles in the pitch-dark. They had no water, no flashlight, no matches, no way of getting food and shelter. They had managed to stop her bleeding, and Pete had bundled her hand tightly by rebandaging her fist as best he could with his T-shirt, already soaked with her blood. Still, she could easily get an infection, if they didn't die of hunger or thirst first, or get eaten by wild hogs or wolves or bears or whatever might be prowling in the woods.

Finally, they were forced to stop. Gemma's ankle was so swollen she could hardly put weight on it.

They slept sitting up between the thick roots of an oak tree. It was still raining. The ground was wet and cold. Gemma leaned against Pete to keep him warm. He had

no shirt. She expected to have nightmares, but instead sleep came to her like the numbing cold of anesthesia: she dropped.

It seemed to her that only a few minutes passed before she woke again, and her dreams—liquid nightmares of dark-beaked birds, sticky with blood—scattered sleekly into memory. Sometime in the night, Pete had moved: he was now curled on the ground like a sleeping animal, his hair lifted by a light breeze.

Calliope was gone.

Gemma's hand was full of a throbbing pain, as if pressure was building up beneath her skin. It took a moment to remember what had happened—her finger, gone. The bullet that had shaved off her finger, the smoke-filled bathroom, the escape. Dr. Saperstein, dead. The replicas, escaped.

And yet the birds were twittering in the trees and shafts of sunlight pinwheeled between branches budding with the pale-green leaves of late spring, and the world was intact.

She let herself cry a little, turning her face into the crook of her arm to muffle the sound. She was cold, and exhausted, and her throat, raw and swollen from all the smoke she'd inhaled, hurt when she swallowed. She was hungry. They'd crawled through a slick of blood and jumped from a second-story window to escape a torpedo

of flame, and she cried because she would have killed for some cornflakes, for french toast with butter.

But she was quickly cried out. She kept hearing her father's voice: *No one ever solved a single problem by shedding tears about it.* It was yet another of his master-of-the-universe pronouncements, like, *the world is full of sheep and lions, and I know which I'd rather be,* but in this case it was probably true. They were out of that awful place, at least, and she knew there must be *something* nearby—why build an airport in the middle of nowhere? Besides, there had been sandwiches brought in, and coffee. They just had to pick a direction and stick with it.

Pete turned over, muttering in his sleep. His lips were purple. His skin looked so pale, so fragile, like tissue paper, and she was suddenly terrified for him.

"Pete." She leaned over and touched his face. "Pete, wake up." She was reassured when he opened his eyes almost immediately.

"Is it time to go to school?" His voice cracked but he managed to smile. Gemma found herself laughing. If she *was* going to die, she was glad that Pete was with her. He sat up slowly. "How's your hand?"

"It's fine," she said, and pulled away when he tried to take it into his lap. She was too afraid to see how bad it was. "Calliope's gone."

"What do you mean, she's gone?" Pete's tone

sharpened. He leaned against the oak tree to climb to his feet, holding his ribs as though they hurt. She saw there were cuts on the palms of his hands, where he must have crawled over broken glass. "Where did she go?"

"I don't know. I woke up and she was gone." Every time she thought of Calliope standing by the car window, staring down at broken Dr. Saperstein, of the look on her face before Calliope managed to recalibrate her expression to something more appropriate—not joy, exactly, but *excitement,* and total absorption, like proof of the entire universe was contained there in that car—she felt a strong pull of hopelessness and nausea. Calliope and the other replicas had planned all of it.

Gemma could understand escape. She could even understand revenge. But that—the massacre at the airport, and whatever Calliope had done to Dr. Saperstein—was something different. That was *pleasure.*

Pete was quiet for a minute. His eyes were almost gold in the early morning sun, and she found herself wishing she could curl up inside them, float away on all that color.

"We can't wait for her," he said finally, and Gemma was surprised by the intensity of her relief. "We need to get help. Christ." His voice cracked. This time, when he smiled, he couldn't quite get it right. "A fucking cell phone, right? My kingdom for a cell phone."

"There must be a town *somewhere,*" Gemma said,

partly to reassure herself. "This is America, not Siberia." That was another thing her father had liked to say. *In America, you can count on only two things. Taxes, and finding a McDonald's.*

"Right," Pete said. "Sure." But his face was like a dying bulb, full of flicker and uncertainty. She hated to see Pete scared even more than she hated being scared herself. She wished she could stuff Pete's fear and pain down inside of her, pack it down her stomach like newspaper, just so he could be okay.

But she hadn't quite forgotten what he'd said to her in the bathroom, how he'd looked at her as if she were at the very distant end of a telescope and he was surprised to find, after all that, how dim and small her light was.

Pete hacked his way into the undergrowth to find her a walking stick; her ankle was still the size of a grapefruit. At a certain point she realized she could no longer hear him moving around in the trees. Suddenly terrified that he had left her, she was about to cry out for him when she heard a shout. In answer, Calliope's voice lifted over the trees.

"It's just me," Calliope said. "It's all right."

They came out of the woods together, Calliope and Pete, like some warped vision of her own life. When Calliope saw Gemma she actually laughed, and ran to her, taking up both of her hands and sending another shock

of pain, like a hot white light, through Gemma's whole body.

"Outside is so big," Calliope said. "I walked for ages before I found a wall."

She was wearing a long cotton dress and slip-on shoes—she'd found new clothes. And she didn't look tired. She didn't even look scared. She looked like the sun had invaded her, glowing beneath her skin. Gemma couldn't shake the feeling that Calliope was somehow feeding off Gemma, siphoning her strength and energy. Taking over.

Gemma jerked away.

"Poor Gemma," Calliope said, but the words didn't quite sound sincere. "You're sick."

"I'm not sick," Gemma said, even though she felt terrible—dizzy and light-headed, as if the smoke she'd inhaled hadn't fully left her. "I'm hurt. I'll be fine."

"You'll be fine," Pete echoed, which actually made Gemma feel worse. Like he needed to say it to make it true.

"It's hungry," Calliope said soothingly. But she couldn't conceal her happiness: Gemma had noticed she messed up her pronouns when she was excited. "I found a wooden house. There's clothing there, and beds. Food to eat. There's a water pump. We can live there, the three of us," she said. "We can make a new Haven, but this time we're

the gods. I can nurse you," she added, because she must have seen Gemma's face. "I know how."

Gemma wanted to recoil when Calliope touched her face. But she didn't. A house meant people, which meant phones, which meant safety. "Can you find your way back?"

Maybe she'd hurt Calliope's feelings. Calliope took a step backward.

"I think so," Calliope said, angling her hand to examine her nails, as if she'd lost interest in the conversation.

"Please, Calliope, we need you." Pete's voice was gentle and made Gemma ache: it was the voice he'd used when he lifted her shirt in the basement and, without blinking, said *beautiful*. She wondered now if that had been put on too, to appease her, as he was trying to appease Calliope.

Was there anything in the world that wasn't just pretend?

Pretend or not, it worked. Calliope smiled again. "I made a path back," she said, addressing Pete directly. "You can follow me."

Gemma went slowly, leaning heavily on her walking stick with every other step. Almost immediately she fell behind, though Pete stopped and waited for her whenever he saw that she was struggling,

Calliope often darted ahead, vanishing among the trees, so they had to call her back. She touched everything: tree bark, slender branches pale and new, even the

pulp of rotten leaves, bending down to run her fingers in the dirt. Gemma couldn't imagine what she was thinking, free at last in a world she didn't know at all, and wondered at how unafraid she seemed.

Gemma had been enclosed too, in a way, bound by her father's rules and her mother's concern, and yet she understood now why people released from prison sometimes wished to go back. She longed for walls, for narrow hallways, for doors that locked. She longed for her old life back, for its sharp angles and clarity: who was wrong, who was right.

In this new world, things doubled and mutated. People had faces beneath their faces. Dr. Saperstein was a monster *and* he wasn't. She was afraid he'd been right about the replicas raised at Haven. Calliope was made of the same material as Gemma was, and she was also a monster. Whenever Gemma caught her eye, Calliope smiled, but always a fraction of a second too late. She remembered what Saperstein had said: *To them there is surviving and not surviving, and that's it.*

Calliope had said she had made a path, left markers so she would be able to find her way back, but if she had, Gemma couldn't see them. It all looked the same to her, and as the sun rose and the insects rose with it, hovering in swarms, buzzing around Gemma's wounded hand, she began to think Calliope was either lost or deliberately

leading them through the same narrow tunnel of trees. Gemma was so exhausted her vision was blinking out, periodically going to black. She didn't know why April was always going on and on about saving the trees—there sure as shit seemed to be plenty of trees already, doing fine.

Just when she was about to call for another rest, Pete shouted. And limping toward them, she saw a low post-and-beam fence, rudimentary and half-rotten, and beyond it: fields. Pastures and farmland. Cows blinking sleepily in the sun.

Farmland meant farms meant *people.* And people meant they were saved.

"See?" Calliope said. "I told you I could find my way back."

Despite everything, Gemma could have kissed her. She laughed, and a group of birds startled, as if they, too, were shocked by the sound. "You're brilliant," she said, and couldn't help it: she put her arms around Calliope, as she would have with April. Calliope tensed, and in her arms she felt so small, trembling slightly, a fine wire coiled and coiled almost to breaking, and Gemma felt terrible and guilty. Calliope just stood there, arms pinned to her sides, and Gemma realized she had likely never been hugged, not once in her life.

It wasn't her fault she had been made this way, forced

to observe and imitate, strange and kind and cruel by turns. Maybe she could be taught. She could learn.

Maybe Gemma could teach her.

As she pulled away, Calliope smiled—a real smile this time, that lit her face all the way to her eyes. And looking at her, Gemma's vision doubled again, but this time she saw not herself but the face of that lost sister, the original daughter, *Emma*. An echo seemed to reach her from a lost world, and she knew then that Calliope was her chance to sew the past and the present together. She could love Calliope, and by loving Calliope she could make up for what her father had done, for the fact that she was alive in Emma's place.

Calliope seemed to know exactly what she was thinking. She put her hand on Gemma's heart. She pressed, and Gemma realized she was reading her pulse, trying to get the measure of her heartbeat: the only way she knew to care for someone else.

"You can be mine," Calliope said. "You can be my replica."

NINETEEN

IT WAS LIKE WALKING INTO a portrait: the red barn, its weathered doors partially open; a tidy white house with faded curtains sitting in a dip of land, an old stone well and a bucket lying next to it on the grass, all bound together in the middle of so many rolling fields Gemma thought of a ship moored to an ocean of green.

Gemma couldn't shake the idea that no one had been home in a hundred years. There were no cars in the driveway. She saw no wires, no satellite braced to the roof, nothing but old-fashioned rakes and shovels, neatly cleaned, as if polished by invisible hands after the original owners had departed. The cows in the pasture stared at them with deep and mournful eyes, and they, too, could have been ancient, could have been standing there for ten decades. Gemma's relief gave way again to anxiety. It was wrong. It was like a photo with a too-obvious filter:

somehow, beneath the brightness, you could see a truth that wasn't nearly so pretty.

Pete veered toward the barn doors, maybe thinking he might find someone at work. But Calliope grabbed his wrist and shook her head.

"Don't," she whispered. For the first time, she looked really afraid. "The barn is where the animals go to die." It was funny, what she knew and didn't know.

"The barn is where the animals go to *sleep,*" Pete corrected her. But he let Calliope pull him toward the house.

Only when they came around the house and saw a buggy did Gemma understand.

"Amish," Pete said.

"There won't be a telephone," Gemma said, fighting down a fear that she couldn't exactly justify. Where was the family who lived here? They hadn't driven off, obviously. They weren't out catching a movie. The fields glimmered in the sun and yet there was no one turning them, raking, planting—Gemma didn't know exactly what, but she knew on farms there was always work to be done.

Calliope was already at the front door. She turned back to gesture them inside. "Come, Gemma-Pete," she said, as if their names were a single thing. "Come see." In her dress, she looked as if she truly belonged. It was as if she learned by absorption, and had, like a chameleon,

changed her skin to match her new surroundings.

"Well, whoever lives here will have to come back eventually," Pete said. "We can rest. Have something to eat. Wait it out." He managed a small smile. "At least we know they aren't on a road trip."

He was right. Besides, Gemma knew she couldn't have gone much farther on foot anyway. Her ankle was so swollen it no longer even looked like an ankle. It wasn't even a cankle—more like a purplish skin-bandage rolled and strapped around where her ankle should be.

The house was unlocked. Inside, it was very neat and full of sunlight. There was a gas stove and, Gemma saw, a small refrigerator cabled neatly to a battery. But no microwave, no digital clocks, no phones or iPads left casually on the counter, no mail, even. The lights were wall-mounted gas lanterns. Again she was struck by the weighty stillness, as if time had turned heavy and dropped like a hand over the whole place.

There was a plate on the table, toast half-eaten, along with a mug of unfinished coffee. This bothered her for some reason—why leave the house so neat but not clear your breakfast?

Calliope caught her staring. "There was a male," she said. "He ran off when he saw me."

"Why?" Gemma asked, and Calliope shrugged. It seemed weird to her that a boy in his own house would

run at the sight of a girl on his land, but then again, she didn't know much about Amish culture. Maybe he'd run for help, and even now there were people on the way who could take them to a town, or point them in the right direction, at least. "He didn't say anything? He didn't speak to you at all?"

"He just ran," Calliope said.

They drank water from a sink that worked with a hand pump and came out cold and tasting deliciously of deep earth. Instantly, Gemma felt better. They ate bread and fried eggs with yolks the orange of a setting sun, and Gemma nearly cried: she'd never been hungry before, truly hungry, in a way that torqued your insides. She couldn't even feel bad about the food they were stealing. They would pay it all back, anyway, she would make sure they did, once she got home.

In a cellar, Pete found an old-fashioned icebox, and in a closet, coarse linen hand towels that he used to make a pack for her ankle.

"We need to wrap your hand again," he said, and Gemma didn't want to but knew he was right.

He crouched in front of her and began to unwind the T-shirt they'd used to stop the bleeding. When it came away, Gemma was shocked by the sight of her missing finger: she couldn't understand, for a moment, where it had gone, still felt it buzzing and tingling.

She bit her lip as tears broke up her vision. Pete said nothing. He didn't look disgusted. He didn't try and make her feel better. He just dampened a clean towel and slowly wiped the blood off the back of her hand, off her fingers. She bit the insides of her cheeks when he touched the wound itself, so hard her mouth flooded with a metal taste. Pain came down on her like a shutter, and then it passed.

"We have to keep it clean," he said, rebandaging it, and she knew that was his way of saying *I'm sorry*.

How could they ever survive what they had seen together? They would be like tumors to each other: a nest of dark things, terrible memories, questions they wanted to forget.

They could never go back to how things had been. If they wanted to go forward, she feared, they would have to cut those tumors out. They would leave all their pain in the past. They would bury it so deep that even their heartbreaks couldn't hurt them.

Still, no one came. It hadn't been long, but Gemma grew anxious and increasingly restless. She desperately wanted to move on, to reach an end point, to hear her mom's voice, to see gas stations and telephone poles and parking lots and all the ugliness of life that now seemed beautiful: maps, grids, roads, wires. She craved fluorescent lights

and boring TV and normalcy. But she also knew it would be risky to leave. They might be ten miles from another settlement, maybe more.

Pete was right: it was better to wait.

He left Calliope and Gemma alone when he went to clean off in the old-fashioned tub, which also functioned with a pump and drew no hot water. She wondered if he felt the same way she did, like they'd been slicked all over with death, like it would never wash off.

In the kitchen she watched the sun turn dust motes in the air, wishing she could shake the feeling of terrible intrusion—a sense that had less to do with being in a strange house and, like Goldilocks, eating and drinking and consuming, and more to do with a feeling that they'd stumbled on a sleepy mystery best not to awaken. She was almost afraid to breathe too hard.

Calliope, on the other hand, moved from room to room, opening drawers, touching everything, marveling at soup spoons and wooden tongs, can openers and mason jars, salad bowls and flower vases, needlepoint pillows and woven place mats. She disappeared and reappeared wearing a second dress on top of the first one, a knit sweater that hit her at mid-thigh, and a wide-brimmed hat. Gemma wanted to say something, to tell her not to, but the words kept swelling in her throat like a sponge. She kept having the crazy thought that Calliope wasn't wearing different

clothes, but different skins; that the clothes were like the discarded shells of long-dead cicadas.

Calliope wasn't sick: it was an obvious realization but one that came late. Calliope was thin, way too thin, and her head was shaven, and she had crooked teeth. But she wasn't like Lyra. Lyra was sick in a way that showed itself even when she was desperately trying to hide it. Gemma knew that the replicas had been given different variants of prion disease, some of them much faster-working than others. There would have been control groups, too.

The idea of Lyra being selected and Calliope being spared made her sick, even though she couldn't say why she cared so much. When it came down to it, she hardly knew Lyra. When it came down to it, she was here because of Lyra. And Lyra had thanked her only once, and probably wouldn't care whether Gemma lived or died.

"You shouldn't touch everything," Gemma said at last, when Calliope crouched, letting her dress pool on the floor, to examine a fat-bristled broom next to the stove.

Calliope threaded a finger through its bristles, then tugged, so some of them came away in her hand. She let them scatter. "Why not?"

Exhaustion now felt to Gemma like a weight, like pressure bearing down on her from outside. "Because these things don't belong to you," she said. "This isn't your house."

A shadow moved across Calliope's face. "Why not?"

Gemma stared at her. She realized she had no idea how to begin answering. *We can live here,* Calliope had said. Did she not understand what belonging meant?

"Because . . . people live here. They're coming back. They use those spoons and cups and hats and . . . and everything."

Calliope removed the hat and turned it over in her hands. "But we used them too," she said after a moment. "So doesn't that mean we own them now?"

"No." Gemma reminded herself that Calliope didn't understand, and that it wasn't her fault. "It's not about who uses what. They just—the house is theirs. They own it."

Calliope frowned. "Why?"

"Just because," Gemma said. "Because the house is theirs, it was always theirs. They probably built it—"

"So if you build something, it automatically belongs to you?" Calliope's voice had turned sharp, and Gemma realized she'd said the wrong thing.

"No," Gemma said carefully. "Not always." Calliope looked down. Her knuckles were very white on the brim of the hat. "You don't belong to Haven, Calliope. You never belonged to them."

Calliope said nothing for a while. "It's just I've never seen so many things before," she said, so quietly the words

touched Gemma like a wind. She immediately felt terrible. "I always wanted, for my own. All of us wanted things. Only people could own anything."

"I'm sorry," Gemma said. She really was. How would she ever be able to fix Calliope? How could she even start? "It isn't the owning that makes a person, you know. It has nothing to do with that."

"Then what?" Calliope said. "What is it?"

Gemma couldn't answer that either. Calliope looked down at the hat, turning it again in her hands.

"At Haven the nurses left things without meaning to. Clips to put in your hair, except we didn't have hair, we weren't allowed. Number forty liked pens. She liked to suck on them. Her tongue was always black with ink. Maybe that's why she was an idiot. I found a whole package of gum, once, and Cassiopeia got a bracelet and I wanted it bad, but she hid it so them wouldn't take it." Calliope shook her head. "But I got even better than she did, in the end. It was because of watching. Most of the other thems never paid attention. But I always paid attention. I saw how the people talked and how they did things."

Wind briefly stirred the curtains, and made phantom shapes: faces appeared in the cloth, rippled, and were gone.

"The nurses hid in the bathrooms to use their cell

phones." She said *cell phones* the way someone else might say *church*: as if the words carried special power. "They weren't supposed to, but they did anyway. I found a cell phone of my own one day. It was just sitting there. I kept it hid. I was very, very careful. When they turned up Ursa Major with Nurse Maxine's wallet, all of us got searched. Ursa Major got hit so bad her face swole up and she had to go to the Box."

A terrible taste soured Gemma's mouth.

"The first day I was so happy. I hid far on the other side of the island and missed Stew Pot and all my testing, and I got in trouble from nurses afterward. But it was worth it. Sometimes the cell phone did nothing, and other times it lit and played music. Once I saw lots of numbers and I pressed all the buttons and I must have pressed at the right time and somebody spoke to me. 'Hello,' she said. 'Hello.' I was too scared to talk back. I liked to listen, though." Calliope scowled. "And then the phone made music too loud and the nurses took it away from me. Nurse Maxine said she would cut my fingers off if she ever caught me stealing again. I was happy when Haven burned," she added abruptly, and her voice sharpened. "I was happy when the roof exploded. I hoped she was inside, I hoped all her skin was burning, her and all the other nurses."

Gemma took a deep breath, fighting the hard tug of nausea. "But think of how many people died," she said.

“And—and all those babies, the infants in Postnatal, the ones you liked to visit? Remember, you told me that?” Calliope’s face didn’t change. “They’re dead.”

Calliope shrugged. “Things die,” she said. “At Haven, things died all the time. The Pinks and the Yellows, mostly all of them died. Browns too. They got sick early and started walking into things. Forgetting where their cots were and being stupid clumsy.”

“So that’s it?” Gemma’s voice was inching into a scream, and Calliope looked up, frowning, as if the tone bothered her. But Gemma couldn’t stop it. She couldn’t calm down. “You don’t feel *bad*? You don’t feel sorry?”

It was like watching a shutter latched tight against a storm: all the expression went out of Calliope’s eyes. For a long time, she stood there, staring at Gemma in silence, still holding the hat she’d found in one of the closets, her long white fingers knuckle-tight on its brim.

“If it isn’t the *owning* that makes humans,” Calliope said finally, and her voice was all knit together, interlaced with tension, “and it isn’t the *making*, either, then maybe it’s the *un*making?”

Before Gemma could stop her, Calliope had ripped the ribbon from the crown of the hat. She tossed it on the ground and began to stomp it with a heel. Her face flattened, like a reptile’s, into an expression of cold anger.

“Stop it.” Gemma struggled to get to her feet. Calliope

swept a hand over the kitchen shelves, crashing mugs, bowls, and plates to the ground. "Calliope, *stop*."

She didn't stop. She turned and darted into the living room. With two hands, she yanked the mirror from the wall and threw it. Gemma had to duck out of the way, folding her ankle again and barely catching herself on the counter. When the mirror hit the wall, the glass slid out of the frame and shattered.

A curse, was the first thing Gemma thought. A curse of bad luck.

"There," Calliope said. Glass crunched beneath her shoes. "Now it's ugly. Now it's ruined. Now no one can have it."

"You shouldn't have done that," Gemma said, tasting blood and tears in her mouth—she'd bit down on her tongue. Calliope lunged for her and Gemma screamed. But Calliope just gripped her by the wrist, squeezing so tight Gemma could feel the individual impressions of Calliope's nails.

"What if they never come back?" Calliope asked, so quietly Gemma nearly missed it. Terror swept down her spine, like the touch of an alien hand.

"What?" she whispered.

Calliope was careful not to look at her. "You said the people who live here will come back," Calliope said. "But what if they don't? What if they stay away forever?"

Dimly, over the thunder of her heartbeat, Gemma heard Pete creaking down the hall. Calliope released her quickly—but not quickly enough.

"What the *hell*?" Pete had changed into a pair of loose drawstring pants and a clean shirt, and there was color in his face again, although his eyes were still too bright, as if he had a fever. Gemma was shocked by how intensely relieved she was to see him.

For a second Calliope just stood there, breathing hard. Then she shoved past Gemma and hurtled out the door, letting it slam behind her.

TWENTY

"SOMETHING'S WRONG," GEMMA SAID. SHE thought of the way Calliope had flown at her, her sharp-fisted hands, the sour heat of her breath.

What if they never come back?

"That's an understatement," Pete said. He smiled, but only halfway, as if he couldn't quite remember how to do it.

"No." He didn't see. He hadn't seen how Calliope looked, and hadn't heard what she'd said. "I mean, whoever lives here should have come back by now. They should have come home. Why haven't they?"

"Hey." Pete had to step very carefully: he wasn't wearing shoes, and the floor was still littered with glass. "Deep breath, okay? You're just scared."

"What if—what if Calliope did something to them—" She choked on the words, on the very idea of it, and Pete

put his arms around her, as if he knew it was the only way to keep her on her feet.

"Come on," he said. "It's all right. Home stretch. You're exhausted."

"You're not listening to me." Gemma pulled away and saw reality for a moment like a fabric sail, blowing away from its mast, straining in invisible currents. "She asked me what would happen if they never came back."

"She's never been outside, Gemma," Pete said. "She has no idea what to think."

Gemma shook her head. Her mouth tasted like vomit. She was dizzy with confusion and fear. "Where are they then? You said yourself—it's not like they went on a road trip."

Pete's hair was wet: when he pushed a hand through it, water sprayed through his fingers. "Maybe they walked into town."

"What town?" Gemma no longer cared that she was shouting. "I haven't seen a town, have you, Pete? In fact, I think the whole reason we're here is that there is no fucking town."

He threw up his hands and let them fall hard, a clapping sound that made Gemma flinch. "So maybe they went to a picnic. Or a ukulele bonfire. Or to make soap out of lye or something. How should I know?" Pete was doing his best to be nice, but she could tell he was losing

patience. His irritation kept showing, like the nub of something sharp rubbing up beneath a sweater, distorting the fabric. "I mean, shit. She doesn't even know what a barn is. What could she possibly have done?"

"She knows what a barn is," Gemma said: a stupid response, but she was on the verge of tears again. "She called it by name. She's smarter than you know."

Pete frowned. She was worried he would tell her she was being crazy again, and that she would start to cry, but he just shook his head.

"Look. I can't imagine what it's like for you—" He broke off, shaking his head. "I mean, being with her. Seeing your *face* . . ." He smiled but only barely. "It's weird even for me. When you're standing next to each other . . ." He reached out and knuckled the counter, like there was an insect there he needed to crush. "I'd be freaking out too."

Gemma felt a chill go through her. She was a cold mist, barely hanging together. "You think I'm freaking out," she said.

He looked at her. Pale eyelashes. Freckles, lips, the coral inside of his nose. She'd studied his face so often—thinking it beautiful, thinking it hers. But the face was just collision, random physical accumulation that meant nothing.

"Anyone would freak out." He tried to take her hand

but she balled her fist, and weirdly enough her other hand, the injured one, pulsed with sudden pain, as if she'd balled that instead. "She's not you. She's nothing like you. You shouldn't be afraid."

"I don't think she's like me," Gemma said. "I don't think she's anything like me."

But she realized, even as she said it, that this wasn't exactly true. Wasn't that the whole point? She could have been Calliope, and Calliope could have been her. People became different bodies by chance or accident or God, depending on what you believed; but if you had the same body, the same voice, the same hair and fingers and eyes and nails, then how did you know the difference? She would have to separate from Calliope, cleave her like some horrible head in a fairy tale, and even then she would have that doubleness inside her.

"Go rinse off," Pete said, in a voice she hated: it was a tone her father used, hooking onto an *I know best* kind of thing. "It will make you feel better. I promise. By the time you get out, what do you want to bet we'll be hitching a ride back to the twenty-first century in a buggy?"

Gemma couldn't smile, even though she knew he was only trying to help. She wouldn't let him help her to the washroom, either, even though she was hobbling on her swollen ankle and had to lean on the furniture for support.

The bathtub was old and spotted with rust. Pete had

left blood behind, too, a faint ring of it where the water had turned color, and more funneling toward the drain. She pumped for water and was shocked by how cold it was. But at the same time she liked it, and liked the smell, too, like spring soil, and dirt newly turned over.

She stripped out of the clothes she'd been issued at the holding center and maneuvered into the tub, trying not to put weight on her ankle and careful, too, not to use her left hand. The shock of cold water even at her ankles made her gasp, and instinctively she went for a knob that wasn't there. Then she wanted to cry again, not for the lack but for all the things she had always used, for how lucky she was and for her life, pure and simple, for the ability to stand naked and hurt ankle deep in cold water. She was alive: she'd made it out. Goose pimples raised the hair on her thighs and forearms. The water took blood from her skin and swirled it into pink. She was ugly and damaged, and for an instant, she didn't care: she was alive. Her ribs held her, her heart held her, the world held her. It bound her like a promise.

Pete was right: she did feel better, infinitely better, once she'd watched a film of soot and dirt and blood wash away, as if it was carrying the memory of what had happened. Still, she was uneasy. She hadn't heard anyone come back. The house was still silent, still wound up, like a coiled spring.

There were towels pegged to the wall, and she took one. In an adjacent room she found a closet full of dresses like the one Calliope had chosen, and she rooted around in a drawer until she found pants, a white shirt, and a dark vest, all of them obviously meant for a guy. But a pair of sandals wedged beneath the simple bed fit her pretty well, and she almost laughed when, feeling something crunch in the pocket of the vest, she fished out a half-empty pack of Marlboro Lights and a Bic lighter decorated with a peeling Steelers logo.

So. There were rule breakers here, too.

Pete wasn't in the kitchen, although he'd swept up the glass. Calliope wasn't back, either. In an instant, all her good feeling was swept away; she stood drowning in the air, in the emptiness. She was alone.

She was suddenly terrified. She launched herself to the door, ignoring the pain in her ankle, crying out: there was something behind her, something too terrible to look at; the weight of her fear had transformed into a monster.

She was outside, and the light was blinding. The cows moving across the pasture calmed her only slightly. She was alone and lost. She was shouting Pete's name without even meaning to, and when she saw movement inside the barn, the shift of color and shadow, she went toward it with her arms outstretched.

"Don't. *Don't.*" His voice stopped her. She'd never

heard anyone sound like that, and in that moment, though she was still standing in the sun, the shadow of the monster behind her reached out and swallowed them. "Don't come in here. Don't."

For a moment he was still invisible. He was corners of himself, an arm and a leg, trying to move out of sticky darkness. And she was drawn toward him, to reach him, to pull him away, and so even as he plunged outside, like someone diving in reverse, she saw behind him the shoes attached to the ankles, and an arm—a small arm, a young arm—held motionless in a slant of light. Even if she hadn't, she would have known by Pete's face: it was as if all the skin had come off, as if the fear had come down and planed away everything else.

The barn is where the animals go to die.

He grabbed her, and this time Gemma felt that he was the one in danger of falling. "We can't stay here," he said. "We've got to get out of here. We have to get out now." There was blood on his shoes.

She couldn't move. Her thoughts had frozen: they were rattling together like cubes in a tray. "What happened?" she asked, even though she knew. But she couldn't quite make sense of it—that pale child's arm reaching into a triangle of sun, and a man's feet fanned apart. *Bodies.*

"Jesus." Pete was crying. He turned away from her and bent to put his hands on his knees, trying to breathe,

retching a little. "Jesus Christ." He just kept saying it, over and over, *Jesus, Jesus,* and Gemma felt the clean brightness of the sky above them, felt all the emptiness of that endless hurtle into space.

"She killed them," she said. The words didn't sound real. Pete just nodded. He was still doubled over. She wanted to put a hand on his back, but she couldn't make her arm obey the command.

The barn is where the animals go to die.

Where was she now? Where had she gone? Gemma was freezing, gripped by fear. In the distance, the woods rippled as a breeze passed through the trees. Was someone shouting? She couldn't think. She thought she heard voices crying out.

"We can't stay here," she said, as Pete had. But neither of them moved. It was like a nightmare. Too bright, too warm, too empty.

Voices. She definitely heard voices now, not the phantoms but real people. In the distance a long trail of orange dust unfurled, and then she saw horse carts, three of them, and a cluster of people. They were coming fast, and for a moment she felt nothing but relief. They were saved.

Pete had her shoulders. He shook her, and her teeth jumped together. "You need to run. Don't you understand? We can't be here. They can't find you here."

"What are you talking about?" Her thoughts were still

frozen into uselessness. The wagons were closer now. The ground shivered under the vibration of so many hooves. She could make out the men inside them, all men, all dressed in black, all shouting. There was a boy, too, maybe thirteen or fourteen. He was standing, balancing like a sailor on a rolling sea deck, scouting for sure. He was pointing.

"Listen to me, Gemma." Pete was shouting, but she couldn't hear him properly.

"Run, Gemma. Listen to me. You gotta move."

She'd already lifted a hand to wave back, to hail the people in the wagon, because they were waving too, because the boy in front, the one who reminded her of a sailor, was pointing at her.

Pointing, shouting. *Angry.*

And suddenly she remembered what Calliope had said: *There was a male. He ran off when he saw me.*

The cooled coffee with milk congealing into a pale skin on its surface. Half-eaten toast.

You can be my replica.

The men were pouring down off the wagons now, shouting, as the boy still stood with a finger raised, trembling and white-faced with fury, and finally Gemma heard him over the rattling of her heart, over the fear that had her in its grip.

"That's her," he was saying. He had the beginnings of

a beard, dark and patchy, and a long, narrow face, but it was his eyes that struck her. They were large and terrible, like holes that had been gouged into his face. "That's her. That one. That's *her.*"

Pete shoved her. The shock of pain when she stepped on her ankle jolted her into her body, into understanding: Calliope had killed people and Calliope had disappeared and Gemma, her replica, would be her substitute. *"Run."*

They were swarming toward her, jackets flapping in the wind like capes, so she was reminded of insects, of biblical locusts coming down to bring punishment.

Finally, Gemma ran.

TWENTY-ONE

SHE LOST SIGHT OF PETE almost immediately.

Pain darkened her vision every time she put weight on her left ankle, and her ankle kept folding, rolling her down to her hands and knees. She lost one sandal. She fell, got up, fell, got up. She could hear the men shouting behind her, tunneling toward her like a wave, but she was too afraid to look and see how close they were.

She was choking on her own spit, blind with pain and panic. Down, up again. In the fields the cows watched her lazily, flicking their tails. The woods were impossibly far. She kept running anyway, up and down the swells of land, falling and climbing again to her feet, swallowing her snot.

Then she had crossed the expanse of green and hit the fence, running into it with hardly a break in her step, simply plunging over it, toppling, rolling on her shoulder and

then hauling herself again to her feet, sheltered in the sudden shadows, ping-ponging from tree to tree, using her good hand. She tripped and slid down a steep embankment, through a mulch of rotting tree bark: at the bottom of the slope, an enormous felled tree wheeled its roots to the sky. An overhanging lip of earth made a kind of tunnel, and she saw at once this was her only chance: to hide, to wait, to hope that the men missed her. She scuttled backward into the soft rot of this long, damp space. The air smelled like moisture, pulped leaves, and decay.

She waited, shivering, her arms around her knees, listening to the distant shouting of her pursuers. At one point they seemed to be almost directly on top of her, and fear turned her stomach to liquid. But then they passed on.

She lost track of time. Her terror turned every second into a swampy hour, a long agony of waiting. Finally, she realized the woods were quiet. She couldn't hear anyone shouting.

She hadn't heard anyone shout in a long time.

Carefully, she shimmied out of her hiding place, still pausing every few breaths to listen for footsteps or the sound of voices. Nothing. Now that her panic had eased up, the pain in her ankle had redoubled. It took her twenty minutes to work her way up the slope she'd tumbled down in seconds.

At the top of the embankment she stood, trying to catch her breath, waving away a cloud of gnats that rose in a swarm. Afternoon sunlight made elegant angles through the trees. That meant hours had passed. She hoped the men who were after her had given up.

She wondered what had happened to Calliope—whether she, too, had made her escape through the woods.

She thought she remembered which direction she'd come from. She would have to go the opposite way, or risk ending up right where she started. If this was farmland, she comforted herself with the idea that she would have to reach another farm eventually—preferably one wired for the twenty-first century, where no one believed that she was a murderer. Even better, she might find a road full of traffic, full of normal people, soccer moms and dentists and teenage drivers with both hands on the wheel.

She swore then that if she ever made it home she would never complain, ever, about being bored. She wanted to be bored every day of her natural life. She wanted to die of boredom, literally.

So she went on, hobbling, limping, leaning heavily on a stick she fished out from the underbrush. She had to stop and rewrap her ankle twice, clumsily because she had only one hand, because she was shaking so hard, and the skin was so enormously puffy it frightened her. Miles of land, tight-knit woods of oak and maple and birch,

dappled sun and the sky held at bay by the canopy of branches, the occasional flash of a deer bounding off in the distance, broken stone foundations that might have existed since the days of Paul Revere. She kept telling herself there had to be a road soon, soon, soon.

The afternoon lengthened. The shadows turned the color of a bruise. More than once, she imagined she heard the noise of traffic—there, over that ridge, just behind that stand of trees, she could swear she heard a horn blowing. She was desperately thirsty, and her head hurt. She'd been crying for an hour without realizing it, and squinting hard to try to make treetops into rooftops or telephone poles. In the thickening shadows, she could almost believe it. She'd lost her second sandal too, without realizing it.

And now it was getting dark.

She began to shout for help, no longer caring who found her, wishing, now, she'd never run in the first place. She shouted until her voice broke and she couldn't bear it anymore. No one came, anyway.

And then she saw, in the distance, deliverance: a stone house, a roof overgrown with green moss, but a *house*. No—more than one house. Three houses lumped next to one another, like faerie houses dropped by some miracle in the middle of the woods.

If she'd been less desperate, she would have noticed the shattered windows, the doors angled off their hinges, the

wood rot, and seen it for a settlement no one had entered in years, possibly decades.

If she'd been less tired, she would have noticed the low circle of stones indicating an old sunken well, with only a flimsy covering of ancient wood to keep animals from falling in.

But she was desperate, and tired, and the woods were dark.

She tripped on the edge of the sunken well and saw, briefly, the small covering of ancient wood, like a trap-door set in the ground. Then she crashed through it and tumbled down into the long, sleek mouth of a thirty-foot hole.

PART III

TWENTY-TWO

AT ALMOST THE SAME TIME Gemma fell, Kristina and Geoffrey Ives arrived at a Bruinsville, Pennsylvania, police station, not ten miles from the old stone well in the middle of the Sequoia Falls Nature Preserve where their daughter now lay unconscious.

They had arrived in Lancaster County the night before, after one of Geoff's many military contacts, Captain Agrawal, had signaled that Saperstein might have mistaken Gemma and Pete for the replicas they were pursuing, only to discover a calamity: an explosion at the private facility where Saperstein had been licking his wounds and trying, without success, to rally new financial support. Kristina refused to consider the possibility that Gemma might be among the dead bodies excavated from the wreckage. She wouldn't even think it.

They were ushered by Captain Agrawal down a narrow

hallway to the locked and windowless evidence room in the back. Kristina had to reach out a hand to steady herself against the file cabinets.

How had she ended up in a police station with her daughter missing and children turned to ashes? There seemed to be a gigantic hole in her life that she couldn't bridge. She couldn't remember her way across it.

A sudden swoon of terror darkened her vision, made her dizzy on her feet: she imagined they were bringing her inside to show her Gemma's body, still and cold and lifeless, her lips dark as a bruise.

Years ago, she and Geoff had refused to accept the death of their only child. They had transgressed the natural order: they had taken their child back, after death had already claimed her.

She couldn't shake the idea that death had come, now, to settle the score.

When the door opened and instead she saw Pete Rogers, bloodless and exhausted-looking and definitely alive, she almost cried out. He was sitting at a table wedged between the metal shelving, which had been cleared of everything but a few cardboard boxes—or maybe that was all the evidence of crime in this part of Lancaster County. He was gripping a Styrofoam cup of what smelled like hot chocolate, and he had a blanket draped around his shoulders. The room was cold and extremely

bleak, with a cement floor and exposed wire-encased lightbulbs.

"It's the only room that locks besides the drunk tank," Agrawal said, as if he knew what Kristina was thinking. "I wanted to be sure he had privacy."

"Pete." Kristina's relief lasted only a second—fear grew almost immediately again inside her, a hard, cold metal thing that stuck in her throat. The night before, she'd gone instinctively for the Klonopin in her purse, only to find that suddenly her throat wouldn't work to swallow. She literally could not get the pill down.

She hadn't been this sober in years. She hadn't been this afraid, either.

"Pete." She went to him and knelt, taking his hands, which were cold, noting the bruised color of his eyelids and the capillaries broken across his cheeks and forehead. "Pete."

He showed no sign of having heard her.

"He's in shock," Geoff said, as though it weren't obvious.

"One of the troopers picked him up right on the shoulder of the turnpike a quarter of an hour ago, near the intersection of Route 72," Agrawal said. "My guy nearly plowed him."

"He needs a hospital," Kristina said. She had a memory of seeing Pete, April, and Gemma laughing together at her birthday party, playing bocce barefoot on the lawn.

Pete's pants were rolled to the knees and Gemma had several paper cocktail umbrellas tucked behind her ear. She was laughing. Could that really have been only four days ago?

"We've got a team from Lancaster General on their way now," Agrawal said. "I wanted to bring you in first. In case . . ." Kristina didn't miss the look Captain Agrawal gave her husband.

"Gemma's still out there." Pete's voice was so raw it hurt just to hear. It was as if he was speaking through a mouth full of thorns. He started to stand up, lost his balance, and sat down again. "I lost her. We have to find her."

"Shhh." She put a hand on his forehead, which was clammy with sweat. She smoothed back his hair. She had met his mother once—a cheerful, round-faced woman who'd arrived with paint still smudged on one cheek. She was a kindergarten teacher, she'd explained, and Kristina had immediately envied her warm, chaotic friendliness. "It's okay. Just tell me what happened."

He was grabbing the table as though he still worried he might fall down, even though he was sitting. "It was Calliope," he said, his voice cracking over every syllable. "She must have had the whole thing planned from the start. Gemma tried to warn me and I didn't listen. I didn't believe her." He was shaking. Kristina reached out and

put a hand on his back, trying to rub some warmth into him. "There was so much blood. . . ."

Immediately, it was as if the cold had flowed into her body as well. "What—what do you mean?" Memories swept suddenly through her head, brightly awful, like dead leaves: Gemma's veins threaded with tubes and needles, like some kind of alien plant; Gemma's mouth leaking blood the first time she'd lost a tooth; the thick Y-shaped scar across her chest, so similar to the incision that morticians made after death.

"There were three of them," Pete said. "One of them was just a kid."

"What are you talking about?" Kristina's voice sounded loud in the little room. "What's he talking about?"

"He means those homicides off Hemlock," Agrawal said quietly, avoiding Kristina's eyes. She knew that something terrible had happened to one of the Amish families in the area, but she had deliberately tried not to listen. She had enough tragedy of her own. She couldn't handle anyone else's. "He was on the scene." But Kristina had the feeling that there was more, that there was something he wasn't telling her.

"I told Gemma to run," Pete said. He wouldn't look at her. He was staring at his fists, balled now in his lap. "They were coming after her. There was no other choice."

The cold made Kristina's fingers and lungs tingle.

"*Who* was coming after her?"

Pete shook his head. It was as if he'd forgotten anyone else was in the room. "They thought she was Calliope," he said. "That was the whole point. That was what Calliope wanted."

Kristina imagined herself freezing, like a pane of glass webbed with frost, filling with tiny cracks. "Who's Calliope?"

Pete met her eyes, finally. "Calliope's one of Gemma's replicas," he said.

"One of . . . ?" Kristina tried to take a step backward and knocked one of the shelving units behind her. There was nowhere to go, no space at all. She couldn't breathe.

"All right, that's enough." Geoff came forward and tried to put a hand on Kristina's shoulder, but she jerked away. "The kid is in shock, Kristina. He needs to go the hospital, like you said."

"Numbers six through ten," Pete said, as if he hadn't heard. Now that he was looking at Kristina, she wished that he would look away. "Five in all. But Calliope wanted to be human."

"He's confused." Geoff's voice seemed to reach her from a distance, as if she really were hearing him through a thick layer of ice. The air had frozen in her lungs. She couldn't speak. She had the sense that she and Pete were alone at the bottom of a lake, that everyone

else, the whole world, was held at bay by thousands of tons of water.

"That's why Calliope did it," Pete said, in a whisper. "She wanted to switch places."

TWENTY-THREE

GEMMA BLINKED INTO CONSCIOUSNESS AGAIN, tossed up by a hand of pain. Something screamed. Or rather, she screamed and it screamed, and it was impossible to tell who started first. Leathery wings swept her face and the tangle of her hair, and her voice reached registers she didn't even know she could hit: a high-C, horror-movie scream that echoed back to her as the bat winged up toward the moon, probably just as scared as she was, knocking against the sides of the well in its effort to get out.

It was silhouetted briefly, a black blur against the sky knotty with clouds and a moon just easing out of the darkness, and then it was gone, and with her terror ebbing, the pain came grinding back instead, and the memory of what had happened: the long, limping escape through the woods, the sudden realization that she was lost. The

house in the glen—now, in memory, so obviously abandoned, maybe for a century—and the soft splinter of wood breaking apart beneath her.

The well.

She was at the bottom of a well, alone, in the middle of the woods.

She was shivering. The well smelled, strangely, like the inside of a dirty produce drawer, like the chill of old vegetal rot. The mud was puddled with old water and debris, with a tangle of tree branches and miscellaneous trash. She was lying in the rot of the old well, and when she shifted, she heard the crunch of small animal bones beneath her. High above her, a portion of the well cover was still intact. It blotted out a sweep of sky and reminded her of a half-closed eyelid.

"Hello?" she whispered. Of course no one answered. She cleared her throat and said, louder, "Hello?" Her voice rolled off the stones and then dropped.

Panic came up from her stomach, sharp-clawed and frantic, like some kind of rodent. She could barely sit up. Her back hurt; everything hurt. Nothing seemed broken, at least.

"Hello!" she tried again. "Help me!" There must be someone out there, someone who would hear. The well tunneled her voice into echoes, so even when her voice began to crack she was momentarily surrounded by the

cascading responses of her own words, *help me.* "Help me! Hello! Help!"

She shouted, over and over, into the thin night air, but her voice, still raw from overuse, gave out quickly. It dropped into hoarse croaks and then into whispers. Finally, she couldn't even do that, and when she opened her mouth, nothing came out but a soft whistling, like a leak from a faulty kettle.

Still no help arrived. No one came. No one answered.

There was no one around to answer, no one for miles and miles. Only the bats, blind and hungry, clicking their way through the dark.

TWENTY-FOUR

IN THE CURDLED LIGHT OF a new dawn, while a hundred police officers from all over the state began to gather in the parking lot outside the Bruinsville police station to smoke cigarettes and drink coffee and blink the sleep out of their eyes, while four bloodhounds lashed to the wrist of their handler sniffed experimentally at shoes and car tires and the crusted remnants of someone's dropped bacon, egg, and cheese, Gemma woke up to the pressure of a light rain that had started hours earlier and to a voice calling softly to her.

She blinked. Rain blurred her vision, and she swiped it from her eyes, disappointed when she realized that the voice, and her name, must have been part of a dream. There was no one above her, no one looking down on her at all: just the sky, a small and narrow mouth, graying above her. Staring up at the knit of clouds, she thought of

the surface of a distant mirror.

A shadow moved: she saw her own reflection peering down at her as she peered up at it.

She blinked again through the long tunnel of rain.

Calliope.

"Hello, Gemma," Calliope said. Then Gemma knew that hers was the voice she had heard calling softly to her in her sleep.

It took Gemma a long time to sit up. An eternity to claw, inch by inch, to her feet. "Calliope." Her mouth was dry. She opened it to the rain. "Please. Help me."

Calliope's face was a small, shifting pattern of shadows. "Don't be afraid," she said in a sweet voice, like the subtle pressure of a razor on Gemma's skin. "Be a brave girl, now."

Calliope disappeared again. When Gemma opened her mouth, when she screamed, she felt as if more fear flooded in, instead of being expelled.

"Please."

Calliope reappeared almost immediately, and Gemma felt a small flicker of hope. Calliope had murdered all those people. Calliope was sick. She was evil. But she was still *someone*. She was a chance. Gemma couldn't stand to be alone. She couldn't bear it.

"Please, Calliope." She licked her lips. "I—I want to help you. If you get me out of here, you can come and live

with me. We can be like—like sisters."

"Sisters?" Calliope repeated the word in a puzzled tone of voice.

"Like friends," Gemma said desperately, realizing Calliope likely didn't know what sisters were. "Like best friends, who share everything."

For a long time, Calliope looked at her. She seemed to be considering it. Gemma allowed herself to hope.

Then Calliope said, "I'm tired of sharing."

This time, when she vanished from the lip of the well, Gemma heard almost immediately the scrape of something heavy on the ground. And then a portion of the sky above turned black. Gemma thought, confusedly, of an eclipse.

"Good-bye, Gemma." Calliope was invisible, hidden somewhere behind the curtain of black that began to inch slowly across the opening of the well.

A door, or some kind of table: Calliope must have found it in one of the old cabins.

She was using it to cover the well.

She was using it to seal Gemma inside.

Terror turned Gemma inside out. "No!" She pounded the walls with her fists, as inch by inch the daylight narrowed to a finger, to a line, to a single point above her. "No! Please! *No!*"

The covering slid into place. Now she could see

nothing but a faint gray web of sky, where gaps in the planks revealed razor-thin slices of daylight. Calliope's voice, when she spoke, was so faint Gemma couldn't be sure, afterward, that she hadn't imagined it.

"Good-bye."

Gemma screamed for hours. She screamed, again and again, calling for Calliope, calling for someone to help. But no one answered—only the rain, scissoring through the rot of old plywood, a quiet shushing.

She slept again. She woke up crying, from a dream of rescuers, of friendly voices drawing closer. Wishful thinking, like people who saw mirages of floating water in the desert.

But then, once again, she heard them.

She sat up as quietly as she could, as if by making too much noise she would frighten off the distant voices. And for a second, she thought she had: she couldn't hear them anymore, and she strained so hard to listen that she felt the effort traveling all the way through her jaw.

Then they came again, nearer this time. She could make out only a few phrases, which carried through the woods and, like water going off a cliff, tumbled down into the well: "clear," "no sign," "radio." Cops. So someone had been sent to find her. In all likelihood, that meant Pete had escaped and found help.

She was saved.

“Down here,” she yelled, and was horrified when instead what came out was a fragmented whisper, like the rough sound of dry leaves skittering in the wind. She could barely hear it over the drumming of her heart. She cleared her throat and tried again. “Help me. Please. I’m down here!”

A whisper. A croak. A fish opening and closing its mouth soundlessly beneath the water.

She’d screamed for hours.

She’d screamed herself hoarse.

Already, the cops were drifting away—their words lost shape and edge, and their voices became tones, low notes of regret and disappointment. She grabbed a piece of wood from the splintered pile next to her and tried to beat it against the stone, but it crumbled moistly in her hand.

Help me.

Please.

Please.

She crawled, digging a hand into the loam of rot at the bottom of the well, until she found a rock. Loosing it from the mud, she drove it hard against the side of the well, again and again, rhythmically, and the sound traveled as a shock from her wrist to her elbow and up to her teeth.

But it was too late.

She was alone again.

TWENTY-FIVE

SHE WATCHED THE RAIN BEAD along the fine prism of a spider's web. The spider, black-bodied with furred white-and-black legs, had been at it for hours, leaping and soaring beneath the splintered remains of two shattered boards, trying to restore what had been lost when Gemma had fallen. It was amazing how pretty the web looked in the rain, in the trickle of light that reached her down here.

She lay there, cheek pressed to the mud, breathing in the smell of rotted wood and leaf rot, surprised that she wasn't afraid, wasn't in pain, wasn't feeling much of anything. She was content simply to watch the spider. She wondered how many times over the spider had seen its own web destroyed, and how many times it had simply begun to reweave. Ten? Twenty? One hundred?

She wondered if Pete was okay, and if he'd made it back

to civilization, whatever that meant. She wondered if he'd managed to convince anyone of the truth, or whether he'd been shunted off into some psychiatric hospital.

She had no idea what time it was, only that it had been hours since the voices had gone, and so far they hadn't come back.

In Chapel Hill, her classmates would be drinking bad coffee in the cafeteria, finishing last-minute homework assignments, sweating through pop quizzes, ducking outside to smoke weed behind the music building.

She had to get up. Her stomach hurt. She had to use the bathroom. There was a bad smell permeating the air; she realized that it was coming from the filthy cloth still tightly wrapped around her hand.

She had to get out of the well. Not tomorrow. Not when—or if—someone found her. Now. Today.

She kicked through the rubble at the bottom of the well. Wood splinters. A soda can—that got her interest, that was good, it meant there were other people who came this way, hikers or picnickers, and she couldn't be that far from help. She found a textbook, too, from someone's history class—the pages warped, the type blurry and mostly indecipherable. That almost, almost made Gemma smile. She and April had hurled their biology textbooks onto the train tracks once, just to watch them get mowed over, even though both of their parents docked them

allowance for the cost of a replacement.

There was no ladder. No booster rocket. No flare gun, or charged cell phone. Big surprise.

The well walls were moss-slicked but studded with rocks that made decent handholds. She wished now more than ever she'd been allowed to participate in gym—her mom had always insisted she be excused, claiming a weak heartbeat, concerned that Gemma might flatline in the middle of a game of dodgeball—and that she'd learned rock climbing during the aerial unit last fall. She couldn't climb one-handed, anyway, but when she tried to use her left hand, thinking that with four good fingers, she'd be okay, the pain was so bad she nearly peed herself and stumbled backward, gasping.

So. She couldn't climb.

She thought of piling all the rotted wood together, stacking it carefully in a cross-hatch pattern, hoping that by some miracle of geometry she would be able to climb the pile like a footstool and reach the top of the well. But the wood was soft and rotten and there wasn't much of it to begin with: it boosted her barely a foot. Her voice was still shot, still coming out in a bare croak, like the throaty wail of a dying frog.

Stretching onto her tiptoes, she managed to get a hand around a root exploding through the rot between stones. Maybe she could climb it, brace her feet against the wall

and get some leverage—it would take her only a quarter of the way toward the top, but a quarter of the way was better than nothing.

But here again, she failed. She could barely support her weight with one arm, and her feet slipped as the wood rot crumbled beneath her. She slammed into the wall with a shoulder and dropped on her knees—remembering, at least, to shield her left hand, so she didn't accidentally put pressure on it.

She sat there, panting, her nose leaking snot into the mud. She was too scared even to cry. She might actually die here. Here, at the bottom of some shitty hundred-year-old well, in a state she didn't even *like*. She would die a virgin, alone, unloved.

Funnily enough, it wasn't Pete she thought of then, or April, or even her mom. It was Lyra, the way she looked when Gemma had last seen her: still fragile but also full of life, something hatching. When Gemma closed her eyes, she could hear Lyra's voice, whispering to her across a distance.

Gemma, her voice said. *Gemma.*

Gemma's heart nearly cracked. She opened her eyes again.

But still she could hear Lyra's voice, louder now.

"Gemma, Gemma." And Caelum's, too, a lower, deeper echo of hers: "Gemma, Gemma."

She climbed to her feet. She couldn't quite believe it. They were so distant, she almost feared she really had snapped, and that what she heard was just the transformation of her memory into sound. But no—there was an unfamiliar voice, too, a man's voice. And how could she remember something she'd never heard?

That meant they were here. Close.

Instantly, she was seized by terror: they wouldn't hear her. They would leave, like the police had left, and no one would ever think to look for her here again.

The rock was still where she'd dropped it, exhausted, after an hour of banging fruitlessly, hoping someone would come. She picked it up again and slammed it hard against the slick wall, and the noise it made was of an old stone mouth, clicking its tongue in disapproval.

Not loud enough. Was it her imagination, or were the voices receding already?

She banged the stone again and again. Now she *was* crying, from terror and frustration. How could they not hear? How could they not *see*? Of course, she hadn't seen it either: the well was separated from the houses by a hundred yards, and tucked behind a stand of trees.

She thought of throwing something into the air, in case they happened to be looking in her direction. But it was no use. She could barely lob the rock ten feet in the air, much less hope to break through the wood that Calliope had used to conceal the opening.

The well smelled like her own sweat, like a hard panic. She wasn't imagining it. Lyra's voice was receding.

They, too, were going away.

She was shaking and burning hot, too. She shook off the wool vest she'd taken from the farmhouse—a sudden vision of the boy, red-faced, enraged, pointing at her, as the wagon crested the swell of the hill, overwhelmed her—and as she did, the cigarettes and the peeling lighter thudded out of one pocket.

Gemma's breath seized in her throat.

Could she . . . ?

It had been raining on and off all night. The wood was damp, although not as damp as it could have been—Calliope had done her this favor by covering the well.

She bent down. The lighter was cool in her hand. She thumbed a flame to life and was shocked by how vivid it was, how bright against the darkness.

Could she . . . ?

It was risky. It was dangerous. She remembered how quickly the airport bathroom had filled with smoke, how quickly she'd felt she couldn't breathe. She had no idea how far Lyra and Caelum had traveled already, and whether they'd even *see* the smoke.

On the other hand, she didn't know how much longer she'd survive.

And what had Calliope said?

In all the stories, there's always a fire.

TWENTY-SIX

AND THEN, WHILE SHE WAS still hesitating, still trying to decide, three gunshots cracked out in the silence.

That settled it. Three gunshots meant a gun and someone to fire it: someone was still near, and she would take her chances that it was someone who would help, and not Calliope or some psycho Amish guy with a rifle from the 1800s. Maybe Lyra and Caelum had even gotten hold of a gun. Maybe they were trying to signal to her.

She hoped and prayed that they weren't on the wrong side of the bullet.

Either way, she would have to take her chance.

Gemma had never built a fire before—three of the four fireplaces at home were electric and functioned at the push of a button—but she'd watched her mom do it a few times, amused that Kristina had once been a tomboy and had spent her summers camping and hiking and

hitchhiking between different beach towns, and amused, too, that Kristina always got so offended when Gemma said she couldn't imagine it.

Quickly, quickly, before they went away.

She tore handfuls of paper from the old textbook, saying a silent apology to the Book Gods for ruining the binding—and was pleased to find many of the pages at the center very dry. They lit up easily, flaming quickly into little bright universes that soon shriveled and burned up to nothing.

The wood was harder. She discarded all the wettest pieces and wound up with a small pile that she layered on top of a pyramid of crumpled pieces of paper. It would have to do.

She was shocked by how much smoke there was right away: smoke curled off the wood as if being planed by an invisible machine. The chemical smell of ink made her cough. She crouched as low as she could, suddenly very afraid. What if the wood *did* burn, so well, so quickly she couldn't control it?

Smoke climbed up the well, rolling from one side to another, like someone rappelling down a cave but in reverse. Gemma tilted her head and gasped with relief: the smoke had sniffed its way to the open air, had begun to trickle through the narrow gaps in the wood and lift toward the trees.

Someone would have to see.

Please, God. Let someone see.

The wood was still smoldering, releasing long tendrils of blue smoke that reminded Gemma of dark hair, that felt like hair in her mouth and in her throat. Her eyes and head hurt. Already, the air was very bad.

Should she put out the fire? Her head hurt so badly, she had trouble thinking through the pain. One more minute. She would wait one more minute.

The wood burst into flame, at last.

Gemma began to cough.

Her head now hurt so badly she couldn't think of anything at all.

She was very tired and thought, maybe, she should just lie down for a while, down in the mud, where it wasn't so hot. . . .

TWENTY-SEVEN

GEMMA DREAMED SHE WAS RIDING on the back of a giant bat, cupped in the soft leather of its wings. She dreamed that a veil had been placed over her face, to keep her from looking down and getting afraid, to keep her from crying out and startling out of the sky. But she couldn't breathe. The cloth was wet from her breathing, and it flowed into her open mouth. It tasted like smoke.

Briefly she woke up to the sound of voices and lights—hands everywhere, leathery hands, unfamiliar, and faces she didn't know—but she hovered there, on the edge of consciousness, for only a few seconds before the bat enfolded her in its wings and once again swept her up, this time loosing itself from the trees and hurtling across the clean, cool night air.

She could breathe again. The veil had come loose. Her sister had unhooked it, because she didn't like how it looked.

That's better, her sister, Emma, said. Except that Emma had Lyra's face, and Gemma knew, in her dream, that all along Lyra-who-was-Emma had simply disguised herself to give Gemma time to adjust to having a sister.

The bat had turned to a trundling donkey, and Gemma rocked back and forth, back and forth, while Lyra, who was her sister Emma, walked beside her. The sky above them was the color of milk. Was she dreaming or not? She was bound up in white sheets, as if prepared for burial, but she didn't feel afraid, not with her sister Lyra standing next to her and whispering to her, over and over, *Shhh. It's okay. You're okay now.*

TWENTY-EIGHT

"IS IT TRUE? DID YOU really lose a *finger*?" April didn't wait for Gemma to answer. "That's so *awesome*. You got your finger blown off. Is it your middle finger?"

"Pinkie," Gemma said.

"Oh, well, thank *God*," April said. "How else would you flick off Chloe DeWitt and the pack wolves? Seriously, that is the most badass thing I've ever heard. You're going to be Instagram famous, like, immediately."

"Sure," Gemma said. "Maybe I'll even become a hand model."

"Uh-huh." April fed a Twizzler into her mouth, then offered one to Gemma. "Maybe I'll get my finger blown off too. You know, so we can be twins."

Gemma rolled her eyes. "You're certifiably insane. You know that? You should be locked up." But the knot in her chest had loosened. April had that effect: like a warm bath

after you'd almost frozen to death.

Since Gemma had woken up—nearly eighteen hours since she'd first been admitted, time enough for April and her mothers to catch a flight to Philadelphia and then make the drive to Lancaster General—April had barely paused for breath.

She told Gemma how her mom Diana had helped her crack into Jake's computer after April admitted the story they'd cooked up about finding it in the library was in fact a fabrication.

"I should have known," Diana said. "When's the last time you two were at the library?"

"It took her, like, two seconds," April said, deliberately ignoring the question. "Meanwhile she can't use Snapchat to save her life."

April had been hoping that there might be information on Jake's computer that would help them locate Gemma. Instead, she had found passwords to HavenFiles.com, lists of bloggers and journalists who'd expressed interest in what was really happening at Haven, hundreds of names and connections, data that Jake, out of precaution, out of fear, had kept secret.

But April, God love her, had never kept a secret in her whole life: she had flooded HavenFiles.com with new uploads, had emailed every single whistle-blower she could find online, had started a Truth Apocalypse, as

she put it. Her mom Angela had even contacted the *New York Times.*

"Some detective talked to me," she said. "He wanted to know all about the Haven Files. All about Jake Witz, too."

"Is April bugging you, Gem?" Diana asked, ruffling her daughter's hair.

"Yeah," Gemma said. "For about the past ten years."

She was kidding, of course, though in truth, she didn't want to think about Jake Witz, or detectives, or the replicas escaped from the airport, and what would happen when the truth about them began to break. That would come later. For now, though, she liked to hear April's voice, and see Angela and Diana bickering over whose turn it was to run down to the canteen for coffee, and sit in the sun with her mother, clear-eyed, sitting next to her.

"Har-dee-har." April made a face through a mouthful of Twizzler. "All I'm saying is, when the shitstorm hits the—" But she didn't finish, because just then the door opened behind her, and Lyra and Caelum edged shyly into the room.

Gemma's heart leapt. They were both wearing hospital gowns, and Lyra was painfully pale, and still far, far too thin. But she was smiling, and alive.

"Looks like you have some more visitors," Kristina

said, reaching out a hand and smoothing Gemma's hair back.

"You're awake," Gemma blurted. She had been asking since she had woken up that morning.

April treated Lyra and Caelum's arrival like she treated everything: as if it was exactly what she had expected all along. "You're *heroes*," April said, and then held out her bag of Twizzlers. "Twizzler?"

Lyra shook her head. Caelum, however, took one, and Gemma couldn't help but smile.

"Come on." Angela put a hand on April's shoulder. "Let's leave them alone for a bit, okay?"

Gemma's mom stood up. "I could use a cup of coffee, actually."

April made a face. *Leaving Gemma alone* was not a concept April had ever been particularly good at. It was one of the things Gemma loved most about her.

"Yeah, sure," she grumbled. "But we'll come back, right? You can't get rid of me that easily." She pointed a Twizzler at Gemma.

"I wouldn't dream of it," Gemma said. Lyra and Caelum exchanged a look. She thought she saw a smile pass between them.

Kristina bent down to kiss Gemma's forehead. "I'll be right back," she said, and Gemma nodded to show it was okay for her to go.

“How are you?” Gemma asked, as soon as everyone else had left. She was worried about how pale Lyra looked. “How are you feeling?”

But Lyra answered immediately.

“We’re fine,” she said. Caelum took Lyra’s hand, and Gemma felt a surge of love for them both. She struggled to find the words to express how she felt—how grateful she was.

“April was right,” she said at last. “You’re both heroes. I can’t believe you found me.”

Slowly, Lyra smiled. It was the funniest thing. Her smile was like something that snuck up on her, like the kind of sun that begins by planting an elbow through the clouds and then begins to push, and push, until the whole sky is exposed.

“That’s what friends do,” Lyra said. “They find each other.”

Gemma knew, then, that Lyra understood. That the terrible things that had happened to her hadn’t, after all, been more important than the love she had found.

“Exactly,” she said.

Suddenly, unexpectedly, Lyra came forward and put her arms around Gemma’s shoulders, and squeezed. They had never hugged before. Gemma blinked away tears. She could feel Lyra’s ribs through her back. She thought of a bird; she thought of the dream of being

carried to safety on a pair of wings.

"Thank you," Lyra said, twice. Then she pulled away, almost as if she was embarrassed. Without another word, she turned for the door.

Caelum lifted a hand, and quirked his mouth into a smile, and waved. Then they were gone.

Not a minute after they left, Kristina was back and fussing over Gemma. "She's going to be okay, isn't she?" Gemma asked, after Lyra had slipped out, promising to lie down. She was consumed by a strange anxiety, a premonition that she wouldn't see Lyra again—or that she wouldn't see her for a long time.

Kristina sighed. She looked down at her hands. "Lyra's very sick, Gemma."

"I know that," Gemma said. "That isn't what I meant." But she wasn't sure what she *did* mean. She was scared all over again, scared and full of love: she knew she couldn't save Lyra, and that was the scariest thing of all.

"I wish I had the answers," Kristina said. That was one of the things Gemma loved about her mom: she wasn't a liar.

Kristina moved to the window and drew the curtains to let in the sun. Gemma blinked. Outside her window, a spider was weaving in one corner, putting the finishing touches on a web that looked like a blown-up snowflake.

"Your father called," she said at last, almost casually.

"He wants to talk to you."

"I don't want to see him," Gemma said. "I don't want to see him ever again."

"Well." Kristina turned away from the window again. She had no makeup on. Gemma couldn't remember the last time she'd seen her mom with no makeup. She looked gorgeous, Gemma thought. "You can't avoid him forever."

"Why not?" Gemma asked.

Kristina bit her lip. For a second, Gemma was sure—sure—she had been about to smile. But she sighed instead, and came toward the bed.

"Listen, Gem." This time, when she brushed the hair out of Gemma's eyes, Gemma nearly cried. She'd missed her mom so badly. She'd been so afraid they'd never see each other again. "I think . . . I want you to know—and I know this will be hard for you—that I don't think I'm going to go home. To your father, I mean. I think I'd like to get my own place. A place for just you and me." Her throat was moving up and down, up and down, as if it was doing double duty just to get the words out. "What do you say? I know things will be different. . . ."

But she didn't finish. Because Gemma started to laugh, and cry, both, imagining a little house where she and her mother would live together, she and her mother and their animals, all covered in pet hair, and nothing white at all.

TWENTY-NINE

DEEP DOWN, GEMMA HAD KNOWN that when Lyra hugged her—their first hug ever—she had meant it as a good-bye. She was right. By the next morning, Lyra and Caelum had vanished.

According to the nursing staff, they must have slipped out around dawn, unseen even by the stubbornest bloggers and tragedy tourists, through a little-used stairwell right by the ladies' room that led down into the parking lot.

They had practice, Gemma knew, in turning invisible.

She couldn't say she blamed Lyra and Caelum. They'd spent so much of their lives in closed rooms, surrounded by charts and IVs and sharp-edged equipment made for cutting. Gemma didn't blame them for not wanting to waste another minute.

"They'll be back," Gemma said to her mother. "They'll find us again, when they're ready. That's what friends do."

She was sure, absolutely sure, that it was true. They just needed to find their own way back.

She was both desperate to see Pete and dreading it, but she couldn't delay it any longer; he was asking for her. Pete had gone into shock soon after being picked up by the police, and for nearly twenty-four hours he'd been in critical condition, floating in and out of consciousness, while they tried to regulate his organ functions and his temperature. His parents had flown up from Chapel Hill, and they told Gemma only after she'd been admitted did he stabilize. Even though he was unconscious, by then, kept under by a course of anesthesia, it was like he knew.

He'd been moved only that morning from the ICU to a recovery floor. Still, the room they had him in was dark, all the blinds sewn up against the light—"so he doesn't get overwhelmed," his mom said, and gave Gemma a hug, before slipping outside with her husband to give Gemma and Pete privacy.

He was propped up on several pillows, but his eyes were closed. She inched toward the bed, scared of waking him, and scared, too, that he wouldn't wake up. He was so pale, even in the dark she could see veins in his forearms and his chest. He was hooked up to an IV, and an EKG, and the sound brought Gemma back to her childhood, and terrified her: What if Pete was sicker than anyone thought?

But he opened his eyes when she kneed the bed accidentally, and smiled.

"Gemma," he said. His voice sounded raw. Just hearing him say her name like that, like it was the name he'd been waiting to say his whole life, made her lose it.

"Oh my God." She started to cry. She couldn't help it. She loved him so badly; she wanted him to know that. It didn't even matter whether he felt the same way. "You look terrible."

"Thanks," he said. He cracked the smallest, faintest smile. "I forgot my mascara at home."

It was the second time in a day she'd laughed and cried at the same time. She managed to adjust the hospital bed, so she could climb in next to him, and he laid his head against her chest.

"I thought I would never see you again," he whispered.

"Shhh." She put her hands through his hair. "I'm right here."

"I was so scared." His voice broke. In the dark, their bodies lost form: they could have been a single person, a single body entangled together in the sheets. "What's going to happen, Gemma? What's going to happen to us?"

Gemma leaned back and closed her eyes. She imagined, somewhere in the woods of eastern Pennsylvania, a spider weaving a web in a well. After rain or wind came to destroy it, it wove. It wove with thread so fine it

was almost invisible, and she wondered if the spider was ever afraid, that its life was bound up in something that could be blown away with a breath. It wove anyway, either way.

Spiders were funny that way. They leapt first, and the web followed. It was a kind of biological faith, that demanded belief and then turned it real.

"It's going to be okay," Gemma said. "Trust me." She didn't know if it would. But she didn't know it wouldn't be either, and that, she thought, was what being human meant. You built your life into meaning, you transformed it into liquid faith, again and again, like a web; you did it blind, by instinct, because to not do it would be to stop living. And the darkness sieved through. It flowed and gathered and dropped, but it wasn't strong enough, wasn't real enough, to touch what you had made.

That was the true gift: to have a story that was still unfolding, like a thread unspooling, and as it did, this single thread separated light from dark, meaning from senselessness, hope from fear.

"It's going to be okay," she repeated. She put a hand on Pete's chest, above his heart, and he put his hand on top of hers, so the rhythm of his heart passed through her palm and back to his. She heard, for a split second, the sound of his life and hers, drawn together along the string of an ancient instrument, and that string

hummed with the sound of a thousand thousand other lives, and when she closed her eyes, she saw a spider buried deep underground, spinning music, pure music, for the world.

Photo by Charles Grantham

LAUREN OLIVER is the cofounder of the media and content development company Glasstown Entertainment, where she serves as the president of production. She is also the *New York Times* bestselling author of the YA novels *Replica*, *Vanishing Girls*, *Panic*, and the Delirium trilogy: *Delirium*, *Pandemonium*, and *Requiem*, which have been translated into more than thirty languages. The film rights to both *Replica* and Lauren's bestselling first novel, *Before I Fall*, were acquired by AwesomenessTV; *Before I Fall* has been made into a major motion picture.

Her novels for middle grade readers include *The Spindlers*, *Liesl & Po*, and the Curiosity House series, cowritten with H. C. Chester. She has written one novel for adults, *Rooms*.

A graduate of the University of Chicago and NYU's MFA program, Lauren Oliver divides her time between New York, Connecticut, and a variety of airport lounges. You can visit her online at www.laurenoliverbooks.com.

FOLLOW LAUREN OLIVER ON

stolen cash rubber-banded in their jeans, and their hair cropped so short it might recently have been shaved, slept together in the very last seat of a northbound Greyhound bus. Who knows what they were dreaming about? A sign announced they were coming up on Philadelphia, but they didn't stir, and the bus didn't stop, and they sailed on.

And then there were the usual cheaters and hookers and lowlifes who came in and out regularly. Guy even knew some of their names. He'd gotten a hand job from one of the working girls, Shawn, who wasn't a girl at all, more like forty-seven. Up close, she'd smelled like barbecue potato chips.

He knew what people looked like when they were sleepless, desperate, guilty, and plain high out of their minds.

Gemma Ives. The girl's ID was all messed up, warped like it had gone through the washing machine, and the picture was scratched. He could tell she'd lost weight, though, since the picture was taken—if it even was her in the picture. The guy didn't have a license at all. He just wrote his name down in the register. It was all about covering your ass, Guy knew, if somebody flatlined in one of the rooms. They just needed to show due diligence. But their debit card matched the ID, and it worked, so he figured fuck it.

"One room, one night," was all the girl had said. She kept looking over her shoulder, and every time the insects pinged against the glass, she jumped.

As if she were being watched.

As if she were being *followed.*

Two hundred and forty miles away, a different girl and a boy, both dressed in stolen clothing, both with a stack of

PROLOGUE

Monday, May 16, 3:19 a.m.

They looked nervous.

"Jumpy, you know," he would say, and each time he saw them clearly in his mind: both of them skinny, with complexions the color and texture of wet clay, and eyes like someone had knuckled holes in their faces when they were still wet. "Like they were on the run."

Of course, plenty of the people who walked into the Four Crossings Motel looked nervous: it was that kind of place. And even if Guy's mom, Cherree, was always telling him to turn away anyone with track marks or the jumpy look of a major addict, he knew they'd only bought the place because she'd wanted to cash in on the pill poppers and dopeheads, a whole new generation of druggies—suburban moms, and men still wearing their ties from the office, and thirtysomething dental hygienists—who needed a place to crash while they got high.

"Erin Bartels has a gift for creating unforgettable characters who are their own worst enemy, and yet there's always a glimmer of hope that makes you believe in them. The estranged sisters in *All That We Carried* are two of her best yet—young women battling their own demons and each other as they try to navigate beyond a shared painful past and find their way to a more hopeful future."

Valerie Fraser Luesse, Christy Award–winning novelist

"*All That We Carried* is so much more than just a beautiful novel—it's a literary adventure of both body and spirit, a meaningful parable, a journey of faith. Erin Bartels creates amazingly realistic characters in two sisters wrestling with their past and with one another. Not only did this story make me want to pull on my hiking boots for my own adventure, it propelled me to search out a deeper faith. Simply stunning. A novel not to be missed!"

Heidi Chiavaroli, award-winning author of *Freedom's Ring* and *The Tea Chest*

Praise for *The Words between Us*

"*The Words between Us* is a story of love found in the written word and love found because of the written word. It is also a novel of the consequences of those words that are left unsaid. Bartels's compelling sophomore novel will satisfy fans and new readers alike."

Booklist

"*The Words between Us* is a story to savor and share: a lyrical novel about the power of language and the search for salvation. I loved every sentence, every word."

Barbara Claypole White, bestselling author of *The Perfect Son* and *The Promise between Us*

"If you are the kind of person who finds meaning and life in the written word, then you'll find yourself hidden among these pages."

Shawn Smucker, author of *Light from Distant Stars*

"Vividly drawn and told in expertly woven dual timelines, *The Words between Us* is a story about a woman who has spent years trying to escape her family's scandals and the resilience she develops along the way. Erin Bartels's characters are a treat: complex, dynamic, and so lifelike I half expected them to climb straight out of the pages."

Kathleen Barber, author of *Are You Sleeping*

Also by Erin Bartels

We Hope for Better Things

The Words between Us

All That We Carried

a novel

ERIN BARTELS

a division of Baker Publishing Group
Grand Rapids, Michigan

Published by Revell
a division of Baker Publishing Group
PO Box 6287, Grand Rapids, MI 49516-6287
www.revellbooks.com

Printed in the United States of America

Library of Congress Cataloging-in-Publication Data
Names: Bartels, Erin, 1980– author.
Title: All that we carried: a novel / Erin Bartels.
Description: Grand Rapids, Michigan : Revell, a division of Baker Publishing Group, [2021]
Identifiers: LCCN 2020019550 | ISBN 9780800738365 (paperback) | ISBN 9780800739607 (casebound)
Subjects: LCSH: Domestic fiction.
Classification: LCC PS3602.A83854 A79 2021 | DDC 813/.6—dc23
LC record available at https://lccn.loc.gov/2020019550

21 22 23 24 25 26 27 7 6 5 4 3 2 1

For Alison, naturally

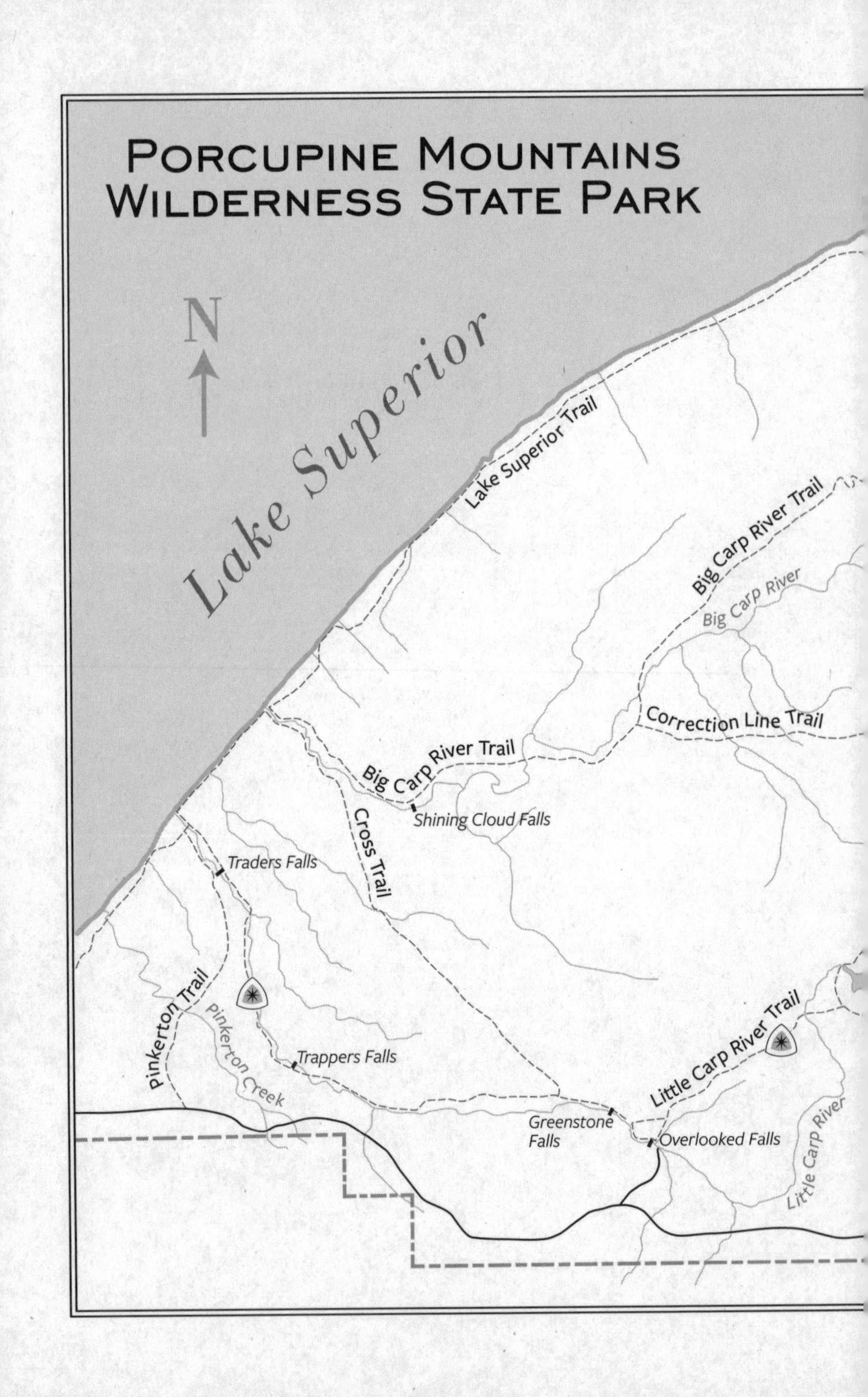

PORCUPINE MOUNTAINS
WILDERNESS STATE PARK
N
Lake Superior
Lake Superior Trail
Big Carp River Trail
Big Carp River
Correction Line Trail
Big Carp River Trail
Shining Cloud Falls
Cross Trail
Traders Falls
Pinkerton Trail
Pinkerton Creek
Trappers Falls
Little Carp River Trail
Greenstone Falls
Overlooked Falls
Little Carp River

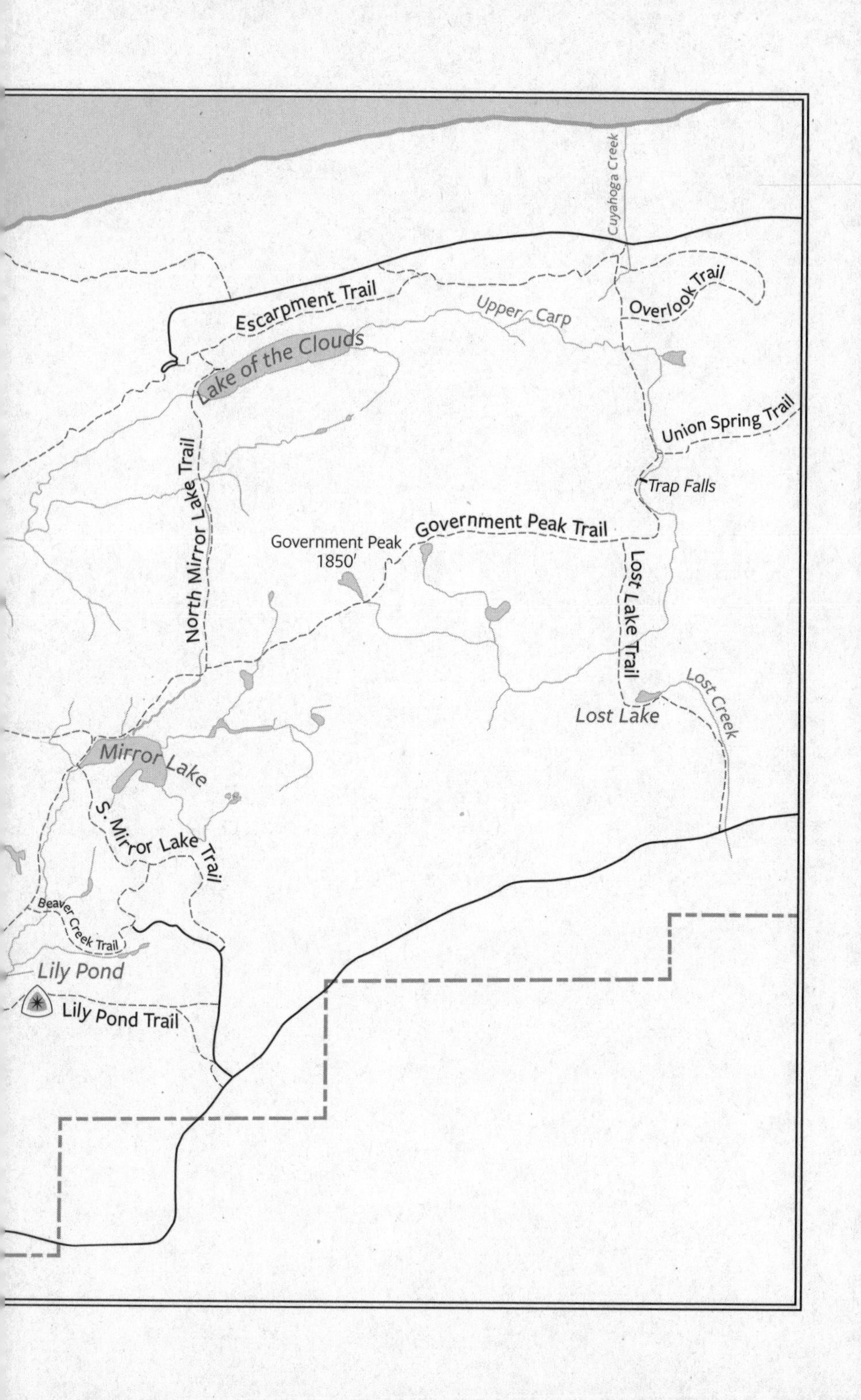
Cuyahoga Creek
Escarpment Trail
Upper Carp
Overlook Trail
Lake of the Clouds
Union Spring Trail
North Mirror Lake Trail
Trap Falls
Government Peak Trail
Government Peak
1850′
Lost Lake Trail
Lost Creek
Lost Lake
Mirror Lake
S. Mirror Lake Trail
Beaver Creek Trail
Lily Pond
Lily Pond Trail

One

MIDWESTERNERS DO DUMB THINGS on the one nice day in March. The thought that winter might indeed have an end makes them giddy, unpredictable, and more than a little bit stupid. They wear shorts, make big plans, believe that this—finally—will be the year they get in shape or go to Paris or write their screenplay. And much like you wouldn't hold a friend to a promise they made while emerging from the effects of anesthesia after surgery, Olivia Greene felt that her sister had no right to hold her to the promise she'd made on that unseasonably warm day seven months ago.

Melanie had called at lunchtime when Olivia would not be in court and would therefore have no excuse for letting the call go to voicemail as she normally would. The sun had just broken through the rushing clouds, lighting the towering smokestacks of the power station south of downtown like columns of a Greek temple. Mists lifted from the low places along the road that were still cradling crusted snow. And at that moment, after an unsatisfying lunch at a mediocre restaurant with two colleagues she didn't much care for, Olivia had felt just restless enough to agree to a weeklong backpacking trip with the younger sister she hadn't seen in a decade.

That Melanie chose a hike, she couldn't quite understand. Hiking had long been ruined for her.

Now as she pulled off the highway and into the gas station lot where they had agreed to meet in Indian River, Olivia wished that day had been as miserable as the rest of March always was. If it had been sleeting, she never would have agreed to this nonsense.

She didn't know what kind of car her sister drove, but she didn't bother looking for her either. Melanie wouldn't be there yet, despite living only a half hour away. Instead, Olivia got out of the car, rubbed her hip, which was sore from the long spate of sitting, and went into the gas station. The sprawling shop had the normal gas station fare—pop, beer, candy, salty snacks—but it also sold accoutrements for three distinct, though at times overlapping, markets: veterans, hunters, and those passionate about right-wing politics.

She made haste to the bathroom, sure that everyone she passed knew she was out of her element. She'd done her hair that morning and put on makeup because that's what she did every morning, and while she was dressed in jeans and a hooded sweatshirt, she suspected they were brands you could not get at any store Up North. She washed her hands and wondered if she should buy a camo baseball cap to fit in. Of course, where she was going it wouldn't matter. She wouldn't be seeing many people, and of those she did see, she guessed that at least half would be young professionals like her, dabbling a bit in nature, thinking that a walk in the woods would solve their problems.

Olivia knew better. Problems like hers couldn't be solved.

She snagged an iced tea out of the cooler and passed a rotating case of hunting knives on her way to the counter. A knife. She'd forgotten to buy a knife at the sporting goods store at the mall when she was stocking up on gear for the trip. She didn't know exactly what she might need one for. She only knew that if she didn't have one, a need would present itself. She looked over the knives on offer, eliminating those with Confederate flags, divisions of the Armed Forces, or nationalist sentiments on the handle, until all that was left to choose from were animals. Whitetail deer, black bear, turkey, wolf, fish. A fish would do.

"Excuse me," she said to the woman behind the counter, "could I get the knife that says brook trout?"

The woman opened the case and extracted the knife Olivia pointed out. "You should get the one with the salmon," she said. "Salmon run's started."

Olivia just smiled and held out her credit card. She'd never cared for that half-crazed look of a spawning salmon—the eyes desperate, the scales turned a bloody red, the upper jaw looking for all the world like the thing would be screaming if only it had vocal cords.

"I guess you want the one with the state fish," the woman said, then she narrowed her eyes. "Where are you from?"

"East Lansing."

She nodded. "Heading to the cottage one last time for the year?"

"Hiking."

The woman looked her up and down and sort of shrugged, as if to say that the fact some suburban girl in designer jeans was going hiking wasn't her business, but she wouldn't be surprised when the front page of next Sunday's paper sported a headline about a dead hiker. Natural selection and all.

"Around here? Or are you headed to the Upper Peninsula?"

"The UP, yes," Olivia said. She wished the woman would just ring up the knife and be done with it. A line was beginning to form behind her, though the clerk didn't seem to notice.

"Pictured Rocks?" the woman said.

Olivia winced. "No." She lowered her voice. She didn't really want to announce to a bunch of strange, burly men what remote place with no cell service she was headed for. "My sister and I are hiking the Porcupine Mountains."

"Hoo! The Porkies!" she all but shouted. "I hope you're ready for that." Then she gave Olivia a look that told her she was clearly not ready for that.

"We know what we're doing," Olivia said more tersely than she meant to. "We've hiked before."

The woman shook her head and finally rang her up. Olivia snatched up her things and headed for the exit.

"Watch out for bears!" the woman yelled.

Back at the car, she tucked the knife into a small compartment in her pack and looked at her smartwatch. 12:18. Melanie had not called or texted. She pulled both packs out and leaned them against the car, carefully so as not to scratch the finish. Though the trip had been Melanie's idea, Olivia had thought it best if she did the planning and the packing. It took her much of the summer, fitting it here and there into the cracks in her frenetic schedule. Mel's pack was lighter for the moment but would weigh more once she added her clothes and food, both of which Olivia would inspect before they set off, to ensure that

Melanie had adhered to the list she'd sent her back in July. She was about to lock the car when she spied the corner of something beneath the seat. She pulled it the rest of the way out.

The map. She had almost left the map behind.

Sure, they would have trail maps at the welcome center, but not like this one. Olivia had ordered it months ago. It was waterproof and tear-resistant, and she'd augmented it with additional details, clearly marking the trails they were going to take in pen. She'd emailed a scan of the map to her boss because she'd read that you should always make it known to others where you plan to hike and when you plan to return, so that if for some reason you *didn't* return, people would know where to look for you.

Her stomach churned at the almost oversight, and she had to sit down. Maybe the woman behind the counter was right to be skeptical.

"Ollie!" came a chipper voice, and Olivia looked up to see her little sister, strawberry blonde curls bouncing as she all but skipped up to the car. "I'm so excited to see you!"

Olivia stood to give Melanie a hug, keeping the map clenched firmly in her hand. Melanie squeezed her so tight her back cracked.

"Yikes!" Melanie said as she pulled away. "We need to take care of that!" She spun Olivia around and began to knead her shoulders. "You're all tied up."

Olivia shrugged away. "No point in fixing it now. I'll feel a lot worse in a few days."

Melanie dropped her hands for just a moment before crushing Olivia in a second hug. "I just can't believe I finally get to see you! It's been way, way too long."

Olivia felt her throat tighten. The last time she'd seen Melanie was during the funeral and the week of dazed shock afterward. Now all of the emotions of that time—the fathomless grief, the exhaustion, the enormity of their shared loss—rushed in like a dammed river reasserting itself against the puny will of humankind. She gripped her sister with a ferocious possessiveness that surprised her—then she remembered the reason she'd avoided Melanie for so long. She let go and took a step back. "Let's get these in your car. Did you already get gas?"

"I've got plenty of gas. I'm only twenty miles from here."

Olivia looked at her watch but said nothing. They lugged the packs over to Melanie's car, and Olivia started pawing through a reusable grocery tote in the back seat. "What's all this?"

"What?"

"This." She dug around. "Where's the cheese? Where are the little packages of chicken salad and tuna I put on the list? And no jerky? How are you going to get enough protein?"

Melanie started tucking things back into the bag. "I'm a vegan. You know that."

"A vegan? No, I didn't know that." Olivia felt herself looking at her sister the same way that dubious clerk had looked at her. "Did you at least stick to the clothing list?"

"I have what I need."

"And everything's in Ziploc bags?"

"No."

"No?"

"I didn't want to use all that plastic. It's wasteful."

"What if it rains?"

"I checked. It's not supposed to rain. Anyway, aren't the packs waterproof?"

"They're water-*resistant*. But if they're outside all night, they're going to get damp. Even if it's just with dew."

"It'll be fine."

Olivia took a deep breath. "Let's just get going. We still have a six-hour drive ahead of us, and we're behind schedule as it is."

"Okay," Melanie said. "I just have to use the ladies' room."

She walked off—no, *ambled* off—toward the gas station. As unhurried as ever. When they were kids, Melanie was forever lollygagging behind, interested in a puddle or a rock or her own belly button. Olivia would be waiting on her little sister to catch up all week.

It felt like an hour before Melanie reappeared, but that was probably just because Olivia checked the clock so many times.

"Okay, let's go," she said when Melanie finally got in the driver's seat. "Just head north on I-75 and I'll tell you where to go from there."

"I know how to get to the Upper Peninsula, Olivia."

"I know you do. Sorry." Olivia shrugged. "Once a bossy big sister, always a bossy big sister."

Melanie pulled out of the parking spot and clicked on her left blinker.

"The highway is right," Olivia said, pointing. "It's right there. You can see it."

"I thought we could go to the Cross in the Woods shrine first," Melanie said, eyes gleaming and expectant.

"Why on earth would you ever want to go there?" Olivia said. "Did you become a Catholic?"

"No, but I try to make it a point to do something Catholic every couple months."

"What? Why? No, never mind. It doesn't really matter. We don't have time for it."

"But it's just three minutes away," Melanie said. "I passed it on the way here."

"Well, maybe you should have gotten on the road earlier so you could see it before you were supposed to meet me, which was at noon, by the way, not 12:45. You obviously didn't even leave your house until *after* noon. Now it's almost an hour later than I had us scheduled to get on the road. And we still have to stop for dinner, and we're not going to get to the motel until after eight o'clock, if we're lucky."

A car honked behind them. Melanie switched to her right blinker and turned right.

"Besides," Olivia said, "there's no popping in with Catholics. You're either in or you're out. No in between. Remember when we'd sleep over at the O'Neils' and have to go to Mass with them? We never knew what was going on, and we weren't allowed to do the bread and wine thing because we weren't Catholic."

Melanie pulled onto the highway and drove in silence for a moment. "I did leave before noon," she finally said. "I had to stop on the way to get a turtle out of the road. And then I had to upload the video to my YouTube channel."

Olivia bit her tongue. While she had been waiting, Melanie had been uploading a video of herself saving a turtle?

"It's already got a bunch of comments," Melanie continued.

And that was why she had taken so long inside the gas station. She'd been checking to see how many people liked her.

It didn't matter, Olivia told herself. What's done is done and can't be undone—the phrase her mother used to say any time

Melanie broke one of her toys or ruined one of her books or tore one of her shirts. The phrase Olivia repeated to herself whenever she thought of what happened to her parents. What's done is done and can't be undone.

"I'm glad the turtle is okay," she said.

Melanie smiled. "Me too."

Two

MELANIE'S HEART QUICKENED when the first tower of the Mackinac Bridge came into view. This would be her seventh time over the bridge, a significant number. Seven days of the week. Seven notes in the diatonic scale. Seven letters in the Roman numeral system. The seven in the Tarot deck was the card of the chariot—the symbol of overcoming conflict and moving forward in a positive direction. Lucky number seven. She'd need luck on this trip if she hoped to move forward in a positive direction with Olivia.

She hit her sister's upper arm with the back of her hand. "There's the bridge!"

To her surprise, Olivia smiled. A good sign. Maybe it would all work out. It had to. Because they couldn't go on as they had for the past ten years. Something had to change. Only time together would do it. Time with no distractions. Time in the forest. Time for Melanie to explain herself. She had seven days to make it work. Seven days was enough. Her seven-day spiritual detox program was her most popular offering on *Meditations with Melanie*. And nothing needed detoxing like her relationship with her sister.

"I know a bailiff who refuses to cross big bridges," Olivia said. "He'll drive miles out of his way to avoid it. If he were going to the UP, he'd have to drive all the way around Lake Michigan and come in through Wisconsin."

"Why doesn't he just use the assistance program?" Melanie said. "Someone who works for the bridge authority will drive your car across for you if you're uncomfortable with it."

"I guess he's too afraid for even that. It's weird. He can't remember anything bad that ever happened to him on a bridge, he's just always been scared of going over them."

"I wonder if he's tried hypnosis to cope with his fears."

Olivia laughed. "No, I don't think he's tried hypnosis."

"It works for a lot of people."

"I'm sure it does." Olivia shifted in her seat. "Man, my hip is killing me."

"What's wrong with it?"

"Nothing. Just sore from sitting so long. It'll be fine."

Melanie slowed to forty-five miles per hour and pulled into the left lane. She would have preferred to drive in the right lane closer to the breathtaking expanse of blue water beneath her, but with big trucks required to go no faster than twenty and with Olivia already touchy about the time, she decided it was better to be fast than fascinated. If she got stuck behind a semi for five miles at twenty miles per hour, Olivia would probably have a stroke.

"You know, bridges are an important symbol in a lot of different belief systems," Melanie said. "They can be about crossing over from life to death. They can be about finding connection with one another. In a Tarot deck they can symbolize spanning the gap between misery and harmony. And they work either way. So if bridge cards start showing up in readings, it doesn't necessarily mean something bad or something good. It all depends on where your life is moving. Either we are moving toward misery or toward harmony in our lives."

"Yeah," Olivia said, "or they can be about the fact that we need one piece of land to connect to another piece of land so we can get a car across it."

Melanie bit the inside of her cheek. "How about some music?"

"Sure."

Olivia punched the button for the CD player. After a moment of silence, the sound of a solo acoustic guitar rang out, joined a moment later by a cello. Then a powerful female voice singing about rain and wind and absence and regret. Mel glanced over at her sister. Olivia's eyes were closed, just the way their father's had always been when he listened to loud music in the living room after a hectic day at work. But the face Mel saw was their mother's. Broad forehead, sensible nose, strong jawline. Olivia had their mother's straight brown hair and solid build. She had her no-nonsense attitude and her drive. She was in all ways fierce and formidable. The ultimate big sister.

Well, almost. The ultimate big sister wouldn't have left when Melanie needed her most.

As the last bittersweet notes of the song rang out, the car left the metal grate of the suspension bridge and the tires hit the concrete. Melanie and Olivia reached out to turn off the CD player at the same time and shared a smile. There were some songs that just needed to ring in your ears for a while.

"I haven't heard that since . . ." Olivia trailed off.

Melanie lowered her window to pay the toll. She handed the clerk four dollars, beat him to saying "Have a nice day," and pulled back out into traffic. She had driven perhaps a quarter mile before she realized Olivia never finished her sentence.

"When was the last time you heard that song?" she prompted.

"Do you have other CDs in here?"

Melanie allowed the deflection. She could guess the answer. "Back of your seat."

For the next forty-five minutes, Olivia played DJ as they drove west along the north shore of sparkling Lake Michigan. The CDs she put into the player had all once been part of their parents' collection, parceled out between the two sisters along with the photo albums, the jewelry, the books, and some of the furniture. Melanie relaxed into the soundtrack of her childhood and entered an almost meditative space, adrift in memories of times lost.

The road continued straight, the lakeshore curved away south, and they headed into the alternating pasturelands and scrub forest of the interior. Here the trees had more color than they did in the northern reaches of the Lower Peninsula. The varied green of the pines, spruces, and firs stood out against a tapestry of yellow and orange, with the occasional red thrown in like a garnish of flame. Fields of grazing dairy cows and wide wetlands playing host to migrating geese and herons occasionally broke up the monotony of the trees. Overhead a pair of sandhill cranes flew low and slow, heading south for the cold season ahead.

It was beautiful.

"I've sent a bunch of people to prison up here," Olivia said. "Not sure it's much of a punishment."

Melanie shook herself out of her reverie. "You look at all this gorgeous nature and that's where your mind goes? Prison?"

She shrugged. "It just popped into my head. It's the only connection I have to the UP."

"No it isn't," Melanie said.

"I don't like to think about that trip."

Melanie paused, picking her next words carefully. "The trip wasn't the problem."

"I don't want to talk about it. I know it helps some people to talk about things like that—I know it helps you—but that's just not me."

"I know. It's fine. We'll talk about something else."

But neither, it seemed, knew what that something else should be. They drove along in silence for a few minutes more.

"This is your turn up here," Olivia said, looking up from the paper map on her lap and gesturing at the upcoming intersection. "Turn right."

Melanie pointed the car north. Overhead, birds of prey soared on thermals. That, at least, was safe to talk about. "Look, a bald eagle. I see hawks and eagles all the time. Every time I leave the house, I see one. I think it must have something to do with my aura. Like they can sense a kindred spirit or something."

Olivia leaned forward and looked out the window. "That's a vulture."

"What? No, it's a bald eagle."

"That?" she asked, pointing.

"Yes."

"That's a vulture. If those are following you around, I think you may want to reexamine your aura. But I'm guessing you just see them a lot driving because of the roadkill."

Melanie craned her neck to keep the bird in sight. It couldn't be a vulture. She saw those all the time. They were eagles.

"Watch the road," Olivia snapped.

Melanie felt a stab of panic when she saw she had veered over the center line, and she overcorrected. She took a breath, let it out slowly, centered herself. Everything was okay.

"Do you want me to drive so you can look at the scenery?" Olivia said.

"No," Melanie mumbled. How could they be vultures? Settling her eyes back on the horizon, she saw a bank of gunmetal gray approaching from the northwest. "I think it's going to rain."

Olivia looked up from the map again. "Yep. Let's gas up at Seney so we don't have to do it later in a downpour."

"How far is it?"

"Not more than ten minutes, I should think."

Melanie looked at the gathering storm. "I hope we make it."

Three

IN ADDITION TO GAS at fifty cents more a gallon than downstate, the little gas station on the outskirts of Seney offered a wide selection of animal pelts slung over the railing by the door. Olivia ran her hand over each one as Melanie pumped the gas. No matter what the animal—deer, coyote, fox, raccoon, skunk—they all had a rough overcoat for protection and a soft undercoat for warmth. Like her and her sister. Melanie the soft and loving, she the stiff and repellent. No matter how she had tried to change that about herself, she always came up short.

She warned the clerk inside about the coming rain. He snapped his fingers at a young man, who sprang into action gathering up the furs and disappearing with them into a back room.

"Sorry," the clerk said to Olivia, "did you want to buy any?"

Olivia politely declined and asked where the bathroom was. When she walked back outside, Melanie was walking in.

"I'm glad he took those pelts away," she said. "I have to go so bad, but I wasn't getting within ten feet of those poor things."

Olivia rolled her eyes, then looked at the sky. "Hurry up. We're going to get dumped on any minute now."

She got into the driver's seat as Melanie disappeared inside the store. The first drops of rain hit hard and fat on the windshield and were quickly followed by more. Minutes later, Melanie ran out and tried to get in the driver's seat before realizing Olivia was already there. She ran around to the other side, shoulders hunched against the steady rain, and practically fell into the passenger seat and slammed the door.

"Sheesh! That came on fast. I'm already soaked."

Olivia looked at her. "It's not that bad."

Melanie shook a shower of water out of her curls.

"Hey!" Olivia said. "You're getting the map wet."

"Relax." Melanie laughed. "We've got GPS."

"Not for long. Can't depend on it where we're going."

"You're driving?"

"What's it look like?"

"Looks like you're driving. Better you than me. I hate driving in the rain."

"Me too, but it's better than having to ride when someone else is driving." Olivia headed west into the storm. Maybe they would get lucky and drive through it rather quickly. "Can you get a radar map on your phone right now?"

"I can try." Melanie started tapping at her phone as the rain intensified. "Not much for a signal."

"See?" Olivia squinted into the curtain of rain and slowed the car. "Never mind. We have to drive through it either way." She looked at the speedometer and sighed. So much for making up time lost to Melanie's turtle.

The CD player remained off as Olivia concentrated on the road. Which was fine with her. It had been pleasant at first to hear all of those songs from when she was a kid and a teenager. From before everything in her life changed irrevocably. But after Melanie mentioned that trip—the last trip she'd taken to the Upper Peninsula, and the last one she had ever meant to take until that stupid warm day in March—she knew she couldn't listen to any more old songs and keep her composure, which she was determined to do. Other people might burst into nostalgic tears at the drop of a hat, but she was not one of those people. What's done is done and can't be undone.

The storm gave her something else to focus on. The closer they got to Lake Superior, the worse the weather got. Olivia could feel the wind trying to nudge the car off the road. She considered stopping to wait it out, but the numbers on the clock had her pressing on.

Not long after they passed through Munising, Olivia saw flashing lights in her rearview mirror, though she couldn't hear any sirens over the pounding rain. She pulled to the side of the road and let a state trooper pass. A minute later it was followed by another. Then an ambulance, then a fire truck. With each emergency vehicle, Olivia's stomach dropped a little further and the lump that had formed in her chest rose up her throat until it was sitting on her voice box.

"Something awful must have happened," Melanie finally said.

Olivia stared straight ahead and put all of her energy into focusing on the gray line of the road that could just be distinguished from the varying grays of the skies above, the lake to their right, and the rain all around. The colorful drive had turned dark and dull, and the only bright spots were the headlights and taillights of other cars and the spinning lights of the first responders.

On a fairly straight stretch of road along the Lake Superior shoreline, Olivia slowed to a crawl of less than five miles per hour. A cluster of flashing lights marked the spot where all of the emergency vehicles had converged. In the center of it all was a motorcycle on its side and a man facedown in the street. Olivia gripped the wheel tighter. Melanie covered her mouth with her hand. Was this what the scene had looked like at their parents' accident? It had been raining then too.

A drenched police officer held up a hand. Olivia stopped the car and waited for clearance to go. With every second that eked by in view of the man in the street, she felt her heart rate tick up, up, up. She risked a glance at Melanie, and the panic left in a whoosh. Her sister was looking into her phone and fixing her hair.

"What are you doing?" Olivia said, incredulous.

"Shh. Just be quiet a minute." Melanie tapped the screen, waited a beat, then started to talk. "Hello out there, my Mellies. This is Melanie Greene at a moment of crisis, coming to you on behalf of a fellow sojourner who needs your help. As I film this, a man lies in the street in the pouring rain. There's been an accident. First responders are on the scene, but it's not clear from where I sit if the man is dead or alive. If he is alive, he is most certainly unconscious. He does not have a helmet on. I'm asking you right now, wherever you are, to stop what you're doing and start to pray. Send your prayers up to heaven, send your good vibes and warm thoughts to this man. Whatever goodness and positive feeling you have, project it out toward Michigan's Upper Peninsula, which is where I am right now, and I'll help channel it all into this man. We may never know the outcome—the officer is telling us to move ahead—but the Universe will. And the Universe works in mysterious ways."

Olivia stared open-mouthed as Melanie made a peace symbol at the camera and then blew it a kiss.

"Remember, my Mellies, you control your destiny. Peace, love, and life to you." She clicked off the camera and started swiping at the screen.

"What. Was. That?" Olivia said.

"Go," Melanie said, motioning to the officer who was now approaching the car.

Olivia waved an apology and crept forward past the flashing lights. Melanie continued to fiddle with her phone.

"We need to get somewhere with better reception," Melanie said. "How far are we from Marquette?"

Olivia struggled to keep her tone even. "What were you doing just now? Were you just using a quite-possibly-dead man to up your YouTube numbers? What is wrong with you?"

"Of course not," Melanie said, obviously offended. "I was using my already very high number of viewers to help *him*. I would have thought that was obvious."

Olivia let out a skeptical little puff of air. "Good vibes and warm thoughts? That's what you think will help this guy? Whatever hope he has of ending this day in a hospital bed rather than in a locker in the morgue is standing around him in uniform. Positive energy from your Mellies, whatever those are, has nothing to do with it."

"Look, I don't want to argue about this right now. Can you please just get us to Marquette? I need to upload this as soon as possible."

"I can't believe you of all people could think that thoughts and prayers have any effect at all."

"I said I don't want to argue about it," Melanie said with more force.

Olivia bit off her next reply. When they were children, she knew just how to get a rise out of her little sister. She'd always loved an argument. It was why she became a lawyer. But she didn't want to fight with her sister now. She wished they got along better, and she knew that a lot of their problems were probably her own fault. She was really the only person she knew who didn't get along with Melanie, the most get-alongable person in the world.

For now, she would put all her energy into getting them to Marquette. For dinner, which she suddenly realized was way overdue, and for whatever flaky purpose Melanie had in perpetuating the archaic belief that there was a god or a force or some greater meaning to the universe, something that cared about what happened to the billions of inconsequential humans walking around on this indifferent planet.

But mostly for dinner.

Melanie sat on the living room floor, hugging her knees in her plaid flannel pj's and staring intently at the glittering pile of reds and greens, golds and silvers. Outside, the world was still dark. Inside, the room glowed with light and anticipation.

"Just tell me one," Melanie said to Olivia, who was seated in the wingback chair, pretending to read the newspaper, pretending not to care about the presents beneath the tree.

"No."

"Come on, Olivia," Melanie pleaded. "If you tell me one of mine, I'll tell you one of yours."

Olivia turned the page. "No."

Melanie picked up a box and shook it. Olivia put the newspaper down on the coffee table and knelt next to her sister. "I know what that one is," she teased.

"Tell me," Melanie said, eyes alight with that special mania that comes over children on Christmas morning.

"No," Olivia said with a smug smile. "You're going to find out soon anyway."

Melanie flopped onto her back. "They're taking forever!"

Olivia tucked the box back under the tree and picked up one of her own.

Melanie sat up. "I know what that *one is."*

Olivia had her own suspicions, but she was trying not to get her hopes too high. If she was wrong and the box didn't contain a Tamagotchi—if it was the cheaper knock-off Giga Pet that would solidify her status in her friend group's second tier, for instance—she'd still have to act pleased when she opened it. She handed Melanie the box she'd just been shaking.

"Okay," Olivia said, her voice as official and older-sistery as she

could make it. "I won't tell you what it is, *but I will answer three yes-or-no questions about it. And then you have to do the same for this one."*

Melanie spun to face her, sitting as close to her as possible without actually landing in her lap. Olivia scooted back a few inches. Melanie scooted up.

Olivia put her hand out to stop her. "Okay, ready?"

"Ready."

"Ask me a question."

"What is it?"

Olivia rolled her eyes. "No, a yes-or-no question. Like, can you wear it, or something."

"Can you wear it?"

"No."

Melanie frowned in thought. "Is it a toy?"

"Yes."

She bounced up and down on her flannel-clad butt. "What is it?"

"No, that's not a yes-or-no question," Olivia said, exasperated. "Ask if it has batteries."

"Does it have batteries?"

"No. That's three. My turn."

Melanie collapsed onto her side and bounced back up again. "No fair!"

"It is so. We said three questions. That was three questions."

"But—"

"My turn."

Melanie scowled. "Fine."

Olivia held up the gift in question. "Is it electronic?"

"Yes," Melanie mumbled.

"Is it Japanese?"

"What?"

"Is it Japanese?"

"I don't know."

"What do you mean you don't know? You said you knew what it was."

"I don't know that.*"*

Olivia huffed. "Fine, that question doesn't count."

"Do you want to know where it came from?"

"Yes!"

"Oh, it came from Meijer."

"Not the store*!"*

"Yes, I was there when Mom bought it at Meijer."

Olivia put her face in her hands. "Never mind. Forget that one."

"Okay, you get one more."

"Two more."

"No, I told you it's electronic and it came from Meijer." Melanie ticked off the short list on two fingers.

"Fine." Olivia thought hard. She needed to ask a question that her little sister would actually know the answer to. "Can it die?"

Melanie laughed. "No! It can't die*. It's electronic, silly."*

"What's going on in here?" Olivia and Melanie's father shuffled into the room, followed by their mother. They were both in robes and slippers, hair mussed, eyes half closed.

"I'll make some coffee," their mother said.

Their father flopped onto the couch. "Do you girls know what time it is?"

"It's Christmastime!" they shouted in unison.

Melanie leaped on top of him. He shot an arm out and wrapped it around Olivia, dragging her into the pile. Both girls squealed and giggled and tried to get away. He let them go and called out to his wife in the kitchen. "Excedrin?"

"On it," she replied.

A few minutes later, Mom and Dad were snuggled up on the couch, steaming mugs in hand, while Olivia and Melanie scrambled around on the floor, finding and distributing presents, setting aside the ones that would be brought to their grandparents' house later that day. When the piles were all made, the girls looked expectantly at their parents.

"Okay," their dad said. "One at a time. Starting with . . ." He moved his finger slowly across the room. "Mom."

The girls deflated for just a moment. Then Olivia grabbed a present off her mom's pile. "Do this one first."

Melanie jumped up. "Yes, we made that one for you!"

Their mother plucked the bow from the box and tore the paper away. Inside the small, square box sat a pinecone stuffed with cotton and adorned with an orange triangle and two black and yellow circles of construction paper.

"It's an owl!" Melanie said.

"I see that. It's lovely!" Their mother held it aloft by the string attached to the top, and it turned slowly in the air.

"It's for the tree," Olivia explained.

"I found the pinecone," Melanie said.

"And I cut out the eyes and the beak," Olivia said. "And I tied the string."

Their mother handed it to Melanie. "Hang it on the tree for me."

Melanie bounded across the room and hung the owl directly in front of another ornament.

"Come here," their mom said, and she gathered them into her arms. "That was so thoughtful of you two. Thank you. I love it."

For just a moment, all four of them were on the couch in a tight, warm ball.

"Okay," their dad said. "Who's next?"

Four

MELANIE SAT IN THE BATHROOM stall and finished uploading her video. Whatever Olivia thought of her motives, she knew they were pure. If Olivia had devoted her life to justice, Melanie had devoted hers to encouragement. And for every criminal Olivia had sent to prison, Melanie could count hundreds of people she'd helped through hard times. For all she knew, one of those people her sister had prosecuted now watched *Meditations with Melanie* to cope with their new situation in life.

Upload complete, she returned to the table where Olivia was perusing the menu.

"Might be a good idea to eat big tonight," Olivia said. "Last chance for real food for a while."

Melanie searched the menu in vain for the *V* for vegan symbol and then started back with the salads. She was used to building her own vegan meals at restaurants. Even though most chain restaurants were quite accommodating nowadays, local joints Up North were still hit or miss unless they were run by Millennials. After Olivia ordered a steak, medium rare, with buttered mashed potatoes and green beans, Melanie started in on her order: garden salad, no croutons, olive oil and vinegar on the side, with a couple lemon wedges and a plain baked potato. Yes, plain, thank you. No, no butter, no cheese, no sour cream. Yes, just plain.

"I can bring you butter on the side," the waitress said. She had a concerned look on her face, as though she was responsible somehow for Melanie's well-being and the only thing that would ensure that well-being was some sort of dairy product.

"No, thank you."

The waitress left, shaking her head, and Melanie was sure that she would bring butter anyway.

When Mel looked back across the table at Olivia, her sister was already looking at her.

"Hey," Olivia said, "I'm sorry I freaked out a bit back there."

Melanie nodded. "It's fine. I know we don't see eye to eye on stuff like that."

"Yeah, but I shouldn't have made that big of a deal about it. You've never come into a courtroom during a trial and given me your two cents about how to do my job, and I shouldn't have put my nose in where it didn't belong in your job. That is your job, right?"

"Partly," Melanie said. "I do make money off the YouTube channel from ads, but mostly it helps me market my detox packages and my life coaching services."

Olivia nodded, but Melanie had had enough experience with this to tell when she was being judged. Her sister thought she was a flake or a hippie or maybe even just garden-variety dumb. But Melanie had seen how her words changed people's lives. She made people happy, and that was all that mattered.

"So is being vegan a part of the detox or something?" Olivia asked.

"It's what I advocate in my program. Some people just do it for a span of thirty or sixty days. Some make a permanent lifestyle change because they lose weight and they just feel so much better and more energetic."

"That can't be why you do it though. You've never needed to lose weight."

"No." Melanie fiddled with her utensils.

"Okay, so is it a moral thing? Like an animal cruelty thing?"

"Not exactly." Melanie smoothed her napkin on her lap. "I started thinking about reincarnation, and I got . . . anxious. About Mom and Dad."

Olivia's eyebrows practically met above her narrowed eyes. "What do you mean?"

Melanie looked her plain in the face. "I didn't want to accidentally do anything to Mom or Dad."

"You mean . . . eat them?"

Olivia was looking at her like she was the dumbest person she knew. She should have listened to the voice inside her that had been telling her to just lie to her sister. But lies brought negative energy and bred more lies, like how one fruit fly somehow led to dozens. It was better to tell the truth, even if it made you look foolish.

"Okay, let me get this straight," Olivia said, and she began counting off on her fingers. "You believe in reincarnation, and that good vibes and positive energy can help people you don't know miles away from you, and also in prayer, and you do Tarot readings, and you try to do something Catholic every couple months. Am I missing anything? I'm not trying to be mean here, I'm just trying to understand. What's the basis of your belief system?"

Melanie leaned back as the waitress put their food on the table. She picked up the little dish of butter next to her potato and handed it to Olivia. "The basis of it?" she said, buying time.

"Yes, what is it based on? Like, Christians base their beliefs on the Bible, Jews base their beliefs on the Torah, Muslims base their beliefs on the Quran, Native Americans base their beliefs on an oral tradition. So what are your beliefs based on? I'm seriously not trying to be mean. I just don't get it."

"No, I know you're not. Believe me, I can tell when you're trying to be mean."

They shared a hesitant laugh, and Olivia cut into her steak.

"I don't know," Melanie said, poking at her salad with her fork. "They're based on a lot of things. Things I've read and teachers I've heard and poems and documentaries and stuff like that."

"So, there's no one set of teachings or documents or traditions. You're just picking the stuff you like from everything that's out there. Like, cafeteria style."

Melanie took a big bite of her salad to give herself a moment to think. No one had ever asked her what she based her beliefs on before. It hadn't seemed to matter to any of her clients or people who attended her workshops or her online audience, her Mellies. Why did it matter to Olivia? Olivia who believed in nothing at all.

Melanie swallowed and took a sip of water. "I guess you could say that."

Olivia put down a forkful of potatoes. "But that's completely illogical. You can see that, right?"

"Why should it be?"

"Because of the law of noncontradiction. If one of those groups is correct, then everyone not part of that group is wrong. If Christians are right about having to believe in Jesus, then any other system of belief with other gods and other ways to heaven can't be right. Or if Buddhists are right about reaching nirvana, then the Christians can't be right. You see what I mean?" Olivia finally put the potatoes into her mouth, but she kept talking right around them. "You can't believe just a little bit of everything. And anyway, why bother? Why not just choose one?"

Melanie let that last question settle into her brain. "Frankly, I've never really seen the need to choose just one."

"But you can see how that doesn't work, right?" Olivia insisted.

Melanie shifted in her seat and changed tacks. "What do you think happened to Mom and Dad? Like, where do you think they are now?"

Olivia frowned. "At some point immediately following the accident, their hearts stopped, they stopped breathing, and their bodies shut down. The potential energy left in their cells after they died was used up as, well . . . as natural processes progressed."

"So in your opinion there's nothing left of them."

"Nothing." Olivia offered her a sad smile. "It's not that I wouldn't love to see them again. I just don't think I see any evidence of an afterlife."

Melanie leaned forward. "Okay, but what if you're wrong?

Then you'd miss your chance to see them again. That's why I try to follow all of these different belief systems. Because wherever they are, I want to be there someday."

Olivia's expression softened. "So, you're just covering your bases."

Melanie gave a little nod. "I guess so."

Her sister said nothing and focused on dismembering her steak.

Melanie finished her salad, the sound of her own chewing deafening in the general silence. One look at the dry baked potato made her feel ill. There was no way she could stomach all of that now. Not with her guts tied up like they were. She had always thought of herself as someone who lived life from a place of generosity and love. It had never occurred to her that something else might lie at the root of her magnanimous attitude toward the spiritual realm. Something that looked suspiciously like fear.

Five

IT WAS PAST 7:30 when the waitress finally came around with the bill. Even though Olivia had her credit card ready, she still had to all but shove the little plastic tray back into the waitress's hand to get her to run it immediately. At the rate they were going they wouldn't make it to Ontonagon until after ten o'clock. Had they been going to a big hotel in a major city, it wouldn't have mattered. But only a few cities in the Upper Peninsula even had big chain hotels, and Ontonagon wasn't one of them.

What awaited them was not room service and down pillows and streaming TV but a tiny one-room cabin with beds that had probably been there for forty years. Or rather, *bed*. They would be sharing, like they used to do on the hide-a-bed in the family room when Mom and Dad let them have a "sisters' sleepover" and fall asleep watching a movie.

Olivia explained their weather delay to the owner over the phone, and he graciously said that he'd be up until at least ten but that his wife went to bed at nine. If he was too tired to stay up, he would just leave the cabin unlocked with the key inside.

Olivia also called the park headquarters to ask about the trail conditions after the rain, but she had to leave a message.

The deluge had let up some while they were eating, and the dash to the car parked on the street outside was easier than the dash inside had been. Melanie's hair was curlier than ever in the wet air. As Olivia checked the rearview mirror for traffic, she saw that hers was flat and lifeless. She'd meant for both of them to take showers tonight so they'd be fresh for the morning and get out of the cabin as early as possible, but the long day of driving had taken a toll on her energy reserves, and she was sure she'd fall asleep as soon as her head hit the pillow.

As they left Marquette, the sky ahead was dark with clouds obscuring an early sunset.

The next two hours on the road were quiet. The rain was light yet persistent, and Olivia found it impossible to relax. She sat upright away from the seat back, gripping the steering wheel in both hands and scanning the edges of her headlights for eye-shine that would indicate a deer that might leap out in front of the car. She was used to city driving, which was never very dark and where the largest animal you might hit was a raccoon. Here in the sparsely populated western UP, even her brights couldn't illuminate enough for her tastes, and any time an oncoming car appeared, she had to turn them off.

She tried and failed to avoid thinking of her parents. It had been dark and rainy then too—for them at least. When it all happened, she and Melanie were far away, sleeping in tents along with four other friends, out of reach and out of touch on the backcountry trails of Pictured Rocks National Lakeshore. It had been warm and dry on the trail, and they were on their second of three planned overnights on the long Labor Day weekend. That day they had explored caves in the sandstone cliffs that had been carved out of the rock by the wave action on Lake Superior. They had splashed in the frigid water, baked in the warm sun, and marveled at the clear blue of the sky and turquoise of the lake. Everything was perfect.

It was sometime after they had roasted marshmallows over the campfire, Olivia figured later, that the accident occurred. That was when the six friends had coupled up—which had been Olivia's plan all along—and edged away from the firelight for a little privacy. She'd carefully chosen the group to include three potential couples with similar interests. She and Eric were both heading into their senior year of college and were into all the same bands. Melanie and Keith were both going to be sophomores and were artistic. And her friends Bryce and Lisa were both junior-year fitness nuts.

She'd never played matchmaker before, but like almost everything else she tried, she found she had a knack for it. It was all about taking what she knew about each person and projecting it into the future. What was cute and quirky now but would get nails-on-the-chalkboard annoying later? Which strengths could balance out which weaknesses? Could at least one person in every couple be reasonably expected to make a decent living? She'd thought of everything.

Before she could see her plan come to full fruition, she was found by a ranger and taken aside along with her little sister. She was startled at first to hear a perfect stranger ask her if she was Olivia Greene, but then she remembered that all of their names were on the campsite registrations for particular nights.

All a ranger had to do was look for her on the right part of the trail, which could be easily deduced by where they had slept the night before and where they planned to sleep that night.

She couldn't recall later exactly what the ranger said. The details were erased by the numb shock. All she knew in that moment was that her parents had been in an accident, that they had been taken to a hospital, and that she and Melanie needed to get home. The six of them silently followed the ranger down a two-mile access trail to his truck. They piled the packs in the back and squeezed seven people into seating for five, then he drove them back to Eric's Explorer.

The logistics of getting Olivia and Melanie home to Rockford and getting everyone else back to campus in Ann Arbor were ironed out with a few phone calls. The hikers would meet Olivia and Melanie's Uncle Craig in Lansing, and he would take them the rest of the way home. The others would continue on back to the University of Michigan. What no one told them until Uncle Craig had delivered them back to their house, where Aunt Susan and Grandma Ann were waiting, was that both of their parents had died from their injuries before they reached the hospital.

They were just . . . gone.

In the week that followed, the gray haze of grief colored everything. It obscured the faces of friends and family, dulled the sounds of conversations and eulogy and hymns. It settled into Olivia's spirit until her dreams, which were inevitably nightmares, felt more real than her waking hours. She felt as though she was slipping silently into a still pond and if she went all the way under she might never resurface.

Her solution was to get back to school as soon as possible. Her classes offered the distraction she needed. Melanie had gone the other direction. She dropped out of school, spent two years emptying and selling their childhood home with Aunt Susan's help, and then fell into a pretty severe depression that Olivia had never truly known the scope of, though Aunt Susan kept sending her emails that hinted at it and suggested that Olivia may want to get in touch with her little sister.

But getting in touch with Melanie meant having to face all of the emotions she had been avoiding. And it meant dealing with her rage over the fact that Melanie had betrayed them all by forgiving the guy who'd caused the accident and who'd walked away unscathed. Using law school as a convenient excuse, Olivia managed to avoid her family and her memories for years. Until Melanie came after her.

The move north to Petoskey helped Melanie begin to break out of the hold depression had on her, but even Olivia had to admit that it was starting a blog that really made the most difference. A blog that became a YouTube channel that became a life coaching business. Melanie got better and had apparently made it her mission in life to get other people better too.

Olivia knew that was what this trip was about. Melanie had arranged just the right combination of things to force Olivia to face the past—a long car drive, a remote hiking trip, music from their childhood in the CD player. In the end, Olivia had acquiesced to Melanie's harping. But she put her foot down on the location. Melanie had wanted to return to Pictured Rocks to finish the hike they had started ten years before. But there was no way Olivia would ever set foot on that trail again. She knew she'd recognize the exact spot where that ranger had appeared out of the trees to tell her the worst news she would ever receive. She would go hiking if it would get Melanie to leave her alone. Just not there. Never there.

They pulled up to the main-office cabin at 10:08 p.m. Though the rain had been lighter much of the way there, they'd hit another downpour a few miles from the motel.

"Stay in the car," Olivia said. "I'll check us in and get the key."

She dashed out, arms above her head to fend off the torrent, then yanked on the front door to no avail. A man of about sixty wearing a robe was rounding the front desk. He hurried to the door and turned the lock, ushering her in.

"Oh, come in, come in! I'm so glad to see you made it." He tugged lightly on Olivia's arm and shut the door behind her.

A woman, also in a robe, came out from behind the counter. "We were so worried."

Olivia wiped the wet hair from her face and was about to speak when she found that she couldn't. A lump had risen suddenly in her throat, and she felt—absurdly—like she was about to cry.

"Oh! You're soaked!" the woman said, rushing into action. She snatched a towel from the cupboard beneath the coffee maker and handed it to Olivia as the man pulled her farther into the room. "And you're limping, you poor thing."

She was?

"Where's your sister?"

Olivia pointed out the door. "Car," she managed. What was wrong with her? She stood in courtrooms with people who had done despicable things to their fellow human beings—deceptions, beatings, rapes, murders—and had never had a problem controlling her emotions. Why was it so hard to check into a stupid little cabin?

She took a deep breath. "We're here. And ready for bed."

"I bet you are," the man said. "Willa?"

The woman pulled a key from the wall behind the counter and pointed. "It's the third one down. The lights are on for you. Wanted you to be able to see it in the dark."

Olivia nodded. "I'm so sorry we kept you up. It wasn't my intention to arrive so late. I had it all scheduled out and—"

"Nonsense," the man broke in. "You can't schedule everything. Weather will have its way."

"Bernie, what about the road? Don't forget that," Willa said.

Bernie shook his head. "No, these girls are going west, to the Porkies, aren't you?"

"Yes," Olivia said, surprised to realize that she wasn't at all upset about this man referring to her as a girl. "What road?"

"It's nothing," Bernie said.

"It's not nothing," Willa protested. "Up in Houghton they've had roads washed clean away today by this storm. Had no rain all summer—dry as a bone out there—then all this rain all at once. Ground can't keep up with it."

"But they're not going to Houghton, they're hiking the Porkies," Bernie said. Willa seemed about to speak again, but her husband cut her off. "The road out there is fine. The trail may be another matter. But maybe it won't be so bad. It certainly was a dry season. Now let's let these girls get some sleep."

Willa gripped Olivia's hand. "Do be careful out there. I worry so much about hikers, especially if you don't have any men in your group."

Olivia laughed at that. "Oh, don't worry about us. We've managed so far without men. I'm sure we'll be just fine." She gave Bernie a wink, which he returned. "Well, I better get back out to my sister. Oh! When do I pay? We'll be getting out early tomorrow morning."

"We're up at six, dear," Willa said. "Now go get some sleep."

"Thank you, again, for staying up so late."

"No problem," Bernie said. He unlocked the door for her, and she rushed back into the car.

"Everything okay with the room?" Melanie said. "You were in there a long time."

"Yeah," Olivia said. "We just got talking. They're a nice couple."

At that moment she knew why she'd found it so hard to speak at first. Bernie and Willa looked to be about how old her parents would be now, and they had been up late, worried and watching for her and her sister to come in out of the storm.

Olivia quickly pulled the car away to where the floodlight could not illuminate her face and then idled slowly toward the third cabin on the left. She parked as close to the door as possible, glad she'd packed a separate bag for this overnight stay so she wouldn't have to lug her pack in through the rain. In less than a minute, she and Melanie were inside with their things, shaking the water out of their hair and taking in their new surroundings.

The room was small, only about the width of a double bed and two nightstands. Along one wall was the door to a tiny bathroom. Another wall was lined with a small refrigerator topped with a microwave, a narrow sink, a two-burner stovetop, and a petite table with two chairs, above which was a laughably out-of-place flat-screen TV. So maybe they did have streaming up here.

Olivia dumped her stuff on the table and turned on the TV. She didn't have to search for the local news and weather channel. It must be what everyone watched before they left for the day's adventures. Footage of the flooding up in Houghton was terrible, but it wasn't what she was looking for. She scanned the ticker for anything that included the Porcupine Mountains. She heard Melanie moving about behind her—using the bathroom, brushing her teeth, changing into pajamas. The ticker repeated itself three full times. Nothing new.

Finally, Olivia turned around to find Melanie snug under the covers, writing in a journal. She could read no anxiety on her little sister's face. In fact, Melanie smiled contentedly as she scribbled away.

"What are you writing?" Olivia said.

"Oh, just notes about the day." Melanie looked up. "Did the news have anything on that motorcycle accident?"

Olivia had nearly forgotten the accident. "I don't think so."

"I tried to see if I could find anything before we left Marquette, but the only articles about accidents were years old. And you know there had to be more than the one accident in all that rain. I don't understand how search engines work. Maybe there should just be one website where all accidents are reported and then followed up on, so you can find out what happened after the accident."

Olivia wished she would stop saying the word *accident*.

"It could be like the Weather Channel. But, like, the Accident Channel, you know?"

"I'm getting ready for bed." Olivia disappeared into the bathroom. Since she was already all wet, she might as well take a shower. The tiny stall was tight quarters for someone as tall as she was, and the well water smelled faintly of sulfur, but the towels were soft. She slipped into clean pj's and took a moment to savor the feeling. Soon she'd be grimier than she had been in many years.

When she came out of the bathroom, Melanie had switched from her journal to a book. Olivia got into bed and tried to look surreptitiously at the cover.

Melanie tipped the cover toward her. "It's about a man who hiked the Appalachian Trail solo after he lost his wife to cancer," she explained. "It's really good."

Olivia turned away and switched off the lamp on her side of the bed.

"Do you want me to turn this off?" Melanie said.

"No, you can read."

"Do you want me to read to you?"

"No. I'm going to sleep."

"Okay."

"Don't stay up too late," Olivia said. "I have my alarm set for seven o'clock. Enough time to check out, eat, and get to the park headquarters to check in when they open at eight. If you have to take a shower tomorrow morning, make it quick." She kneaded her pillow, laid her head down, and closed her eyes. Tomorrow would come quickly.

Sleep would not.

Six

MELANIE THREW THE CAR into park in the small dirt lot at the Government Peak trailhead and turned to her sister. "Here we are! Right on schedule."

Per Olivia's desires, they had rolled in to the Porcupine Mountains Wilderness State Park visitor center at 7:58 a.m. and were waiting outside the door when it opened at 8:00. They checked in, received their backcountry camping permit, and got an update on the weather—fine but on the cold side—and trail conditions—a bit soggy in places. The rivers and waterfalls would be running high, but nothing insurmountable. Melanie made the four-mile drive to the trailhead in silence as Olivia frowned over her map and made some last-minute notes. And then they were there.

"This is so exciting," Melanie said as they unloaded their packs and poles. Olivia had insisted they both have a set of hiking poles because they would technically be hiking in mountains, though anyone who had hiked in any major range would laugh at what Midwesterners considered mountains. According to Olivia, they'd scale one of the highest peaks in the park today, at a measly 1,850 feet.

An orange hatchback roared into the small gravel lot, parked at an obnoxious angle, and spit out three loud people and an empty beer bottle, which none of the three stooped to pick up. Two guys and a girl in their early twenties, dressed as though they were going to be Instagramming their trip.

"Day hikers," Olivia said with just a touch of derision. "Let's get moving fast so we don't have to hike near them."

The hatchback opened, revealing three brand-new packs. Not day hikers.

"Maybe we should let them go on ahead of us," Melanie suggested. "They look pretty fit."

"And we're not?"

"I mean, we're not decrepit yet, but it's not like we're running marathons or anything. And you were complaining about your hip."

Olivia approached the noisy trio. "Excuse me." No one heard her, or if they did they were ignoring her. "Excuse me!"

They stopped talking and looked at her like they'd never seen another human being before. "Yeah?" the girl said, challenge in her voice.

"Are you hiking the backcountry?"

"Yeah," one of the guys said.

"I'm just wondering if we might be going the same way," Olivia said, pulling out her map.

The guy gave his friends an eye roll and leaned in. "This where you're going? The stuff in pen?"

"Yes."

"We're going that way too. At first. Then we're skipping over this way to the lake." The other two already had their packs on, and the girl handed him his while never taking her narrowed eyes off Olivia. He pulled it on and snapped the belt across his stomach. "Why?"

"Just curious," Olivia said. She folded the map and headed back to Melanie's car.

The girl whispered something to the guys, and they all laughed. Then they headed into the forest.

"I guess that settles that," Olivia said. "We'll hike behind them and hope we don't catch up."

Melanie picked up the beer bottle and tossed it in the back of her car. "Little early in the day to be drinking, wouldn't you say?"

"Your car's going to smell like beer when we get back," Olivia warned. "But I guess there's no trash can, so . . ." She trailed off.

Packs were hoisted and straps were clicked into place, then Melanie locked the car and tucked her keys into a side pocket.

"You have your water, right?" Olivia said.

"Yes."

"And your food."

"Oh! No, wait."

Olivia sighed and dug Melanie's keys out of the pack. "What were you going to eat?"

"Calm down, we didn't leave it."

"We almost did." Olivia quickly transferred the food to the food bag and the food bag to the pack that was still on Melanie's back. "What about this box back here? What's in there?"

Melanie opened the other back door and grabbed the box before Olivia could open it. "Nothing. Just some stuff I wanted you to go through after the hike." She shoved it across the back seat, where it landed next to the beer bottle.

"What is it?"

"Just stuff. You'll see. Later. Let's get going. This trail isn't going to hike itself!"

Olivia locked the car and stuffed the keys back into the side pocket of Mel's pack. "Okay, disaster averted. Let's go." She started down the trail.

"Wait!" Melanie said, pulling out her phone. "We have to get a start-of-the-hike selfie."

"We do?"

"Yes, of course we do. Stop being so difficult. Take your sunglasses off."

"This better not end up on your website."

Melanie snatched the sunglasses off Olivia's face and positioned her by the sign for the Government Peak Trail, which indicated several destinations, including where they would sleep that night: Mirror Lake, 8 miles.

Melanie snapped several pictures, then swiftly thumbed through them. "Come on. Act like you want to be here." She snapped several more, pronounced them "workable," and turned off her phone to save the battery.

"Okay then, let's go. Sun sets at 7:32."

With Olivia in the lead, they started walking. The trail led gently up beneath a canopy of yellow birch and burnished maple. The forest floor was already littered with a mosaic of fallen leaves, and the underbrush was heavy with berries of red, white, and nearly black. Melanie took in the glorious colors, breathed in the sweet scent of decay, and felt lucky—no, blessed—to be in this exact place at this exact moment. A moment that would never come in exactly this way again.

On any other day, she would have stopped right then to record it in her journal—what she saw, what she heard, what she felt—so that she could go back to it someday when the darkness came creeping in from that place where it always lurked just outside her field of vision. Not that all of the moments she recorded were pleasant. Some were downright painful. In fact, of all the pages of the first journal she'd filled after her parents' accident, Melanie could count on one hand those that testified to anything other than complete despair. She wasn't sure she'd ever be able to return to that journal for solace, to relive those exhausting days of grief mingled with pragmatism, the bouts of crying over some item in the house and then having to decide what to do with it. Save, donate, discard. The slow dispersal of goods dragging out her grief along with it.

But then, journals weren't just about the happy days, and anything of significance got written down. Or perhaps some moments only became significant by virtue of being recorded. The particular patterns and colors of the leaves at this hour of this day probably weren't important in any sense that Olivia would understand. But to Melanie they marked the beginning of a sparkling new chapter in her relationship with her sister. The one in which Olivia would finally forgive her for the event she recorded at the end of that first journal. The unforgivable sin that had forever rent the fabric of their relationship.

Melanie hadn't noticed him at the committal service in the cemetery that day until Olivia pointed him out.

"What does he think he's doing here?" she'd said, her voice like granite.

Melanie followed her gaze to a young man standing in the

open passenger door of a car whose windshield still sported the neon-yellow price sticker typical of a certain echelon of used car lots. He was wearing sunglasses, though the day was cloudy, but Melanie recognized the wiry build, tattooed arms, and buzzed dark hair of Justin Navarro. Uncle Craig began walking toward the car, presumably to ask him to leave. But he didn't have to. Justin got into the car, and whoever was in the driver's seat drove away.

Later, on the pages of her journal, Melanie wondered why Justin had thought it appropriate to come and how long he had been there, skulking along the edges of their sorrow. She saw him the next week at the other end of the medicine aisle in the grocery store, and then at the thrift store the week after that, when she dropped off several bags of her father's clothes. He was thumbing through shirts, and she wondered if she might run into him someday in a parking lot and realize that he was wearing something of her dad's.

She'd decided right then that she needed to speak to him. That she couldn't go on seeing him in town, pretending nothing had happened when both of their lives had changed forever. Yes, it was awkward at first, and Melanie had to work hard to keep from crying, but that first tentative conversation ended with an agreement to meet for coffee the next day. One coffee led to another, which led to meeting once a week, during which the two of them would update each other on how they were doing emotionally and what was happening in their lives.

Over the course of the next few months, Melanie came to realize that she could not hate Justin Navarro the rest of her life as Olivia intended to. She had to let go in order to move on.

She told him she forgave him, and she recorded the moment later that day on the final pages of that first journal. Then she called Olivia at school to tell her and to encourage her to do the same. After a stunned silence followed by some sharp words, Olivia hung up on her. That was when Melanie knew that Justin didn't only take her parents from her, he took her sister as well.

Until now, if Melanie had anything to do with it.

The climb continued for maybe another thousand feet before it leveled out and they crossed a small wooden bridge.

"That's Cuyahoga Creek," Olivia announced. "The next bridge will be over the Upper Carp River."

From behind her, Melanie could barely make out the words, but she didn't really care all that much what the creek was called. It was sweet and talkative, and that was all that mattered. Jeweled trees leaned in toward the water, as though listening to the creek tell its particular story. She looked up to say as much to Olivia, but she was already several yards away, climbing up the next little hill.

Melanie followed, though at a deliberately slower pace. Olivia may have a schedule, but she did not. She was determined to enjoy every moment of this walk in the woods in her own way, at her own speed. It was how she had determined to live her life as well, one of the reasons she had moved north to the artsy little town of Petoskey, where she celebrated every season's unique offerings. The hot, windblown summers when the cries of seagulls mixed with the sounds of children on the beaches and the cracks of baseball bats in the park. The crisp, colorful autumns when the city emptied of tourists and the gales started out on Lake Michigan. The long, snowy winters of firelight and candlelight. And the fresh green springs when she would comb the beaches in search of the stones of fossilized coral that gave the city its name.

Here in this moment, in the Porcupine Mountains, Melanie celebrated the transitions she saw all around her, from the trees preparing for winter to the berries and seeds that would fatten up the birds and bears and stock the squirrels' larders. Everything was beautiful and magical. The only thing keeping it from being absolutely perfect was the fact that Olivia was walking too fast to notice it.

They traversed relatively even terrain for about a half mile until they came to an open space and the second bridge, where Olivia finally stopped to let Melanie catch up. "Grab my water for me?" she said.

Melanie pulled one of Olivia's two 32-ounce water bottles from the side of her pack and handed it to her, then she turned to let Olivia return the favor. Olivia drank sparingly. Melanie gulped down a third of the bottle in a matter of seconds.

"Whoa, slow down there," Olivia said. "Conserve."

"You have a filter, right?"

"Yes, but you can't get water just anywhere."

"We're literally standing above a river."

"Well, we're not stopping to filter here. We're not stopping until Trap Falls, where we'll take a short snack break, then we'll lunch on Government Peak, and you can't get water there. I wasn't planning on having to refill the bottles until we make camp tonight."

"If I need some when we stop at Trap Falls, we can just do it there."

Olivia sighed and held out her water bottle to Melanie to put it back in her pack.

"What's the big deal?" Melanie said, handing hers over. "If we're stopping anyway."

"I just don't want to spend a lot of time there, that's all."

"Why wouldn't you want to spend time at a waterfall?"

"Because it's only a quarter of the entire distance we have to travel today, and I don't want us to get off track so early in the trip. We're well rested, we're fresh, our muscles don't hurt yet. We need to make the most of that today because tomorrow we're not going to be feeling quite as good."

"Fine, but if you're not careful, you're going to catch up with those other people, and you clearly don't want to be anywhere near them."

Olivia said nothing, but her expression grudgingly acknowledged that Melanie was right. She started walking again, a little slower. Melanie retrieved her phone, took a few shots, and turned it off again. Then she soldiered on but still managed to focus on the positive. She was out in the beauty of nature with someone who sorely needed such beauty.

Not long after the bridge, they began a steady climb. The trail soon converged with the river they had crossed, which ran rushing and gurgling along in a gorge to their left in the opposite direction of their hike. The sound of it filled the air so that Melanie could no longer hear any breeze in the trees. She listened closely for patterns and variations, trying to discern what it was the river wanted to say to her. It had no schedule, no agenda. It ran and jumped and danced its days away with joyous abandon, whether anyone was there to see it or not.

Melanie felt a sudden and unexpected yearning to feel that free, to be utterly unaware and unconcerned with the results of her labors—to forget about views and likes and comments in order to make room for the sheer joy of being. It was the attitude she advocated for others but found difficult to cultivate in herself. With each step, each deepening breath that came with the effort of the constant uphill climb, Melanie felt more keenly the weight of the expectations she had placed on herself over the past ten years. The weight of being the perfect bereaved daughter, the manager of the estate, the dispenser of good advice, the bubbly online personality. She could feel her cheeks and ears getting hot, could feel her heartbeat in her temples, a trickle of sweat running down her neck. And still the top of the hill was out of sight and out of reach.

Just when she thought she couldn't take another step and would have to call out to her sister to stop so she could catch her breath, she ran into Olivia, who had already stopped ahead of her. Both of them were breathing hard, unable to speak. Wordlessly they retrieved the water bottles, and this time they both gulped, though Olivia still stopped herself before Melanie did.

"You're going to be all uneven," Olivia said. "Give me your other bottle." She reached into the matching pocket on the other side of Melanie's pack, then poured from one of the bottles to the other until the water was evenly distributed. Then she put both back in Mel's pack without asking if she was done drinking.

"Here, give me yours," Melanie said.

"No, it's fine. Just put this one back."

Melanie did as directed while Olivia consulted her map.

"We're about a third of a mile away from Trap Falls. We'll

take the packs off there and stop for a fifteen-minute break and have a snack."

"Good," Melanie said.

Olivia looked across the narrow river that was now at about the same elevation as they were. "This must be the way you go for the skiing and mountain biking trails."

"Which way?"

Olivia pointed across the river. "This way. That's Union Spring Trail across there."

"The bridge is out," Melanie said.

"No, there's no bridge. You have to ford it." Olivia turned to her. "You did bring water shoes like I told you to, right? They were on the list."

Melanie shook her head. "I didn't see the need."

"They wouldn't have been on the list if they weren't needed."

"I just figured why buy special shoes when I would never use them again. I'll just go barefoot."

Olivia squeezed her eyes shut. "I didn't want anyone slipping on slimy rocks and going down in a river, that's all. But, whatever. It can't be helped now." She hitched the pack up onto the top of her hips and tightened a strap. "Let's go."

They walked alongside the water, in and out of trees, the occasional leaf drifting down from the canopy to land on their path. Then they veered away from the river back into the woods. In a little while, Melanie could hear the waterfall—a rushing, murmuring *shhhh* off to her left that promised rest and peace and beauty. Then it was up ahead, tumbling white and black down a cascade of moss-covered rocks and ending in a swirling pool of water, foam, and yellow leaves.

[illegible] quickened her pace, unbuckling her pack as she [illegible] dumping it next to a crude wooden bench. She stood [illegible] of the pool, stretched her arms over her head, and brea[illegible] deeply, unfettered by the weight she'd been carrying. "This is gorgeous," she proclaimed, turning to Olivia. "I wish we could camp right here."

Olivia carefully leaned her pack on the other side of the bench and sat down. "It's supposed to be the best waterfall in the eastern half of the park. But we'll see lots more in the next couple days. That's how I chose our route. I wanted to see as many of them as we could. By the time we're done we'll have seen eight named falls. This will be the only one today."

She prattled on about the itinerary, but Melanie hardly heard her. She was taking off her shoes and socks and edging toward the water. Though it couldn't be more than fifty degrees out, her feet were hot and sweaty. She dipped them into the frigid flow of the Upper Carp River and closed her eyes, breathing slowly in through her nose and out through her mouth three times. Mesmerizing.

When she opened her eyes, she spotted movement up above the falls. A tawny back, a muscled leg, a long, ropelike tail. She stopped breathing. She looked again, harder. The shape was moving away. Melanie got to her feet, crouching, and put a finger to her lips to silence her sister.

Olivia stopped talking for a moment. "What?"

"Shhhh!" Melanie beckoned her with a finger, then held up a hand. A second later she straightened up. "Shoot. It's gone."

"What?"

"I think it was a cougar."

Olivia closed the distance between them. "It was probably a deer."

"No, it had a long tail."

"It was probably a deer," Olivia said again. "A cougar would have taken off running the second it heard us walking up, and if not, then definitely when we started talking."

"And a deer wouldn't?" Melanie challenged. "I know what a deer looks like and moves like, and this wasn't a deer. It was definitely a cougar."

"A second ago you said you *thought* it was a cougar. Now it's definitely a cougar?"

"It was a cougar."

Olivia looked at her a moment, then shrugged and turned back to the packs. "I guess, maybe. Anyway, whatever it was, it's gone now and we need to eat something."

Melanie looked back to where the creature had been. She had seen a tail, hadn't she? Olivia had already ruined her theory about hawks and eagles always showing up when she was around. Her sister was not going to ruin the fact that in the first hour and a half of the first day of their hike, she had been visited by an elusive big cat that had been the stuff of legends until the Department of Natural Resources finally confirmed that they were indeed reestablishing themselves in Michigan. Melanie decided to take it as an omen that her idea for the hike and for reconnecting with her sister and helping her to heal was the right one. That cougar was Olivia—powerful and solitary and elusive. Yet she was courting Melanie, slinking around the margins, wanting to be seen. All Melanie had to do was not scare her off.

She took some pictures of the falls, then put her socks and shoes back on and joined her sister on the bench. Olivia ate a little container of diced pears and a handful of trail mix while Melanie sampled from her bag of vegan granola. They sipped some water and watched the waterfall tumbling down the rocks.

"This is nice," Olivia said. She stood up and tucked her trash bag into her food bag and her food bag into her pack. "Let's get going."

Melanie reluctantly followed suit. She wished Olivia had planned less walking and more looking. That's how she would have planned the trip. But even though the hike had been her idea, Olivia had taken over the logistics. Just like when they were kids and Melanie had wanted to have a lemonade stand one summer. Olivia took over production and pricing and took all the fun out of it. Or when Melanie decided to go to the same college as her sister and Olivia took over registering her for classes and planning out what she should take each semester to get in all her requirements. Or when their parents died and Olivia took over the funeral planning, thus ensuring it would end up being embarrassingly short and strangely uncomforting. That was the one good thing about her abrupt return to college—it allowed Melanie to deal with the estate at a far healthier pace without her big sister's interference.

Soon Melanie's thigh muscles were burning again with the steady climb. The river arched to the left as they veered to the right, deeper into the golden woods. Melanie kept thinking of that cougar and all of the reasons it hadn't been a deer—the height, the heavily muscled back leg, the tail. It irritated her that Olivia didn't believe her. Did she think she was stupid? That she didn't know the difference between a cougar and a deer? Between predator and prey? Or that she was making it up entirely?

Finally, the argument got so heated inside her head that it boiled over to her mouth. "It's possible that the cougar didn't run off because it couldn't hear us over the sound of the waterfall."

Ahead of her, Olivia turned her head slightly but kept on walking. "I don't know about that. They have excellent hearing. I mean, they have to be able to hear their prey over the sound of water and wind and stuff. It seems really unlikely that if one was at that spot it wouldn't have heard us. And smelled us. And probably seen us with our completely non-camouflaged clothing."

"Okay, but a deer has even bigger ears," Melanie said between labored breaths. When would this incline end? "And a deer wouldn't have slunk away like this thing did. It would have bounded away, and I would have seen the white tail sticking up."

Ahead of her, Olivia tripped on a root but caught herself. "The deer might be used to seeing people."

Melanie pushed a branch out of the way. It snapped in the air behind her and hit the back of her pack. "In all these woods? I don't know about that."

"The wildlife use the trails," Olivia said. "Deer would likely come into contact with people, and certainly they would hear and smell them. And that loud little group had to have gone by not long before we did. I'm sure that would have scared off just about anything."

"It is completely plausible that I saw a cougar," Melanie persisted.

"Possible," Olivia corrected. "I wouldn't say plausible. More likely, if it wasn't a deer it was a coyote."

Melanie caught her foot on a rock and pitched forward, catching herself with a hand on a tree trunk. "Cougars and coyotes are nothing alike. Coyotes are dogs. Cougars are cats. You couldn't make up two more different creatures."

"Watch out," Olivia said as she pushed a branch out of her way and it came swinging back toward Melanie's face. "Man, it's getting close out here. This trail must not be used much."

Melanie stopped a moment and looked around. "Yeah, this is much narrower than before." She looked at her smartwatch. "We've gone over three miles since we started at the parking lot. Almost three and a half. How much further to this mountain peak?"

"It's 4.8 miles from the parking lot."

Melanie started walking again. "I'll definitely be ready for a break."

The trail had leveled off while they were arguing, and now as Melanie decided to let the cougar thing drop, the trail did the same, heading steeply downhill. She groaned. If they were heading up to one of the highest peaks in the park, they would most certainly be going back up just as steeply at some point. She was about to say as much when she heard Olivia far ahead of her say, "What the heck?"

Melanie quickened her pace and caught up to her sister, who was standing on the edge of a river, looking from the map to the river to the map again.

"This shouldn't be here," she said. "There's no river crossing before the peak."

Melanie took the map from her hands. "What do you mean?"

Olivia took it back. "I mean, there's no river crossing before the peak."

"Well, obviously there is," Melanie said, spreading her arms in front of her to indicate what was clearly a river they must cross.

Olivia poked at the map. "No, there is not. Look."

"That's what I was trying to do before you snatched it out of my hands." Melanie reached out for the map and Olivia handed it over. "Where did we park?"

"Here," she said, pointing. "And this dotted orange line is the trail we took to the falls. See how it leads to Government Peak? And see how it also doesn't lead us over a river?"

Melanie traced the line with a finger to where it met a dotted black line labeled Lost Lake Trail. A dotted black line that led to a river crossing a full mile south of the point at which the orange line of the Government Peak Trail turned sharply west.

"Um, we never made a right turn," Melanie said, indicating the spot where the trails converged.

"What?" Olivia leaned in.

"Right there. We should have turned right."

Olivia took the map back and stared at it, mouth open. "We're a mile off course. And it's not even lunchtime." She rubbed a hand over her face from forehead to chin and back up over her mouth. She looked like their mother did whenever they'd done something without thinking, like when seven-year-old Melanie had decided to wash the car with Brillo pads.

Melanie looked at her with a pained smile. "I think we need to turn around."

Seven

THE WALK BACK to the junction of Government Peak Trail and Lost Lake Trail was made in silence. Partly because the climb back up that last hill was arduous and putting a strain on Olivia's sore hip, and partly because she didn't trust herself to speak. She kept repeating to herself that it didn't matter—what's done is done and can't be undone—but it did matter. She should have been paying closer attention to the sign that surely had to have been there. She shouldn't have argued about what Melanie thought she saw because Melanie was always seeing things that weren't there—spirits and ghosts and miracles and signs, of what, Olivia was sure Melanie decided completely arbitrarily.

When they finally got back to the junction, there was indeed a sign. In fact, it was embarrassingly obvious.

Olivia tried to put a smile on her face. "Well, here we are. Back on track." She avoided looking at her watch, though she'd stolen glances at it over the past mile. "Let's get as far as we can before we stop for lunch."

Melanie merely nodded. She didn't apologize. There was no reason for her to; Olivia had been leading the hike so far, so it was her responsibility to keep them on the right path, no matter how distracted her sister might have made her.

Thankfully, the ground was fairly level here, with only gentler rises and falls over ridges and small creeks that were probably dry during the summer but were flowing with rainwater now. There were soggy spots, but the hiking poles helped them navigate without too much trouble.

Still, they weren't going quite as fast as Olivia would have liked. The underbrush leaned in close, scraping at their arms and packs and slowing them down. For nearly a mile, Olivia saw nothing but the ground in front of her feet as she watched for roots and rocks and focused on forward movement to the exclusion of all else.

They'd already gone nearly six miles that day, and Olivia was getting hungry. If Melanie felt the same way, she did not say. In fact, she said nothing at all for so long that Olivia began looking back over her shoulder every so often—hard to do with a pack—just to make sure she was still behind her. She was—right behind rather than lagging, as she had been before their unfortunate detour.

Just when Olivia was starting to feel her energy wane, the trail relaxed and came to a marshy area surrounding a lake. She paused and took out her map. "There," she said, pointing to a little red triangle by the pond. "We can eat there if no one has set up camp yet. I don't know about you, but I need to eat before I climb a mountain."

"Yes!" Melanie proclaimed. "I'm so glad you said that. I'm starving."

"Why didn't you say something?"

Melanie raised her eyebrows. "Seriously?"

Olivia shifted her footing and folded the map. "You can say when you're hungry or thirsty or have to stop and pee, you know. This isn't the army." Melanie made a "yeah, sure" face that made Olivia equal parts angry and ashamed. "I'm just trying to get us where we need to go."

"Okay, well, where I need to go right now is anywhere I can sit down and eat."

"Right."

Olivia led the way to the campsite, which was indeed empty at the moment, though the warmth coming off the fire ring suggested it had been occupied earlier. They dumped their packs against a couple tree trunks and stretched their shoulder muscles. Olivia cracked her neck. Melanie caught her ankles in turn behind her back and stretched the muscles on the front of her thighs, then she looked at her watch.

"No wonder I'm so hungry. It's nearly two o'clock!"

"Yeah, I know," Olivia said.

"How much further do we have to go from here?"

Olivia examined the map. "The peak is right here behind us. After that it's about three and a half miles more."

Melanie dug around in her pack. "That doesn't sound so bad."

"Well, I don't expect we'll make great time climbing the mountain."

"Oh, it's barely a mountain," she said, pulling out her food bag. "How hard can it be?"

"With packs? Plenty hard." Olivia retrieved her own food bag and pulled out a stick of cheese and a stick of beef jerky, which she alternated eating bite by bite.

Melanie chomped off the end of a carrot stick. "Why don't we just leave them behind and pick them back up when we come down?"

Olivia almost laughed out loud. "Melanie, the trail goes *over* the mountain. It's not, like, a side excursion. When we come down, we'll be on the other side."

"Oh."

"And I hope you're eating more than just that."

Melanie polished off the carrot stick and followed it up with another. "I told you, don't worry about my food. I've got it covered."

They both chewed quietly for a few minutes, the silence of the famished. Olivia savored the taste of the meat and cheese and followed it up with a few dried apricots. She watched her sister consume some nuts and dried cherries and another carrot stick and marveled that anyone could willingly give up meat and dairy products. And who in their right mind would give them up because they were worried that they might accidentally eat their own parents?

"How does reincarnation work?" she said before she could stop herself. "I mean, isn't it, like, if you're bad you come back as some lower life form, and if you're good you come back as a higher one?"

"Sort of. It's more like you accumulate good and bad karma throughout your life, and then what you have when you die would determine if you were going to be born into a higher or lower caste if you're Hindu. Eventually the goal is to reach moksha, but you have to not want it in order to attain it. For Buddhists, you attain enlightenment through the eightfold path—correct view, correct intention, correct speech, correct action, correct livelihood, correct effort, correct mindfulness, and correct concentration. Until you get it right, you are continually reborn."

"Sheesh." Olivia took a drink of water. "So, you think that Mom and Dad accumulated enough bad karma to come back as subhuman? They always seemed like pretty good people to me."

"Well, no. I wouldn't think so."

"Though, I guess if you have to get everything perfect, no one would make the cut." Olivia regarded her sister. "Actually, you always seemed like you'd rather come back as an animal than a human."

Melanie laughed and pushed the air out of her food bag. "Yeah, probably."

Olivia chewed on an apricot. It made some sense that human beings had developed religious systems that had such high standards they were impossible to reach in practice. Scare people with the thought of eternal damnation or continual rebirth as a slug or a centipede and they'll work hard to avoid it, which in turn would make for a more ordered society.

But then, not everyone who broke the law meant to. Justin hadn't. Even so, Olivia wished there were some kind of eternal consequences awaiting him. He ought to come back as a mosquito or a fly, something universally despised and likely to get swatted.

"So," she continued, "for someone who's not Hindu and not living where there's a caste system, what's the next step up? Being born into a richer family? That's basically the higher class in America. But then that doesn't seem like something the Buddhists would be real into. Kind of materialistic."

"I don't pretend to know how it all works," Melanie said. "It's just a nice philosophy to live your life by. It keeps you mindful of how your actions and attitudes affect others."

Olivia stood up and stuffed her food bag back into her pack. "Fair enough. But if you're doing good things so that you'll be freed from the cycle of death and rebirth, aren't you doing it for selfish reasons? Doesn't that kind of negate your altruism?"

Melanie crossed her arms. "Why do you do good things? If it's not because a spiritual belief system requires them or encourages you to do them, then why do them?"

Olivia had to think for a moment. "Because it's good to help people."

"Why?"

"Altruism makes for a kinder and more unified society, which is good for everyone."

"Oh, come on. You don't do good things for the sake of society. You do them because it makes you feel good to do them, doesn't it?"

Olivia furrowed her brow. "I guess, ultimately, you could say that."

"And what evolutionary purpose does that serve?" Melanie said. "If we're all just a collection of atoms and molecules and chemical reactions concerned solely with our own survival—which is your view, right?"

Olivia nodded slowly, unsure of where Melanie was about to take this.

"Then what do we have to gain by, say, helping an old lady with her groceries? If she isn't fit to carry them, she shouldn't eat. She should be picked off by natural selection. Or what about people who train seeing-eye dogs? They're training a natural predator to help the blind rather than eat them like they would in the wild. How does that make sense in your worldview? How do hospitals make sense? Or food banks? Wouldn't you have a better chance to pass your genes on to the next generation if there were fewer people to compete with?" Melanie swung her pack onto her back. "When you can answer those questions, then you can criticize my beliefs." She started walking.

Olivia snatched up her own pack and hustled to keep up. "I wasn't criticizing."

"Yes, you were."

"I wasn't, honest. I was just trying to—hang on a minute, would you? I have to get my straps snapped."

Melanie stopped, hip out of joint. Olivia quickly buckled her straps, then reached out to grab Melanie's arm.

"I didn't mean for that to come off as combative. I just don't get it, is all. It just doesn't make any sense to me."

"It doesn't need to. It just needs to make sense to me."

Olivia put her hands up in a "you win" gesture, but she wasn't really ready to let it drop entirely. "All right, I'm sorry." She raised her eyebrows. "Friends?"

Melanie smiled thinly. "Of course."

They started up the path with Melanie in the lead. The going was steep much of the way, and by the time they reached the top, Olivia was sweating. Up there the breeze off Lake Superior was no longer blocked by land or trees. It wicked the moisture from her neck and hairline, and she put her arms out. She turned slowly around, taking in the view: rolling hills as far as she could see, covered with orange, brown, red, yellow, and green. Above, the sky was blue with a few clouds drifting by. Below, the earth was a carpet of leaves. This was the best of what Earth had to offer. And it was plenty.

Melanie spoke up. "Hey, why don't we just camp here tonight?"

"We can't camp here."

"I saw some of those triangles here on the map, so there must be campsites."

"There are, but we didn't reserve a campsite here. You can't just pick any site you see. It's not first come, first serve. I reserved our sites months ago."

Melanie stepped off the stones. "But we could share with someone else if they came."

"No, we can't. Those are the rules. What if, when we got to the site we reserved, those people from the parking lot had already set up camp?"

"So?"

"And they took the flattest spot for their tent and left us only slopes with a bunch of roots for our tent. And they were loud and annoying. And they left a mess. And you came out in the woods so you could be alone, but instead you're forced to spend the night with strangers. Anyway, if we camp anywhere closer than where I reserved for tonight, it will make tomorrow's hike that much longer."

"I don't think any of that would bother me."

"Well, it would bother me, so we're not going to do it. Come on. We need to keep moving."

Without waiting to see if Melanie was ready, Olivia started her descent.

"Race you to the top!" Olivia blew by, a flurry of swishing snow pants and trailing turquoise scarf, dragging the sled behind her.

Melanie trudged on, slower than she had to. You can't rush climbing Mount Everest. She'd already been on the climb two days. Her Sherpa kept on, a few paces behind, but the rest of the team had fallen away, one by one, unable to take what the mountain threw at them. The blinding snow, the biting wind, the thin, cold air, the emptiness—ah, the horrible emptiness.

"Come on!" Olivia screamed from the top. "I'm not waiting for you much longer!"

Melanie sighed behind her bright pink scarf. Imagining was so much easier without Olivia around. She focused back on the task at hand, digging one spiked boot and then another into the icy path, stepping over the frozen body of some poor soul who didn't make it up and now wouldn't make it down.

"I'm going!" Olivia shouted. She knelt on the two-person sled and heaved herself off the top of the hill.

Melanie watched her sister shoot down, narrowly missing two other kids on saucer sleds, then faced the looming summit with renewed determination. The mountain would not defeat her. Not this time.

"You really are the slowest person alive," Olivia said, coming up from behind her and matching her pace. "It does not take this long to climb a hill. Do you want to go home?"

"No," Melanie said.

"Are you too cold?"

"No," she said again.

"Then what is taking you so long?"

"I'm climbing Everest."

Olivia threw back her head. "Ugh. Just walk up the stupid hill and get it over with. At this rate you're only going to get to go down it a couple times before we have to go."

"Mountains are hard to climb."

Olivia huffed out a sigh and started running up the hill. At the top she yelled down, "I scaled Mount Everest before you did!"

But to Melanie the sound was just some strange groaning on the wind. She pushed on through the storm, finally reaching the summit on the third day. After that triumphant moment, Everest seemed to shrink. The rocky ground smoothed into slick snow packed down into ice. And she joined her sister on a two-person sled, careening down to where her father sat on top of a picnic table, sipping hot cocoa out of a Styrofoam cup.

"Three more times and then we're done," he said. "Mom's got chili on the stove and it's starting to get dark."

Eight

THE LIGHT WAS JUST BEGINNING to falter when Melanie caught the first sight of Mirror Lake. Seeing it ahead, she felt her spirits rise for the first time since Trap Falls. She was more than ready to stop walking. The trail from Government Peak was muddy much of the way, and the close underbrush made a constant scraping sound on their nylon packs. And though she took walks on most days, rain or shine, Melanie hadn't realized just how different it would feel to walk all day, up and down many inclines, with fifty pounds of gear on her back.

"We made it!" she said, quickening her flagging pace a little. "Where's our site?"

"It's not too far. Maybe just another half a mile or so."

Melanie stopped. "Half a mile?"

"It's on the other side of the lake."

Melanie groaned. Of course Olivia had chosen one on the other side. She always had to make things more difficult than they needed to be.

"I just figured that it would give us a leg up tomorrow morning if we were already a little further along the trail."

"I'm not going to be able to even lift my legs if I don't get this thing off my back soon."

"Then I guess we better keep walking."

They passed a cabin. And then another. And, cruelly, another. Why couldn't they have stayed in the cabins? The forest around them dimmed as the sun slipped down the other side of the modest mountains. Melanie struggled to keep up with her sister's pace. Finally, they came to a little wooden bridge across a river that drained slowly out of the lake.

"It's just on the other side," Olivia said.

But just on the other side, the first site they came upon was already occupied. Had someone done what Melanie had wanted to do and just picked a site? Olivia kept walking right on by. Where was this stupid campsite?

Thankfully, she stopped at the next numbered spot and unbuckled her pack straps. "Let's get the tent up quick."

The moment Melanie got her pack off she realized how badly she needed to pee. "Where should I go to the bathroom?"

"Wherever you want." Olivia looked around and pointed. "I suggest that way, away from our neighbors. The toilet paper and the shovel are in the front pocket of my pack, and there's hand sanitizer in there too."

Melanie hurriedly retrieved the items and started picking her way through the trees. But no matter how far she went, she could still see Olivia unrolling the tent. Using a large tree trunk as a shield, she bent down and started to dig a hole. The ground was thick with fibrous roots, and it took her a moment to realize that she had to stab the plastic trowel straight down to cut through. She had dug little more than a depression in the dirt when she just couldn't hold it any longer.

She piled leaves over the spot, used the hand sanitizer, and then tucked everything back into the plastic bag. When she got back, Olivia already had the tent up and was unrolling the fly.

"Okay, what do you want me to do?" Melanie said.

"I'm almost done with this. Why don't you go gather firewood and I'll get the sleeping pads inflated and the bags laid out."

"Don't you need to go to the bathroom?"

"It can wait."

Melanie dutifully walked back into the trees in search of firewood. But coming as they had at the end of a long summer season full of hikers, the pickings around the campsite were slim. She managed several handfuls of sticks for kindling, but larger branches were nonexistent. She dumped her meager offerings into the fire ring and said to Olivia inside the tent, "I'm going to have to go a little further afield for wood."

"There's a flashlight in the bottom left pocket of your pack."

Melanie looked around at the darkening woods. "I shouldn't be that long."

She walked out past the pee tree, as she decided to refer to it, and up a small rise, marking her path by taking note of particular saplings and bushes. She found a long stick next to a rotting log, another caught in the branches of a bush covered in clusters of tiny blue-black berries. One here, one there. Steadily the bunch grew until it took two hands to hold them. She'd have to go drop them off, then come back out for more.

Melanie turned back to where she had come from and

scanned the trees. She could see her breath. She couldn't see Olivia or the tent. Suddenly she realized that she had stopped making a point to mark her progress. And even if she had continued to purposefully notice this tree or that, she was surrounded by trees. Trees that had all started to look the same, especially as the light, which had seemed sufficient when she left without a flashlight, began to fade. She felt a spike of panic stab up her spine and almost called out to her sister—she couldn't have wandered out of earshot—but no. She was an adult. She should have been more careful. Olivia should never know that she got herself all turned around and quite possibly lost.

She'd been moving so slow she couldn't have gone far. And she had been going slightly uphill. The campsite, therefore, had to be downhill. Keeping a firm grip on the sticks and branches she had gathered, Melanie walked swiftly in the direction that felt the most downhill. The long branches trailing behind her caught themselves on a bush. She wrenched them free, stepped into a sudden depression, and nearly twisted an ankle. When she stopped for a moment to right herself and pick up a dropped stick, she thought she heard movement to her left.

Olivia? Or something else?

Sudden fear froze her to the ground. What was it? A bear? A wolf? Had the cougar from Trap Falls been tracking them all this time?

Melanie's breath came in little white clouds of vapor, puffing out of her open mouth in swift succession. What was she doing out here? She didn't know anything about the woods. She'd been on just one hike—the one—and it had been led by Olivia's friend Eric, who had been an Eagle Scout. That trail had been in a far more populated area and was visited by many more hikers and tourists. On that hike, a ranger had found them easily. Out here in sixty thousand acres of wilderness covered in a blanket of trees, who would find her? Who would find her if she really was lost?

Melanie nearly screamed as something leaped across the leaves right in front of her feet. She breathed once, twice. A chipmunk. Just a chipmunk rushing to get ready for winter. She had to get ahold of herself. And she had to get back to camp.

“Mel?” Olivia’s voice came from a little ways away, behind Melanie’s right shoulder.

She’d been going the wrong way.

She rushed in the direction of the voice. “Coming!” After a minute, she could just see the blue and gray tent through the trees, and relief flooded her body. She broke through the underbrush back into the campsite, dragging her sticks and branches behind her.

“Nice job,” Olivia said, taking in Melanie’s haul. “How far did you have to go?”

“Not far,” Melanie said with a carefully placed smile.

“You should have taken a flashlight.”

“I needed both hands to carry the wood.”

Olivia and Melanie set to work breaking the branches down into sticks for the fire ring.

“I found the bear pole so we can hang the food bags after we eat,” Olivia said.

At the word *bear*, Melanie stiffened. “Maybe we should eat in the tent so bears won’t be attracted to the smell of food out here.”

Olivia leveled a look in her direction. "That's absolutely the worst thing anyone on a hiking trip can do—other than start a forest fire. You never, *ever* bring food into a tent."

"Okay."

"Not even gum or mints in your pockets. Nothing. Understand?"

"Yes."

"A tent isn't going to mask the scent of food to a bear. That's why there are bear poles, so you can store your food far away from your tent and up off the ground where bears can't get to it."

"Okay."

"Melanie, I'm serious. Don't ever bring food into the tent."

"Okay! I got it!" Melanie snapped a large branch under her heel. "You don't have to talk to me like I'm an idiot."

Olivia began making a tepee of sticks in the fire ring. "I'm not trying to make you mad, but the people you read about getting attacked by wild animals, usually they *are* idiots. They do dumb things that could easily have been avoided if they'd just educated themselves a little. I'm not saying you're dumb," she hastened to say as she struck a match, "but bringing food into a tent is dumb."

"Yes, I'm well aware of that now. Thank you."

It took a few tries, but the fire finally caught. They stood on either side of it, alternately warming their hands and the backs of their legs, and eating their supper in silence. Melanie didn't know what Olivia was thinking about, but she could not stop the thought that was rampaging through her own brain over and over and over—that were it not for her sister saying her name, she would have been lost in the woods in the cold at night with no food, no water, no shelter, no compass, no flashlight.

She *was* dumb. She *was* one of those idiots who might end up on the news someday. She, quite simply, had no idea what she was doing. She never really had. She'd been walking through life dealing with each day as it came, never planning, always reacting. She'd stumbled onto some things that made her happy, at least on the surface—but she'd always admired how Olivia set about conquering a task, how she always seemed to know what was coming next and what to do about it. Melanie would give almost anything for that kind of certainty.

When they were done eating, Olivia hung the food bags on the bear pole and went out into the woods with the trowel and the toilet paper—and a flashlight. The fire had died down, and after they brushed their teeth and washed their faces, Olivia smothered the remaining embers. They took turns in the tent changing into their pj's—not so much for modesty's sake but because changing clothes in a small tent required so much contortion that only one person could comfortably do it at a time. Once they were both inside, Melanie could feel Olivia assessing the level to which she'd adhered to the command on the packing list to bring warm pj's, but to her credit Olivia said nothing.

Melanie brought her journal and a pen into the tent, but once she'd crawled into the downy sleeping bag, a wave of exhaustion overtook her. She set the book aside, turned off her flashlight, and snuggled down into the reassuringly constrictive warmth of the mummy-style bag and zipped it up from the inside.

Day one was done, and it hadn't gone as well as she'd hoped.

Tomorrow was a new chance to connect with her sister. A new chance to help her heal. A new chance to gather enough courage to tell Olivia what she could no longer avoid telling her.

Melanie closed her eyes and listened to the silence outside the tent. And within minutes, she was asleep.

Nine

OLIVIA LAY ON HER STOMACH, flashlight trained on the map in front of her. Compared to today's, tomorrow's walk looked easy. The black dotted line of the Little Carp River Trail led south and west of Mirror Lake on what looked to be fairly level ground much of the way. Two and a half miles to the bridge at Lily Pond, where they would break for snacks. Another half mile to the spot where they would ford the Little Carp River. Two more miles to Greenstone Falls, where they would eat lunch. Then a pleasant afternoon along the river until they forded it again and made camp at Trappers Falls.

Or should they eat lunch earlier?

A small snore from her sister told Olivia that Melanie was not about to be engaged in conversation about when and where to lunch the next day. She glanced at her watch. 9:30. Today had been kind of a mess, but they had managed to deal with the unpleasant surprise of going the wrong way. The tent had been up before dark. They were fed and safe and warm in the sleeping bags she had purchased expressly because they were rated for five degrees Fahrenheit. She folded the map, clicked off the flashlight, and zipped herself snugly into place, pulling the bag's built-in hood over her head and cinching it shut until only her eyes, nose, and mouth were showing.

It felt good for a moment to lie so flat on the ground, which was hard despite the sleeping pad beneath her. Within the confines of the mummy bag, she rotated her feet to stretch her leg muscles and pulled her shoulders down and in, stretching her upper back. Her spine decompressed, her bones settled into place, her breath came slow and regular.

But she didn't fall asleep. It was too quiet. Too dark. Too still. She opened her eyes but could see nothing at all. Wrapped as she was, flat on her back, hands crossed over her stomach, she began to feel as though she were in a casket. Like she was not *on* the ground so much as *in* the ground.

Olivia sat up with effort, bringing the sleeping bag with her. If she could sit up, she was not in the ground. She tried to think of something else, anything else, before her mind could go to the last caskets she saw—those of her parents. But trying not to think of them only made her think of them all the more.

It had been a closed-casket funeral. They hadn't had a will that specified end-of-life matters, so circumstance chose for them. The accident had been bad. Their bodies were not in good shape. Olivia wanted them to be cremated and the ashes scattered—no keeping them in a jar on the mantel or in a box in the closet. She didn't want the memory hanging about. Melanie wanted them buried so there would be a place to visit them and to bring their grandchildren someday.

In the end, Olivia conceded, and her parents were given a Christian funeral at the church they had attended for Christmas and Easter and at which her father had tutored refugees in reading and writing in English. The service, though well attended because of the tragic nature of the accident and the relatively young age of its victims, offered Olivia little comfort. Her parents had never talked about their religious beliefs. They had never prayed before meals or before bed. Never taught their daughters to. She knew they'd both grown up going to church, but other than the holidays, they'd never taken their own children. If God hadn't mattered all that much to them, why should they matter all that much to God?

And yet the minister seemed to say that they did matter and that they were safe with God and all the saints who'd gone on before. Did he know something about them she didn't? Or was this just the standard thing he said at all funerals? She'd wanted to ask him then, but there was no time. Over the years she'd thought about calling up the church to talk to him, but the longer she waited the less it seemed to matter. Until one day she realized it had all been for show. Nobody knew what happened after death except what you could observe from this side of it—that the organs shut down and the body broke down into its component parts according to predictable patterns. Religion was just there to give people something to do, to keep their minds off death, or at least to make death seem not so permanent.

The only thing, in fact, that had stuck with Olivia from the service was a snippet of Scripture the minister read. Something about doing justice, loving mercy, and walking humbly. He'd said her parents did those things, and she guessed that at least was true. But so what? It hadn't kept them from harm.

Olivia lay back down and twisted herself and the mummy bag onto her side like a worm. Oof. Not that side. She turned over. That was better. She could fall asleep like that. She lay there listening to Melanie's soft breathing and tried to match hers with it, to slow her body down and trick it into sleep. Whether she actually did fall asleep before she heard the scream was anyone's guess.

It came from somewhere back in the forest, back where Melanie had been searching for wood for the fire. Every hair on Olivia's body stiffened, and she stopped breathing for a moment, listening intently to the silence. Listening for some other sound to make sense of the first one. But there was nothing.

"Melanie?" she whispered. But Melanie was asleep. How? How could someone sleep through that unearthly scream?

Olivia wrenched her hand up inside the sleeping bag and unzipped it enough to get her arm out. Outside the bag the air was cold. She turned her wrist and her watch glowed out the time. 11:45. Had she really lain there awake for two hours? She must have slept. Must have been dreaming.

But there it was again. It had to be an animal. Maybe a screech owl? Didn't they make terrible noises? Or maybe it was a rabbit that had gotten caught by something. She'd heard that terrified rabbits screamed. And weren't cougars said to scream? Hadn't she read that in some book as a child? Whatever it was, Olivia now understood why the woods used to frighten people, why so many fairy tales involved witches or creatures of malice lurking in the shadowy spaces between the trees at night.

A third scream rang out, exactly the same as the others. It was an animal, she decided. A person being attacked wouldn't scream three separate times in exactly the same way. This was an animal noise, whatever it was.

"Melanie?" she tried again. But still her sister slept soundly.

Olivia zipped herself back into the mummy bag and listened, but there were no more screams. Eventually the adrenaline that had been coursing through her body dissipated and she was able to breathe normally again. She shut her eyes and tried to settle her heart. She tried not to think of how tired she was going to be the next morning if she couldn't get some sleep.

Somehow, miraculously, she did manage to drift off. And she could only be sure of it because she was definitely awakened sometime later by another sound. If the scream had been loud and sharp and distant, this sound was low and lumbering and close. This sound was breathing. And footsteps. And it was right outside the tent.

Instantly Olivia's mind pinpointed the exact location of the knife she had purchased back at the gas station in Indian River. It was in the little zippered compartment on the front of her pack. Outside. Her pack was outside, hanging from the broken branch of a pine tree about six feet off the ground. Why hadn't she brought the knife in with her?

More footsteps. More heavy breathing. Olivia waited for the sound of a zipper, the sound of their tent being opened. Those screams had been a person. They might have been three people. Someone was going campsite to campsite, murdering people. She struggled to get to the zipper of her bag again, to get an arm free, to get out of the bag so she could protect her little sister. But what could she do? She had no gun, no knife, not even one of her hiking poles. And if somehow she survived whatever was about to happen, she couldn't call for help because there was no cell signal. She felt her heartbeat tick up another notch. Her breath was coming faster. She had to keep her head. Had to stop herself from hyperventilating. She braced herself and waited for something to happen.

But the sound of the tent being unzipped never came. The footsteps had stopped.

The breathing had not. In fact, it was closer than ever, just inches away from her face on the other side of a few microns of nylon. Something was there, outside the tent. It was not leaving, but it also was not coming in. In fact, it sounded like it had lain down.

It wasn't a deer. The heavy footfalls and heavy breathing weren't in the least deerlike. It wasn't a porcupine or a raccoon—they slept in trees, and this sounded bigger than that. The footfalls were too loud to be a fox, a coyote, or even a wolf. And a cougar, if there were any around as Melanie believed, would have been completely silent. The only thing left was a bear.

There was a bear on the other side of the tent fabric. Its head had to be less than a foot from her own, because she could clearly hear it breathing, deep, capacious breaths.

Had Melanie brought food into the tent despite Olivia's stern warning? Did her own fingers smell like beef jerky? She snuck a hand to her face. It just smelled like hand sanitizer.

Olivia waited another minute for something to happen. But the breathing outside the tent never changed, except perhaps to get slower. She settled back down into her mummy bag as quietly as possible, drawing the zipper closed again. Even if there was a bear outside, it wasn't doing anything. It wasn't nosing at the tent, wasn't scratching at the food bags. Maybe it was just chilly, and their tent, with its two warm bodies inside, was a smidge warmer than the cold black woods. Maybe it was lonely and just needed a friend. Someone with whom to share the dark night.

Olivia slowed her breathing to match the pace coming from outside the tent. And finally slept.

Ten

"RIGHT HERE, SEE?"

Melanie bent over the spot that Olivia pointed out.

"You can see the lines where his claws dug into the ground," Olivia said. "Maybe when he was getting up."

Melanie studied the marks while Olivia got out her phone and took a few pictures.

"If it was a bear, it was a small one," Melanie said.

"It sounded big," Olivia said. "Well, it sounded heavy and slow, and that says big to me."

Melanie stood up and poked through the ashes in the firepit, looking for any leftover heat. It was cold. She could see her own breath, and her hands and nose were freezing. "And what about the scream?"

"Oh," Olivia said, standing straight, "that was just unearthly creepy. I've never heard anything like it before. I'll have to look it up later. I can't believe you slept through all of this."

Melanie couldn't believe it either. She wasn't allowed to have her cougar, and now Olivia got a bear and a . . . whatever that was? The double standard was irritating enough, but what really needled Melanie's mind was the fact that the bear had gone to Olivia's side of the tent rather than hers. She'd always prided herself on her connection with the animal world. Animals could tell she was a kindred spirit. They were drawn to her. They weren't drawn to Olivia. Olivia who once pushed a pony away at a petting zoo. Olivia who had said her eagles were vultures.

"I'm going to get the food bags," Melanie announced.

"I'll start rolling up the pads and bags, and then we can break down the tent," Olivia called after her.

"I'm eating breakfast first."

Melanie stalked off to the bear pole. The long, hooked pole with which she was supposed to get the bags down was surprisingly heavy and hard to maneuver into the loop of the bag ties. Once the first bag was finally on the hook, Melanie lost control, sending it to the ground with a thud. She hoped it was Olivia's. The next one came down more softly, but Melanie's arms were so tired it took her three tries just to hang up the hook.

She retrieved the bags from the ground. It had been Olivia's that fell so hard. It was significantly heavier than her own bag, and she wondered for a moment if she hadn't brought enough food along. Or maybe vegan food was lighter than Olivia's jerky and cheese and whatever else she had in there.

Olivia had the pads and bags rolled, stuffed, and strapped to the packs by the time she got back, and was already breaking down the tent. Melanie sat on a half-rotted log and pulled a vegan protein bar out of her food bag.

"Just have something to eat first," she said.

"I'd rather be ready to go once we've eaten," Olivia said.

Melanie retrieved one of her water bottles. It was full. She checked the other one, also full. "You already filtered our water?"

Olivia shook out the tent fly and laid it on the ground. "Yeah. I did it this morning while you were getting dressed."

"And you did the pads and the sleeping bags."

"I want to get started early. We'll be going by some really nice features this afternoon, and I don't want us to feel rushed when we get there."

Melanie stopped chewing and tried to swallow the lump of protein bar. She hated protein bars on a good day. As she saw now how childish she was being, this one was making her feel ill. She swished some water around in her mouth and swallowed the chunks like a mouthful of pills. "You could have woken me up earlier. I must have gotten way more sleep than you."

"I feel strangely okay," Olivia said as she slowly and tightly rolled the fly, brushing off every speck of dirt with a dry washcloth as she went. "I'm actually kind of excited about tonight. We'll be camping near a waterfall, and we'll be the only ones there. And, I don't know, there's something about knowingly going to sleep next to a bear that's just kind of invigorating."

Melanie frowned. She put the rest of the protein bar back in her bag and stood up. "What do you want me to do?"

Olivia pointed. "Grab those ties for me?"

Melanie retrieved two strips of nylon fabric and handed them to her sister.

Olivia swiftly tied the rolled fly and set it aside. "Can you pack up the tent poles and pegs? The rubber bands are in the bag there."

As Melanie did as directed, Olivia straightened, folded, and rolled the tent in the exact same manner as the fly. Then she strapped tent, fly, and hardware bag to the top of her pack.

"I'll be right back," she said, retrieving the toilet paper and shovel.

When she disappeared behind a tree, Melanie picked up Olivia's pack with her right hand and her own with her left hand.

"Why is your pack so much heavier than mine?" Melanie asked when Olivia returned.

"They're about the same."

"No, they're not. Yours is way heavier."

"Maybe a little."

"How much does the tent weigh?"

Olivia shrugged. "I don't know."

Of course she knew. Melanie could all but guarantee Olivia had added up the weight of every item on her calculator app as she walked around the sporting goods store. "Shouldn't I carry at least part of it? Or if you carried it yesterday, I should carry it today?"

"No, it's good. I'm trying to lose some weight. This will help me."

Melanie didn't argue further. It was never profitable to argue with Olivia when she had her mind made up—she pitied the defense lawyers who had to face her in the courtroom. She'd just have to find a way to even out the load later.

Once they'd eaten, they headed out. The ground was level, but that was about the only good thing one could say about it. The rains had turned many low spots into bogs that sucked at Melanie's hiking shoes, and even once she got moving at a good clip she just couldn't get warm. The sleeping bag Olivia had gotten was great for the cold night, but her leggings, tee, and fleece jacket just weren't cutting it in the crisp morning air.

Every few hundred feet, Olivia veered off to the left or right of the trail to avoid mud or standing water. Melanie followed. They struggled through the brush, up little hills, around fallen trees, and then they were back on the trail, looking for the next reassuring blue blaze painted on a tree trunk. A bit farther and the whole process repeated itself.

Melanie poked her hiking poles into the sludge and tried to step on rocks or rotting sticks or logs rather than in the muck, but every surface was slick with mud and she slipped off about half the time. Off trail, she tripped over everything in her path. She cursed and growled under her breath. Her brand-new vegan hiking shoes looked like the feet of a filthy extra in a documentary about the spread of the plague in medieval Europe.

When they stopped to pull out each other's water bottles, Melanie looked up at the blank gray sky that had been so blue the day before and released a bitter sigh. Even the colorful foliage on the trees seemed dry and dim, where yesterday it had felt like she was walking through a million suncatchers. By the time they reached the bridge over the river at Lily Pond, Melanie was in what she had always thought of as a brown mood—her signal to herself that she needed to change things up before she sank further down into black.

"After lunch, why don't we see who can spot the most varieties of mushroom," she said.

Olivia raised her eyes from her pack. "Wouldn't the person in the lead have an unfair advantage?"

"We'll switch on and off every fifteen minutes, how's that?"

Olivia shrugged. "Okay."

They sat on a bench built into the wooden bridge and faced the pond. It could have been so beautiful in the sunshine. For about a minute neither spoke. They just stared ahead at the trees mirrored in the still water and framed with browning cattails. A young couple with a friendly shepherd mix approached from the right, the direction they would soon be heading.

"Morning," the man said.

"Morning," they said in unison.

Melanie wished they would stop so she could pet the dog, whose paws were as muddy as her shoes—not a promising sign about what they were soon to face—but the couple didn't even slow down. She retrieved her bag of carrot sticks. Olivia pulled out a can of SpaghettiOs.

"What. The heck. Is that?" Melanie said.

Olivia turned the can's label toward her. "SpaghettiOs."

"Yes, I can see they're SpaghettiOs. But why? Why on earth would you bring SpaghettiOs hiking?" Melanie gagged a little. "You're not eating those cold, are you?"

"Do you see a microwave out here?"

"Blech! Gross!"

"Settle down," Olivia said as she peeled back the aluminum lid.

"That is so disgusting." Melanie turned away. "Ugh. I can't even look at you."

Olivia started laughing. "You sure you don't want some?"

"Sick. No."

Olivia leaned closer and waved a spoonful of the cold canned pasta in Melanie's face. "Hmmm?"

Melanie swatted her away, sending SpaghettiOs flying over the bridge and into the water.

"Hey!" Olivia said, still laughing. "Man, you are just as easy as ever to annoy."

"Well, you're just as annoying as ever."

Olivia snickered. "So sensitive."

Melanie knew Olivia was just giving her a hard time, but the word *sensitive* got under her skin. Because she wasn't being sensitive. She was just being herself. And she didn't like being told that she was somehow more delicate than everybody else. It wasn't her who was sensitive—it was everyone else who was callous. Especially Olivia, who'd never given Melanie the satisfaction of falling for a prank or doing anything but shrugging when criticism was leveled at her. If anything, Olivia could stand to be more sensitive.

"That explains why your food bag is so heavy," Melanie said. "How many cans are in there?"

"Just two. I had a hankering for SpaghettiOs when I went shopping."

"Weirdo."

Olivia kept smiling and shoveling SpaghettiOs into her mouth. Melanie foraged around in her bag for a few more morsels. She was already missing salads and roasted veggies and smoothies and almond milk protein shakes and pan-fried tofu with rice and lentils. She chewed on a granola bar and followed that up with a handful of almonds. Eventually she wasn't hungry anymore, but she wasn't satisfied either.

It was the first time she went to dinner with Justin that she'd decided to become a vegan. Right there in a dark corner booth of a Mexican restaurant on East Paris Avenue in Grand Rapids. It was a terrible place in which to become a vegan. Even the bean dip wasn't vegetarian. She and Justin had been emailing each other for weeks, talking about what had happened the night of the accident and what happens after you die—what might have happened to her parents, what might eventually happen to him. He was reading a New Testament someone had given him at a support group, even though he admitted to being a scoffer in the past. But now it felt like he really had something for which he needed to be forgiven. They'd covered a lot of ground in those emails, and Melanie had started thinking through the ramifications of reincarnation. Seeing the couple at the next table chowing down on tacos, ground beef spilling out the other side, she felt almost sick. That night she'd eaten a salad of just lettuce, tomatoes, and onions.

"Ready?" Olivia said when they had both tucked their food bags back into their packs.

"Sure."

"You want to lead first?"

"Hmm?"

"The mushroom thing. You want to be in front first?"

"Oh, yeah. I guess so."

Olivia caught her eye. "Hey, what's wrong?"

Melanie shook her head. "Nothing. I'm just . . . it's just kind of gray today, you know?"

"Yeah. Not as nice as yesterday."

"And I can't seem to get warm. All I can think about is getting back in that sleeping bag." When she saw the concerned look on Olivia's face, she added, "For the warmth."

Olivia nodded, but Melanie worried she had tipped her hand. When she'd been in the throes of depression after the accident, she'd spent most days in bed. Olivia wasn't there, but Melanie knew that her aunt had tattled on her. It was good she did. If Melanie had been left to herself, she'd probably still be in that same bed. It was good to have people who cared about you. Though, if she was honest, it wasn't either of them who'd gotten her out of it. It was Justin.

"Why don't you go first," Melanie offered. "And you can't just say 'there's one' when you see it. You have to describe it. Like 'the one that looks like white oyster shells' or 'the one that looks like earwax.'"

"Lovely," Olivia intoned. "All right. Let's get a move on."

For the next fifteen minutes, Olivia led the trek and the mushroom count. It was a silly game, but it helped Melanie focus on something other than her brown mood. She did manage to spot some that Olivia had missed, including a rather phallic purple mushroom that looked nearly black against the leaf litter. When they got to the spot where the Little Carp River Trail met the Lily Pond Trail, they switched off, Melanie leading the way west toward the first place they would have to ford the river. As she searched out mushrooms, she saw not only the seemingly endless variety of fungi—tall and short, skinny and fat, ones that looked like open umbrellas and ones that looked like closed umbrellas, red, orange, yellow, white, solid and spotted and striped—she also saw so much she might have otherwise missed. Lichens and ferns of various types, and so many different and delightful varieties of mosses.

Melanie was fully entranced. She'd never dreamed her

manufactured distraction would be so good for her soul. Whatever creative force was behind this world, he/she/it never seemed to run out of ideas. There was no real reason for so much variety, was there, other than that it was meant to enchant those who looked upon it?

Behind her, her sister snagged a mushroom she hadn't seen as she was musing. What did Olivia see when she looked at the multitude of species in just this small parcel of land? No doubt there was a scientific explanation for it all. Something that didn't want a divine designer. But Melanie just couldn't understand how anyone could think there was nothing more to this life than survival of the species.

"Why is it you don't believe in God? Or some kind of higher power?" Melanie asked when they came to the Little Carp River crossing and started to change out of their hiking boots and socks.

Olivia shoved her feet into her water shoes. "I guess I just don't see any evidence for it. Or need for it."

Melanie rolled up her pant legs and slipped her hands through the loops on her hiking poles. "I see evidence everywhere I look."

"Believe me, I know," Olivia said. "Don't forget your boots."

Melanie silently chided herself for nearly leaving the most essential part of her hiking gear behind and decided to drop her line of questioning until she'd thought of a better response.

"Ready?" Olivia said.

Melanie nodded. "Want me to go first?"

"I can. That way if there's a problem you can avoid it."

"Why should you have to find the problem?"

Olivia stopped at the water's edge. "I don't know. Maybe

because I'm the one who remembered water shoes. Plus I'm the oldest. Just used to doing things first."

Melanie stepped up beside her. "I don't think that's necessary anymore." Without waiting for Olivia's response, she stepped into the water. She sucked in a breath at how cold it was but didn't hesitate to take the next step. The water was fast moving but shallow, not even reaching to Melanie's calves. The poles helped her brace and balance, but she immediately regretted not purchasing the water shoes. The submerged rocks were slimy beneath her bare feet. Even so, she was across in less than thirty seconds and turned back to give Olivia a triumphant look. But Olivia was right behind her, looking down at her own footing, totally missing Melanie's conquest of the watery obstacle.

Melanie dried her feet on the hand towel Olivia had instructed her to bring, put her socks and shoes back on, and shoved the towel back into her pack without much thought to where it should go.

"My turn in front," Olivia said. "How many do you have now? I have twenty-four."

"I don't know. I wasn't really counting."

"What? This was your game, Melanie."

Melanie took a sip of her water and looked around. "Is this a campsite?"

Olivia took out her map. "Yes. Two of them."

"Too bad we can't just camp here. My feet are freezing."

"Well, we can't. We've barely gone three miles anyway. Hey, what is with you today?"

Melanie felt herself fighting back sudden tears. She would not cry, not in front of Olivia. Especially when she had no idea what she would be crying about. It had been so long since she'd felt this way. Was it simply being with her sister that had yanked her back?

"Do you need a break?" Olivia said, not unkindly.

Melanie whipped her emotions into submission and put her water bottle away. "No, I'm fine. Moving will help me warm up." She wrenched her pack—which was getting heavier by the moment—onto her back and shoved her arms through the straps.

"Okay, if you're sure."

"Totally. Let's go. And I have thirty mushroom species. So I'm winning."

Olivia smiled. "How about we say you won. I don't think at this point I could tell the difference between what I see and what I've already seen. So you win the mushroom game. We'll have to think of something else for the next leg."

Melanie scowled. She knew she must look like a petulant child who'd been put off by a playmate who was tired of the game. But she couldn't stop herself. "Don't patronize me, Olivia. If you don't want to play, that's fine. I'm fine." With that, she found the next blue blaze on a tree and started walking away.

They walked in silence for ten minutes. Twenty. The ground got wet again, and Melanie was now the one who had to look for the driest route around the muck. Small puddles alternated with what in some cases looked to be a hundred yards of sludge pockmarked with the soggy footprints of hikers who had gone before. It was slow going and frustrating. Kind of like recovery. Good days and bad days. Serenity and struggle. Wanting to quit but pressing forward because that was the only way out.

After quite some time focused only on the ground directly in front of her, Melanie looked up and stopped. Where was the next blue blaze? And when had she last seen one?

"What's wrong?" Olivia said behind her.

Every fiber of Melanie's being wanted to lie, wanted to keep walking and miraculously stumble back upon the trail. Yet overriding her fear of looking stupid for leading them astray was the greater fear of being lost in the woods where no one would find them.

She turned to her sister and said in a calm voice that belied the mounting anxiety within, "I think we've lost the trail."

Olivia gripped Melanie's hand tighter. "Stop pulling."

Melanie pulled harder. "I see it!"

Olivia yanked back on her arm. "It's not going anywhere. It's bolted to the ground. And Mom and Dad said we have to stick together."

The Ferris wheel loomed up ahead, lights flashing, music singing from tinny speakers. A sea of people lay between them and it, a sea in which Melanie seemed determined to be lost.

Pulling her like the husky she kept asking for but never received, Melanie propelled Olivia forward, slamming her into strangers, who wheeled and yelled things like "Hey!" and "Watch it!" and a few things she knew she was not supposed to say—ever.

They made it to the entrance, but the line stretched back twenty feet or more.

"Do we have to do the Ferris wheel?" Olivia asked as they tacked themselves onto the end of the line.

"Yes!" Melanie whined. "It's my favorite part and Mom and Dad said I could and they said you had to take me, so there."

"Fine, but then you have to come with me to play some of the games."

"Dad says those are fixed and a waste of money."

"He said the whole fair is a waste of money."

They waited as the current group of riders exited out the little gate and then shuffled forward as the line did. The conductor emptied and filled four seats, sent the wheel around three times, then repeated the process. Finally, it was their turn to board. Olivia handed their tickets to an unsmiling woman who never looked at them and led Melanie to the open seat. A scruffy man smelling of cigarette smoke secured the bar across their laps, and the wheel began to spin, slowly lifting them higher and higher above the crowd.

"Olivia!" came a shout from below.

She waved to the figure on the ground.

"Ooooh," Melanie teased. "There's your boyfriend."

Olivia punched her in the arm. "He's not my boyfriend."

"I bet he is. I bet you kissed him." Melanie puckered her lips and closed her eyes.

Olivia punched her again.

"Hey! Knock it off. I'll tell Mom."

"And I'll tell her how annoying you're being and she won't blame me."

Melanie crossed her arms but could only maintain the sulk for a few seconds before she pointed and screamed, "There's Mom! There's Dad!"

Olivia joined Melanie in waving maniacally for a moment, and then they were making the next circle. When they next reached the top, the wheel stopped. The sun was setting and the moon was rising, and Olivia could see for miles in each direction. Farm fields and clusters of trees and long, straight roads leading off to the horizon. It felt like . . . possibility.

"Melanie, what do you want to be when you grow up?"

"I want to work at the fair."

"You want to be a carny?"

"Yeah. It would be so fun. I bet they get to ride all the rides for free."

Olivia rolled her eyes. "Yeah, they all look like they're having loads of fun."

"What do you want to be?" Melanie asked.

Olivia looked west toward the brilliant setting sun. "An explorer."

Eleven

OLIVIA GAZED OUT into the unending parade of tree trunks, her eyes searching for a spot of blue amid the brown and orange and yellow. She wasn't really concerned just yet. They couldn't have gone that far off the trail in their quest for dry ground. But as each slice of forest was ruled out, her mind clicked into problem-solving mode.

She was prepared for this. She had the map. She had a compass. She had her instincts. She'd simply formulate a plan and everything would be okay.

"I'm so sorry, Ollie," Melanie said.

"It's fine. Don't worry. It will all be fine. Just let me think."

Olivia examined the map. She looked again at the lay of the land. Had they been going mostly uphill or down?

"Well, do we know which side of the trail we're on?" she said. "Did we last go right or left to get around the mud?"

"Right," Melanie said. "Wait. No. Maybe left? I don't know. We've been weaving all over the place. I don't know why they don't keep up this trail more."

"Mel, it's wilderness. That there's a trail at all, wet or dry, is pretty much the only thing they could do. They can't control the weather."

Olivia chewed her lip. If they'd gone to the right, getting back on track should be rather simple. If they went south, they'd hit the trail. But if they'd gone to the left, going south would bring them farther away from it. They'd eventually hit the river, but they'd be miles off course. At that point they might be better off crossing the river to get to South Boundary Road so they could hitchhike back to their car. The hike would be over and they would have missed all the best features of the park—most of the waterfalls, Lake Superior, the escarpment, and the Lake of the Clouds.

"The compass is in the bottom right pocket," Olivia said, turning. "Can you get it out for me?"

Melanie dug around a bit, then she started removing things and handing them to Olivia—flashlight, a skein of thin rope, a baggie with matches in it, the ridiculous brook trout knife. "Let me try the left side."

But Olivia knew it wasn't in the left side. The left side was for first aid, not tools. She unbuckled the straps on her pack. "Let me look."

For the next few minutes, Olivia carefully removed every single item in her pack, one by one, and then put them back. With every pocket she emptied, she felt just a bit more panic tickle the back of her neck. Where was it? She knew she'd bought it along with all the rest of the gear. She remembered the price, the label. She remembered throwing the packaging into the recycling bin. She remembered puzzling over what seemed like needlessly complicated instructions and bringing it to bed with her to watch YouTube videos of how to properly use it.

And then she could see it clearly, sitting on her nightstand the night before she left. She'd already packed the car. She told herself she'd remember to grab it in the morning, repeated her mantra for the next day: keys, cell phone, compass, keys, cell phone, compass. Only, while she had remembered the first two items, she had forgotten the third. It was still there, sitting on the nightstand, completely useless.

"I don't have it," Olivia said.

"Did you put it in my pack?" Melanie said.

"No. I mean I left it at home. On my nightstand."

Melanie began unstrapping her own pack now. "Are you sure? Don't you think we better just check mine?"

Olivia agreed, but she knew they would not find it. And they didn't. They were lost in the woods with no compass. With the sun hidden behind a blanket of soft gray clouds, they couldn't even tell what direction they were facing. They put everything back into place in their packs and stood up.

"Now what?" Melanie said.

Olivia looked at the map again. The squiggly lines marking off the changes in elevation blurred. She pulled herself together and wiped at her eyes. "Okay, here's the deal. Wherever there's water, you're going to be going down to it, right? The river cuts through and wears away the rock below. So we need to go downhill to get to the river. You see all these lines really close together?" Olivia pointed to two unnamed peaks on the map. "If we get to this steep incline, we're going the wrong way." She pointed to another set of lines. "And I don't remember going up any areas like this. Now, being that we're both right-handed, I think it's likely we're on the right side of the trail."

"I'm left-handed."

"What?"

"I'm left-handed," Melanie said again. "How could you not remember that?"

Olivia frowned. "And you were in the lead."

"Yeah, thanks for pointing that out. I had forgotten how this whole mess was my fault."

"I didn't say it to point that out. I just said it because it might mean that you tended to go around things to the left rather than the right. It matters to the solution, Melanie. You need to stop being so sensitive."

Melanie threw up her hands. "There's that word again! Sensitive. I've always been too sensitive. Well, sorry, but I don't think I'm being too anything. We all know this is my fault. We all know you're going to fix it. And then you'll have something else to be smug about, some other story to tell about your flaky little sister and how you always have to get her out of scrapes."

Olivia stepped back and waited for Melanie to exhaust the geyser of words that had obviously been hovering near the boiling point for a while. It had been so long since they'd spent concentrated time together, she'd forgotten how volatile her sister's temper could be. Melanie spent so much energy trying to get along with people and agree with them that she never opened the tension valve until she was at the point of exploding.

"Are you done?" Olivia asked. "Because that sort of thing isn't going to help this situation at all. We both should have been looking for the next blue blaze. I'm as at fault as you are. And I'm the one who forgot the compass."

Melanie pressed her lips together.

"Okay, then," Olivia continued. "Let's start moving with the assumption that we're on the left side of the trail. We'll head to our right for a bit. And if we start climbing steeply uphill, we'll assume we're going the wrong way and turn around. How does that sound?"

Melanie nodded and ran a hand over her curls, which were looking limp and greasy. Olivia was sure her hair looked even worse.

"Let's take a picture," Olivia said.

"What?"

"Let's take a picture for your blog or whatever. The time we got lost in the woods."

Melanie managed a small smile. "Okay, sure." They got her phone out of her pack and turned it on. "What face should we make?"

"I don't know. The face you were making a minute ago when you were so mad at me would do."

Melanie let out a little laugh, but Olivia knew she was embarrassed. Mel snapped a picture, then turned off the phone without looking at it.

"Now then," Olivia said, "we better move."

Melanie looked at her. "You're much calmer than I would have thought you'd be in this situation."

Olivia shrugged. "What's done is done."

"And can't be undone," Melanie finished.

"Except we're going to try to undo it now by getting back on the trail."

She started picking her way through the trees to the right, not at all confident that this was the correct action in their situation. But what else could she do? They couldn't just stand there. They had to do something with the knowledge they had, which admittedly wasn't much.

It was slow going. Neither Olivia nor Melanie said anything. All of their concentration was on feeling the ground beneath their feet and scanning the trees around them for a shock of blue. If only the sun would come out, that would be something at least, but no matter how Olivia strained her eyes against the flat gray sky between the treetops, she could not discern any difference in the light.

Every time she felt that the ground was leading them down, it would begin to go up, and every time she felt it going up, it would begin to go down. Looking again at the squiggly elevation lines on the map, she could rationalize this pattern no matter what side of the trail they might be on. She could also see that it would be better for them to be lost on the left side, closer to the road and eventual rescue, than the right side with its mountains and trees that stretched on for miles until they ended abruptly at Lake Superior.

She looked at her watch. They had been walking for twenty minutes or more. Surely if they were going the right direction they would have hit the trail by now. But without a compass or the sun, they couldn't even be sure that they were going in one direction rather than in circles.

Unbidden, thoughts of news stories of lost hikers and lost children crowded in. People who had wandered off a trail and over a cliff, who'd gotten stuck in canyons or attacked by wild animals. She remembered a heartbreaking story about a toddler who'd wandered away from his grandmother's house only to be found dead weeks later, less than a mile from where searchers had been on the first night of the search. That story had haunted her for months after she'd read it, and now it was back, running rampant through her mind.

That would be them. They would run out of food. Someone would be injured and leave a delectable little trail of blood behind them. They'd be tracked by Melanie's cougar. They'd eat poisonous wild mushrooms in a doomed bid to stay alive, or they'd freeze under the first snowfall, which wasn't that far off.

"Hey, doesn't moss grow on the north side of trees?" Melanie said.

Olivia shook herself back to reality. "What?"

"Moss grows on the north side of trees, right?"

"That's not just an old wives' tale?"

"I don't know. I don't think so." She walked around and looked at several of the larger tree trunks nearby. "Well, these have moss on both sides, but there's more on one side than the other."

Olivia examined the trees. "Yes. Maybe."

"We don't have anything better to go on, do we?"

Olivia shook her head and looked again at the map, hoping, she supposed, that everything would all suddenly fall into place and make sense. "If that's true, I think we've been going west, more or less. And we haven't hit the trail. If we were on the left side, we probably should have hit it by now. We could be going along right here where there's not a lot of elevation change overall."

Melanie leaned over the map, and Olivia ran her finger along a short section.

"If we kept going this way—if this is the way we're going—we would eventually start going downhill, but we wouldn't reach a trail for miles, and it would be this Cross Trail here, not the Little Carp River Trail we want."

"You think we should turn south?"

"Or what we think is south, yeah."

Melanie nodded. "That sounds like a good idea."

"I think it's our best bet—as long as we're actually on this side of the trail and actually going this direction."

They shared a resigned look and then turned what may or may not have been south.

"You know," Melanie said as they picked their way through the trees and underbrush, "this all goes to show that you can plan all you like using the facts you know, but at some point you're going to run into something you just don't have the data for, and you're going to have to go with your gut and trust the Universe to send you in the right direction. Not all of life can be mapped out."

Olivia rolled her eyes, knowing Melanie couldn't see her face. "That from one of your videos?"

"No, but it will be."

"If we ever get back to civilization."

"Don't say that. You're such a pessimist."

"Experience has led me to what I think is a reasonable view of the world," Olivia said, "and it's not necessarily negative."

"Well, what would you call it?"

"Indifferent. The world is indifferent. The universe doesn't want one thing or another. It's just running along according to the natural laws that were put into motion billions of years ago when the universe started expanding. It doesn't care whether I have a good life or a bad life, a long life or a short life. I don't matter to it. You don't matter to it. And that's okay."

"That doesn't sound okay to me. That sounds horrible."

"Luckily, you are not bound to it. I'm not interested in proselytizing and getting everyone to agree with me. I'm not a militant atheist or anything. It makes no difference whether others agree or not. Believe what you want."

"So at this moment, as we wander around, lost in the woods, the only hope you have is in yourself? In your ability to find the trail again?"

Olivia didn't answer.

"That seems like a sad way to go through life, is all I'm saying," Melanie said. "And a hopeless one."

Olivia stabbed a hiking pole into the ground. "Yeah, well, a lot of good hope does you. Hope doesn't save people. Hope didn't save—"

She didn't finish her sentence. She didn't have to. They both knew what she was talking about.

They were quiet for a while as they struggled on. Olivia scanned the trees for moss now, as well as blue blazes. She checked her watch again. They had eaten at Lily Pond at 11:00. It was now nearing 1:30. The sun would set in six hours, and it would start to get dark earlier than that, especially if this cloud cover didn't break.

Just as Olivia was beginning to let her fears get the best of her again, she felt the ground change. The balls of her feet started stinging a little, and her toes pressed up against the insides of her shoes. Her knees felt achy, and the muscles on the front of her thighs were sore. They were finally going downhill. Thirty minutes later, she could hear water. She stopped and motioned to Melanie to listen.

"The river," she said.

Olivia picked up the pace, crashing through bushes and tripping on rocks and roots, ignoring the pain in her hip. A moment later she could see it. She wanted to cry, but she just kept stomping through the ferns and fungus to the water's edge. Melanie caught up with her a few seconds later. Olivia gripped Melanie's upper arms and pulled her in for a hug made awkward by the packs.

"We did it!" Melanie said. "We found the river!"

Olivia threw her pack to the ground and felt her legs buckling as she came down from her heightened state of anxiety. She sat down hard on the ground and felt the tears of relief that she couldn't stop anymore slide down her face. Melanie plopped down beside her and put an arm around her shaking shoulders.

"Are you okay?"

The voice didn't belong to Melanie.

Twelve

MELANIE LOOKED UP to see a man coming up out of the water. He wasn't particularly tall or particularly fat or particularly handsome or particularly anything at all—except wet. Water dripped from his olive-green waders and a beige canvas bag slung across his body, and trickled down his bare forearms beneath the rolled-up sleeves of an orange-and-green-plaid button-up flannel. His hands were empty.

Melanie was about to stand up when he knelt down to their level.

"You're a bit off the path, aren't you?" he said.

He had a kind face that somehow looked both concerned and unsurprised, as though he had expected them to tumble out of the forest miles from any trail but was nonetheless troubled by the state they were in. They must look quite a sight after hours pushing through the undergrowth.

"We lost the trail for a while, trying to avoid the muddy parts," Melanie said.

Olivia seemed at last to be able to pull herself together. "Is this the Little Carp River?"

"Yes," the man said. "But if you're looking for the trail, you're about a mile away from it at the moment. Maybe more."

Melanie pulled out a water bottle for her sister and unscrewed the top, but Olivia was focused on the map she'd retrieved from her back pocket.

"Can you tell me where we are on this?"

The man edged closer, took a moment to orient himself to the map, and pointed. "Right about here."

Melanie pushed the water bottle into Olivia's hand. "What are you doing way out here?"

He looked down at his waders and smiled. "Fishing. Downstream it's a bit overfished, so when I come out here I like to visit these upstream areas off the beaten path."

"We're supposed to be on the Little Carp River Trail," Olivia said, getting to her feet and brushing the dirt off her rear end. "I'm assuming we can just follow the river downstream and we'll get there?"

"Might take a while, but yes."

Olivia sighed. "I don't know what to do about our campsite tonight. There's no way we'll make it before dark now."

"Which one are you staying at?"

Olivia quickly folded the map up and tucked it into her pocket. "We'll figure it out." She yanked up her pack and slipped her arms through the straps. Melanie saw her tuck the knife into her pants pocket.

She understood why Olivia didn't want to tell a man they'd just met where they were sleeping that night, but she didn't have to be so brusque about it. "Thank you for your help . . ."

"Josh," the man supplied.

"Thanks, Josh. We appreciate it. Best of luck on your fishing." Melanie struggled to stand with the heavy pack still on her back. The man—Josh—held out a hand. She took it and he helped her to her feet.

"You're welcome to use my campsite tonight," he said. "I'm right on the river, just past the Greenstone Falls cabin where the Little Carp Trail meets the Cross Trail. It's not too far. And if I have that site, I imagine yours is quite a ways further since the backcountry sites are so spread out in this section." He looked up at the sky. "You're right that you'll be hard-pressed to get where you're going before dark."

"Thanks, but—" Olivia began, but Melanie cut her off.

"Just a minute." She pulled Olivia aside and turned her to face away from Josh, who politely took a few steps away to give them some privacy.

"What?" Olivia whispered harshly. "We are not staying with some strange man out in the middle of nowhere."

"He seems very nice, and he's willing to help us."

"We don't need any help. We found the river on our own and we'll find the trail on our own and we'll camp on our own."

"How far is our site?"

Olivia said nothing.

"Let me see the map."

Olivia sighed. "If he's right about where we are on the river, it's at least six miles away."

"Are you crazy? We can't hike six miles in"—she checked her watch—"five hours. And eat. And rest. And set up the tent. And—"

"Okay, I get it," Olivia said. "But we can't just trust this guy.

We know nothing about him. We can't go to sleep with him just outside the tent."

"You slept with a *bear* outside the tent."

"That's different."

"Yeah, this is a person, not a large carnivore. Someone who is polite and doesn't look like a serial killer and who seems genuinely concerned about us."

"We're as close to the road as we are to his campsite. Maybe we should call this trip what it is—a bit of a disaster—and just see if someone can take us to our car."

"You mean hitchhike? How is hitchhiking with a stranger—who then has us in his car and can take us anywhere he wants—better than pitching a tent at this guy's spot? And no, I don't want to call it quits. This trip is not a disaster. And we haven't even seen the best spots yet. You said there would be waterfalls—"

"We saw a waterfall."

"One waterfall! You promised me eight. And Lake Superior. And the Lake of the Clouds. And the overlooks. All the best stuff is yet to come. I am not giving up halfway through just because it got hard."

The look on Olivia's face told Melanie the barb had hit a tender spot. Maybe Olivia's only tender spot.

Her sister narrowed her eyes. "What's that supposed to mean?"

"I think you know."

"You're such a child."

"I'd rather be a child than whatever it is you've become." Even as she said it, Melanie regretted it. She didn't even mean it. But she was in it now. "You go ahead and hitchhike to the car if you want. I'll take my chances with Josh."

Olivia gaped. "That's not fair."

"Oh, you want to talk about fair?"

Olivia planted her hands on her hips. "Sure. Hit me with your best shot."

"Was it fair that you just left and went back to school when Mom and Dad died, leaving me to sort everything out on my own?" Melanie started, holding up one finger. "Was it fair that you never called Grandma Jean and Grandpa Lou or Grandma Ann or Aunt Susan and Uncle Craig or even sent them a card for ten years?" Two fingers. "Is it fair that you've never come to see me in Petoskey? Or that you didn't invite me to your graduation?" Three, four. "You can't just quit when things get hard. You can't just quit your family. That's not how it works."

Melanie hadn't exactly meant to say those things. They were things she'd thought—for years—but she never imagined she'd just blurt them all out like that. She waited for Olivia to say something. She could see her sister gathering up the words in her mouth, like the pulling back of an arrow in a bow.

"Maybe I did leave. Maybe I did quit my family—what remained of my family. But at least I didn't betray Mom and Dad by getting all chummy with the guy who killed them."

Melanie could feel her face beginning to crumple. She'd known that Olivia wasn't happy that she'd forgiven Justin for the crash. But she'd tried to keep her relationship with him a secret. It was why they met in Grand Rapids rather than Rockford, which was too small a town with too big a gossip network. It was why the move to Petoskey had worked out so well. No one there knew them, knew their history, knew their secret.

There their odd friendship could grow, unscrutinized. There they could both try to move on with their lives.

Melanie took a slow, cleansing breath. She would not let Olivia drag her into defending herself. "I'm finishing this trip, with or without you." She turned to tell Josh that they would camp at his site, but he'd disappeared. "Nice going," she said to Olivia.

"Me? You're the one who's freaking out here."

Melanie walked down to the water and looked first downstream and then up. Josh was standing in the middle of the river in water up to his knees, casting a fly into a still spot downstream. Melanie waved to him, but he was focused on the water. A moment later the line caught and tightened. Josh alternated between reeling it back in and letting it run out until suddenly a huge fish leaped out of the water. Another dance between drawing in and letting go until finally the fish could not resist the pull any longer. Josh held it firmly in his hand and removed the hook. Melanie assumed he would put it back into the water, but instead, he slipped it into the canvas bag at his side.

She waved again, but now it seemed superfluous. He was already walking toward her through the water with a smile on his face, like he knew what she was about to say.

"Decided to take me up on the offer?" he said when he reached the shore.

"How'd you know?"

"If the answer was no, you'd already be gone."

Melanie smiled and held out her hand. "I'm—"

"Melanie." He took her hand and gave it one firm shake.

"Yes." Had she told him her name? He must have heard Olivia say it. He must have heard a lot of things. "Please forgive us if we didn't seem grateful for your offer. We've had a rough day. Actually, between you and me, we've had a rough decade. My sister's not so keen on the idea, but I believe in fate and there's no such thing as coincidence, and for us to come out of the woods right here, where you were randomly fishing way off the trail? Well, that's fate."

Josh smiled. "That's not quite what I'd call it, but you certainly are right where you need to be, and right on time." He indicated the bag at his side. "A fish this size is really too much for just me."

"Oh, thank you, but I'm vegan."

He raised his eyebrows and gave her a little nod as Olivia walked up. He held out his hand to her. "Olivia."

Had Melanie told him *her* name? They must have been arguing a lot louder than she thought. How embarrassing.

Olivia gave his hand a cursory shake and pointed to the map. "Is this the spot?"

"Yes," Josh said. "I'm already set up there, but there's plenty of room for your tent."

"We won't be imposing on you?" Olivia said.

"Of course not. Meeting people along the way is one of the best parts of any journey. And I had a feeling I'd have company tonight."

"Oh, I get feelings like that too," Melanie said. "Once I found a dog wandering around and I had a feeling its name was Sadie, and then when I found the owners and they came to pick her up and told me her name, it *was* Sadie."

"So when do we start?" Olivia said.

Josh shrugged. "I'm ready if you are."

"Lead the way."

Thirteen

OLIVIA COULDN'T BELIEVE she was doing this. Following some strange man deeper into the woods. If Josh had been a woman or a young couple or even those three loud people from the parking lot, it would be totally different. But no. The one person out in the woods they run into is a bearded man in a plaid flannel shirt with an unsettlingly calm demeanor. If she saw this in a film, she'd walk out, disgusted with how stupid the heroine was. Likely their story would be made into a movie someday—one of those poorly acted TV movies about tragic unsolved mysteries. It would be called *Who Killed the Greene Girls?*, and she and Melanie would be painted as simpletons lured to their brutal deaths by a man played by a C-list actor with one expression, and the expression would say *I lure simpletons to their brutal deaths.*

The one saving grace in all of this was that Josh's campsite was not nearly as remote as many of the backcountry sites. If anything happened, anyone staying in the two nearby cabins would hear their screams, and they were close enough to the road that they could run there if needed to find someone who would pick them up and take them to their car.

They walked along the river, Josh in the lead, Melanie in the middle, Olivia bringing up the rear. Every so often, Josh would look back to make sure they were keeping up with his brisk pace, and if they were lagging he would stop to let them catch up. He even offered to carry a pack. Olivia would have liked nothing more than to be relieved of her heavy burden, but allowing Josh to carry it would have made him more of a hero than he already was. She did not want to be dependent on the kindness of this stranger, and to let him carry her pack would be admitting that she needed his help. But she didn't. She could take care of herself.

Despite the less-than-ideal situation, Olivia tried to enjoy the walk. The river's gurgling flow was a constant pleasant drone. The breeze whispered through the browning trees. It was beautiful out here. But it was hard to focus on these good things. Because once she stopped obsessing about how dumb it was to follow Josh, she started obsessing about how awful the fight with Melanie had been. Olivia had had no idea that Melanie felt so . . . abandoned. She had always figured that they were both coping in their own unique way and that Melanie was happy with her choice to stay behind, just as she had been happy with her choice to move on. Yet all these long years Melanie had been quietly building up a pile of grievances and accusations.

Was that what this trip was about? Getting her alone in the woods, where she'd have to listen to her sister berate her for her conduct for the past ten years? Did Melanie actually think anything she said could not be trumped by the fact that she'd befriended Justin Navarro? If Melanie thought Olivia was just going to hand her a free pass for that, she had another thing coming.

It was already late afternoon when they saw the first sign of the trail—a straight wooden bridge crossing the river in the distance.

"There it is!" Melanie said, turning back toward Olivia with a huge grin across her face.

"That's the spur trail," Josh said. "It connects the main trail with the parking area off the road."

Despite her fatigue, Olivia quickened her pace. "How far is the parking lot?"

"Another mile," Josh said.

"Is there a ranger stationed there or anything?"

"No. Just a gravel lot and a pit toilet," he said. "By the way, whenever either of you needs to stop, just let me know."

Olivia frowned. She hadn't thought of peeing out in the open anywhere near this guy. "Are you parked in that lot?"

"No, I'm way down at Pinkerton Creek."

They reached the bridge, and Olivia took a moment to appreciate the feel of a man-made structure beneath her feet. Strange how a level surface was so foreign to the natural world. Just another reason to doubt that the world had been made specifically for humans, who had to do so much to alter the environment to make it more to their liking. If God had created everything for them, wouldn't he have created it to suit them more?

"We're coming up on Overlooked Falls," Josh said. "It's just a few hundred feet down this way. Why don't you drop your packs here and we'll take a quick break."

He started walking before they could answer. Melanie leaned back against a tree and unbuckled her straps, then let the pack slide down to the ground. She waited for Olivia to do the same.

"I'll keep mine on," she said.

Mel shook her head and practically skipped after Josh. Olivia struggled on behind. They had been walking so long through wild terrain that the path here felt wide and luxurious. Dead pine needles beneath her feet cushioned her steps and softened the sound of her footfalls. In a moment, she couldn't see Melanie or Josh ahead, but when she came over a small rise, she caught sight of them down by the water. Josh, in his waders, was standing in the river, and Melanie, a couple feet away on land, phone in hand, was taking pictures of the falls. Then she turned the lens on their new companion and took a picture of him. Olivia could imagine what Melanie would put on her blog about their benefactor. Then her heart sank at the thought of what she might write about her cantankerous sister.

Olivia stepped off the path and over large boulders down toward the river. The falls were nowhere to be seen, though she could hear them.

"Aren't they sweet?" Melanie said when Olivia reached her.

Olivia turned to look upriver, and there they were. A series of small waterfalls tumbling over resistant rock. At the topmost level, the river split in two around a large outcropping of rock, and the water leapt down in two falls, joining back up for a distance of perhaps fifteen or twenty feet, only to split again around an immovable stone. The bedrock was brown, etched with cracks and faults and peppered with moss and fallen yellow leaves. It was truly a beautiful sight. The kind of thing Olivia had been most looking forward to seeing on this trip out into the wilderness. A moving postcard.

Could Melanie have been right when she claimed that Olivia had never even sent a card or a letter to anyone in her family for the past ten years? What kind of a person did that? What would her parents have thought if they knew?

But they didn't know. Olivia made a mental note to send apologies to her neglected relatives. She'd fix it, and then she wouldn't need to feel guilty.

Beside her Melanie sighed. "I'm so glad we didn't miss this."

Josh looked back to them and smiled. "It's nice, isn't it. And it's not even the best one, in my opinion."

"Have you seen all the falls in the park?" Melanie said.

"At one time or another."

"Do you live up here?"

"I'm from Paradise."

"Oh," Melanie said, "so these falls must seem pretty puny to you after Tahquamenon Falls."

Josh sloshed through the water back to shore. "They're not better or worse. Just different. Sometimes you need the kind of powerful experience you get from the big falls like Upper Tahquamenon, and sometimes you need something quieter than that. Just like sometimes you want a nice big crackling campfire and sometimes all you need is a single candle."

"Well, I need a big crackling campfire," Melanie said. "I've been cold all day. How far is it to the campsite?"

"Just about a mile," Josh said.

"Are you ready to go, Ollie?"

Olivia didn't care for Melanie using her childhood nickname

in front of a stranger, but she nodded. Watching two people walk around unfettered by packs had her feeling truly exhausted.

They walked back up to the wooden bridge where Melanie had left her pack.

"Could you hold this a second?" Josh asked her, handing over the fly rod.

"Sure," Melanie said.

Then Josh scooped up her pack and swung it onto his back.

"Oh, no, you don't have to do that."

"It's no problem," Josh said, loosening the straps to fit around his larger frame. "I don't mind at all."

"Well, okay," Melanie said. She picked up her hiking poles in her free hand. "Do you want to use these?"

"You keep those. I'll take back the rod. It's not easy to walk through a forest with a fishing pole and not get it all hung up on branches. It would be easier for me to carry it."

With the pack on his back and the canvas bag with the trout in it hanging just below his right hip, Josh led the way across the bridge and down another trail on the opposite side of the river. This time, Melanie motioned to Olivia to go next, but Olivia declined.

"You go first," she said. "I'll be slower."

"Want me to take your pack for a while?"

"No. Let's just go. It's not far now."

They hugged the river most of the way, and Olivia watched the fallen leaves speed effortlessly by on their way to Lake Superior a little less than seven miles downstream. There were several more petite drops with unnamed falls and cascades as the river hurtled itself down the resistant bedrock.

Twenty minutes later, Josh stopped and pointed toward the water. "Greenstone Falls."

They followed him a little farther downstream and down to the river, where again they had to turn back to look in the direction they had come from in order to experience the beauty. Perhaps fifteen feet wide, Greenstone Falls was a picturesque cascade dropping a gradual six feet over rounded rocks and boulders into a swirling pool of foam and leaves. Though it was still cloudy, the yellow trees that framed the waterfall seemed to shine with a light of their own.

Beside her, Melanie was taking more pictures.

"Why don't I take a picture of the two of you?" Josh offered.

"Oh, yes! Thank you," Melanie said, handing over her phone. She sidled closer to Olivia. "Take that pack off, for goodness' sake. It'll be a better picture without it."

"But then I'll have to put it back on again."

Melanie snapped open the waistband strap. "Just take it off. I'll carry it the rest of the way." She was yanking it off before Olivia could do much to stop her.

Josh took the pack from her with one hand and leaned it against a rock.

Melanie pulled Olivia close. "You're all sweaty."

"Of course I am. You would be too."

"Turn this way," Josh commanded. He framed the shot. "Smile."

Olivia obliged, but the smile felt fake. She had utterly lost control of this trip that she had so meticulously planned. Wrong turns, lost trails, uninvited guests. And now she was being told to smile.

Josh handed the phone back to Melanie. "Not much further now."

Olivia tried to snatch her pack back up, but Melanie beat her to it. She stumbled a little under the weight. "Holy cow. This is so much heavier than mine. Olivia!"

"It's just because you've been walking without one for a while. It always feels heavier to put it back on."

"No, it's because you've taken more than your fair share of the weight. No wonder you're limping. Either you let me carry the tent tomorrow or at least break it up half and half. And what else is in here that's so heavy—besides your other can of SpaghettiOs?"

Josh laughed. "SpaghettiOs?"

Olivia rolled her eyes. "I don't need any further critique on those, thank you very much." She walked back up to the trail and took the lead position. Melanie and Josh followed.

A moment later, they passed the first cabin, followed by a wooden bridge leading across the river to the second cabin. Less than ten minutes later, Olivia came upon a cleared area right on the river's bank with a fire ring.

"Here we are," Josh said as he and Melanie came up behind. "See, plenty of room."

"But where's your tent?" Olivia said.

"I don't have one." He pointed off toward the woods. "I'm a hammock guy."

There, strung between two sturdy trees, was a lightweight green-and-black zip-up hammock. Beside it, hung on a tree and nearly blending in with it, was a compact backpack.

"You travel light," Olivia said. "Where's the bear pole?"

Josh indicated a spot in the trees. "Over there, but I don't use it."

"What do you do with your food bag?"

"I don't have one. I just fish and do a bit of foraging."

"But what if you don't catch anything?" Melanie said, dumping Olivia's pack at her feet.

"I have some flatbread in my pack. But when I go fishing, I always catch something."

"And you don't worry about bears?" Olivia said. "You know you're supposed to hang that stuff on the poles. It's super dangerous to keep it in your pack."

"Oh, I just hang the pack a ways away at night. I've never had a problem with bears." He slid Melanie's pack off his back and leaned it on a makeshift log bench by the fire ring. "Need some help setting up your tent?"

"Sure," Melanie said at the same time Olivia said, "No thanks."

"We've got it," Olivia said.

"Suit yourself. I'll get a fire going and prep this fish." He walked into the trees and down toward the river.

"That was rude," Melanie said.

"Listen, we're perfectly capable of setting up our tent—I did it on my own last night—so why would we need his help?"

"He was just being polite."

"I'm not interested in feeding his ego or his hero complex. We're not two damsels in distress."

"We kind of were," Mel broke in.

"No," Olivia said as she started to unpack the tent, "we figured out what we needed to do on our own with limited tools and resources. We found the river, just as I thought we would, and we would have been perfectly fine without this guy. Other than carrying your pack, which he didn't have to do, he's done absolutely nothing for us, which is fine because we don't need any help anyway."

"Oh? How much further is it to our reserved campsite?"

Olivia unrolled the tent in one violent motion and laid it on the most level piece of ground. "Three miles, which we could have done."

"We would have been setting up the tent in the dark," Melanie said, pulling out the poles and stakes.

"I have no doubt that we would have managed just fine."

"I don't think I would have been collecting firewood in the dark. So we would have been eating in the dark, in the cold, and then we would have just gone right to sleep. Sounds super fun."

"I don't want to argue about this anymore. You got your way. Here we are, risking our lives with some random guy, just like you wanted."

Melanie threw up her hands. "Random? Of all the places we could have reached the river, of all the possible times we could have reached it, we come out of the woods right there, right then, when a nice, helpful person is there, way off the trail. How can you think that was random?"

"Because how could it not be?" Olivia pushed a pole through a sleeve on the outside of the tent. "There's no other logical explanation than that it was a coincidence."

Melanie caught the pole from the other side and affixed it to the metal eye ring attached to the corner of the tent. "Can't you see how crazy that is? If everything is just coincidence, you know the mathematical chances of anything existing at all? Let alone a planet as full of diverse, complex, interrelated life as Earth is?"

Olivia stuffed another pole through another sleeve, jabbing it toward her sister but saying nothing. She clipped and tied and pulled and adjusted.

"It's just strange," Melanie continued, "that someone as smart as you are, with all those expensive degrees, wouldn't see how unlikely it is that all this came from nothing on its own with absolutely no guiding force."

Olivia snapped open the fly and fixed Melanie with a look. "So, you don't think anything at all is just a coincidence?"

Melanie shrugged. "No."

"You believe *everything* that happens is something God or the Universe or whatever has orchestrated?"

"Yes."

Olivia gave the fly another snap and picked up the last pole. "You realize that if that were true, it would mean that this same God or force or whatever orchestrated the accident, right? That it *wanted* our parents to die."

Melanie caught the pole on the other side of the sleeve and stared at Olivia.

"You can't just believe in the good stuff without dealing with the bad, Mel," Olivia continued. "If fate sent you to meet a guy in the woods because he uses a hammock and therefore has plenty of room for your tent at his campsite, then fate also sends one car on a collision course with another. It's not exactly an accident if it was planned out from time immemorial. And I can't believe in any kind of God who would do that."

They finished setting up the tent in silence. Olivia was sure that Melanie must be running through arguments in her mind, but so much time passed that it was clear she couldn't think of any retort. Because there wasn't one. Believing in nothing was better than believing in something that brought comfort when it was convenient but left you out in the cold when it came to the hard stuff in life. Her parents had died because of the unfortunate fact that they were in the wrong place at the wrong time. Nothing more.

When she had pounded the last stake into the ground, Olivia stood up. Josh had gotten the fire going. Melanie was nowhere to be seen.

Fourteen

MELANIE LEANED AGAINST the rough trunk of an enormous pine tree and shut her eyes. Why did every conversation with her sister have to be like that? It hadn't always been that way, had it? They had once had so much fun together. They used to tell each other secrets and laugh until their stomachs hurt and conspire with each other against babysitters. Olivia used to stand up for her. Now it just felt like she was stomping all over her.

The worst of it was, Melanie had never actually thought through the full implications of her belief that there were no coincidences, and now, without all the online friends and followers who stood at the ready to buoy her spirits, she didn't know what to do. Anytime she ran into something hard in life, she'd just post about it on Twitter or Facebook and her community would pounce on her with encouragement and positive vibes, even quoting her own words from her coaching videos back to her. Justin too had largely been supportive—even if he'd seemed less apt to agree with her on the finer points and more likely to stay silent on spiritual matters since he started attending a church. No one ever just came right out and told her she was dumb for believing what she did as Olivia had.

As she had to Olivia.

Why had she done that? It was breaking her one rule—never go negative. Negative statements hurt, no matter how well reasoned or carefully delivered. She never told her clients they were wrong. How was that helpful? And here she'd told her sister—the lawyer—that she hadn't thought something out. When the truth was it was Melanie who hadn't thought something out.

Had the Universe chosen her parents for destruction? Her kind, civic-minded parents who never hurt anyone? Could some things be coincidence and other things not? That didn't seem very consistent. Though consistency had never concerned her before. She believed a bit of everything because a bit of everything felt true and right.

"There you are."

Melanie jumped and put her hand over her heart.

"I think your sister's worried about you." Josh stood a few feet away to the right. He had removed his waders and his hands were in his pockets. "We're about ready for dinner. Just waiting on the flames to die down a bit. Are you hungry?"

"Oh, sure." Melanie stood straight and brushed off the back of her pants. "Though you're wrong about Olivia. We're kind of in a thing right now. She's probably happy for a few minutes without me."

Josh stepped aside to let Melanie pass. "If you don't mind my asking, what's the problem?"

"Oh, nothing," she said as she picked her way back toward the tent. "Just sister stuff."

"I know we just met," he said, "but can I make a suggestion?"

"Fire away. I will always take a bit of advice."

"Assume the best about her."

Melanie stopped walking. "I always assume the best about people. And anyway, I don't think she's a bad person. We just don't see eye to eye on something and we're arguing about it."

"I'm not talking about whether she's a good person or a bad person. I'm talking about how she's feeling inside."

"I don't really get what you mean."

"Whatever you're fighting about, where is she coming from? Is she coming from a place of pride, where she feels she has to be right?"

"Definitely."

"Or," Josh continued, "is she coming from a place of fear, where she's afraid to be wrong?"

Melanie thought for a moment. She couldn't imagine Olivia being afraid of anything.

"Because in my experience, when it comes down to it, most people are ultimately operating from a place of fear, not a place of assurance. It makes them defensive, makes it hard to listen to other points of view. Just food for thought. And speaking of food . . ." Josh swept his hand toward the fire, inviting Melanie to continue the walk back to camp.

As they came out to where Olivia could see them, Melanie examined her. Her hands were planted firmly on her hips and her mouth was set in a line. When they got closer Melanie could see the two deepening wrinkles between Olivia's eyebrows that had been there since college. She didn't look afraid. She looked irate.

"Where were you?"

"I was just over there," Melanie said, pointing, then she continued on to her pack and got out her food bag and a water bottle.

"I don't have plates," Josh said as he poked at the fire and positioned a small folding grill rack over the glowing coals, "but I do have pita bread that works just as well." He laid the two fillets of the fish he had caught and dressed on the grill and then pulled out a compact travel salt-and-pepper shaker.

"Melanie doesn't eat meat," Olivia said.

"I'm fine with what I've got in my pack, thanks," Melanie said.

"What about you, Olivia?" Josh said.

"Oh, she eats meat," Melanie offered.

"Great. Have you ever had fish that was caught just a couple hours ago?"

"I can't say that I have," Olivia said.

"You'll love it," he said.

Josh tended the fish, then got out the pita bread and passed it around. Melanie took some to be polite, though she normally tried to be gluten free in solidarity with those who had celiac disease. Their host parceled out some fish between Olivia and himself and looked in Melanie's direction once more to offer it to her. She shook her head and smiled.

"Tell him why you're a vegan," Olivia said.

"She doesn't have to explain herself to me," Josh said.

"It's because she believes in reincarnation and she doesn't want to accidentally eat our—anyone she knew."

"That's not—" Melanie started.

"Oh, and also just in case animals have souls. She's covering her bases."

Melanie stared hard at Olivia until her sister met her eyes.

Olivia stared right back and raised her eyebrows as if to say, *Am I wrong?*

"What do you believe about that, Olivia?" Josh said.

Olivia broke away from Melanie's stare. "I don't believe in reincarnation. And I don't believe animals have souls. Or people, for that matter."

Josh nodded, but not in agreement. Melanie knew that nod. It was a noncommittal nod, one that said "I hear you but I don't agree with you, and I don't want to get into it right now." She got that nod from people a lot.

They ate in silence for a minute. Melanie waited for Josh to add his opinion to the discussion, but he remained quiet.

The light was beginning to dim a little. Night was approaching. Their second night on the trail. Not where they were supposed to be. Not sharing their deepest thoughts and longings like she'd hoped. Just sitting on a log, a foot away from one another. A foot that might as well be a mile.

"Why do you come out here all alone?" she heard herself asking.

Josh put another chunk of fish into his mouth and chewed thoughtfully for a moment before swallowing. "I like to spend time out in God's country."

"But why don't you come out with friends or family?"

"That's a rude question," Olivia said.

"No it isn't," Josh countered. "I enjoy spending some time alone now and then. And like I said, I always meet new people out here."

Melanie tore a small piece of pita off the whole. "What do you do? Like, your job."

"I do a bit of everything. I build things, I fix things, make things beautiful."

"Like houses? Do you build houses?"

"Sometimes. I build tables and mantelpieces. Cabinets. I fix plumbing and engines."

"You do all that in Paradise?" Olivia said. "Seems like too small of a town to sustain that kind of business."

"Most of my work is outside of Paradise. I travel all over."

Melanie spoke around the pita in her mouth. "Do you have a website? I could look you up when we get back to civilization."

"No website."

"How do you run a business without a website?" Olivia said.

"It's mostly a word-of-mouth thing. People just tell other people about me."

Melanie laughed lightly. "It's like you're from another era. My whole business is online."

He waited for her to continue.

"I'm a life coach. I do it mostly through my blog and videos on YouTube and social media and stuff. Just sending out encouragement to people, you know?"

"And what do you do, Olivia?"

"I'm a prosecuting attorney."

"She's very good," Melanie piped in. "You know that story a while back about the guy who had swindled a bunch of old ladies out of their life savings, pretending to be investing for them? She sent that guy to prison. And a bunch of others. She hasn't lost very many cases."

Olivia looked at her. "How do you know?"

Melanie shrugged. "Just because you don't know what's going

on in my life doesn't mean I don't know what's going on in yours." Even as she said it, she hoped it was true. If Olivia really knew what was going on in her life, it would get real ugly real fast.

Soon the last bites of dinner were eaten and night was closing in. Josh put some more wood on the fire and blew on the embers. It flared up, and Melanie basked in the heat. Olivia went off to hang up the food bags, brush her teeth, and use the facilities, such as they were, before it got pitch-black, then she disappeared into the tent. Melanie stayed close to the fire. She didn't want to go into the tent with her sister. She didn't want to start fighting again. Being near Josh was better. He seemed like the calm center in their sisterly hurricane. Across the fire his face glowed a warm orange in the darkened woods. She couldn't decide if he was handsome or not.

"How long are you out here for?" Melanie asked.

"This time, I think at least two more nights."

"Where are you going tomorrow? Or will you stay at this camp the entire time?"

"Tomorrow I'm heading down the Cross Trail to Superior for one night, then I'll be heading up the Big Carp River for the salmon run."

Melanie frowned. "So you're not going the same way we are?"

"No. The Cross Trail takes me directly to where I need to be. But you're in for some nice hiking tomorrow. It's one of the best hikes in the park. Besides being up on the escarpment."

"It'd be nicer if you were with us," she said, then immediately regretted it. She didn't want him to think she was flirting with him. She just really liked his company.

Josh smiled at her across the fire. "I'm sure we'll meet up again sometime."

"I hope so." Then it felt like it was time to call it a night. Melanie always tried to follow those gut feelings. And to stay one moment longer would make it awkward. She stood up and waved. "I better get to bed before Olivia wonders what's happened to me again. I'll see you tomorrow."

Josh returned the wave. "Good night."

Melanie dispensed with the evening rituals and climbed into the tent and over Olivia, who was lying in the dark, still but obviously not sleeping. She changed into her pj's as quietly as possible, trying not to kick her sister, then slipped into the sleeping bag Olivia had prepared for her without her asking or knowing or even really thinking about the fact that a sleeping bag needed to be prepared. Olivia, ever the older sister. Melanie lay there in the blackness and wondered if she could fall asleep with her eyes open since it was just like having them shut.

Olivia's voice rose out of the dark somewhere near Melanie's feet. "Hey, Mel?"

"Yeah?"

"I'm sorry." It was quiet for a beat. "I was kind of a jerk today."

Melanie waited for her to continue. But it was apparently all she had to say.

"Miss Crabapple! The papers, if you please!"

Olivia sat at one end of the dining room table, wearing her father's old glasses and ringing a small gold bell. At the other end of the table, Melanie tore a sheet of paper from an electric typewriter found at a neighbor's garage sale the day before and rushed it over to her sister.

"Your speech, Mr. President!"

"Madame President," Olivia corrected out of the side of her mouth. Then loudly, "Miss Crabapple, how do you ever hope to be secretary of state when you can hardly manage being secretary of this office?"

"Yes, Mr.—Madame President. Yes, of course."

Olivia strode to the window, gripped her nonexistent lapel, and stared into the middle distance, which was really just the lilac bush in the backyard. Then she ran her eyes over the speech she had just been handed. "Miss Crabapple, the fate of the country is at stake and you hand me this gibberish?"

"You didn't give me enough time," Melanie said in her own voice.

"Shh," Olivia hissed. "Go get the hat and sit in the living room. You're a reporter now."

Melanie took off the elbow-length gloves and shawl she had donned as Miss Crabapple and put on a fedora from the dress-up trunk.

"Pad and pen," Olivia directed.

Melanie slid the legal pad and a black fountain pen from the table and sat in the wingback chair.

"No, you're on the couch," Olivia said.

Melanie sighed and changed places. "Come on, just give the speech."

Olivia walked to the center of the room and pretended to rest her arms upon an invisible lectern.

"Friends, countrymen"—she nodded at Melanie—"reporters from all the most important papers in the world."

Melanie nodded back, her invisible mustache twitching.

"I come to you today not just as your president but as your friend. We stand on the brink of war. The aliens that—" She looked at Melanie. "Does it have to be aliens?"

"Yes. You said they could be from anywhere."

"Fine." Olivia addressed the rest of the living room. "The aliens that have invaded Earth can only be stopped if we put aside our differences and join forces. The very human race is at stake! But we must also be aware that these aliens can take on human form, masquerade as one of us."

"Hey, I didn't write that," Melanie said.

"I'm improvising."

"But—"

"They may look like someone you've known for years. Like your own parents." She pointed a finger at Melanie. "Like your own sister!"

Melanie shot up from the couch. "I'm not an alien!"

"That's exactly what an alien would say!"

Melanie threw down the legal pad and the pen. "I'm not playing anymore."

"Wait!" Olivia said, grabbing her arm to keep her from leaving the room. "Okay, you're not an alien. You're not an alien."

Melanie allowed Olivia to turn her toward the kitchen, where her parents were washing and drying the dinner dishes to the sounds of eighties pop music.

"But maybe they *are," Olivia whispered.*

Melanie stifled a giggle. "Okay."

Olivia removed the glasses and Melanie took off the hat. They dug around in the trunk for the two thick sticks that served as swords, magic wands, and conductors' batons, depending on the need. Now they were laser guns. They crept slowly, quietly, toward the kitchen's swinging door. The song ended. They stood stock-still, like statues, until the next one on the CD began. They flanked the door. Olivia pushed it slightly open with her gun.

There they were. Aliens. At the sink. Not washing dishes. No. They were developing a toxic chemical soup that they would unleash upon an unsuspecting planet within minutes. They must be stopped.

Olivia charged into the room, Melanie at her heels, both screaming and waving their laser guns in the air.

The alien that looked like their dad dropped a wet dish, and it shattered on the floor.

The girls stopped shouting. Looked from the shards on the floor to the faces of their stunned parents.

"Out!" their mother said.

They scurried out of the room. Melanie began to cry. Olivia quickly disposed of the sticks and closed the trunk while Melanie stood in the dining room, tears streaming down her face.

"Shhhh," Olivia soothed. "Shhhh."

She could hear the pieces of the broken plate being collected. Then she thought she heard another sound.

"Shhhh," she said again, this time to quiet her blubbering sister.

Melanie swallowed hard and wiped her nose on her sleeve.

Was that . . . laughter?

Olivia peeked through the swinging door again. Her parents were sitting on the kitchen floor, faces red, mouths stretched in mirth, practically crying as they tried to suppress the laughter. She opened the door the rest of the way, and her mother schooled her features, but her dad couldn't stop.

"Sorry," Olivia offered. She felt Melanie come up behind her.

Their mother motioned them into the room with one arm and elbowed their father with the other. "Would you stop?" she said to him. Then to the girls, "Come here."

They shuffled forward into the room, the door swinging closed behind them.

"I don't think I have to tell you that was not a good idea, right?"

The girls shook their heads.

"You shouldn't sneak up on people, and you shouldn't shoot at them, and you really shouldn't do those things when they have wet dishes in their hands, right?"

The girls nodded.

Having recovered for the moment, their father added, "You're lucky that wasn't one of the good dishes."

They nodded again.

"Okay, come here," he said.

Olivia and Melanie walked into their parents' open arms. They sat there in a giggly pile on the wet kitchen floor. And all was forgiven.

Fifteen

OLIVIA OPENED HER EYES. She could make out the tent around her in the gray light of almost dawn. How long had she slept? She felt the reassuring hardness of the gas station knife in her hand, ready to be flipped open and used to defend herself and her sister should the need arise. Her sister. She struggled to unzip the mummy bag from the inside and sat up. Melanie was there. On her side. Still asleep.

Olivia lay back down. But then she needed to pee. This was the worst part of backpacking. Having to get up off the ground after a day of hiking and go out into the cold and drop your pants. Guys had it so easy.

Every joint creaked and every muscle screamed in protest as she slid out of the tent and into her shoes. Blisters on her heels and the tops of her two littlest toes felt like lightning rubbing against the inside of each shoe. With some effort, she pulled herself into a standing position and zipped up the tent door, then stumbled out from under the extended roof of the fly and into the murky morning. Her breath came in clouds as she searched her pack for the toilet paper and shovel.

She walked a few dozen feet into the woods and then looked around to make sure Josh couldn't see her, but she couldn't even see his hammock from where she was. She quickly dug her hole, did what she'd set out to do, and covered everything up. Back at her pack she used the hand sanitizer and ran her eyes over the surrounding trees. Where Josh's hammock should have been, there was nothing. No pack hanging up, no foldable grill rack standing over the ashes in the fire ring. Had he already left? Had she imagined him?

Olivia quickly took stock of their things and found nothing missing. She retrieved the food bags and filtered the water, and then she realized that she was incredibly cold. She climbed back into the tent and snuggled back down into her sleeping bag just as Melanie was waking up.

"It's freezing out there," she said.

Melanie groaned. "I told you we should have done this in the summer."

"I'd rather be cold than sweating and swarmed by mosquitos."

"I guess."

They lay in the gray light, Olivia trying to warm up, Melanie moving and flexing inside her sleeping bag.

"My back is killing me," Melanie said.

"It'll be fun putting those packs back on."

"Wrong."

"We should get going as soon as possible. Get a jump on things. We have a lot of ground to make up."

Melanie groaned again.

"Hey, I gave us an out yesterday. We could have hitched back to the car and slept in the little cabins again last night. You wanted to keep hiking."

"And I still do," Melanie said. "I just need to get moving and I'm sure I'll be fine. Maybe Josh can make another fire this morning."

"He's gone."

Melanie sat upright in her bag. "Gone?"

"Gone. I find it a little strange that he didn't say goodbye when he seemed so friendly yesterday. But then, there you go. He was a weirdo after all."

Melanie slumped over.

"You look like you're a larva about to pupate in that thing," Olivia said.

Melanie unzipped the bag and let it fall away. "Holy mackerel, it's cold out there!"

"I told you it was."

"Crap. I have to pee."

"You just gotta do it. Get up."

Melanie crawled over her. "I'm borrowing your shoes. Mine are too far away from the door."

"Whatever."

Olivia helped push Melanie out the door and into a semi-standing position, then zipped up the tent and started changing into her clothes. Two days in and she was feeling grimy and smelling ripe despite using deodorant and wet wipes. She ran a hand through her hair. "Ew," she said out loud to no one. "I'm never going hiking again."

She pulled it into a ponytail, put on a ball cap she'd had since college, and started rolling the bags and deflating the pads. She'd gotten hers done and had started on Melanie's by the time she came back.

"Give me my shoes, would you?" Olivia said. "I need to stand up. I'll finish the bags in a minute once I can stretch my legs."

"I can do my stuff," Melanie said.

"You have to do it really tight to fit it in the stuff sack."

"I know."

"Okay, be my guest."

She left Melanie in the tent and rummaged through her food bag for the second can of SpaghettiOs. She sat on the log and ate the nearly frozen pasta while staring out across the river, completely spaced out and mind blank, only coming to when the plastic spoon came back out of the can empty. She stood and rinsed the can in the river, then added it to her trash bag. She had some pears and drank some water. Then finally Melanie was unzipping the tent to come out. Olivia pushed her shoes toward her with her foot.

"What the—there's something in my shoe," Melanie said.

Olivia leaned over to see under the fly. "What?"

Melanie held out a round black object. Olivia took it from her and opened it. "It's a compass."

"There's a note," Melanie said. "'So you can find your way in the wilderness. Josh.'" She looked up at Olivia. "What a sweetheart. I hope he doesn't need that."

"He seemed like he knew where he was going," Olivia said. "Did he leave his phone number or anything? I'd like to return it at some point or at least pay for it."

"No, and anyway, I think he meant it as a gift, free and clear."

"Are you about done in there? I want to pack up the tent, and you need to eat something."

Melanie held out her hands, and Olivia pulled her to her feet. "Pack away. I'm starving."

Twenty minutes later, they were ready to leave. Melanie rubbed her arms while Olivia consulted first her watch and then the map.

"How many miles?" Melanie said.

"Let's just start walking and not think too much about it. It should be easy, anyway. All we have to do is stick to the river. It's all downhill from here to Lake Superior."

"And we get to see some more waterfalls, right?"

"Right."

They headed west out of the campsite, following the blue blazes of the North Country Trail, a 4,600-mile footpath stretching from the eastern border of New York to the middle of North Dakota. Altogether their trip would take them on just nine miles of the NCT, and most of it they'd hike that day. One hundred and seventy-five miles to the east lay the only other stretch of the NCT Olivia had ever hiked—the trail she'd been hiking when the ranger had found her to tell her of her parents' accident. So even though this was one of the nicest hikes in the Porkies, according to both Josh and the always authoritative word of the internet, there was a part of Olivia that wanted to get it over with. She felt a strange buzzing in the soles of her feet with every step, as if the memory ran through the trail like electricity through a power line.

They made good time despite the cold and their aching muscles, which did loosen up a bit as they walked. Other than a quick stop for water, they didn't slow down—and didn't speak—until they reached the first ford of the day, which would bring them to the spot where they had meant to camp the night before. They wordlessly removed their hiking boots. Olivia's feet were hot and red and one of her blisters had burst, but she forced her water shoes on and waded across the shallow but quick-running river. On the other side, shoes and boots were exchanged once more, and Melanie wandered over to the campsite fire ring, presumably in search of residual warmth.

"There's not going to be any fire left," Olivia said. "This was supposed to be our spot, so no one slept here last night."

"Oh yeah?" Melanie said. "Come see."

Olivia strode over, skeptical. But Melanie was right. It did feel warm. Olivia poked the ash with a stick, releasing the banked embers, which sent up a little flame.

"Ooh! Get some sticks," Melanie said.

"We're not making a fire. We're leaving in a minute. You can't make a fire and leave it. These people should have completely extinguished their fire before they left. And," she added more indignantly, "they shouldn't have even been here!"

"Don't you see though?" Melanie said. "Someone else needed this site. Maybe they got lost too. Or maybe someone turned an ankle and needed to stop for the night. But we got lost and ended up with Josh so that these people could use our open site. So it all worked out."

"Or," Olivia said, "there were just some people hiking who didn't make reservations ahead of time and thought they could do whatever they darn well pleased and take any site they wanted. I bet it was those three we saw at the trailhead where we parked the car." She started looking around the campsite for evidence to support her theory.

Melanie threw up a hand. "Why do you always think the worst of people?"

"Because, in my experience, people are pretty much the worst. You don't know because you live in a happy little echo chamber full of rainbows and unicorns, but I deal with the worst humanity has to offer on an almost daily basis. My whole job is about making people who break the law pay for their crimes. Sometimes it's heinous, like rape and murder, and sometimes it's just people being selfish jerks and not caring about anybody else because all they can think about is themselves and what they want. I have no respect for people who have no respect for the rules. The rules are for the good of everyone."

Olivia realized she was ranting and stopped, though she had much more to say on the topic. She bunched all the embers together with the stick and poured some of her water on them, sending up a plume of smoke, then she spread the whole mess out. "You want to eat lunch at a waterfall?"

Melanie said nothing.

"What?" Olivia prompted.

"My life isn't all rainbows and unicorns."

"Fine. But my point stands." She shifted her weight off her sore hip. "Ready?"

Melanie lifted her hands and her eyebrows in the universal sign for *duh*. Olivia bit back a sigh and started walking.

Just a minute away from the campsite flowed Trappers Falls, which looked more like a waterslide than a waterfall. Olivia and Melanie silently dumped their packs and pulled out their food bags, which were lighter now after two days of hiking. Positioning herself on a stone ledge littered with yellow leaves, Olivia pounded some string cheese and jerky, then started shoving handfuls of nuts into her mouth. She was ravenous, and she wasn't sure why.

"I never really thought about the fact that your job was so negative," Melanie finally said.

"It is what it is."

"It must wear you down though. Day after day dealing with the worst people can do to one another."

"It's definitely a drag sometimes," Olivia said. "But it is satisfying when you know you've gotten a dangerous person off the streets. You feel like you're doing some good. Of course, it doesn't always work that way. There are guilty people that go free. And there are people who get lighter sentences than you wish they would. You see some of the same people come through the court system again and again." She stopped talking for a moment and stared at the water. "It's frustrating, really. What do we have if we don't have a society of people that can function? I mean, it's hard to say if our prison system even works at all except to keep some dangerous people out of the general population. But there are so few who come out of it and seem to be able to make something of their lives. It's not always their fault—society doesn't make it easy for them to reintegrate. It's like, once you've been branded this way, you can never escape it. There's no forgiveness. You're just . . . out."

Melanie nodded. "It sounds like you're under a lot of stress with your job."

"Don't tell me I should meditate or drink special teas or anything."

Melanie laughed. "I wasn't going to."

"Okay, see that you don't." Olivia tied up her trash bag and shoved it back into her food bag. "I'll say this—it's not always fun, but it is necessary. And it seems to be something I'm good at, so there you go."

"You are good at it. You're good at everything. You always have been."

Olivia shook her head. "No, I'm not."

"Yes, you are. You played every sport, you got all A's, you were always getting some leadership award or going on some special trip to somewhere or other because you were one of the smart kids."

Olivia put a hand on Melanie's knee. "You want to know the truth? I wasn't good at everything. I just immediately quit the things I wasn't good at. You don't remember them because I didn't do them long enough."

Now Melanie was shaking her head. "No, I don't believe that."

"It's true. You know I tried out for the fall play my freshman year of high school when you were still in junior high?"

"You did?"

"Yes, and when I didn't get the lead role, I quit. I wasn't going to play some background character with no lines."

"That's crazy. Why would they give you the lead as a freshman? That's not how it works."

"It's how I thought it should work!" Olivia laughed. "And did you know I took piano lessons for a week, and then I quit because I thought playing 'Mary Had a Little Lamb' was infantile and the teacher wouldn't let me jump ahead into better songs because she said I wasn't ready for them?"

Olivia was enjoying the incredulous look Melanie was giving her, so she kept going.

"I quit doing anything artsy when nothing I painted looked like it did in my head. And I never sewed anything after I sewed a little pillow top I was embroidering onto the pants I was wearing. And I never helped Mom cook because I once burned a pan of snickerdoodle cookies and was so angry at myself I cried." Olivia was really laughing now.

Melanie smiled. "I loved cooking with Mom."

Olivia pulled up short. She hadn't meant to mention her mother. And now the memory of that ill-fated attempt at baking became the memory of her mother handing her a freshly laundered softball uniform, which became the memory of her father's ecstatic face the first time she hit a home run, which became the memory of the four of them at a Detroit Tigers game, where she caught a foul ball with her bare hands, chipping a bone in her finger. She didn't know she was crying until Melanie wiped at her cheek.

"It's okay to talk about it," Melanie said. "And it's okay to cry about it."

Olivia looked at her sister, whose eyes were red and shining, whose smile was a little shaky at the corners. Then she stood up and wiped at her own eyes and nose. "We should get going again."

She picked up her pack and her hiking poles and took a few steps up from the river and back onto the trail. In her peripheral vision, she saw Melanie put her face in her hands for a moment before standing up and brushing the dirt off her pants.

"We're three miles from Lake Superior," Olivia said.

Wordlessly, Melanie put her pack back on and walked up to her. Olivia silently implored her not to say anything. To just drop the whole thing, forever and always.

Melanie touched her arm. "I'll lead for a while." She held out her hand for the map. Then she headed into the yellow glow of the trees.

Sixteen

MELANIE HAD BEEN SO CLOSE. So close to breaking through to the other side of grief. After ten years. As close to a breakthrough as Explorers Falls was to being an actual waterfall. To Melanie it just looked like someone was draining their pool down the driveway for the cold months. They didn't even stop walking to look at it.

Her spirit felt just as drained. Olivia knew what was good for everyone else, but she couldn't see what was good for herself. It was hard for Melanie to do all the grieving for the both of them, all alone with no one in her life who really understood. Aunt Susan was a support, but she lived so far away. And losing a sister wasn't quite the same as losing both your parents so young. Just when you feel so utterly lost in the world and in need of guidance. And anyway, Melanie knew what it was like to lose a sister too. Olivia wasn't dead, but she may as well have been.

Though, there was Justin. He understood something of what she was going through. His grief wasn't the same as hers, but it was grief nonetheless.

Propelled by her frustration and aided by the lay of the land along the river, Melanie walked faster than she had the previous two days, and especially faster than earlier that morning when the unannounced departure of Josh had her feeling deflated. She knew she should slow down a little and intentionally enjoy the old-growth hemlocks and the maples that glowed yellow and orange all around her. But her feet were following her racing mind.

Now that Olivia had been on the cusp of crying, it would be that much harder to get her back to that vulnerable place. The conversation on the banks of the river had no doubt inoculated her to further discussion about all they had lost, like getting a flu vaccine. But there was still hope. Melanie just had to find a different strain, a different way in, something that Olivia could not stay silent about.

She needed an argument.

The only question was, about what? Melanie had to choose carefully. Not every subject would lead them to their shared loss. And there was a plethora of subjects about which Olivia was more knowledgeable than her. Melanie had to be able to hold her own and keep things going. And it couldn't seem like she was baiting her. As a lawyer, no doubt Olivia knew how to spot leading questions.

She was still contemplating the best way forward when she felt Olivia's hand on the back of her arm. She was about to ask what was up when she saw that her sister's finger was over her lips. Melanie looked at her hard. Olivia turned Melanie's shoulders around a little further, stepping back so that she could see what was behind them.

Melanie felt her breath catch. Perhaps thirty or forty yards away, a black bear was casually ambling toward them. Melanie tried to ask Olivia what they should do, but no sounds could get past the jagged lump of ice in her throat.

"Don't move," Olivia whispered between labored breaths. "Don't move and don't run. It's been walking behind us for a few minutes. Or at least, I noticed it a few minutes ago. It looks young. Maybe it's the one that slept by our tent."

Melanie found her voice. "What do we do?"

"Nothing. For now."

"But shouldn't we scare it away? Aren't you supposed to make loud noises and stuff?"

Olivia shrugged and breathed deeply, which became a yawn. "Yes. I thought you'd want to see it first though. You were walking so fast it was hard to catch up to you without running, which you don't want to do in a situation like this."

Melanie was equal parts touched that Olivia had thought of her and confused by her own reaction to the bear. She'd always thought she had a psychic connection with wild animals. But this was real. This was terrifying. And here Olivia was yawning at it, as though being followed by a bear out in the woods where no one would hear your screams as it ripped you to pieces was as normal as walking out to get the mail.

The bear seemed to notice that they had stopped walking, and it too stopped. Melanie silently prayed that it would turn around and go in the other direction. Instead, it stood up on its hind legs and bobbed its head, sniffing the air. Young or not, on its hind feet it was as tall as a man. Melanie's heart rate ticked up another notch.

"What is it doing?" she whispered.

"It's just smelling us."

"Us? Or our food?"

The bear dropped to all fours again and took a couple steps toward them.

"Should we leave something for it?" Melanie said.

"That's pretty much the worst thing we could do. Then it will see us as a source of food. Us and every other hiker who comes by. That's the kind of thing that makes bears dangerous."

"This one already seems dangerous."

Olivia laughed lightly. "Whatever happened to Dr. Melanie Dolittle? I thought you'd be thrilled. You seemed so disappointed about missing it the other morning."

"Being visited by a bear and being followed by a bear are two very different things."

"That or you're just a lot of talk." Olivia whacked her hiking poles together and yelled, "Hey!"

"Don't do that!" Melanie ground out. "You're going to make it mad."

"You want to get rid of it or not?" Olivia said at a normal volume. "You were the one who brought up making loud noises. And you're right. You're supposed to make noise the whole time you're hiking. It's our fault for being so silent for the last mile. And the needles have softened our footsteps. Really, we should have a bell on one of our packs, but I didn't want to have to listen to a bell ringing incessantly. Just be ready, okay?"

"For what?" Melanie said incredulously.

"Not running. Don't run. Just be ready with your poles to jab at it if it comes too close."

Before Melanie could stop her, Olivia took several long, quick strides toward the bear, smacking the poles together and shouting, "Get out of here! Go on! Get out!"

The bear took a few quick steps backward and then looked at them as if it was all some big misunderstanding.

Olivia stomped toward the bear and then stopped short and let out three sharp barks like a dog. The bear skittered away, looking back twice more, and then disappeared over a ridge.

Olivia turned back to face Melanie with a grin. "How about that?"

Melanie's legs quivered. She wanted to dump her pack on the ground, lie down on her back for a few minutes, and take some big, slow, calming breaths. But more than that, she wanted to get as far away from that bear as humanly possible.

"You all right?" Olivia said.

"I'm fine."

"Gosh, I did not expect that kind of reaction from you. I thought I'd have to keep you from going up and hugging it."

"Well," Melanie started. But she didn't know how to finish. She hadn't expected that reaction either. She started walking again, looking back over her shoulder every minute or so. But all she saw was her sister.

Within ten minutes they reached another backcountry camping site.

"No wonder that bear was headed this way," Olivia said, pointing to a little pile of garbage in the fire ring. "Someone has apparently never heard of 'leave no trace.' And I bet I know who." She picked up a beer can with her fingertips.

"Why would they leave their trash here?"

"Probably thought the next people would just burn it in their campfire. Stupid, stupid, stupid." Olivia dropped her pack and fished out her garbage bag.

"You can't take that with us if that's what the bear was after," Melanie said.

"I have to. It's what they should have done. You think we should leave it so that the next people at this site have a bear to contend with?"

Melanie tried to cross her arms, but the pack straps made it difficult. She settled for clenching her fists at her side. "Well, I don't want a bear to contend with."

Olivia stuffed the trash into her bag. "This is the right thing to do. You should never be afraid to do the right thing."

"That's rich," Melanie mumbled. Olivia looked up, but Melanie turned away and pretended she hadn't said anything. Then she remembered that she had wanted to get into an argument with Olivia before they were interrupted by the bear. "I think it's perfectly rational to be afraid of a bear."

"Of course it is," Olivia said. "I just didn't think you would be."

"You think I'm not rational?"

Olivia made a face. "You really want me to answer that?"

Melanie's hands went to her hips.

"Anyway, that's not what I meant," Olivia said. "I mean you love animals. Like, *love* them. You used to pet everything you laid eyes on—stray dogs, injured squirrels, that disgusting pet millipede in Mr. Fletcher's classroom. You once had a funeral for a dead toad."

"I remember that," Melanie said. She started down the trail and Olivia followed.

"Something had pulled out its entrails," Olivia said. "It was so gross. And you picked it up with your bare hands. And *kissed* it."

Melanie smiled at the memory. "I felt bad for it."

"That's what I'm saying though. You have such deep feelings for animals. It was just odd to see you scared by a bear. Totally rational, don't get me wrong. Just surprising."

And just like that, Melanie had her in. "You know, now that I have a moment to think about it, it surprises me too. A lot. But I guess we can't choose our reaction to things sometimes. Our fight-or-flight instinct kicks in, and that's all we can do."

"What I saw back there was not fight or flight. That was fright. That was freeze. Freeze into a solid block of ice."

"Yeah, I guess it was," Melanie said. "It felt a little like my first dance recital. I don't know if you remember that."

"Oh yes, I remember. You came out on stage and then just stood there, completely still, while all the other little girls danced around you."

"Yeah, well, this felt like that." She chose her next words carefully. "What sends you into fight-or-flight mode?"

It was quiet for a moment. All Melanie could hear was the constant whoosh of the river, the soft squeak of her pack, and the sound of her own feet.

"I suppose I fear the unexpected. That's why I wanted to be the one to plan a trip that was your idea."

"And why you're glued to this map," Melanie said, waving it at her.

"Exactly," Olivia said. "In the courtroom, I never want to be taken unaware by a surprise witness or a new piece of evidence.

It's all about knowing ahead of time what people will say and having a ready answer."

"I guess that makes sense," Melanie said. "But the bear was unexpected—twice—and you didn't seem like you were afraid of that."

"It wasn't unexpected. I knew from researching the park that black bears were a factor. And I knew from reading up on bear behavior what to expect should we encounter one. So the one we saw today didn't feel unexpected at all. Even the one that slept by the tent—I was only really afraid when I thought it might be a person out there. Because a bear will generally behave according to its instinct, so you know what to expect. But a person might do anything, especially if they were intoxicated or on drugs."

Melanie considered this. It was obvious to her where this fear came from—from their parents' very unexpected deaths. If Olivia were one of her life coaching clients, she would just go ahead and say that to her. And if Olivia were one of her clients, she would nod thoughtfully and say, "You know, you're right, Melanie. You're absolutely right. All of my problems can be traced to that one event." Melanie heard stuff like that all the time. She was good at her job.

And Olivia was good at hers. Some of that surely could be traced back to what had happened to their parents. Melanie wondered not for the first time what their lives would be like had the accident never occurred. She would have finished school, earned a degree in art history, and been working at a museum in London or Paris or New York. Olivia would still be a lawyer, but maybe she and Eric would have gotten married. Maybe she'd have a baby.

And what about their parents? They'd be deciding what to do in their retirement. They'd stay close to home to see their grandchildren, of course, but with frequent trips out to see Melanie in her glamorous big-city life.

"What about you?" Olivia said, breaking into Melanie's thoughts. "Besides bears, I mean. I know you got over your stage fright."

Melanie didn't say anything for a while as she tried to pin down what exactly it was that she was afraid of.

"Do you want my help?" Olivia said. "Because I think I know the answer."

"Okay, what?" Melanie said.

"You're afraid of being wrong."

Melanie stopped walking and turned around. "What?"

"Why else would you believe in every religion and fad spiritual system out there except that you're afraid to commit to one? And why would you be afraid to commit to just one? Because what if you're wrong? What if you choose one, just one, forsaking all others, and you choose the wrong one?"

Melanie shook her head and resumed walking. "That's silly. No matter what I chose, there would be millions of other people who believed the same thing. I wouldn't be alone in that belief, so why should I be worried about what other people think of my choice?"

"No, that's different. I didn't say you were afraid of *looking* wrong. I said you were afraid of *being* wrong. If you pick the wrong one, well, there are consequences, right? There's hell or being reincarnated as a lower life form, or even just missing out on having a fun life because you were part of some religion that was all about renouncing the pleasures of this world and taking vows of silence and eating just bread and water and wearing only scratchy clothes."

Melanie said nothing.

"Anyway, that's just my educated guess," Olivia said, and Melanie could hear the smirk in her voice.

A moment later, the trail led straight to the riverbank. Across the shallow water Melanie could see another blue blaze. The second crossing of the day. As she removed her hiking boots, she argued with Olivia in her head. She wasn't afraid of being wrong. Why, she only barely believed in the concept of wrong. She didn't like to tell people they were wrong about anything because everything was about perception and the lens you saw the world through. Who was she to say something was wrong? Unless it was, well, murder or cheating or stealing or stuff like that. Some things you *did* were right and wrong, but a person's private beliefs? Melanie didn't believe in imposing on that with a value judgment.

She didn't fear being wrong. Her fear went deeper than that. She had felt it when she saw the bear on the trail. She had felt it three years ago when she had such terrible food poisoning that she couldn't get up off the bathroom floor to reach the phone and call Justin to come take her to the hospital. She had felt it as a small child when she'd jumped into a neighbor's pool without a life jacket after seeing Olivia do just that, only Melanie couldn't actually swim and had to be saved from drowning by her mother.

Melanie wasn't afraid of being wrong.

She was afraid of dying.

Seventeen

OLIVIA SHOULD HAVE KEPT her mouth shut. Even if she did believe it. And even if she wasn't the one who'd started them down this uncomfortable conversational path to begin with. She leaned against a tree, pulled off her hiking boots and socks, and tried to think of something funny and self-deprecating to say that might break the tension that expanded within Melanie's silence. But nothing came.

Melanie pulled her pack back on, picked up her boots and her poles, and stepped into the steady stream of water.

"Seems kind of strange that they would have us cross the river back there just to recross it downstream, doesn't it?" Olivia said. "I mean, how hard would it have been to cut the trail along just the one side?" She was about to put her pack back on when she heard a scream, then a splash. "Mel!"

Olivia ran into the water after her sister, who lay on her side, water piling up against her pack and flowing over her legs. Olivia grabbed her hand, but the pack was taking on water, making it impossible to right her from that angle. Olivia stepped over Mel's legs so she was upstream and yanked up on her pack. Melanie struggled to get her bare feet back under her. Then she was standing in the river, water dripping from everywhere except for one dry shoulder and half of her hair. Her hiking poles hung from her wrists and tapped against Olivia's side as she helped her to the far shore.

"Are you okay? Did you twist an ankle?"

What would they do if one of them couldn't walk out? They were more than three miles from the nearest trailhead. Melanie's cheeks were pink, her teeth were chattering, and her lips had an unsettling purplish cast. It was still only around forty degrees.

"We have to get you out of these clothes." Olivia snapped open the waist strap of Melanie's pack and helped her out of it. "Take them off, right now," she said as she unzipped the pack and began pawing through it. But the contents of Melanie's pack were wet as well. Olivia wanted to scream at her for not packing everything in Ziploc bags as she'd instructed her.

What's done is done and can't be undone.

Without a word, Olivia left the pack there in the dirt and rushed as quickly as she dared back over the slippery river rocks to her own pack. She pulled it on, grabbed her boots and poles, and crossed the stream once more, then dumped everything onto the ground and found her hand towel.

Melanie was still fully clothed. Olivia started stripping her down from top to bottom. She wrung out her hair, pulled off her coat and her shirts, and dried her as best she could with the small towel. She gave Melanie one of her own T-shirts and the jacket off her back. Then she got to work on the lower half. Her pants were too big around Melanie's slim waist, but she pulled the drawstring tight. She dried Melanie's boots as best she could and checked the size. Despite being a bit taller than Olivia, Melanie wore a size nine to Olivia's nine and a half. Olivia thought but a moment before putting another pair of socks on Melanie's feet, followed by her own completely dry boots. Melanie was still in such shock from the cold, she didn't seem to notice.

Olivia looked intently into her eyes. "Are you okay?"

Melanie managed to nod.

"Are you still cold?"

She nodded again.

"But nothing is broken or twisted?"

Melanie took a few small steps.

"Okay, here's the deal. We need to get you moving. I'm going to pack this stuff up so we can keep going. In the meantime, I need you to just walk around in a little circle to get the blood flowing. I think we're close to the lakeshore. Maybe someone will have a fire going where we can warm you up some more, okay?"

Melanie nodded again but did not move.

"So start walking," Olivia said.

There wasn't a lot of room, but Melanie dutifully obeyed, making a tight oval around the spot where Olivia knelt in the fallen leaves squeezing as much water as possible out of everything in Melanie's pack before refolding, rerolling, and repacking it.

"Okay, we're ready," Olivia finally said. She handed her dry pack to Melanie, then pulled Melanie's wet pack onto her own back.

"Wh-what are you doing?" Melanie said through her shaking.

"You said you wanted to carry the tent," Olivia said.

"B-but—"

"No buts, let's go." She held her hand out for Melanie to go first, which she did without further argument.

For a few minutes they walked between the Little Carp River to their left and a steep wooded hill to their right before the trail opened up and the land beneath their feet spread out to the northeast. It wasn't more than twenty or thirty minutes before they could hear the sound of another waterfall. Traders Falls was about halfway between the river crossing and the shore of Lake Superior. The falls were small and picturesque, but neither Melanie nor Olivia slowed their determined pace to admire them.

"Are you warming up?" Olivia called up to Melanie.

"A bit, yeah," Melanie said.

Her voice was no longer shaking, and Olivia took that as a good sign. Now she turned her worrying over to the next problem. Everything in Melanie's pack was wet. Her clothes, her underwear and socks, her towel, and quite possibly her sleeping bag, though Olivia hadn't had time to check it out. They still had two nights and two days left on the trail before they got to their car, unless they could find someone who would give them a ride from the Lake of the Clouds to the Government Peak trailhead where they had started. If it stayed cool and cloudy, there was no way the stuff would dry out enough to use. Olivia had one more set of clothes left, which meant they'd both be wearing the same clothes for a couple of days. That in and of itself was not a big deal. They'd just be extra gross and grimy when they got out of the woods.

What worried her was what they would do during the cold

nights on the cold ground. One person could barely fit into a mummy bag, let alone two. If Melanie's sleeping bag was wet, of course Olivia would give Melanie her bag. But then what would she do? She wouldn't even have much for extra clothing to put on.

The farther they walked, the more she ran over this problem in her mind. And the more she ran over it, the more the hard truth came to the surface—they couldn't spend another night out on the trail. In her obsessive poring over the map earlier, Olivia had located the spot where Josh had said he parked, the trailhead at Pinkerton Creek. That was their last chance to cut the trip short before they were locked into at least eleven more miles of hiking—and more than fifteen if they couldn't find a ride at the Lake of the Clouds. Surely at this point Melanie would agree that it would be better to take their chances hitch-hiking than walk into certain hypothermia for at least one of them.

When they came to a small wooden bridge leading off to the left, they finally paused. A sign indicated that the North Country Trail continued over the bridge, as did the Pinkerton Trail, which would lead them to the parking lot and South Boundary Road. If they continued going straight, they would be on the shore of Lake Superior. Already the wind was picking up, reminding Olivia that of course the lakeshore would be even colder than the woods.

Melanie pulled one of her water bottles from her pack on Olivia's back. "We should have done it this way the whole time."

"Me with your pack?"

"No, just carrying each other's water bottles. Then they

wouldn't be changing hands so many times because we can't reach our own when our packs are on."

Olivia pulled one of her bottles from the pack Melanie was carrying. "I hadn't even thought of that."

They both took a few long swigs. This close to the lake, there was no reason to scrimp. They had three quadrillion gallons of fresh water at their disposal—enough to cover the entire land surface of both North and South America with a foot of water.

"So where are we?" Melanie asked.

"Well, that's what I wanted to talk to you about. I've been doing some thinking, and considering the present state of things, I want to propose a change in plans."

Melanie got a little wrinkle between her eyebrows and waited for Olivia to continue.

Olivia pointed down the trail. "That way is Lake Superior, where we might find someone with a fire where you can warm up some more and maybe, if we could find some way to hang things up near it without catching anything on fire, dry a few things out." She pointed at the bridge. "That way is the road. And the lot where Josh said he was parked."

"Okay," Melanie said slowly.

"Here's the thing. Everything in your pack is wet. Luckily I was carrying the tent, so that's dry. But all your stuff is wet. And it's going to be cold again tonight. And that's dangerous. When people die out in the woods, it's not usually because of a bear attack or starvation, it's because of hypothermia. Well, the leading causes are falling, drowning, and heart attack, but in our case those aren't really an issue, because we're not rock climbing or canoeing down dangerous rapids and we're youngish and at least passably fit. So if something gets us, it's probably going to be hypothermia."

"Where did you get that list?"

"Backpacker.com. I think the article was called 'A Dozen Ways to Die.'"

"Oh."

"Anyway"—Olivia patted her pockets—"I think we need to admit that this is the point at which we should throw in the towel and call this trip finished." She twirled her finger at Melanie. "Turn around, would you?" She started digging through the pockets of her pack. "I know you're going to want to keep pushing forward, but sometimes . . . huh . . ."

"What?"

"I can't find the map." She spun Melanie around again. "Did you see what I did with it?"

Melanie twirled her finger now. "I think I had it last."

Olivia turned her back to Melanie. "I just emptied out your entire bag and repacked everything. It wasn't in there."

"Did you look in every pocket?"

"Yes." Olivia spun back around to face her sister. "Oh no."

"What?"

"You had it."

"That's what I said."

"No, you had it. In your hand."

Melanie shook her head and mouthed *no*, but she didn't look at all like she believed herself.

"You dropped it," Olivia said.

Melanie nodded slowly.

"In the river."

Melanie nodded again. "Olivia, I am so, so sorry. I had it under my arm because I couldn't hold it and my poles at the same time."

It must have fallen when Melanie did and been washed downstream when Olivia was preoccupied with getting her sister out of her wet clothes. It was gone. The map was gone.

"Well, that settles it," Olivia said. "We have to stop. We have to cross this bridge and take that trail out to the road and hope that someone comes by before dark. What day is it?"

"Now, hold on," Melanie said. "Let's just think a minute."

"That's all I've been doing for the last half hour, Mel. Trying to think our way out of this mess. And this is it. This is the plan."

"Just hang on a second."

"No, it's over. What is it, Saturday? Sunday? Is it still the weekend?"

Melanie looked at her watch, but it had been in the water too long. No matter how she shook her wrist, it would not wake up.

Olivia looked at hers, noting the low battery symbol in the corner. "Monday. Crap. No one's going to be here on a Monday in October. Tourist season is over, and people coming up to see the fall colors would come on a weekend, not a Monday. Everyone's back at work."

"Not Josh," Melanie said.

"Right, and he said he was parked at this trailhead. We should get down there as fast as we can so we don't miss him."

"Wrong. I mean, yes, that's where he said he parked, but he won't be there. Last night he said he was going to the salmon run on the Big Carp River."

"He left so early in the morning though. He probably already finished fishing and headed back to the car."

Melanie was shaking her head again. "I don't know. I got the feeling he'd be around for a little while. He didn't seem like he was in any hurry. And he did say something about running into each other again on the trail, didn't he?"

"Melanie! We have no map! All of your stuff is soaking wet! This is ridiculous! We can't go wandering around in the woods with no map and no idea where Josh is. Even if we found him, how is he going to help us? All the guy had was a hammock. He's not going to suddenly have an extra dry sleeping bag."

"He gave us a compass."

"A compass can't keep us warm!"

"Stop!" Melanie held up her hands. "Just stop. You're freaking out because this has all been really unexpected. This wasn't in your plans. But I'm the one who fell in the river. I'm the one who's cold. I'm the one who made a blunder. And I will be the one to figure out my situation. You think you have to fix this, but you don't. You think you have to run everything because no one could run it as well as you can, but you don't. I am an adult. I have been running my own life for ten years without your input. I think I can manage to make my own decision about how to handle this."

Olivia pressed her lips together and planted her hands on her hips. "Well?"

"Just give me a second!"

Olivia looked down at her feet, which were aching in Melanie's damp, too-small hiking boots.

"Okay, how far is it to Lake Superior?" Melanie finally said.

"I could tell you—if I had a map."

"Oh, please. How do you not know that map by heart now? Ballpark?"

Olivia sighed. "I don't know. We're probably less than ten minutes away."

"What time is it?"

"It's already past three."

"Here's what I want to do. I want to keep going to the lake and just see if there's anyone there who might be able to help us or who might have an extra map or something. If there's anyone there, we can ask if they've seen Josh, and then that might help us decide what to do. If it seems like we're alone out there, then maybe we think about taking that other trail to the road."

Olivia raised her palms to the sky. "Don't you see that the later it gets, the less likely it is that anyone will happen by in a car? That hitchhiking in daylight and hitchhiking at night are two very different activities? Every minute we spend out here makes it less likely that we'll get picked up at all."

"Thirty minutes isn't going to make much of a difference. We've already wasted ten minutes just standing here doing nothing."

Melanie had her there.

"Fine. Thirty minutes and no more. If we haven't found anyone who can help us in that amount of time, we bail."

"Fine."

"Here." Olivia shrugged out of Melanie's soggy pack. "You can take this back." She bent to untie the boots. "And these torturous things."

"Why are you wearing my boots?" Melanie said, looking down at her own feet.

"Because they were wet and mine were dry." Olivia stepped out of the boots and stretched her toes.

"You didn't have to do that."

"But I did, didn't I?" She motioned to Melanie to take off her boots. "But my feet can't take much more, so give me mine back."

When they were both reequipped with their own stuff, Melanie grasped Olivia's upper arms and looked into her eyes. "You're a good sister."

Olivia pulled away. "Let's get this over with." She headed for the next marked tree down the path.

Eighteen

MELANIE COULD FEEL the power of the lake even in the woods. The wind was high and cold, and the rhythmic waves crashing against the shoreline quickened her pulse and her pace. When they came out of the trees, she caught her breath. Superior was a deep gray-blue, flecked with the white of breaking waves all the way out to the horizon, where it merged seamlessly with the cloudy sky. The smooth tumbled stones that made up the beach were a darker gray, slick and wet and adorned with the occasional orange leaf that had lodged there. Large bodies of boulders hunched in the surf, and the skeletons of dead trees and driftwood lay like petrified lightning.

This was what she hadn't realized she'd been longing to see. The waterfalls were pretty and the fall colors were dazzling, but Lake Superior was something altogether different. It was power. Raw power, gathered up and gathered up and then released in a relentless onslaught as it battered the shore. People thought of fire as the most powerful of the four elements, but to Melanie it had always been water. She could see it at home in Petoskey on the shores of Lake Michigan, but Superior was in a category of its own. It was constantly cold, even at the height of summer. It was treacherous, as the many shipwrecks littering its bed attested. It seemed almost to be calculating, as though it worked a will known only to itself. On a still summer morning it might be glassy and serene, but now as the cold season began it felt delightfully malicious.

To her life coaching clients, Melanie was always advocating things that would bring them peace and serenity—fountains, gardens, meditation, therapeutic massages, walks in the forest—because of course that's what they needed. In an anxious world, her clients were the stressed-out, the burned-out, and the down-and-out. They came to her looking for balance and a sense that everything was going to be okay.

But Melanie had begun to think that she had perhaps just a bit too much serenity in her life. Her predictable, comfortable life. Her days that started with green tea and ended with chamomile-peppermint. Her wardrobe of earth tones. Her house with its tastefully minimalist, Zen-like atmosphere. Her collection of yoga-friendly music that had no hooks, no rise or fall, just a constant, insistent middleness. So on the few occasions she was met with something like Lake Superior in October, she savored it with an almost guilty sense of pleasure, like she was flirting with a dangerous man.

For a moment as she stared at the writhing lake, Melanie forgot about everything else. She forgot about Olivia and the map and her plans for her sister's spiritual awakening. She forgot how cold she was, how sore her muscles were, how dirty her hair felt. She forgot about the decision they would have to come to in twenty minutes. She stood facing the wind and the water and felt supremely thankful. Though to whom, she was not quite sure. Not the lake itself, for it seemed either indifferent to her or bent on her destruction. If not that, then to something bigger. To whatever had made the lake. Or to whatever had made the glacier that carved out the lake. To whatever force or spirit ultimately controlled all of this. For she was sure that there had to be something or someone out there. Someone she was always kind of searching for in her own haphazard way. But never quite finding.

Eventually she became aware of another sound above the waves, insistent, harsh. Olivia was saying her name.

"What?" Melanie finally said.

"Your teeth are chattering. Come on. We need to check out the other campsites and see if we can get you out of the wind."

As she looked at her sister, Melanie felt another, smaller wave of gratitude overwhelm her. Maybe Olivia hadn't been there for her when their parents died. Maybe she'd shut her out when she'd forgiven Justin for his part in it. But she was here for her now. She meant well, even if her brand of love was more of a shove toward safety than a hug amid the trial.

On the way to the lake, they had passed three empty campsites near the mouth of the Little Carp River. Olivia thought there might be half a dozen more scattered along the mile or so of shore between there and the mouth of the Big Carp River. All they needed was for one of them to be occupied by someone and Melanie knew she could convince Olivia to stay on the trail. She didn't have answers to all of Olivia's practical objections—the possibility of a wet sleeping bag was the greatest obstacle—but she never really spent a lot of time worrying about practicalities. Things would work themselves out. They always did.

"You know, we could go a lot faster without the packs," Melanie said. "We can come back for them if we need to, or if we don't find anyone they'll be waiting for us on the way back to the bridge."

"That's a good idea," Olivia said.

They leaned the packs up against a birch tree and started walking again. Without a pack weighing Melanie down, it felt like floating. She thought that as much as she enjoyed hiking, she could enjoy it so much better without shouldering such a heavy burden of worldly goods. Josh did it right. He didn't carry around a tent or a sleeping bag or even much food. He simply went along his way and trusted that there would be enough for him.

A few minutes went by before they saw the next site, which was empty, the fire ring cold and dead. Just on the other side of a small creek there was another. Also empty. Several minutes later there was another. Same story—no people, no tent, no fire. At any moment, Olivia would say that the allotted time was up and they needed to turn around and get themselves to that trailhead parking lot.

"Let's just try one more," Melanie said to preempt her.

"Okay. Just one," Olivia said.

They crossed another creek on a wooden bridge and resumed walking. Melanie couldn't get the time from her malfunctioning watch—and she sure wasn't going to ask Olivia and therefore remind her that they were running out of it—but it felt like they had walked nearly twice as long as the distance between the last two sites when they finally came upon the next one. Melanie's heart sank. It too was empty, the only sign of previous human habitation one of those plastic on-the-go flossers she felt like she had seen dropped in every parking lot for the past five years.

"Gross," she said.

"That's it. We tried. Now we have to face facts. Let's go get our packs. I only hope we haven't missed our ride."

A flash of blue between the golden trees caught Melanie's eye. "I think I see someone. Come on."

She didn't wait to see if Olivia would follow her. In a moment she was back on the rocky shoreline, where thirty or forty feet away, a man stood looking out at the water just as she had been not half an hour ago. She said hello, but the wind blew the sound back down her throat. She tried again, but he did not hear. Finally, she was near enough to tap his shoulder, but before she had a chance to, he looked her way with a smile.

"Melanie."

When he said her name, she recognized that it was Josh.

"I thought we'd see each other again." He looked past her and called out, "Olivia," and waved at her to join them. "Have you set up camp nearby?"

"No," Melanie said.

"Where are your packs?"

"We left them back down at the Little Carp River," Olivia supplied.

"Oh?"

Melanie shared a glance with her sister. "Are you camping around here?"

He pointed farther down the shore. "I'm the last site before the cabins. It's maybe five minutes from here."

"Do you have a fire going?" Olivia said. "Mel's had a chill today and she could use some warming up."

"I hadn't started it yet, but I've got all the wood gathered. You're welcome to join me."

"It's not too windy for a fire out here?" Olivia said.

"Not at that site. It's off the shore a bit, back in the cedar trees. They block the wind." He started walking. "Follow me."

"So, you're not going to leave the park tonight?" Olivia said as they followed behind.

"I hadn't planned on it," Josh said. "I was upstream earlier today and the salmon are running thick. Not too many other fishermen out right now. It's a great time to fish and just enjoy the quiet."

They stepped back onto the trail. Josh strolled along with his hands in his pockets. "Where are you two camping tonight?"

"Our site is quite a bit further up the trail that runs along the Big Carp River," Olivia said. "Near a crossing, I think. Before you climb the escarpment."

"I know the spot," Josh said. "That's around where the few other fishermen I've talked to are staying. Most of the spots on the lakeshore here are pretty cold and windy in the fall. Your site is about four and a half miles away. Though, if you have to go back and get your packs, that's going to add almost three more miles. No way you'll get there tonight."

"Right," Olivia said. "We know that."

"Once you get off track it's hard to get back on," Josh said.

"This whole trip has been harder than I expected," Olivia said.

Josh looked back and smiled, but it wasn't a smug smile like

Melanie thought they might see from such an obviously accomplished outdoorsman. He wasn't laughing at how unprepared they were. He wasn't pitying them either. His smile reminded her of her father smiling at her when she fell off her bike and skinned her knee. Caring, concerned, but also showing her that he was proud of her for trying, for doing something she hadn't been sure she could do. It was the kind of smile that helped you get back up.

"You're welcome to stay with me," he said.

Just then they reached his spot back a bit in the woods. There was indeed significantly less wind. Josh's hammock hung between two trees, barely swaying every so often. Wood and sticks were piled up next to the fire ring. He immediately started making a little tepee of dry leaves and pine needles and the smallest sticks, over which he made another of slightly larger sticks. Blocking what breeze there was with his body, Josh leaned over the fire ring and scraped a couple pieces of metal together. A moment later a flame was shivering in the midst of the kindling. He moved a stick here and there, and the fire caught, stronger, licking up to the second layer of fuel.

Melanie held her hands over the flames. To someone who had been so cold, the feel of actual heat was nearly miraculous. "What was that?"

Josh held out the device. "Flint fire starter. Never hike without it." He carefully added a few larger pieces of wood to the fire. "So, what happened today? Why are you so cold?"

Melanie looked to Olivia, expecting her to relay the story of her klutzy sister who fell into a river. But Olivia raised her eyebrows and dipped her head, indicating that it was Melanie's blunder so it was Melanie's story.

"Well, most of the day went pretty well. The morning anyway. We crossed the river and had lunch at Trappers Falls."

"Where we were supposed to camp last night," Olivia interjected.

"We saw—was that Explorers Falls?"

Olivia nodded.

"Right, Explorers Falls. And then just a bunch of hiking. Everything was going really well until we got to the second crossing. I slipped somehow, I don't know how, I guess the rocks were slimy or something. Anyway, I fell, and even though the water was pretty shallow, of course everything got soaked. Like, completely soaked. I had to change my clothes, but everything in my bag was wet because I didn't put my clothes in Ziploc bags"—she nodded at Olivia—"even though she told me to, so she gave me some of her clothes and even switched shoes with me. I've been cold ever since, and we were hoping to find someone with a fire so I could warm up."

Josh had been listening and nodding as Melanie relayed her story. Or, most of her story. She couldn't bring herself to say that she had also lost their map. Olivia could add that detail if she wanted.

"So it's good that we happened upon you," Melanie said, by way of wrapping things up.

"That's a rough day for sure," Josh said. He looked like he was deliberating what to say next. "So why did you leave your packs behind?"

"Here's the thing," Olivia jumped in. "Back at the junction with the Pinkerton Trail, I suggested that we needed to just call this trip a disaster and hike out so we could find a ride back to the car and stay in a motel tonight. Somewhere she could get a hot shower and sleep in a warm, dry bed. Because, sorry, but I think we're flirting with something really dangerous if we stay out here in the cold, and I think you'd agree with me because you obviously know what you're doing out here."

She paused, ostensibly for Josh to acknowledge the correctness of her opinion, but he merely waited for her to continue.

"But Melanie didn't want to do that and thought that if we could find someone to help us out—I don't know how, beyond having a fire to warm up at—then we could keep going. And it was quicker to check that out without packs on than with, so we left them and were going to just go back for them on the way out of the woods."

"Or," Melanie interjected, "we would just grab them and bring them back to wherever we ended up. So I guess that's what we'll do since we found you."

"But," Olivia said, her voice a little louder, a little more insistent, "Melanie is forgetting that we have a bigger problem to address. All her stuff is wet, so she's not prepared to go any further on this hike, and she can't even sleep out here tonight because her sleeping bag is wet. And while I'll give myself a few extra blisters wearing her shoes so that she has dry feet, I will not knowingly subject myself to death via hypothermia just so she can stubbornly continue a trip I didn't even want to go on in the first place."

Melanie clenched her jaw. She had no response to Olivia's practical arguments, but she wanted to lash out at her for being . . . well, her. No one had ever had the ability to make her feel small and stupid like Olivia did. Melanie took a few deep breaths and then turned her back on the fire to warm the other side of her. And also so she didn't have to look at Olivia.

"You obviously know your way around the woods," Olivia continued behind her. "What would you do in this situation?"

Melanie braced herself for Josh's assessment, which would surely fall in line with Olivia's.

"I guess that depends," he said.

Melanie turned around again so she could see him. He was already looking at her.

"Why are you on this trip?" he said.

"What?" Olivia said. "What kind of question is that? It's a hiking trip. We're here to hike."

"Okay, but there are much easier places to hike. You're not avid hikers, right?"

Melanie laughed. "That's pretty obvious, isn't it?"

He smiled. "Right. So why here? Why now? Why a hiking trip and not some other kind of trip, like a visit to a city with museums and restaurants and shops? It's a lot more trouble to plan and execute a wilderness hike than it is to spend a weekend in Chicago. So why here?"

"Why are you here?" Olivia snapped.

"I'm fishing," Josh answered calmly.

"Okay, why are you fishing here instead of somewhere else?" she pressed.

"Stop it, Olivia," Melanie said.

"What? I'm just asking what he was asking."

"This is where the fishing is good at the moment," Josh said, "so this is where I am. But my mission out here is not what's in question. Why are *you* here?"

"Why does it matter?" Olivia said. "Why we're here makes no difference in whether it's smart to continue or not."

"It makes a difference in whether you're willing to face hardship to see it through. For instance, if you're out here because you thought it would be fun and neither of you is having any fun, then there's no real reason to persevere, is there? If the point is to have fun and you're miserable, then the decision is easy. Abandon ship."

Olivia crossed her arms and looked about to say something, but Josh continued.

"But if the point of the trip is something else altogether, then you need to weigh that purpose against the trouble you're running into and decide if it's worth it to push forward anyway. Trouble, in and of itself, isn't a reason to quit something."

Melanie found herself nodding.

"So, my original question stands. Why are you on this trip?"

Melanie took a stab. "To reconnect. With each other."

"Which you could do a lot of places, I suppose," he said.

"Okay, true. But it's easier to reconnect in a place like this where there are no distractions than in a city where there are shows and exhibitions and stuff."

"So it was your idea." Josh poked at the fire with a piece of driftwood, then dug the smoking end into the ground to put it out.

"We've barely spoken for ten years," Melanie said quietly. "It felt like we had some catching up to do."

"What happened? If you don't mind my asking."

"Hmm?"

"Sisters not talking for ten years? Something must have happened."

Melanie looked at her sister, whose face was set like stone. "Our parents died ten years ago in a car accident. We were on a hiking trip when it happened."

"That's horrible," Josh said, his brow knit with what seemed like real concern.

Melanie nodded and stared at the fire. "It was really hard. We were both in college. After that we kind of went our separate ways. I quit school to take care of stuff at home, and Olivia . . . left."

"This is a waste of time," Olivia said. "This whole trip has been a waste of time. We need to go, Mel. We can't stay out here and you know it. Whether or not you've gotten what you wanted from me, it's time to leave. We can talk in the car on the way home, if that's what you want."

"That's not what I want," Melanie said. "I mean, it's not the only thing I want. And anyway, you'd find it just as easy to change the subject in the car as you have here. You're right that this has been a waste of time. You've made sure of it."

Olivia scowled. "Excuse me? Who got us lost in the woods? Who got herself completely soaked in cold water because she didn't want to buy water shoes, and whose clothes got wet because she didn't want to buy plastic bags, making it fundamentally dangerous to keep going? If anyone's trying to sabotage this trip, it's you. You've made everything harder. You completely destroyed my itinerary. You even managed to lose the map! I'm just trying to get us out alive at this point. I figured out where to go when we were lost. I scared away the bear that was following us. I sacrificed my feet so yours would be dry. I've been doing everything in my power to make it so you can take this stupid hike that you think will miraculously heal our relationship and make me feel better about my parents dying and you chumming around with the guy who killed them, even though that's utterly ridiculous to the point of being insulting."

Melanie squeezed her lips together and counted to five. She would not cry. "Go on then," she said, her tone measured. "If you're having such a bad time, take one of the packs and hitchhike to the car. You can sleep in a motel, and I'll see you in a couple days if you're not too high and mighty to come back and pick me up. Or I'll get an Uber, if they have any up here. Or maybe Josh can drop me at a bus station. Just leave the tent and the dry sleeping bag and some food. I'll do the rest of the hike myself."

Olivia came around the fire to where Melanie stood, resolute. "That's absurd."

"Why? Because it wasn't your idea? Because it's not part of your plans?"

Olivia threw up her hands. "No, because you're inexperienced, you have a terrible sense of direction, as we have established, and you have no map."

"Josh knows where he's going. I'll follow him."

Olivia stepped closer and lowered her voice. "That's the stupidest thing you've said yet. You don't even know this guy."

Melanie made no effort to talk quietly. "He was pretty helpful yesterday and nobody got raped or murdered. I'm pretty sure it'll be okay."

Olivia punched her in the arm. "You idiot," she hissed. "It's a lot harder to overpower two women than it is to overpower one. You have no idea what he's capable of."

Melanie looked to where Josh was standing, eager to draw him into the argument just to make her sister squirm. But he wasn't there. She gave Olivia her own punch in the arm. "You're the idiot." Then she stalked off to find Josh, Olivia hot on her heels.

They found him back on the rocky shore at the water's edge, standing just out of reach of the waves.

"Did you figure it out?" he said without turning around.

"I'm going on," Melanie said before Olivia could say anything.

He looked at Olivia. "What about you?"

She picked up a rock and flung it into the churning water, where it vanished. "I don't know what to do here. She won't listen."

Josh looked at each of them in turn. "How about this. Olivia, what if you and I go back to where you left the packs. Melanie, you stay by the fire and keep it going and keep warm. And if, when we get to the packs, you want to keep going to the road, you can go ahead and I'll bring the other stuff back here to Melanie. Otherwise, we each grab a pack and come back here."

Olivia shook her head. "No, Melanie needs to come too, that way we can both leave if we choose to."

"I think Melanie's already made her choice though."

Melanie nodded vigorously.

"You just need to make your choice. Quit or push on."

"This is totally none of your business, and you're not getting it anyway," Olivia said. "The choice has already been made for us. She can't sleep in a wet sleeping bag."

"Did you ever actually pull that bag out to see if it was wet?" Melanie asked.

Olivia hesitated. "No, but everything in the pack was wet. All of your clothes were wet. Of course it would be too."

"But it's in a separate stuff sack, which, for all we know, might be waterproof. I mean, I can't imagine you getting anything less than top-of-the-line equipment."

Olivia was silent, and Melanie knew she had her. She had actually out-argued the lawyer for the moment. Olivia was all about evidence-based beliefs, and now she found herself lacking evidence. She'd have to go get the sleeping bag in order to prove her point.

"Fine," Olivia finally said. "Josh and I will go back to the packs. If the sleeping bag is dry, I'll come back and we'll finish this hike together. If it's not . . . you're on your own."

Nineteen

STU-PID, STU-PID, STU-PID. With each stride, the word ran through Olivia's brain. Left, right. *Stu-pid.* Sometimes it was directed toward Melanie. Sometimes it was directed toward herself. Either way, it was an accurate description of both of them. Melanie was being reckless. She was being belligerent. Both of them were being stupid. And a bit selfish. Now that word took the place of *stupid* in her interior monologue, one syllable per step. *Sel-fish.*

"What do you get out of this?" she asked Josh, her tone almost accusatory.

"Pardon?" He slowed his pace and moved over as much as he could to allow her to come up almost beside him.

"Why are you walking nearly three miles you don't have to, to carry a load for someone you've only barely met, after watching her and her sister fight like children about whether or not they should cut a pointless trip short?"

"The trip doesn't seem pointless to me. Your sister said it was to reconnect."

"That's her reason, not mine."

"Then what's yours?"

"Ugh, stop changing the subject. I ask a question and you ask a question. Just answer. Why are you helping her?"

"I thought I was helping both of you."

"You're not. You're helping with her plans and hindering mine."

"See, but there's the reason for my question: I thought you shared those plans."

Olivia gave him a puzzled look.

"To reconnect."

She rolled her eyes. "Oh. No. That's not what this trip is about for me."

"Why not?"

She picked up the pace a bit. "I don't feel some gaping hole in my life that needs to be filled. She might, but I don't."

This was not entirely true. Olivia felt an enormous hole where her parents had been. But Melanie couldn't fill that. Nothing could.

Josh matched his stride to hers. "Why did you agree to the trip?"

"For two reasons. First, because Melanie is like glitter." Olivia wiggled her fingers in the air. "You know how you can never really get rid of glitter once it enters your house? That's what Mel is like. She's that one annoying Christmas card you pull out of the envelope that's just covered with glitter, and it gets all over the place and you're picking it off yourself until Easter. She just keeps calling and texting and emailing. I had to say yes to stop her."

Josh was smiling. Olivia wanted to be irritated by this, but he had a pleasant smile.

"And what's the second reason?" he said.

"Because I knew I'd have to plan it. I mean, I could have been nicer about it, but everything I said back there was true. She'd fall off a cliff if I wasn't watching her. She's too distracted for hiking in the wilderness. She doesn't pay attention to details. She thinks everything will just work itself out." She shook her head. "Probably just the natural result of her being the baby in the family."

"And you being the oldest."

Olivia shrugged. "I guess. She's always had someone watching out for her, and a lot of the time when we were young, that was me. If something happened to her, I was the one in trouble."

Josh grinned again. "Gee, I wonder how she has survived without you for nigh on a decade."

He was right. Melanie had survived. She'd made a lot of big decisions on her own: distributed an estate, sold a house, moved to a different city, created a career out of nothing but a lot of mumbo jumbo. Maybe Olivia wasn't giving her enough credit.

"What are your religious beliefs?" Josh asked.

"That's a super-weird-bordering-on-rude question to ask someone you just met."

"I only ask because of what you've been through with your parents. And it's pretty clear your sister believes in something."

"She believes in everything. Questions nothing. Just sucks it all in like a cosmic vacuum cleaner picking up all the junk out there."

"And you? What's your motto? Question everything, believe in nothing?"

"I definitely don't believe in God."

Josh glanced over. "Sure you do."

Olivia stopped walking. "Excuse me, but I think I know my own mind. I haven't believed for a long time."

He stopped and looked at her, a thoughtful turn to his mouth. "Let me ask you this: to what in your life do you devote the most time, effort, and passion?"

She didn't even have to think about the answer. "My job."

"And in what do you find your sense of self-worth? Where's that rooted?"

Olivia shrugged. "In my job, I guess."

"So if you do your job well and guilty people are convicted and serve their time, you've done a good job and you feel good about yourself."

"Right."

"What if they aren't convicted? What if you know without a doubt in your mind that someone is guilty, and they get off on some technicality, some procedural thing that went wrong? Then what?"

"I feel angry," she said.

"At what? The system? The jury?"

"Well, partly, I guess. But I'm upset with myself too because I always feel like there could have been something I missed or something I could have hit harder during questioning or cross-examination."

"So, your job is where you spend your time, energy, and passion, and when something goes wrong you feel like you're at fault and your sense of self-worth suffers?"

"Yes, I suppose that's accurate."

"Easy. Your job is your god. Or one of them. Let's try another."

Olivia started walking again. "I don't like this game."

Josh followed. "Who is the final arbiter of truth in your life?"

"What?" she threw over her shoulder.

"How do you decide if something is true?"

"I look at the evidence and use reason to deduce the truth."

"There's another one then. Reason. The human mind. Your own human mind. So, you. You are your god."

"I see what you're trying to do. Let's just say I don't believe in a higher power, some divine being out there puppet-mastering all of this. I believe in science. Observable fact. Nothing more. Nothing less."

"And yet you didn't trust me when you first met me. You hadn't observed anything about me, yet you made a judgment."

"That's not true. I observed that you were a man, and I deduced from what I know of men as a sex that you might be dangerous. That's completely reasonable. And, I'll add, I trust you more now than I did at first because I gathered more firsthand information about you as an individual—namely that you didn't steal anything from us or attack us when we were sleeping, and also you shared food with us. And gave us a compass—thanks for that, by the way."

Despite herself, Olivia was enjoying this conversation. She loved to argue. But arguing with Melanie was like trying to play tennis with a golden retriever. She could never get a good volley going. Josh, on the other hand, was a skilled partner. He had a lot to say and wasn't afraid to hit hard. It wasn't mansplaining—she'd had plenty of experience with that in both law school and the courtroom. It was more like talking to an expert witness who was confident that what he was saying was true and accurate to the best of his knowledge, that it was true whether or not anyone else believed it.

This was also what was beginning to bother her about the whole thing. He was just as confident as she was. And they couldn't both be right.

"However, despite beginning to trust you, I don't entirely like you."

Josh laughed. "And why is that?"

"You have the irritating habit of not answering my questions even though I've answered a ton of yours."

He tipped his head to the side. "Or is it just that you don't like my answers?"

Olivia laughed then. "Nice try. You still have not answered my only real question, which is, what are you getting out of helping us? Besides, perhaps, not having our deaths on your conscience when you get back to civilization and read about two inept lady hikers gone missing in the wilds of the Porcupine Mountains."

He smiled. "I think maybe you've answered your own question." He pulled a hand out of his pocket and pointed at the two packs still leaning against the birch tree. "And don't be so conceited as to think you two are the first people I've put on the right path. I'm always looking for opportunities to do what my father would have me do."

"What does that mean?" Olivia knelt down by Melanie's pack and started pulling at the straps that held the sleeping bag in the stuff sack to the frame.

"My dad was a ranger in this park. His job was to prepare people for what they'd face, to give them the rules and enforce them. But he was also called upon to rescue them. To track down those who had strayed from the trail. Sometimes he had to physically carry people out to safety."

Olivia unsnapped the compression straps on the sack and pushed the tightly packed mummy bag out. "I guess that's why you're so comfortable out in the woods."

"And it's why I'm helping you. I do what he would want me to do."

Olivia unfurled the mummy bag and ran her hands over every inch of it, front and back. Then she shoved her arms inside and searched for wet spots. After a minute she groaned out loud. "Dang it."

Josh smiled down at her like he knew what she was going to say next.

"It's dry."

"I called the top bunk before we even got in the car this morning."

Olivia stood in the doorway, hands on hips, frowning up at Melanie, who was sitting cross-legged on the top bunk and hugging her once-white stuffed bear, Bruno.

"You had it last year," Melanie said, squeezing Bruno tighter.

"But I called it. You have to call it."

"Nuh-uh. It's my turn."

Olivia expelled a lungful of air and spun around. "Mom!"

Melanie lay down on her side and buried her nose in Bruno's matted fur. He smelled kind of bad, but in a good way. A way that reminded her of all their picnics outside, when she'd take him and a snack in the wagon up the sidewalk until she reached Mr. Barkley's house and lay a blanket out right by the chain-link fence that kept his rottweilers in. Mr. Barkley wasn't his real name—at least she didn't think so—but it was what she called him because of the dogs. She would sit there most summer afternoons with Bruno, passing bits of cheese and crackers through the fence and wiping the dog slobber off her fingers with the blanket.

Right now she had to pee. Bad. But she couldn't leave the top bunk if she hoped to keep it. They didn't have bunk beds at home, so their week renting the cabin on Lake Michigan each year was her only chance to sleep in one.

Olivia stomped back into the room. "Come on, Melanie."

Melanie smiled. Olivia hadn't quoted Mom saying anything. Which meant Mom either didn't care and wanted them to work it out themselves or that she was on Melanie's side.

"No, it's my turn," she said sweetly.

Olivia reached up and grabbed Bruno by a leg.

"Hey!" Melanie pulled him back.

Olivia yanked again and Bruno almost slipped out of Melanie's hands. She wrapped her arms around his squishy middle.

"I called it!" Olivia said, pulling harder.

Melanie felt herself being pulled to the edge of the bed. But she would not let go, she would not give in. She locked her teeth onto Bruno's ear like one of Mr. Barkley's rottweilers with a bone.

"Melanie!"

Olivia yanked once more, and Melanie felt herself going over the side. She was falling face-first to the cabin floor below. Then the room spun and she was looking at the ceiling. Her tailbone connected with the hardwood, then her back, but not her head. Olivia was standing next to her, one arm extended, rigid, eyes as wide as Melanie had ever seen them.

Bruno's ear still clenched between her teeth, Melanie took big breaths of air through her nose. Olivia pulled her arm back and knelt at Melanie's side.

"I'm sorry, I'm sorry, I'm sorry, I'm sorry," she kept saying.

Melanie sat up, dazed. She opened her mouth and scraped a few strands of Bruno's fur off her dry tongue.

"Are you okay?" Olivia said.

Her mother appeared in the door. "What happened?" Then she saw Melanie on the floor. "What happened?" she said again.

Olivia opened her mouth, but Melanie spoke up first. "I fell off the top bunk. Olivia was just helping me up." She stood and rubbed her backside.

"Oh my goodness, are you okay?" her mother asked, turning her around to inspect the damage.

"I'm fine," Melanie said.

"I think maybe you're not ready for the top bunk, sweetie," Mom said.

Melanie nodded. After a little more fussing, their mother left to finish unpacking. Melanie went to use the bathroom. When she came back in, Olivia was sitting on the bottom bunk with Bruno in her lap.

"Thanks," she said, holding the bear out to her sister.

Melanie nodded and took Bruno by the paw.

A few minutes later they were in their swimsuits. The afternoon flew by in a flurry of sandcastles and rock collecting and diving into the waves on the big lake. Then dinner and showers and a game of Sorry! Then it was bedtime. Melanie slipped under the covers of the bottom bunk and listened to Olivia trying to get comfortable on the top. Their parents came in for kisses and good nights. When they left, all was quiet except the sound of crickets through the open window.

Melanie tried to fall asleep, but Olivia kept moving around, making the bed shake and creak. Finally, Melanie saw her sister's legs silhouetted by the night-light, and Olivia dropped to the floor.

"Want to switch?" Olivia said.

"No, it's fine."

Olivia stood there for a moment. Melanie scooched back toward the wall and pulled back the covers. Olivia slipped in beside her and pulled the covers up over her shoulders. Their faces were inches apart, Bruno shoved into the space between them.

"Thanks for saving me," Melanie said.

"Huh?"

"Your arm. You flipped me on my way to the floor."

"Oh. Yeah. I didn't even think about it. It just happened."

"Well, thanks."

Olivia let out a little laugh. "I guess it's the least I could do. I did pull you off in the first place."

"Mom told you it was my turn, didn't she?"

Olivia sighed. "This bear smells terrible."

Melanie giggled and turned the other way, bringing Bruno with her.

"Next year," Olivia said from behind her. "Next year, it's yours."

Twenty

MELANIE PLACED ANOTHER broken branch on the fire and shifted it around with the stick Josh had been using. The tip flickered and smoked, and she dug it into the dirt as he had. She eyed the dwindling pile of sticks and logs with some measure of anxiety. She didn't want to use up all of the fuel, and she was afraid of leaving the fire untended to find some more. The thought of getting lost—again—kept her by the sputtering flames, giving them just enough of a nudge to keep going.

She kept checking her watch and then remembering for the twentieth, the thirtieth time that it wasn't working. How long had Olivia and Josh been gone? And when Josh finally returned, as she kept reassuring herself he would, would Olivia be with him? Or had she finally had it up to here with her little sister as she so often had when they were kids, when Melanie wasn't playing by the rules and Olivia would stomp off and leave her in the basement with a board game or on the lawn with their Barbies and model horses?

If she didn't come back, would it be weird to be here alone

with Josh, a strange man she'd only met the day before? If Olivia did come back, would that mean suffering through two more days of her bad attitude?

Melanie tried to reconcile the woman who had rushed to help her at the river with the one who had so thoroughly belittled her in front of a third party. But if she thought about it, of course that's how it had always been. Olivia the protective older sister had to take care of Melanie the flaky baby sister. Olivia the judgmental critic had to point out all the ways Melanie fell short of her expectations.

Why had Melanie wanted to see her so badly? She had been doing just fine on her own for years. She felt good about herself, mostly. She had plenty of friends and followers to connect with. She had Justin. Why had she invited Olivia back in—no, insisted, dragged her kicking and screaming—when Olivia had so clearly wanted nothing to do with her? When she would have been better off without her?

Right at that moment, Melanie decided that she hoped Josh would come back alone. She didn't want to see Olivia again—not on this trip and maybe not ever. Possibly when they were old ladies. But maybe not even then. Olivia could walk right out of the woods and catch a ride with some lunatic out on the road. She could pick up the car and . . .

Oh. It was her car though. Olivia wouldn't drive Melanie's car back home. She'd wait for her, probably at those little cabins they'd stayed in, and meet her at the trailhead a couple days later, all clean and smug and well rested, while Melanie would probably have to be practically carried out by Josh. And then Melanie would have to listen to her I-told-you-so's all the way back to the carpool lot in Indian River. Melanie would be rid of her for two days and then be stuck with her for at least eight hours with stops—more if they stayed somewhere overnight to break up the trip.

Melanie put another stick on the fire and poked at it. Why was having a sister so hard?

She checked her dead watch again. Then, voices. She strained her eyes toward the sound. Movement. A laugh. Olivia's. She saw them through the trees, Josh and Olivia, packs on, grinning and looking like an Eddie Bauer catalog. All they were missing was the wire hair fox terrier leaping after a stick. Melanie was simultaneously relieved and irritated. Relieved to see them—yes, even Olivia—but irritated that they seemed to be having such a good time together without her. That Olivia was having a good time at all.

Josh caught sight of her and waved. Then Olivia quieted down, as though she was what they had been talking and laughing about and now they had better hush up.

"Looks like you kept the fire going nicely," Josh said as they drew near. He removed Melanie's pack from his back and leaned it against a cedar tree. "Also looks like we're going to run out of wood before long, so I better scare up some more." He shared a look with Olivia, who nodded and took off her own pack, then he strode off into the trees.

"What was all that about?" Melanie said.

"What?" Olivia said.

"That little knowing glance."

Olivia made a face. "There was no glance."

"Mmm."

Olivia held out her hands in a "what gives?" gesture. "You're not happy to see me?"

"I didn't really think you'd bail."

"Well, anyway, it turns out the sleeping bag is fine. I kind of wish I'd taken the time to check it earlier. It would have saved a lot of stress. And walking." She busied herself removing the tent from her pack and beginning the ritual of unrolling and setting it up. "Want to give me a hand?"

Not especially, Melanie wanted to say, but she strove not to be a petty person. Pettiness was so often a factor in her clients' unhappiness. Not being able to let go of little snubs or unintended insults. She routinely gave out a mantra for people struggling with this smallness of spirit: *What I cannot free rules over me.* She'd read it years ago on the inside of a Dove dark chocolate wrapper. She needed to let go of the tiny seed of bitterness she'd allowed to burrow into the soil of her heart and instead embrace her sister's change of mind without suspicion or resentment.

She leaned over to take two corners of the tent and shook it out with Olivia, like shaking out the blanket onto the hide-a-bed for their long-ago sisters' sleepovers.

"I'm glad you're back," Melanie said. She was fairly certain she meant it. Because the Olivia who returned was not quite the Olivia who had walked away a little while ago. "So, what were you and Josh talking about when you got back? You actually looked like you were enjoying yourself."

Olivia smiled. "You know, I was. It's interesting. He must be our age or pretty near to it, and yet there's something about him that seems older. I don't know if it's the way he talks or what he talks about, or if it's just a result of him growing up out in the middle of nowhere up here—his father was a park ranger—but I don't know. That can't be it. He sounds too educated."

"That's kind of judgy—implying that it's surprising that someone raised up here wouldn't be educated."

"That's not what I mean, exactly. It's just . . . well, you'd know if you talked to him much."

"I guess I'll have plenty of time the next couple days."

Olivia pushed a tent peg into the ground. "Oh, I don't think it's really necessary to make him walk with us the rest of the way. He was just offering that as a favor if I didn't come back. We shouldn't hold him to that. He was just being a good guy."

"So let him be a good guy. I think it would be better with him. You looked like you were having a nice time when you walked up. What did you say you were talking about?"

"We were . . . well, I guess we were arguing more than talking."

"It didn't sound like an argument."

"It was. It was just . . . it was philosophical. It wasn't personal. He didn't flip out when I disagreed with him."

"Oh, I get it," Melanie said. "He wasn't *sensitive*."

"Exactly."

Melanie shoved a tent pole through a sleeve toward her sister.

"Hey! Careful!"

"Don't take it personally."

Olivia rubbed her arm where the pole had hit her and bent down to guide it into place. "What is with you? I thought you'd be happy I came back and that I was getting along better with Josh, and here you're jabbing me with sticks."

"It was an accident."

"Sure it was."

Before Melanie could respond, Josh walked up with an armful of wood. They put up the rest of the tent in silence. When it was done, Olivia reached into her pack, retrieved the skein of nylon rope, and tossed it at Melanie. Harder, Melanie thought, than she really needed to.

"What is this for?" she asked.

"Clothesline."

Melanie stomped around the campsite for a moment looking for a suitable spot, then began tying one end to a tree branch.

"Not there," Olivia said. "Closer to the lake."

Melanie glared at her and walked to the side of the site that was closest to Lake Superior, then started to wrap the rope around the trunk of a sapling.

"No, I mean way closer," Olivia said. "Like as close as you can get to the edge of the woods. Where there's lots of wind."

Melanie spun around. "Perhaps you would like to do it?"

Olivia approached with her hand held out. "Sure."

Melanie shoved the rope into her hand.

"And I'll just take your pack too so I can hang up all your clothes for you," Olivia said as she lifted the pack onto her back. "Maybe by the time I get back, you can have the beds made in the tent. Can you handle that?"

Melanie's face burned as she realized that off in the periphery, Josh had seen this whole childish exchange. "Fine," she said.

When Olivia was out of sight, she threw the pads and bags through the open tent door. Then she followed them in and zipped the door shut behind her. Sitting cross-legged on the cold, hard ground, Melanie whisper-screamed into her hands and then punched a sleeping bag. She felt just like she had when she was twelve and Olivia had embarrassed her in front of the neighbor boys when they were playing Truth or Dare. Olivia had dared her to French-kiss one of them, and Melanie thought that a French kiss was licking another person's mouth because Olivia had told her it was kissing with your tongue. She couldn't look Kyle Wilson in the eye for years.

"Knock knock," came Josh's voice from outside the tent. "You okay?"

"Yeah."

A pause. "You sure?"

"Yeah, I'm fine, Josh." She started unrolling the sleeping pads as if to prove that she was indeed okay. Would someone who was not okay be able to inflate two long blue rectangles? She took a deep breath and began to blow into one of the valve stems.

"Listen," Josh continued, "Olivia and I talked a bit about your parents' accident on the way back."

What? She had talked to Josh, a complete stranger, rather than her sister?

"I think maybe she's ready to talk to you about it. She just doesn't really want to argue about the afterlife stuff at this point."

Melanie stopped blowing. "Is that so? Is that what she was talking to you about? 'The afterlife stuff'?"

"A bit."

"And I suppose you don't believe in anything either? Is that why you're telling me this?"

Josh unzipped the tent door partway. "No. I'm telling you this because she was ready to talk to you when we got back, but then you started picking at each other like children. I thought you said you wanted to reconnect. It's just, this doesn't seem like reconnecting, is all," he said. Then he zipped the door shut.

Melanie could hear his footsteps head off toward the lake. She finished blowing up the sleeping pads and unrolled the bags. He was right, and it annoyed her. Why was she suddenly shooting herself in the foot just when it seemed Olivia might be taking a few steps to meet her in the middle? She needed her journal so she could try to make sense of her jumbled thoughts.

Her journal! Had it gotten wet when she fell in the river? And where was her phone? It had been in her pants pocket.

She stumbled out of the tent to find that she was alone again. How long did it take to hang up some wet clothes? Was Olivia out there reading her journal? Going through her texts to Justin?

As much as she didn't want to leave the warmth of the fire, she could not stand idly by while Olivia pried into her personal life. Melanie would have to tell her what was going on eventually. But in her own way, at the right time.

And this was not the right time.

Twenty-One

OLIVIA SNAPPED A PAIR of Melanie's leggings in the air and laid them over the makeshift clothesline she'd strung between a quaking aspen and a dying white birch tree. The wind off the lake blew them back toward the forest like a flag. It was the last of the clothes in the pack, but not the last of the casualties of Melanie's fall. Olivia had found her phone in a pocket. She took the battery out and arranged the pieces of the phone on a wide, flat stone to dry. It might power on later, or it might not. But even if Melanie had to get a new phone, she'd likely still have all her pictures on the card or in the cloud somewhere.

The thing that she knew Melanie's heart would break over was the journal. If she'd used a pencil it would have been fine. The pages would have dried wrinkled, but they'd still be readable. But she'd used pen, and all along the outside margins her loopy cursive letters bled together into an illegible mass. It was like their relationship. Like someone had been writing their story, and some dumb accident, a momentary shift in balance, had wrecked it. No amount of wishing could undo it.

"How's it going out here?" Josh's voice hit her ear like a soft breeze.

Olivia lifted her head from where she crouched over the journal. "Okay, I guess." She held up the journal. "This will never be the same."

Josh took the book from her as she stood. He riffled the damp pages and shook his head. "That's a shame."

"She's going to be really upset about it."

Josh handed the journal back to Olivia. She turned a few pages.

"There are some in the middle that didn't get it too bad. She might be able to read some of it and figure out what she was saying." Opening to a page, Olivia caught sight of her own name. She shut the book before she could read any more—not because she wasn't curious about what Melanie was saying about her but because she was. She deliberately placed the book on the rock next to the pieces of Melanie's phone.

She felt the corner of a T-shirt flapping on the clothesline. "Do you think this will be enough?"

Josh felt the leggings. "Should be. It's good she brought pants other than jeans. Denim takes forever to dry."

"Probably we should have gotten hiking-specific clothing that dries super fast. I could have done that. I don't know why I wasn't prepared for something like this."

"You can't be prepared for everything."

"You can try," Olivia said.

Josh regarded her with a thoughtful twist to his mouth. "And that's what you normally do, isn't it? You want to be ready for anything."

"Doesn't everyone? No one likes being caught off guard."

"Always being on guard against what *might* happen to you seems like kind of an exhausting way to live. When you block out the possibility of bad surprises, don't you lose the possibility of good surprises too?"

"You sound like Melanie."

Josh laughed. "She may be onto something there. Let me ask you this: when's the last time you were pleasantly surprised by something or someone?"

Olivia bit the inside of her lip a moment. "When we found you. Both times, I guess."

"Okay. And you wouldn't have had those pleasant surprises if you hadn't had a couple things go wrong, right?"

"If we hadn't had those accidents, we wouldn't have needed your help at all. You would have been just another person on the trail. Actually, we wouldn't have even crossed paths because we would have made our campsite that night while you were still out on the river fishing. You would have been inconsequential."

Josh sat on the rock next to Melanie's journal. "But you did have those accidents. You did get lost and we did cross paths."

"So? If we hadn't lost the trail, it would have made no difference if we never met at all."

"How do you know that? Can you see every contingency into the infinite future? How do you know you weren't meant to meet me all along?"

Olivia put her hands on her hips. "Because nothing is *meant*. Not in the sense you're using the word. I thought we'd been over this already."

"All right. Let's look at this from a different angle. Cause and effect. Do you think you and Melanie would have had all the same conversations you've had in the past couple days if you hadn't gotten off the trail? Would you have even had the same thoughts in your own mind if everything had gone according to your plan?"

"Of course not. I will allow that my thoughts and our conversations were affected by what happened."

"You might say they were *e*ffected by it. Caused, not just influenced."

Olivia tipped her head in concession. "Perhaps. But the fact that there is a cause and an effect doesn't mean there is a mind behind the cause. Every part of the planet might be said to eventually affect every other part of it, but that doesn't require a mind or a will. There are laws of nature that behave in predictable ways that are interacting with one another." Josh opened his mouth, and Olivia rushed on. "And don't give me that crap about an ultimate cause or an unmoved mover. I've heard that argument before."

He closed his mouth and smiled. "And you avoid talking about it because you've already decided it doesn't fit into your worldview."

Olivia shook her head. "Don't pretend like you know my inner thoughts. Don't think that because I told you a little bit about my life, you somehow have any authority to say anything about it."

Josh didn't respond. Just kept smiling that knowing smile. Who did he think he was? Pretending to know what she was thinking. She was trying to think of what else to say to get that look off his face, to jab him like she jabbed unreliable witnesses on the stand, when he stood and brushed off the back of his pants.

"I've got wood to carry and fish to fry," he said. "I'll see you back at the campsite."

Olivia watched him disappear into the trees, then squatted down to rummage through Melanie's pack again even though she knew there was nothing else in there. A moment later she heard footsteps coming up the path.

"Look, I don't want to talk about it anymore, all right?" she said without looking up.

"Well, excuse me," came Melanie's voice. "I was just coming to see if you needed any help."

Olivia stood. "Sorry, I didn't mean you. I thought you were Josh."

"Oh." Melanie glanced at the full clothesline. "Do you need any help?"

"No. All done."

"Okay."

They stared awkwardly at each other for a moment.

"Hey, did you see my phone anywhere?" Melanie said.

Olivia pointed to the rock. "I didn't try to power it on. It needs to dry out first."

"My journal!" Melanie snatched up the book and cast Olivia a suspicious glance.

"I didn't read it. It's unreadable anyway."

Melanie opened it and frantically flipped through the pages. "No! No, no, no!"

"I'm sorry, Mel."

"I had something really important recorded in this one." She sat down hard on the rock. "Now it's gone. All of what happened, all I felt about it."

Olivia said nothing, and she especially did not say that this wouldn't have happened if Melanie had put the journal in a plastic bag as directed.

Melanie dropped the journal on the ground and put her face in her hands.

Olivia sat down and put an arm around her shoulders. "You still know it happened though, right?" she tried. "You still know how you felt."

"Right now, maybe. But what about twenty years from now? I'm not going to remember it as clearly."

"Gosh. Twenty years? What's so important you want to remember it perfectly twenty years from now?"

Melanie's teary eyes met hers for just a moment, then she looked at the journal on the ground. "Nothing." She straightened her back and stared out at the lake, her limp curls blown back from her blotchy face by the wind. "This trip sucks."

Olivia laughed. "Yes. Yes it does." She rubbed Melanie's back. "But we're going to finish it anyway. Who knows? Maybe it'll get better."

"It's gotta be all uphill from here, right?"

"Sure. I mean, yes, literally it's basically all uphill from here because Lake Superior is the lowest elevation in the park."

"Oh, Ollie," Melanie said, giving her a half-playful shove. "You're the worst sometimes."

Olivia smiled. "I know. It's an art, really—exasperating people." She stood up. "Speaking of which, did you see Josh when you came out here?"

"No. You exasperated him?"

"Other way around. He's apparently imperturbable."

"What were you two talking about?"

"This and that. How I'm too concerned about being prepared for every contingency and how I'm suppressing evidence of a god to fit my own agenda. Your standard light conversational fare for someone you've just met."

Melanie laughed. "I swear I didn't put him up to that."

"Right."

"Honestly. I'm just glad you weren't out here talking about me."

"Oh, Melanie. You're not as interesting a topic of conversation as you think you are." She pulled Melanie to her feet and handed her the food bag from her pack. "Come on. Let's go eat dinner. We can come back for this stuff later."

They started up the path.

"First thing I'm going to eat when we get out of these woods is a giant burrito smothered in cheese and sour cream," Olivia said.

"That actually does sound kind of good," Melanie admitted.

"Well, get your own. I'm not sharing."

Twenty-Two

MELANIE PICKED THROUGH the contents of her food bag. When she'd chosen this stuff at the grocery store, she'd been excited to eat it. Now it was just a random jumble of disparate items that had no business being in the same bag. Like the weird off-brand Halloween candy left, sad and unloved, in a plastic pumpkin come December. Not one thing looked like it could satisfy her hunger. These were snacks, not meals. She'd just been snacking all this time. She needed something substantial.

Next to her the firelight flickered across the pale pink flesh of the trout on Olivia's makeshift pita-bread plate. Josh had caught and grilled up two small fish: one for Olivia and one for himself. When he'd extracted the pita bread from the bag in his pack, Melanie noted there were only five pieces. That would leave only three after tonight, and Josh had said he was staying in the woods at least one more night, with a long hike back to the car after that. She couldn't very well ask him for a piece. So she sat silently by the fire, muscling down another protein bar and wishing she was in her kitchen at home.

Nothing was going right. She'd been a fool to think a ten-year rift could be solved in just a few days. To think that Olivia's heart of stone would soften if she could just say the right words and pull on the right heartstrings. Nothing short of a divine act could make that happen.

Now her journal, her backup plan, was destroyed. If she was going to tell Olivia about what was going on in her life, she'd have to say it out loud. And even though she'd practiced saying it in the bathroom mirror in the days leading up to this trip, she was never confident she'd be able to get the words out of her throat when the time came.

Melanie felt herself slipping into a pit, like she'd slipped on those rocks in the river. She was going down, not into cold, rushing water but into a still, dank darkness she knew all too well. She closed her eyes and tried to focus on something else. The cool air at her back. The heat from the fire on her face. The feel of the ground beneath her feet. The sound of leaves dropping from the trees. The physical world. But the most physical thing she felt at that moment was still the gnawing hunger in her gut.

All at once she became aware of Josh standing beside her, extending a pita that cradled several large chunks of cooked fish.

"What? No," she said by reflex. "I'm—"

"You're hungry," Josh said.

"I have plenty."

"So do I."

"No," she said, shaking her head. "Then you won't have enough."

"I always have enough, and then some," he said, offering it again to her.

This time Melanie took it. She knew these fish were not her

parents. She'd always known it, she realized. They had not come back as animals of some kind, or even other people. She knew it as plainly as she knew that it would never be the right time to tell Olivia about Justin. That she just needed to get it over with. She lifted the fish to her mouth and took a bite, savoring the taste, remembering the big family meals they'd had with their parents. Then she swallowed it down and stared hard at the fire.

"Justin asked me to marry him."

She winced as she said it, as though expecting a blow. But nothing happened. Nothing was said. She risked a glance at her sister. Olivia was staring at her. Glaring at her. Lips slightly parted, fire dancing in her eyes.

"I haven't told him anything yet."

Melanie didn't want to hear the kinds of things Olivia was undoubtedly lining up in her brain to shout out at any moment. All of the anger that was building up inside of her. Even so, she wished she'd get it over with. The silence was somehow worse.

"I said I needed to talk to you first."

At that, Olivia stood up and threw the pita bread with the fish to the ground. "You're sick," she spit out. "You're seriously sick. How have you let him gaslight you like this? Are you out of your mind? Or are you just stupid?"

Olivia's words fell like hailstones on Melanie's battered spirit, and she felt herself shrinking beneath them.

"What am I supposed to say to you right now?" Olivia continued. "What did you think I would say? 'Oh, hey, that's great, sis, congratulations, when's the big day'? 'If only Dad was alive so he could walk you down the aisle'?" Her voice rose another register. "He's the reason Dad will never walk you down the aisle! He's the reason Mom will never cry joyful tears on your wedding day! He's the reason I couldn't stand to talk to you or even look at you for the past ten years! And now you're going to marry him?"

"I didn't say I was going to—"

"The fact that you're close enough to him that he would even dream of asking you that question—it's just unbelievable! I knew you moved up there to be near him. I knew it! I knew where he went when he left Rockford. And then a couple months later you move up there too and you think I'm not going to figure it out?"

Olivia took a few sharp steps away from the fire, then turned around and came back, stopping at Melanie's feet, looming over her like a vulture over a deer carcass on the side of the road.

"If you thought I was done with you before, you have no idea what you're in for now. When I get into my car in Indian River, that will be the last time you see me. Ever. Understand? I don't want to have anything to do with you ever again."

Olivia stalked off to the tent and zipped herself up into it. Melanie crumpled. Hot tears stung her chapped cheeks. Her breath came in choking gasps. She felt the pita bread with the fish on it being removed from her hand. Josh settled down next to her on the log and put an arm around her shoulders. It felt like her heart was imploding, like it was being sucked in on itself until it was a single small, hard piece of gravel stuck in the wall of her chest.

How was it that this was both exactly what she'd expected and yet simultaneously so much worse? How could she have imagined for one moment that Olivia would give her a chance to explain herself? To explain that no one in the world understood her as well as Justin did. That no one knew her sorrow like he did. That he was so, so sorry for the pain he had caused in both their lives. That he'd agonized over it. That he'd considered suicide, even going so far as to plan it out and write a note. That he credited her forgiveness with stopping him from taking his own life. That he'd finally found his peace with God and realized that his life was still worth something. That while he could never undo what he had done, he could move forward.

But Olivia would never listen to all of that. She didn't want to forgive. She'd wanted him to stand trial all those years ago for manslaughter, but no one else in the family agreed. No charges were filed, and she'd never forgiven them for it.

Slowly, Melanie ran out of tears. She wiped her eyes and nose on the sleeve of Olivia's jacket, only realizing then that she was wearing it. She looked up at Josh, embarrassed by how long she had been in his arms, embarrassed by the spectacle he'd just witnessed, feeling she owed him some sort of explanation but knowing she didn't have the energy to offer one.

He rubbed her upper arm and let out a breath. "You want to borrow my hammock tonight?"

In spite of herself, Melanie managed a laugh. "Yes." She sniffed. "But no. Of course not."

"Why 'of course not'?"

"Then you'd have nowhere to sleep."

"I'd sleep in the tent."

"With Olivia?"

"Presumably, yes." Josh stood and tossed the remains of Olivia's discarded food into the fire. "I think at this point, between the two of us, she'd rather have me in there, right?"

Melanie stood. "I guess." She brushed off the back of her pants.

Josh reached for her food bag. "I'll take care of all of this. Why don't you head down to the beach and see if your stuff is dry?" He fished a compact flashlight out of his pocket and tossed it to her. "It'll be getting dark soon."

Wrong, Melanie thought. Things were clearly already as dark as they could get.

She started down the path that led to the lake, still trying to regulate her breathing after her sob session. It had been six months or more since she'd cried that big for that long, and at the moment she was having trouble recalling what the last one was all about. With her journal destroyed, she wasn't sure if she'd ever remember.

Why hadn't she listened and put everything in plastic bags as instructed? Why was Olivia always right? Was she right about Justin too? She certainly knew him better than Melanie did. All of the personal revelations over the years—about his family issues, his problems in school, his years of dabbling in drugs—Olivia had already known all of it and never divulged any of it to Melanie. She'd kept Justin's secrets for him. It was what best friends did, after all.

When they'd found out that it had been Justin driving the other car, Melanie expected Olivia to show at least some concern for him. Instead, she'd burned him out of her life for good, just as it seemed she was now ready to do to her own sister. How could Melanie ever hope to have a relationship with someone who allowed no room for mistakes, no room for repentance?

The rocky shoreline of Lake Superior was littered with blobs of black and gray and blue. Her clothes, blown off the line and now strewn along the beach. She crisscrossed the stones, snatching up pants and shirts and sports bras, hoping she'd manage to get it all, hoping that a hiker would not stumble upon a pair of her underwear at some later date. The task took her far enough afield that she lost track of the clothesline and the large flat rock that held her journal and the pieces of her cell phone.

She scanned the trees for the line of rope. When would she ever stop getting herself lost?

Her arms full of clothes, she stumbled over the wave-rounded stones, willing herself in the right direction. Or what she thought might be the right direction. It did cross her mind that if she were out here long enough, Josh would eventually come looking and find her. But she didn't want to be found. She wanted to find her own way.

What she needed was to start thinking like Olivia. She stopped walking. The wind blew her limp hair across her face, and she noted the direction. If her clothes had been blown off the line, that was the direction they would have gone, and she'd already gathered them all up, so she started walking the other way down the beach, sticking near the trees, scanning up and down. Twenty or so yards ahead a flash of white caught her eye. The ink-stained pages of her journal flapping in the wind.

She quickened her pace. There was her phone in pieces on the rock, the clothesline hanging rather limp between two trees, and her pack, blending in with the general brownish-green of a nearly denuded shrub. She folded her clothes haphazardly with no regard for what was clean and what was dirty. At this point in the hike, did it really matter? The second a clean article of clothing touched her body, it would be dirty. She zipped up the pack and put her cell phone back together but resisted the urge to try powering it up. Maybe tomorrow.

Lastly, she picked up her journal. The pages were mostly dry but so wrinkled she couldn't close the book all the way. Was it even worth taking? Melanie almost left it on the rock before remembering Olivia's reaction to the trash in the fire ring and her "leave no trace" rule. She'd bring it with her and find some appropriate way to dispose of it later.

She sat down on the rock and stared out at the lake. The wind was dying down and the sky was dimming. Melanie hugged herself tightly against the cold. What would it be like to see Olivia the next morning? Would she even talk to her? Look at her? Would Josh have to be their go-between and mediator for the rest of the hike? That at least might make things tolerable. Then there'd be the long, agonizing drive back to Olivia's car.

And after that? Nothing? If she told Justin yes, certainly. But what if she told him no? Could Olivia get over the fact that she'd even considered marrying him? She'd have to choose: Justin or her sister. Or had she already lost her sister for good?

Melanie stood up. It was time to get back to the campsite.

She was buckling the straps of her pack when she noticed something being pushed up onto the shore by the waves. More trash. She picked it out of the water, turned it over, and laughed out loud. The Universe certainly had a sense of humor.

Twenty-Three

OLIVIA HAD ENTERED a nightmare and couldn't wake up.

Justin? Justin Navarro? Did the man have some sort of sick fascination with destroying her? If he'd followed Melanie to Petoskey, she'd have to say the answer was a definite yes. But it was Melanie who had followed him. He must have manipulated her somehow. Starting with the day of the funeral when he'd shown up at the cemetery in a new car that had to be driven by someone else because his license had been suspended. A day he knew she would be vulnerable to emotional exploitation. But marriage? That was too far. That was sick and twisted and spiteful. It was clearly designed to hurt her.

Olivia knew the accident had been just that—an accident. Unplanned. Unfortunate. But Justin knew her well enough to know she'd have no sympathy for him. Who could?

Melanie.

Simple, trusting Melanie. If he couldn't have Olivia, he'd have Melanie.

"He's your oldest friend," Melanie had said that horrible day when she'd called to tell Olivia she'd forgiven Justin. "Don't you think he's sorry?"

"Sorry? Sorry is something you say when you miss someone's birthday or shut a door in their face! Sorry is for breaches of etiquette, not manslaughter!" she'd screamed at the phone as her college roommate looked on, eyes wide and jaw slack. "You can't be friends with someone after they kill your parents!"

And now ten years later she was forced to have the same basic conversation. Marriage? How could Melanie do this to her? To the memory of their parents, which she so obviously tried to honor in the most ridiculous ways. Or was that all a ruse? Just a way for her to get sympathy and attention from other people? How often had she trotted out her personal grief in front of her followers and subscribers so she could get their thumbs-ups and their trite little messages of fake encouragement?

Olivia felt like she was going to throw up, though there was nothing in her stomach to come out. She hadn't had a chance to take one bite of Josh's fish before Melanie sprang this insanity on her. Now they were out there together. Melanie undoubtedly crying, Josh undoubtedly offering a shoulder to cry on. And what did she have? Why should Melanie get comfort while she got nothing?

"Hello?" came Josh's voice from just outside the tent. "Olivia?"

"Go away." She listened. No footsteps. "I said go away."

"How do you know I haven't?"

"I mean it."

"Yeah, here's the thing though," Josh said, undaunted. "Melanie is going to sleep in my hammock tonight."

"So?"

A slight pause, then, "So I'm wondering if it's okay to bunk with you."

"No."

"I don't snore. Much."

"I said no."

Olivia could hear Josh shifting positions, and when he next spoke, the sound was closer to her ear, as close as that bear's breath had been.

"Would you rather have Melanie in there with you tonight?"

"I'd rather have no one in here with me tonight."

Josh sighed. "I know. But here we are."

Olivia sat up and rubbed her burning eyes. "Fine. But no talking."

"Thanks."

"Wait. What do you sleep in?"

"I thought I'd try a sleeping bag."

She unzipped the inside of the tent door so she could look at him through the screen. "I mean on your person."

"T-shirt and shorts?"

"That'll do." Olivia zipped the window shut again. "Just stay out there until I say, all right?"

"Right."

Olivia unzipped the door enough to reach into her pack and get her pj's. She peeked through the small opening for Melanie, but she was nowhere to be seen. She thought of her sister's clothes and cell phone and wrecked journal on the beach and almost told Josh to remind her to get them. Then she didn't. Let her remember her own stuff. If she didn't, that was her problem.

Ten minutes later the light was dimming outside, and Olivia zipped herself into her mummy bag.

"You can come in now."

Silence. Hushed voices. The sound of a long zipper twenty feet away where the hammock hung. Then footsteps. Josh unzipped the tent and carefully climbed over her in the twilight. He leaned over her to zip the door up again, then took a moment to slide into Melanie's mummy bag and zip himself up into it. Olivia could hear his soft, regular breathing. As directed, he didn't speak.

Olivia tried to settle into the silence. Tried not to think of the fact that she was now sharing her tent with a strange man she'd stumbled upon in the woods. Tried not to think of her sister out in Josh's hammock, exposed to whatever dangers might lurk outside the tent. What if the bear came back? What if there really was a cougar?

She twisted in the mummy bag, but no position was comfortable. Her back hurt, her feet hurt, her hip hurt. The silence was so loud. She had to get her arms out or she was going to lose it. She contorted and pulled at the zipper, but it didn't budge. She sighed and pulled harder, but the stupid slidey thing would not move along the teeth. She grunted and sighed again and waited for Josh to ask her what was wrong.

"Hey," she finally said.

He shifted but said nothing.

"Can you unzip this thing? It's stuck, and I feel like I'm in a straightjacket."

She heard his own zipper and felt him moving in the almost black next to her. His hands found the zipper, manipulated it a moment, and pulled it down from the spot near her left cheek to just above her elbow. She stuck an arm out and let out her breath.

"Thank you."

Josh zipped himself back up.

"You can talk, you know," she said. "I mean, not a lot. But you can say things like 'sure' and 'you're welcome.'"

"Just trying to follow the rules," he said. "I know this is an imposition, and a good houseguest knows how to make himself invisible."

They were both quiet a moment. Olivia tried to fall asleep. But she wasn't tired.

"I'm sorry you had to witness that," she said. "You'd understand if you knew the history here. But it was bad manners anyway, to fight like that in front of you."

"Not that it's any of my business, but—"

"Oh, I know you won't let that stop you."

Josh laughed. "But I kind of got the idea that your sister was talking about the guy who caused your parents' accident?"

"Bingo."

"Hmm."

Olivia waited for more, but Josh said nothing else.

"Am I out of line here?" she challenged. "Thinking maybe my sister shouldn't marry the guy who killed our parents?"

"Well, no, maybe not. It's certainly not the normal way people might get together."

"Don't joke about this, okay? If you want to sleep in this tent and not outside on the ground with the wild animals, you will not joke about this."

"Loud and clear," he said.

Olivia took a deep breath. "It's worse than that. The guy was my best friend all through elementary, junior high, and high school. And then I went to college and he didn't. I was going to be a lawyer and he was going to be a mechanic. And whatever, that's fine. I have no problem with that. But he kept telling me I'd changed and I was too serious, and he was all jealous that I was meeting new friends and new guys at school. We had a big fight when I was home one summer. Then I went back to school. A week later I'm on a Labor Day weekend hiking trip with my college friends, and he takes a blind corner too fast and hits my parents' car. Flipped it over down an embankment."

She paused to tamp down the emotion that was starting to manifest itself in her voice.

"Then Melanie calls me to say they've been having dinner together and hanging out, and oh, by the way, she's forgiven him? And she acts like I'm supposed to be okay with that and like I'm supposed to forgive him too."

She paused so that Josh could interject some appropriate word, like "Wow" or "Seriously?" or "That's ridiculous!" But still he said nothing.

"Then she forces me on this trip so she can corner me with the fact that Justin asked her to marry him? And she somehow expects me to give her permission or my blessing or some such nonsense. So you can see, she's the one who's out of line here, not me."

Silence.

"Right?"

Silence.

"Say something, man. Anything."

Josh's voice emerged from the darkness on the other side of the tent. "That's tough."

Olivia waited for more.

"That's it?" she said. "'That's tough'?"

"It is. What do you want me to say?"

She sat up. "That it's ridiculous. That it's insane. That clearly this guy just gets off on manipulating women's emotions and that he couldn't have a more willing victim than my supremely naïve sister, who believes everything that's ever said to her so long as she can put a positive spin on it."

"I'm not going to say any of that."

Olivia expelled a little puff of exasperation. "Why not? It's true."

Josh unzipped his bag again and sat up. "You don't really want to hear what I think."

"Yes, I do," Olivia said, though she wasn't sure she meant it.

"Look, clearly there is a complicated history here. There's a lot of hurt. Real hurt. It's totally valid that you're angry. But have you ever looked at it from his point of view?"

Olivia bit her tongue to keep from shouting at Josh to get out of the tent.

"If you were friends that long, he must have known your family, known your parents. Right?"

"Yeah."

"Spent a lot of time at your house? Maybe even at your table?"

"Yes," she conceded. Indeed, their house had been a second home to him, especially when his parents were going through a nasty divorce.

"So—and I'm not saying this to diminish your pain in any way—he lost your parents too. And he had the double burden of being the cause of that loss."

This was irritatingly similar to what Melanie had said to her on the phone all those years ago. And what her friend-but-maybe-someday-hopefully-more Eric had said later that year which drove a wedge between them, leading to the end of their relationship before it even had a chance to begin. What her roommate had said, propelling her to find her own apartment.

Four witnesses, all with the same story.

But she couldn't be wrong about this. This was easy, wasn't it? This was a crime that had never been paid for. This was the scales of justice all out of balance. Did people just expect her to forgive him?

"It's hard, I know," Josh said. "Don't think I haven't had to forgive plenty of people who didn't actually deserve forgiveness. I mean, at the end of the day, who does? Everyone falls short. Everyone crosses lines. Everyone makes mistakes. Sometimes restitution can be made and sometimes it can't. Justin can't bring your parents back, so you'll never be satisfied with any length or intensity of punishment for him. There's no such thing as justice in a case like that. Unless you think he should be executed. Life for a life. That would be a certain kind of justice."

"I didn't say that," Olivia said. "Obviously I don't think he should be executed. It was an accident. I know that. But is it so wrong for me to want him to stay out of my life? Out of my sister's life?"

"Probably not. But you can't live your sister's life for her. You've got one life to live. Yours."

Olivia sighed and lay back down. Her arm was cold. Her chest was cold. Her heart was cold. And sad. And lonely. "I can't do this. I just can't do this anymore."

She felt Josh's warm hand on her shoulder. "You don't have to."

She shrugged it off. "What is that supposed to mean? Just let it go? Pretend it's not happening? Live in some delusion like my sister? A problem doesn't just solve itself if you ignore it."

"Did I say you should ignore it?"

"Well, no. But . . . I don't even know what you said. 'You don't have to.' Don't have to what?"

Josh took a deep breath and let it out. "Let me ask you this: have you been carrying your pack around in the woods for three days?"

"Obviously, yes."

"Have you been carrying your sister's pack?"

"I carried it some of the way."

"The same time you were carrying your own pack?"

"No, that would be practically impossible."

"Why?"

"Because it would be too heavy." She almost added "duh" but refrained. "What's your point?"

"I think you just made it."

Olivia sat with that for a moment. "Has anyone ever told you you're super annoying?"

"I have my detractors, yes." Josh chuckled. "But when people take the time to get to know me, they generally come around to see that I only have their best interest at heart."

Olivia sighed. "I don't know why you care at all. You just met us. You've been stuck sharing your food and watching us act like jerks to one another. And after a day or two that will be it—you'll never see or hear from us again."

"I hope that's not true," Josh said as he settled back down into his sleeping bag. "I'm kind of fond of you two."

She scoffed. "We've certainly done nothing to endear ourselves to you."

"It's nothing you've done, that's for sure," he quipped. "It's just who you are."

Olivia thought for a moment. Who was she, anyway? Apart from what she did. And if she met herself somewhere along the way, would she want to be her friend? Would she even give herself a second glance? She couldn't avoid the fact that the answer was a resounding no.

"Josh?"

"Hmm?"

"Why are you so nice?"

Josh yawned. "Just my nature, I guess."

"I wish I was nicer," she admitted.

"Well, practice makes perfect, as they say."

"Yeah."

"Good night, Olivia."

"Good night."

A moment later, Olivia heard Josh's breathing deepen and slow in sleep. She lay in the dark, trying to unravel a decade of sadness and anger and resentment, trying to discover what she was without that tangle of bitterness squeezing in on all sides. She couldn't carry both her pack and Melanie's. Carrying just her own load was exhausting enough.

As she drifted off to sleep, the thought occurred to her that it would be nice if there was a God after all. Someone who could deal with the justice that needed meting out so she didn't have to. Someone who would carry the load once in a while. Someone who would calm her spirit and challenge her intellect and just be there alongside her in the dark.

Maybe someone like Josh.

Twenty-Four

MELANIE HAD LAIN AWAKE half the night. Though she was warm enough and far more comfortable in the hammock than she had been on the hard ground, she couldn't get her brain to turn off after Josh went into the tent. For a while she could hear voices murmuring in the dark, though she could not make out any words. She could imagine what Olivia was saying. Melanie only hoped her sister hadn't won Josh to her side.

As they went about their morning tasks, she tried to read his face and his mannerisms. Had anything changed? Did she detect a bit more brusqueness? A little less eye contact? Or were those her own doing as she looked down at the ground and answered questions or responded to comments with as few syllables as possible?

They ate breakfast in shifts as sleeping bags, tents, and hammocks were packed, water was filtered, and teeth were brushed. Olivia never looked at her, never handed her anything, never spoke. When they started down the trail, Olivia took the lead, with Josh next and Melanie bringing up the rear. So angry, Mel thought, that Olivia couldn't even bear to look at her back.

The wind was cold and the sky still clouded as they walked along the lakeshore. A gull hovered silently over the water in an invisible air current, body quivering, wing dipping slightly to stay balanced. Waves reached their fingers onto the shore and rattled the rocks, knocking stone on stone, wearing each other down bit by bit. Melanie squatted awkwardly under her pack, picked up two stones, and rubbed them together. They looked almost identical. But if one was comprised of harder minerals than the other, that would be the one to survive the eons of constant clashing. The softer one would succumb, grain by grain, until nothing was left of it but some sand scattered by the wind.

Melanie tossed the stones into the lake one at a time.

Their party soon hit the mouth of the Big Carp River where it drained into Lake Superior. The trail came to a bridge crossing and made a sharp right to follow the river upstream.

"That's our turn," Josh called up to Olivia. They were the first words anyone had spoken in an hour.

They crossed the bridge and picked up the Big Carp River Trail on the other side. This path would take them inland—away from the lake, away from the cold north wind, and ever closer to the end of their hike and the beginning of the drive home. Olivia had originally planned for one more night on the trail, but Melanie was sure that once they reached the parking lot at the Lake of the Clouds, they'd be hitching a ride the rest of the way to the car.

For the next half mile, the river rambled over rocks to Melanie's right, but the sound held no pleasure for her. Where just a couple days ago she had stopped and leaned in close to hear what a creek had to say to her, now she was sure she was utterly deaf to such things. After years of reading signs and messages in everything, Melanie felt like a sojourner in a foreign land where she didn't speak the language. The rustle of the leaves, the call of a bird, the whisper of the breeze—she could interpret none of it. Maybe the Universe wasn't trying to speak to her through these things. Maybe the Universe wasn't sending hawks into her skies. Maybe they were all just vultures. Maybe there was no Universe at all. Just a universe. An infinite black void made up of nothing more than chemical reactions, where life was an accident. Just as death sometimes was.

Maybe her parents weren't out there somewhere. Maybe they were just . . . gone.

Melanie was so lost in these bleak thoughts that she didn't realize Olivia and Josh had stopped until she was practically on top of them. They were looking at the river, where a series of small ledges and inviting pools created a little paradise. A nearby sign said "Bathtub Falls."

"Nice, isn't it?" Josh said.

Melanie nodded.

"You should get your phones out," he said. "The next half mile or so there are more than a dozen cascades and falls—all unnamed but worth remembering—culminating in Shining Cloud Falls. One of the best spots in the park."

Melanie took out her phone and pressed the power button. After one heart-stopping moment of nothing, the screen lit up. She waited until all the little icons appeared, then tapped the camera and held the phone out toward the falls. But where normally she'd experience immense pleasure capturing a moment—one that would never come again in exactly the same way—she felt nothing as she hit the button. She turned her phone off and waited for Olivia and Josh to start walking again. Olivia, she noted, hadn't bothered to get her phone out at all. Of course not. She wanted to forget this trip ever happened. Just like the last hiking trip they'd been on.

The scenery for the next twenty minutes or so was achingly charming. But Melanie couldn't enjoy it. She took no more pictures, nor could she do so very easily if she had wanted to. Olivia walked so fast she was soon out of sight, and Melanie's heavy steps had her lagging so far behind that she often lost sight of Josh as well.

She should have been using this time to think through what to say when they were alone again in the car. She cared about Justin. Deeply. When they spent time together, she felt understood, known, loved. In the time she had spent with Olivia the past few days, she had often felt misunderstood, occasionally felt that she was only barely tolerated, and certainly felt judged at every turn. The choice should have been easy.

But Olivia was family. Or . . . maybe not. Family was there for you. Family supported you. Family sacrificed for you. Family loved you.

Did Olivia love her? Did Olivia love anyone?

As Melanie turned this over in her head, she came upon Josh standing in the middle of the trail.

He pointed down toward the river. "Shining Cloud Falls. Better vantage point down there."

Melanie hesitated.

"Come on. We're all going down there for a break and a snack."

She reluctantly stepped off the trail down a depression that had clearly been made by many other hikers over the years hoping for a better look at the falls. She slipped out of her pack and stretched her back muscles, keeping some distance between her and her sister, who was standing near the river. She busied herself retrieving a snack from her dwindling food supply, found a flat spot on the ground, and sat. Olivia's body obscured the view, but Melanie said nothing. Eventually her sister too took off her pack and settled down to eat, and Melanie could see the falls clearly.

Shining Cloud was not one fall but two, crashing down side by side, separated by an outcropping of rock. The one on the right fell straight down off a ledge before it hit more resistant rock and bounced off of it and into the basin below. The one on the left cascaded lazily down a more gradual decline like the flowing white hair of some wise woodland wizard. Strange that so many of the park's waterfalls were actually two falls, split by hard rock. Melanie might have found the idea friendly a few days ago. Now it seemed lonely.

As though he knew what she was thinking about, Josh said, "A couple days ago right after all that rain, I bet you couldn't see that rock in the middle there."

"Really?" Melanie said.

"Sure." He took a swig of water. "A higher volume of water can change a river's behavior dramatically. During the spring thaw this river is pretty wild. At the end of summer, it's usually calmed down a bit. Except when you get a big weather event like we just had. The more pressure you put on the waterway with extra rain or snowmelt, the faster and harder it all flows down out to the lake. Makes for some nice white water and waterfalls. But of course it makes the crossings trickier."

"Are we crossing the river today?" Melanie said.

"Twice," Josh said. "In about two miles and then again in a little less than that."

"Why don't they just keep the trail on one side of it?"

"Well, when you're cutting a trail, you're probably taking a few things into account. One, the lay of the land. Some spots are just easier to tame than others. Two, the trails may have already been there in some form long before this was a state park. There was commercial copper mining going on here before the Civil War, and before that the Ojibwe were mining with hand tools. Even the wildlife makes trails. By the time park rangers were cutting and maintaining trails, some of this was already mapped out."

"There was mining way out here?" Melanie said. "It's hard enough to get around with a backpack. I can't imagine trying to get supplies in and copper out."

"They sure tried. The mines in this area weren't nearly as successful as those up near Houghton and Calumet. Most of them couldn't make the numbers work. But there are several marked mine shafts scattered around the park. And dozens more unmarked. You'll be near one today before you get up on the escarpment."

Melanie didn't care for the way he said "you" rather than "we." She knew he intended to fish the salmon run today, but naturally they would accompany him, wouldn't they?

All this time, Olivia had sat with her back to them. Surely she'd say something now, just to clarify the plans for the day.

Or did she already know? Had she and Josh talked it over in the tent while Melanie lay awake in the hammock?

Olivia said nothing. Just tucked her food bag back into her pack and strapped it on her back. Josh, Melanie now realized, had never taken his pack off, nor had he eaten anything.

"Do you want a granola bar or something?" Melanie offered.

"Nah," he said. "I'm good."

Olivia was already heading back up to the trail, and Melanie scrambled to ready herself for more walking. Trudging, really. Putting one miserable foot in front of the other until they hit pavement. Then it would be over. Mostly.

They left the picturesque river and ascended a steep hill. Over the next hour they made their way over fairly level, if often soggy, ground beneath towering hemlock trees. When they had stopped in at the visitor center before starting the hike, Melanie had read in one of the displays that the Porcupine Mountains contained the largest stand of virgin hardwood and hemlock forest left between the Rockies and the Adirondacks. Trees saved from the clutches of the country's insatiable hunger for lumber by the rugged landscape beneath her feet. Some of these trees must have been standing watch when the Ojibwe were extracting copper from the rocks.

As she passed by some of the bigger trees, Melanie laid her hands on them, trying to feel the life and the memory within, trying to reclaim her sense of oneness with the natural world. Trying to see eagles where Olivia saw vultures. Yet all she felt beneath her hands was the rough texture of the bark, a completely practical and unmagical covering that protected the tree from bugs and fungus.

They made the first crossing, which was more difficult than any of the others had been despite Josh's steadying hand. More than once Melanie might have gone down were it not for his help. On the other side they ate a quick lunch and carried on, following the river upstream until they entered a low-lying area that was quite wet and rather unpleasant because of it. This section seemed to stretch on forever, and as Melanie slogged through she tried to make up her mind what to do about Justin.

Finally, after what seemed like hours, they reached the river again for the second crossing.

"Last time you'll have to do this," Josh said brightly as Melanie and Olivia removed their boots.

Rather than cross barefoot this time, Josh pulled on his waders before helping Melanie across. As she dried her feet and pulled on her socks and boots, he gave Olivia's hand a firm shake.

"Well, this is it," he said. "This is where I leave you."

Olivia's father pulled a large blue cooler from the back of the Explorer. "You got that, Justin?"

"Yep."

Olivia watched her dad watch Justin lug the cooler down the sandy path toward the beach.

"He's fine, Dad," she said, hoisting a beach chair under each arm.

"I still think he should see a doctor."

Olivia followed Justin's footsteps down the path but couldn't help overhearing her mother say, "He probably doesn't have insurance."

And, *Olivia thought,* he doesn't want anyone poking around in his life. *He'd told her the truth, but when her parents asked her about his limp, she told them he'd come off a dirt bike. They didn't need to know that he didn't even own a dirt bike. They didn't need to know that his dad had reappeared after six months of unexplained absence and attempted to rob his own house for drug money. That Justin had fought him off with nothing but the baseball bat he'd won at a Whitecaps game her parents had invited him to last year, twisting an ankle in the process.*

Olivia gave her head a firm shake. Forget about that now. Today was just supposed to be fun.

Melanie ran past her toward the beach, carrying nothing at all. She peeled her shirt and shorts off, kicked off her flip-flops, and high-stepped it over the scalding sand into the endless blue of Lake Michigan.

With no help from Melanie, who was busy diving through waves and occasionally screeching, the rest of the family—and Justin—laid out blankets and chairs and towels. Sunscreen was applied, handing off the tube and getting each other's backs. Mom and

Dad. Olivia and Justin. As always. Only this year there was something about Justin touching her bare back that sent little chills up Olivia's neck.

"Go get your sister and tell her to get out of there and put on some sunscreen," her mom said as she settled into a chair with a book.

Olivia dutifully headed for the water, though at an unhurried pace. Justin went down the beach in search of flat stones for skipping.

"Mom says come in and get sunscreen on," Olivia said when she finally reached Melanie on the sandbar.

"When are you just going to date him already?" Melanie said.

Olivia put her hands on her hips and waited for Melanie to comply with orders.

"He's obviously in love with you."

"When are you just going to mind your own business already?" Olivia said. "Now come on. Mom said to go in."

"He can't stop looking at you, you know."

Olivia resisted looking toward the beach to see if what Melanie said was true. "Do you want me to tell Mom you refuse to come in?"

Melanie stalked off, then dropped suddenly into the water when the sandbar ended. Olivia laughed.

"Shut up!" Melanie said, and she started to the shore with a slow breaststroke.

Olivia chanced a look at the beach. Justin stood squinting out at the water, hands on his narrow hips. Olivia couldn't tell what he was looking at exactly. There was, after all, an entire beautiful vista to view. She waved. He waved back. Then he walked into the water and headed straight for her.

Twenty-Five

OLIVIA WATCHED JOSH make his way upriver and out of sight with a measure of sadness that baffled her. All told, she had spent less than forty-eight hours in his presence, and she could count on one hand the number of hours spent talking to him. He'd helped them out in a pinch, or two, and now he was going on his way and they were going on theirs—that was it. Even so, the loss of his company sent a cloud of melancholy straight to her heart.

Just knowing he was walking the path with her had set her mind at ease. Then everything wasn't on her shoulders. She didn't have to know the way because he did. She didn't have to think about every contingency because he'd probably already experienced them all and would know what to do. It felt like having her father back, his steady footsteps somehow reassuring her that everything would be okay. That she and Melanie would get through this. Not just the hike, but all the other stuff too.

Her conversation with Josh in the tent hadn't been long, but it had been enough to nudge her thinking in a new direction. It wasn't that she didn't know Justin had lost something. It was simply that she hadn't considered it relevant given the magnitude of what she had endured. There might be any number of extenuating circumstances in a court case. But they didn't negate the fact that a law had been broken, that someone had been victimized, that justice must be satisfied.

And yet, this wasn't a court case. Her family had made sure of that by refusing to press charges, given that it was an accident and that Justin had been such a big part of their lives for so long. Facts that had seemed irrelevant to Olivia until last night. But this wasn't a trial and she wasn't acting as a lawyer, so perhaps not all the rules applied. Or perhaps there were different rules altogether.

At this point she was sure of three things. First, that it had been cowardly and selfish to abandon her family after the accident. Second, that no matter how angry she was at Melanie, eliminating her from her life was not the answer. Third, that she could not forgive Justin. Not yet—maybe not ever. But perhaps she could talk to him.

Olivia looked at her watch and then turned to face the sister she had not spoken to all day. "It's five miles to the Lake of the Clouds. We better get going."

Over the next few hours they would be struggling to climb four hundred feet up from the Big Carp River valley to the rocky cliffsides.

For half a mile or more, she sorted through her thoughts as she forced her tired legs to carry her step by agonizing step up the mountainside. The trail was uneven, the left side rising up to the summit, the right dipping down toward the river. Soon Olivia's left hip was screaming, and she tried to compensate by forcing her right leg to do more of the work.

This was what had been happening all those silent years. Melanie pulling more than her fair share of the emotional weight of their loss. She'd needed someone to lean on. In Olivia's absence, she'd found Justin. Even if Olivia tried to do her part now, it wouldn't make up for past neglect. It wouldn't get Justin out of her sister's life. And Melanie was clearly still hurting. She needed attention and rest and time to heal. She needed a break.

"Want a breather?" Olivia said, suddenly unable to keep climbing.

Melanie nodded and twirled her finger to tell Olivia to turn around. Instead, Olivia reached around to get Melanie her water bottle first. They drank long and deep. No need to be too stingy even though there would be no spots to filter water from here on out. They would be spending no more nights on the trail. They could fill up at the visitor center on the way out if it was still open. Barring that, the nearest gas station would be well stocked with far more than water.

All around them, brown needles carpeted the forest floor. Giant fallen trees blanketed in soft green moss invited weary travelers to sit and rest awhile. Overhead a breeze whispered through the lofty hemlocks. It gave Olivia the feeling of being in a church. The living trees were the columns of a great cathedral, and the fallen ones were the pews. They were even situated, incredibly, in generally parallel rows. Olivia knew from her summer research that this must be a spot that had been affected by the great blowdown of 1953, when straight-line winds came ashore from Lake Superior with the force of a tornado and left a two-mile-wide swath of destruction behind. A completely logical and scientific reason for the uncanny arrangement of logs.

Olivia unbuckled the straps of her pack and let it slide off her back. "Let's sit a moment."

She sat on a log, and Melanie settled down on another. Olivia stood, walked around to where Melanie was, and sat down next to her.

How did she start this conversation? "Sorry" was not enough. "I was wrong" was the understatement of the century. "I'll do better" felt like an empty promise.

Melanie's eyes met hers. She held her gaze for a moment, then wrapped her skinny arms around her big sister's sweaty neck. "I'm sorry," Melanie said into her shoulder. "I'm so sorry."

Olivia pulled back. "No, Mel."

Melanie hugged her again. "No, I am. I don't know what I was thinking."

Olivia gently pushed her away. "Stop. Let me say something."

Melanie leaned back and rubbed her nose with her sleeve.

"Gross, Mel. Don't forget that's mine," Olivia said with a laugh. "You're just borrowing it."

"Oh." Melanie gulped. "I can wash it and mail it to you."

Olivia waved that away. "Never mind that. I have something I need you to hear." She paused. Why was it so hard to say?

Melanie looked at her, eyes guarded, apparently ready for another blow. Shame coiled around Olivia's throat like the too-tight turtleneck her mother had forced her to wear for her fourth-grade school portrait. She'd done this to her sister. The years of verbal sparring had been nothing more to her than practice for her chosen profession, honing her skills and sharpening her tongue. But to Melanie, they'd been deeply personal—and she had been on the losing end of every single one.

Olivia took a breath. "I have not treated you fairly. Not during this trip, not during the past decade. Not after the accident, not before the accident. I've always had to be right, even when it didn't really matter, which is probably most of the time. I've treated you like an opponent, not a sister. It's not fair to you and it's not good for me." She paused to brush a small, pale-colored moth off the toe of her shoe. "I don't know why I'm like this. I've often wondered how we could possibly have had the same parents."

"Is that why you used to tell me I was adopted?" Melanie said.

Olivia laughed. "No. That was just to make you mad. You see what I mean though? You would never do that to me. It would never even occur to you to say something like that, something designed to make another person feel bad."

Melanie shrugged. "Nature versus nurture, I guess."

"It would seem so. Though we basically had the exact same nurture situation, so you must be naturally good and I must be naturally . . . evil?"

"I wouldn't say *evil*."

"Okay," Olivia said. "Maybe not evil, but definitely not good."

"Contentious?"

"Perhaps." Olivia felt something tickle the back of her hand and brushed it off absentmindedly. "Anyway, what I'm trying to say is that I'm sorry for the way I've treated you, and I'm going to make a concerted effort to do better." She turned to face Melanie head-on. "I know that you and Justin are close."

"Olivia, I—"

"No, let me finish. I know you're close, and I understand why. He was there for you when I wasn't." She forced the next words out of her mouth. "I know I should have been more sympathetic, not just about your relationship but about him directly. He had a really hard life—probably you know even more about it now than I did when we were friends, and I know a lot—and the accident made it much, much harder. I could have handled his involvement better."

Something like hope lit Melanie's watery eyes.

"I'm not saying I forgive him," Olivia hastened to say. "But I want you to know that I'm going to be reaching out to him to at least have a conversation. Someday."

"That's really good to hear, Olivia."

She smiled at her sister and flicked a fluff of seed off her shoulder. "But I wouldn't expect much to come of it, okay? It's just . . . a start. Maybe. Though, I guess I am almost kind of glad you badgered me into taking this trip. *Almost.*"

"Me too." Melanie smiled as she said it, but then Olivia saw her smile melt away.

"What?"

Melanie reached up to the brim of Olivia's baseball cap. "What is all this stuff? It looks like snow." Her eyes danced.

"It's not cold enough for snow."

"It is much warmer today than it was yesterday," Melanie agreed. "I mean, I'm not soaking wet either, but still."

Olivia stood and sniffed the air. "Mel, this isn't snow." She caught a piece in her hand and smudged it across her palm with her thumb. "This is ash."

Melanie rose to her feet. "Someone with a campfire nearby?"

Olivia took in the flecks of white drifting lazily through the forest around them. "I don't think so."

They locked eyes.

"Get your pack," Olivia said, her heart beating frantically against her ribs. She hoisted her own pack up with strength she didn't know she still had after days of practically nonstop physical exertion.

Melanie was ready just as quickly. "How many more miles?"

Olivia started walking, ignoring the pain in her hip. "Three? Maybe four? We didn't pass the mine yet, right?"

Melanie followed close behind. "I didn't see a mine. But I don't know that I'd know one if I saw it."

"Probably there'd be a sign. And it wouldn't be right on the trail. Off a ways maybe. Keep your eyes open."

"We're not going to stop to admire an abandoned mine," Melanie said incredulously.

Olivia turned to her sister. "No, but it might come in handy—if we need somewhere safe to hunker down."

Melanie's eyes widened. "No. We're not stopping anywhere. We're getting out of the woods. Today. Let's go."

Twenty-Six

AS MELANIE MARCHED along the trail, synchronizing her steps with the swift swooshing of her blood in her ears, the fear of a possible forest fire was mollified somewhat by the fact that her sister had actually admitted she had been wrong about something. About a lot of somethings. It was the type of breakthrough Melanie had been hoping for. How much further could they have gotten had they not been so rudely interrupted by the prospect of a natural disaster bearing down on them? She knew Olivia would not have gone so far as to offer her blessing when it came to Justin's proposal. But maybe, just maybe, she'd get there at some point if she was willing to at least talk to him.

Ahead, Olivia stopped abruptly. "I'm sure we should have already passed the mine, and I've seen nothing. No sign, no evidence anywhere that humans were ever here, let alone blasting holes in the ground."

"Maybe it's just nothing at this point," Melanie suggested. "It doesn't take long for nature to take over once people are out of the picture."

"You're right. Even if it were still here, it's better to be out of the woods altogether than stuck in a mine shaft in the middle of a forest fire. Whatever safety we might find from actual flames wouldn't really matter if the fire sucked all of the oxygen out of our hiding spot."

"I hadn't thought of that," Melanie said. She looked at the canopy overhead. "Do you actually see any ash here? I mean, is it possible what we saw was just from one person's fire?"

"I think that's pretty unlikely, don't you?"

"Yeah," she admitted. "But—"

"There are no campsites along this part of the trail. The last ones we passed at the river were empty. There are a few up ahead on the escarpment—we were supposed to stay at one of them last night. There are also a few spots along the lakeshore. You know where we went upriver with Josh this morning? If we'd kept going on the same trail we would have stayed on Lake Superior for miles and miles. If someone started a fire out there where it's so windy—"

"And then left it unattended—"

"Exactly. Remember that one site where the people hadn't put their fire all the way out?"

Melanie felt her jaw drop. "Those same people—"

"Yeah. And I bet I know who it is."

"But I don't feel any wind today," Melanie said, looking for a reason Olivia could be wrong.

"That's because we're on the other side of a whole line of little mountains that block it. And we're going up those mountains."

"Doesn't it seem like maybe that's the worst thing we could do? Maybe we should turn around and go back to the river. And what about Josh? He's down in that valley fishing right now. Shouldn't we find him and warn him?"

"I'm not worried about Josh," Olivia said. "I'm one hundred percent sure he can take care of himself. But the fastest way for us to get out of danger is to get out of the woods. And the fastest way to do that is to keep going the way we're going. Besides, we need to get to somewhere we can report the fire."

She started walking again. Melanie followed behind as quickly as possible, all the time wishing that life had fewer complications. If someone was in charge of this whole enterprise, why didn't they just make good stuff happen? Why were there forest fires and car accidents and broken relationships? If there was an all-powerful God, that meant he had the power to do good things all the time—but chose not to. Or perhaps he was completely good and wished good things to happen, but he wasn't all-powerful. Olivia had said she couldn't believe in a God who would cause their parents' accident. But maybe God hadn't done that. Maybe he was just as powerless to stop two cars from colliding as they were to stop a forest fire.

Maybe Olivia was right. Maybe religion was just there to make people feel like there was more meaning to life than just chemical reactions. Maybe she'd been wasting her time with her constant dabbling in spiritual things. Maybe there were no spiritual things.

After what felt like more than a mile of steady upward progress, the trail leveled out. Melanie scanned the forest for falling ash but didn't see any. Could they have imagined it? Could Olivia have been mistaken? Or perhaps she had purposefully led Melanie to believe there was a reason to rush through this last leg of the trip just so she could get it over with. Had she regretted her contrite words on the log and so cut them short with an outright lie? Had Melanie really seen ash in her sister's hand?

They emerged from the dense trees onto an outcropping of resistant bedrock with unobstructed views of the Big Carp River valley below. An unending carpet of orange and yellow unfurled beneath them, bisected by the river snaking its way through the trees. There was no smoke rising from the valley. Melanie strained to see if Josh was down there in the water, but they were too far away to spot a single man.

This high up, she could feel some breeze. But it certainly wasn't what she'd call windy. She lived on Lake Michigan. She knew windy.

Olivia motioned to a wooden bench set back from the cliff. "I think we should stop here for a few minutes and eat something. I'd like to keep pushing on, but my energy is really lagging. What do you think?"

Melanie was surprised to be asked her opinion on the matter. "Sure. I'm really hungry. And tired." She pulled out her last protein bar and unwrapped it. "You know, I haven't seen any ash this whole time we've been walking. I think we're worried about nothing."

Olivia opened a pouch of tuna salad. "It would be nice if that were true."

"It must have been something else. Some kind of fungus maybe?"

"Hmm. I have heard of some kind of invasive pest that's been a problem for hemlocks. Some kind of parasite. Woolly something-or-other." She squeezed the tuna salad into her mouth. "Something that lays eggs in white sacs."

"There you go," Melanie said. "I bet it was just some of those coming loose and falling to the ground."

Olivia didn't look convinced. She took another bite of her tuna then a swig of water. "So, what are you going to tell Justin?"

Melanie nearly choked on a bite of protein bar. She chased it down her throat with some water and coughed. "I don't know."

Olivia raised her eyebrows. "Oh, come on."

"I actually always thought you two would get married," Melanie deflected. "Then you just threw him away when you went to school."

"I didn't throw him away. He was never my boyfriend or anything."

"I think maybe he thought of himself that way."

Olivia shrugged. "I can't help that."

Melanie frowned at her.

"I'm sorry, but I never thought of him that way. So if that's what has you unsure—like I'd be angry you stole my first love or some such thing—that's not my issue with it."

"That's not it."

"Well, what is it then? Look, I'm not actually going to cut you out of my life. I shouldn't have said that. I was just surprised and angry and . . . I mean, I'm still angry and I don't forgive him, but I'm not going to make you choose between us. I'm not going to be celebrating holidays with the two of you or anything, but I'm willing to work on you and me." She paused. "I mean, you love him, right? You uprooted your life in Rockford and followed him to Petoskey."

"Yeah."

"Okay, so . . ."

Melanie sighed. "I'm not—I just—" She tried again. "I need to be sure I love *him* and not just the idea of . . . making up for you."

"What?"

Melanie twisted a little on the bench, trying to find a more comfortable position. "Like, the reason I was so nice to him at first was because you were so mean. He wanted to talk to you, not me. But I was the next best option. I felt bad about how you treated him, so I was extra nice. I listened to him like I thought you should. I became his friend because you stopped being his friend. I did all the things I thought you should be doing. And we have become real friends. But . . . do I love him like that? Or is it just that I think someone *should* love him like that?"

Olivia tucked the empty tuna pouch into her trash bag. "You know, Josh said something last night. I won't say it as well as he did, but here's the gist of it: you can't live someone else's life for them. I can't live your life the way I think you should live it, you know? And you can't live mine. Or Justin's."

Melanie nodded and looked at her muddy hiking boots.

"You're carrying a lot of weight around," Olivia continued. "You're trying to make everything right for everyone else. Maybe you need to think about yourself once in a while."

Melanie felt tears building up behind her eyes. She was exhausted by all of it. Physically and emotionally depleted. Worrying about so many other people. Not just Olivia and Justin, but all of her followers and clients. Worrying that they were eating right and breathing right and living right. Worrying that if she didn't constantly think about them and anticipate their needs, their lives would spiral out of control. That if she was gone too long from their screens, she'd lose them. And she'd have no one left to worry about. Except herself.

"Thank you for saying that," Melanie said, swallowing down the lump that had lodged in her throat. "I just want everyone to be happy and live good lives."

Olivia put her hand on Melanie's shoulder. "You don't have to answer to God for anyone else. If we mess up, it's not on you. You just have to answer for yourself."

"God? Excuse me?"

Olivia dropped her hand to her lap and looked rather sheepish, as though she'd let slip that she was taking Melanie to a surprise party. "Eh, I'm trying the idea out today. We'll see." She stood up. "Come on. We're not going to figure this all out right now. And we still have a mountain to climb."

Twenty-Seven

OLIVIA LED THE WAY forward along the trail, silently chastising herself for using that word. God. It would only get Melanie's hopes up for her when the entire notion was still strange and alien and likely to wear off the minute they were safely out of these woods and on the way back to real life. People under pressure often made bad assumptions and faulty decisions.

She remembered her father telling her about her great-uncle Gordon, who had been an altogether rotten man. Beat his wife and kids, shot the family dog after it urinated on a sofa, couldn't hold a job down because of his temper and his drinking. Bedridden with bone cancer and given six weeks to live, he'd made a bargain with God. If God got him out of that bed and made him walk again, he'd be a changed man. He did get out of that bed. He did walk again. In fact, he lived six more years.

Her father had told her that story as an argument for the existence of God, but she could read between the lines. Great-Uncle Gordon hadn't actually changed, of that she was sure. If he didn't abuse his family anymore, it was because he wasn't fast enough or strong enough after the cancer had ravaged his body. And if he didn't shoot another dog, it was because they'd sold his guns while he was in the hospital. And he used his weakened condition as a new excuse not to look for a job. The doctors were just wrong about the timeline, that's all.

So no, she reasoned, she didn't really believe in God. She'd been momentarily taken in by a fisherman, like a catch on the end of his line. Now she was wriggling her way back into the water.

She checked her watch. Nearly four o'clock. They'd lingered too long on the mossy logs beneath the hemlocks, too long at the overlook. Without her map she couldn't be sure exactly where she was, but she did know that they could make no more stops if they hoped to make the parking lot before sunset. If they missed getting a ride, they were sunk.

"How does your watch still have power?" Melanie said from behind her.

"Solar charger. It was full when we started hiking, and it's still not totally depleted."

"You think of everything."

Suddenly aware of how hot she felt, Olivia took off her ball cap as she walked and wiped her forehead with her arm. Sure, it was the hottest part of the day, but in the UP in October, that shouldn't be more than fifty degrees or so. And for the past ten minutes, they had been walking on level ground. If she felt like this now, the big climb up to the escarpment was going to be brutal.

She fanned her face with her hat and turned back to her sister. "Are you hot?"

"Oh my gosh, yes! I thought it was just me."

Olivia stopped walking, looked ahead, looked behind. For what, she wasn't quite sure, but she saw nothing out of the ordinary. For the past quarter mile on the right-hand side, the land rose up from the valley to meet them and continued far above their heads on the left. Up ahead, she could see that the land tapered down toward their level. They must be coming to some kind of gap in the mountain ridge. After that, they should begin their climb.

She started walking again. Felt the breeze pick up. Then she saw it, dancing through the trees about twenty yards ahead. Ash. She picked up the pace, urged Melanie on with a silent wave. The trail curved to the left, and the ground spread out before them, level and radiating heat through the soles of Olivia's shoes.

Melanie gasped. "Look!"

Three deer, then four, then three more bounded out of the trees and across their path, crashing through the underbrush down the hill toward the valley. Chipmunks scurried in their wake. Jays cried out and zipped through the trees.

"We need to move," Olivia said.

"Wait!" Melanie whispered.

Olivia wheeled on her to argue, but Melanie was pointing and smiling like a maniac. Olivia followed the invisible trajectory of her outstretched finger to the spot the deer had just been. A cougar stood there looking at them, body taut, eyes wide, one ear turning back toward the place it had just come from. It sniffed the air once, twice, then jogged off in the same direction the deer had gone.

For a split second, Olivia considered following it. Animals knew where to go during a natural disaster, right? They had some special sense for things like this. But she would not change course now. She was getting out of this forest. And out was up, not down.

"I told you," Melanie squealed.

"Not now," Olivia warned.

She pushed forward along the trail, speed-walking only because she couldn't run with a pack on her back. Should they ditch them in the woods? The ash was getting thicker and the heat was intensifying. She felt like she was rushing into the fire rather than away from it, but the blue blazes on the trees dictated her route.

After a few minutes that felt like much longer, the trail made a sharp right and began to rise. Another switchback, and then they were climbing what felt like straight up.

Olivia's muscles burned. Her hip cried out in protest. Her blisters screamed against the insides of her boots. Behind her, Melanie was coughing.

"Just a little further," she lied. She had no idea how much further, how long it would take them to reach the top. Or what they would find when they got there.

Despite herself, Olivia began a silent chant, much as she had when she was walking behind Josh to get the packs they'd left leaning on the birch tree. It was far less critical than her earlier chant of *stu-pid* or *sel-fish*. Those were directed at herself and at her sister. Now she directed her words skyward. *Save us, save us, save us.*

The trail made another turn, and Olivia's muscles were given a short reprieve.

Melanie got her cough under control. "Can we just stop a second? I need some water."

Olivia didn't want to stop, but her throat was parched too. "Okay, but quick."

They grabbed and gulped and shoved the bottles back into the packs.

"How much further?" Melanie said.

"How should I know?" Olivia said. "I have no map."

"Yes, you do."

"What?"

Melanie spun around. "I forgot. Front zipper pocket."

Olivia unzipped the compartment. "How—?"

"It washed up on shore near where we hung the clothes out."

This was too much. She snatched the map out of Melanie's pack. The ink indicating her plans was gone, but she could still see the depressions her pen had made in the surface. It really was her map. Impossible.

"There. We must be there, where the trail winds back and forth up the mountainside. And there," she said, pointing, "is the open spot between the peaks where the heat got so intense and the animals were running through." She looked toward the shoreline on the map. "The fire could have started at one of these campsites."

"So how much further?" Melanie repeated.

"A little more than a mile and a half and we'll be at the parking lot." She looked at her sister. "We can do this."

Melanie gave a resolute nod. Olivia rolled the map up until it resembled a relay baton, then pressed forward up the hill. One more big push and they'd be on the escarpment. From that point, it was a straight shot on level ground and they could move fast.

Just a few minutes later, they reached the top. Unobscured by trees, the valley opened up below them and the sky opened up above. But they didn't stop to admire the view. They pushed on past three empty campsites. Smoke was rising in the west to join the clouds, and the air smelled like a campfire. Were there rangers out on the trails right now, looking for backcountry hikers? Would she be met on the path by a stern-faced man bearing bad news as she had so many years ago? Were all her hiking trips doomed?

Olivia checked her watch again. 4:50. She attempted to open the map without slowing down and tripped on a tree root. She went down hard, her right knee striking a rock, sending a lightning bolt of pain up her femur, like the feeling she used to get up her arms if the bat hit the softball just wrong. She struggled to stand.

Melanie was on her in a breath, helping her to her feet. "You okay?"

"Yeah," Olivia said through clenched teeth. She was not okay. She took a faltering step and let out an involuntary yell.

"Olivia!"

"I'm fine. You take the lead. I'm fine."

Melanie hesitated.

"Go!" Olivia shouted. "I'm right behind you."

Melanie started walking, looking back at Olivia every third step.

"Stop looking at me," she said. "You're going to trip too."

Olivia struggled on, chiding herself for such an avoidable mistake. She was slowing them down. Melanie kept looking back, but now it was only every sixth step. The trail curved slightly right along the top of a ridge that had so little tree cover that for the first time they could see in the other direction, all the way to Lake Superior. Olivia stopped and stared.

Smoke rose from an ever-widening swath of forest, starting at the lakeshore and reaching inland. The fire was big and the wind was strong, but Olivia was comforted by the fact that it wasn't actually upon them. Yet.

Next to her, Melanie was holding back tears.

"We should keep moving," Olivia said. "It's got to be less than a mile. Less than a mile and we can get out of here."

She took the lead, breathing through the pain radiating up and down her leg. Every step was a fight with herself to keep moving forward. She could do anything as long as she knew there was an end point she was working toward. If her great-uncle could walk off bone cancer, she could walk off a fractured kneecap or a bone bruise or whatever this was. She could walk off the pain in her hip. She would walk out of these woods on her own two feet, blisters and all.

Fifteen minutes later, they came to another overlook where they could see the Big Carp River. Unlike earlier when it was far off in the distance, here it flowed practically to the foot of the cliff they were standing on. The water churned and boiled with salmon jockeying for the best spots in which to spawn, and there, down among them, stood a man in olive-green waders flicking a fly rod.

"Josh!" Melanie shouted. She cupped her hands around her mouth. "Josh!"

"He can't hear us from up here," Olivia said.

"We have to tell him about the fire. Josh!" She walked closer to the edge. "Josh!"

Olivia grabbed her arm. "Melanie! What do you want to do, fall off a cliff to get his attention? Back up!"

Olivia placed herself between her sister and the drop-off she'd been walking toward. Melanie took a step back. Olivia turned around to see how close her little sister had gotten to the edge. But when she pivoted on her left foot to avoid putting too much weight on her right knee, something in her hip snapped, her leg buckled, and the weight of her pack threw her off balance. She heard her sister scream.

And then she was falling.

Twenty-Eight

IN THE SPACE of one strangled breath, Melanie heard her own scream echo off the hills on the far side of the valley. Then branches breaking and her sister's body connecting with the side of the steep embankment.

"Olivia!" Melanie dumped her pack to the ground in a second and scrambled up to the edge on all fours. "Olivia!"

About twenty-five feet below, she could see the maize M on her sister's navy-blue hat, the straight line of one of her hiking poles, the boot on one of her feet. She wasn't moving.

"Olivia!" she screamed through tears. "Olivia!"

Rope. She needed the rope. She scrambled back to her pack and began emptying pockets. Where was it? Where was it? Where was it? The answer came in a sickening flash. On the beach, still strung between two trees where they had dried her wet clothes in the wind. The same wind that was now sending a forest fire ever closer.

Okay. Okay. No rope. Help. She'd have to go for help. The parking lot was close. Less than a mile. Maybe less than half a mile. With no pack she could cover it fast. But how could she leave Olivia? What if the fire jumped the ridgeline and started burning the dry autumn vegetation where her sister lay?

She crawled back up to the edge and tried to gauge the distance. She would have to climb down there herself and bring her up. Olivia's pack still had rope. She could tie it to the pack on her sister's back and drag her up the cliff.

Melanie searched the edge of the escarpment for a gentler way down, but there was none. She moved about five feet to the left of where Olivia had gone over so she wouldn't land on her if she fell, then slowly rolled over on her stomach, pushing herself back until her legs hung over the edge. Her feet searched for a spot to rest. Nothing. She pushed a little farther. A little farther. Then slipped too fast, scraping her stomach and rib cage over the rock. She fell for only a foot or two before her feet hit the ground. She grabbed wildly at a prickly bush anchored in the rock and caught it, keeping herself from sliding any farther but puncturing the meat of her hand.

Melanie got her bearings and looked for another handhold, another foothold. Inch by painstaking inch—and sometimes foot by startling foot—she made her way down to where Olivia lay against the dirt-packed root structure of a fallen tree, her face and arms scraped and bleeding. Terrified of the answer she might receive, she put her cheek against her sister's open mouth and pressed two fingers against her neck. Breath. A pulse. Thank God.

Melanie unzipped one of the side pockets of Olivia's pack and found the rope. She unwound a portion of it and tied it around the metal frame of Olivia's pack. She knew nothing about knots, so she just kept making more and more of them. They couldn't all fail. Then she looked back up the cliffside. They were much farther down than she'd thought. But it didn't matter. She would get her sister up there and get her to the parking lot and get her to a doctor. She had to.

Next to her, Olivia groaned. Melanie was on her in a second.

"Olivia! You're okay. I'm going to get you out of here, and you're going to be okay."

Olivia groaned again and tried to move.

"Just stay there," Melanie said. "I'm going to pull you up. Just stay there."

Hugging the steep slope, Melanie made her way back up the escarpment, unwinding the rope as she went and praying it would be long enough to reach the top. Three times she slipped, losing precious time and distance before her hand found a grip or her feet found a rock or root. Just as she was fearing that her strength, already sorely tested by their near sprint through the woods, would fail, Melanie finally reached the top. Gripping the rope, she lay for a moment on the rocky outcropping, catching her breath. She shouted over the side, "I'm going to pull you up!"

Now came the hard part. Olivia had always weighed more than Melanie, and the most Melanie lifted in everyday life was a bag of groceries. How would she do this?

Incline, lever, pulley. Weren't those the simple machines she'd learned about at the children's science museum during their fifth-grade field trip? She looked around for a tree. A tree could act like a pulley. But there wasn't enough soil up on the escarpment to support big trees. There was nothing up here but bushes and shrubs.

Instead, Melanie positioned herself behind a low boulder, bracing her feet against the rock. She started to pull. The rope went taut. She pulled harder. But the blood from the wound on her hand made the rope slippery. She wound some around her hand and pulled as hard as she could. Her fingers started to turn purple.

Then the rope finally budged. She'd moved her. Maybe only a few inches, but she'd moved her. Melanie pulled with renewed strength, drawing in another few inches of rope and wrapping it around her forearm. Pull, wrap. Pull, wrap. Pull, wrap. She had heard of people under duress performing great feats of strength in order to save another human being. She used to think that must be due to some otherworldly power infusing a human body with extra strength. But surely it was just the power of adrenaline, a completely explainable biological process. Melanie didn't care at this point. All that mattered was that it was working.

Pull, wrap, breathe.

Pull, wrap, breathe.

Pull, wrap, breathe.

Finally, she could see the top of Olivia's pack over the edge of the escarpment.

Almost. There.

Almost. There.

Almost. There.

There was Olivia's hat. Then her tortured face, twisted in pain. Then . . . Josh's face?

In her shock, Melanie almost dropped the rope. But she managed to keep hold. In a few seconds, Josh, with Olivia on his back, was over the edge and laying her down on the ground.

Melanie hurried to disentangle herself from the rope and get much-needed blood to her fingers.

"Olivia!" she said, rushing over. Olivia coughed and moaned and held her side.

"She probably has some broken ribs," Josh said. "Maybe a concussion."

"Where did you come from?"

"From the river. I heard screaming and saw her fall. I climbed up from below."

She stood and fixed him with a glare. "You shouldn't have left us. If you'd been here, this would never have happened." She knelt by her sister. "Is she going to be okay?"

"We need to get her to a hospital." He began unbuckling the straps of Olivia's pack. "Help me get her out of this thing. Careful."

Though every movement clearly sent spasms of pain coursing through Olivia's body, Melanie and Josh managed to get the pack off. A minute later Josh was half bent over with Olivia on his back, her right arm coiled around his neck, her left pressed against her side, where a troubling blotch of red was growing.

"What about her pack?" Melanie said.

"We'll send someone back for it."

"But there's a fire—"

"Leave it, Melanie. We can't take it with us."

He started down the trail, quickly but smoothly. Spent, Melanie struggled to keep up. Down an incline, around a wide curve, past another overlook, down another incline, around another curve, up another hill. Josh never slowed. Melanie seemed to stumble with every other step. Occasionally she heard a sharp intake of breath from her sister, but otherwise Olivia was silent. Finally, they hit a boardwalk and Melanie got her first glimpse of the Lake of the Clouds. But only a glimpse. Immediately they veered off to the parking lot, where rangers were directing traffic back down the road and out of the park.

After a quick conversation with one of the harried rangers, Olivia was carefully placed on blankets in the back of a Suburban and checked over. The ranger pulled her hand away from her side. The bleeding was clearly worse. A first aid kit appeared, and the ranger quickly bathed the wound with isopropyl alcohol and pressed a wad of clean cotton gauze against it.

"You," she said to Melanie, "get in here and maintain pressure on this."

Melanie climbed into the back of the truck beside Olivia and pressed her hand where the ranger indicated. Josh reached up to close the liftgate.

"Wait—you're coming, aren't you?" Melanie said.

"No, I need to stay here. There are a few hikers unaccounted for on the Lake Superior Trail. I just volunteered to lead a search party."

"But—"

"She'll be okay, Melanie. And I'm needed here. I'll grab the backpack and have someone take it to the hospital for you."

Then he closed the back of the truck. Melanie watched through the tinted glass as he jogged off in the direction they had just come. A second later someone got into the driver's seat.

"Ready back there?" the ranger's voice called.

"Yes," Melanie managed to croak out.

"It's thirty minutes to the hospital. I'll try to get you there in twenty. Try to keep her from moving, especially her head. It's a curvy road."

Keeping one hand and then the other pressed against Olivia's side, Melanie removed her pack and leaned over her sister. She rolled up some of her dirty clothes and tucked them on either side of Olivia's head to keep it from moving back and forth with the motion of the truck.

"Olivia, it's going to be okay," Melanie said. But Olivia's eyes were squeezed shut, and Melanie wasn't sure if she was getting through to her.

"I'm Serena," the ranger shouted back. "What are your names?"

"Melanie. And this is my sister, Olivia."

"She's going to be okay."

How did she know that? How did Josh know? What if she wasn't? What if Melanie had badgered her sister into taking a fatal trip with her? What if she lost her too?

"How long have you two been on the trail?" Serena said.

"I don't know. Three days, maybe? Four?" She looked to Olivia for confirmation but got nothing. Olivia's face was scrunched in pain, her breathing slow and deliberate, as though if her concentration lapsed she would forget to breathe.

"Beautiful time of year for it. I mean, normally. This fire . . . I just can't believe it."

Melanie didn't respond. She didn't have the energy for a conversation. But that didn't stop Serena, who probably thought she was helping her keep her mind off her troubles.

"I've been working here for nine years. Love it here. Especially in the fall and winter. Beautiful country. Before this I was down cutting trails in Columbia. But I missed the seasons. Where are you from?"

Melanie wished she would stop talking. "I live in Petoskey."

"Love that town. Kind of artsy, isn't it? I'm from Chicago originally."

She needed to concentrate, to focus her mind on her sister, to channel her energy. She couldn't lose her.

"You both live in Petoskey?"

Argh. Shut up. "Olivia's a lawyer in East Lansing."

"And you? What do you do?"

Melanie sighed. She normally loved that question. Loved sharing what she did with people, even when they didn't quite get it. But she didn't want to explain her job to Serena. She didn't want to explain it to anyone anymore. It should be simpler to say what it was she did. If it was a real thing, it would be one word that wouldn't require a long explanation. Lawyer. Plumber. Writer. Nurse.

"I'm a counselor," she said.

Vague enough to be both true and false at the same time. Kind of like her beliefs, she thought wryly. According to Olivia, at least. Did it matter that she couldn't explain what she believed in one word either? Did she have to have a label for it to be real?

"That's good. You probably have some great coping strategies for what you two have been through out there."

They all had a label. Jewish. Christian. Muslim. Buddhist. Atheist. And as Olivia said, they couldn't all be right. A thing couldn't be both true and false. And one true thing couldn't contradict another true thing.

"About ten more minutes," Serena said after a short silence. "How are you doing back there? Not too bumpy?"

"Not too bad," Melanie said. Still maintaining pressure on the wound on Olivia's side, she leaned toward the front seat and lowered her voice. "Can I ask you something?"

"Of course," Serena said, matching her volume.

"Do you believe in God?"

Serena stifled a laugh. "Oh, man. That's a big one. I thought it was going to be something about the park or the fire or something. Um, yeah. I believe in God. Why?"

Melanie collected her thoughts. "Do you think the fire was part of his plan?"

"Part of God's plan? Gee, I don't know. That's above my pay grade. There are lots of ordinary reasons a fire starts. Unattended campfire, fireworks, cigarette butts."

"People," Melanie said.

"A lot of the time, yes. But one of the main sources is lightning—that's what started the Duck Lake Fire back in 2012. My first year up here. I suppose someone could make an argument for God being involved somehow, but I don't know. Some things just happen. Lightning is a natural occurrence."

"I remember hearing about that fire. That went on awhile, didn't it?"

"Weeks. It took the DNR twenty-three days to contain it. Burned more than twenty thousand acres. That'd be like losing one third of the Porkies." She was quiet a moment. "I hope they can contain this quickly. They're predicting rain tonight. That would really help. It's a godsend we had that rain a few days ago or it might be spreading even faster. It was such a dry season."

Melanie glanced back at her sister. Olivia had been so angry when they came upon that fire ring that had been left with live embers. When she'd put the fire out, was she just delaying the inevitable? If God was all-powerful, wouldn't he just find another way to get a fire started?

"So you think this one was just an accident?" Melanie said. "Just dumb luck?"

"I think it was negligence," Serena said. "And if they can determine who is to blame, they could press charges."

Those three loud hikers at the Government Peak trailhead. Olivia clearly blamed them. But was that fair? It might have been anyone. "How would they figure that out?"

"If it started at a particular campsite and they can narrow down the time, it's easy enough to figure out who stayed there and left a fire burning. As long as they registered."

"So at least justice could be served?"

"Right. But that doesn't get the trees back."

What's done is done and can't be undone.

Someone had started a fire. Olivia had fallen off a cliff. Justin had killed her parents.

None of them could be undone. All of them were accidents. If there was a God, he had allowed all of them to happen. Didn't it follow then that he must have let them happen for a reason? That, as Olivia had said, he must have wanted their parents to die? Or even if he hadn't arranged the accident specifically, that he hadn't cared enough to keep them alive?

Did he care enough about Olivia?

Melanie leaned back and looked down at Olivia's face, which was beginning to bruise beneath the abrasions. She didn't believe in God. Certainly hadn't believed in more than a decade. Yet, just a couple hours ago she had let slip that she was entertaining the notion. One day she was an atheist, the next she was questioning that. Why? What had changed?

Olivia stirred beside her, tried to speak.

"We're almost to the hospital," Melanie said.

Olivia mumbled something.

Melanie stroked her hand. "I can't quite understand you."

"Josh," Olivia managed.

"He's okay," Melanie said. "He stayed to help find some missing hikers." Hikers who might have been the ones to start the fire.

"Josh," Olivia said again.

"He's not here right now. I'm sure he'll come by the hospital though. Just relax."

From the front seat Serena said, "We're here."

The next several minutes were a blur of gurneys and nurses and doctors and questions Melanie couldn't answer. What was Olivia's blood type? Who was her primary care physician? Was she allergic to any medications? Had she had any previous serious injuries or surgeries? Melanie didn't even know her sister's current address—Olivia's license, along with her insurance card, was in her pack in the middle of a forest fire.

Melanie's hand was cleaned and bandaged, and she was checked over for injuries and smoke inhalation. Then she waited as Olivia was poked, prodded, scanned, x-rayed, and sewn up. She haunted the front entrance, looking for Josh. She ate a garden salad from the hospital cafeteria. She texted Justin to let him know they were out of the woods and in Ontonagon in case he saw news about the fire and began to worry. Then she walked out to the parking lot to get her phone charger before she remembered that, of course, her car was still back in the gravel lot at the trailhead. She wanted to consult the map to see if her car was in the path of the fire, but she'd given it back to Olivia. Who knew where it was now? Probably at the bottom of a cliff.

A couple hours later, a doctor updated her on Olivia's injuries. A concussion, three cracked ribs, a fractured kneecap, multiple scrapes and abrasions, and a puncture wound just an inch away from her left lung.

"That in itself is a miracle," the doctor said. "As is the fact that she seems to have suffered no traumatic brain or spinal injury. But there's something else you should know."

"What?"

His face was grave. "Is there any family history of osteosarcoma? Bone cancer?"

Melanie felt her stomach drop. "Our great-uncle died of bone cancer."

His frown deepened. "The nature of Olivia's injuries concerns me. Anyone might crack a rib or two in that kind of accident. But the injuries to her legs are different. The patellar fracture—that's the kneecap—is odd because she doesn't remember hitting her knee during the fall."

"That wasn't from the fall. Or, not from *that* fall. She tripped earlier and landed on her knee. But that was when we were rushing because of the fire, so maybe she didn't remember it."

"Mmm. And the damage to her hip was not a result of anything during your hiking trip. It seems to have been giving her trouble for a while now, judging by the scar tissue there."

"She was limping. Even before the hike."

The doctor nodded thoughtfully. "Osteosarcoma is an aggressive cancer. If it's caught early enough, the survival rate is around seventy percent. But if it spreads beyond that localized spot, the survival rate drops to thirty percent. I'm not certain she has it, but she needs to make an appointment with her primary care physician as soon as possible after she gets home. And that's another thing. When she is cleared to leave, she can't drive herself. I assume you can drive her?"

"Of course," Melanie said without a thought. She would drive Olivia to East Lansing even if it meant she'd have to hitchhike back home afterward.

"And she is likely to need some help at home for a while. She won't be walking right away. She'll need the dressing on her wounds changed. Won't be able to lift things, not even a gallon of milk."

Melanie nodded, letting the magnitude of the situation sink in.

"Does she have a family?" he asked.

"I'm her family."

He pursed his lips. "Could be a big job for one person."

"Whatever I need to do."

He stood up. Though she was physically and emotionally exhausted, Melanie followed suit.

"Doctor . . . what do I tell her? About the cancer?"

"Tell her she's lucky she ended up in the hospital with a bunch of broken bones. Otherwise, it might have gone undetected until it was too late. Someone must be looking out for her."

Twenty-Nine

OLIVIA OPENED HER EYES, then shut them again immediately. She had hoped she'd wake up in her bed at home. More than that, she didn't want Melanie to realize she was awake. She wasn't ready for inane questions like "How are you feeling?" and "Can I get you anything?" She wanted to be alone and quiet and just *there*. To revel in the joy of being there instead of not being anywhere. Instead of being dead, which she was sure she should have been.

"Olivia?" came Melanie's voice anyway. "Everything okay?"

No, everything was clearly not okay. This stupid trip. Why did it have to be such a nice day when Melanie had called her? This never would have happened if it had been crappy and depressing like it was supposed to be in March.

"Are you in any pain?"

Where should she start? Her head throbbed, her side hurt, her arms stung, her hip ached, her knee felt like electrodes were being applied to it. The pain must have registered on her face, because Melanie left the room and came back with a nurse, who fiddled with an IV.

"When can I leave?" Olivia asked the nurse.

"Tomorrow morning, most likely."

"It's not tomorrow yet?"

The nurse smiled. "Not quite. Anyway, we can't let you go until we're satisfied that you won't conk out on us, can we?"

Olivia scoffed. "I just survived a forest fire and a fall off a cliff. Clearly I cannot be killed."

The nurse laughed, but Olivia knew what she'd just said was a smoke screen. Between the fire and the fall it was clear that if God was real, he was after her. She didn't know what to do with that.

"Any news about the fire?" she asked.

The nurse hung in the doorway a moment. "There were some other people brought in—smoke inhalation—but I think they may already be gone." She disappeared, off to some other patient.

"I wonder if it was those three," Olivia said. "Did Josh ever show up?"

"If he did, I missed him," Melanie said. "And it wasn't because I wasn't watching for him."

"Guess they need all the help they can get out there."

"News said they've got planes dumping water from the lake on it. And the coast guard is spraying it from boats. And it did start raining."

Melanie handed Olivia her nearly dead phone so she could read an article about the efforts to contain and extinguish the fire, which had burned through a swath of secondary-growth forest on the shoreline but had so far spared the old-growth hemlocks and pines. It was cautiously optimistic in tone, anticipating containment by the following day if the weather cooperated. Thinking of that cathedral of trees that had so unexpectedly moved her, Olivia felt like maybe she should pray they'd be unharmed. But really? Pray for trees? That was something she'd laugh at Melanie for doing. And did she really think anyone was listening? Or cared?

Olivia rested the phone on her leg above the apparatus that was stabilizing her knee. "Hey, did anyone ever bring in my pack?"

"Not yet."

"I'm just now realizing that it has my wallet and my car keys in it. I'm not going to get very far without those."

"Look at yourself. You think you can drive like that?"

Olivia sighed. "How long is this thing supposed to be on?"

"I don't know. Weeks, probably. But I've figured out a way to get you home."

"How?"

"I can get someone to meet us in Indian River so they can pick up my car there. Then I'll drive you home in yours."

"And then how will you get home from there? Fly?"

Melanie scooted closer. "Let's not worry about that until the time comes."

"I think the time is coming tomorrow if that nurse is right."

Melanie took her hand in a motherly way.

Olivia tugged it away. "That's weird."

"Olivia!"

"It is! It's weird to grab my hand like I'm a six-year-old. Just say what you need to say."

Melanie crossed her arms. "Fine. The doctor told me you'd

need help when you got home, so I'm going to stay with you and help you out."

"I don't think that's such a great idea."

"Why not?"

"Are you kidding? Think of everything we've argued about in the last few days. Do you really want more of that? Do you really think I'd be a good patient? I'll be horrible and you'll drive me crazy, and you know it."

"But you need help," Melanie insisted.

"Let's let me be the judge of that, shall we?"

"But—"

"Ms. Greene?" came the nurse's voice from the door.

"Yes?" Olivia and Melanie answered in unison.

The nurse chuckled. "I meant you, Miss Melanie. Can you come out here a moment?"

Melanie stood up. "This conversation is not over."

"I can't do even one more day of this, never mind weeks," Olivia said aloud to the empty room when the door had shut.

She swiped at Melanie's phone still in her hand. The lock screen appeared. Olivia thought for half a second and then connected the dots to make an M. It didn't work. She switched the phone over to her left hand and tried again, making the M backwards. Bingo. She began swiping back through Melanie's photos. Several of various waterfalls and colorful fall leaves and mushrooms. The one from after Melanie fell in the river. The one where they were lost in the woods. One of the tent. Some of Olivia's back as she led the hike. The one from the beginning of the trip at the Government Peak trailhead.

But none of Josh.

Melanie came back into the room carrying Olivia's pack. "Special delivery."

"Who brought it?"

"Serena."

"Who's Serena?"

"She's the park ranger who brought us to the hospital earlier."

"Oh." Why hadn't Josh brought it? "Hey, did you not take any pictures with Josh in them?"

"Huh? No, I took a picture of him."

Olivia waved Melanie's phone at her. "I don't think you did."

Melanie snatched the phone and started swiping furiously. "I know I did. I took a picture of him at those Overlooked Falls or whatever." She swiped the other way. Slowly her face fell, and she sat down hard in the plastic chair next to the bed. "Where did it go?" She kept swiping, unwilling to give up.

"Maybe something got messed up when the phone got wet. Or maybe you took it with my phone?" Olivia offered, even though she knew it was absurd. "Speaking of mine, can you get it out of my bag for me?"

Melanie looked at first like she hadn't heard her. Then she came to. "What?"

"My phone. Can you get it for me? It's in the right-hand pocket there."

Melanie did as directed, then settled back in the chair to swipe through her pictures once again. Olivia powered on her phone and blanched at all the notifications. Emails, appointments, task reminders. She had to be in court on Monday. She thought of the kinds of notifications Melanie would have after so long off the grid. Were people still sending positive thoughts to the man in the motorcycle accident? Were they still sharing the video of Melanie rescuing the turtle?

She tried to imagine how Melanie would put a positive spin on their hiking trip for her blog. Wrong turns, lost trails, bear encounters, forest fire. A fall in a river and one off a cliff. Near-constant bickering. There was not one part of this ill-fated trip that was redeemable. Not one reason for it to have happened at all. A total waste of time, energy, and resources. It hadn't really fixed anything fundamental in her relationship with her sister, despite Melanie's best intentions and their conversation among the hemlock trees. It was a start, but not much more than that. It had not gotten Melanie to leave her alone as she'd hoped it would. Indeed, Melanie now seemed determined to move in with her for an indeterminate amount of time.

"So," Olivia said, "I'm happy to pay for your flight back if someone can pick you up at the Traverse City Airport and drive you back to Petoskey."

Melanie put down her phone. "Olivia, we need to talk."

"We are talking."

"This is serious."

"I know. I'm seriously offering to pay for a plane to take you home so I don't end up killing you." Olivia smiled to take the sting out of what she said, but when she saw Melanie's eyes tearing up, the smile faded from her lips. "What is it? What's wrong?"

Melanie took a deep breath. "The doctor thinks you might have cancer."

She paused as if to give Olivia a chance to talk, but Olivia found that speech was quite beyond her at the moment. Even putting one coherent thought together felt like a skill she'd never mastered, like playing the cello or speaking Portuguese.

"He's not sure," Melanie went on, "but you need to get tested when you get home."

"Cancer?" Olivia managed finally.

"Osteosarcoma. Bone cancer."

"Why?" The word sounded like nothing more than a wisp of air coming out of her mouth. "Why would he think that?" she said, stronger now.

"Your hip."

"Oh." Olivia relaxed. "It was just sore from hiking."

"No, you were complaining about it in the car on the way up."

She was? Olivia thought back. How long had her hip been hurting?

"He said they saw scar tissue built up in the X-ray. And your knee fracture bothered him."

"I fell off a cliff!"

"That's not what happened to your knee though. That was just you tripping and landing on it. That shouldn't fracture the knee of a woman your age."

Olivia's mind raced for another explanation. Not enough calcium or vitamin D or something. Didn't everyone in Michigan suffer from vitamin D deficiency because of the cloud cover?

"He said you were lucky," Melanie said. "That if you hadn't had to come in for X-rays from that fall, it could have gone undetected until it was too late to do anything."

Olivia felt like she was going to throw up, but she also couldn't remember the last meal she'd eaten. "How old was Great-Uncle Gordon when he died?"

Melanie's face turned ashen. "Forty. I think. Maybe forty-one." She rushed on, "But he doesn't *know* you have cancer. He just thinks you should get checked out as soon as possible."

Olivia worked to regulate her breathing.

"I know you'll pooh-pooh this," Melanie said, "but clearly this is fate. If you hadn't come on this trip, you'd never have known."

"We don't even know if there's anything to know, Melanie. Maybe I injured it previously and it didn't heal correctly. Maybe I have early-onset osteoporosis. If that's a thing. And until we know if there's anything to know, we're not going to talk about fate or cancer or any of it. All we're going to do is get out of here as soon as possible so we can get me home as soon as possible, so *you* can go home as soon as possible."

"Fine," Melanie said.

"Fine," Olivia said.

Melanie stood up and dug her keys out of her pack. "First I have to figure out how to get to my car."

Thirty

OUT IN THE hall, Melanie glanced at the large clock above the nurses' station. 1:17. In the morning. She'd never find someone to take her to her car at this time of night. Still, she walked down to the lobby to see what options might be open to her. The little gift and flower shop near the entrance was closed. Other than the woman sitting behind the information desk typing away at a computer, the place was empty and quiet.

"Excuse me," she said to the woman. "Do you guys have, like, Uber up here or anything?"

A pained smile spread across the woman's face. "Not really, no. Do you need a ride somewhere?"

"My car is at a trailhead in the Porcupine Mountains. I need to get it before I can drive my sister home tomorrow. Well, today, I guess."

The woman nodded, still wearing that smile that said *I can't help you*. "There's a shift change at seven o'clock," she offered. "Perhaps it would be better to wait until morning. Maybe you could find someone to take you to your car then."

Melanie tried to remember if she knew anyone in the western

UP. Where was Josh? Maybe trying to get back to his own car at Pinkerton Creek.

"Hey, can you tell me whether or not someone came in here tonight?"

"Do you have a name?"

"Josh— Oh. I don't know his full name. He was tall, early thirties, brown hair, beard, in a plaid flannel and maybe fishing waders?"

"I haven't seen anyone like that, I don't think. But I just got here at eleven. He may have come in earlier. Apparently they had several people brought in from the Porkies because of the fire. The police were even here."

"Did they arrest anyone?"

The woman shrugged. "Don't know."

Melanie thanked her for her time and headed outside to watch the rain from beneath the portico at the patient drop-off area. The wet parking lot sparkled like Christmas lights under the tall light fixtures. It would be Christmas in just a couple months. She'd put up a small tree, decorate her house, invite Justin over to watch Christmas movies and drink hot cocoa. Another year gone. Perhaps the last one she'd spend unmarried. The Christmas after that, she could be trimming the tree and baking pies with a big pregnant belly running into tree boughs and countertops. And all the Christmases that followed could be brightened by the sound of children's laughter and storytelling and wide-eyed wonder. Then grandchildren. A family. A real family.

"Melanie, right?" came a voice to her left.

She turned to see Ranger Serena standing there in the doorway.

"Oh, hi," Melanie said. "I thought you'd gone."

"I would have, but a nurse heard me coughing and wanted to check me over."

"Are you okay?"

"They let me out, so I guess so."

Melanie thought fast. "Hey, you're not going back toward the park tonight, are you?"

"You need a lift somewhere?"

"I do. My car is at the Government Peak trailhead. I don't suppose you could drop me off there, could you?"

"Of course."

"I know it's late and you probably just want to get in bed."

"It's no problem at all. In fact, it's good I happened by. They'll let me into the park, but I'm not sure they'd let just anybody in. It's closed and the roads are blocked off. As a precaution." Serena started walking out into the rain and motioned for Melanie to follow her. "I'm just over here."

They trotted out to her truck, and Melanie settled herself into the passenger seat. "You're sure this isn't too much trouble?"

"Nonsense," Serena said as she turned the key in the ignition. "When I was a teenager I hitchhiked from Chicago to Yellowstone and back, so I always give people rides when they need them. Just paying it forward."

They pulled out onto the street.

"That's incredible," Melanie said. "Chicago to Yellowstone?"

"It was stupid, is what it was. But I didn't think about that at the time. One of the best times of my life."

"There were a couple times on our hike that my sister wanted to call it quits and hitchhike back to the car. I thought she was crazy. Now I wish we had."

Serena glanced at her. "How is she?"

"Pretty banged up, but she'll pull through. Actually, it's a really good thing we didn't quit."

"Why's that?"

Melanie filled her in on Olivia's injuries and all that the doctor had said about the possibility of cancer.

"Oh my," Serena said when she was done. "God was certainly looking out for her, wasn't he?"

"You think so?"

"Well, sure. Don't you?"

Melanie stared out at the spot of road illuminated by Serena's headlights. "I do. It's just—this may sound weird and conceited, but I don't mean for it to—I'm not quite sure why God would bother himself—or herself—about Olivia. She doesn't believe in God. She doesn't believe in anything. If God was going to arrange all these events to save someone's life, why her? Why not someone who actually believed?"

Serena moved her hand slightly on the wheel to keep the truck in line with the road's sinewy path. "Don't you think that maybe someone like your sister is the one who needs that kind of intervention the most though? It's the sick person who needs the doctor, not the healthy person. The one who doesn't believe that needs convincing. And what better way to get her thinking in the right direction than sending her that kind of a sign?"

Melanie sat with that a moment. "But that's not fair. I'm always looking for signs. And then she's the one who gets them?"

"Oh." Serena sounded surprised. "I thought from our earlier conversation that you already believed in God."

"I do. I mean, I believe in lots of stuff. I believe in way more than her. Way more. I follow all sorts of belief systems."

"Hmm," Serena intoned.

"What?" Melanie said.

Serena gave her an apologetic shrug. "Maybe quantity isn't the point."

Melanie slumped back against the passenger seat and crossed her arms. Something was off about this whole thing. She was the one who searched for signs, so she should be the one who got them. She was the one who'd given Josh a chance first, so she should have been the one having the long, intimate conversations with him, the one laughing with him along the trail. She was the one who had stepped up to the edge of the cliff, so she was the one who should have fallen down it and been saved from cancer because of it.

She strove to do everything right and was rewarded with yet more work to do. Olivia did nothing at all and good things just fell into her lap, unearned.

After several quiet minutes of driving, Serena pulled up to a roadblock, spoke to an officer, and was waved through. A few moments later, she put on her blinker. "Here we are."

She pulled into the gravel parking area. Melanie's car was the only one there.

"I'll wait to make sure it starts," Serena said.

"Thank you," Melanie said. "Thank you for everything today. For getting Olivia to the hospital so quickly, for bringing the pack to the hospital—oh, hey, do you know the guy who gave you the pack? Josh?"

"Another ranger gave it to me."

"A ranger? Not a guy with a beard and a plaid flannel shirt?"

"No, it was my friend Mike. Handed me the pack and asked me to take it along to the hospital when I was about to bring in a few more hikers after you guys."

"Oh, okay," Melanie said, disappointment lacing her voice. "I was just hoping I could figure out how to get ahold of him. He helped us out a lot on the trail." Then, more hopefully, "He was the guy who put my sister in the back of your truck."

Serena shook her head. "Sorry. My superior told me someone was in there that needed to get to the hospital fast. I didn't take the time to introduce myself to anyone standing around there."

Melanie opened her door. "No big deal. Just thought I'd ask. Thanks again!" She jumped out, shut the door, and trotted through the light rain to her car. It started up with no trouble. She gave Serena one more wave, then the truck disappeared into the night.

Rather than pull out onto the road and drive back to the hospital, Melanie plugged in her phone and then leaned back, closed her eyes, and listened to the rain pinging off the car. She was exhausted in every way a person could be exhausted, and all she wanted to do was sleep. She opened one eye and peeked at the gas gauge. Not a good idea. She sat up straight, put the car in reverse, then put it back in park. She dug around in the glove box for the paper map of the Upper Peninsula Olivia had brought along to supplement the GPS. She found the Porkies and squinted at the lines indicating roads. At the far western end of the green blob that was the park, she found it.

The Pinkerton Creek parking lot was thirty miles away. Driving there and back would mean adding more than an hour to the twenty or so minutes it would take her to get back to the hospital. It was already past two o'clock. And what was her plan, really? If Josh's car was there, would she just sit around in the parking lot until he appeared? What did she plan to say to him if she did see him? And how could she possibly know which car was his anyway?

She looked at the gas gauge once more, then pulled out onto the road.

Melanie followed Olivia out of Macy's after a fruitless search for the perfect anniversary gift for their parents. Everything Olivia liked was too expensive. Everything Melanie liked Olivia hated. They'd driven down to the mall without permission to use the car for nothing. All Melanie wanted to do was get home—fast—so they wouldn't get caught.

Out in the parking lot, Olivia unlocked the door. "Oh, wonderful! Someone hit us with their door!"

Melanie came around to the driver's side where Olivia was trying to scratch red paint off the white door with a fingernail. It wouldn't come off, and even if it did it wouldn't have mattered. The little dent was plain as day.

"Well, that's just great," Melanie said. "Now we're going to get it."

Olivia unlocked the door. "Relax. Justin can fix it."

The drive back up the Beltline was quiet. Olivia had just gotten her permit and wasn't supposed to be driving without an adult, so she insisted on no distractions. Not even the radio. And the only thing Melanie had to say was "I told you so," which she sure as heck wasn't going to say to an already angry and stressed-out Olivia.

Thirty minutes later, Olivia pulled up in front of Justin's house. "Stay here," she commanded.

Melanie watched her go up the rickety wooden steps to the front door. She'd never seen the inside of Justin's house, though he was over at their house all the time. Frankly, it looked like a house her parents wouldn't want her to go into. Bad neighborhood. Unkempt yards. Cars parked on the lawn that were never actually driven.

Movement at the door. Olivia was talking to someone. Then the door closed and Olivia got back in the car.

"So?"

"He said to bring it up to the garage."

Olivia pulled the car up the gravel driveway, stopping as close to the garage as possible. Difficult, because the driveway seemed to be a dumping ground for unwanted items. Car parts, a kiddie pool, a pile of old bricks. Melanie wondered if her fastidious parents had ever seen the place.

Justin came out the back door in jeans and a hoodie but no coat. Olivia got out, so Melanie got out, though she would rather have stayed in the warm car.

"What do you think?" Olivia was saying to Justin.

"Easy. Twenty minutes."

He acknowledged Melanie with a nod and disappeared into the garage. A moment later he was back with a toolbox and an extension cord. He plugged a hot glue gun into the extension cord and pulled a strange-looking tool out of the box. He popped a little black disk into the tool and covered the flat part with hot glue, then stuck it to the car where the dent was.

"Umm," Melanie said, looking to Olivia. She had expected Olivia to flip out, but her sister's face was completely calm.

Justin slowly squeezed a trigger on the tool. It braced against the car, pulling back the glued disk. Then the disk popped off, leaving a round pad of dried glue on the door, which Justin peeled off. He repeated the whole process with two smaller disks, then ran his fingers over the spot.

"All good," he proclaimed.

Olivia ran her fingers over it as well. "What about the paint?"

He pulled a couple cloths and a small tub of something out of the toolbox. After a few seconds of rubbing whatever was in the tub onto the spot on the car; the red paint was gone. He handed Olivia the other cloth. "The compound has to dry. Buff it when you get home."

"Thanks," she said, giving him a hug. "You're amazing."

Something crashed inside. Then there was yelling.

"Want to come over for dinner tonight?" Olivia said casually, as though she'd heard nothing.

"Better not," Justin said.

They shared a look that Melanie couldn't read.

"Next time," Olivia said. "Let's go, Mel."

Melanie waved at Justin. "Thank you."

He nodded and watched them pull down the driveway. Then he trudged back to the house.

"Why wouldn't he come to dinner?" Melanie said.

"None of your business."

Melanie slouched low in the seat.

"Since we can't seem to agree on anything, let's just get them a gift certificate to a restaurant or something," Olivia said. "They could use a night out."

"Okay."

After a moment, Olivia said, "Sometimes he has to stay home to help his mom."

"Oh." She didn't ask for more explanation. It was easy enough to put two and two together. And Melanie would bet green money that the next time she saw Justin, the way he'd helped his mom would be written all over his face.

Thirty-One

OLIVIA WINCED as she pulled at the seat belt.

"I told you I'd get it," Melanie chided. She reached into the car over Olivia's body and blindly searched for the spot to click it in.

Olivia pushed her away. "That's even worse. I've got it. I'm not going to be able to avoid being in some pain, so I have to just work through it."

Melanie stood in the light drizzle, waiting for Olivia to get settled, then firmly shut the car door and walked around to the driver's side. It was nine o'clock. If they kept their pit stops brief, they'd be in Indian River by midafternoon and Olivia would be back in East Lansing for dinner. She thought of how good it would feel to be showered—no matter how complicated the process—and sleeping in her own bed and managed to smile through the pain.

"What day is it, anyway?" Olivia said as Melanie pulled out of the parking lot.

"Wednesday. I think."

"Strange. The whole time we were hiking, we were falling behind, and here we are going home a day ahead of schedule."

"That is a little strange."

Olivia chuckled ruefully and let out a long, low sigh. "Not one thing went as I planned it."

Melanie laughed. "Your plans were literally wiped off the map."

"Don't think I didn't notice the irony in that. If I had known any of this was going to happen, I would never have said yes to this trip."

"I know you wouldn't have. And frankly, I don't think I would have even suggested it."

Olivia eyed her little sister. "I don't know about that."

Melanie flashed a smile. "It certainly will go down as one of the worst hiking trips anyone has ever taken. Somewhere down the list from that guy who had to cut off his own arm."

And their last hiking trip, Olivia thought but did not say.

Melanie looked back at the road, and Olivia studied her sister's face. She looked tired. When Olivia had woken up that morning at seven o'clock, Melanie was not there. When she still hadn't appeared an hour later, Olivia called her phone. She knew from the amount of time it took Melanie to answer and the low, breathy quality of her voice that she'd just woken up. But she told Olivia she was out getting gas and breakfast and she'd be back soon. She appeared with a McDonald's bag at the moment Olivia was signing discharge papers. Melanie brought all of their stuff to the car as an orderly wheeled Olivia, McDonald's bag on her lap, down the halls and out the door.

Now Olivia dug into the bag and pulled out greasy, paper-wrapped breakfast sandwiches. "Is one of these yours?" she asked incredulously.

"Yeah," Melanie said.

Olivia examined them. "Which one? They look the same."

"They are the same. Sausage, egg, and cheese McMuffins."

"Umm."

Melanie held out her hand. "I'm cheating."

Olivia plopped a decidedly non-vegan sandwich in her hand. "Don't they have oatmeal?"

"Hard to eat that while driving. Just this once won't hurt. Anyway, I've been reevaluating some of that stuff the past couple days."

"You've had time to evaluate the merits of veganism when we were trying to outrun a forest fire and you were busy saving me when I fell off a cliff?"

"I didn't save you. Josh did."

"Which, by the way, what is going on with the fire? And what ever happened to Josh?"

Melanie took a massive bite of her sandwich and commenced chewing. Olivia waited.

"From what I could glean from the hospital staff talking," she finally said after swallowing, "the fire containment is going as well as it could be. We should see if we can get anything on the radio about it." She took another bite.

"What about Josh? Did he ever even come by the hospital?"

"No. I asked Serena about him—she's the ranger."

"Right."

"And she couldn't remember ever seeing him."

Olivia frowned. "I really wish I knew he was okay. I mean, I'm sure he is, it's just, the whole thing feels kind of unfinished. Like he's this big loose end just hanging out there."

Melanie nodded. Olivia bit into her own sandwich. For the

next few minutes, there was only driving and chewing, until finally Melanie said, "I went out to where his car was supposed to be parked last night."

"Yeah?"

"No one was there."

"No cars?"

"None. So I can only assume he got out fine and either drove home or is staying in some motel somewhere around here."

"Is that why you look so tired? When did you get back into town?"

"I went and looked for Josh and then drove back until I hit a twenty-four-hour gas station," Melanie said. "Gassed up then parked the car there and slept for a few hours until the phone woke me up."

"Oh man. I wish I could drive part of the way for you."

"Me too."

Olivia spun her head around and recoiled at the sudden pain. "Oh, I should not have done that."

"What?"

"Nothing. Just my neck. But I was going to say that there's no way you can drive me all the way back to East Lansing today on just a few hours' sleep."

Melanie squeezed the wheel at ten and two. "I'm not."

Olivia sighed. "I was really looking forward to being in my own bed tonight."

"You will be."

"How?"

"Well, I know you weren't keen on the idea of me coming along with you anyway."

"Yeah . . ."

"And I'm sure you have friends and coworkers who could help you out a bit during your recovery."

"Okay . . ."

"And if you don't, you'll hire help, right?" she said severely.

"Mel, who's bringing me home?"

Melanie glanced at her. "Don't be mad."

"What? Who?" Olivia said impatiently. Then it dawned on her. "No . . ."

"You said you were planning on talking to him anyway, so I figured this would give you time to do it and it would give me time to rest and—"

Olivia buried her face in her hands and groaned. "I wish you'd asked me first. That's all. I just wish you'd asked me." She took a deep breath. "I don't know if I'm ready to do this yet."

"Well, you've got at least six hours to get ready." She reached into the back seat and produced a small box, which she set on Olivia's lap. "This might help."

It was the box Olivia had asked about at the beginning of their trip. She wiped her hands on a napkin and stuck it in her pocket, then removed the lid and stared into the past. Ticket stubs from movies. Notes folded into paper footballs. A dried corsage from homecoming. A cheap imitation silver locket. And a handful of photos.

She and Justin on a trampoline. The two of them Rollerblading on the rail trail. Being dropped off at camp. Splashing each other in Crystal Lake. Eating ice cream on a bench and squinting into the sun. Her dad had taken these photos with his camera back before they all had smartphones. Olivia was intimately familiar with each one. Small holes attested to where pushpins had held them to the bulletin board in her bedroom. Her mind filled in the time on either side of the moment that had been captured. Moments that would never come again.

When she came to a picture of her and Justin at age four or five standing in the backyard in just their underwear, his tanned bare arm slung over her tanned shoulders, Olivia stopped. Starting at age seventeen, Justin would cover his arms in tattoos. In this picture, they were peppered with bruises. It had taken years of friendship before Justin divulged the things that were going on in his house as his unhappy and often intoxicated parents took out their misery on each other and on him. Despite that, in every photo of the two of them together, Justin was smiling.

At that moment, Olivia understood that her mother's refrain of "What's done is done and can't be undone" had been wrong. Or at least, it was not universally applicable. What had been done to Justin, Olivia and her loving family had, in part, undone. For many years, they had shown him how a family could be, how it should be. They hadn't removed his bruises, but they'd helped them heal.

Then Olivia left him behind. And he drifted away. And she forgot about him. Until he came crashing back into her life.

"I wondered what had become of this stuff," she finally said.

"You had to know I wouldn't have gotten rid of it."

"You have always been rather sentimental."

"I hardly think it qualifies as terribly sentimental to keep hold of a few childhood memories."

"No, I suppose not." Olivia returned the lid to the box, shrouding the past in darkness. "Music?"

"Your pick," Melanie said.

"Nah. You choose."

"You sure?"

"Sure."

Melanie retrieved a CD from her visor and popped it in. Olivia recognized it immediately as one of their mother's favorites—the first disc of Paul Simon's 1991 concert in Central Park. She had attended it with her sister Susan while pregnant with Melanie.

Olivia sank a little lower in her seat, closed her eyes, and let her mind drift back to better days. She imagined her mother singing along to the songs she'd grown up with. Imagined her father teaching her and Justin how to throw a baseball. Imagined Melanie's face when she finally got the kitten she'd been begging for. All of the photos that had been taken. All of the beautiful days that had passed by without photographic evidence to prove they'd happened. So many more happy memories than sad ones.

It was a good life. And even if that part of it was over, life could still be good. It could be better than she had allowed it to be. She could be better than she had allowed herself to be.

As she slipped into sleep, Olivia saw one more face in her memories. Josh's. And she felt sure in that moment that she would see him again someday.

Thirty-Two

MELANIE DROVE EAST, back toward Marquette, back to the scene of the motorcycle accident nearly a week earlier. What had happened to that man? Had he been treated and sent home as Olivia had? Or had his funeral been held sometime when they were tromping through the woods?

Life was so strange. The way it could go on for one person and end for another. If there was a life force out there, why was it always ebbing and flowing so capriciously? Who chose who got to live and who must die, and by what criteria? Why was Olivia's life saved by falling off a cliff and their parents' lost while driving down a familiar street?

Attempting to fathom one being arranging all of this for billions of people all over the planet for all of time was like trying to untangle all of the neurons in all of the brains of all those people. To lay them all out in such a way that you could see all the connections simultaneously, so you could see exactly which cause created which effect.

Impossible. She used to be comfortable with that—with

the impossibility of knowing, the inscrutability of it all. When coaching clients asked her for specifics, she deliberately fuzzied things up and encouraged them to relax into the not knowing, into the nearly knowing. Specifics didn't matter. What mattered was how you felt, and any combination of ideas that made you feel some happiness in the midst of a troubled life was what was right for you.

Melanie thought about this as the names of tiny towns ticked by—Three Lakes, Imperial Heights, Beacon, Humboldt, Greenwood. Little outposts of civilization in the vast wilderness Longfellow had made famous in his "Song of Hiawatha," a tediously long poem Melanie had been assigned to read in high school, and which she discovered her father still knew by heart from his own school days. How very western these towns all sounded, as though the people who established them were assuring themselves that they could tame the dangers they might face—the fevers from the marshes, the pestilential vapors, the poisonous exhalations of Longfellow's poem—as they cut lumber and drained wetlands and platted out farmland.

At the junction for M-28, she should have turned left to stay near the lakeshore. It would have taken her right past the site of the motorcycle accident and given her the chance to see if a roadside marker had been put up, indicating the man's fate. Indicating whether or not her plea for positive vibes had been effective. But when it came down to it, she didn't actually want to know.

Instead, she followed M-41 south through nearly fifty miles of nothing but trees. The sky cleared as she got farther away from the big lake. Beech and birch trees shone bright yellow against the pines and firs, and shocks of red sumac rose like waves along the roadside. Summer's wildflowers were brown and spent. Life was winding down like an old clock. In a few weeks, daylight saving time would end and it would be dark before Melanie sat down to dinner. On the nights Justin could come over to eat or to watch a movie, it wouldn't be so bad. On the nights she was alone . . .

But she didn't have to be alone anymore. She did love Justin. And she knew he loved her. Not just the role she'd played in the wake of Olivia's rejection. Her.

It wasn't until Melanie slowed the car to take a left on US-2 that Olivia stirred. "Where are we?" she asked.

"A little over halfway to Indian River."

Olivia stretched and groaned. "Ugh. I forgot I was all messed up for a minute there."

"Do you need to take something for the pain?"

"Maybe. And I need to get out of this car and move. I'm all stiff."

"We can stop in Manistique for lunch and bathrooms."

"You mean Munising?"

"No," Melanie said. "I took a different route."

"Oh. How far to Manistique?"

Melanie checked the GPS, which had started working again as they approached the southern shore of the peninsula. "This says thirty-eight minutes."

"I don't think I can wait that long."

Melanie tapped the GPS. "Here. There's a gas station just south of this little lake. We'll stop there."

For the next twenty-five minutes, Olivia shifted and sighed

in her seat. She fiddled with the radio, flipped through CDs, never landed on anything. When they finally arrived at the gas station, Melanie helped Olivia get out of the car—not an easy feat—and hobble to the bathroom. She stocked up on water and snacks in lieu of lunch, then helped Olivia back to her seat. She was walking around to the driver's side when two women walked out of the gas station.

"That was incredible," one said.

"It really was," said the other. "I thought it would be a huge waste of time, but I think it's my favorite part of the trip so far."

"Excuse me," Melanie broke in. "What are you talking about?"

"The big spring," the first one said.

"Kitch—Kitch-ipi—oh, I can't say it. It starts with a *K*," the second one said.

"It's just north of here."

"What is it though?" Melanie said.

"It's . . . well, it's this spring."

"It's a really still pool of blue, blue—"

"Turquoise."

"Yes, turquoise water."

Melanie waited for more.

"It's hard to explain," the women said simultaneously. Then they laughed uproariously.

"You just have to see it," the first one finally said. "It's worth the drive."

"How far away is it?" Melanie asked.

"Oh, what do you think it is?" she asked her friend. "Fifteen minutes up the road?"

"If that."

"Which road?"

They pointed.

"This one here—149. It jogs, but there are signs."

"It starts with a *K*?" Melanie confirmed.

"Yes. Kitch-something. They call it the Big Spring."

"Thanks," Melanie said. The women went on their way and Melanie got in the car.

"What was all that?" Olivia said.

"Nothing. We just need to make one little detour before we go."

The walk from the parking lot to the viewing platform at Kitch-iti-kipi was slow and, if Olivia's expression was any indication, painful. When the water first came into view through the trees, Melanie felt a twinge of disappointment. It just looked like a pond. A blue one, sure, but a pond nonetheless. They came to a large deck. Through a wooden gate set in the railing, one could step onto a large covered rectangular raft, which they did. A sign indicated that if she turned a large metal wheel, the raft would move along a cable strung across the length of the spring, bringing them out to the middle.

"Oh!" Olivia said. "You can see clear to the bottom here."

In the center of the raft behind a wooden railing was a hole, a rectangle within the rectangle of the raft, and indeed you could see through the crystal-clear water to the bottom, which was crisscrossed with the remains of fallen pine trees. Melanie pulled the wheel and the raft moved a little. Pull by pull, first with her left hand, then her right, and as she tired, with both of them, Melanie slowly moved the raft to the middle of the pond, where there was nothing on the bottom but pale sand.

"Look," Olivia said, pointing into the hole in the raft.

Swimming lazily through the water were large, dark bodies of fish. A sign by the rail said that they were mostly trout—lake, brown, or brook—much like the fish Josh had been grilling for them, the fish on Olivia's knife. Another sign explained how meltwater and rainwater filled one permeable layer of rock that sat beneath another layer of rock, which was impermeable except for a few cracks. At these cracks, the pressurized water shot up into the spring at a rate of more than ten thousand gallons a minute. Where the water came up out of the ground, the sand looked as though it was boiling, though the water was only forty-five degrees Fahrenheit year-round. All quite practical and scientific and unmagical.

Maybe that was how the world really was. One vast machine. Nothing more than a collection of predictable, measurable processes. It was bleak, but that didn't necessarily mean it was not true. And if it was true, if this was the only life she'd ever have, Melanie didn't want to spend the rest of it on her own.

She looked out across the achingly blue water to the trees, which were reflected perfectly on its glassy surface. For every tree right side up, its twin was upside down. Each had a partner. Not one of them was alone.

"I'm going to tell Justin yes," Melanie said. She glanced at Olivia's face for her reaction and was surprised to see a smile there. A small one, perhaps strained, but a smile nonetheless. Melanie gave a resolute nod and looked back out at the trees. "This is pretty."

Olivia joined her at the rail. "Yeah." She pulled Melanie's phone out of her back pocket. "One more picture?"

Melanie took the phone from her. "Sure." With their backs to the outer rail, Melanie framed their faces on the screen. "You can't see much of the spring behind our fat heads."

"That's okay," Olivia said. "We know it's there."

Melanie snapped the photo, then looked at it. "You look really happy in this one."

Olivia tipped the screen toward her. "You don't."

"I'm just tired. It's been a long day already."

"So what are you going to do with this trip on your blog?" Olivia said.

"I don't know yet. Maybe nothing."

"Nothing? That hardly sounds like you."

Melanie shrugged. "It's a lot to process. And it's a lot to keep up, you know? The blog, the videos, the social media. It's been kind of nice to have a break from that this week. The thought of diving back into it all . . . well, it's exhausting really."

"What about your following?"

"I dunno. They'd get on without me. It's kind of arrogant of me to assume I'm really necessary, right? Anyway, some of the stuff I've been saying to them all these years is ringing a little hollow to me the last couple days. Maybe I need to take some time to myself." She motioned to the bubbling sand forty feet below. "I don't have that sort of thing. I am feeding and feeding other people, but nothing's really filling me back up. I just feel a little . . . empty."

Melanie could feel Olivia looking at her.

"Do me a favor, Mel?"

"What?"

"Anytime you're feeling that way, let Justin know, okay? Or

send me a text. Or call. I'll be more responsive than I have in the past. Just don't keep it to yourself."

Melanie blinked hard and nodded.

"Hey," Olivia said, turning Melanie to face her. "I love you, Mel. And I'm going to be a better sister to you from here on out."

"Okay," Melanie whispered.

Olivia pulled her into a gentle hug, and the tears Melanie had been holding in slipped out through the cracks and cascaded down her cheeks like twin waterfalls.

"Hey, hey," Olivia said. "What's wrong?"

Melanie hiccupped a sob, then sucked in a deep, quavering breath. "I don't know. I just feel so . . . so empty all of a sudden. Which is stupid. I've gotten what I wanted. I reconnected with you and I'm going to have you in my life, and I'll have Justin too and I won't have to choose."

Olivia rubbed her back. "Well, maybe that wasn't the only thing you were hoping for. Maybe that was just the stuff you could see on the outside."

Melanie wiped her nose with the back of her hand. "I miss Mom and Dad so much."

Olivia pulled her in for another hug. "So do I."

They stood there on the platform in the middle of the turquoise water, ringed in on all sides by pines and cedars and silence. Melanie pulled away and searched Olivia's eyes.

"Do you really think we'll never see them again? Do you really think there's nothing left of them?"

Olivia frowned. "I don't know. I hope not."

Melanie slumped back against the outer railing. "I'm just so tired."

"It's been a long week."

She threw up her hands. "No, I mean my whole life. I can't do this anymore, covering my bases. There are too many things I have to do, and it's all on me to do them, and what if I mess up? And you're right. You're right that they can't all be true. That one thing has to be it, the real thing. And if that one thing is true, then the things that aren't it can't be. I don't know, maybe there's nothing. Nothing beyond this life. Maybe—"

"No," Olivia said. "Don't say that."

"But you—"

"I know what I said, but . . . I don't know. Maybe I've been wrong. Frankly, I'm not even sure how much I truly believed what I was saying or if I was just saying it because it didn't require anything of me. I did nothing, you did everything. I believed nothing, you believed everything. But maybe we're both wrong. Maybe there's just one thing. One real thing."

Melanie swallowed and wiped her eyes.

"Okay?" Olivia said.

"Okay. Yeah."

Olivia smiled. "Now we just have to figure out what it is."

Melanie laughed despite herself. "Easy, right?"

"Yeah, easy."

The sun had dropped below the trees, but it hadn't quite set. The purple-gray sky was stained with tangerine at the horizon. Almost twilight, but Olivia could still make out the ball as it swished through the bright white net. She palmed it briefly and sent it over to Justin.

"One more and you're out, P-I,*" she said.*

"I know. I know how to spell."

She could hear the smile in his voice even if it was getting hard to see in the dark.

Swish.

She set up her next shot, took it, and missed.

"Now you're in for it," he said. He dribbled up the driveway, spun to the right, then the left, then passed the ball between his legs before going for a right hook. But the ball bounced off the rim and into Olivia's waiting hands.

"Ha!" she shouted. Her laugh echoed in the August night. "You're always trying that fancy stuff, and it never works. It never works, my friend!"

"Oh, you mean this?" He hit the ball out of her hands and proceeded to dribble it step-by-step through his legs as he danced around her. "Or this?" He spun it on his finger and popped it up with his elbow.

"Or this," Olivia said flatly, hitting the ball out of his hands.

It bounced onto the grass. After a beat, they both tore after it, jostling, pushing, shoving. Then they both had their hands on it, trying to wrench it away. Justin pulled with his entire body weight and they crashed onto the lawn, legs tangled, both still hugging the ball. Olivia gave it one more giant twist, and Justin let go.

"You win! You win!" he said.

Olivia could hardly breathe she was laughing so hard, lying flat on her back, smelling grass and dirt and summertime.

Justin lay next to her, his chest rising and falling. "You win," he said again. "I'm done."

Olivia sat up. "The game's not over. You just have P-I. *You need your* G *or you'll never be a real pig!"*

Justin put his hand on his stomach. "I'm done."

"Quitter."

He popped the ball out of her hands again, and it went rolling back onto the pavement, hit the garage, and reversed course, rolling faster and faster down the driveway and into the street.

"You're going to go get that," Olivia said.

Justin didn't move. Olivia lay back down next to him. A few of the brightest stars had appeared as the sun retreated beneath the gentle curve of the earth. The grass felt prickly beneath her bare legs and arms. Summer was coming to an end. Soon she'd be leaving for her freshman year of college. It was only a two-and-a-half-hour drive from Rockford to Ann Arbor. But she knew in her heart she would not make it often. Nights like this were running out.

"You know you can use this hoop whenever you want, right?" she said. "And you can still come over here for dinner any night of the week. You can keep an eye on Melanie for me."

Justin looked at her for a long time. Too long. Then he stood up and walked across the street to get the basketball. Olivia tamped down the tears that wanted to come, thankful it was too dark for him to see her face anymore. Then he was standing over her, offering a hand.

"Get up, O. It's your turn."

Thirty-Three

IN THE TWO AND A HALF HOURS it took to get from the crystal waters of Kitch-iti-kipi to the gravel ride-share lot next to the Shell station in Indian River, Olivia tried to prepare herself to see Justin Navarro for the first time since she'd spotted him at the cemetery ten years ago. She looked again through the photos Melanie had saved, pulled those good memories to the front of her mind, silently practiced what she would say to him. She deliberated between a hug, handshake, or hands-free greeting. She breathed in, breathed out. When Melanie pulled in to the station, she thought she was ready.

She spotted him immediately, leaning against the wall outside. His hair was longer, and he'd exchanged his stubble for a neatly trimmed beard. The tattoo sleeves that had made him look like a drug dealer back when he was wearing oversize basketball jerseys with baggy jeans made him look like the quintessential Millennial entrepreneur now that he was sporting slim-fitting pants, a button-down shirt with rolled-up sleeves, and brown suede loafers with no socks. But he wore the same guarded expression she'd known so well. The one that had only ever relaxed into a smile when he was with her.

Melanie stopped at the gas pump. "Are you going to be okay with this?"

Olivia nodded, though she suspected it was a lie. Melanie got out of the car, ran over to where Justin stood, and gave him a long hug but no kiss. Then she disappeared into the store. Olivia pretended to be busy with her phone to avoid eye contact with Justin as he walked up to the gas pump, slid his credit card in, and lifted the nozzle.

All at once Olivia felt tremendously childish and realized that she needed to get out of the car. To use the bathroom, yes, but also because when she did finally say hello to him, she wanted it to be at eye level rather than him standing and her sitting. She removed her seat belt and opened the car door, but the apparatus keeping her knee immobilized meant she could not get out without help. She closed the door and decided to wait for Melanie, but almost as soon as it was shut, somebody opened it.

Olivia looked up to see Justin looking down at her.

"Need a hand?"

She muscled down her pride. "Yeah."

Justin took her elbow. Leaning the weight of her upper body in his sure grip, she twisted enough to get her leg out and let him lift her gently out of the car. Much smoother than when Melanie had gotten her out earlier that day. The moment she was stable, Justin dropped his hands and hooked his thumbs on his pockets. They looked at each other for one pregnant moment.

Olivia felt her heart rate tick up, and she forced herself to breathe slowly, deliberately.

She pointed into the car. “Can you grab those crutches? I need to use the bathroom.”

“Of course.”

He sprang into motion, and a moment later Olivia was hobbling toward the door. Inside, the clerk gave her a long, hard look. It was the same woman who had sized her up five days earlier. Olivia turned away.

In the bathroom, she caught sight of herself in the mirror and wished she hadn’t. Her hair was in a greasy ponytail beneath her sweat-stained baseball cap. Her chin was scraped. A long purple bruise stretched from her temple to her jawline. A zit was brewing at the corner of her nose. She’d have to go to work like this. To explain to everyone what had happened on her big hiking trip. She wondered if her new look would work for or against her in the courtroom.

A few minutes later, Olivia gathered up her wounded pride and her crutches and headed back out into the store. Melanie was at the counter, buying iced tea and a bag of salted cashews. Olivia grabbed a Coke and plucked a newspaper from the rack near the door. Above the fold was an aerial shot of the fire in the Porcupine Mountains, accompanied by the triumphant headline “CONTAINED!” Olivia scanned the article for names, hoping she wouldn’t see hers, hoping she would see Josh’s. But the only people mentioned by name were park rangers. Everyone who had been in the park was accounted for, the cause of the fire was still under investigation, and the old-growth portion of the forest remained unspoiled.

"You gonna buy that?" the woman behind the counter asked. "'Cause this ain't a library."

Olivia plunked the paper down on the counter next to the Coke.

"Crazy, isn't it," the woman said, indicating the paper. She rang up Olivia's items, then fixed her with a look. "What happened to you?"

Olivia wordlessly tucked the receipt in her pocket and reached for her items, but Melanie, standing nearby, beat her to it. The woman behind the counter turned to the next person in line as they made their way outside, where Justin was now gassing up Olivia's car.

"I gave him your keys," Melanie said. "He's already got the packs in the back—I took my stuff out of mine. So I think you should be all set." Melanie put a hand on Olivia's arm. "Listen, I haven't told him yet."

"Does he know I know?"

"No. Let's not make this about me and Justin. This is about you and Justin. You'll get a few hours in the car to talk, he'll get you settled back in at home, then he'll stay the night at a hotel and fly home tomorrow, and I'll pick him up in Traverse City. He's already bought a ticket."

Olivia started toward her own car, which was dusty and covered in maple seeds. Melanie helped her into the passenger seat, handed over the Coke and the newspaper, then stood in the open door.

"Hey," she said. "I know this didn't turn out like either of us planned. But believe it or not, I think things are going to get better from here."

Olivia nodded. "They will."

Melanie frowned. "Promise me you'll call your doctor first thing tomorrow morning."

"Promise."

"And keep me updated."

"Okay."

Melanie shut the door. Justin closed the gas cap and came around to where Melanie stood. Olivia couldn't hear what they were saying, but she could see them in the side mirror. They ended the short conversation with a tight embrace and a quick kiss. Then Melanie knocked on the window, blew Olivia a kiss, and walked away.

Justin got into the car and started it up. "Where to?"

"East Lansing."

He indicated her University of Michigan ball cap. "They let you in there with that?"

"I don't wear it during football season."

"Ah." Justin pulled out of the parking lot and onto I-75 South.

Olivia stared out the window and tried to think of something appropriate to say, but nothing was coming to her. How did you talk to a friend you'd abandoned? How did you talk to the man who'd stolen away your parents and hoped to marry your sister? How did you begin to dig yourself out of a decade of bitterness?

She waited for him to break, to say something first. But he didn't.

"What do you do in Petoskey?" she finally said. Inane, but safe.

"I do custom bodywork on cars. Restore them, soup them up. Engine work. Detailing. Stuff like that."

"You have your own garage?"

"Yeah." He glanced at her. "It's a good living."

She nodded. "I'm sure it is."

The agonizing silence set back in. There was no way to start this conversation. Not without sounding like the prosecuting attorney she was.

"Get to the beach much?" Olivia tried.

"Just say it," Justin said.

"Excuse me?"

He looked at her. "Just say it."

"Say what?"

He looked back to the road. "Whatever it is you've wanted to say to me all these years. Just say it."

Olivia scowled. "What do you think I've wanted to say to you?"

He didn't answer.

"You think I had anything good to say to you? Any words of forgiveness or reconciliation? 'Let's let bygones be bygones'?"

"No."

"Then what the heck do you think I should say to you?"

Olivia sighed and shifted in her seat. Her foot hit something on the floor of the car. The shoebox of memories. Of course Melanie would put it right there where Olivia would see it. She rubbed her forehead and softened her tone.

"I've had a lot of time to be angry. A lot of time to wish things had been different. But they aren't. And there's nothing I can do about it."

She reached into her pocket for the used napkin from her breakfast to blow her nose, but her fingers found something else.

Something hard and round. She pulled it out. Josh's compass. How did that get there?

So you can find your way in the wilderness.

Forgiving Justin had never been part of her plan. She was off the path she'd marked out for her life, slogging through the muck and the underbrush, directionless. She opened the compass. The needle swung around to point north, back where they'd just come from, back where, for a moment at least, Olivia had allowed herself to imagine that there might be a God after all. One who called on people to do justice, love mercy, walk humbly. She'd been all hung up on the first part, had made it central to her identity. But she'd never been very good at the other two.

She flipped the compass closed. Despite all of their missteps and mistakes while hiking, they had made it out alive. More than that, if the doctor was correct, Olivia might have that hiking trip to thank for saving her from cancer. That wasn't really justice. She and Melanie were unfit in the Darwinian sense and should have been eliminated from the gene pool. If it hadn't been for Josh—guiding them along the river, sharing his food and his shelter, dragging her back up the escarpment and out of the woods—they might still be out there. Maybe caught in a forest fire.

Josh had put his own life on the line, for her and for others when he went back in with a search party. The paper had said everyone was accounted for. No one had been left to fend for themselves amid the flames. He'd found everyone he was looking for—including the people who must have been responsible for the fire. He loved mercy.

"Listen, Justin," she began tentatively. "I know it was an accident." She swallowed down the emotion she felt rising in her throat. "I know you lost them too."

Olivia could see his jaw clench beneath his beard. Did he give himself headaches that way like she did? Had he been as tightly coiled all this time?

"I haven't been a very good friend through all of this. Or a good sister." She pushed the reluctant words past her teeth. "I'm going to try to do better."

Justin nodded a little. "It's been hard—knowing you were out there hating me all these years." He glanced her way. "You were my best friend. My only friend."

"I know."

"When you left it really sucked, you know?"

Olivia pressed her lips together. "Yeah. I know."

"And then the accident and everything fell apart . . . and I had no one."

"You had Melanie," she offered, and for the first time she truly understood what her sister had been trying to tell her all those years ago. Justin had needed forgiveness. And Melanie had needed to forgive.

"Yeah, she helped. A lot. I don't think I'd still be around if it weren't for her."

Olivia tucked the compass back into her pocket and took out the napkin she'd been after in the first place. "She told me you asked her to marry you."

Justin looked at her, the question he was afraid to ask written across his brow.

"I'll admit I didn't take it so well," Olivia said.

His face fell.

"But I'm slowly coming around to it. It makes sense."

Relief washed over Justin's face, but it was quickly replaced with concern. "She hasn't told me yes or no."

Olivia smiled. "She told me."

He waited for more.

"It's not my business to say," she said. "And Melanie didn't want this ride to be about the two of you. Though, I don't know what we're supposed to talk about if we can't bring her into it. She's the only thing we really have in common at this point."

Justin passed a semi and returned to the right lane. "We've got practically twenty years of history together, just you and me. That's two-thirds of our lives."

"We did have some pretty good times." Olivia stared at the road ahead. Those times were all behind her now.

Just like the accident. Ten years in the past but still fresh, still raw. Still permanent. Why did that hang on, a parasite on her soul, when the good stuff faded like mist beneath the heat of the sun?

"Melanie said you've been going to church."

Justin nodded.

"You believe all that stuff?"

"Yes, I do."

He tightened his grip on the steering wheel, but his face relaxed so that Olivia saw something there she'd never seen before. It wasn't just happiness like in the old photos in the box at her feet. It was something more. It was peace. It was serenity. In fact, it wasn't unlike Josh's face.

"What do you think they'll say to you if you see them again?" she mused. "Do you think they'll forgive you?"

"Your parents?" He shook his head. "They won't have to. When my life ends, I'll be carrying nothing with me into the next one. No sins, no mistakes, no guilt. There's nothing to forgive in heaven."

"So that's it, then? All the transgressions of our lives on Earth are just gone and no one has to pay? How is that fair?"

"It isn't. Just like it isn't fair that nearly twenty years of friendship can be destroyed by three seconds of reckless driving."

"Careful."

"Just like it wasn't fair that my dad beat me and spent the grocery money on drugs and alcohol," he barreled on. "You've got to stop thinking in terms of *fair*. Fair is the bare minimum of happiness. It's zero. It's not positive, it's not negative, it's just zero. You want to live your life striving to achieve zero?"

Olivia shifted uncomfortably in her seat.

Justin softened his tone. "When has something being fair ever made you happy? When Melanie said it wasn't fair that you took both drumsticks when your dad brought home fried chicken, he took one of them from you and gave it to her. Did *fair* work for you then?"

"It worked for Melanie," Olivia quipped.

"When the two of you couldn't agree whose turn it was to pick the Friday night movie, what happened?"

"Mom picked."

"And what did she always pick?"

Olivia sighed. "*Dead Poets Society*."

"Which you *hated*."

"You hated it too."

"What about how angry you used to get because your parents

were so much stricter with you than they were with Melanie? That her curfew was later than yours was at the same age. That she got her kitten when they wouldn't let you get a husky puppy. That you had to get a summer job at an office while she got to babysit kids at the country club pool every day."

"What's your point?"

"That your obsession with things being fair hasn't brought you any joy. All it's produced is bitterness." He glanced her way. "And by the way, I never said that no one had to pay."

Thirty-Four

MELANIE SAT by the stone fireplace in the lobby of the tiny Cherry Capital Airport in Traverse City and watched the spot where she knew Justin would appear. The day before, she'd gotten home, taken a shower, and collapsed into bed. She'd woken up at six o'clock, savored a hot cup of tea, and sat down with a blank journal, thinking she'd process some of the events of the past week. To her surprise, she could not quite bring herself to write anything down.

She relocated to the computer to start working through what she had missed during her time off the grid, starting with the comments on the video from the scene of the motorcycle accident. They were largely what she'd expected—notes of support and declarations that thoughts and vibes were going out and prayers were going up. But there were also a few along the lines of what Olivia had said—that she was using someone else's tragedy to get clicks. Her fingers itched to respond to those comments as she had responded to Olivia's criticism, but she refrained.

Instead, she deleted them. She couldn't do anything about

the thumbs-downs—there were always a few of them—but she didn't have to let false accusations go unchecked. After she finished with that video's comments, she clicked to the previous video she had posted and did the same. It felt good. It felt like scraping the sad remains of a failed recipe from her plate and shoving it down the garbage disposal.

Once she got started, it was hard to stop. Comment by comment, video by video, she rejected every criticism of her or her motives until everyone who disagreed with her was silenced. Then she sat back and looked at the clock. If Justin's flight was on time, she was going to be late. Again.

The drive down to Traverse City was always lovely, but today especially. The rolling green hills had burst into fall color while she was gone. Every tree had become an individual rather than just an anonymous part of the collective. The blue sky was studded with fluffy white clouds playing peekaboo with the sun. Lake Michigan and Grand Traverse Bay sparkled to her right. Lake Charlevoix, Torch Lake, and Elk Lake glittered to her left. Every charming tourist town along US-31 was now empty of its summer traffic snarls. It was for moments like these that she lived Up North.

Plus she was on her way to see Justin. To take him home and tell him she would marry him.

She'd meant to text him the night before to see how everything went, but then she'd fallen asleep so quickly and completely. She'd been a little annoyed when there wasn't a text from him this morning to update her on the situation with Olivia. No text letting her know he was boarding his plane. No text letting her know it had landed.

Now she stood up to check the status of the flight, but as she did people started filtering into the lobby. She spotted Justin immediately. He was talking on his phone, a wide smile on his normally stoic face. Melanie's gut twisted at the sudden thought that perhaps Justin had not stayed at a hotel that night. That maybe he'd stayed with Olivia. But the thought fled when Justin saw her, said "I gotta go" into the phone, dropped his backpack, and pulled her into his arms.

"Oh, I missed you," he said into her neck.

"I missed you too."

He kissed her long and slow, the kind of kiss she'd wanted back in Indian River but hesitated to give him in front of Olivia. He shouldered his backpack and steered her toward the door.

"So how did it go?" Melanie asked.

"Rocky start. But ultimately better than I expected."

"That's good," she said. "What did you talk about?"

"Oh, lots of stuff. We talked about old times. I got her set up at her place. Got us some Chinese food while she took a shower. We watched a movie. Then I took an Uber to the hotel. Took another to the airport, and here I am."

A movie? They'd watched a movie?

Melanie unlocked the car, and Justin tossed his bag in the back seat. "Did you talk about the accident?"

"A bit." He got into the car.

Melanie got in and fastened her seat belt but did not start the car. "What did she say? Did she forgive you?"

Justin scrunched up his brow. "She's not quite there yet."

"But she watched a movie with you?"

"She's on the right path, I think. Give her time."

Melanie frowned and started the car. "She's had ten years."

Justin put his hand on hers where it rested on the shifter. "Don't be like that. This is progress." He sat back. "She seemed like a different person in a lot of ways. And I guess in others she seemed exactly the same."

Melanie put the car in reverse and then studied his face, which seemed lost in a memory that did not include her. Just as all those photos had not included her. Was there a piece of him that would never quite be hers? A piece that would forever belong to her sister?

"What's up?" Justin said.

"What?"

He looked around. "We're not moving."

"I just thought . . ." She put the car in drive. "I don't know what I thought."

She could feel him watching her, but she pasted a smile on her face and headed for the highway.

"So who were you talking to back there?" Melanie said after they'd been on the road for a few minutes.

"Back where?"

"The airport. Before you saw me. Who were you talking to?"

"Oh, that. That was Dale. The guy with the '55 T-Bird I was telling you about a couple weeks ago. Said he might have a couple more cars coming my way this winter. Wants them ready for the summer car shows."

"That's great!" she said, masking her relief that it was not Olivia with extra enthusiasm.

"It'll be good money. Which is great if we're going to be paying for a wedding." He let the word hang there in the air a moment. "So what do you think? Are we going to be paying for a wedding? I kind of got the idea from Olivia that maybe we'd be paying for a wedding."

"Olivia said that?" Melanie snapped. What gave Olivia the right to tell Justin yes or no?

"Not exactly. She said she knew I'd asked you."

"And?"

"And she said she knew what your answer was, but she wouldn't tell me. She didn't seem like she was upset about it or anything, so I kind of thought—I mean, that was your reservation, right? That she'd be angry and you'd have to choose, her or me. But now it doesn't seem like that's the case." He fell silent.

Melanie pulled off to the side of the road. "I can't have this conversation while driving." She parked by a stretch of sandy beach that separated US-31 from the waves on Grand Traverse Bay and swiveled in her seat to face Justin. She reached for his hand. "I've given this a lot of thought since you asked me, but also a lot just this week. And I do want to say yes."

He frowned. "But?"

"I just have to ask—when you were with Olivia yesterday, did any of your old feelings for her pop up?"

"What do you mean?"

"I think you know what I mean. I just have to be sure that when you saw her yesterday, you weren't thinking about what might have been if things had gone differently."

Justin relaxed his face and put a hand on top of hers. "That was a really long time ago, Mel. God led me away from Olivia. And he led me to you. You were there for me. You cared. You showed me love and mercy and friendship. And you're the one I want to marry. Not Olivia. Okay?"

Melanie sniffed and felt a tear escape her eye. "Okay."

"You believe me?"

She nodded. "Yeah. Okay."

He dipped his head and caught her eye. "So will you marry me?"

Melanie straightened in her seat and smiled through her tears. "Yes."

Later that night when Melanie returned home, she sat back down with her new journal. She had lost the record of Justin asking. She would not miss recording her answer. She scribbled away for ten or fifteen minutes, reliving the emotions from the car. But she only chronicled the joy. None of the suspicion or second-guessing would make it into the official record of her life.

Afterward she scanned her emails and social media notifications. So many people looking to her for encouragement and guidance. So many people taking without offering anything in return beyond an ego boost. She scrolled through months of posts and comments, and rather than feeling accomplished as she usually did, she felt mildly irritated. Nothing she said actually meant anything. She had just been saying things that people wanted to hear, feeding their ideas back to them, a slightly shined-up version of what they already believed.

What was the point of it all? Was she even helping anyone? Or had it all been about her all along?

Suddenly she wished she had not deleted all those negative comments. She wanted to think about what they said. Wanted to look herself in the face with a more critical eye, to see if maybe there were some things she was just plain wrong about. But she couldn't undo it.

She got up and searched the fridge for something edible, but she'd emptied it of all but condiments before leaving for the hiking trip. Anyway, it wasn't food she was craving. Not physically, at least. She needed something to nourish her soul. And before that, she needed to detox it.

She turned on every light in the kitchen and dining room, settled into a chair, and picked up her phone. She fixed her hair in the screen, centered herself, then hit record.

"Hello, my Mellies! I'm back from my hiking trip in Michigan's glorious Upper Peninsula, and I have to tell you that I am just filled to overflowing with stories I'd love to share with you. Getting lost and encountering bears and escaping a forest fire—no, really, all of that happened and more!"

She paused, knowing that even now she was putting on a front. She relaxed the practiced smile on her face and took a breath.

"The thing is, I'm not really ready to talk about it. I need some time to process. Some time to think through what this trip really meant to me. For that reason, among others, I'm going to be signing off for a while. It's time to clean my mental house, to reevaluate. Over the next few weeks, you may see content disappearing from my channels as I sort through the kind of person I want to be and the kind of messages I want to send. It may be that I close up shop online altogether and start something completely new. I don't know yet. But there's one thing I do know: life is about more than just being happy or being liked or being self-actualized. It's about more than just me. It's about more than just you.

"Now, I'm not saying I know *what* it's about. But I know it's about *something*. Something bigger. Something real. Something mysterious, yes, but also something that wants to be known. So that's what I'm going to be looking for. You know me: I'm all about the journey. But what's a journey without a destination?

"So goodbye for now, my Mellies. Peace, love, and life to you. And may we all find what we're really looking for."

Melanie blew a kiss at the camera and stopped the recording. A few minutes later, it had been uploaded to all of her platforms. Before she could see any comments, she shut down her computer and uninstalled the apps from her phone. Then she texted her sister.

How are you holding up?

Epilogue

THREE YEARS LATER

OLIVIA PUT THE CAR in park in a handicapped spot in the lot at Tahquamenon Falls State Park and pulled a red knit cap over her short brown hair. She opened the door, slowly turning her entire body to the left before she stepped out of the car. Deliberate movements like this had become second nature to her. She had to be careful not to wrench her new titanium hip, still had to concentrate to stand on her prosthetic without her cane. It had been a long, agonizing road to get to this point, but she was determined to reassert her independence.

This was why she was here. Or at least, that's what she told herself.

The amputation of her right leg from just above the knee had been difficult to come to terms with, though she felt that the recovery from the hip replacement on the other leg was more tedious. The chemo was no picnic either. But she had come through. Next week she'd be back to work full-time. For now, she had just one goal: walk unassisted from her car to the falls.

She drew in a deep draught of the crisp autumnal air. It smelled of pine needles and decay and cedar trees, a welcome relief after so much time breathing the sterile air in hospitals and rehab centers and her apartment. It crossed her mind that her sister got to smell air like this all the time. Perhaps she ought to reconsider Melanie's invitation to come live with her and Justin. But no, she'd only be in the way. Especially since Melanie was pregnant with number two.

She stepped up onto the sidewalk gingerly, giving the task her full attention. When that feat was accomplished, she began to make her way up the paved walk toward the trees. With each step, she felt more confident, more at ease. There were few people there this late in the season, and those who passed by gave her little notice. In long pants it was hard to tell she had a prosthesis. In summer she'd had to contend with staring children and people thanking her for her service. At first she tried to explain that she was not a veteran, merely a cancer survivor. But it got complicated and took forever, especially if the hiking trip somehow slipped in there, so she stopped correcting people and merely made a point to always thank actual veterans and soldiers anywhere she encountered them.

She could hear the crash of the forty-eight-foot falls getting stronger, sneaking past the trees on her left, drawing her down the walkway. At one point the railing by which she'd been hovering—just in case—made a sharp left turn toward an opening in the trees, where she'd be able to see the falls in the gorge far below. Did she follow the rail? Or meet back up with it when it returned to the straighter path in fifteen feet? Perhaps she should have brought the cane after all.

She opted to follow the rail. Safe was better. At the opening in the trees she paused to watch the foam drift away from the basin of churning water. White foam tinged with brown from the tannins that leeched from the cedar trees, like a river of root beer. A little farther and she could see the falls in the middle distance.

She lingered at the rail, trying not to think of anything in particular, trying to experience something without making any plans or doing any mental calculations about time or distance or efficiency. It was a skill that was hard to master, one that had been suggested to her by the therapist she saw during her recovery. When she found herself wondering exactly how much water went over the falls each day, she moved on.

A few minutes later, she stood at the precipice of a very long flight of stairs—the sign said ninety-four—twisting down toward the brink of the falls and broken every ten or twelve steps by landings with benches. She was sure she could get down them if she took it slow. Coming up, though, could be another matter. Yes, she was cleared for normal activity, but this wasn't exactly normal. Given the choice, even an able-bodied person might opt for an elevator rather than climb that many steps. And she was less able-bodied than most.

Disappointed, she slowly retraced her steps toward the car. She'd have to settle for the lower falls today. She drove four miles down a winding road hedged in by forest to another parking lot, repeated the slow ritual of exiting the car, and headed down another long, paved path.

After several minutes of careful walking, she stepped off the paved path and onto a boardwalk leading to a deck she was sure had not been there when her family had visited Tahquamenon when she and Melanie were small. On the other side of the wooden rail, the lower falls tumbled and crashed over rocks and downed trees, eventually ending up at a wide basin downstream. For just a moment, she thought of nothing at all, allowing her basic senses—sight, smell, hearing, touch—to simply receive data without using that data to come to any conclusions.

She felt the reassuring shape of Josh's compass in her pocket and thought of the last time she'd seen a waterfall before today, of that cursed hiking trip in the Porkies that had turned out to be the most bizarre of blessings. She'd tried to dismiss it for a while, but when the diagnosis came in she couldn't deny it any longer. There were too many coincidences, too many times she'd been ready to quit but had been thwarted. The man in the river right where he needed to be, the borrowed campsite, the dry sleeping bag, the fire driving them on, the stumble that cracked her kneecap, the fall off the escarpment. Even that overly warm day in March that started it all. Every little thing pushing her a little further along to where she needed to be in order to save her life.

She took out her phone, snapped a picture of the falls, and examined it to see if the phone's mediocre camera had managed to capture the dynamic movement of the water. It hadn't, but something in the top left corner of the shot caught her eye. A small blotch of blue and olive green standing out against the autumn trees.

Olivia looked at the actual river above the falls where the

blotch had been but saw nothing. She moved to the left and stepped up onto the wood slat at the bottom of the rail to gain a better angle. At first there were only trees and water. But then . . . yes, that was a person up there. A man in a blue shirt and olive waders with a canvas bag slung across his body, waving his fly rod back and forth, back and forth, in what seemed like a familiar rhythm. For the barest moment, he turned her way, and Olivia could swear he looked right at her. Then he went back to his fishing.

With a strange sense of urgency, she made her way to the edge of the viewing platform. There was a narrow path that ran along the river, strewn with rocks and roots. A harder path to take than the wide, paved one that would take her back to her car. But it was, she suddenly knew, the right path.

With nothing in her hands, Olivia set her jaw, stepped off the smooth, man-made platform, and took the hard way. The way that would lead her home.

Author's Note and Acknowledgments

I HAD BEEN SITTING on my butt for more than a decade when I decided I wanted to do some backcountry hiking with my sister, Alison. With equipment mostly borrowed from my father-in-law, we spent several days and nights in June of 2012 hiking Pictured Rocks National Lakeshore in Michigan's Upper Peninsula. In the years that followed, we hiked the Grand Sable Dunes, Tahquamenon Falls, the Manistee River Valley, the Jordan River Pathway, and Sleeping Bear Dunes. We did start a hike in the Porcupine Mountains that we did not finish due to the miserably high level of mosquito activity (I'm talking, like, eleventh plague on Egypt here). But we've never gotten lost, fallen off any cliffs, or run from a wildfire. We've never even had an argument while out on the trail. We did sleep next to a bear one cold October night. Our hiking trips are chronicled at www.erinbartels.com. Just look for the blog posts in the Travel category tagged "hiking" or click through the Photos page.

Alison and I spent most of our twenties thinking that we were very different people. As it turns out, we're not so different after all. Somewhere along the way, we each took a step toward the other, and eventually our paths met. We have been enjoying each other's company on the journey ever since.

Thank you, Alison, for being game to follow me out into the woods. For the companionable silences. For the conversations we probably wouldn't have had anywhere else. Thank you for never complaining. Thank you for eating disgusting, cold SpaghettiOs on the trail. Thank you for knocking down those insufferable little cairns with me. There is a special kind of contentment I know we both experience when we are far from civilization, ensconced in trees and wind and water and sky. I'm so glad I get to share those blessings with you.

Thank you to my publishing team at Revell for your work on this book. To Kelsey Bowen, Andrea Doering, Jessica English, Michele Misiak, Karen Steele, Gayle Raymer, Mark Rice, and everyone else who has had a part in its journey from concept to contract to completed product. Thank you to WFWA, especially Orly Konig and Jennie Nash for the 2018 writing retreat at Hotel Albuquerque (my home away from home), where the idea for this book went from nebulous to certain. Thank you to my agent, Nephele Tempest, and my husband, Zachary, for reading the manuscript and offering both encouragement and helpful critique.

Most of all, thank you to the God who made this world that I so dearly love, the author of all beauty and wonder, who beckons me to walk the narrow, winding path of life by faith. May you be my compass when I stray, my helper when I stumble, and ever the object of my deepest devotion.

LOVED THIS STORY?
READ ON FOR A SNEAK PEEK OF
ANOTHER CAPTIVATING STORY FROM ERIN BARTELS!

• • •

Coming Soon

One

THE SUMMER you chopped off all your hair, I asked your dad what the point was of being a novelist. He said it was to tell the truth, which I thought was a pretty terrible answer.

"Nothing you write is real," I said. "You tell stories about made-up people with made-up problems. You're a professional liar."

"Oh, Kendra," he said. "You know better than that." Then he started typing again, as if that had settled things. As if telling me I already had the answer was any kind of answer at all.

I don't know why he assumed I knew anything. I've been wrong about so much—especially you.

There is one thing about which I am now certain: I was lying to myself about why I decided to finally return to Hidden Lake. Which makes perfect sense in hindsight. After all, novelists are liars.

"It will be a quiet place to work without distraction," I told my agent. "No internet, no cell service. Just me and the lake and a landline for emergencies."

"What about emailing with me and Paula?" Lois said, practicality being one of the reasons I had signed with her three years prior. "I know you need to get down to it if you're going to meet your deadline. But you need to be reachable."

"I can go into town every week and use the Wi-Fi at the coffee shop," I said, sure that this concession would satisfy her.

"And what about the German edition? The translator needs swift responses from you to stay on schedule."

We emailed back and forth a bit, until Lois could see that I was not to be dissuaded, that if I was going to meet my deadline, I needed to see a lake out my window instead of the rusting roof of my apartment building's carport.

Of course, that wasn't the real reason. I see that now.

The email came from your mother in early May, about the time the narcissus were wilting. For her to initiate any kind of communication with me was so bizarre I was sure that something must be wrong even before I read the message.

Kendra,

I'm sorry we didn't get to your grandfather's funeral. We've been out of state. Anyway, please let me know if you have seen or heard from Cami lately or if she has a new number.

Thanks,

Beth Rainier

It was apparent she didn't know that you and I hadn't talked in eight years. That you had never told your mother about the fight we'd had, the things we'd said to each other, the ambiguous state in which we'd left things. And now a woman who only talked to me when necessary was reaching out, wondering if I knew how to get in touch with you. That was the day I started planning my return to the intoxicating place where I had spent every half-naked summer of my youth—because I was sure that in order to find you, I needed to recover us.

THE DRIVE NORTH was like slipping back through time. I skirted fields of early corn, half mesmerized by the knit-and-purl pattern that sped past my windows. Smells of diesel fuel and manure mingled with the dense green fragrance of life rushing to reproduce before another long winter. The miles receded beneath my tires, and the markers of my progress became the familiar billboards for sporting goods stores and ferry lines to Mackinac Island. The farm with the black cows. The one with the quilt block painted on the side of the barn, faded now. The one with the old bus out back of the house. Every structure, each more ramshackle than the last, piled up in my chest until I felt a physical ache that was not entirely unpleasant.

In all our enchanted summers together on the lake, there had been more good than bad. Sweet, silent mornings. Long, languid days. Crisp, starry nights. Your brother had thrown it all out of whack, like an invasive species unleashed upon what had been a perfectly balanced ecosystem. But he hadn't destroyed it. The good was still there, in sheltered pockets of memory I could access if I concentrated.

The first step out of the car when I arrived at the cabin was like Grandpa opening the oven door to check on a pan of brownies—a wave of radiant heat carrying an aroma that promised imminent pleasures. The scent of eighteen summers. A past life, yes, but surely not an irretrievable one.

On the outside, the cabin showed the effects of its recent abandonment—shutters latched tight, roof blanketed by dead pine needles, logs studded with the ghostly cocoons of gypsy moths. Inside, time had stopped suddenly and completely, and the grit of empty years had settled on every surface. The same boxy green-plaid sofa and mismatched chairs sat on the same defeated braided rug around the same coffee table rubbed raw by decades of sandy feet. That creepy stuffed screech owl still stared down from the shelf with unblinking yellow eyes. On tables, windowsills, and mantelpiece sat all of the rocks, shells, feathers, and driftwood I'd gathered with my young hands, now gathering dust. Grandpa had left them there just as I had arranged them, and the weight of memory kept them firmly in place.

Each dust mote, each dead fly beneath the windows, each cobweb whispered the same pointed accusation: *You should have been here.*

For the next hour I manically erased all evidence of my neglect. Sand blown through invisible cracks, spiderwebs and cicada carapaces, the dried remains of a dead redstart in the fireplace. I gathered it from every forgotten corner in the cabin and dumped it all into the hungry mouth of a black trash bag, leaving the bones of the place bare and beautiful in their simplicity.

Satisfied, I turned on the faucet for a glass of cold water, but nothing happened. Of course. I should have turned on the water main first. I'd never opened the cabin. That was something an adult did before I showed up. And when I went out to the shed to read the instructions Grandpa had written on the bare pine wall decades ago, I found it padlocked.

Desperate to cool down, I pulled on my turquoise bikini and walked barefoot down the hot, sandy trail to the lake. Past Grandpa's old rowboat. Past the stacked sections of the dock I had only ever seen in the water—yet another task adults did that I never paid any attention to because I could not conceive of being one someday. At the edge of the woods, I hesitated. Beyond the trees I was exposed, and for all I knew your brother was there across the lake, waiting, watching.

I hurried across the sandy beach and through the shallows into deep water, dipped beneath the surface, and held my breath as long as I could, which seemed like much less than when I was a kid. As I came back up and released the stale air from my lungs, I imagined the stress of the past year leaving my body in that long sigh. All of the nervous waiting before interviews, all of the dread I felt before reading reviews, all of the moments spent worrying whether anyone would show up to a bookstore event. What I couldn't quite get rid of was my anxiety about The Letter.

Out of all the reviews and emails and tweets that poured in and around me after I'd published my first novel, one stupid letter had worked its way into my psyche like a splinter under my fingernail. I had been obsessing about it for months, poring over every critical word, justifying myself with logical arguments that couldn't take the sting out of what it said.

Kendra,

Your book, while perhaps thought "brave" in some circles, is anything but. It is the work of a selfish opportunist who was all too ready to monetize the suffering of others. Did you ever consider that antagonists have stories of their own? Or that in someone else's story you're the antagonist?

Your problem is that you paid more attention to the people who had done you wrong than the ones who'd done you right. That, and you are obviously completely self-obsessed.

I hope you're happy with the success you've found with this book, because the admiration of strangers is all you're likely to get from here on out. It certainly won't win you any new friends. And I'm willing to bet the old ones will steer pretty clear of you from here on out. In fact, some of them you'll probably never see again.

Sincerely,
A Very Disappointed Reader

Maybe it was because the writer hadn't had the courage to sign his name—it had to be a him. Maybe it was because it had been mailed directly to me rather than forwarded on from my publisher, which could only mean that the writer either knew me personally or had done a bit of stalking in order to retrieve my address. It hurt to think of any of my friends calling me a "selfish opportunist." But the thought of a total stranger taking the trouble to track me down in order to upbraid me gave me the absolute creeps.

But really, if I'm honest with myself, the letter ate at me because deep down I knew it had to be someone from the small, private community of Hidden Lake. Who else could have guessed at the relationship between my book and my real life?

Whoever this Very Disappointed Reader was, he had completely undermined my attempts to write my second book. I knew it was silly to let a bad review have power over me. But this wasn't someone who just didn't like my writing. This was someone who thought I was the bad guy. He had read my novel and taken the antagonist's side—your brother's side.

Now I closed my eyes, lay back, and tried to let the cool, clear water of Hidden Lake wash it all away. But the peaceful moment didn't last. The humming of an outboard motor signaled the approach of a small fishing boat from the opposite shore. Hope straightened my spine and sent shards of some old energy through my limbs and into my fingers and toes. And even though I knew in my heart that it wouldn't be you, I still deflated a bit when I saw your father, though in almost any other context I would have been thrilled.

He cut the motor and came to a stop a few yards away. "Kendra, it's good to finally see you again. I was sorry to hear about your grandpa. We wanted to make it to the funeral, but Beth and I were out of state."

"Yes, she told me."

He looked surprised at that, then seemed to remember something. Perhaps he knew about the strange email.

I swam to the boat—not the one I remembered—and held on to the side with one hand, using the other to shade my eyes as I looked up into his still handsome face. I didn't ask him where you were that day, and he didn't offer any explanation. More likely than not, he didn't know.

"Beth's in Florida now," he continued. "It's just been me since Memorial Day. I was hoping to catch your mother up here before she put the place up for sale."

"It's not going up for sale."

"No? Figured she would sell it."

"It's mine. Grandpa left it to me."

"That so?" He glanced at my beach. "I can help you put the dock in tonight, around five? I'd help now, but I'm off to talk to Ike."

"Ike's still alive?"

"Far as I know."

I smiled. "That would be great, thanks. Hey, I don't suppose you've heard from Cami yet? No chance she'll be coming up this summer?"

He looked away a moment. "Nothing yet. But I've seen Scott Masters once or twice this month. And Tyler will be up Friday."

He waved and headed out across the lake to Ike's. I tried to separate the thudding of my heart from the loud chugging of the outboard motor that receded into the distance.

Of course Tyler would be there. Every paradise needed a serpent.

Erin Bartels is the award-winning author of *We Hope for Better Things*—a 2020 Michigan Notable Book, winner of two 2020 Star Awards from the Women's Fiction Writers Association, and a 2019 Christy Award finalist—and *The Words between Us*, which was a finalist for the 2015 Rising Star Award from WFWA. Her short story "This Elegant Ruin" was a finalist in *The Saturday Evening Post* 2014 Great American Fiction Contest. Her poems have been published by *The Lyric* and the East Lansing Poetry Attack. A member of the Capital City Writers Association and the Women's Fiction Writers Association, she is the current director of the annual WFWA Writers Retreat in Albuquerque, New Mexico.

Erin lives in Michigan, a land shaped by glaciers and hemmed in by vast inland seas, where one is never more than six miles from a lake, river, or stream. She grew up in the Bay City area, waiting for freighters and sailboats at drawbridges and watching the best Fourth of July fireworks displays in the nation. She spent her college and young married years in Grand Rapids feeling decidedly not-Dutch. She currently lives with her husband and son in Lansing, nestled somewhere between angry protesters on the capitol lawn and couch-burning frat boys at Michigan State University. And yet, she claims it is really quite peaceful.

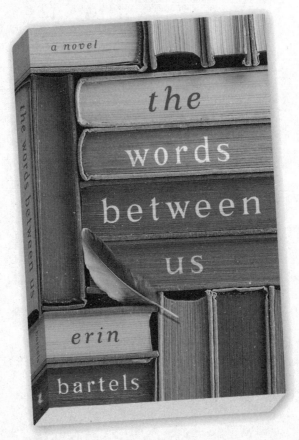

Check out her newsletter, blog, podcast, and more at

ErinBartels.com

@ErinBartelsAuthor 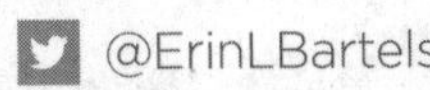 @ErinLBartels  @ErinBartelsWrites

Author Photo: © Matthew Mitchell Photography

Be the First to Hear about New Books from Revell!

Sign up for announcements about new and upcoming titles at

RevellBooks.com/SignUp

@RevellBooks

Don't miss out on our great reads!